T

"You didn't give a _____"

Nate ran a hand over the taut muscles at the back of his neck. "So why don't you tell me now, Callie? Why'd you take off like that, never to be heard from again?"

"I don't know," she said softly.

For a moment he simply stared at her. After all these years, *this* was her answer.

"I don't know," he mimicked. "Bullshit!"

Callie flinched and he realized he'd never raised his voice to her before. He took in a ragged breath, leaning his forehead against the door frame. Callie was one of the most intelligent women he knew. Intelligent women didn't abandon someone without a reason.

So what was hers?

Dear Reader,

People often act in ways that they can't explain. For instance, I have spent my life hopping from task to task, doing a little here, a little there, until the jobs are done. I thought I was a master multitasker—which I am. I also recently learned that ADD runs in our family and I'm a classic case. I adapted to my particular challenge without knowing what it was. Such is the situation with my heroine in *Always a Temp*.

Callie McCarran has a problem staying in one place long enough to put down roots. Like her father, she's a traveler. She works as a journalist and takes temporary jobs when she needs additional income, moving from city to city, job to job. She avoids permanence in all aspects of her life and accepts this as part of her makeup. What she doesn't know is that there may be other reasons she acts the way she does.

Nathan Marcenek, whom Callie had unceremoniously dumped the day after high school graduation, is a stayer—or so he thinks. He's convinced himself, after suffering a devastating accident, that he's happy living in his small hometown and editing the local paper. Then Callie comes back into his life and suddenly he finds himself questioning his decisions and the reasons he made them.

I hope you enjoy Nate and Callie's journeys in *Always a Temp*. Please stop by my Web site at www.jeanniewatt.com or drop me a line at jeanniewrites@gmail.com. I love hearing from readers.

Jeannie Watt

Always a Temp
Jeannie Watt

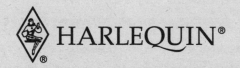

TORONTO • NEW YORK • LONDON
AMSTERDAM • PARIS • SYDNEY • HAMBURG
STOCKHOLM • ATHENS • TOKYO • MILAN • MADRID
PRAGUE • WARSAW • BUDAPEST • AUCKLAND

Recycling programs
for this product may
not exist in your area.

ISBN-13: 978-0-373-78373-1

ALWAYS A TEMP

ABOUT THE AUTHOR

Theater usher, gymnastics instructor, grocery store clerk, underground miner, camp cook, geologist, draftsman, executive secretary, groundskeeper, ball-field mower, janitor, teacher, artist, cowboy gear maker, writer. Jeannie Watt has worn many hats, some temporary, some more permanent, during her life. Because of this she knows how to politely ask a parent with a crying baby to step into the lobby without also making the parent cry, how to coax a cranky copy machine into operation, how to jack a loaded mine car back onto the tracks, and how to make breakfast for thirty in a wilderness setting. The skills learned from her many occupations have now become invaluable resources for her favorite job—writing.

Books by Jeannie Watt

HARLEQUIN SUPERROMANCE

Don't miss any of our special offers. Write to us at the following address for information on our newest releases.

Harlequin Reader Service
U.S.: 3010 Walden Ave., P.O. Box 1325, Buffalo, NY 14269
Canadian: P.O. Box 609, Fort Erie, Ont. L2A 5X3

Many thanks to Kimberly Van Meter and Victoria Curran for straightening me out on a number of journalistic points.
Any remaining errors are my own.

I also want to thank Victoria for her patience and insights during revisions.
I knew I needed something more in the story.
Victoria knew what it was.

CHAPTER ONE

THE BOY SCRAMBLED UP and over the fence just as Callie McCarran opened the back door. Sun glinted off his short, silvery-blond hair before he dropped out of sight into the vacant lot next door.

"Hey," Callie called, but it was too late. The kid couldn't be more than seven or eight, but he was a quick little guy. It was the second time she'd seen him in the yard in the two days she'd been back in town, which seemed odd, since there was nothing of interest back here.... But then she noticed the baseball-size hole in the porch screen, which was quite possibly related to the baseball lying under the wicker chair.

Callie bent down to get it.

"I found your ball," she called. Nothing. Shaking her head, she went out into the over-grown grass and set it on the empty birdbath.

"It's on the birdbath," she yelled, in case the kid was crouching on the other side of the fence. "I'm going in the house now." She walked a few steps, then added, "And I'm not mad about the hole." The entire porch needed to be rescreened before she could sell the house, so no big deal.

Callie went back into the classic 1980s kitchen, complete with country-blue ruffled curtains at the windows and cow-decorated canisters on the cream-colored countertops. She poured a glass of tap water and drank it all without setting the glass down. She'd cried a lot during the past few days and no matter how much water she drank, she felt dehydrated. But she had held up during the memorial service, thank goodness, because if she had broken down, the good townspeople would have added "hypocrite" to her list of epithets. They were already treating her like a leper.

Okay, leper was probably too strong of a word. People had been pleasant enough, offering the obligatory condolences, but she'd been aware of the undercurrents, the why-the-hell-weren't-you-there-for-your-foster-mother-in-her-time-of-need undercurrents. And no one spent much time talking to her. A few murmured words, then off to join other more legitimate mourners standing in small groups near the buffet. Following the service, Callie had spent most of the time alone beside the podium, waiting for the moment when she could leave. Grace's accountant had stood with her for a while, but Callie had a feeling that was only because she was paying him, or rather the estate was paying him, to take care of the final bills. Even he eventually drifted away.

Damn it, I would have been there for Grace, if I'd known how sick she was.

She hadn't known…and she hadn't exactly tried to find out, either. Instead she had stayed with her once-in-a-lifetime trip through Kazakhstan. Attached to a geologic field tour, she'd been chronicling the economic growth and environmental pitfalls since foreign companies had been allowed to mine there.

She was still quite angry with Grace for not telling her she was terminal. That while treating her for a chronic stomach disorder, the doctor had discovered an inoperable malignant growth. But really, Callie hadn't wanted to know the truth.

She'd been afraid to know.

The worst part was that she'd ignored the biggest red flag of all: Grace had asked her to come back to Wesley when she returned to the States. She hadn't been home in twelve years, and in hindsight, Callie could see that Grace wouldn't have made such a request without one hell of a good reason— such as being in the process of dying.

Callie refilled the glass and walked to the back door, peering through the window. The ball was still perched on the birdbath. She wondered if the kid would come back or if this was the last she'd see of him. If he did come and get the ball, she hoped he'd play with it somewhere else.

Not that she'd be here.

But then again, maybe she would. For the first time in a long time, Callie felt no desire to move on. No need to find the next city to explore, the next story to write… maybe because she hadn't written anything except her contracted Kazakhstan article since receiving news of Grace's death.

Callie pressed the cool glass to her cheek. This was the second time she'd suffered such a loss, and it wasn't any easier than the first. Just different.

Her father had disappeared when she was six, leaving her with Grace, his distant cousin and only relative. A business trip. Except he'd never returned. Now she'd lost the only other parent she'd even known.

She set the glass in the sink and went to her old bedroom, now a guest room, and pulled her dark blue knit dress over her head and tossed it on the bed. None of her clothes wrinkled. She traveled too much to buy anything that couldn't be crumpled into a ball and shoved into a suitcase. She traveled with only a carry-on bag whenever possible, because she hated dealing with extra baggage. No extra belongings, no extra people. Just the bare minimum.

But Grace hadn't been extra baggage.

Callie sank down onto the bed and stared at the wall opposite. She should have made more of an effort. *Should have, should have, should have…*

The room had been pale green when she'd lived here. She'd wanted lavender, a color Grace could not abide. Callie had begged, but the room had remained green, because

Grace said there was no way she was having that much lavender in her house.

Now the walls were apricot.

Which meant…?

Nothing. It meant that it had been time to paint and Grace had chosen a different color.

Restless, Callie got up and paced back into the living room in her underwear. It was hot and no one was likely to stop by to visit the ungrateful foster child.

A magazine lay folded back on itself on the maple end table next to Grace's blue velvet recliner. Her slippers were on the floor next to the chair. Grace was everywhere and nowhere.

And the house was so freaking quiet.

Callie had to get out. Regain her equilibrium so she could deal with stuff that two weeks ago she had no idea she'd be dealing with.

A few minutes later, dressed in cropped khaki pants, flip-flops and a light pink T-shirt, she all but bolted down the walk. There weren't many places to go in Wesley, Nevada, but she'd find somewhere.

"Callie!" Alice Krenshaw was standing on her porch next door, still wearing the black muumuulike dress she'd worn to the memorial, a copper watering can in her plump hand. "Are you all right?" she asked, probably out of a sense of duty, because she hadn't been friendly at the funeral.

"Fine," Callie called back, not slowing her pace. Maybe later she'd talk to Alice, but right now she didn't want to talk to anyone. She saw her shake her head as Callie got into her borrowed Neon, read the disapproval in the gesture.

She started the engine and pulled out onto the street, having no idea where she was going. For the first time…ever…she wasn't entirely sure that being accountable to no one but herself was a good thing.

Right now Callie wouldn't mind leaning on someone, and there was only one person in town who might agree to prop her up, but she had fences to mend there first. A minor repair, she hoped. After all, twelve years had passed, and surely by now Nate would have come to the conclusion that what she'd done had been for the best.

"DID YOU HEAR ME, Mr. Marcenek?"

Nathan Marcenek took off his glasses and

rubbed a hand over his eyes, his vision blurry from staring at a computer screen for too long. When he focused on Joy Wong, the receptionist for the *Wesley Star* newspaper, she blinked at him expectantly.

"Callie's here?" He hadn't seen this one coming. In fact, he'd been surprised to hear she'd come back for the service, since she hadn't set foot in Wesley since abruptly leaving town, and him, the day after high school graduation. Even Grace's illness hadn't brought her home.

"Send her in," Nathan said, wishing he'd had the foresight to hide a flask of whisky in his desk drawer for occasions such as these. He had a feeling he might want a stiff belt after this unexpected meeting was over.

Joy nodded and disappeared into the hall. He heard her say, "First door on the left," and then a moment later the woman he could have quite happily gone the rest of his life without seeing again walked into his office. And if anything, she was more striking than he remembered.

Her dark blond hair was shorter than it'd been in high school, curving along her shoulders instead of falling down her back, and the freckles over her nose had faded. But her eyes were the same. Closer to aqua than blue; her gaze direct and candid. Or so it seemed. Nathan had learned the hard way that Callie was a master at hiding things.

"Hi, Nate," she said, her voice husky.

"Callie." He stood, his leg protesting the movement less than usual. Adrenaline mixed with testosterone was amazing stuff. "It's been a while," he said, uttering the understatement of the year. He sat back down without offering his hand or cheek, or whatever one offered to an ex-friend/girlfriend who'd proved to be less than trustworthy, and gestured to the chairs on the other side of the desk.

Callie appeared unfazed by his lack of warmth. She would have been a fool if she had expected him to welcome her with open arms and Callie was anything but a fool.

She took a seat on the only chair that didn't have papers or books stacked on it, and set her small leather backpack on the tiled floor next to her feet. When she focused on him again, her expression was more businesslike, as if she'd changed tactics, which instantly put him on edge. Tactics meant a mission, and Nathan wasn't going to be involved with any Callie missions.

"I was surprised to hear you were editing the *Star*," she said as she folded her hands in her lap, obviously more comfortable with this reunion than he was. "The last I'd heard you were working as a reporter in Seattle."

So she knew something about his career. Nathan waited, wondering if she was also aware that he'd been injured on that particular job. Rather spectacularly injured, in fact. The story had gone national, but the incident had been followed almost immediately by a huge government scandal that had stolen the headlines for weeks.

Callie waited for his reply to her small-talk opening, and after a few seconds he began to relax. She didn't know. There would be no token murmurs of sympathy. No suspicions that he'd tried to live in the fast lane and had gotten the snot knocked out of him. Callie was the last person he wanted to know about that, since honestly, the way she'd dumped him without ever looking back had been part of the reason he'd tried to be less boring.

"I took this job fourteen months ago."

"Where were you before that?"

"Here and there. How about you?" he asked, trying to figure out what was going on. Surely she wasn't here cashing in on old-friend status? If so, she was bordering on delusional. Friends were people you could trust. Friends didn't do what she'd done. "Where've you been working?"

The better question would have been where *hadn't* she been working? Callie never stayed in one place long. He hadn't consciously followed her career—pretty much the opposite, in fact—but Grace had been proud of the foster daughter who never came to visit, and made sure everyone knew where Callie was working.

"Same places as you," she replied. "Here and there. Funny we didn't meet." She didn't exactly smile, but the dimple appeared near the corner of her mouth. Even now it charmed the hell out of him, which in turn ticked him off.

"Yeah." The polite game was over. He didn't smile back, but instead held her gaze, waiting for her to explain the reason for her visit as he absently rubbed the muscles of his right thigh.

Callie sat in stubborn silence on the other

side of his desk, studying him. He wondered how he was stacking up to the guy she'd dumped after graduation. Finally, he gave in and said, "I'm sorry about Grace."

"Thank you. It was a shock."

Nathan didn't try to hold back the snort. The culmination of a terminal cancer diagnosis had been a shock? That pissed him off. "She'd been sick for a long time," he pointed out none too gently. "Where were you?"

The color left her cheeks, but her eyes flashed. "I didn't know about the cancer, all right?"

He guessed he shouldn't have been surprised, although he found it hard to believe that none of Grace's friends had tried to contact her. "Did you try to find out?"

"She told me she was doing fine, that they'd just changed her treatments. I thought I had time to finish the project I was working on." Callie cleared her throat, the first indication that perhaps she wasn't as cool and collected as she wanted him to believe. "If I'd had any idea how serious it was, I would have been here."

Nathan wondered. He took off his reading glasses, holding them by the bow. "So," he said briskly, making the change of topic sound like a brushoff, "once the estate is settled, where are you heading off to?"

"Nowhere."

His jaw tightened. He didn't want her in town, didn't want to be around her. Didn't like being reminded of those days when he'd gone through hell wondering why she'd left. Why she wouldn't take his calls. Not the best of times for a kid who was struggling with self-image issues, issues his dad wasn't exactly helping him with.

"You're keeping the house?" His voice was amazingly cool considering what his blood pressure was doing.

She drew back at the suggestion. "Of course not. I just want some…" Her voice trailed off as she made a small gesture. A fire opal set in an asymmetrical gold band on her left ring finger caught the light. An engagement ring? Somehow he doubted it. "I want some time to go through Grace's things. Tidy up the place to sell. I don't have any pressing commitments."

"I see." And he now had an idea of what was coming next. If she wasn't here as an alleged friend, then…

"I need a temporary job, Nate. I don't want to live solely on savings."

Bingo.

She leaned forward in her chair, her expression intent. "I thought I could freelance for you." When Nathan didn't answer immediately, she added, "I might even improve circulation."

Heaven knew she'd improved his circulation more than once. Nathan shoved the thought aside. "Yeah, you would do an excellent job. There's just one problem."

"That I'll be leaving?"

He set his glasses on top of a stack of papers, rubbed his eyes again. "That's not the problem."

"Then what, Nate?"

He hesitated for a moment before he said, "I don't want to work with you, Callie, and I don't want to publish your articles."

Her eyebrows, a few shades darker than her hair, rose higher. "You're kidding."

He shook his head, watching Callie's expression change as she realized he meant what he said. He was passing up work from a writer of her caliber.

"Because of what happened between us,"

she said. He nodded. "But that was twelve years ago."

"That doesn't make what you did any less crummy."

Callie showed no emotion as she said, "I'm not here asking for friendship, Nate." But he had a strong feeling that had been exactly what she'd been there for. Callie didn't have any friends left in town. He was all that remained of their small high school group. "I just want to submit some freelance work."

"Isn't going to happen."

"I can't believe you're letting personal matters interfere with professional."

"Believe it, Cal."

"Would you at least give me a chance to—"

"What would it matter?" he asked sharply, cutting her off. "If you had something to explain, maybe you could have answered one of my calls twelve years ago. You know, back when I cared?"

Callie rose to her feet and slung her leather bag over her shoulder so hard it made a noise when it hit her back.

Nathan also stood, and again his leg cooperated.

"Well, I guess I'll see you around." Her voice was cold.

And he probably would see her around for a few days, because she'd make certain he did, but he'd bet his next paycheck she'd be gone within a matter of weeks. Or days. She'd find a new assignment, let the real estate agent sell the house, the accountant handle the estate.

"Goodbye, Callie."

She left without another word, the distinctive sound of her flip-flops echoing on the tile in a weird staccato rhythm as she returned to the main office. Nathan sat back down, stretching out his bad leg, feeling the familiar deep ache as his scarred muscles protested. His nerves were humming.

He'd done a decent job of pushing Callie out of his mind over the years, filing their relationship away under Rugged Learning Experiences. He rarely read her articles and he'd had no intention of ever seeing her again.

Now here she was, back in Wesley, ready to let bygones be bygones. He reached for his glasses.

As he'd said, it wasn't going to happen.

CHAPTER TWO

THANKFULLY, JOY WONG wasn't at her desk when Callie left Nathan's office, because, thick-skinned as she was, Callie didn't think she could handle any more rejection today—not even a dismissive smile. Joy had been one of Grace's friends, although Callie had never known her well, and it had been obvious from her politely distant demeanor at the memorial service that Joy was in the Callie-is-a-rotten-person camp.

Callie quickly skirted the receptionist's desk, crossed the foyer and escaped out of the building into the heat. The big glass door closed behind her with a muffled click.

Safe.

She couldn't believe how off base she'd been about Nate.

The plan had been simple when she'd entered the *Wesley Star* office. She would apologize to Nate for running scared, explain that she'd been overwhelmed by things she still didn't fully understand. And then Nate, realizing that she'd been young and confused, and obviously had a reason for not contacting him, would forgive her. After all, twelve years had passed. Time heals all wounds and all of that. But two seconds into the reunion Callie knew she'd better come up with a different plan. The young Nate she'd jilted was nothing like the older Nate sitting behind the editor's desk. Oh, they looked almost the same—dark-haired, blue-eyed, with glasses—but they weren't the same guy. So she'd saved face and pretended she was interested in free-lancing, which she was, never dreaming that Nate would reject her there, too.

She felt like crap.

Heat waves danced on the asphalt as Callie crossed the lot to her car. She didn't even look at the man loading equipment into a minivan two spaces away from where she was parked. He seemed vaguely familiar, but she wasn't going to submit herself to more rampant disapproval.

Callie opened the car door with a little too

much force, making the old hinges squeak, and climbed into the two-hundred-degree interior, cranking the windows down as soon as she shut the door. Since she rarely needed a car, unless she happened to be making a trip across the Nevada desert to a place with no airport, she didn't own one. The Neon belonged to a friend of a friend in Berkeley, who'd had no qualms about lending it to Callie indefinitely in exchange for two hundred dollars—which was approximately twice the value of the cranky little car, as near as she could tell.

Callie pulled the neck of her shirt away from her damp skin before she reached for the ignition. The no-frills Neon lacked AC, and she was getting a quick refresher course in just how hot Nevada could be in August. Even the high desert, where Wesley was located, had long stretches of days in the hundred-degree-plus range, and wasn't she lucky that they were having one now?

As she pulled away from the building, she glanced at Nate's window. He was sitting there staring at his computer. It killed her how much he looked the same, yet how different he was. Of course, there were small

changes that came with maturity. His face
had become leaner, making his cheekbones
more prominent, his chin more angular. And
his body was harder, more muscular. Ironically, he'd been dressed almost exactly the
same the last time she'd seen him, on graduation night, right down to the sleeves of his
oxford shirt rolled up over his forearms and
his shirt tucked into jeans rather than pants.
He'd once told her that the only thing that
stood between him and complete nerddom
was that he refused to give up his Levi's.
She'd never thought of him as a nerd, but
rather as the quiet brother sandwiched in
between two hell-raisers. Safe, dependable,
understanding Nate… Scratch understanding.

Yeah, Nate had changed.

A few minutes later she parked her car in
front of Grace's house, which, once the
estate was settled, would be hers.

Callie McCarran. Home owner.

What a joke. Houses were for people who
liked to put down roots, form relationships.
Other people signed mortgages and long-term
leases. Callie paid rent on a mouse-proof
storage unit to store the few things she trea-

sured and could not bring with her on her travels.

A house would be wasted on her.

CHIP ELROY POKED HIS shaved head into Nathan's office. "Hey, was that Callie McCarran I saw leaving the building a while ago?" He had two cameras hanging around his neck and a large black lens bag in one hand.

"In the flesh," Nate muttered, looking back down.

"Wow. I haven't seen her since high school." Chip gave a slight cough. "She, uh, filled out nicely, wouldn't you say?"

"Yes," Nathan said in a conversation-stopping tone. "Do you have something you need to discuss?"

"Nope," Chip answered, emphasizing the *p* and taking the hint. "I'm heading out to take photos of the new bridge." He pushed off from the door frame, his baggy pants dropping an inch as he did. He hiked them back up with his free hand.

"Are you done with the BLM story?"

"I will be by tomorrow morning."

"See to it." Nathan shifted back to the

piece he was editing. It would be so great if Chip had a clue when to use an apostrophe. At least he took decent photos.

Two hours and one headache after Callie had left, Joy came into Nathan's office carrying a cup of green tea. She insisted he drink one cup a day to help combat stress. Nathan actually thrived under pressure and hated green tea, which tasted like boiled lettuce, but he was wise enough not to mess with Joy. The office would implode without her.

"Thanks," he said absently as she set the cup on the one clear spot on his desk—the spot he kept clear for this purpose—close to the potted plant. He was beginning to think that there might be something to the purported medicinal properties of green tea, since the dieffenbachia had put on an amazing growth spurt.

"You should have hired her to freelance," Joy said. There was no doubt which "her" she meant, since with the exception of Millie, the advertising salesperson, there had been no other woman in the office that day.

Nathan looked up. "You were listening?"

"Not on purpose. You didn't close the

door and I was in the supply closet taking inventory. You should have given her some work."

"But I didn't."

"It would have reduced the load here."

"She's going to be gone in a few weeks, Joy."

"How do you know?" Joy challenged.

Nathan moved his mouse, bringing his screen back up. "Trust me. I know."

"We'll see," she replied on her way out the door, which she closed behind her, leaving Nathan free to dispose of his tea and to wonder why she was defending Callie. Since Joy and Grace had been friends, he hadn't expected that. And he hadn't made a mistake.

Vince Michaels, the owner of the *Wesley Star* and several other rural papers scattered throughout Nevada and western Utah, would not agree. He'd be totally pissed if he discovered that Nathan had refused to hire Callie, since she'd won a few awards and people knew her name.

Was that why he felt like hell?

"WHAT ARE YOUR SKILLS?" Mrs. Copeland, the woman who managed the only temp agency in Wesley, propped her fingertips together as she asked the question. Tech Temps catered almost solely to the gold mining industry, the number one employer in northern Nevada, but Callie was more than willing to take on a mine job, which ranged from secretarial to truck driving. Two days had passed since her unsettling conversation with Nate, and she still had no idea what she was going to do in the future. But if she was going to stay in Wesley for an undetermined amount of time, then she needed to work, because at the moment, writing wasn't cutting it.

If she had to, she could write the service articles her magazine contacts were asking her to take on, but Callie's strength was her voice. She wrote about people and places and her unique style had earned her both a name and a steady income.

Now, not only was her writing off, her voice was MIA and she was getting concerned. She hoped that if she got out into the workforce, met new people, had new experiences, something would spark, as it always had before, and the words would flow once again.

Grief was a bitch.

"I can do just about anything." And she had, having supported herself with temporary jobs, between travel writing and other freelance gigs, since she'd left college. Indeed, the list of Callie's skills, noted on the résumé sitting in front of Mrs. Copeland, was long and detailed. Maybe that was why the woman wasn't looking at it.

Mrs. Copeland puckered her mouth thoughtfully and turned to her computer. She clicked her mouse and made a face. "Diesel mechanic?"

Callie couldn't help smiling. "No, that's one area where I'm lacking, but I did work in a tire store once."

"Accounting?"

"At first, but one of the regular guys got sick for a week, so I mounted tires and fixed flats."

Mrs. Copeland clicked through several more screens, her expression not exactly reassuring.

"Anything?" Callie had already checked the local paper, which was her only source of employment information. A remote town like Wesley had no short-term job listings on the Internet boards.

"Doesn't look good. Most temp jobs are seasonal and you're here at the end of the summer rather than the beginning."

"I was hoping someone had become conveniently pregnant and needed time off."

"It happens," Mrs. Copeland mused. But it didn't look as if it was happening now. Callie felt a sinking sensation when the lady took her hand off the mouse and turned to her, propping her elbows on her desk and clasping her fingers under her chin. "I see you have a college degree."

"In journalism." But she had a sneaking suspicion there wasn't a big call for journalists in the mining industry.

"I suggest you go to the school district office. They're crying for subs."

"Subs?"

Callie's horror must have shown. Subbing involved kids, and she hadn't spent much time around kids. Like, none. The woman smiled. "It's not a bad job. They pay close to a hundred dollars a day. You work from eight to three forty-five."

"Then why are they crying for subs?" A justifiable question, considering the high pay and the short hours.

"They require two years of college to get the license and not many people here meet that requirement. If they do, they usually have full-time jobs."

"A hundred dollars a day."

"Almost a hundred," Mrs. Copeland corrected her, her chin still resting on her clasped hands.

"I was hoping for something steadier." Even a serial temp worker needed a little security in the short term.

"Trust me, it's steady. My brother teaches and I know." Mrs. Copeland picked up Callie's résumé and slid it into a manila folder. "If you're not interested in subbing," she said, after placing the folder on a high stack on the rolling file cabinet next to her, "you can check back every few days, or check online. Maybe something will open up."

"Okay. Thanks." Callie left the office and walked to her hot car. Subbing…did she want to get back in the workforce that badly?

She gave herself a shake. Okay. The idea of trying to control a class of kids was intimidating, especially since she had zero notion how to do that, but…if it didn't work out, she didn't have to go back. Heck, if it didn't work out, she probably wouldn't be allowed back. She would go with Plan B then—taking the magazine contracts. She didn't want to do that just yet because a small part of her was afraid that was all she'd ever do from that point on. She might never write anything worthwhile again.

Callie got into the Neon and drove the half mile to the school district office, where they practically hugged her for showing up with a bona fide college diploma and the desire—although Callie wasn't quite certain that was the correct word—to substitute teach. These people were desperate.

After filling out forms and getting instructions on what to do with transcripts, she went to the sheriff's office to be fingerprinted—a requirement for the sub license application. She'd looked around cautiously when she arrived, since once upon a time Nate's father, John Marcenek, a man who'd never particularly cared for Callie, had been sheriff. But surely he'd retired by now. He had to be over sixty.

"Who's sheriff?" Callie asked the brisk

woman wearing too much perfume who took the prints.

"Marvin Lodi."

Callie wasn't familiar with the name. "John Marcenek retired then?" She was actually kind of hoping he'd been voted out of office.

"Yes. He's chief of the volunteer fire department now."

That sounded like the perfect retirement gig for Nathan's dad. Something where he could be in command and throw his weight around.

Callie left the sheriff's office and went back to Grace's house, where she ordered her college transcript online, requesting that it be sent directly to the State Department. The extreme shortage of subs in the district meant her application would be expedited, according to the district office secretary. As soon as the paperwork was approved, all she had to do was wait for a call.

And in the meantime, she could try to force out some words.

Callie went into the kitchen with its sparkling linoleum floor, waxed in a bout of insomnia the night before, and glanced out the back window at the grass she needed to mow as soon as it cooled off. Then she smiled.

The baseball, which had disappeared from the birdbath a few hours after she'd put it there two days ago, was back, next to her bottom step. She went outside and picked it up, wondering if the owner was anywhere nearby.

The fence separating her property from the alley and the vacant lot next door was solid wood, but on the other side chain-link divided the backyards, so Callie was able to see Alice Krenshaw pruning her bushes near the corner of her house.

"Hey, Alice," she called, her first voluntary contact since the memorial. She figured if they were going to be neighbors, however temporary, then they needed to develop a working relationship.

Alice looked up from under the brim of her gardening bonnet, her pruning shears still open, prepared for the next snip. "Do you know a little white-haired kid in the neighborhood?"

"He lives in the rental on the other side of the vacant lot. The Hobarts." Alice pointed to the two-story house, which was a bit ram-shackle, with worn paint and missing screens.

"Thanks. I need to return something." Callie held up the baseball and Alice nodded before returning to her pruning.

Callie went through the back gate into the alley, half expecting to find a kid crouched in the shadow of the fence, waiting for the opportunity to retrieve his ball. She walked along the buckled asphalt to the house Alice had pointed out. The backyard wasn't fenced and the weeds of the lot that separated the house from Grace's were encroaching into the dried grass. A few toys were scattered about—a yellow dump truck and bulldozer, a half-deflated plastic swimming pool. Dead bugs and leaves floated on the remaining water.

No kids.

Callie looked up at the second floor windows and clearly saw two children looking down at her—the white-haired boy and a darker blonde girl. Callie held up the ball and they both instantly disappeared from view. But they didn't come out the back door as she expected. She waited for several minutes, and when it became obvious that she could be cooling her heels for nothing, she walked down the alley and around to the front of the house, where she rang the doorbell. The bell made no sound, so she knocked. And knocked again.

Nothing happened.

Okay... Then it hit her. The kids must be home alone and had been told not to answer the door. It made perfect sense. Callie set the baseball on the weathered porch boards and headed back to her own house.

Maybe she could do a piece on latchkey kids....

NATHAN MOUNTED THE road bike and expertly locked his shoe cleats into the clipless pedals, then started down the road leading out of town. It had not been a good day, with deadlines stacking up like cordwood and a phone call from the big boss, Vince Michaels, insisting that Nathan put Vince's high-school-aged son, Mitch, to work again. Mitch had worked as an intern the previous semester and had been about as useless as a screen door on a submarine. Then to complicate matters, Nathan found out Mitch had been harassing Katie, the part-time billing clerk, with sexual innuendos. Nathan had put a quick stop to that and had called Vince, who hadn't taken the matter seriously until Nathan mentioned the potential for a harassment suit. Then he'd taken notice. Mitch had sulked and stayed away from Katie, but he'd continued to be as useless as ever.

Nathan didn't need Mitch hanging around again, doing nothing and upsetting the people who were actually working, but he had him. Another Vince-related headache. Nathan had a lot of autonomy working at the *Star,* but there were areas where the boss needed to back off and keep his fingers out of the pie.

Nathan geared down as he approached the first big hill, and the tension on the pedals eased as revolutions per minute increased, allowing him to maintain speed as he climbed. The first time he'd ridden after getting out of the hospital, he'd gone all of a mile. His good leg had had to do the work; his injured leg had been along for the ride, the foot locked onto the pedal by the cleat mechanism in his shoe, the leg doing little more than bobbing up and down as the pedals turned. But as time passed, the remaining muscles in that leg started doing their job, and now he rode fifteen to twenty miles a night, sometimes thirty, depending on how late he left the office and how stressed he was. Despite the deadlines, he'd managed to get out relatively early tonight, before seven o'clock, anyway, because Chip had turned in two decent articles, proofread and well written for once.

It was twilight by the time Nathan had completed the loop around the edge of town, dipping down near the river, then back through the older section of town, where he lived. When he rounded the last corner before his house he saw his younger brother, Seth, backing out of the driveway. Seth caught sight of him and pulled the truck forward again.

"Good ride?" he asked, getting out. He had on his wilderness clothes—a light green microfiber shirt, khaki pants, hiking boots. His hat was jammed in his back pocket instead of on his close-cropped, dark blond hair. Out to commune with nature, no doubt. Or to rescue someone. He was driving the official beaten-to-death truck with the SAR—Search and Rescue—insignia on the door.

"Every ride's a good ride," Nathan answered, pulling off his helmet and shaking his sweaty hair. For a while he'd been afraid that he'd never ride again. "What's up?"

"I'm on my way out of town and needed to borrow your GPS." He held it up. "Mine's on the fritz."

"Help yourself to my stuff anytime," Nathan said as he pushed the bike into the garage with one hand on the seat. "You know how much I like it."

"Oh, I will," Seth said with a laugh. "Has Garrett talked to you at all?"

"About?" Nathan hung the bike on a set of supports attached to the wall, hooked his helmet over the bar extender, then peeled off his gloves.

"He's all ticked off about some fight he had with Dad. Don't tell him I told you." Seth started for his truck.

"Hey, he's the one who wanted to live next door to Dad." Nathan was surprised that his dad had fought with Garrett, though.

Usually he saved his arguments for Nathan, the kid he didn't understand.

"No. He's the one who wanted to live rent free," Seth corrected, and he had a point, since their father owned the house next door and didn't charge Garrett rent in return for minor property upkeep. "Want anything from the city? I'm stopping in Elko on my way to Jarbidge."

Nathan shook his head. "I'm good. What's going on in Jarbidge?" The isolated mountain community boasted a population of less than a hundred.

"Probably a party, but we're going up for specialized search and rescue training starting early tomorrow morning." Seth got into the truck and was about to close the door when he said conversationally, "You aware that Callie's still in town?"

"I am." His brothers were the only people who knew the truth about what Callie had done to him. As far as everyone else knew, they'd parted by mutual agreement.

"Just wondering," Seth said casually.

"No big deal." Because it wasn't—except that whenever he thought about her coming into his office, cool as could be, his blood pressure spiked. He was really looking forward to the day she put Wesley behind her. Then the coronary he was working on would result from deadlines alone.

As his brother swung out onto the sealed blacktop, Nathan lifted a hand, then went into the house through the side door, hitting the switch to close the garage as he went in. He'd barely peeled out of his sweaty shirt when the town fire siren blew. He grimaced and put the damp shirt back on again. He hated going to fires, but Chip was leaving town for two days, so he was the only one there to cover the story.

He really had to hire another reporter.

But it wouldn't be Callie. He didn't care if she stayed for a decade.

CHAPTER THREE

CALLIE WOKE to the smell of smoke. She pushed her hair back from her forehead as she sat up, disoriented until she realized that, despite the noise of the antique cooling system churning in the window beside her, she'd conked out on the sofa. That would teach her to wax floors at midnight.

She got to her feet, rubbing the crick in her neck as she went out on the front porch. The neighborhood was quiet, but the smell of smoke was strong. She walked out to the middle of the street, where she could see over the tops of the houses, and sure enough, a column of dark smoke rose into the rapidly darkening sky on the north edge of town, where housing developments encroached on the desert and Bureau of Land Management property. It was the season for wildfires, but black smoke meant a structure was burning.

Maybe she'd find something to write about.

Callie went back in the house, ran a comb through her sleep-flattened hair, then grabbed her car keys. By the time she'd followed the smoke to the outskirts of town, about a mile away from Grace's house, several vehicles bearing volunteer firefighter license plates had sailed by her.

A crowd of onlookers gathered on the last street of the development, which had new tract houses on one side and vacant lots on the other. Maybe seventy yards away, on the undeveloped side of the street, firemen were dousing flames that had engulfed a derelict trailer parked in a weed-choked lot.

Ever conscious of not getting in the way of people who had a job to do, because that tended to get one banished from the scene, she parked her car several yards from the closest vehicle, hugging her wheels to the ditch to keep the roadway clear. She left the car and casually walked up to the knot of by-standers, wanting to blend in as she took in the scene.

"Any idea how it started?" she asked the teenager next to her, a sandy-haired kid with baggy pants. The sky was clear, so if the fire had been caused by lightning, it was a freak strike.

The teen shrugged without looking at her, but the middle-aged man standing slightly in front of her turned, frowning as if he was trying to place her. Probably not too many strangers showed up at neighborhood fires, so Callie couldn't blame the guy for thinking she might be a firebug there to enjoy the results of her handiwork.

"I'm Callie McCarran," she said, saving him the trouble of trying to memorize her face or get her license plate number.

"Doug Jones." He turned back toward the action, but Callie caught him watching her out of the corner of his eye.

Callie gave the teenager another shot. "Have you had many fires this summer?" Fire seasons varied. Some years would be fire-free and during others it would seem as if the entire state was ablaze.

"We've had a few," the boy said without looking at her. His focus was on the firemen—or rather, on one particular fireman who looked as if he might be a she. The only she, as far as Callie could tell.

"Do you know the name of the female firefighter?"

The kid shrugged again and ignored her.

Oh, yeah. She was going to do well substitute teaching. Couldn't get kids to answer the door. Couldn't get kids to answer a question. And speaking of kids… Callie saw a distinctive white head at the edge of the crowd. Her across-the-lot neighbor. This little guy got around. Callie craned her neck to see who was with him, but the crowd shifted and she lost sight of him.

The breeze was light and it didn't take long for the firefighters to get the blaze under control and stop it from spreading to the desert, where it could have taken off in the dry grass, sage and rabbit brush, causing major damage. The crowd started to disperse as the flames died, some people going to cars, others to nearby houses, and Callie once again caught sight of the boy as he tried to resist his sister's efforts to pull him down the street. No adult was in sight and it was nearly nine o'clock. What would two kids that age be doing so far from home?

Unless they had sneaked out to see the action without their parents knowing. Kids did do things like that, or so she'd heard. She'd been too afraid of the wrath of Grace to have tried.

The girl finally got her brother to cooperate, even though she wasn't much bigger than he was, and he began trudging down the street beside her. Every now and then he looked over his shoulder at the firefighters.

Callie wasn't about to offer them a ride, being a stranger and all, and no one else seemed concerned by their presence, so she decided that Wesley was indeed a very small town and the rules were different than in a more urban area. She watched until they pulled their tired-looking bicycles out of the ditch near a streetlight and started riding off along the sidewalk. Okay. They had transportation home. But it still disturbed her to see kids out that late without an adult.

Doug Jones gave Callie one last suspicious look, then headed to a nearby house. *Bye, Doug.* Callie stayed where she was, hoping to get a chance to talk to the female firefighter, who was still dealing with embers near what was left of the trailer.

As she waited, a big Dodge truck and a panel wagon pulled out of the throng of vehicles belonging to the volunteers, giving Callie a better view of the fire engines. She also had a better view of Nathan and his older brother, Garrett, standing in the headlights of one of the engines, deep in conversation.

She hadn't realized Nate was there, though it made perfect sense—his staff was probably so small that he had to report as well as edit—and she certainly hadn't realized that the deputy she'd spotted a few times on the fringes of the crowd was Garrett Marcenek. Go figure.

She'd known Garrett for years, and had no idea he'd ever thought of pursuing a career in law enforcement. How ironic. Now instead of being arrested, he'd get to do the honors. So what might Seth Marcenek be doing? If the rule of opposites applied, he'd pretty much have to be a priest.

"Hey, Garrett," someone behind her called. "I'm taking off."

The brothers both looked up, catching Callie midstare.

Damn.

She instantly started walking toward them, as if that had been her objective in the first place. If she was going to stay in this town for a while, then she wasn't going to try to avoid the Marcenek brothers.

"Garrett, good to see you," Callie said before either man could speak. She firmly believed that whoever spoke first had a psychological advantage. "Nathan."

"Callie." He revealed no emotion. No coldness, no warmth. Nothing.

"Welcome back," Garrett said, shifting his weight to his heels. Callie wondered if he was resting his hand on his holster on purpose, or if it was just a habit.

"Thank you."

"I need to check something out," Nathan said to his brother, his eyes focused behind Callie. He left without another word, brushing past a burly volunteer firefighter carrying a Pulaski ax. Nate favored one leg slightly, making Callie wonder just how many miles he was putting on the bike. Five to ten a day had been the norm when they'd been in high school, but he'd ride as many as twenty when he was stressed. She had gone with him on the short rides, but when he needed to put his head down and pedal, she'd found other things to do.

The man she'd seen unloading equipment

from the minivan in the parking lot that morning was there, taking notes as he talked to one of the firefighters. He lowered his pad as Nathan approached, and the two fell into conversation. An old memory jarred loose. Chip Elroy. From her sophomore geometry class.

"So how long have you been a deputy?" Callie asked, turning back to Garrett.

"Since about a year after you dumped Nathan." He held her gaze, his expression cool and coplike.

"Eleven years then." She wasn't surprised by Garrett's response. The brothers had wildly different temperaments, with Garrett looking for trouble, Nathan trying to keep him out of it, but they were tight.

"Give or take a few months." He shifted his weight again. "What're you doing here?"

"You mean at the fire?" Obviously, since he had to know why she was back in Wesley. She glanced over at the trailer's smoldering metal ribs. "Just seeing if there's a story." She cocked her head. "Who's the female firefighter?"

"Denise Logan."

Ah, from high school. She would have been in Seth's graduating class.

"Was this arson?" When Garrett didn't respond, Callie added, "Pretty clear night. No lightning."

"How long are you staying in town?"

"Awhile."

"And then?"

She shrugged.

"Must be nice," Garrett replied, "having no ties. Going where you want, when you want."

"It's great," she agreed, refusing to rise to the bait. "You should try it."

"Can't. I prefer to be there for the people who matter to me."

"Oh, do you have some of those? People who matter to you? Because I remember you dumping girls right and left, without much regard for hurt feelings."

"At least I told them it was over, instead of taking the coward's way out and running away without a word."

She wasn't touching that one, and Garrett knew it. He smiled without humor, then muttered, "I have some things I need to take care of." Nodding in dismissal, he strode past her toward two older men checking gauges on a truck.

Callie turned away and headed for the

Neon. She got in without looking back, slamming the stubborn old door shut.

She fought the urge to rest her forehead on the steering wheel in defeat, and instead turned the key in the ignition, carefully pulling back out onto the road and then executing a three-point turn. She followed the route the kids had taken, to make sure they'd gotten home.

A few minutes later she turned down Grace's street and cruised by the house where the neighbor kids lived. It was dark inside, except for the distinctive glow of a television set, but the old bikes were propped against the porch. They were home. She debated stopping, but it was late, almost ten now. Maybe she'd try to catch the parents at home tomorrow and mention that the children had been at the fire. Parents who cared simply did not let kids ride across town—even a small town—after dark.

"SO WHAT'S THE DEAL HERE?" Nathan asked, indicating the burned-out trailer with a jerk of his head. He'd rejoined his brother after he'd made certain that Chip, who'd thankfully put off his trip when he saw the smoke, would get his photos in before he left the next day. "Two fires in a week, no lightning."

Nathan hated fires. He hadn't had a problem until the explosion, when the world around him had erupted into a fireball. That was after the shock wave had thrown him back against a brick wall and driven shrapnel into his leg and torso. His partner, Suzanne Galliano, had also been injured, but her wounds had been superficial, which was why she was still reporting in Seattle, while he was back here in good old Wesley, Nevada.

"What do *you* think the deal is?" Garrett asked. He was careful what he said around Nathan in an official capacity, having been quoted as an "unnamed source" enough times to get him in trouble with the brass, who had no trouble figuring out the identity of the unnamed source.

Nathan rubbed a hand over his head, loosening his matted hair. "If it turns out this fire was man-made like the last one, then someone could be setting fires."

"That's a big leap, junior," Garrett said, careful not to be quotable. "A field and a structure."

"Or the fires may not be related and this one came about because old man Anderson wanted to get rid of his rusty trailer without paying to have it torn down and hauled away."

"Talk to Dad," Garrett said, jerking his head to where their father was conferring with another man near the front of an engine.

"Oh, I will. Later." Not that it would do a lot of good. Fifteen years of being sheriff prior to taking over command of the fire department had made John Marcenek a master at avoiding a direct answer.

"My gut reaction is that the two incidents aren't connected, and you're probably right about Anderson," Garrett finally said, before giving Nathan a fierce look. "*Do not* quote me."

"Unnamed source," he agreed with a half smile. The brothers fell into step as they walked back to Nathan's car.

"Law enforcement officials are uncertain whether the incidents are connected," Garrett corrected. "You didn't seem too surprised to see Callie at the fire."

"Probably looking for a story. She showed up at the office and asked me for freelance work a couple days ago."

Garrett glanced at him. "No shit?"

"I turned her down, but if Vince Michaels hears about it, he'll be an unhappy camper."

"Or rather, you'll be an unhappy camper."

Nathan grinned for the first time all evening. "In your words, no shit."

As soon as Callie got home, she fired up her laptop and started to write. Words appeared on the screen, but something was lacking: decent writing. Disgusted, she ditched the file and turned off the computer. She'd try again tomorrow.

The next morning was no better, nor was the afternoon. Finally, as the sun was setting and Callie had accomplished nothing except for an industrial cleaning of the bathroom, she faced reality. She couldn't keep cleaning bathrooms and waxing floors. She had to do the one job she did not want to do, the task that was constantly lurking at the back of her mind, and then maybe she could settle and write a few words.

She needed to go through Grace's belongings.

Callie opened the bedroom door and stood in the doorway, taking in the neat little room.

Grace's reading glasses were on the nightstand, along with an empty water glass, and a box of tissues set on top of a library book. Callie should probably return that before the library police came after her.

She went to the closet and opened the door, the squeak of the wheels in the tracks instantly bringing back memories. When the closet had squeaked, it meant Grace was awake, getting her robe. It meant Callie would smell breakfast soon and that the house would be warm when she got up.

The closet smelled of spice. Grace had loved cinnamon and had sachets everywhere. Callie had always loved cinnamon herself, but at the moment the scent was too poignant, too much.

Sorry, Grace...

Callie did her best to shut herself off as she pulled armloads of clothes out of the closet and laid them on the bed before going back for more. If she didn't think about what she was doing, she wouldn't get sucked down. And once she got this chore done, the worst would be behind her. She'd be able to write.

After the first closet was empty, she shook

open a trash bag and shoved the clothing into it, hangers and all. If she stopped to sort and fold, she wouldn't make it through the process without breaking down. The most practical approach was to make everything disappear into black plastic as quickly as possible.

But Callie wasn't quick enough. She slowed down for a few seconds and the next thing she knew, she'd pulled an oversize cardigan she'd always associated with Grace out of the pile of clothing on the bed. And, instead of shoving it into the bag, she held it up, then bunched it to her, breathing in the scent of the only mother she'd ever really known.

Her throat closed.

Callie resolutely blanked her mind, folded the sweater and set it inside the swollen bag before tying it shut. She shook open another bag and headed for the dresser, planning to quickly sort through Grace's unmentionables so she didn't accidentally throw away or donate something of value. Grace had had a habit of hiding things in her underwear drawer, as if placing something here would keep it safe from prying eyes—those of a young girl trying to peek at her Christmas presents, for example. Sure enough, when Callie opened the drawer, something solid slid across the bottom. She pushed aside the cotton undergarments to find a fancy lingerie box.

She set the box on the bed and for a moment just looked at it, wondering what on earth it could contain that was worthy of hiding in the underwear drawer. The corners of the lid were worn and the cardboard had grown brittle with age. She gently eased the top off.

Photos. Tons of photos. And her school-work. Award certificates. Callie's life in a box.

She lifted out a photo of herself taken on the first day of junior high, wearing low-rider flared pants and a body-hugging, long-sleeved shirt. The shirt had been too hot for August in Nevada, but Callie had wanted to wear it, and Grace had acquiesced. Beneath that were more photos—showing her rabbit at the fair for 4-H. Callie riding her bike. Grace had bought it used, but it had been one of the cool bikes. A Trek 920, like Nathan's. Not that Callie had been concerned about that kind of stuff.... She smiled slightly. She'd pretended not to be, anyway, but she had loved having a bike that was as nice as everyone else's. Grace hadn't made a ton of money working at the grocery store, but she'd taken care of Callie.

Callie had not taken care of Grace.

She put the lid back on the box and set it on top of the dresser, then went back to the clothing, checking all the drawers before quickly dumping the contents into trash bags. No more sorting, because everything was going to charity. People who hadn't abandoned their foster mother could sift through her stuff.

By the time she finished, despite her best efforts to keep the self-recriminations at bay, Callie was a wreck.

She should have come home and she hadn't.

She'd shut everyone she'd ever been close to out of her life over the past decade, for reasons she didn't quite understand.

Well, damn it, she didn't want to be alone anymore.

CHAPTER FOUR

NATE WAS SLOUCHED on the sofa, his feet propped on the coffee table and his laptop on his thighs, when the dog next door started yapping. Since Poppy's owner went to bed at approximately sundown every night, Nate put his computer on the coffee table and went to the window to see what had disturbed the little rat.

"You've gotta be kidding me," he muttered as he dropped the curtain and went to the door. Callie was already on the bottom step when he pulled it open. Twice now he'd seen her and twice he'd felt the odd sensation of having a missing part of his life back again—which was ridiculous, since this missing part had blown him off and disappeared for a dozen years without a word.

"Why are you here?" It was late and he was too tired for niceties.

Her eyebrows lifted as she said, "Because I want to make peace."

He rested a hand against the door frame. "Make peace?" They weren't at war. He just didn't want her around.

"Over ten years have gone by, Nate. I'm sorry I took off, but we're different people now. Surely we can start new."

Start new. Yeah. So easy. He didn't feel like making it easy on Callie, so he continued to block the door, even though she obviously wanted to come inside.

"I went through hell after you left. I was afraid something had happened to you, until Grace told me you were all right." It had taken him a couple of days to get hold of her foster mother, since she'd traveled to Boise immediately after the graduation ceremony to attend a wedding, giving him and Callie the freedom to almost consummate their relationship, emphasis on *almost*. Her trip had also given Callie the freedom to blow town the next day.

His fingers gripped the door frame. He would never forget how he'd felt when he'd realized she'd gone without a word. He loved her, thought she'd loved him, yet she disappeared after their first awkward and unsuccessful attempt to make love. He'd felt like such a freaking loser.

"I did what I had to do," Callie said now, an edge of frustration creeping into her voice.

Nate ran a hand over the taut muscles at the back of his neck. "You didn't give a reason for leaving. So why don't you tell me now?"

"I don't know," she said softly.

For a moment he just stared at her. After all these years, this was her answer.

"'I don't know,'" he mimicked. "Bullshit!"

The word echoed through the night. Callie flinched, and he realized he'd never raised his voice to her. He drew in a ragged breath, leaning his forehead against the doorjamb. Callie was one of the most intelligent women he knew. Intelligent women didn't just abandon someone without a reason. And more than that, deep down he'd wanted her to have a concrete reason for leaving. Maybe something he'd done or said. Maybe his inexperience. Something they could have worked out, given a chance. He'd always believed she'd had a reason.

"We're not going to be friends and you're never writing for the *Star,* Callie. Not while I'm editor." He looked up at her. "Got it?"

She stared him down for a few seconds, then muttered something under her breath that sounded a whole lot like "We'll see," before she abruptly turned and crossed the lawn back to her wreck of a car. It started with a puff of blue smoke. She pulled away from the curb before she snapped the headlights on. Nathan watched her disappear around the corner.

What kind of a jerk treated someone who'd recently lost her only relative that way? Especially when he knew exactly how it felt to lose a parent?

But did Callie *ever* feel anything? He was really beginning to wonder.

THE NEON GAVE A COUPLE of ominous coughs as Callie drove home. Par for the course. Everything else in her life was going to hell. Why not the borrowed car, too?

Nate was still angry with her. And he wanted answers she didn't have.

Why had she left?

Why does a horse bolt at a loud noise?

Instinct. It was the way she was. She couldn't put a name to the reason if she tried, since she didn't fully understand it herself, but she did accept it. She panicked when she felt as if she was being tied down, and according to Grace, her father had been the same way. Hard to fight genetics.

So what had made her think she could explain tonight? Or that after their first encounter in his office, that Nate would listen? What had made her even try?

The need to be with someone who, even if he didn't understand, might accept her as she was. After all, he was Nate. He'd once loved her. She'd thought.

Callie bit her lip as she considered all the things she should have said and hadn't, because she needed more time to get them out.

She'd wanted to explain that he'd always been on her mind after she'd left, that ending their relationship had nearly ripped her apart, too, but the panic had been stronger than her feelings for him. How could she get that across to him?

She couldn't.

Yet.

But with time… With some time, maybe he'd come around. She missed him and she needed a friend.

When she got home, the Hobart house was still dark inside except for the flickering glow of the television. No car was parked in front of the house or in the carport.

Was someone home with those kids?

A television also glowed in Alice Krenshaw's living room, and there was no car parked in her drive, either, which was because Alice's husband worked the night shift at the mine and they owned only one vehicle. The Hobart family probably had the same circumstances. One car and shift work.

No matter how she twisted it around, though, it still bugged the heck out of Callie that those kids had been out so late without supervision. Twice.

Uncaring adult? Zero supervision? Or were the kids masters at sneaking out?

Was it any of her business?

And here she was, sitting in her car, spying on the house next door. How creepy was that? Callie got out of the little Neon, trying not to slam the stubborn door too loudly.

She'd left the lights on in Grace's house, but it looked anything but welcoming. Kind of a theme here in Wesley. Maybe that was the reason she hadn't come back sooner.

But deep down, she knew it wasn't.

CALLIE HAD DRIVEN AWAY half an hour ago and Nate was still keyed up, unable to focus for more than a few minutes, which was disturbing to a guy notorious for his ability to hyper-focus. He put the laptop aside and then absently ran his hand over the numb area of his thigh.

So what exactly did Callie want from him? Friendship? Forgiveness? Physical intimacy during a rough spot in her life? Perhaps all three. Who didn't want comfort when life took a devastating turn?

Him. Physical intimacy had been out of the question after the explosion nearly destroyed his leg. He'd had no desire to share his battered body, and even when he finally had, it had been with the woman who was his nurse during the latter part of his hospital stay, a woman who was accustomed to seeing trauma and injury. The relationship hadn't lasted long. Nate's heart hadn't been in it and he'd had a sneaking suspicion she was laying him just to get his confidence back up. He didn't need mercy screws.

Again he ran his hand over his leg, felt the twisted tissue and deep dip where the destroyed muscles had once been.

No. Even though he wouldn't mind showing Callie that he was no longer the inexperienced kid suffering from performance anxiety, there'd be no physical intimacy. He wasn't the guy to give her comfort, because he wasn't ready to put himself out there—especially with someone he couldn't trust.

In fact, it really pissed him off that she was back, acting as if nothing had happened, wanting to pick up where they'd left off before she'd abandoned him.

We're different people now, Nate.

In more ways than she knew.

Nathan got the laptop, settled it back onto his thighs and resolutely finished the article. He'd just shut the computer down and was ready to call it a night when his cell phone rang.

His leg had stiffened and it took a few minutes for it to cooperate as he crossed the room to the buffet table where the phone was plugged in, charging. He glanced at the number, expecting it to be one of his brothers, since it was so late, then smiled.

"Hey, Scoop." Suzanne Galliano had been his best friend in Seattle. They'd collaborated on several stories and had been together the night Nathan's investigation into the illegal import of pharmaceuticals ended in an explosion and warehouse fire. Fortunately for Suzanne, her hospital stay had been only two days, her recovery from the mostly superficial wounds rapid. Nate's recovery, on the other hand, not so much. Hell, in a lot of ways he'd yet to recover from the blast.

"Are you still stuck in the middle of nowhere?"

"You mean my charming hometown? Yeah. I'm here."

He could almost see her rolling her eyes. "Well, maybe I'll be able to do something to save you. The paper just lost a reporter and they're hiring. You'd have to throw some stuff together fast, get it up here, but honestly, I think you have a good shot."

"No thanks."

"Nathan…!" she whined. "Come on. You know you don't belong where you are. You

should be writing and reporting, not editing. I bet you'd make more money in this job than you do now, and it could be a springboard to bigger and better things."

"Thanks. I'll think about it."

"No you won't. I know that tone."

"I will. Honest."

She blew a raspberry into the receiver. "Fine. But you're throwing away an opportunity."

"I like being near family."

"The same members of your family who tried to kill you more than once as a child?"

"The very same," Nathan agreed as he shut off the living room lamp and walked into his bedroom. His brothers might have made a career out of attempting to do him bodily harm as a youngster, but he'd returned the favor. In spades. He might be the quiet brother, but he wasn't a wimp.

"You need to rethink your priorities, you masochist. If I don't hear from you by Wednesday, I'll assume it's a no and arrange for counseling."

"Thanks for the heads-up."

"No problem. I'll make you see the light one of these days. How's the *physical* therapy?"

Nathan smiled. "Over for the most part. I ride my bike. It keeps the leg strong and flexible." Plus, he'd been able to buy a bitchin' bike with the money he saved once the therapy stopped.

"There's some good bike riding here," Suzanne said in a sincere voice. "And I kind of miss you."

"I'll think about it. Hey, how's Julia?" Her significant other, who had never fully forgiven Nathan for dragging Suzanne down to the warehouse with him that fateful night.

"She's doing well. Just got a promotion to design manager."

"Tell her congratulations from me."

"Maybe you can tell her yourself when you come for the *interview*...." His ex-partner's voice trailed off hopefully.

"I'll think about it. Good night, Suze. Talk to you later."

Nathan tossed the phone onto the dresser and went into the bathroom, where he stared at himself in the mirror for a few seconds before turning on the water to brush his teeth.

It had been nothing short of a miracle when, after Nathan had returned to Wesley,

Vince Michaels had bought the paper and promptly fired the editor. Newspaper jobs in a town the size of Wesley were nonexistent. Nathan lived near his dad and brothers, in the town he'd grown up in, doing the job he'd trained for. If he felt as if he was just going through the motions day to day, it was from the inherent stress of an editor's life. Survival mode.

He just needed to ride his bike more, take the edge off.

This was where he belonged.

CALLIE WOKE UP SHEATHED in sweat, the light cotton blanket that had covered her in a tangle at the end of the bed. She sat up, swung her feet onto the floor and then sat for a moment, her face in her hands.

Her heart was still hammering.

Crap. She'd thought she'd moved past the dream years ago.

She took slow, deep breaths until her heart rate slowed, then turned on the night table lamp and went to the bathroom. When she returned, she shook out the comforter and sheet, then lay back down. It was three-thirty. The dream never came twice in a night, so once her adrenaline level dropped, she might go back to sleep. Maybe.

It was unusual for the dream to come during such deep sleep. Usually it happened when she was nodding off, startling her fully awake, frightening her with…she had no idea what frightened her once the first images, recognizable in the split second when the dream struck, were forced back. A burning sensation in her nostrils, then terror would overwhelm her. Not shrieking, sheet-clutching terror, but a deeper fear that threatened to suffocate her. A feeling that she was going to be dragged into a dark unknown.

Over the years she'd learned not to panic, to breathe slowly through her nose, and the burning sensation, along with the terror, would pass. They already had now, leaving Callie to wonder, as always, what it was in this dream she would not allow herself to recall. What terrified her so much?

When she awoke again, sun was shining in through the window and the comforter was still covering her. No more dreams, no restless sleep.

Callie hated the dream, but she'd learned to live with it.

Now she wondered what had triggered it. She could usually link it to stress, but the greatest stress in her life—Grace's death—hadn't brought it on. So what was the cause tonight?

Nate. Had to be.

NATHAN WENT TO WORK and disappeared into his office, closing the door behind him. Between Callie's visit and Suzanne's call, he hadn't slept much, and he was not in the mood for socializing. Barely ten minutes passed before Joy was there with the boiled lettuce juice.

"I heard there was a bit of a scene at your house yesterday."

Nathan looked at her from beneath the hand that was propping up his head while he read.

"Yes," she continued, placing the cup on his desk near the dieffenbachia, "I talked to Ed Nelson at the café this morning and he said you were yelling at some good-looking woman on your lawn."

"I wasn't yelling." *Much,* he amended to himself, remembering how Callie had flinched when he'd shouted "bullshit." He'd had no idea that Ed, his neighbor across the street, had been listening.

Joy clasped her hands together over her shapeless navy blue dress. "Was it Callie you weren't yelling at?"

"Yes." He had the feeling from her body language that Joy had something to say on the matter, and out of curiosity, he waited, wondering if she was going to mention the fact that Callie had not come home to be with Grace when she was dying. But Joy didn't say anything.

Finally he gave in and asked, "You were a friend of Grace's. Did she ever mention anything about what happened between Callie and me at the end of high school?" *Do you understand that your normally sane employer had a reason for yelling at a woman on his front lawn?*

And had Callie gone with Grace's blessing? He'd never been able to figure it out the few times he'd talked to her after Callie had disappeared. Grace had simply assured him that her niece was fine, and had obviously wanted him to let the matter rest.

He'd been so frustrated. Callie was safe, but for reasons unknown, did not want to talk to him. His brothers were the only people he'd ever spoken to concerning the matter, and he hadn't said much. Since he'd left town himself for a summer job shortly after graduation, and went on to college in the fall, he figured no one cared what had happened. So what if nerdy Nathan Marcenek had been blitzed by tornado Callie? But Wesley was a small town and gossiping was a hobby for some.

Joy contemplated him as if looking for signs of a hangover. "I vaguely remember people wondering why she took off like she did." She shifted her mouth sideways in a thoughtful manner. "And it was kind of obvious a few days ago that you didn't want her back in your life."

He really was going to have to remember to close the office door.

"So Grace never said anything?" He felt ridiculously like an insecure teenager as he asked the question.

"Grace was protective of Callie," Joy said after a tactful pause.

"That didn't work in the other direction, did it?" he asked darkly, truthfully. Callie hadn't been protective of Grace.

"No." Joy shook her head, the fluorescent light glinting on the few strands of gray in her black hair. "It didn't."

The phone rang, and ironically, Joy, who'd planted herself in his office without invitation, appeared relieved to have a reason to escape. He didn't blame her. "Do you want me to close the door?"

"Please."

A moment later, she sent him an e-mail, apparently not wanting to risk a continuation of their previous conversation. Mitch Michaels would be showing up for his first day of work next Monday. Did he want her to reschedule Katie's office hours so they didn't coincide?

Nathan considered it. Then he came up with a better idea. He wrote a quick reply, telling Joy to leave Katie's hours as they were. Mitch would be working in the basement on the archives. The kid wouldn't see the light of day while he was in the office. Vince might be able to force Nathan to babysit his son and try to teach him a work ethic, but he didn't have much say in what the kid actually did.

SINCE CALLIE ALWAYS FELT unsettled and basically rotten the morning after the dream, it seemed a perfect time to dive into Grace's personal files. The accountant had phoned the day before and had reported the estate was all but settled, so now it was up to Callie to finish her end of the deal so that she could move on.

She soon came to realize, though, that no time was perfect for diving into personal files. Grace had kept everything, from the warranty on her new kitchen faucet to the property deed, in a tall, wooden, three-drawer file cabinet. Callie sorted for two hours, keeping the documentation that would be handy to the new owners of the home, tossing paperwork on items that were long gone.

In the back of drawer number two, she found a file with her name on it. Even though it held the paperwork on the foster care arrangements, this was much less distressing to her than finding her schoolwork and certificates in the old lingerie box in Grace's dresser had been.

The folder contained duplicate immunization records, her high school transcripts and SAT scores, among other things. She glanced over the foster care papers, then closed the folder and stashed it in the box she was putting in storage back in California. Someday. She wasn't sure when. It was going to take some time to go through the house single-handedly, and she was going to take that time. She needed it, to make peace with herself for not being there when Grace needed her.

She finished the third and final file drawer just before noon. She had a giant bag of paper to be shredded or burned, and a giant headache. Time for iced tea and a peanut butter sandwich, even though it felt as if a stiff belt of vodka would come closer to hitting the spot.

She dragged one of the wicker porch chairs out into the tall grass under the elm tree and ate in the shade. It was hot, but she wanted to be out of the house, away from the memories.

The kids next door were playing in the vacant lot that separated their houses. Callie could hear them arguing about who was pitching and who was hitting, and wondered if a ball would soon come sailing over her fence, perhaps followed by a white-haired kid.

She clinked the ice in her glass. The grass desperately needed to be cut. She'd put the job off twice because she hadn't wanted to tackle the mower. Although she'd done well with her tire store job, she was not the most mechanically inclined person, and was fairly certain the mower would win if it came down to a battle of wills. When she'd been a teen, Grace had beaten the mechanical monster into submission, somehow managing to get it started every weekend so that Callie could mow the lawn and earn her allowance. Now she was on her own.

In this corner, Callie McCarran, and in the other, Lawn-Boy...

But maybe Grace had a new mower. Callie got out of the wicker chair and walked to the shed, flipping open the latch with a quick movement of her thumb. It took a moment for her eyes to adjust, but as soon as they did, she recognized her old opponent lurking in the far corner.

Okay. Maybe she'd hire a kid to do the job—one with his own mower.

Feeling better about the lawn situation, she was about to close the door when she suddenly recognized the weirdly shaped dusty object with garden tools leaning against it. Her old bike, her once beautiful Trek, with a coil of hose hanging off the handlebars. Callie swung the door open wider and stepped inside, amazed that Grace hadn't donated the bike to charity years ago, and ridiculously happy that she hadn't. Callie removed the hose and laid it on the useless lawn mower, gathered the rake, hoe and shovel and jammed them into the corner.

After a quick spider check, she wiped the cobwebs off and lifted the bike, coughing as she accidentally inhaled some of the dust that had settled on the frame. She hauled the Trek out of the shed and laid it on the lawn, then turned the hose on it. Years of dirt and spiderwebs washed into the grass and disappeared.

Her baby was a wreck.

The tires were flat, the chrome pitted and the seat cracked. The chain hung sadly. She found the hand pump in the shed under the tool bench and tried to put air in the tires, but it was no use. The inner tubes were goners, having endured extreme temperature changes over the past decade. Callie propped the bike against the shed door and considered what she'd have to do to make it operational. Everything. A complete overhaul and tune-up were in order, but for the moment new tubes and tires and an oiled chain would probably suffice.

She'd never been a cycling maniac like Nathan and his brothers, but she'd loved her bike and had enjoyed getting from point A to point B under her own steam. She still liked the idea, and with the Neon acting up, an alternate mode of transportation was quite possibly a godsend.

And maybe a way to connect with Nate, because damn it, she wasn't giving up. Her old friend was in there somewhere, and truthfully, the man he had become was very, very attractive. He also appeared to be lonely, and if he would just listen to reason, he and Callie could solve both problems at once.

CHAPTER FIVE

"IT'S YOUR TURN TO FORCE Dad to go to the doctor," Garrett said over the phone in his commanding cop voice.

Nathan was not one bit impressed. "I'm behind schedule," he answered, changing computer screens to pull up his calendar. "And it's not my turn."

"It is, too, and you're always behind schedule."

"The news never stops."

"Come on, Nate. You're better at this than I am."

"You're a cop. Coercion is part of your business. Anyway, it's Seth's turn."

"Hey…" Nathan could hear his brother flipping through his desk calendar. "You're right. It's your turn in October."

"Can't wait," Nathan said drily. His other

line lit up. "Gotta go. Call me if you need backup."

"I can't imagine not," Garrett said succinctly before hanging up.

John Marcenek had had no problems with doctors until he started having health issues related to high blood pressure, which culminated in a ministroke that he sneeringly called "the episode." After that, he developed a strong dislike of those in the medical profession—especially those who told him to stop drinking and lose weight if he wanted to avoid future "episodes."

The truth was hard to handle, especially when it involved changing a lifestyle filled with manly habits such as eating bags of chips and pork rinds during the televised game and drinking too much. He'd left law enforcement after more than thirty years— fifteen spent as county sheriff—when he hit the mandatory retirement age. After that he poured his energy into being chief of the volunteer fire department. John Marcenek was accustomed to command and didn't take well to being ordered around. Even for his own health and well-being. Garrett and Seth were very much like the old man, with he-man occupations John approved of and he-man hobbies. Nathan had always been the odd man out—the son his father didn't understand. The son who wrote and drew. Because of that, Nathan actually was the best candidate to strong-arm his father to the clinic. Since they had never seen eye to eye, he was used to his dad's bellowing, and took it in stride. If he hadn't developed that ability, he would have imploded long ago.

The only time he'd seen a different side to his father was after his accident. John had hovered uncomfortably near his bedside in Seattle, while Seth and Garrett held down the fort in Wesley. His dad hadn't said much about the injury itself, talking instead about sports and stuff, but after that Nathan was convinced his dad loved him in his own way. John would never understand his middle son, and wasn't going to try and Nathan had learned to accept that.

CALLIE CLOSED HER LAPTOP and pressed her fingertips against her forehead. She'd been back for three weeks, had sorted through all of Grace's belongings. The estate was settled and still…nothing. No words. She would start writing, then suddenly feel the need to wash walls, sort out stuff in the basement, escape the keyboard.

Her last finished piece had been the Kazakhstan article, written after her trip had abruptly ended, when she'd gotten word of Grace's death. Callie had composed the contracted article in a numb haze. She'd written in airports and hotel rooms on her fractured journey here, since getting a quick flight home from central Asia wasn't exactly a piece of cake. She'd been practically finished by the time she'd gotten to the States, did the last editing the night before leasing the Neon from the friend of the friend to drive to Wesley, and had submitted by e-mail.

She couldn't remember a word she had written. She didn't know if what she'd sent in was a piece of crap or up to her usual standards, and she hadn't been able to bring herself to open the file on her computer, for fear of what she might find. So when the check arrived in the mail, forwarded from her San Francisco post office box, she decided the piece must have been adequate, because the payment was unusually rapid.

Now she had some money to tide her over until she received her substitute teaching license or Mrs. Copeland called from Tech Temps. Callie was hoping for the latter. She still wasn't certain how she felt about subbing, but what concerned her more was the lack of spark in her writing. Something had to change. Or else she was going to have to change her occupation, perhaps even take up something permanently.

Callie didn't want to do that. She needed the freedom to get up and go when she felt the urge.

She did have an idea niggling at her that she thought would make a very nice submission to the *Wesley Star.* Maybe she'd write it, submit and see how Nathan reacted. Perhaps now that he'd vented the frustrations he'd had bottled up for ten years, he'd be more reasonable.

Callie certainly hoped so, because that was an integral part of her plan.

It wasn't difficult to hunt down Denise Logan, the female firefighter. Callie asked about her in the grocery store, and the clerk, not knowing that Callie was a horrible person who had abandoned her foster mom, told her a few things about the woman. Like where she lived. With that information Callie was able to dig up Denise's phone number and arrange a coffee and an interview at the new café.

Callie was waiting in a red upholstered booth when Denise came in at exactly two-thirty—a time when the place was nearly empty, and they could talk and not worry about taking up a table. Denise smiled and raised a hand when she spotted Callie. Her long blond hair was pulled back in a ponytail and she was wearing almost exactly the same outfit as Callie—a formfitting T-shirt, denim skirt and leather sandals. She looked nothing like the all-business firefighter Callie had seen the previous week.

"Thanks for coming," Callie said as Denise slid into the booth.

"Hey, thanks for asking me. I've never been interviewed before." Denise waved help at the waitress who came out from behind the counter. They ordered iced tea, and then Denise settled back in her seat and waited for the questions to begin.

Callie pulled out her small tape recorder. "Do you mind if I record your answers?"

"Not at all."

"You grew up around here," Callie said. She remembered the Logan kids, all several years younger than herself. The junior and senior high schools were combined. "Did you always plan to stay in Wesley?"

"Oh, no," Denise said with an easy smile. "I went to the University of Nevada, Reno, got my degree in fire science at their school near Carlin. But—" Denise held up her palms, her expression philosophical "—there are no jobs, so I moved home."

"Why did you get a degree in a field where there are no jobs?"

Denise's eyes brightened. "Because when there is a job opening, I'm going to get it."

Callie laughed. "I like the way you think. How do you support yourself while you wait for that job?"

"I'm a bookkeeper at the junior and senior high."

"And they give you time off when you get a fire call?"

"That's one reason I work there."

"Are there other reasons?"

"Well, the hours are good. I work from seven to two. Also—" she smiled ironically before sipping her iced tea "—I didn't have a lot of choice. The school district is one of the main employers in the county. If there's a non-mining-related job to be had, there's a good chance it's at one of the schools."

"That's what I discovered," Callie said, then told the story of her own search for a temp job.

"So you *only* work temp?" Denise seemed surprised.

"I've never been on a job for longer than six months."

"Wow. I don't know whether to be impressed or appalled," the blonde said candidly.

"Working temp allows me to write for a living. Travel. Fun stuff like that."

"Sounds cool, actually, so I guess I'll go with being impressed. I subbed for a while before I got the bookkeeping position."

"What's substitute teaching like?" Callie felt compelled to ask the question, hoping for a reassuring answer.

"Like holding thirty corks underwater." Denise laughed at Callie's horrified expression. "Sorry," she said with a shrug. "But it's true. Be prepared to be busy."

"Tell me about fire school." Callie changed the subject back to research, and made a mental note to pop in and see Mrs. Copeland at Tech Temps on the way home.

"It's rigorous, but so worthwhile…." Denise answered questions for almost twenty minutes before the café door swung open and a group of high school boys traipsed in, laughing and pushing one another, obviously glad to have made it through the school day. Thankfully, they settled at a table across the room from Callie and Denise, but one kid smiled at Denise in a confident and blatantly wolfish way before turning his attention back to his buddies. Callie was amazed at the balls of the kid. Denise worked at his school and should command a degree of respect rather than the once-over he'd just given her.

"Tyler Michaels," Denise said, sipping her iced tea. "He lives on the hill above my house and his dad owns the newspaper and some other businesses."

"He's confident," Callie said, her eyes on the boys, who were now teasing the waitress.

"You should see his brother, Mitch. Unfortunately, they have looks, lots of money, no respect, and they think they're God's gift to women."

"That kid must be all of fourteen. Kind of young to be God's gift to women."

"Fifteen. Doesn't slow him down one bit. And Mitch is even worse. I had to smack Mitch down at the school and now I guess his little brother is taking a shot."

How nice. Denise's carefree attitude had evaporated as soon as the teens arrived, so Callie decided to wrap things up.

"One last question." The most important one. "How does the old guard feel about a young female firefighter with a college degree joining the ranks?" *How is it working for that ass, John Marcenek?* Callie couldn't count the number of times she'd tried to talk to him and had gotten gruff put-downs for her efforts. It was as if she wasn't good enough for Nate, or had been somehow leading him astray.

Denise rolled her eyes. "Where do I begin?"

"At the beginning?"

She hesitated, then leaned forward, placed her palms on the table and said seriously,

"Before I answer, promise me you won't write anything that will get me in trouble with the guys I work with."

"I'll be tactful."

"Well, let's just say it was a while before they took me seriously."

"In other words, you had to prove yourself."

"Yeah," Denise said, relaxing against the red booth cushion, her smile returning. "If you put it that way, it sounds all right."

"How long did it take…?"

When Callie left the restaurant, she felt confident that her writing slump was over. She was already composing the article in her head, had her lead, so the question now was how was she going to sell this article when the editor of the local paper had told her in no uncertain terms that he wouldn't publish anything she wrote?

That was a toughie.

Callie unlocked the Neon, pausing to watch the teens leave the café and pile into a car parked on the other side of the lot, before climbing into the stiflingly hot interior and rolling down the window to let some marginally cooler air circulate inside.

The kids drove by and Callie glanced over in time to see Tyler Michaels smile at her. The kid did think he was something.

Callie wondered if the dad, the owner of the paper, was the same way. She would soon find out.

On a hunch, she returned to the small grocery store where she'd found out how to track down Denise. As she had hoped, the same bored clerk was behind the register. Callie picked up a few items and set them on the counter. As the young woman started scanning the bar codes, Callie asked in a conversational tone where she might find Vince Michaels. The clerk glanced up. After explaining exactly where Vince Michaels lived—this clerk was truly a stalker's dream—Callie asked if he could be found anywhere in town. Like, in an office.

No office, but he played golf.

Interesting. Especially to a woman who for one entire season was the worst player on the Wesley High School girls' golf team.

JOY TAPPED ON THE DOOR and came in with the tea. Nathan had already dumped one cup that day, so he frowned at the second.

JEANNIE WATT 95

"Callie's here."

A day full of surprises. It made him wonder what kind of magic the evening might bring. "Send her in," he said with a sigh of resignation.

She paused in his office doorway a few seconds later, looking wonderful. He hated that she looked wonderful, hated that he still reacted to her.

"Good to see you, Callie."

She stretched her lips into a humorless smile. "Gee. With a little practice, you could sound like you mean that."

"I'll work on it," he said drily.

"I ran into Vince Michaels on the golf course."

Instant headache. "*You* were playing golf," Nathan said flatly. Callie was awful at golf. She'd all but been kicked off the girls' team the one year she'd played.

"I was practicing my swing with my old clubs, hitting a bucket of balls the same time he was."

"How'd you manage that?"

"I'm not without resources."

Yeah. Nate imagined that Jesse Martinez, the golf pro, would have provided a wealth of information if approached in a proper manner. By an attractive female.

"Shouldn't you be mourning Grace instead of playing golf?"

"I am mourning Grace," Callie said in an intense voice.

Nathan felt a twinge of guilt at the low blow, but still—sucking up to his boss? He hadn't seen that one coming.

"Anyway, I mentioned this great idea I had of writing a series of articles while I'm here. Unique career choices in a small town. Doll maker. Lady firefighter. Geriatric kindergarten teacher. He seemed quite interested. He's heard of my work, you know." Callie idly fingered the fabric of her blouse. "Of course, the final decision is up to you."

"And we both know what that decision will be."

"Look, Nate." Her chin jutted out. "I was with you after your mom passed away. I admit I had no idea what you were going through until now, and you didn't talk much, but I was there. I'm just asking you to return the favor."

"You're blackmailing me into being your friend?"

"I'm blackmailing you into letting me

write for you, and if I really need to, to talk to you. Friendship will come later."

"That ship sailed."

"Nothing's saying it can't come back to port."

"I'm saying."

"Okay, we'll hold off on the friendship clause. What about the articles?"

She spoke offhandedly, but Nathan was probably one of the few people on earth who was aware that Callie hid her vulnerabilities that way. She was hurting.

He'd been dead honest when he'd said they wouldn't be friends again, because friendship involved trust. He no longer trusted Callie, but he felt for her. He couldn't help it, having lost his own mother.

He gritted his teeth as if trying to hold back the words he knew were coming.

"Write one article on spec."

She didn't exactly break out smiles, but she seemed satisfied with the small concession.

"And the other...?"

"I'll listen if you need someone to talk to," he replied gruffly. But that was all he was going to do, and only because he owed her. "Once or twice. Plan accordingly."

"Another thing."

"There's more? What do you want? My car?"

"You're close. Can you give me the name of a decent auto mechanic in town?"

"I go to R&M."

"How about bikes?"

Nathan frowned.

"I found my old bike," she explained. "It needs a tune-up and new tires."

"Elko."

"The Neon won't make it to Elko and the bike is my transportation while the Neon's in the shop."

"Bring it over to my place. I'll see what I can do." He leaned back in his chair, folding his arms over his chest.

"Tonight?"

"Tomorrow around six. What size rims? Twenty-six?"

"I don't know."

"Measure them when you get home. If they're not twenty-six inch, call me."

"Great. See you then." She turned, looking so happy that Nathan almost hated to ruin the moment. But he did.

"This is a one-time deal, Cal. I'll help you

out because of circumstances." His mouth tightened before he added, "Because I owe you for being with me after Mom died. But you owe me, too."

She was no longer smiling. "What do you want me to do about it?"

"Nothing. And I mean that from the bottom of my heart."

THE HOBART BOY DASHED across the empty lot to his house just as Callie turned onto their street. It was dark. The library had just closed and she was on her way home with a folder of research on unusual occupations people had held in Wesley over the years, gleaned from the special collections. So what was the kid doing out at nine o'clock again? Alone this time.

What disturbed her most was that the Hobart house was once again dark. This time there wasn't even the glow of a television showing through the windows.

Was that kid in there sitting in the dark? Surely if an adult were home, the house wouldn't be pitch-black.

Callie forgot all about minding her own business and marched up to the front door and knocked. No answer. She knocked again. Nothing.

So now what? Was she nuts? Did she or did she not see a white-haired kid? Was he inside or hiding in the thick foliage that surrounded the house?

Slowly, she walked down the buckling sidewalk toward her own house, then on impulse walked past her gate to Alice's.

Her neighbor answered on the first knock. "Hello, Callie," she said stiffly.

"Hi. I, uh…" She pointed down the street. "Do you know if there's an adult home at the Hobarts'?"

"There must be."

"No one answered when I knocked and there's no car."

"It looks dark," Alice said helpfully. "Maybe they aren't home."

"I saw the boy go into the house." Or at least she thought she had.

"Oh, my. Well, Callie, I don't know what to tell you. The mom works downtown at the Winners Casino, but…" Alice's plump face brightened. "I think her mother lives with them. Yes. I seem to remember hearing that at club."

"Well, if she's there, she's fond of the dark."

Alice cocked her head, then stepped out onto the porch to look at the Hobart house. "Maybe the electricity got turned off. That does happen, you know. And I don't believe the family is well off financially. Single mom working at a casino…" She shook her head.

Callie moistened her lips thoughtfully. "So you think everything is all right?"

"I think I wouldn't go sticking my nose in their business. They can be a cantankerous bunch."

"Didn't they just move here?"

"From the Bellow's Ridge area. The family has been up there for generations." Bellow's Ridge was an extremely rural ranching community forty miles from Wesley.

"I see." Callie nodded as she digested the information, then attempted a smile, even though she wasn't reassured. The smile must have come off as genuine, though, because Alice smiled back. "Thanks," Callie said.

"You bet. Good night, Callie." Alice

started closing the door, then stopped and asked, "How long do you plan on staying?"

"I don't know," she said truthfully.

Alice's fingers tightened on the half-open door. "Why didn't you come home when Grace was sick?"

Callie's shoulders rose and fell as she inhaled, then exhaled. "Poor planning on my part," she finally answered. "Good night, Alice."

Callie stayed up past midnight, reading, jotting notes, staring into space.

Every now and then she would go to her side window and look out at the Hobarts'. It was still dark. No television glow. Nothing. That bothered Callie immensely.

She thought about calling the police, but...what if she didn't have her facts right? What if she'd strung a bunch of minor incidents together and come up with a scenario that was blown all out of proportion because of her own experience having a working parent—not that her father had neglected her. He'd always seen that she was cared for.

Callie was still not certain what her dad had done for a living, why he'd traveled so much. She'd been very young when she'd been with him, and he couldn't exactly take her on the road with him—especially after she'd entered kindergarten and then first grade. She had few clear memories of who she'd stayed with, for how long or why, but she recalled being with many different people. She'd even stayed with Grace a time or two before that fateful trip when her father had dropped her off, never to return.

She'd asked Grace what her father had done for a living exactly twice. The first time she'd been in elementary school and had been curious, since all the other kids were spouting off about what work their dads did. Grace had told her he was a traveling salesman. Years later, Callie had asked again, thinking that "traveling salesman" might have been a euphemism Grace had used for a seedier occupation—such as drug dealer or something. But the answer had been the same.

Callie had pushed a little more, asking if he was involved in any kind of criminal activity that may have gotten him killed. Grace had replied that to the best of her knowledge, Callie's father had been a salesman or unemployed, as finances allowed. And he'd loved traveling. No. He'd needed to travel.

Callie understood the need to travel, and because of what Grace had told her, knew that she came by her inability to settle in one place honestly. Yet…here she was in Wesley, where she had been ensconced in Grace's house for a couple weeks now, and she hadn't yet felt the tug to move on, to see what was around the next curve in the road.

The tug would come.

It always did.

CHAPTER SIX

MITCH MICHAELS WAS well dressed and personable, a kid meant to manage—as long as it didn't take a lot of effort on his part. Nathan was willing to concede that maybe Mitch would be all right if he was doing something he actually wanted to do. And there were no women around. Truthfully, Nate despised the kid and resented being saddled with him at the paper. He didn't have a much higher opinion of Mitch's younger brother, Tyler, who thankfully was not yet an intern. That day was coming, though. Nathan was certain of it.

"Hey, Mitch," he said when the young man swaggered into his office later that day. "Have a good summer?"

"It was all right." Once upon a time, the statement would have been accompanied by a charming smile. Not anymore. Not since

Nathan had set Mitch straight on the matter of sexual harassment last spring. "It was nice to get out of this hellhole town for a while."

Mitch and Tyler had been urban transplants five years ago, when Vince had moved to Wesley from Salt Lake City after his divorce, and built a mansion in the foothills of the Jessup Mountains. He wanted his sons to grow up in a less complicated environment, he'd said, but Nathan suspected that he wanted to get his boys as far away from his flaky ex-wife as possible.

Whatever the reason, Mitch was being groomed to follow in his father's footsteps and take over either the newspapers or the trailer manufacturing business Vince was developing near Elko.

Last spring Nathan had had the kid answering phones and doing office work, which had proved to be a disaster. It ended in Nathan's explanation to Mitch that if the kid persisted in harassing Katie, Nathan would personally make sure she pressed charges.

"My dad wouldn't like that." Mitch had worn an expression that made Nathan want to smack him, which was what the kid had probably been angling for.

Nathan had merely shaken his head, unfazed. "Your dad has nothing to do with it. What you're doing is illegal."

Mitch had shown no sign of believing Nathan. But it was possible that he'd discussed the matter with his father later, because for the last three weeks of the internship, he'd shown up, sullen and withdrawn, and had kept to himself, doing the smallest amount of actual work possible and making everyone feel uncomfortable while he was there.

When the school year ended and he headed off for the summer with his mother, Nathan didn't know who was happier, Mitch, Katie or himself.

And now Mitch was back, but this time he was going to be where nobody had to deal with him—in the basement, scanning and digitalizing the archives, thus killing two birds with one stone. Vince had purchased the equipment the previous year, but no one in the office had time to do it. Perfect solution for everyone.

Nathan explained to Mitch what he'd be doing while the kid stared back at him stonily. "Do you understand?" Nate finally asked.

"Yeah."

"Chip's already down there printing photos. He'll show you how to run the equipment and then you're on your own."

Nathan watched Mitch descend the basement steps with the air of someone who was going to have to do something about this situation. Though he understood very well why Vince wanted Mitch to work, Nathan truly wished he wasn't the lucky guy in charge of transforming Prince Mitch into a hardworking employee.

Mitch paused three steps down and looked back. "This'll be my only job this semester?"

"Yeah."

"I'll sure learn a lot about running a paper," he said snidely.

"You want to run a paper, Mitch?" Nate had heard that the kid actually wanted to be a doctor, probably for the prestige and the money.

"Not really."

"Then I guess this'll work for both of us."

As soon as Mitch had disappeared, he returned to his office. He'd barely brought up the screen when Joy came in with a typed article in one hand.

"Callie McCarran just dropped this by. You might want to take a look," she said in a tone indicating she was aware of the possibility that he wouldn't. "It's pretty good."

Nathan gazed at her over his glasses. Joy held the article out. "Read it."

He leaned back in his chair and did as she asked, reading Callie's take on Denise Logan. It was well crafted, but he expected nothing less from Callie. She'd caught the essence of what it was like to be a formally trained, young female firefighter on a volunteer crew of older men. He knew for a fact that his father, as fire chief, had given Denise fits and she had done the same to him.

"Good article," he agreed. His dad was going to hate it.

"You're going to reject it."

"No." He tossed the article onto a side table and went back to his computer. Joy stood where she was for a long moment, but when he refused to look up, she finally retreated.

THE PHONE RANG at 6:30 A.M. It had to be a wrong number. Callie had lain awake deep into the night and had finally fallen asleep sometime in the early hours of the morning. The last thing she needed was some jerk who couldn't dial right waking her up. She grabbed the phone to stop the ringing, rolling over onto her back as she said hello in a voice that sounded as if she'd been out carousing for most of the night.

"Miss McCarran?"

Callie's eyes popped open. Not a wrong number. "Yes?"

"This is Nelda Serrano from Wesley High. Would you be available to sub today?"

"I…uh…don't think I have the license yet."

"It came into the district office yesterday. Your personal copy should arrive soon."

"Okay. Sure." This was what she'd signed on for. "What time do I get there?"

"You'll be subbing for Mr. Lightfoot, one of our English teachers, and you'll need to be here no later than seven forty-five. Come to the office when you arrive."

"Will do. Bye."

Callie got out of bed and went into the bathroom, squinting at herself in the mirror. Was this really a good idea?

It was a paycheck and she wouldn't mind one of those. Besides, as a serial temp, she was used to jumping in and fearlessly doing jobs with which she had only a passing familiarity. She couldn't remember a job, though, that caused her such anxiety prior to arriving on-site. Usually she needed to see equipment she had no idea how to run—state-of-the-art copy machines and such—before she felt any real anxiety.

It was the kids.

What did she know about handling kids? And it didn't help matters when she recalled classes during her own school days where the sub had been rather viciously terrorized. Had she taken part in those attacks? She certainly hoped not, but her memory was hazy. She did remember enjoying the spectacle…*oy.*

What had those subs done to provoke attack? she mused as she brushed her teeth. They'd shown vulnerability. Callie wouldn't do that. No vulnerability.

An hour after the call, Callie parked the sputtering Neon in the faculty lot, hoping she qualified, and walked through the nearly empty halls to the office. Mrs. Serrano was waiting for her.

"Thank goodness. If you hadn't been available, then the principal would have had to cover the class, which would have put me in charge of entertaining the discipline cases until he got back to the office."

"You don't like being the hammer?" Callie asked as she accepted a stack of papers from Mrs. Serrano.

"Not one bit." The woman took a set of keys out of a metal cabinet and handed them to Callie. "You turn these in before you go home. Dismissal time for teachers is three-thirty."

"Got it."

"I'll introduce you to some teachers in the neighboring rooms who can help you out. You went to school with Tanya Munro, I think, and your neighbor across the hall is Dane Gerard. The kids call him Great Dane." Callie was curious to see what a guy called Great Dane looked like.

They stopped at a door around the corner and down the hall from the office—the room where Callie had had history class back in the day. Mrs. Serrano let Callie open the door, perhaps testing to see if she could manage, because the old lock was a touch sticky. Callie prevailed and entered the room.

Chaos. There were messy stacks of paper on every available surface. Piles of books. Old newspapers. Contents of the basket marked Turn In were heaped almost as tall as Callie, it seemed.

"Mr. Lightfoot is one of our more free-form teachers."

"I, uh, can see that." Callie started toward the desk that would be her home base for the remainder of the day.

"And, well…" She turned back to see Mrs. Serrano still hovering near the door, as though she wanted to get away quickly after delivering more bad news. "I'm not sure there's a lesson plan."

Callie's eyes must have filled half of her face. A step-by-step plan was an absolute necessity. "I…" She couldn't back out now. Could she? She might be able to push past Mrs. Serrano and outrun her down the hall….

"No worries," the woman said quickly. "All the teachers have contingency plans in their file cabinet in case of unexpected absences such as this."

"Was there an emergency?"

"Just a touch of the flu." Callie got the

feeling that Mrs. Serrano wasn't buying Mr. Lightfoot's story. "He plans to be back tomorrow."

"Is it normal not to have a lesson plan?"

Mrs. Serrano let out a telling sigh. "It is for Mr. Lightfoot, but in general, no. Why don't you just…" she sucked in a breath through her teeth "…check the top file drawer. There should be a red folder in there."

Callie could almost hear the woman's silent plea *Please be there, please be there* as she slid the drawer open. The red folder was there. Callie pulled it out, held it up. The secretary let out a sigh, then walked across the room to the cluttered desk.

"Wonderful. Now here's the lesson-plan book." Mrs. Serrano pulled a light green binder out from under a stack of creative-writing journals on the corner of the desk. "And there's the grade book. Take attendance in that. The symbols are marked in the front." The secretary's head jerked up as the phone in the office started ringing. "I need to get back to the phones. Tanya and Dane aren't here yet, but when they do arrive—"

"I'll introduce myself. Thanks, Mrs. Serrano."

A moment later, the secretary was gone. Callie opened the red folder. It contained word search puzzles. Okay. So far so good. She checked the lesson plan book and found the pages were blank for that week. Not so good. The grade book thankfully had names written in it, but no seating charts. She remembered hating them as a student, but right now they seemed like a very good idea. No luck.

Callie sat down behind the messy desk. She had no idea what grade she was teaching, but she had word searches, a grade book with names in it and the will to survive. What more did she need?

Dane Gerard, a tall man with sandy hair and a handsome face, leaned in the door to introduce himself. When he saw Callie he came on into the room. Callie was familiar with the drill. Small town, new single woman.

"Do you need help with anything?" he asked, shaking his head in commiseration as he surveyed the room.

"What grade am I teaching?"

His blue eyes came back to her. "Sophomores. They're harmless."

Harmless to him maybe. He was used to them.

"How about seating charts?"

"Phillip doesn't believe in them."

Good for Phillip. "Any helpful hints?" She was certain she'd have many questions as soon as the school day started, but she didn't know the specifics yet.

"Watch your back?"

Callie smiled in spite of herself. "Thanks."

"Just take attendance using these slips," he held up a pad that had been sitting on the podium, "hand out the word-search puzzles and watch them work. That's all you have to do." There was a glint in his eyes as he said "It'll be fine. Honest. The first time is the hardest, but once you get to know the kids, it's a snap."

"I have no choice but to believe you." She leaned back against the white board, determined to relax. "So what do you do around here?"

Dane settled a hip on the desk and explained that he coached both boys' and girls' basketball and used to be a player himself. Now he taught algebra and calculus. He was also quite full of himself, but considering the circumstances, Callie thought it best to disregard that. She might need him soon.

The bell rang and Callie jumped. Dane pushed off from the desk.

"Give a yell if you need help," he said as he crossed the classroom. The first student came in the door just as Dane went out. "Ready or not, here they come."

"Or not," Callie muttered to herself.

She went to stand by the door because it seemed like the thing to do. The students continued to file into the room, eyeing her as if taking her measure. Callie was careful not to appear perky or enthusiastic, which she remembered as being sub-attack triggers. Instead she did her best to radiate quiet confidence.

Almost all of the boys were taller than she was and the majority of the girls better dressed. Callie's yellow camp shirt and denim skirt seemed bland next to heeled ankle boots, skinny jeans and tops that in many cases were cut just a wee bit low. And everybody smelled good. She'd forgotten the maintenance that went into high school.

"Are you a sub?" a boy with two lip piercings asked as he sauntered past without waiting for an answer.

"You're new," commented a girl with a

stylishly draped scarf who plopped down in the desk next to the door. She inspected Callie's outfit as if she were Heidi Klum judging a runway contest.

"Actually, I went to school here."

"Oh," the girl replied, obviously less than impressed. Callie couldn't really blame her, but she felt deflated.

By the time the second bell rang to start class, most of the students were in their desks, but a few were still milling around, talking to each other.

"Take your seats," Callie said, remembering hearing her own teachers say that about a million times. What else had they said? The kids settled and she stared out over approximately thirty expressionless faces. Everyone was waiting for her to do something. Oh, boy.

"Mr. Lightfoot left some work," she said with authority.

"Word searches?" one of them asked.

"You got it," Callie replied.

"Who are you, anyway?" a tall girl near the front said.

"I'm…uh…Ms. McCarran." She'd forgotten to write her name on the board and she wasn't going to do it now. She knew better than to turn her back on them.

"You'd better take attendance." The only boy in the room shorter than she was pointed to the pad Dane had showed her.

"Right." Attendance. Callie began, sometimes having to repeat names two and three times before she heard the response. She was beginning to think they were doing it on purpose. *Quiet confidence.* She handed the word searches to the short boy and asked him to give them out. He'd barely gotten started when the classroom door burst open and a big kid in baggy pants and a black T-shirt strode in. He dropped his books on the desk with a loud bang and then jammed himself into the seat, his legs sprawling in front of him. He was a good five minutes late.

"Excuse me," Callie said sharply, before she noticed a couple of kids in the front row shaking their heads.

"That's Junior," one of them whispered, as if it explained everything.

"Oooh-kay," Callie said softly. Junior sat and stared into the distance while the rest of the students either got out pencils and started the word search or took a cue from their gigantic classmate and stared into space.

With the exception of Junior's grand entrance, the period passed without incident and Junior left more quietly than he had arrived, but Callie remained on edge, waiting for…she didn't know what. But whatever it was, she wanted to be ready.

The rest of the classes proved livelier, with chattier kids, possibly because they were finally waking up, and more personal questions, which she deflected with dry replies before she managed by some miracle and a lot of bluffing to get the students working or quiet. She had a few behavioral problems, but faced them down; a few boys who tried to hit on her, which she ignored. One helpful girl told her she didn't need to be so jumpy. Callie hadn't realized it showed, and made an effort to tone down her jumpiness.

Tyler Michaels, the guy who'd leered at Denise Logan in the café during Callie's interview, was in one of her classes. Other than acting like an overly confident rich-kid-chick-magnet, he hadn't been any kind of problem. But seeing him reminded her that Denise worked at the school in some tucked away office. Callie would have said hello earlier if she'd remembered, but she'd been thinking of little except surviving the day when she'd first arrived at the school.

When the teacher dismissal bell rang at three-thirty, Callie returned her keys to the office.

"Did you have a good day?" Mrs. Serrano asked politely.

"Pretty good," Callie replied. Would she rather be a temp in an office? A seasonal store worker? A gofer/number cruncher during tax season? A backup butcher in a slaughter-house? You bet. Unfortunately, those jobs were not available. So subbing it was. At least for now.

"Is Denise Logan here today?"

"She was," Mrs. Serrano replied. "Her day ends at two o'clock."

"Oh, that's right."

"Can I give her a message?"

"No," Callie said. "I'll see her next time I'm here."

The Neon barely made it across town. And Wesley was not a very big town. She would have been sunk had she been in San Francisco or Denver. Callie had to get the car in to R&M Auto soon. Her two-hundred-dollar lease was turning out to be a bad investment.

When she got home, she took off her school clothes and tossed them in a heap in the closet. The school had no air-conditioning and the denim skirt and yellow cotton camp shirt were gross. She slipped into her tech pants, a cami and sandals, then went out the back door to get her bike. It wasn't exactly where she'd left it. Either gremlins or Hobarts had been here. Shaking her head, she wheeled the contraption out the back gate into the alley and started the ten-block walk to Nathan's house.

She'd walked only a few blocks when a car came up behind her, traveling slowly. Callie automatically moved up onto the sidewalk, but the engine continued to purr behind her. She cast a glance over her shoulder and saw a teenager driving one hell of a sports car.

"Hey," the kid called out the passenger window. "Didn't I see you at the school today?"

"Maybe," Callie said without slowing. The car edged closer to the side of the street, still shadowing her.

"It's hot." He said the word *hot* in a way that set Callie's teeth on edge. "I can give you a...*ride* to wherever you're going."

Oh, yeah. This kid thought he was a smooth one. "No, thanks."

"You sure?"

"I'm sure." Callie looked over at him again and suddenly recognized the kid—or rather she recognized him as being related to the boy who had annoyed Denise during their interview. This had to be Tyler Michaels's older brother, Mitch. Well, he wasn't going to harass her—even if he was Vince Michaels's kid.

"Positive," Callie called, putting her head down and walking as fast as she could with the disabled bike. The car continued to follow her.

"It must be hard pushing that bike. How about I push the bike and you drive the car?"

"How about you drive away and leave me alone?" Callie replied sharply.

To her surprise, Mitch Michaels laughed appreciatively.

"Have it your way. I'll see you around."

"Not if I see you first," Callie muttered as the blue sports car cruised down the street and around the corner.

NATHAN WAS IN THE GARAGE, cleaning the grease off a gear. The radio was on, playing oldies, and he hadn't heard her walk up the cement driveway in her rubber-soled sandals. She stood for a moment, watching him work, a frown of concentration pulling his dark eyebrows together. In spite of the heat, he was wearing long pants. She recalled the days when all he wore were cutoff jeans, slung low on his hips. He'd thought he was such a twig, but Callie had appreciated the long lean muscles that came from hundreds of miles put on his bike. And though he was still lean, he was anything but a twig. The muscles in his forearms flexed as he worked, making her even more aware of just how attractive he'd become.

And then he looked up, his blue eyes connecting with hers and for one brief second she felt as if she was eighteen again and in love with Nathan Marcenek. But his expression clouded and the moment was lost.

Callie wanted it back. She felt an odd welling of sadness and regret, very much like she'd been feeling as she mourned for Grace. She started pushing the flat-tired bike into the garage, her own muscles flexing with the effort. Somewhere in that tall, muscular body was her old friend Nate Marcenek. Yeah, she'd screwed him over, but she wanted to make amends. She wanted her friend back.

CALLIE MANHANDLED THE BIKE with its two flat tires into the garage, a V of sweat between her breasts and damp, dark blond tendrils curling around her face. She brushed the hair away from her forehead with her wrist.

"You pushed it all the way from your house?"

"I needed the exercise."

He didn't think so. She was fit and firm. Every part of her.

"Thanks for doing this," she said, with a tentative half smile. She must have noticed his lack of response, though, because after a few seconds the smile faded.

He felt crummy, treating her like this, but he needed to stay in control. He needed to stop feeling this pull toward her, as if she was the Callie he'd fallen in love with. He studied her old bike. And it was indeed Callie's old bike. The Trek 920. He probably still had parts for it in his heap of extra bike paraphernalia.

"It's been in the shed for over a decade," she said.

"A rough decade from the looks of it."

"The shed isn't totally weatherproof," she agreed. "Dust in the summer, moisture in the winter."

He put a hand on the tattered bar extenders and Callie let go as he examined the patient.

"I'm going to have to order some parts."

"All right. Just tell me how much it costs."

"You can count on it." Twelve years ago he wouldn't have dreamed of charging Callie. But that was twelve years ago and so much had changed.

Callie wandered over to the wall where he had his bikes hanging—two mountain bikes and a road bike. "These are nice. You've come up in the world, Nate."

"One of the perks of being steadily employed."

"I wouldn't know about that."

He looked up from the gears, which were impacted with dried grease and dirt. "Have you ever been steadily employed?"

She shrugged. "Not that I recall."

"So just freelancing and temp jobs."

"I haven't gone hungry yet."

"Amazing."

"I like to be able to move on when I need to." The comment hung in the air and for a moment they stared at each other, Callie silently daring him to go ahead and say something snide about her moving on, and Nate wondering if he should.

"Must be nice," he said instead, taking the high road, since lately he'd been spending too much time on the low.

"No complaints," Callie replied hollowly. She fixed her gaze on the bikes, but he didn't think she was seeing them.

Oh, well. He went back to the gears. He'd have to take the assembly apart and clean one component at a time.

"Speaking of temporary jobs, I substitute taught today," she said conversationally.

"No kidding?" He'd had no idea she'd been considering something like that. "What class did you sub for?"

"Sophomore English." She gave the front tire of the road bike a lazy spin, then turned back to him. "I'd say of all the jobs I've had, subbing is one of my least favorites. I've never had to watch my back like this before. Kids are scary."

"What else *have* you done?" Nate asked, reaching for the tool kit, remembering how she'd evaded this question the last time he'd asked.

"A little of everything."

She was good at evasion. "Do you need the bike soon?" Nathan asked. "I'm going to have to order a new derailleur."

"Whenever you have time."

He got to his feet—pretty smoothly, he thought, considering the trouble he some-times had when his damaged muscles seized up. He crossed to his big tool kit.

"What'd you do to your leg?" Callie asked from behind him.

Nathan hoped his spine didn't stiffen visibly. "What do you mean?" he asked casually, opening the lid and plunging a hand inside.

"You were moving stiffly when I saw you at the fire, and you're still stiff."

"Just a muscle problem."

"You know, I found a product that really helps…." When he turned, her voice trailed off, telling him that he was failing in his bid to appear casual and unconcerned. "But I guess you have your own ways to treat muscle injuries."

"Yeah. I've had some experience. Look, Cal," he said, tapping the wrench lightly in his palm. "I'm probably going to have to put your bike aside for tonight. I have some work to edit and I won't be able to do much until I get the parts." *And I want you out of here in case you can still read me as well as I can read you.* He didn't want her asking about his leg. He didn't want to deal with her finding out.

"Well, then, I guess I'll be going."

"Guess so."

Callie smiled with false brightness, then started walking down the driveway. Nathan watched her go, thinking that once upon a time he might have offered her a ride.

CHAPTER SEVEN

NATHAN'S PHONE RANG at midnight, waking him up from a sound sleep. He answered without checking the number.

"Well, you missed out." Suzanne sounded ticked.

"I kind of thought I might have," he agreed, rolling over on his back in bed and dropping an arm over his eyes.

"Because you didn't send in an application packet?"

"Yeah. That's pretty much why."

Suzanne sighed. "Aren't you even tempted to get back into the game?"

Nathan's mouth twitched. "I'm in the game."

"You're in the minors. Will you at least come up to the city to visit for a few days sometime?"

"Like when the paper doesn't need to be edited?"

"Like when you take a vacation." There was a pause before she said suspiciously, "You've been there over a year. You do take a vacation, don't you?"

Nathan let his silence answer. "Damn it, Nathan. You *are* nuts."

"Let me know if something else opens up."

"When haven't I?" Suzanne asked with a sniff. "For all the good it does. A lot of wasted time and effort—"

"So how are *you* doing?" Nathan cut into her rant before she warmed up.

"Fair to middling," Suzanne responded in a normal tone. "I take a vacation every now and then, you see…." And the rant was on again.

Nathan hung up a few minutes later, smiling in spite of himself and having promised to consider the vacation idea.

Truth be told, he wouldn't mind getting away. He was busy here in Wesley, and near family, but…he was restless. His dad would tell him he was a damned fool for questioning a near-perfect situation, but Nathan couldn't shake the feeling that maybe he wanted more than the same old stressful thing, day in and day out.

At one time he'd wanted a more adventurous life, less certainty in his days—right up until the world had exploded around him. Did he still want that?

What would he have done if the Wesley job hadn't opened up while he was recuperating?

CALLIE SPENT THE NEXT two days at the high school, substituting for shop class. She'd almost backed out when she'd discovered the subject, but Mrs. Serrano informed her that shop became a study hall when the instructor was absent. Apparently the teacher, Mr. Carstensen, who'd been there when Callie had attended school, didn't want the uninitiated supervising kids armed with power tools. Callie appreciated his farsighted approach to substitute teacher safety.

The Neon had made the trip to the high school grudgingly both days, but thankfully, Callie managed to snag a cancellation slot at R&M Auto. She just hoped the car lasted the two more days until the appointment so she didn't have to hire a tow truck.

Shop class was easier to manage than the other classes she'd subbed for at the high school—perhaps because of the teacher fear factor. Fear of Mr. C., not herself. She spent the time watching kids pretend to study—although a few actually did appear to be focusing on the words in front of them—and outlining some ideas for her next interview. The doll maker. He was a guy who'd learned to sew in the military, during the Vietnam War, though she didn't know in what capacity. Now, with the help of the Internet, he was making a living selling the folk dolls he'd once made as a hobby.

Her article about Denise had appeared in last week's paper, and Callie had yet to catch up with her to find out if she'd been satisfied. Callie had hoped to see her the last day she subbed for shop class, but Denise had been gone by the time she'd dropped the keys off.

Dane had been in the office, though, and walked Callie to her car, where he asked if she wanted to stop at the café for a malted. She'd laughed, but turned him down.

"I'll have you know," he said with a glint of humor in his blue eyes, "I don't give up easily. I'm a competitor."

"I'll keep that in mind," Callie said drily as she yanked the Neon's door open.

"See you next time you're here, which will probably be when? Tomorrow?" Dane propped a foot against her tire.

"As a matter of fact, yes."

"Then I guess," he said with a charming smile, as he stepped away from the car, "I'll see you soon."

Callie pulled out of the lot a few seconds later, not exactly certain how she felt about the Great Dane. But it was nice to have a guy treat her well for a change. Too bad it wasn't the right guy.

"Whose piece of crap bike is this?" Seth edged around the bike as if he might catch a disease from it.

"Callie's," Nathan said from where he was working on his own bike.

Seth squinted at him from across the garage. "Why do you have Callie's bike? You two hooking up again?"

"Hardly."

"Hey, no one would blame you for taking a shot," Seth said, frowning as he ran a finger over the tattered rubber on the bar ex-

tenders. "I mean, yeah, she burned you, but
you know the score now, so you can—" he
shrugged "—score."

"Maybe I don't want to score."

"Then I feel very, very bad for you."

Nathan opened the door to the kitchen and
Seth followed him inside, going straight to
the fridge for a beer. He was there to discuss
their father's last doctor's visit, as soon as
Garrett arrived.

Seth popped the top and drank deeply
before wiping the foam off his mouth with
the back of his hand. He looked as if he
wanted to give advice on scoring, but fortunately, Garrett showed up then, tapping on
the side door before coming into the kitchen.
Being the older, more mature brother, he
actually nodded at the fridge and asked,
"May I?" before opening it.

"Help yourself," Nathan said as his
brother emerged with two bottles, one of
which he pressed into Nate's hands.

Fortified by Stella Artois, the brothers
settled at the kitchen table for the John
Marcenek powwow.

"I'll be surprised if he goes back to the
doctor willingly," Seth said. "I had a bitch of

a time getting him there, because he hadn't been taking his medication and he was shifty about it." He took a pull from the bottle. "I'm glad my turn's over."

Nathan muttered a curse. "Maybe we'll have to start double teaming."

"Maybe," Seth agreed. "Anyway, he's not been taking his meds because they make him tired. And the one he really needs leads to constipation. The old man isn't putting up with that shit—no pun intended—so he quit taking them. His blood pressure is through the roof. I think the doc shamed him into going back on the meds, but short of handing him the pills and doing a finger sweep after he takes them, I don't know what we can do."

"Well, that is good news," Garrett said, setting his beer aside. "Where's the Scotch?" He pushed his chair back.

"Don't you have shift tonight?" Nathan asked as Garrett opened the cupboard above the fridge.

"I traded." He pulled out the Laphroaig.

"No," Nathan said. "That's for me. Go for the cheap stuff."

Garrett reluctantly put the bottle back and pulled out the Speyburn.

"Better," Nathan said, turning back to Seth, who was watching Garrett.

"You're the one who went for the free rent," Seth said. "With privilege comes responsibility."

"Bite me." Garrett set the bottle down along with three shot glasses. He'd jumped at the chance to live in the house next door that had been a rental unit while the brothers were growing up. John had rented the house cheap to anyone who passed muster—and agreed to watch the boys while he was on night shift. After Seth had graduated high school, John had stopped renting the second house, tired of the repair work that was part of being a landlord, and when Garrett had come back to town after police academy, he'd happily moved into it.

Now he wasn't so happy.

"I can't handle Dad single-handedly."

"We're not asking you to do that. We're asking you to see that he takes his meds every day."

"Fine." He looked up at Nathan. "Whose crappy bike is that in the garage?"

"Callie's."

"You aren't—"

"None of your freaking business. All right?"

"He's not," Seth said, as he turned his shot glass upside down. Like their father, he was a beer man through and through.

Nathan muttered a curse. "Okay, here's the deal. Garrett, you make sure he's still on his meds. I'm going to drop by and explain that if he doesn't do as the doctor asks, then there's no way he's passing next year's physical and he's off the fire crew."

No one argued with him. Nathan was always the guy who handled the rough stuff with his dad, because he was the one who was used to being yelled at.

"What does Seth do?" Garrett asked after taking a slow sip from the shot glass.

"Seth stops by daily to cheer him up."

"Cool." Seth lifted his beer.

"And to make him lose thirty pounds."

Seth sneered. "Oh, yeah. I can do that."

"Make him walk with you. Maybe we can buy him a bike."

"With a jumbo reinforced frame," Seth said morosely.

"Whatever it takes."

CALLIE RECEIVED HER FIRST substitute request from the elementary school, and discovered that sixth graders weren't as intimidating as sophomores, but they were more exhausting. In an odd way, though, they seemed more mature than the sophomores. Maybe it was because they were still kids for the most part, acting their age instead of trying to act like they were Callie's peers.

The sixth-grade teacher, Mr. Jones, had left copious notes. Callie knew what time to start a lesson, what time to finish it. And if she hadn't had notes, she would have had Sienna, the Helper Girl. Helper Girl was fine in the beginning, but by the end of the day she was beginning to grate on Callie's last nerve. Callie sucked it up, though. She had a feeling that any kid who acted like this had issues elsewhere in her life. Who was Callie to add to them?

After school she had dismissal duty, which involved standing on the play field and encouraging the kids to go home. Sienna was there by her side.

"What grades are the Hobart kids in?" Callie asked, spotting her little neighbors playing on the swing.

"Lucas is in fourth and Lily is in fifth.

They're weird," Sienna added conversationally.

Do you mean weird like hanging with a teacher after school instead of going home?

"We're all a little strange," Callie said drily, making Sienna laugh.

"You're not. You're nice."

Not according to the people at Grace's memorial service.

"Oh," Sienna said excitedly. "There's my mom!" A shiny pickup pulled up behind the school. "Bye, Miss McCarran! I hope you come back!"

"Bye, Sienna. Thanks for the help today."

The girl spun around to wave, then ran to the truck. The woman driving looked sane and happy to see her daughter. Okay, maybe it was hard to tell who had issues and who didn't. Maybe Sienna had been born helpful and needy.

The Hobart kids had disappeared while Callie was waving to Sienna, and the rest of the students were beginning to drift off the playground, meeting parents or walking home. Callie glanced at her watch. Five more minutes to freedom.

A long five minutes. It was blazing hot

standing out on the play field, but eventually Callie got into the oven that went by the name of Neon, and the little car coughed its way to the repair shop. She had a brief consultation with the mechanic, who promised to call as soon as he had a diagnosis, then she declined his offer of a ride and walked home. Quite possibly one or two of her sub checks would be going toward the repair of a car she didn't even own. That was foolish, but she would be even more of a fool to head out across the Nevada desert in a car that sounded like the Neon. When she left town, that was.

The house seemed quiet after spending the day with twenty-four sixth graders. Callie shucked off her school clothes and put on a tank top and khaki shorts. She dropped ice cubes into a glass, filled it with water and headed out to the shade in the backyard rather than turning on the noisy old air-conditioning unit.

She could hear the Hobart kids playing in the lot on the other side of the cedar fence. They didn't have many toys scattered in their yard, but they did seem to get a lot of mileage out of the baseball.

Callie had yet to see an adult on the

premises other than the very blonde woman she assumed was the mother, although she had to admit that was probably because she only had a view of the side of the house unless she was out on the street. The front lawn and porch were obscured by thick honeysuckle bushes, and the carport was on the opposite side.

Funny, though, that she saw the kids a lot and the adults hardly ever. And it still bothered her, especially after she'd once again seen the boy out after dark and the house completely dark. Again she'd knocked and again got no answer.

AFTER FED EX DELIVERED the bike parts to Nate's office, he took an early out and went home to fix Callie's bike. He'd worked until ten the previous evening and took files home with him today, so it wasn't as if Vince Michaels wasn't getting his money's worth and the paper wouldn't come out on time.

It was peaceful tinkering in his garage, with no phones or machines in the background. Plus he was looking forward to getting the bike back to Callie and being done with the obligation.

He loaded it in the back of his small truck

and drove over to Callie's a little after four o'clock. She was walking down the sidewalk from the direction of town when he pulled onto her street. They arrived at Grace's house at the same time.

"Where's your car?" he asked as he hefted the bike out of the truck and set it down. It bounced on its tires.

"Still in the shop. You weren't the only one who had to order parts. The bike looks like new."

"You subbed today." She was wearing makeup and her hair was down.

"Yeah."

"You should have told me," he said, holding the bike by the seat.

"Oh? Why?" she asked innocently. "Would you have given me a ride?"

"Maybe."

"Well, walking isn't that big a deal to me. I just left a half hour early."

"When's the car done?"

"Tomorrow."

"Are you subbing tomorrow?"

"No."

"All right."

"Careful, Nate." He looked up at her. "You sound like you might care."

He just shook head.

"Did you write me up a bill?"

"Not yet."

"Well, until you get round to it, how about dinner or something?" She smiled that old Callie smile, which in turn made him want to smile back.

"I don't think so."

Her face fell. "I won't walk out on you."

"I have work to do, and if you're going to have that next article in on time, so do you."

"It's done. I e-mailed it. Didn't you get it?"

"Uh, no." He didn't want her to know he'd taken off a couple hours early, planning to make up the time tonight, in order to fix the bike once the parts came in. "I've been busy."

She studied his face for a moment, as if trying to figure out what he was thinking. Her eyes shifted to the house behind him as a car with a worn muffler pulled up in front.

"Are you familiar with the Hobart family?" she asked. Nathan glanced over his shoulder to see a tall man in a cowboy shirt and jeans get out of the car.

"They're from up north," he said, turning back to her. "They have a bit of a rep."

"A Hobart family lives in the house across the lot there. The kids come into my backyard sometimes."

"Casing the joint?"

"I hope not. They're nine and eight."

Nathan nodded politely, wondering why he was getting a neighborhood update.

"I don't think their parents take very good care of them."

"Why's that?"

"Because I see them out at night a lot. And the house is dark. I've been wondering if anyone is even home at night with them."

"You've been watching them that closely?"

"I noticed the little boy at the fire where I saw you and Garrett. His sister was dragging him home from it, so yeah, I've noticed."

"Did you talk to the parents?"

"No one answered the door that night."

"You're sure the kids were in there?"

"Yeah."

"But you have no way of knowing whether or not there was an adult."

"Alice said there's a grandma, but I've never seen her."

"That doesn't mean she doesn't exist."

Callie was still staring at the house, a tiny frown drawing her eyebrows together. "I guess."

"Callie?" She glanced back at him, her eyes distant. He recalled some of her crusades in junior high and high school. Once she bit into a cause, she refused to let go. "The Hobarts are not people to mess with."

"Damn, Nate. Are you saying I should ignore what's going on?"

"No. I'll be the first in line to turn someone in for child abuse. I'm saying be sure of your facts. Are the kids overly skinny? Do they have marks on them? Wear raggedy clothes?"

"There are other forms of abuse. Like, say, neglect."

The man who'd gone in the house came out again, with the two kids bounding around him, healthy and energetic. Nathan turned a serious gaze back on Callie, wondering what she saw.

"On a one-to-ten scale, how sure are you that the kids are being neglected? By sure, I mean hard evidence."

Callie pressed her lips together momentarily. "Four," she said grudgingly. "Going by hard evidence."

"Be careful here, Cal."

"Thanks for tuning up the bike for me. I'm looking forward to riding." It was pretty obvious that she wouldn't have minded having someone to ride with. Nate didn't make the offer, because part of him really wanted to and he didn't totally trust that part of himself.

When Callie was like this, when he was able to push past issues aside, then he could see being friends again—or rather, he could if they hadn't once moved beyond friendship. He still felt the sexual attraction to her. Strongly. Had she just come back right after dumping him, yeah, maybe he would have swallowed his pride and tossed his hat back in the ring. Enjoyed the moment. But now when he thought of being her lover, trust issues reared their ugly heads. Logically, he could tell himself that his leg didn't matter. But honestly? It mattered to him. His head was messed up about it. He was ashamed of something out of his control, and he couldn't help feeling that way.

Callie seemed distant as he left, quite possibly because he'd done his best to make her that way. He didn't want to go to dinner with her and he didn't buy her theory that the kids next door were neglected. He'd seen them playing in the lot and they looked like healthy, happy kids.

He had to admit, though, that it bothered him to see Callie distressed, since it didn't fit with his idea of a selfish Callie. Selfish Callie made it easy to stand back, keep his distance. He didn't particularly want that to change.

When he got home, just in case she was onto something, Nathan called Garrett and asked him what he knew about the Hobart family. His answer was exactly what Nathan had expected. They kept to themselves, and if no one bothered them, they didn't bother anybody.

"Callie's concerned about the kids." Nathan opened a cupboard. He hadn't shopped lately and didn't have much selection. Instant macaroni and cheese, or soup.

"How so?"

"She says they spend a lot of time unsupervised." He pulled out a can of soup, then put it back. He didn't want to go out and eat alone. Maybe he should have gone to dinner with Callie.

"So did we."

"She seems to think these parents are leaving them alone while they work at night."

"Evidence?"

"That's the sticking point. I think it's all just gut feeling, but if these kids are being left to their own devices…" Nathan pulled a Chinese dinner out of the freezer and popped it in the microwave.

"Remember when she talked you into trying to set the pound dogs free when you were eleven?"

"These are kids, Garrett."

"I'll ask around unofficially, see if anyone's heard anything. I'll check with the school, too. Talk to their teacher."

"Thanks."

"So…spending much time with Callie?"

"I fixed her bike."

"Don't get suckered in again, Nathan."

"Your faith in my common sense is overwhelming." He punched the microwave buttons with unnecessary force.

"I know the power of the double X chromosome."

"Shove it."

CHAPTER EIGHT

WHEN CALLIE GOT HER CALL from Mrs. Serrano, asking her to sub for Dane Gerard while he was away for a basketball game, she made it a point to get to the school early enough to stop by Denise's office and say hello.

"I loved the article," Denise said the moment she saw Callie standing in the doorway of her tiny office. "You did such a good job of getting across the difficulties of my situation without making anyone look bad or me look like a whiner. Very matter-of-fact. I loved it."

"Great," Callie said. Heaven knew she'd written a few articles in her time that weren't so appreciated. And Denise's warmth and sincerity were a nice change from the reception she'd received from many people in town. Although she had to admit that people seemed to be forgetting about her now. She'd bumped into one of Grace's club friends and actually got a cool hello.

"By the way, who are you today?"

"Mr. Gerard. Algebra and calculus. I sure hope he left some word search puzzles…."

Denise laughed. "I doubt you'll have to teach calculus. So you're doing all right with the subbing?"

"Right now I have the utmost respect for people who do this for a living." Callie adjusted her leather backpack on her shoulder. "I'd better be going so I can gear up for the day. I just wanted to say hi."

She'd started toward the door when a thought struck her and she turned back. Denise cocked her head curiously. "Do you notice much about the gawkers when you fight fires?"

"Sometimes."

"Have you ever noticed some young, very blond kids there? Around eight or nine years old?"

"You know, I have. I figured their parents must be serious fire groupies to bring the entire family, but I don't know who they are."

Callie felt a surge of anger. "Thanks."

"Hey," Denise called after Callie had left the office. She reversed course and stuck her head in the door. "Would you like to come out with the staff to The Supper Club Friday after school for decompression?"

"Isn't that for real teachers?"

"It's for anyone who survives a day with kids."

Callie laughed. "I'll probably try to make it."

"No probably. Plan on it. The more teachers get to know you, the more jobs you'll get."

After that day, however, Callie wasn't sure how many more jobs she wanted to get at the high school. Algebra went fine. The sophomores and freshmen were familiar with her, and she'd identified the players.

Calculus, on the other hand, was her first ever upper-classman group. For the most part it was quieter, the kids more on task as they worked on problems Dane had left. But Mitch Michaels was in the class, and he obviously recalled her as the woman with the bike who he'd tried to pick up. He kept making eye contact and smiling in a not-so-innocent way.

At first Callie ignored him, thinking maybe he'd get the hint, but by the end of class she'd had enough. When the bell rang, dismissing school, Mitch left with the rest of the kids, but five minutes later he came sauntering back in.

"Hello, Mitch," Callie said pleasantly, even though she was speaking through her teeth.

"Miss McCarran." He perched his butt on one of the desks, an indication he was in no hurry to leave.

"Do you need something?" She cringed inwardly as the words left her mouth, and for a moment she thought he was going to tell her exactly what he needed. The kid exuded confidence, but it was an unsettling kind of confidence. The kind with sexual overtones that stood the hairs up on the back of her neck.

"No. I just thought I'd drop by and talk. I know subs don't have a lot to do between three and three-thirty."

"Oh, I'm fine all by myself."

Mitch shifted his gaze to the floor for a moment, a slight smile playing on his lips. Then he looked up with a suggestively arched eyebrow. "I'm graduating at semester."

"Then what?"

"School in California. Cal Poly."

"What are you majoring in?" *And what do I have to do to make you go away?* She was getting an uncomfortable vibe.

His leg swung back and forth casually. Callie recognized the brand on his shoe. A pair of those would set her back a couple sub checks. "Premed probably."

"How nice." Callie folded her hands in front of her and stared at him.

"I guess what I'm getting at is that I am eighteen. Legal."

Callie raised her brows in mock confusion and waited. He shifted slightly, but it wasn't out of discomfort. The boy was too comfortable.

"I know your father," Callie finally said. "We played golf together." Kind of. But she was sticking with the half-truth, because what kind of kid hit on someone who'd played golf with his dad?

This kind of kid. One corner of his handsome mouth curved up. "I play golf, too."

"You'd better leave, Mitch."

He didn't argue. Instead, he acted as if that was part of the game. Maybe it would be part of the game if they were living in a 1960s Sandra Dee movie. They weren't, so Callie continued to apply her stony stare until he left the room. When the door clicked shut behind him, she exhaled. No wonder Denise had been so creeped out by Mitch's younger brother, if she'd already had to put up with this.

Callie finished her note and dropped the keys off at the office, glad the day was over and she was done with students. But she wasn't. Mitch was sitting in his shiny blue sports car, parked a few spaces away from the Neon. The driver's side window was open and he smiled at her when she walked past.

If he followed her out of the lot, she was driving straight to the sheriff's office…but he didn't. Callie watched her mirror the entire way home.

Okay, he hadn't done anything except sit in his car, but he'd sure gotten the message across. He wanted to play.

Fat chance.

When Callie pulled onto her street, glad to

be far away from Mitch Michaels, the first thing she noticed was the car parked under the carport of the Hobart house. It would have been hard not to notice it, since it was a hot pink Mustang. The paint was chipped, the bumper dented, but at one time it had probably been a sweet ride.

Later that night there were lights on in the Hobart house. It wasn't exactly lit up like a Christmas tree, but the ground floor had lights on in two rooms. That was promising.

She hoped.

SETH BOUNCED HIS helmet off his thigh as he waited for Nathan to finish the last-minute adjustments to his bike. Nate's Saturday morning ride with his younger brother inevitably became a race, and he needed every advantage.

His injured leg had recovered more than the doctors had hoped, but the nerve and muscle damage were extensive enough that his left leg still had to do more work when he rode. As a result, Seth almost always beat him when they raced around the loop by the river, and being a total brotherly jerk, he also crowed about it. That more than anything endeared his younger brother to Nathan. No sympathy from the kid. Nathan was as uncomfortable with sympathy as he was with his injury.

"Come on," Seth said. "I have a shift later and I want to eat before I go."

Nate popped the wrench back into his tool kit and put the bike back on its wheels. Together they walked to the road and mounted, clicking their shoes into place.

"I have to go back to the office myself."

"You work too many hours."

"Look who's talking. One paying job and two volunteer."

"Yes, but I use my jobs to meet women. Can you say the same?"

No, he couldn't.

"You know," Seth mused, "since you're falling down on the job, maybe I'll find you a woman."

"Yeah, why don't you do that," Nathan said as he put his head down and started to seriously pedal, leaving his brother behind.

"Blonde, brunette or redhead?" Seth called as he caught up and then sailed past.

"Surprise me!" Nathan yelled after him. He heard Seth give a bark of laughter and began to think that perhaps he'd just made a major error. "No blind dates!" he shouted into the wind.

"Too late," Seth called back. "I'm setting something up and if you back out, you'll hurt her feelings."

"Don't…"

Seth slowed until the two bikes were side by side. "Trust me, Nate. It's for your own good. Time for you to get back on the horse."

"No." It had taken almost a year for Nathan to finally accept the twisted and scarred flesh on his leg as part of him, but he still wasn't wild to share. His leg was ugly, and that was a generous assessment, but it worked and Nathan was alive. For that he'd be ever grateful. But he wasn't ready to put himself out there for anyone.

Head down, Seth started pedaling, acting as if he didn't hear him. Nathan poured everything he had into the pedals and finally pulled ahead of the kid as they reached the city limits. They both slowed, Nate sitting up and drinking from his water bottle, squeezing the rest over the back of his neck and chest.

He didn't mention blind dates as he and Seth rode side by side down the nearly deserted street leading to his house. He wasn't going on a blind date; he'd made that clear. And he didn't want to draw any more lines in the sand, because Seth was a guy who dearly loved to cross lines.

CALLIE DIDN'T KNOW WHAT to make of the situation with the kids next door. During the four days the pink Mustang had been there, the lights and TV went on and off during the appropriate hours. But this morning the car was gone and the house was once again dark in the evening. But the kids were there, playing outside until the sun went down.

Was that nine-year-old girl babysitting her brother all night while the mother worked an evening shift at the casino?

So what should Callie do? When did none-of-her-business shift into her moral duty? She was seriously considering calling Child Protective Services, but maybe there were circumstances she wasn't aware of. Maybe the kids went to a neighbor's house evenings. That would explain the dark house and also let Callie believe these children were being cared for. She needed to believe that.

Callie hadn't been able to find someone to mow her lawn, so in a fit of desperation, she dragged Lawn-Boy out and fought a few rounds with him, losing on a TKO when she pulled the starter cord for the umpteenth time and the handle broke into two pieces, sending her flying back onto her butt with a piece of plastic clutched in her hand. The other part of the handle was still attached to the rope, preventing it from disappearing inside the engine, and Callie decided to admit defeat before she ended up paying to fix something else.

But if she was going to sell this house, she had to mow the lawn. Alice was no help, with her xeriscape gravel, rock and succulent landscaping. Callie was going to have to suck it up and go ask the neighbors for recommendations. What happened to kids who put flyers up at the grocery store? Were they all home playing video games and surfing the Web?

And then to add to the joy that was her life, Mitch Michaels had actually called her landline and asked her on a date that morning, pointing out that when she wasn't working, it wouldn't be a conflict of interest. After turning him down flat and suggesting he never call again, she wondered whether he'd asked her on a dare from a friend, to make fun of her, or whether he really wanted a date.

Didn't matter. If he kept bugging her, she was going to call either his dad or the cops. He was eighteen…maybe Garrett could scare some sense into him. Yeah, Garrett, who liked her so much.

Or maybe Mitch had actually gotten the message and was just saving face.

And maybe it was time to leave, to head back to San Francisco. She could drop the Neon off on the way, before it cost her more money. There'd be no Mitch Michaels, no worries about the kids next door, no battles with Lawn-Boy.

No more unsettling attraction to Nathan, who wanted nothing to do with her.

Tempting. Callie leaned her palms on the edge of the sink and looked out the window at the overgrown lawn. Very tempting. But she wasn't going to let a bunch of grass, a cranky hunk of machinery, a horny kid and her ex-boyfriend drive her away before she was damned ready to go.

She raised her gaze to the Hobart house across the lot. Nope. She was staying a while longer.

NATHAN RUBBED HIS FINGERS over his eyes, pushing his reading glasses up on top of his head before tossing them carelessly onto the desk.

It was late. He needed to get home. He'd forgone his evening bike ride to finish up at the office, and now his stomach was growling and he was getting a headache, though he couldn't tell if it was work related or Callie related.

Seth called as Nathan was leaving the building. "I have your blind date set up."

Nate shut the phone and shoved it in his pocket. It wasn't going to do him much good in the long run, but perhaps he could get his hands on some aspirin or Scotch before Seth found him in person.

No such luck. Seth was parked in front of his house when he got there.

"Turning the phone off isn't going to help. There's nowhere you can hide."

"I don't recall giving the blind date an okay," Nathan said, shouldering his way past his brother to unlock his door.

"You said, 'Surprise me,'" Seth countered with a crooked smile. "Surprise!"

"Who is she?" Nathan dumped his day pack, which he used in place of a briefcase, next to the door.

"New girl at the mine. Her name is Gina."

"Do you know her at all?"

"I've talked to her."

"Then why aren't you dating her?"

"She refuses to take me seriously."

"I wonder why?" Nathan said as he went into the kitchen and opened the fridge. "Could it be the Gumby insignia on your hat?"

Seth shrugged as he accepted a beer. "Honestly, she's not my type, and yeah, Gumby may figure into it. She's more serious than the girls I date."

"Why's she at the mine?"

"She's the new human resources person. And she is good-looking."

Nathan twisted off the beer cap, took a long drink, watching his brother the entire time for some kind of tell.

"Brunette. Smart. *Really* good-looking." Seth glanced away, then back at his brother, all playfulness gone from his expression. "It's time, Nate. You need to get out, even if you don't end up in the sack. You can't use your leg as an excuse forever."

"It took *me* a year to get used to it. How can I expect someone else to…" Hell, he didn't even know how to finish the sentence. "It's not an excuse," he muttered, going to the table to flip through the mail. "But it is damned ugly." And the last Nathan had heard, wild one-night stands were about attraction. The Igor leg would surely throw a damper on that kind of an evening. His wild one-night-stand days were over.

"Wouldn't know. I haven't seen it since it was bandaged up."

"And you're not seeing it tonight."

"Rats." Seth punctuated the word with a quick clench of his fist.

They went into the living room and Seth turned on the TV, watching the Food Network as he finished his beer.

"Man, I love Cat Cora," he said as he tossed the remote over to Nathan and stood. "I need to find a woman who cooks. I'm getting tired of living on Oreos and canned soup."

Nathan had dozed off during the final minutes of the *Iron Chef,* so he had no idea whether or not Cat had dominated. He also didn't care.

Seth stopped at the door. "Here's the deal about the date. It's a group thing. The mine bought two tables at the Lions Club Crab Feed. You're invited, and Gina will be there."

"Anybody else showing up stag?"

"You're not stag, Nate. You're with Gina. You'll show up?"

"I guess." Maybe his brothers were right. Maybe it was time to get back on the horse. Or to at least spend some time in the pasture getting reacquainted with the animal.

JOHN MARCENEK WAS WORKING on his pickup when Nathan went to see him on Saturday after putting in a half day at work.

"Here to check on me?" John said from beneath the chassis, when he heard the footsteps come into the garage. He rolled out from under the truck on his mechanic's board and sat up, wiping the grease off his hands with the rag he pulled out of his coverall pocket. "Thought you'd be at work. Isn't it Seth's turn to babysit?"

"Are you taking your pills?"

"Yes." He looked shifty, but Nathan had no choice but to believe him.

"Then I'm not here to babysit. I thought you might want to grab a bite."

"Can't. Chester's coming over." John smirked. "That lets you off the hook and now you can go do whatever."

Nathan hooked his thumbs in his belt loops. "I'm not on the hook, Dad."

John stared down at the wood he was sitting on for a long moment. "Look. I appreciate what you guys are doing, but back off, all right? I can take care of myself. I'm only sixty-five, for cripe's sake."

"Yeah."

John got to his feet, his movements awkward because of his bulk. "I heard you're sniffing around Callie McCarran again."

His father had always been a master at changing topics. His favorite technique was to touch a sore spot if he could find one, thus putting his opponent on the defensive.

"Where'd you hear that?" Nathan asked

evenly. Because if it was from Seth or Garrett, he was going to have to rearrange their faces.

"Around."

"If it's true, then it's none of your business. And if it's not…same thing, Dad."

"I don't want to see you make an ass out of yourself," John grumbled as he walked over to the workbench and put the ratchet on its place on the Peg-board. "It's one thing to do it when you're eighteen. Another when you're pushing thirty."

Nathan clenched his teeth. He was not going to rise to the bait. It was one thing to get pushed around by your old man at eighteen, another to be pushed around at thirty.

"Besides that," John said, his back to his son as he pumped waterless hand cleaner into his palm, "I don't think she's the kind that'll take the leg well. It'll take a special woman to deal with that."

Nathan just stared at his father's back. What the hell? That was pretty much the last thing he wanted to hear.

"Bye, Dad." He headed for his rig. John said nothing, and Nathan figured his dad had gotten his wish. He was alone. No more babysitter. Had it been Seth who'd stopped by, they would have ended up playing cribbage. Garrett would have dived into the truck engine with him. Nathan got a lecture on why no woman would want him.

He went home, changed into his bike clothes and took off. Why did his dad still bother him so much?

His dad was his dad, and Nathan was going to have to live with the fact that he was not the favorite son. Or the second favorite.

He rode an extra five miles up the soft dirt of the river road, blissfully alone and out of sight of the highway, before he turned around at the party spot where he and his brothers had done things their sheriff father wouldn't have been thrilled about. He came to the fork where the left turn led down to the campsite by the river, and the right one led up a steep hill to the highway. He started up the hill, glancing down at the river as he climbed, then stopped pedaling when he saw the bike lying on its side, abandoned in the middle of the campground.

It looked like Callie's.

He coasted back down the hill. It *was*

Callie's bike. Lying on its side near the stone fire ring. He came to a stop next to it, looked around, his heart beating faster.

He laid his own bike on the ground next to hers, dropped the helmet beside it and headed for the trail leading to the river.

At first he didn't see anything, but then he spotted her in the water, next to the rickety old fishing dock, her head tilted back and eyes closed, her hair floating out behind her.

She was safe and she was beautiful.

Callie had always been beautiful, maybe even more so because she'd always seemed unaware of it. Or perhaps she didn't care. She'd rarely worn makeup when they'd been together, did little more to her hair than pull it into a braid or a ponytail. Now it was shorter, more stylish, but except for the time he'd dropped off the bike, and the first meeting in his office, it had been tied back.

He stood perfectly still on the bank, watching her. Finally he cleared his throat. Startled, Callie spun around in the water. Her expression cleared when she saw it was him.

"What are you doing here?" she asked, standing and wading closer to the shore. As she walked into shallower water, he could see that she was wearing her biking clothes—Lycra shorts and a body-hugging top, which, interestingly, was transparent when wet. He felt ridiculous standing on the shore fully dressed in long athletic pants, too hot for the weather.

"Come on in. The water is wonderful."

"Normal people don't swim in October," he pointed out. The water lapped at her thighs, which were firm and fit from all that walking, biking and trekking she did in the line of duty.

"Thank global warming. It's not usually this hot in October. Why're you here?"

"I saw your bike lying on its side and got concerned."

"It doesn't have a kickstand so I had to lay it down."

"Really?" he asked, as if receiving new and vital information. She hit the heel of her palm on the water, splashing him.

Nathan took a few steps toward the water's edge, leaned down and picked up a flat stone. He tossed it and it skipped six times before sinking.

"You've lost your touch."

"Think you could do better?"

Callie started toward him, water running in rivulets off her body. She stopped in the shallows, considered the pebbles at her feet, then leaned down and picked one up.

He really wished her tank top left a little something to the imagination. Nathan idly dropped his hand and did his best to arrange himself before she looked up.

She smiled at him once she had her stone, and it was hard to tell whether it was in answer to his challenge or because she was aware that she was turning him on. She pulled her arm back, then let the stone go. One, two, three, four, five, six…and a blip.

"I win."

"That last one wasn't a full skip," Nathan said.

"But you didn't have anything past six."

He couldn't argue with that. "Do you have a shirt or something with you?"

"Why?"

"Your breasts are showing through your top."

Callie glanced down abruptly, then looked slowly back at him, checking him out in the process. He hoped by some miracle she missed his hard-on. He knew when her eyes finally hit his face that she hadn't. She smiled.

"Nothing you haven't seen before," she said.

"I thought you might not want anyone else to see them."

"I have a shirt. It's by the dock." She took a step back. "Come into the water, Nate."

Again he shook his head, knowing he was being invited to do more than simply come for a swim.

"You can strip down to your shorts like you used to. I'll never tell."

But she would see a whole lot more of him than he was willing to show.

"I need to get back to town."

"Fine." She took a few steps toward him, slipped and regained her balance without going under. She held out her hand for stability, and the second he reached for it he realized he'd just fallen for the oldest trick on record. The next thing he knew he was off balance and being yanked forward. He landed with a giant splash and then surfaced, spitting water.

Callie laughed. "Man, Nate. You need to sharpen your instincts."

"Maybe I just let you do that," he sputtered.

"I'd like to believe it." She reached to cup his face, smiling up at him as tiny streams of water ran down from her hair. She was going to kiss him. She was going to see just how far she could push this moment.

He put his hands on her wrists before she could press herself against him, held her at a distance.

"I've felt wood before, Nate."

Fine. Let her think he was being modest. Anything was better than her pressing her gorgeous thighs against his wet nylon pants and feeling his hard, twisted wreck of a leg.

Callie took a step back and he released her wrists. "You are going to have one hell of a lonely life, Nate, if you find yourself so unable to forgive. People make mistakes. I made a mistake. I'm damned sorry about it."

"Me, too, Callie." Because if she hadn't made that mistake and hadn't kept making it by refusing to answer his calls and letters, they might have settled down and had a family. Or they might have gone their separate ways, but with closure. And if one of those circumstances had prevailed, he had a feeling he'd be a whole man today—in every way.

As he walked out of the river, his hair and face were already drying, but the nylon clung to his leg. He hoped the damp fabric didn't show too much, or that Callie was too pissed off to notice—which she might well be, since she stayed in the water.

Or so he figured, because he walked up the trail and around the bend to the campsite without looking back.

CHAPTER NINE

CALLIE SAT ON THE DOCK and dried in the late afternoon sun. It was past time to get to work on her research for the next article, but still she sat, hugging her arms around her knees, trying to contain an aching sense of loss that had come out of nowhere when Nate had walked away.

She was going to have to cry uncle on this one. It was beginning to hurt too much, beating herself on the rock known as Nathan Marcenek.

She'd honestly believed that, given time, Nate would come round to her way of thinking, that they could be friends. Maybe even more…in a friendly ships-that-pass-in-the-night sort of way. Except that Nate wasn't going to let it happen.

Today she'd gotten a glimpse of the old Nate, the one she'd loved. A tiny peek, just enough to make everything she'd ever felt for him burst alive again, and then he was gone, leaving her emptier and more alone than ever.

Damn it, she was used to being alone. She thrived on it.

Or rather, she had. Alone didn't feel so good anymore, and that bothered her. A lot.

She'd made some superficial friends since arriving back in Wesley—Denise Logan, Dane Gerard and some other teachers at the high school. Superficial friends were the only kind she ever had. They demanded nothing of her and she returned the favor.

But she had hoped for something different with Nate. She'd wanted him to be a real friend, as he'd once been, maybe a lover, as he'd almost been. And she'd wanted him to ultimately understand when she had to leave, to recognize that wanderlust was part of her and that she simply couldn't stay put very long. Six months had been her record.

What she wanted was selfish, really, and she was simply going to have to give it up.

Callie rose to her feet, brushed the sand and weathered wood splinters off her Lycra shorts and started climbing the trail to where she'd left her bike. She'd call the real estate agent tomorrow, get the ball rolling on the house. The market was dead at the moment, so a sale could take a while. She'd have a place to live while she finished the articles for Vince Michaels—and they were for him, since Nate wouldn't have bought them if she hadn't gone to his boss first. Nate honestly wanted nothing to do with her and it had taken her this long to get the message, loud and clear.

CALLIE WAS WRITING THAT night, late, when she saw headlights pull into the carport at the Hobarts' place. Lights went on inside the house before the car beams were turned off. Someone had been inside waiting.

Callie went to the window. Her living room was dark, the only light coming from her computer monitor, so she wasn't concerned about being caught spying. Mrs. Hobart got out of the pink Mustang, wearing black pants and a white long-sleeved shirt, the casino dealer's uniform, and climbed the stairs. The boy stepped out into the light, holding the screen door open for his mother, who seemed to be halfheartedly scolding him—maybe for being up so late. It was 1:30 A.M.

Callie went back to her computer, but didn't put her hands on the keyboard. What was the best way to handle this? She didn't want to hurt the family, but it was wrong for these kids to be alone at that age until this early in the morning.

The next afternoon Callie walked over to the Hobarts' and knocked on the door. The car was still at the curb, so the mom must be working the five-to-one evening shift. Callie automatically reached for the doorbell, then remembered from her previous visit that it didn't work. Instead, she knocked on the screen door. A dog started yapping, the noise getting closer as footsteps approached. The blonde woman opened the door, weary and far from welcoming.

"Hi. I'm Callie McCarran. Your neighbor across the lot."

The woman nodded, waiting, the frown still pulling her overly plucked eyebrows together.

"I wanted to introduce myself."

She nodded without offering her name, looking out from around the door as if it was a protective barrier. She wasn't making this easy.

"I substitute teach and I've seen your kids at school and in the neighborhood." This wasn't going well, judging from the woman's expression. "If you ever needed a babysitter or anything, I'd be happy to let them stay at my place while you're working."

"Why're you offering to babysit my kids?"

"I just noticed that sometimes they're home alone, and if they needed a place to stay while you were at work—"

"Have you been spying on my kids? How the hell do you know they're home alone?"

Callie couldn't help drawing back at Mrs. Hobart's aggressive tone. Oh, yeah, this was going great.

"Look," the woman continued, "you stay away from the kids and you keep your nose out of my business, or I'll call the sheriff on you."

And wouldn't Garrett have a field day with that?

"My kids are just fine and I *do* have someone who baby sits them when I work—

not that it's any of your business. My mom is here!"

Callie backed away a few steps, but the woman wasn't done. "The last thing I'd ever do is to let them stay with someone who's been watching them! If I..." Her mouth worked for a moment, but words failed her in her rage. Finally she simply slammed the door shut. Callie could hear her heels on the hardwood floor, followed by muffled shouts of "Lily! Lucas! I want to talk to you!"

Callie walked back to her own house, numb and embarrassed and...damn, she didn't know what she was feeling, but it was bad. And if there was a grandmother in that house, she loved the dark.

The next morning, the dream came as it usually did, when Callie wasn't quite fully awake. There was the sharp burning in her nostrils, the images and sensations that she was on the edge of recognizing before fear took over and blurred everything except her need to escape. Hands. Once again she had the impression of hands.

After the first surge of fright brought her to sit up in bed, Callie took slow, steady breaths through her nose until the sensations faded.

Who had triggered the dream this time? Nate or the neighbor? Both encounters had been unsettling, but Nate had hurt her, while the other had merely put her on the defensive. Her bet was on Nate again.

She pushed the covers back and got out of bed.

She'd hoped to write that day, since there'd been no sub call, but the dream always made her writing suffer. She could put words on paper, but there was no flair. It was as if she was afraid to let her mind go, in case it stumbled on a dark secret behind the nightmare. If there was a secret, the original trigger, it had happened before her father's disappearance, because she'd had the dream before she came to live with Grace.

Callie had considered hypnosis at one point, but ultimately decided against it. The dream came and went. If she was dealing with an actual memory, though…well…once recalled, she'd have it forever. Nope. She was going with head in the sand. If her mind was protecting her, she was going to let it do its job.

Half an hour later the landline rang. She

assumed it was the real estate agent, and hoped it wasn't Mitch Michaels again. He hadn't called after she'd shut him down, but he had hung around her room at school the last time she'd subbed, had tried to walk her to her car. He didn't get the concept of no means no.

She picked up the phone and said hello, ready to put the receiver back down again if it was Mitch. Thankfully, the voice on the other end of the phone was deeper and vaguely familiar.

"Hi, Callie. It's Dane Gerard."

"Oh. Hi, Dane." Relieved, she wondered why the heck he was calling. Mrs. Serrano handled the sub calls.

"So, did you enjoy calculus class?"

Callie laughed. "Oh, yes. Tons of fun."

"The kids said you did a great job watching them suffer through their test."

"I'm an educational sadist. What can I say?"

"I was wondering…the Lions Club crab dinner is coming up in a few days and we have an extra chair at our table. An educational sadist would be a wonderful addition."

"Uh…" Did she want to go out with the Great Dane? A picture of Nate walking away from her at the river popped into her head. "Sure. Sounds good."

"Pick you up at, say, six-thirty?"

"How about I meet you there?"

After the briefest of hesitations, Dane said, "That works for me." Callie had a feeling it didn't. He'd been friendly at school and, unlike Mitch, he seemed to understand when to back off. He must have sensed this was one of those times.

That afternoon Callie saw Mrs. Hobart get into her Mustang wearing her casino dealer outfit. The kids continued to play outside after she'd left. Callie kept checking on and off as it grew dark, and eventually the kids disappeared. She didn't see them go inside because her view of the back porch was blocked, but about the time the kids disappeared from the backyard, the television came on inside the dark house. Deduction? Kids were inside watching TV. Another deduction? There was no adult home, regardless of what the mom had said, because there'd been no lights on until the kids had gone inside. The kids were on their

own until their mother got off shift at about
1:30 A.M.

This was wrong.

Callie rebooted her computer, which cast
an eerie blue glow as it came to life in the
dim room. It only took a moment to find the
phone number and address for Child Protective Services in Wesley, and a form to
download.

If Denise hadn't mentioned seeing the kids
at several fires, and if Callie wasn't going to
leave soon, then maybe she would have
waited. Or if the mom hadn't lied. But Callie
knew from asking at school that it could take
weeks for a nonemergency home visit, since
there were only two social workers in the
county. She wanted the kids to have someone
looking out for them after she was gone.

It didn't take long to fill out the form and
print it for delivery the next day. She felt
crummy, because she honestly didn't want
to cause the family trouble. She simply
wanted to make sure a couple of kids were
not being left uncared for.

CALLIE SPENT MOST of her life in casual
clothing, but she could dress up if the

occasion called for it. The Crab Feed was a major Wesley social event, ranking right up there with the high school's annual community harvest dance fundraiser. She'd waitressed at the Crab Feed twice during high school as part of her Honor Society community service, and recalled that people had dressed up. So she would.

She slipped into a black knit shift, one of her classiest travel-proof garments. It wasn't clingy, but it did hug her body, skimming over her curves and ending a couple inches above the knee. The wide boatneck gave the dress an Audrey Hepburn look. Callie put on the same string of fresh-water pearls she'd worn to Grace's memorial, and slipped her bare feet into black ballet shoes. She wished she had her red ones with her, but they were in storage in California.

Hair. Up? Down? Did it really matter? She wasn't trying to entice the guy. She just didn't want to disgrace herself. Down.

Callie took one last look in the mirror before heading out to the Neon. She forced the corners of her mouth up. Oh, yeah, that looked real.

She tried again. Better. The smile disappeared.

Okay, so she wasn't wild about going to a social event right now, but Dane was a nice guy and he wasn't asking for a commitment. It was just a night out.

The parking lot was full when she arrived at the community center, but she managed to squeeze the Neon into a space between a sedan and the grass at the edge of the lot. She was legal. Almost.

Now all she needed to do was find her date, which proved to be no problem at all, since Dane was the tallest guy in the room. He was standing with a small crowd just inside the door, a drink in his hand, wearing a corduroy blazer and khaki slacks, his sandy hair combed to the side. He looked exactly like an ex-jock. Comfortable in his skin, yet ready for a challenge. She really hoped she wasn't that challenge. He spotted her as soon as she walked in, excused himself from the man he was talking to, a local lawyer she couldn't remember the name of, and went to meet her.

"I paid for your ticket," he said with a half smile.

Callie bit back the "that wasn't necessary." He had asked her, after all, and the tickets were outrageously priced. The money went to charity, though, so Callie had been ready to fork it over. "Thank you," she said.

Dane's gaze traveled over her, but he offered no compliment—aloud, anyway. He let the smile in his eyes do the talking. He approved.

"Would you like a drink?"

"Not yet."

"Then why don't we go sit down? I think you know most of the people at our table," he said, putting a light hand at her waist and directing her past the portable bar, where two guys in the Lions' yellow vests were mixing drinks. "Just a few spousal introductions and you're set."

"Great."

They stopped to talk to several people as they traveled to the table, and Dane's hand settled permanently at her waist.

The microphone whistled and the group turned to see Pete Domingo, the high school principal, adjusting the height of the stand. He cleared his throat, then invited them all to be seated. Dinner would be served by lottery and the last table served would receive a bottle of pricey wine.

"Which means we'll be the second-to-last table served," Dane murmured with a touch of humor as he again put his hand on Callie's waist and guided her through the maze of chairs and large round tables to the center of the room, near the dance floor.

As he said, Callie was already familiar with the three high school teachers there—Mr. Lightfoot, the king of chaos, Mrs. Simms and Mr. Carstensen, aka Phillip, Susan and Rick. They would always be Mr. and Mrs. to her. She smiled and said hello as Dane introduced their respective spouses, then took her seat. Dane pushed in her chair, made certain she was comfortable, his fingers brushing along the bare skin of her shoulders more often than necessary.

The first numbers for the buffet line were announced over the loudspeaker and the people at the table next to Callie stood, laughing and congratulating themselves on choosing the correct seats. Callie moved her chair to give them room to file past, and as she did so her gaze zeroed in on Seth

Marcenek two tables away, laughing uproariously. And across the table from him, very preoccupied with a rather beautiful brunette, was Nate. *Oh, good.*

Callie quickly looked away. She should have known he'd be here. The crab dinner was a community-wide social event. She brought her attention firmly back to Mr. Lightfoot, who was telling the story of his recent illness, and feigned rapt interest in blood test screwups.

Did she know the woman sitting with Nate? Was this one of their classmates who had blossomed? If so, she'd done a good job of it. When Callie casually glanced over while arranging her purse on the back of her chair, she saw Nate's dark head tilted toward the woman. When she finished speaking, he laughed, his eyes never leaving hers.

At one time Callie had made Nate laugh and had been on the receiving end of that particular intimate gaze. A long while ago.

A decidedly unwelcome thought came to her. Maybe this woman was the reason he'd backed off at the river. Maybe he was getting involved with someone.

And maybe Callie's stomach shouldn't be tied up in a knot.

Nathan said something to the brunette then, and she smiled and touched his hand. Callie clenched her teeth.

"Wine?"

Dane—*her date,* she reminded herself sternly—was holding the carafe. "Please." She smiled gamely, took a sip and then, as he poured wine into his own glass, she took a larger, more bracing drink.

"So, Callie," Susan Simms said, and all eyes turned to her. Dane's hand slid along the back of her chair and this time his fingers settled lightly on her shoulder. "You're selling the house? Mrs. Serrano said something to that effect today."

"I just called the Realtor."

"Will you be buying another place here?"

Callie almost laughed, but didn't. "No," she said matter-of-factly. "I'll be leaving." Dane's fingers were now firmly gripping her shoulder, his arm around her as if she was his girlfriend. Which she wasn't.

"I'd hate to see you go," he said with an I'm-as-good-off-the-court-as-I-am-on-the-court confidence that made Callie's hackles rise. Dane was different when he was off school property.

"Oh, I'm kind of looking forward to new vistas," she said as she twisted her chair toward him, making it impossible for him to keep his arm around her shoulders.

"And just when I found a dependable sub," Mr. Lightfoot said as the microphone squeaked behind him, calling another table to the buffet line. Dane met Callie's eyes and once again she saw good-humored laughter, as if he thought she was playing hard to get.

What was it with the guys in this town? Couldn't hook up with the one she wanted, and the others were creeping her out.

NATE HATED TO ADMIT that Seth had chosen his blind date well, but he had. Gina Flores was indeed an attractive, intelligent woman whose company he enjoyed, so it seemed unfair that his attention kept wandering over to where Callie sat with that tall teacher/basketball coach. Nathan therefore made certain that his focus was solely on Gina and their tablemates as they waited for their buffet number to be called. He couldn't say that sparks were flying between him and his date, but she was comfortable to talk to and had a great laugh, soft yet throaty.

She explained what she did in human resources, occasionally looking across the table at Seth, who was doing really bad impersonations, as if wondering how he and Nathan could possibly be related. Sometimes Nathan wondered, too, as his brother butchered his attempt at Jack Nicholson. Everyone could do Jack Nicholson.

The time passed pleasantly enough as they waited forever for their food, except once when he gave in and looked at Callie—and saw the basketball coach sliding his hand possessively along the back of her chair. Nate had never particularly liked Dane Gerard and wondered what the hell Callie was doing here with him.

Okay…maybe he wasn't totally over Callie, but he could fake it until she left town, which according to Joy would be soon, since her cousin, the real estate agent, had just been asked to sell the house.

Their table number got called second to last. Nathan kept his attention on Gina as they went through the line, resisting the urge to watch Dane and Callie. When they sat back down with their plates and started cracking crab, Gina asked why he'd chosen journalism when his brothers were both involved in "less cerebral" occupations. Nathan appreciated the way she phrased the question, making it seem for once as if he was the sane one in the family. Definitely the one with brains. He glanced over at Seth, wearing his beat-up Aerosmith T-shirt under a corduroy blazer, and understood why his brother was getting nowhere with Gina.

"My mom wrote," Nate said, surprising himself with the answer.

"Was she published?"

"Oh, no. Journals. Lots and lots of journals." He'd often sat with her and doodled in his own notebooks as a child, and later, after her death, had started journals of his own. Living in terror that his brothers would find them and blackmail him. Or worse.

Gina smiled and worked the last bits of meat out of a claw. "It's funny how our parents' interests shape our lives. Did you ever consciously decide to be like her and write?"

"Uh…no." He hadn't really thought about the connection before, but yeah, writing did make him feel closer to her.

"She must be proud of you."

"She would have been." He supposed. More so than his father, though, who was raucously entertaining the troops on the other side of the room. "She passed away when I was twelve."

"I'm sorry." Gina focused her soft brown eyes on him. "That might be even more of a reason you pursued it."

"Yeah. Maybe." Again, he'd never thought about that before.

"SO HOW'VE YOU LIKED substitute teaching?" Mr. Lightfoot asked. Callie wondered if he was aware of what a chaotic mess his room was and how a simple seating chart would make a sub's life so much easier. She'd found out from the students that he didn't bother with seating charts. They sat where they wanted, and when they had a sub, they also took on whatever identity they wanted. Juvenile, but apparently amusing to sophomores.

"There's more to it than I'd first anticipated."

Dane laughed. "Well phrased. It's more than babysitting."

"So tell us about being a journalist," Mrs. Lightfoot said, leaning closer. "I hear you've traveled all over the world."

"I've been a few places."

"You've written for some well-known magazines. I'm surprised the newspaper isn't taking more advantage of your presence than just those few piddling articles."

"Damned good piddling articles," Dane said.

"Is there some reason you aren't writing more for them?" Mrs. Lightfoot pressed, looking first at Callie, then over Callie's head to where Nathan sat.

Someone had been listening to gossip.

"I have other things to fill my time," she answered, carefully wiping dripping butter off her wrist.

"Like subbing." Mr. Lightfoot chortled as if he'd just told a joke.

Callie smiled weakly, reaching for her water glass, wishing it was gin, when the fire siren sounded, cutting off Mrs. Lightfoot just as she was about to speak. About a dozen pagers went off a split second later.

The room erupted into activity as members of the volunteer firefighters sprang into action. Wives and girlfriends exchanged looks. Yet another evening shot.

"A field near the old feed plant," John Marcenek called to the men sitting at another table, before flipping a cell phone shut. Chairs scraped back. One fell over as the guy struggled with it.

Callie abruptly set down her waterglass. The feed plant wasn't that far from her house, just on the other side of the river. Was her little white-haired neighbor going to be there? She pushed her chair back, too, without conscious thought. She didn't know if the social workers had investigated yet, but just in case, she wanted to make sure the little kids weren't at this fire. If they were, she was turning them over to Garrett.

"I'll go with you," Dane said. Callie realized he probably thought she was looking for a story. "We'll take my car," he added.

"No." Callie cut a sideways glance his way as they followed a group of men out the front door. "I like to have my own transportation." But Dane wasn't put off.

"Suit yourself," he said easily, once again pressing his hand to her waist, but she side-stepped and then walked faster so he couldn't do it again. *Hint, buddy. Take the hint. You're too pushy for me.*

The air smelled of burning sagebrush when they walked out to the dark lot, where pickup trucks and cars with volunteer fire department license plates were pulling out of parking spots. There was an orange glow on the edge of town, across the river from Callie's house.

She got into the Neon and followed several cars across the river, where she parked on the highway above the feed plant. She'd have an excellent view of the action and still be far enough from the fire that the authorities probably wouldn't send her on her way. Other cars parked along the highway, some driven by firefighters, some by people who simply stopped to watch.

Dane pulled his shiny BMW in behind her. Flames shot high from the dead elm trees that had once formed a windbreak around the plant, and two engines were already in position, shooting jets of water onto the trees. Another was attacking the rapidly moving line of fire in the field between the plant and the river.

Smoke rolled over the highway as Callie walked back to Dane's car, where she could get a better look at the small groups of people. He waved his hand in front of his face. "Man, this is nasty."

"One of the side effects of fire," Callie said as she searched for the Hobart children.

Nothing. No children at all. Yet. Most of the people gathering to watch were residents of the housing development above the highway. Callie had seen several of them pull into their driveways and then walk down to the edge of the road.

She turned her attention back to the fire, watching the firefighters spray water on the flames. A truck with a blade was digging a line around the structures. Unlike the previous fire Callie had witnessed, the volunteer force wasn't making much headway. The fire was still relatively small, but vegetation was dry after a month with no rain and the wind kept shifting direction.

A fluorescent-green BLM fire truck rumbled from the highway down the river road to the plant. A second later another followed.

"Bringing in reinforcements," Dane said.

"The plant must abut BLM land." The BLM wouldn't fight a fire on city or county property, but they would stand ready in case the flames spread onto federal land.

Callie once again searched the crowd lining the highway. Still no kids. She was starting to feel better.

NATHAN HAD CAUGHT A RIDE to the fire with his father, getting a free pass to the action. Gina had understood and sent him on his way. Seth had indeed chosen well in the date department. He just hadn't chosen what Nathan really wanted. Nate hated to think about what that was, because once he admitted it, he was going to have to deal with it—until she left town. And then he had a sneaking suspicion he was still going to be dealing with it.

"You all right?" the old man mumbled without looking at him.

"Yeah." But his fingers were unconsciously kneading his thigh. He shoved his hand in his jacket pocket. As soon as they got to the fire, John jumped out of the pickup and headed toward the fire truck, pulling on equipment as he walked.

Garrett stopped next to the pickup in the sheriff's office vehicle. "Shit," he said in a low voice. "They'd better not lose this one." He looked behind him, up toward the highway, where people were already parking, some firefighters, some not. "Keep an eye on Dad. I've gotta do crowd control… Oh, cool. Look who's here."

Nathan could tell from Garrett's tone exactly who was there. Callie. He wondered if Dane was with her. A quick backward glance, and yeah. He was there. Even at this distance Nate could recognize the two of them standing side by side, near Dane's pricey car. But the Neon was parked next to it.

Nathan felt a sense of grim satisfaction. Dane had followed her. They hadn't arrived together.

IT TOOK ALMOST half an hour for the firefighters to get enough of a handle on the blaze to send one of the BLM trucks back to the bay. The other remained, just in case. An older and heavier John Marcenek was directing the crews. It had taken Callie a while to recognize him, but once she zeroed in on Nate, she'd realized who the man with him was. She did not like that man, pretty much because he made no secret of not liking her.

Denise was also there, geared up and in the center of the action. Callie was impressed at how efficiently she worked, appearing to know exactly what needed to be done and where at every step of the operation.

"Are you going to stay much longer?" Dane asked with a glance at his watch.

That was her cue to agree that the fire had been diverting entertainment, but it was now time to leave. "Afraid so," she said. "Why don't we call it a night?"

Dane raised his eyebrows. "Are you sure?"

"Yeah." Callie smiled up at him, although the smile didn't quite reach her eyes. "Can't help myself. I'm a journalist to the core and I want to be where the action is."

And she didn't want to leave with him.

"Can't fault you there," Dane said. And since it was pretty obvious there would be no good-night kiss or make out session or whatever he'd hoped for, he smiled awkwardly before turning and walking back to his car.

Callie was so damned glad she had the Neon. Dinner with the group had been… unusual, but she wasn't ready to spend the rest of the evening with Dane.

Single women might be few and far between in Wesley, but she didn't need him all but planting a flag on her and claiming "mine."

CHAPTER TEN

THE FIREFIGHTERS FINALLY secured a perimeter around the abandoned feed plant and then, aided by a wind shift, they began to get the upper hand on the blaze. The smoke now rolled toward town, away from where Nathan and Garrett stood beside the idling BLM truck, but his eyes and nostrils continued to burn. A few yards away, Seth was performing his paramedic duties, treating one of the firemen who'd stepped in a hole and wrenched a knee, and his father was in rare form at the engines, bellowing orders and running his crew.

Garrett suddenly cursed and Nathan turned to see that a number of fire groupies were edging closer. Some of the residents of the small housing development on the hill above the plant, most of whom had been at the Crab Feed, had made their way down to the parking lot and were standing in a scraggly line where sage met gravel.

Callie was there, too, off to the side. It occurred to Nathan that that was how she led her life, observing from the periphery. The basketball coach was nowhere in sight. She hunched her shoulders and wrapped her arms around her middle as he watched, rubbing her palms over her upper arms, her gaze shifting from the fire to the crowd, which was growing rather than shrinking. The night air was sending chills up Nathan's back even though he was wearing a blazer, and Callie only had on a sleeveless black dress. Yet still she stayed, shivering. Why? And it was crazy, but he felt an urge to walk over to her and simply wrap his arms around her, warm her by holding her close. Many years ago he could have done that. It killed him to admit it, but he missed those days.

She glanced over at him then, and for a moment they studied each other across the distance that separated them. He had never known anyone else who could connect with him like she could. As if they could read each other's minds if they tried hard enough.

"I'm pushing the crowd back," Garrett said, breaking into Nathan's thoughts. "Go shoo Callie home." His brother smirked as he spoke, telling Nathan that he'd caught the two of them staring like star-crossed lovers. Shit.

Nathan crossed the distance to her.

"You need to go home. There's the potential for volatile substances to react with the fire."

She twisted her mouth sideways in a dubious expression. "For real? Or are you making that up to get me out of here?"

"Both."

Callie held her ground. "Is the fire man-made?"

"We don't know yet." Nate gestured to where the Neon sat on the highway above the parking lot and asked, "Where's your dinner date?"

"He went home."

"Separate cars?"

"You know me," she said. "Sharing a car is too much of a commitment."

"Why're you here, Cal? All these other people have houses close by." Part of him wondered if she'd come to escape her date.

She hadn't appeared to enjoy her companion for the evening as much as he'd enjoyed his.

"I came to see if those little kids next door showed up."

"You're kidding."

She shrugged. "Denise told me she's seen them at other fires and this one is close."

Nate tilted his head. "Do you think they're junior arsonists or something?" he asked, trying to see where she was going with this.

"No. Like I told you before, I don't think anyone is taking care of them at night. I think they do as they please and I think the boy is interested in either fire or firemen."

"So you're gathering evidence?" Or attempting to, since the kids weren't there.

"I'm concerned."

"Just because you haven't seen the grandma—"

"There are no lights on in that place, Nate. Except the television every now and then. And the kids show up at fires."

"So do a lot of people."

"I guess."

"Go home, Callie." She was shivering even worse in her skimpy dress, and there was no reason for her to be there. "The kids aren't here."

"Nate!" Seth sounded uncharacteristically panicked. Nathan stumbled as he turned toward the voice, his injured leg giving out with the unexpected movement. Searing pain shot through his knee, but he didn't stop moving. Garrett raced past him from the direction of the parking lot and Nathan followed as quickly as he could, wincing with each step. Their father was leaning heavily against the fire truck, halfheartedly fighting off Seth and another paramedic.

"Are you all right?" Callie asked from behind Nate. He hadn't realized she was following him.

"Fine," he replied without looking at her.

"Go back to the parking lot, Callie," Garrett commanded when she and Nathan reached the small group of people surrounding his father.

Callie ignored him. "What's wrong with John?" she asked Nathan.

"Blood pressure." He hoped. "Controllable *if* he takes his medication."

"Why *wouldn't* he take it?"

"Makes him irritable," Nathan muttered.

"One would never notice," Callie murmured, as John cursed Seth and the other paramedic, trying to push them back.

"Go home, Callie." Garrett stepped between her and Nathan. "I'll walk you to your car."

"No need," she said through her teeth.

"I insist."

"Call him off," she said to Nathan, then turned and stalked across the lot and up the trail to her car.

"DAMN IT, I'M FINE." John took a few steps toward the rear engine, looking very much as if he was about to wrestle control of the fire crew from his second in command. Nathan took his arm, stopped him cold in spite of his dad outweighing him by a hundred pounds.

"You're not fine," Nate growled. "You're going to the emergency room." His father sent him a baleful look and attempted to snatch his arm away. He failed, which worried Nathan. "You have to go. You'll need a medical release to continue fighting fires after this."

Seth nodded in agreement, quickly backing away from their dad. The air seemed to go out of John Marcenek. His shoulders dropped as the reality of what Nathan had said sank in.

"Dr. Kitras owes me a favor," Garrett said. "We'll see if we can get you in tomorrow, but tonight we're going to the E.R. and making sure everything is okay."

"Whoopee," John muttered, but he started walking toward the passenger side of his truck. There wasn't much else he could do. Garrett opened the door, earning another cranky look, and Nathan got into the driver's seat.

"Seth and I'll be there as soon as we can," Garrett said.

John turned his head as if he didn't hear a word. Nathan started the truck and they drove to the clinic in silence.

The doctor had John checked over before either Garrett or Seth arrived, and pronounced him out of any immediate danger. However, if he didn't stay on his medication, he was looking at a possible heart attack or stroke. Not what John Marcenek had wanted to hear. Nathan called his brothers and they agreed to meet at the house. Their trucks were there when Nate and John pulled up.

Together the three followed their dad into the immaculate kitchen. John had never been particularly tidy before, but apparently retirement did strange things to people.

"You can go home now," he said to Nathan. "I'm going to bed, so one watchdog will be fine." With that he walked down the hall to the room he'd once shared with their mother.

Garrett and Nathan exchanged silent looks, then Garrett went to the cupboard over the refrigerator and pulled down the bottle of Scotch. Nathan shook his head. "Not tonight," he said. "I twisted my leg and I might opt for a painkiller instead."

"This kills pain," Garrett muttered, pouring a shot.

"Yeah. You might want to save some for after you take Dad to see Kitras tomorrow."

"Will do," Garrett said glumly. "How bad's your leg?" The limp was obviously getting worse.

Nathan ran a hand over the thigh, even though it was his knee that had been injured. "It'll be fine. When you have only a few muscles to begin with, it really has an effect when you strain one."

"I guess. Let me know if I need to finagle two appointments tomorrow. I'm sure Kitras will see both of you at once."

"Can't. Too much work to catch up on."

Nathan's leg was throbbing when he got home, but he decided against the bottle of white pills in his medicine cabinet, and followed Garrett's lead. He splashed two fingers of amber liquid over a single ice cube in a crystal glass, then on impulse added another finger. What the hell. This stuff couldn't make him any groggier tomorrow than the conventional painkiller. And it tasted better. He probably should have shared a drink with Garrett, but his brother really would need all of that bottle to deal with their father.

Nate was so thankful right now that Garrett was the brother living next door to their dad.

He picked up a framed photo Seth had given him last Christmas, taken on a father-son fishing trip in Alaska when the brothers had been in their early teens, six months after the death of their mother. They each held a humongous salmon. Garrett was smirking at the camera, looking like the hellion he'd been at the time, and Seth beamed like a puppy dog, the look that hid his natural propensity toward getting into every kind of trouble imaginable, some innocent and some not so much. Nathan looked like the brother who wanted to please. The brother who tried to hold things together in a family that had just lost their mother.

Carelessly, he set the photo on the coffee table and then settled on the sofa, staring across the dark room.

What was going to happen if he decided to leave town? Was it right to leave his brothers to take care of their dad? Would his dad even care if he left?

Why did he feel this urge to move on? Was this how Callie felt? Did she just get the urge, and instead of weighing pros and cons slowly, as he did, simply act on it?

He wasn't that way. He wanted to know what he had available to fall back on. He liked to plan.

He'd heard that that very afternoon Callie had called a real estate agent—Joy's cousin—for a consultation. The wheels were in motion to sell the house, which meant she would probably be leaving town. It wouldn't be long before Callie was out of his life. Out of his thoughts.

Yeah. He really could fake not caring until she left town. No sweat. He took a sip of Scotch, feeling the burn as it hit the areas of his mouth and throat still irritated from smoke inhalation. He didn't mind the burn.

What an evening. He'd started out nervous about going out with a woman, even if it was a lame group date, and had ended up stinking of smoke and going home as alone as he had left. Not that he'd planned to go home with Gina, because as pleasant as it had been talking to her, it wasn't going anywhere. There was no spark. And he'd been thinking about Callie and that freaking basketball coach the entire time. Insane.

Callie made him insane. He sipped again.

He saw a flash of headlights in the window and then heard the sound of an engine turning off. Nathan put the crystal glass to his forehead. He recognized the distinctive knocking noise in the Neon's engine.

"It's open," he called when Callie knocked, adding in an undertone, "Come on in."

She did, pausing for a moment, taking in the scene—Nathan sprawled on the sofa, the drink in his hand.

"How's your dad?" she asked as she closed the door.

"He'd gone off the meds again. I think this time he learned a lesson."

She walked the rest of the way across the room, stopping inches from his toes. He glanced down at his jeans, wondering if she could see the difference between his thighs under the worn fabric. She followed his gaze momentarily before bringing her eyes back up to his face.

"You hurt yourself at the fire."

"I wrenched my knee."

"Can I sit down?"

"It's late."

"It's not even midnight." He didn't invite her to sit, though.

"I heard you put the house on the market."

"I'm in the process. It's time."

"Do you always know when it's time?"

"Always." She picked up the photo he'd left on the coffee table and studied it.

"So, it was time when you left here last?"

She looked up from the photo, obviously uncomfortable. "That was different."

"How?"

"I was reacting to something I didn't understand back then."

"Do you understand it now?"

"I understand it's the way I am. The way I'm wired. My father was the same way—"

"—according to Grace." Nate finished the sentence with her. They'd been over this before, back in high school, only at that time, Callie hadn't thought she was wired the same way as her father. She'd needed to believe then that he hadn't been able to help himself. Now she was telling herself she was the same way, giving herself an excuse to leave whenever she felt the urge. Avoid any kind of commitment.

Maybe she *was* wired the same way as her father. Nathan didn't know. He stared at what was left of his Scotch, which he was now drinking too fast. "So you're just going to spend your life moving from place to place?"

"I guess I am now, once I sell the house." She glanced away, making Nathan wonder if she was nervous about that—having no home base. He couldn't imagine not having one himself. Even if he didn't want one, it seemed to find him, in the form of two brothers and one disapproving father. But it was a form of security. A form Callie would never know, having no family.

"Did they ever figure out what happened to him?" Nathan asked. "Your dad?"

A shadow crossed her features. "No."

Callie carefully set the photo back where she'd found it, then wiped her palms down the sides of her black dress. Their eyes met and once again Nathan felt that silent connection he found with no one else.

"What do you want, Callie? Why do you keep coming here?"

"Is that woman you were with tonight your girlfriend?"

A perfect chance for escape. Nathan didn't take it. Instead, he looked wearily into her beautiful aqua eyes and said, "No. Blind date. How about you?"

"Sucky date. We should have been together, Nate."

His mouth tightened as he looked away. Right. They should be together, then he could fall in love with her again, and then she could leave. Great plan.

"We're driving each other crazy," she said. He couldn't argue with her there. "Why can't we push all this crap aside and simply *be* together while I'm here? You know you feel as drawn to me as I am to you. In some ways it's like we've never been apart in spite of everything that happened."

Nathan got awkwardly to his feet, his knee buckling slightly, and Callie stepped aside, giving him room to move. He limped past her into the kitchen, where only one low-watt bulb burned above the sink. He poured another splash of Scotch over what was left of the ice cube. Warm Scotch, cold Scotch. He didn't care.

"Be together," he said after taking a healthy swallow. "Like being friends…only friends who can't trust each other."

"I will always be up front with you. Before, I didn't know what was happening. I panicked. I thought a clean break would be easiest for both of us. I handled it so poorly, but I was afraid I would give in if I stayed in touch."

And would that have been so bad?

Apparently so.

"How would it be different this time?"

"We both need different things now than we did back then."

"What about sex?" Nathan asked in a low voice. "Is that part of the package?" He reached down with his right hand and absently touched the numb muscles of his thigh, felt the ugly divot, and could not imagine making love to Callie this way.

"The attraction is there and you can't tell me it's not. I think sex would be good for us. In fact, I think we're overdue after what happened the last time. As long as we understand the situation."

Nathan put the glass on the counter with such force that a small amount of Scotch sloshed out, pooling gold on the white counter.

"Listen, Callie. I don't want to have sex with you because it would be good for us or for old time's sake or because you 'care' enough to have sex before you blast out of my life again. I don't want you to make up for the past, and I don't want to be on the receiving end of sympathy."

"Who said anything about sympathy?"

Right. Who had said anything about sympathy? Nathan muttered a curse. "I don't want to have sex because you feel bad about the past. How's that?"

"Very clear," Callie said, her eyes revealing no emotion. "I can't help the way I am, Nate."

"And I can't help the way I am, either." But it sure seemed stupid that at one time they'd been soul mates and now…now this chasm.

"I think you still care about me."

"Even if I did, Callie, I wouldn't do anything about it, because there's no future in it."

"Is that what you're looking for? Is that one of the prerequisites? The guarantee of a future?"

"No. The possibility of a future. With you there isn't even that. I've lost before I start. I won't do that again. I won't waste the time again."

She looked stunned by his last words. She said nothing for a moment, then abruptly turned and walked back through the living room to the front door, where she let herself out. A moment later the Neon pulled away from the curb, leaving Nathan very much alone. Again. Just as he'd been before she'd shown up, but now it felt even worse.

It felt final.

I WON'T WASTE THE TIME.

Callie parked at the curb in front of her house five minutes later, Nate's harsh words circling through her mind.

Just forget about him. You can't keep beating your head on the wall. Just give it up.

She was so preoccupied talking herself down that she completely missed the guy sitting in the shadows on her porch steps. When he moved she jumped a mile, then went into instant defense mode before she recognized him, and even then she didn't drop her guard.

"Mitch. You scared me." She kept her distance as she pressed a hand against her chest in an effort to still her hammering heart.

"Enjoy your evening with the coach?"

"It was an evening." What was going on? Why was this kid here and what did he want? No, it was obvious what he wanted. To what lengths would he go to get it?

"And then you went to see Marcenek. Think Coach knows about that?"

Callie's eyes grew round. "You were following me?"

Mitch shrugged. "So what's wrong with me? I mean, if you're seeing two guys, why not three?"

Callie drew herself up. "Because the third one is too immature and arrogant for my tastes."

And he was also a big kid. Much stronger than she was and probably a lot faster.

"You'd better go now, Mitch…before you *disturb the neighbors!*" Callie shouted the last words, noticing that Alice's windows were open and the television was on. The Hobart house was as dark as always.

Mitch smirked at her and stepped forward, but Alice's porch light snapped on and he jumped back. Callie could see his face, and what she saw unnerved her. Cold determination.

"Leave," she told him.

Alice opened her door and peered out.

"Hey, Alice," Callie called, her eyes fixed on Mitch's face. "So help me, I'll have her call the cops if you don't get your ass out of here."

"Are you all right, Callie?" Alice called.

"I will be in a few seconds," she said through gritted teeth as she stared the kid down. Mitch gave her a look of hatred and stormed off to his car. He fired up the engine and pulled away from the curb with a screech of tires.

Alice came out onto her porch in a wild floral print robe, her hand over her chest. "Are you all right, Callie? Who was that?"

Callie crossed her arms over her chest, hugging herself as she watched the taillights disappear around the corner. "Mitch Michaels."

"Really!"

"Yes." And now what did she tell Alice? That she was seeing another much more intimidating side of this kid that wasn't nearly as charming as the one she'd shut down at school? "It was nothing, Alice. He's just a little persistent."

Even across the distance that separated them, Callie could see her neighbor's shock.

"Trust me, I haven't encouraged him. I, uh, should be getting into the house."

"Are you sure you're all right?" Alice asked in a dubious voice.

"Oh, yes. Everything will be fine now. Good night, Alice."

"Good night."

Callie went into the house, grabbed the phone book and looked up the number for the sheriff's office dispatch. Thankfully, the deputy who called back a few minutes later was not Garrett.

She briefly explained that Mitch Michaels had followed her that evening and had been waiting for her at her house, where he'd behaved in a threatening manner. The deputy sounded rather pleased with the situation, making Callie wonder if he had something against the rich Michaels family or if he'd had dealings with Mitch before and was looking to take the kid down.

"I'll have a talk with him tonight if I can locate him," the deputy promised. "Tomorrow, if I can't. If he persists, then you'll have to consider taking stronger measures."

"Should I have reason to believe he's going to persist?" Callie asked.

"Your guess is as good as mine, but just in case, keep that in mind."

How very helpful, Callie thought as she

hung up the phone. *Your guess is as good as mine.*

She locked all the doors and windows and then went to bed, more creeped out by the situation than she wanted to admit.

CHAPTER ELEVEN

NATHAN WAS JUST OPENING the garage door to go to work when Garrett pulled up to the curb in the sheriff's office SUV. Curious, since this looked a lot like an official visit, Nathan walked toward him. Garrett got out of the car and met him halfway up the drive.

"I wanted you to hear this from me, rather than through the very efficient grapevine."

Nathan didn't like the expression on his brother's face. "Hear what?"

"Callie made a complaint against Mitch Michaels. I guess he was following her last night. Followed her here, in fact, and then confronted her at her house."

Rage unlike anything Nathan had ever felt before exploded inside him. He turned and started back toward the garage without another word.

"Don't do anything stupid, Nate."

He turned back. "Me? I'm the calm, quiet brother. Remember?"

Garrett looked heavenward for an instant. "Just make sure you stay that way. We had extra patrols driving by her place last night. She was safe."

"You didn't go talk to the little asshole?"

"We did. A deputy found him in the café with some friends who swore he'd been with them all night."

"So Callie just imagined it."

"Exactly."

Nathan ground his teeth. "Well, perhaps I'll help Mitch imagine a few things today."

"Watch yourself. If you assault him, it won't endear you to your boss and it won't keep Callie safe."

Oh, yeah. He'd watch himself. "I don't care if Callie isn't your favorite person," Nathan said to his brother, "you continue to make damned sure nothing happens to her, understand?"

"I understand," Garrett repeated wearily. "Just don't do anything to that kid. Let us handle it."

Nathan released a long breath. "I'll try,"

he muttered. It was the best he could do. He wasn't making any promises.

He spent the morning in his office with his door closed, debating how he was going to continue to work for Vince Michaels when he wanted nothing more than to eviscerate his son. And there was another asshole son coming up through the ranks.

Nate had cooled down slightly by the time Mitch showed up for his intern hours that afternoon—enough so that he didn't grab the kid by the lapels and slam him up against a wall. His burning rage had turned into more of a cold, controllable anger.

"I'd like to talk to you." Nathan gestured for the young man to step into his office. There was no doubt in his mind that Mitch knew why. He smirked and walked by him with his distinctive rolling swagger.

Nathan closed the door and leaned back against his desk, folding his arms over his chest as he studied the kid, who stared back insolently. Finally Nathan spoke, slowly and clearly.

"If you go near Callie McCarran, or any other woman, for that matter, I'll cut your nuts off."

Shock crossed Mitch's face, replaced almost immediatcly by the smirk. This kid felt so freaking safe.

"I'm also reporting Katie's concerns from last spring."

"Big deal."

"Last I heard, med school doesn't encourage the admission of students with histories of blatant sexual harassment and stalking."

Mitch's face went purple. He didn't wait to hear another word, but instead wrenched the door open and stormed out, then out the front door. A few seconds later, Nathan heard rubber peeling in the parking lot. He had a feeling that nothing good was going to come of this, but if he had it to do all over again, he wouldn't change a thing.

CALLIE WAS ON THE front porch showing the repairman the window screens she wanted replaced when the county vehicle pulled to a stop in front of the Hobart house. The pink Mustang was there, so the mom was home. Callie wondered if CPS had warned her they were coming, or if they simply swooped in unannounced.

Either way, she felt better knowing someone was finally checking into the situation. She hated sticking her nose into other people's business, but the Hobart kids couldn't continue staying alone at night. It was wrong. Flat out wrong.

After lining the repairman out, she went inside and finished up her last article for the paper on the twice-retired woman who had then got her teaching certificate and was now teaching kindergarten even though she was in her mid-seventies. It had been a fascinating interview, since the woman had done so very much. Having never married or had children, she spent her life following whatever career path interested her at the time.

Although she didn't foresee teaching kindergarten anywhere in her future, Callie identified with the woman. The thought was surprisingly dissatisfying.

There were some weird things going on in her brain these days.

Callie paced through Grace's nearly empty house, feeling almost as empty inside. At every other point in her life when issues had sprung up, she'd been quite satisfied to move along, leaving them behind. Maybe she'd reached a stage where she realized walking away wasn't a solution, but rather a cover-up.

Callie finished the article and e-mailed it to the *Star,* then shut off her computer. She was in the kitchen making tea when there was a knock on the front door. Mrs. Hobart. Through the gap in the front window curtains, Callie could see her standing on the porch.

In spite of all her instincts telling her not to answer the door, that this could not in any way be good, Callie sucked it up and un-latched the door lock.

"You bitch." She had barely opened the door when Mrs. Hobart, hands planted firmly on her nonexistent hips, let fly. "What in the hell were you thinking, calling CPS on me? *You bitch!"* She repeated it in case Callie hadn't received the message the first time.

"I thought your kids were out at night without supervision. That the house was dark when you were gone, and they were home."

"My mom has an apartment in the basement. That's where the kids spend their evenings. I leave the lights off upstairs to save money. Maybe you don't have to worry about electric bills, *inheriting* like you have, but I have to support my mom and my kids."

Callie felt the blood rising in her cheeks. She had no way to see basement lights. She hadn't even known the house had a basement. There were no windows, no door. Nothing.

"And now you know what you've done? You've opened the door for my asshole ex-husband to come in and try to take the kids from me."

"I, uh—"

"If—and I mean it from the bottom of my soul—he gets custody of my kids, then you are going to so deeply regret ever putting your nose in my business…."

Callie swallowed, knowing there was nothing she could say to defend herself that she hadn't already said.

"I'm sorry. I was concerned about your kids."

Mrs. Hobart sneered. "Well, maybe you'd better be concerned about your ass from now on." And with that she stormed down the sidewalk and out the gate, which banged shut behind her.

Callie watched the woman go, her face feeling first hot and then cold. Her heart beat in a slow, heavy rhythm.

She walked back into the house and closed the door, leaning her forehead against the cool glass.

Nate had told her to be careful. But she had truly believed there was a problem in the family, that the kids were being neglected—and she had reacted at gut level. Why? Why had the idea of those kids being left alone struck such a cord?

Yes, her own childhood must play a part, but she'd accepted her childhood.

Or thought she had.

Of course she had.

Her head was throbbing. Was there anything in her life that wasn't screwed up? Anything at all?

"WHAT'S UP?" Nathan said into his cell phone as he saved his files on the computer.

"Want to grab a beer?" Garrett asked. He'd taken their father in for a follow-up physical late that afternoon.

"Anything I need to be mentally prepared for?"

"No. Better than I'd hoped, but Dad's mad."

"The Supper Club or Fuzzy's?"

"Fuzzy's."

Nathan was still at the office. The only person at the office, since normal people were home with loved ones, or out and about. "Be there in ten."

He was actually there in five. Garrett was waiting at a table with a beer in his hand and two unopened bottles in the middle of the table.

"Did you call me from here?"

"Yeah." Garrett nudged a beer toward him. Nathan took it and drank deeply. Fuzzy's was a classic dark bar. No live music, just a dated selection on a jukebox that no one bothered to play. No waitresses. No bar food. People who came to Fuzzy's were there to drink. They also tended to mind their own business.

"What's the deal with Dad?"

Garrett launched into a bunch of medica-lese from which Nathan deduced what they already knew—that if John stayed on the medication, he'd be fine. If he went off, he wouldn't be. "Well, to make a long story short," Garrett concluded, tilting the top of his beer bottle in Nathan's direction, "he can't be on the firefighting squad anymore. He can do logistics, but he can't physically fight the fires."

"That's a hell of a lot better than the alternative."

"Not to Dad. All or nothing." Garrett looked over his shoulder at the bar, then back again. "Want to move into the rental?"

"Oh, yeah. Dad and me living side by side. Good idea. Like his stress level isn't high enough right now."

"Just thought I'd throw it out there," Garrett said morosely.

"I wouldn't last a week."

His brother peeled a strip off his label. It twisted into a curlicue. He let it fall and pulled off another.

"Besides..." Nathan said slowly, "...if Dad really is all right...I don't know if I'm even going to be around."

Garrett's chin popped up. "Why's that?"

"You remember Suzanne, the woman I worked with in Seattle? She called me a while back. There was a job at her paper, but I didn't apply. The next one that opens up, I will."

"You're going back to Seattle?"

"Well, it isn't like I'm going to get blown up twice. That was kind of a freak thing, you know."

"Do you know what a miracle it was that the editorial job opened up here in Wesley when it did? That you had the skills to take over?" Garrett stopped peeling and took a drink.

"Yeah. I do."

"And now that you've done the impossible, landed a journalism job in your hometown, you're throwing it away."

"I can't keep working for Vince Michaels and I don't feel as if I belong here anymore."

Garrett stared at him, his bottle poised in midair. "I can understand about Vince," he finally conceded. "But wait a few weeks, see what happens."

"I still feel like it's time to move on to something else. I'd rather write than edit."

Garrett's eyes narrowed. "Is it because of Callie? Are you following her when she leaves? Because if you are, it's the stupidest move you—"

"No." Nathan cut his brother off. "I have no idea where she's going or what she's doing." And he wished he didn't care. "Maybe having her around made me think a little more, but she's not the reason."

Garrett clearly didn't believe him. Well, Nate wasn't going to justify his decisions with his brother.

"When you came back here, Dad was happy," Garrett finally said.

"I saw him doing those back handsprings across the lawn."

"He was happy." Garrett drained the rest of his beer, then held up two fingers and the bartender nodded.

Bringing over two more, the guy didn't even bother to pick up Garrett's empty. Nathan was only about a quarter of the way into his first one.

"Speaking of Callie, she called CPS on the Hobarts."

"You're kidding." Nathan put his bottle down. "Any idea what came of it?"

"Officially, no. Unofficially, they made a home visit. The kids tend to run around the neighborhood, but they have a grandmother who lives with them in a basement apartment. That's where they spend their evenings. Or where they're supposed to spend their evenings. The thing is, they have adult supervision."

"Anybody actually see the grandma?" Because he knew Callie didn't believe she existed.

"Interviewed her. She doesn't get out much and…" Garrett shook his head. "Callie can't see the basement door from her house when she's spying."

Nathan took a long pull. So there really was a grandma. Callie had spent all that time worrying for nothing. He wondered how she was handling it. And he was also concerned about the possible ramifications.

"Do the Hobarts know it was her?"

"I think it won't be too hard for them to figure it out."

"No." Nathan cupped his hand around his beer, hoping they didn't enact some kind of hill justice. Why had Callie been so certain those kids weren't being cared for? "Any more uplifting news?"

"I thought it was good news that the kids were being taken care of and that Callie was wrong."

"You like the Callie was wrong part the best."

"Listen, she screwed you over royally. You went into a funk for months. Then you ended up getting your leg nearly blown off."

"Why do you blame Callie for that?" Nathan asked quietly. Had his brothers figured out that when he'd first taken the reporter job, he'd been trying to be more dynamic? Trying to be that guy who would impress the Callies of the world? Was he that transparent?

"Never mind."

"No." Nathan put his bottle down with a thump. "Explain."

Garrett shook his head. "Sorry. Got carried away. I'd better get home to the parental unit," he said, after finishing his beer.

"Better you than me," Nathan muttered, pulling out his wallet and flipping a few bills onto the table.

CALLIE WOKE to the smell of smoke wafting in through her bedroom window. It took her a minute to identify the odor as she fought her way to consciousness, and then, when she opened her eyes and saw flickers of orange light reflecting off the window glass, she shot out of bed.

Her back fence was on fire.

She ran out of the house barefoot, wearing only the gym shorts and T-shirt she'd slept in, and cranked on the garden hose, pulling it across the dark lawn. She was almost to the flames when the hose suddenly stopped uncoiling, yanking her back as she hit the end. Crap.

"Fire!" she screamed as she ran toward the house and her phone. "Alice! Fire!" A light snapped on in the house to her left, and then in the one behind her. Callie dashed onto her porch and through the kitchen. She snatched up her cell phone off the coffee table and punched in 911. When the operator answered, Callie gave her address, and told him there was a fire in the alley, as she once again went out the back door. The fire siren went off and she could see her neighbor across the alley stringing hoses together. The old cedar boards of her shed were burning hot. Callie turned her hose on and started spraying it down so that it wouldn't catch fire, too.

Her throat was dry and her heart hammered. There was only one way a cedar fence would end up ablaze in the middle of the night. Someone had set it on fire.

CHAPTER TWELVE

THE SIREN YANKED NATHAN up out of bed, followed almost immediately by a phone call from Garrett.

"Someone torched Callie's fence," his brother snapped. Nathan's pulse jerked. "The fire crew just got here."

"Is she okay?" he asked as he juggled the phone while pulling on a T-shirt and then ramming his feet into his running shoes.

"Yeah."

He slapped the phone shut and went out the side door to the garage, shoving it in his pocket as he walked to the small truck. He got inside and started the ignition in one movement.

Blood pounded in his temples as he drove the ten blocks to Callie's. He pulled to a stop on the opposite side of the street from her place, parked facing the wrong direction and jumped out of the truck. He crossed the street and skirted the house at a frustratingly slow and painful, limping jog. A single engine sat in the alley. The fire was out and people were gathered close by, talking to Garrett. Callie stood next to her back step, apart from the crowd, staring at what was left of her fence.

Nathan immediately went through the side gate, his only thought to make sure she was all right. He was almost to her when her gaze suddenly jerked sideways toward him. She did not look happy to see him.

For a moment she simply stared at him, slightly shell-shocked, and then she tilted her chin at a defiant angle. "Are you here to waste your time?" she asked.

"Shut up, Callie." He wrapped her in his arms, not caring if she felt his twisted leg through his sweats as her thighs pressed against his. Not caring about anything except that she was safe. Callie stiffened for a moment, and then with a small exhalation, she melted into him. He buried his nose in her hair. She smelled like wood smoke, felt warm and alive. He was so damned grateful.

"Somebody lit my fence on fire," she whispered against his neck.

"I can see that," Nathan replied gently, his arms tightening even more.

"They stacked trash next to it and lit it." Her fingers gripped his shirt as she spoke.

Son of a bitch. He truly wished she'd kept her nose out of Hobart business. "Have you talked to Garrett yet?"

Callie shook her head against his chest.

As footsteps approached, Nathan lifted his head to see his brother with a stern expression on his face. Callie cleared her throat.

"I'm okay," she said as she stepped back, out of his embrace.

I'm not.

But Nathan let go.

"THIS IS SERIOUS," Garrett said, his tone matching his words. Callie had the oddest feeling he was more concerned about Nate being with her than the fire.

"No shit," Nate shot back. "Have you talked to the Hobarts?"

"I will. The kids were in the alley."

"By themselves?" Callie asked sarcastically.

"The old lady has trouble getting around. She pretty much stays nested in that apartment." Garrett shifted his weight into cop stance. "I wanted to talk to you first."

"Not much to tell," Callie said, feeling Nate move closer to her. He didn't touch her, but he was there. "I woke up and smelled smoke. The hose wouldn't reach the fire, so I called 911."

"Do you know of any reason someone might do this? Any hostile contact with anyone?"

Wow, if he'd asked that after Grace's memorial, she would have had quite a list. But right now she only had one.

"Mrs. Hobart came to see me. Told me I was making it possible for her ex to gain custody," Callie said stonily. All because of her knee-jerk reactions. "She was very upset."

"When was this?"

"Today."

Garrett put his hands on his belt. "Okay. Just so you know, there'll be extra patrols through this area for a few days."

Callie bit her lip. She was probably going to see if the motel had a room. "I—"

"Great," Nathan interjected.

"Lock everything. I'll be in contact tomorrow."

"I'm staying with her tonight." Nate met his brother's eyes.

Garrett nodded, then glanced back at the smoldering remains of the fence. "Good idea," he said expressionlessly. "I'll see you two tomorrow."

Nate touched Callie's shoulder. "Let's go inside."

He led the way into the house through the back door.

Callie stopped in the kitchen, which looked so stark now that she'd sent almost everything to charity. "Nate…I…" She halted. She what?

Nate didn't give her time to waffle. "Do you want to come to my house or have me stay over?"

"Your place," she said. "I want to get away from here." When in doubt, run.

"I'll wait while you get whatever you need."

All Callie needed was her purse, a few personal items and a change of clothes, which she shoved into her day pack. "I'll follow you," she said once they were outside.

"Fine." Unlike Dane, he apparently didn't mind if she kept her freedom. He got into his small truck, which was facing the wrong way, and did a U-turn in the street. Callie followed him to his house, where she parked at the curb. Why was he doing this? Friendship? Guilt? Something more?

Nate stood and waited for her in the bright light of the garage, then, his hand against the small of her back, he guided her into the house.

"You want something to drink?" he asked once they were inside. Callie glanced around at the kitchen, having seen it only once before. It was a man's space, with buff-colored walls, dark cabinets, brushed chrome appliances. A few dishes on the drain board, a newspaper on the table, but other than that, everything in its place.

"Just a glass of water."

He filled a blue highball glass with ice water from the fridge and then poured himself two fingers of Laphroaig. He held up the bottle. "You sure?"

She took a sip of water. "I'm sure. I don't

think alcohol will help. I don't know if anything will help. Damn, Nate. They lit my fence on fire."

He lifted the whisky, hesitated, then set the glass back on the counter untouched. Callie took another swallow of water, then she, too, put her glass on the kitchen island that stood between them.

"Why'd you come?" she asked. After their last conversation, he'd been the last person she'd expected to see.

"Garrett called me."

"He must have told you I was okay."

Nathan let out a long breath. "I had to come."

"Why?"

"Because regardless of everything, I care. All right?"

"All right," she repeated, as she tried to make sense of her jumbled thoughts. He cared. He wouldn't let her near him, but he cared.

"It's just that there are some things we have trouble with," Nate said.

"Like talking? We never used to have that problem."

"Maybe something happened," Nate replied darkly.

Callie let her chin dip toward her chest. Something had happened all right. "Since I've come back," she said, "I've been pretty universally despised by those who knew me way back when."

"I—"

She held up her hand to cut him off. "I'm not saying I didn't deserve it, but I never meant to hurt anyone with the things I did. And now…" The intensity of his expression caused words to momentarily escape her. She swallowed. "Now…" She tried to form the words, tried to make some sense of what had happened. To digest the fact that someone hated her enough to risk burning down a neighborhood. To keep from being affected by the way he was staring at her.

"If you start crying…"

He sounded both gruff and desperate. Callie couldn't help herself. Nate cursed and moved around the island as she wiped the back of her wrist under her eyes. She thought he was going to hold her again, let her get his shirt all wet.

Instead he took her teary face in his hands and kissed her. Deeply, his fingers threading through her hair, making her want to melt into him even though their bodies were a good ten inches apart.

It was crazily erotic to have him holding her face, with only their mouths touching. He showed no signs of ending the kiss anytime soon, but Callie needed more. She wanted to feel him against her. She reached for him, trying to press closer, but he ended the kiss, taking hold of her wrists and confusing the hell out of her. He released her and backed away, slowly dropping his hands, his expression oddly unreadable.

Callie stared at him, not understanding what had just happened. Finally she asked, "Are you doing to me what I did to you?" It was the only explanation she could come up with.

"No."

She almost wished he'd said yes. "Stop playing this game, Nate. You say you don't want to waste time with me, then you show up like a knight errant. You kiss me like that and then back off. I've had one hell of an evening. I don't need this on top of it."

"I'm not doing this to hurt you, Callie."

That was the last straw. *Not doing this to hurt her.* "Then what's the deal, Nate?

What is wrong with two people, two freaking lonely people, because I know you're lonely—I recognize the signs—giving each other some comfort? I did an awful thing to you, but I was eighteen. You're thirty." She let out a shuddering breath. "If you're not doing this to purposely hurt me, then I'd like to know what the hell the deal is."

He didn't answer, so Callie persisted, partially sobbing as she said, "Tell me!"

"You want to know what the deal is?" he answered, suddenly angry. "The deal is that I all but blew my leg off a while ago. I used to be whole but part of me is pretty damned ugly now and I'm still trying to come to terms with it, okay? How's that for a deal?"

For a moment Callie simply stared at him, trying to process what he'd just told her. Then she tilted her head. "Well, at least you're talking to me," she said matter-of-factly. But she was shocked. Her eyes went to his thighs, trying to see…whatever.

"You want to see?" he dared her.

"Yeah." Her eyes came back up and what she saw in his face belied his challenging tone. "If you can handle it," she added, knowing those few words would guarantee he'd follow through. He was, after all, a guy.

Nathan popped the buttons on his jeans and pushed them down, letting them drop around his running shoes.

Callie felt sick as she studied what was left of his right leg. She couldn't look away, not after goading him into showing her. So she did her best to keep a clinical expression as she took in the long, jagged scars, shiny white with pink edges, twisted over the remaining muscles of his leg, a divot missing from his quadriceps and an oddly shaped calf where the muscles had been stitched together around missing tissue. The still-angry burn scars on his calf and ankle. Once again she felt tears welling, thinking of what he had gone through, but did her best to hold them back.

Silently, Nathan lifted his black T-shirt to show similar jagged scars on the right side of his torso. She simply shook her head, unable to find the words. He dropped the shirt back down, then leaned to hoist his jeans up over his ruined leg.

"How?"

"Shrapnel from an explosion."

"Shrapnel," Callie repeated solemnly. "Of course. I should have known." She sent him a sharp look. "Have you been living some kind of double life?"

He shifted his weight. "I worked as an investigative reporter when I was in Seattle. This was my first investigation and ended up being my last. I arranged to meet a contact in a sting operation. Instead I got set up. My partner and I were lucky. It was an incendiary bomb. We should've been killed."

"Your partner? How is he?"

"She. Suzanne Galliano. She was behind me. She got only a few burns from falling material and one minor shrapnel wound to the face. She's still working in the Seattle area. I spent quite a bit of time in the hospital because of the threat of infection, then eventually came here to finish healing. The *Star* editor job opened up while I was here, and I took it."

"Why didn't you tell me any of this?"

"I don't talk about it." Nathan stared out the dark kitchen window. A moment passed and it became obvious he wasn't going to talk anymore about it now.

"Nate…"

"Maybe we should call it a night." He didn't wait for her reply, but picked up her pack where she'd set it at the base of the island, and limped out of the kitchen. Callie considered staying right where she was, but what would that accomplish?

She found him waiting at the end of the hall. He opened a door and set the pack inside. Callie didn't obediently step into the room and close the door, even though she could tell just how badly he wanted her to do that. Instead she reached out to lightly run her fingertips over his T-shirt, where it hid the shrapnel scars. His abdomen tightened.

"Is this the only reason you won't sleep with me?"

"No." The word came out without any hesitation, and hurt a hell of a lot more than it should have.

Okay. Game over. She couldn't take another minute on the emotional seesaw. Not tonight anyway.

Callie reached into the room to pick up her pack, and then retraced her steps back down the hall.

You are so flipping used to rejection. Occupation—writer, remember?

But this wasn't an article.

Nate didn't say a word until she reached the kitchen. "Where are you going?"

"None of your business."

"Stop the drama, Callie."

She rounded on him. "No drama. I'm going to a motel for tonight."

He sucked in a breath. "Stay." She stared at him. "Please stay."

"Why are you doing this?"

He pushed both hands into his hair in a gesture of frustration. "Because I'm afraid, all right?"

HE COULDN'T BELIEVE he'd just said that.

Callie still stared at him, probably wondering for the tenth time that evening why he was such a jerk. And then she swallowed and said, "Me, too."

Nathan drew in a slow breath. "What are you afraid of?"

"That I'm going to leave this town with you still hating me."

Oh, man. "I don't hate you, Callie. I just don't know what making love to you would accomplish."

"Healing," she said softly.

"Healing what?"

"Me. I think I need some healing."

"Okay." He didn't ask for clarification. If she needed healing, then she did. And damn, in spite of everything, he wanted to help her to do just that. He took a couple slow steps forward, bringing them almost toe to toe, but he didn't reach out for her, as much as he wanted to.

"Have you made love to anyone since the…explosion?"

"Yes."

Callie waited.

"She was a nurse…. My nurse."

"Oh."

"Kind of a mercy thing, I think."

Callie hooked her fingers in the waistband of his jeans, putting his manhood on instant alert.

"The relationship didn't last long," he added.

She tugged and he stepped forward.

"So you haven't made love with anyone who wasn't in the medical profession. Someone who isn't used to traumatized body parts?"

"Uh…no."

"I think you should do that. I think you would feel better."

"Maybe," he conceded.

"I may not be able to offer you a future, but I can offer you a very pleasant here and now."

Nathan figured he had two seconds of sanity left. Maybe three, max. He really had to—

"Take off your shirt," Callie said against his mouth before rolling away so that he could actually do as she asked. "I'll take care of the briefs."

After that they didn't talk. Callie explored, touching Nathan's body in the way he'd fantasized about as a kid, with her hands, her lips. She was hesitant when her fingers skimmed over his scarred torso, so she explored him with her mouth instead.

"Is this okay?" She traced her tongue over the sensitive skin between the scars, making him swell almost to the bursting point.

He closed his eyes and nodded. "Fine. It feels fine."

He rolled over on top of her, before she could get to his leg. He was still sensitive about the leg. "I haven't made love to anyone in over a year."

"So you're saying—"

He managed to crack a smile. "If the first time is quick—" he touched his forehead to hers "—I'll make up for it the second time."

"I don't know, Nate. You're older now. Are you sure you're up to two in a row?"

"Oh, I'm up all right." And there'd be no teenage jitters getting in the way tonight.

She pulled his lips down to hers, kissing him aggressively. Making him wonder how long it had been since she'd had a lover. "How about number three?"

"That would be the one that happens before number four," he said roughly.

She laughed. This felt good. Playful. Not overly serious. "I like the way you think."

THEY DIDN'T MAKE IT to number four. The minds were willing, but the flesh was weak. At least until light started spilling in through the windows and Callie reached over for Nate.

He pulled her up on top of him, guiding himself into her, and they made love slowly, one last time. It had to be the last time. Callie could lose herself in the darkness, pretend that making love was all about the here and now, which it was, but making love to Nate in the daylight, watching the reaction in his eyes, feeling him build to climax, his fingers curved around her waist as she rode him… that was different. It was harder to keep the feelings in check.

Damned light.

Callie collapsed against him after they came, then she rolled off.

"And reality comes rushing in," Nathan said, watching her as she put space between them before she turned onto her side, propping her head on her hand. Her hair fell into her eyes and Nathan gently brushed it back.

"How do you feel?"

"Like I love making love to you," she said matter-of-factly.

"For today."

"For as long as I'm here."

He stared down at her, then brought his hand up to tangle in her hair, cupping the back of her head, wanting to pull her onto his chest and kiss her. Then maybe go for number five.

Instead he moved his hand from her hair to gently touch her face. "Promise me one thing, Cal."

"What?" she whispered warily.

"Don't disappear on me, okay? If you're scared, tell me. I'll back off. Just…don't leave."

Callie smiled. It wobbled slightly, but it qualified. "All right," she said, her voice huskier than usual. "I told you I'd be up front with you, so, yeah. I promise."

CHAPTER THIRTEEN

CALLIE HAD BEEN HOME for only a few minutes when there was a knock on the door. She was sore in interesting places, and crossing the living room brought back flashes of the night before. Healing sex with Nate had turned out to be amazing sex.

And now his disapproving older brother stood on her porch.

Normally she wouldn't have been that wild to see Garrett, but today she hoped he had some information on the fire. She invited him in and closed the door behind him. "Would you like some coffee or something?" All she had was instant, since she'd gotten rid of the coffeepot, but cops were supposed to be used to substandard coffee.

"No, thanks. I came to ask a few questions." He was studying her as if she'd committed the crime herself. "Have you had any more dealings with Mitch Michaels since you called Dispatch about him?" he asked sternly.

Callie's eyes widened as she realized what he was getting at. "Do you mean he's the one?"

"Have you had any dealings with him since then?"

"None." Garrett made a note. "Is he the guy who burned my fence?" she repeated.

"The boy next door saw someone that fit the description."

"The Hobart boy?"

"The same. So I asked around and a couple of people two blocks over mentioned a car similar to his parked in their alley at a time that would correspond with the fire."

"What happens now?"

"We'll question him."

Callie put a hand on either side of the base of her neck as she digested what Garrett was telling her. "How sure are you?"

For a second she didn't think he was going to answer, then he said, "I'm sure," before he started toward the door.

"Let me know what happens, will you?"

"Yeah." Garrett's mouth worked for a

moment, as if he had something else to say and was trying to hold it back.

"Yes, I left Nate in one piece," she said. Satisfied and exhausted. In that order.

Garrett's eyes narrowed. "I don't think he always makes the best decisions where you're concerned."

"They're his decisions to make."

"Do you know about…" His eyes remained hard as his voice trailed away.

"The bomb. Yes. I know." So there.

"I think he took that job to impress you." Callie drew back. "No way."

"You dumped him because he was boring, so he decided to become un-boring."

"I did not dump him because he was boring."

"That's not how he saw it. He saw it as not measuring up. Not even being worthy of a phone call."

"You're…you're not putting this guilt trip on me, Garrett."

"I don't have anything against you personally. I just don't want to see you tie my brother in knots again."

It was all Callie could do not to slam the door after Garrett had left. She didn't believe that Nathan took that job because of her. If he was proving he wasn't boring, the only person he had to convince was himself.

NATHAN SETTLED AT his desk, wishing he could spend the day with Callie, and knowing that was impossible, even if his work schedule would allow such a thing. Which it wouldn't.

Callie wanted him to be there for her, but he didn't think she'd counted on the intensity of feelings between the two of them the night before. What she'd had in mind was comforting sex between friends. Sex to help her forget the fire. Sex to make Nate feel better about himself. She probably hadn't counted on mind-numbing sex. Even Nate had been surprised, and he'd wanted Callie for a long, long time. He just hadn't been able to admit it to himself.

His cell phone rang before he'd managed to address even one of the multitudes of tasks awaiting his attention. He flipped it open.

"Finally turned your phone on?" Garrett asked snidely, making Nathan believe that his brother knew exactly why he'd turned it off last night.

"Do you know something about the fire?"

"I think Mitch Michaels started it, but I don't know why he did it last night instead of when Callie turned him in. Maybe he just needed time to stew."

Oh shit. "How sure are you?"

"On a scale of one to five…six.'

Nathan brought his hand up to his forehead. "I ripped him a new asshole when I found out that he'd tried to intimidate Callie."

"And that would have been…?"

"Two days ago." Nathan had no problem believing the kid was that vindictive. "He hit on little Katie here at work last spring and I threatened him with a harassment charge. He backed off, but when I found out he was at it again…"

"You kinda lost it."

"Yeah."

"And Callie was involved."

"Yeah," Nate answered flatly, in a you-want-to-make-something-of-it? tone. "How do you know it's him?"

"Eyewitnesses. Two saw him and one is over the age of eighteen, so he's a little more reliable than my other witness. I've found three people who saw his car parked in an alley a few blocks away at the time of the fire."

"Have you questioned him?"

"Sure have. Just one problem."

"What's that?"

"His frigging family gave him an alibi."

Nathan sat straighter in his chair. "So what are you going to do?"

"I'm going to continue to investigate, see how much evidence I can put together."

"Get something concrete, will you?" There were too many small things that a big-name attorney could seize upon in a circumstantial case—and Nathan could almost see the lawyers lining up outside Vince Michaels's office door.

"Oh, I'll do my best," Garrett said. "I've been wondering about other *incidents*.... I have some people to talk to."

Nathan knew exactly what his brother wouldn't say out loud over the cell phone. Maybe Mitch was involved in some of the recent manmade fires, if not all of them.

"I would very much like you to get him by the short hairs if you can."

"Yeah," Garrett agreed. "And then shake him. I'll work on it."

Nathan hung up as Joy slipped into the room and set an emergency cup of green tea on his desk. She left again without saying a word. He tried to call Callie, to touch base on this Mitch Michaels development. Her voice mail kicked in.

She's all right, he told himself. Garrett had talked to her a few hours ago. *She just needs some time alone.*

Either that, or she'd already panicked and bolted because they'd made love.

No. She'd said she would be up front with him. He believed her. When she left this time, he'd know about it in advance. That would certainly dull the pain.

He thought about calling the house phone, then decided he needed to get his work done. He'd go over after and see her in person. He had a feeling that was the only way he was going to know what was going on in her head.

THE LANDLINE RANG and Callie jumped. *Nate?* She grabbed for it. "Hello?"

"Callie, I know you're leaving, but can you give me one more day at the school?" Mrs. Serrano. Sounding absolutely desperate. "I already have Principal Domingo covering a class and I don't know what I'm going to do with Mr. Lightfoot's."

"I can't. I'm sorry, but…I can't."

"If it's because of Mr. Gerard…"

Callie rolled her eyes to the ceiling. She'd barely thought of him over the past few days. "No, it's the fire behind my house. I need to be available to investigators."

"The, uh, person in question is no longer in school."

Damn. Word traveled fast in this town. But Garrett had been questioning people in the neighborhood about the car.

"I can't. I'm sorry." Callie hung up after a quick goodbye. She felt for Mrs. Serrano, but she was going to spend the time she had left in town with Nate.

NATE LOOKED UP, surprised to see Callie leaning against the door frame, studying him. He'd been so involved in the story he was working on he hadn't heard her come in.

"Hey," he said in a low voice, feeling ridiculously better because she was there. Safe and…*there*.

She held up a white bag. "You want to partake in some clucks and fries?"

Nathan had a thing for chicken strips—clucks, as they'd called them when they were in high school.

He glanced over at the clock, then saved his story. He was caught up for the day, which was nothing short of a miracle, considering how much he'd had lined up when he'd gotten there, and how shot his concentration was because of Callie and Mitch Michaels. He'd simply put his head down, shut off all thought and forced himself to focus. It had paid off, because now he got to leave with Callie.

"Want to go eat them at my place?"

"You know—" she gave a crooked smile "—I do."

He turned off the monitor, pushed his chair in.

Again Callie followed him to his place in the Neon. She went with him through the side door into the house, and as soon as she had deposited the bag on the table, she was in his arms, her mouth on his. Nathan's leg nearly buckled.

His hands closed over her waist as he regained his balance. Within seconds Callie was unbuttoning his shirt, mumbling something about "always oxford." She peeled it off his shoulders and pushed it down his arms to the cuffs, which she'd forgotten to unbutton. Nathan arched his eyebrows and managed to unbutton himself through the fabric.

"Masterful," Callie said as his shirt hit the floor, followed by her own shirt. And bra. The last time they'd made love it had been dark. Nathan had been hiding his leg. He might still hide his leg, but he was doing better about his less-damaged torso, and right now his attention was on Callie…or rather, her breasts. He boosted her up onto the counter to where he could do them justice. Callie laughed as he lifted her, then sighed as his tongue circled first one nipple and then the other. Her hand clutched his hair.

"Too many clothes," Nathan muttered, unzipping her pants.

"It seems you're more interested in me than in dinner," Callie murmured with a smile.

He considered her, his expression very serious. "Yes, I am."

She laughed again. "Can we go to your bedroom? I like cushioning better than counters."

"We can go anywhere you like." Nathan kissed her. "I'd carry you, but…"

"No need." She jumped down off the counter and walked to the door leading to the hall, her unzipped jeans sliding lower on her hips with each step until her thong showed.

They didn't quite make it to the bedroom. They made it to the carpet, and it was a nice carpet. Plush. Perfect. But neither of them was thinking about carpeting when Nathan pulled off her thong and nudged her legs apart. Callie clung to him as he thrust into her, wishing they'd made peace weeks ago. So much wasted time.

It wasn't until later, when they lay side by side on the floor catching their breath, that Callie ran a hand over the rug and asked, "Did you pay extra for double padding?"

"Yeah, I did."

"Good planning."

He stood and held out a hand to help Callie to her feet. "Shower, then chicken?"

"Will the shower involve creative use of suds?"

He grinned. "Doesn't it always?"

Afterward they ate the chicken and fries without bothering to warm them, and talked about the old times, the good times, every-thing except the present.

It was Nathan who finally brought it up, after they'd abandoned the kitchen and made love yet again, in his bed. Garrett had con-tacted Callie that afternoon, so she knew about Mitch and the alibi. She did not know how concerned Nathan was.

"If it hadn't been an alibi, he'd be out on bail," Callie pointed out.

"True." Nate propped his head on his elbow. "Maybe you should stay here."

"I, uh…"

"Is that scarier than facing Mitch?" he asked, watching her expression shift from wary to warier.

"No. Of course not. It's just that I've never really depended on anyone for anything, except for Grace."

He reached out and pulled her to him. It took her a moment to settle at his side, her head on his chest, but her muscles weren't fully relaxed. "What do you do when you fall in love?"

"I try not to do that," she said softly, her breath teasing his skin.

"Why?" he asked. Why couldn't she let herself fall in love with him?

"It's the way I am."

He was getting tired of hearing that answer. Nathan didn't buy absolutes.

"Do you think it has something to do with being a foster kid? With security?" he ventured, tossing out the obvious theory, the one he'd always believed was at the bottom of Callie's wanderlust.

She settled her head again. "Grace gave me all the security I needed. If she hadn't, then I wouldn't exactly be the type to gallivant around the world, would I? Especially with my father being an unsolved missing person case."

They'd discussed her father and the possibilities innumerable times as teens. She'd always seemed so matter-of-fact about the situation, so accepting of what she couldn't change, even if that meant accepting that her father had probably been murdered. Even now her tone was dispassionate.

"And you don't think what happened to him might affect your sense of security?"

"Whatever happened to him had nothing to do with me. He was in the wrong place at the wrong time, or maybe even involved in the wrong profession. The only thing that possibly relates is he needed to travel. Just like me, so I guess I inherited that trait from him."

Funny that the trait never showed up until graduation, after Nathan had told her he loved her.

"No offense, Callie, but I'm not buying it."

Her fingers curled on his chest and he felt her inhale deeply, then exhale. "Don't psychoanalyze me, Nate. Does it really matter why?"

"If you know the reason, then you can change."

She brought her head up suddenly. "Who says I want to change?"

"Is it healthy to run every time someone gets too close?"

"I don't run because people get too close."

"Then why? And I don't want to hear it's the way you are. There's a reason and I don't for one minute believe it's in your DNA."

Callie's expression was a mixture of anger and pain. "Why are you ruining things? Why can't we just enjoy what we have?"

Because we could have so much more.

Nathan bit back the words. For now. After he'd remained silent for a few moments, Callie finally relaxed and curled up against him again, her cheek and her lightly clenched fist resting on his chest. She stared pensively off across the room until finally her eyes drifted shut and she slept.

CHAPTER FOURTEEN

NATHAN AND HIS BROTHERS took their father out for an early breakfast before work. At first John acted as if the breakfast was a setup, but eventually he let down his guard—right up to the point when Garrett reordered for him, nixing the country fried steak, fries and gravy for an egg white omelet and fruit.

"He's supposed to be the killjoy," John grumbled, stabbing a finger at Nathan. Nate shrugged it off. As always. He'd developed a fairly thick skin over the years, which had proved handy in a journalism career.

"I want to be the killjoy next time," Seth declared. John growled at him and picked up his glass of ice water.

They discussed the fire at Callie's place, which John had not been involved with, until the food came, then launched into the parts of the investigation Garrett could discuss. In other words, the parts that Nathan was free to print. Garrett mentioned that he'd arranged for additional patrols in that neighborhood, then shot a look at Nate before adding that he wasn't entirely certain they were needed.

"She slept at her place last night," Nathan said, not mentioning that he'd been there, too. They hadn't discussed the past or the future. They'd simply given each other as much pleasure as possible. In fact, they'd barely spoken. Things had changed since he'd told her he didn't buy the genetic wanderlust theory, and Nathan had no idea what the outcome would be. He was certain, however, that he and Callie would never have any chance of a future until she faced whatever it was that made her run.

John jerked his gaze up from the fruit he'd been pushing around the bowl. Nathan waited for him to say something—anything—disparaging, because this time it was not going unchallenged. His dad pulled in a deep, disapproving breath, but said nothing.

All in all, it was a crappy father-sons meal,

and Nathan was glad to escape to his stress-ful job. He'd been there almost five minutes when Joy brought in a cup of tea—the caf-feinated kind—and two aspirin. Nathan hadn't asked for aspirin, so his sleepless night coupled with breakfast with his dad might have showed. He thanked her and she left, after giving him one final worried look. A few seconds later she buzzed him.

"Mr. Michaels on line one."

Nathan wished he had that flask of Laph-roaig. He pushed his hair back off his forehead, then picked up the office line.

"Marcenek."

"Nathan, I wanted to touch base concern-ing these unfounded accusations against Mitch."

"There were witnesses." And Nate had already written the story.

"One of whom was eight years old. And we both know the veracity of eyewitnesses. What they saw was someone who looked similar—if they saw anyone at all. Mitch was home with the family."

Funny how rich people's sight was more dependable than other people's. And Nathan wasn't going to bring up the distinctive sports car Mitch drove, which several people had spotted in the area. There were only two in town and Garrett had checked the other one out, too.

"Your boy needs help, Vince."

"One more remark like that and you're no longer an employee of our news family." Which was very likely going to happen whether Nate made another remark or not. He was so ready to move on.

"You want me to pretend this didn't happen."

"There is no concrete proof it did happen."

The guy sounded as if he was practicing a speech.

"I have to report the news. If the sheriff questions a person of interest in a felony, it's news. It's up to the sheriff whether or not he releases the name."

Vince's voice became flintlike. "Keep Mitch out of this. He wasn't involved. Not a word." Vince ended the call without saying goodbye.

Nathan set the phone on his desk and brought up his computer screen. He started to type but his fingers stilled on the keyboard after a couple of sentences.

So what did he want to be when he grew up? He should probably make a decision on that, because he would eventually be printing Mitch's name, if Garrett was correct in his assumptions, and then he'd no longer be the editor of the *Wesley Star*.

He reached for his cell and found Suzanne's work number.

"I need a job," he said without a hello.

"It's about time. Too bad you didn't need a job last month."

"Things have changed. Got any leads?"

"I might. The guy they just hired isn't going to last."

"Why not?"

"Because the editor is going to kill him. He writes like a dream, but he's all ego. Real prima donna and it isn't going over well. The guy is oblivious."

The wonder of the superego. "Is it wrong of me to hope for the worst?"

"Naw," Suzanne said. "The guy is digging his own grave fast. I'll call when there's a development, and in the meanwhile… maybe you could get away for a day, come and meet some people?"

"Yeah. I can do that." And, while he

waited for a job opening, he had some resources to support himself. He'd received an injury settlement for his leg, which he'd invested. His house payment was low enough that he could rent the place for the cost of the payment and then some. If he wanted to head off to the city to try his hand at freelancing—either editing or writing—until something permanent opened up, well, he could do it.

So…what did he do about Callie?

NATHAN WAS A QUIET GUY, but tonight he was too quiet for Callie's peace of mind. They were in his bed, where they seemed to spend most of their time together, laughing, talking, making love. Only tonight they weren't laughing or talking.

Something was on his mind. Something more than what they'd just finished doing, which was uppermost in her mind at the moment.

"What's up?" she finally asked, tracing a pattern in his chest hair until he caught her fingers and brought them to kiss his lips.

"I'm trying to get a job in Seattle."

Callie's head came up. "When?"

He continued to hold her hand loosely in his own. "As soon as I can."

She settled her cheek back onto his chest. They'd discussed Vince threatening to fire him and she really hoped Nathan sued for wrongful dismissal if that happened. He had an article coming out in this week's paper, but the sheriff's office hadn't officially named a suspect. They figured Nate would be employed right up until a suspect was named and Nate reported it.

"What do you think about Seattle?" he asked.

She frowned. "What do you mean?"

"I was thinking that maybe you wouldn't mind going there."

"I…uh…"

"It wouldn't have to be a big commitment, Callie."

She moistened her suddenly dry lips. He wanted her to go with him. It would be like it was now. Only in Seattle.

Why was that so scary?

Because he was talking as if they would live together and maybe depend on each other and…

"I don't think that would be good."

"Why?" he asked in a no-nonsense voice.

"Because if I wanted to leave and we had gone there together…"

"Then I imagine you would just do it." He rolled over and took her face in his hands. "Do you care about me, Callie?"

"You know I do," she whispered back. "You're my best friend."

"But you don't trust me."

Or was it that she didn't trust herself?

Callie pulled away from Nate and got out of bed. She needed to move, to do something. "I have to go."

Nate didn't try to stop her. She put on her clothes while he lay in bed watching her, his expression blank, as if this was exactly what he had expected.

"You can't run forever. We need to talk about this."

"Talk about what?"

"What makes you run."

"I know what makes me run, whether you believe it or not."

Nate got out of bed and started getting dressed himself.

"Sometimes I wonder which of us is

more scarred," he muttered as he stepped into his jeans.

"I am not scarred. You just can't accept who I am."

"But I do love you."

Callie froze for a split second, then forced herself to shove her feet into her shoes, her arms into her jacket sleeves. She couldn't remember the last time she'd heard words that frightened her more.

"YOU ARE THE LUCKIEST SOB I know," Suzanne said.

Funny, but he wasn't feeling all that lucky since having his Seattle conversation with Callie the night before. But the paper had come out with the article about the unnamed arson suspect, and Vince hadn't fired him for that, so maybe he did have a little luck going his way.

"Did they get rid of the ego guy?" Nathan asked, shuffling through some hard copies on his desk.

"No. Jessica McCrae quit. She got accepted into law school and she's outta here."

Nate let out a low whistle.

"She gave notice today and they want to

fill the position immediately." Suzanne paused before saying, "I, uh, took the liberty of tossing your name into the ring. Reynolds would like to see a résumé and a warm body if you can swing a quick trip up here."

"Marcus Reynolds?"

"The same."

Marcus had been Nate's immediate boss before he was injured, and they had always seen eye to eye. "Give me a date and time and I'll work something out."

"Fax a résumé and I'll get back to you."

Nathan hung up the phone. He was fond of Wesley, understood the people, and he liked living close to his brothers. But he wasn't an editor at heart. He was a writer and reporter.

Which left the question…did he quit? Or wait to get fired? Because he had no doubt he was going to be fired in the near future. Vince trusted him to do exactly as he was told—that point was driven home when his boss hadn't demanded to see the last edition of the paper before it came out—so Vince was going to be furious when Nathan eventually defied his orders and printed Mitch's name as a suspect. On the plus side, if he got fired he'd get severance, but just how much of an effect would that have on his chances in Seattle?

Reynolds would understand.

The phone rang just as Nate turned back to the keyboard.

"Day after tomorrow," Suzanne said. "Can you do it?"

Chip could take over his job for two days. Three if he had to, and Nathan probably wouldn't be working for Vince Michaels by that time.

"I can do it."

NATHAN HADN'T SEEN CALLIE in two days—not since he'd told her he loved her—when he stopped by her house. There was a For Sale sign on the lawn, but the Neon was still out front. He knocked on the door.

Callie answered almost immediately. When she saw it was him, her lips compressed, but she stepped back to let him in.

He looked down at her, wishing there was some magic way to get beyond this barrier Callie didn't believe in.

"I'm going to Seattle."

Callie's mouth dropped open. "Travel safe," she finally said.

"Will you be here when I get back?"

"I don't know. I had an offer for a travel story that might last two weeks. Argentina."

"Is that what you want, Callie?"

"It's what I *do*. I travel." She tilted her chin defensively.

"You're just like your father," he said softly.

"I know."

"He abandoned everyone, and you do the same thing."

Callie's head jerked as if he'd slapped her. "My father didn't abandon me!" she snapped. "He always came back, until the trip when he *couldn't* come back."

"You know that how…?"

"I…" Callie closed her mouth.

"Even if he *was* a crime victim, the fact remains your father dumped you with whoever was available, while he went off to wherever he used to go. That's abandonment. You aren't hardwired to travel, Callie. You're hardwired to protect yourself. You live this way because it helps you believe your father was an okay guy. It helps you feel close to him."

"My father *was* an okay guy."

"Okay guys don't dump their kids with whoever's available and take off. Why do you think you were so upset about the Hobart kids?"

She turned her head sideways, looking away.

"All I'm saying is that maybe you're trying to justify your father's actions by living them. And maybe you don't have to do that anymore."

Callie pushed her hand up over her forehead as if she had a headache.

"Callie—" He reached to touch her face, but she stepped away.

"Go on your trip, Nate."

Nathan let his hand drop back to his side. "Will you be here when I get back?"

"I don't know, and that's as up front as I can truthfully be right now."

Ten minutes later, Nathan made the turn onto the highway to Elko, his mind absorbed with Callie—as it would be all night. And the next day. Smooth. Really smooth.

He wondered if he'd ever see her again.

CALLIE CLEARED EVERYTHING out of the house in preparation for the sale. She boxed up the dishes she'd been using, the teapot and extra towels, and took them over to Alice, who was planning a yard sale and was quite thrilled to have additional items.

"Are you sure you don't want me to give you the money they bring in?" she asked for the second time. The kitchen was now empty except for paper plates and plastic forks.

"No. This is a thank-you for being such a good friend to Grace," Callie said. Then she went back to rake the backyard, which she'd finally gotten mowed. The man across the alley, who'd also rebuilt the fence for a reasonable sum in less than half a day, had taken care of the job.

She threw herself into the work. It gave her body something to do while her mind ran wild. Try as she might, she could not shut out the things Nate had said to her.

She wanted him to be wrong. She didn't want her father to be a guy who abandoned her. She wanted him to be the same kind of gypsy she was.

And Nathan had no reason to question the theory that her dad had been the victim of foul play. Grace had believed it, and Grace was one of the most intelligent women Callie had ever met. She was a woman who liked to learn things. She read broadly and when she didn't know about something, she researched.

She must have done the same in the situation with Callie's father. Callie couldn't imagine Grace doing less. She also couldn't imagine her not prodding the police to find answers.

Yet Callie didn't recall any information in Grace's extensive files, the ones that had taken her most of a day to sort, on unsolved police cases. And Grace had told her she hadn't known where her father was headed on that fateful trip.

Did that make sense? Would Grace take Callie without knowing where her dad was going? What if there had been an emergency? What if Grace had had to get hold of him?

That didn't add up.

Damn Nate for bringing this up. Callie had dealt with the loss of her father long ago. She didn't need to be obsessing about it now.

But she had a feeling that it was, indeed, at the bottom of everything.

CHAPTER FIFTEEN

NATE WOULD HAVE ENJOYED his stay in the city more if he'd been able to get Callie off his mind.

Would she be there when he got back? Or was he going to have to hunt her down? Because he would this time.

"What's going on?" Suzanne finally asked over drinks on his last evening there. It was after ten on a weeknight, but the hotel bar was still busy. The meeting with Marcus had gone well, and Nate was fairly certain he'd be called back for an interview. He wanted the job. He also wanted to keep Callie.

"Unfinished business," he said.

"I'm sure the paper will get along just fine without you."

Nate nodded, swirled the ice in his almost empty drink.

"Another?" Suzanne nodded at the glass.

He surveyed the assortment of liquor displayed on backlit glass shelves behind the sleek curve of the ebony bar—a far cry from the haphazardly arranged bottles on the homemade wooden shelves in Fuzzy's Tavern—then shook his head.

"I think I'm good." Nathan preferred to do his thinking while sober, and right now he had some things to work out.

"You're a lot of fun on vacation."

He smiled then and she smiled back. They did well together, he and Suzanne. "I'd like to work for Marcus," he said. "I'd like to move back to Seattle."

"But…"

"No buts. I would."

"But…"

"I think I'm in love."

"When will you know for sure?" Suzanne asked drily.

"The thing is," Nathan said, ignoring her last comment, "she has a problem."

Suzanne pantomimed lifting a bottle to her lips, and Nathan frowned. "Wouldn't you feel stupid if that was the problem?"

"Is it?" she asked, her eyes growing wide.

"No. She's afraid of commitment. Her

father disappeared when she was young and I think that's why she's always on the move."

"I don't get the connection," Suzanne said. "If her father left, don't you think that would make her more clingy?"

"I think she's validating his abandonment somehow in her head."

"What are you going to do?"

"No idea. I don't even know if she'll be there when I get back."

"Don't waste your time on a flake."

"She's not a flake."

Suzanne tilted her head. "Maybe you are in love. I've never seen you in love before."

Nathan made a face at her, then finished the last of his drink. Suzanne glanced at her watch.

"Better get home to Julia," he said, wishing he could go home to Callie right now instead of waiting for his flight the next day.

"You could have stopped by the condo, you know. She doesn't blame you anymore."

But she had at the time of the accident and Nate knew how ingrained a certain behavior could become. Being the good brother because it was the only role your father halfway understood. Or letting memories of a long-dead father control the way you lived.

"Maybe next time."

"I'll hold you to that."

Nathan grinned. "You do that."

THE DREAM CAME BACK full force that night, scaring the bejeezus out of Callie. It was the closest she'd come to remembering—and for one terrifying moment she thought she had. There was a flash of strong recognition, an overwhelming sense of "of course!" followed by the withdrawal, the terror.

Callie jumped out of bed, pacing the floor, hugging herself.

Oh, man. Oh, man.

This had to stop. She had to get out of Wesley and away from Nate.

But this time Nate hadn't triggered the dream. She was certain of it. And the Hobarts probably weren't guilty, either. The kids were cared for in the family's own way.

That left…questions. Lots of questions about the dream and, quite possibly, her father.

So who did she ask?

Who would know about her dad? No one in

this town. They'd lived in Elko, sixty miles away, and before that Reno, and before that…who knew? Somewhere along the line her mother had died. Callie had been four at the time. The story was she'd drowned, but right now Callie didn't believe anything anymore.

Okay, when she came to live with Grace, CPS would have been involved, but it would have been the Elko CPS. Would they still have files that old? And law enforcement would have been called when her dad hadn't returned from his trip.

Twenty-two years ago, so most if not all of the deputies would be retired. Maybe she could find the case file in Elko?

Or maybe she could ask the only person she knew who'd been involved in law enforcement at the time. And wouldn't John Marcenek be thrilled to have a visit from her?

John was not thrilled. He didn't even try to fake it. He opened the door and, when Callie told him she had a few questions, he gruffly waved her into the house, as if she were interrupting high tea with the queen.

"Why are you here?" he asked, easing his bulk down onto a sturdy captain's chair.

"I want information about my father."

"I didn't know your father. He wasn't from around here."

"Do you know of him?"

John shook his head stubbornly.

"Grace never had you look into his disappearance?"

"She did."

"And…?" Callie prompted, growing impatient.

"Nothing came of it."

Callie's jaw tightened, but she'd questioned too many difficult people over the course of her career to let John Marcenek buffalo her.

"But you helped Grace with some kind of foster care issue. I once heard her tell a friend about it."

"All I did was help the Elko authorities track Grace down," he said dismissively.

Callie stared at him. "Why would they have tracked Grace down?" She felt a numb premonitory chill spreading through her. His statement made no sense. "My father left me at her house."

"Your father left you in the Elko K-Mart."

Callie blinked, not comprehending.

Surely she'd heard wrong. After all, blood was pounding in her ears to the point that she was starting to feel light-headed. She swallowed hard. "No. He left me with Grace."

"The night crew found you asleep under a clothing rack after the store had closed." He glared at her impatiently. "You were six years old, for cripe's sake. Don't tell me you don't remember?"

Callie wanted very much to tell him she didn't remember, but her voice didn't seem to be working. Neither did her brain. She stared at him for a long, long moment before she managed to get control of her vocal cords. "Does Nate know?"

John Marcenek gave her a disgusted, of-course-he-does look.

Callie jumped to her feet then, knocking the chair back and walked blindly to the door.

"Wait a minute!"

Callie ignored him and headed out the door, down the path to her car. She didn't know at what point she'd started running, or even how she got the car started. John was lumbering toward her when she squealed away from the curb.

Stay or go? The question circled in Callie's brain as she started to drive. Her suitcase was already in the car. Heck, everything she owned was in the car.

Stay or go?

THERE WAS SOMETHING WRONG with the old man. When Nathan got home he went over to his dad's house to see him before going to the office, since both Garrett and Seth were on shift. John was sitting in his chair at the table, a solitaire game laid out in front of him. But he had yet to turn a card.

"Are you feeling all right?" Nathan asked.

"How was the trip?"

"Interesting."

"Are you going to leave?" he asked bluntly.

"When the right job comes along."

"No idea when that might be? Or where?"

Nate shook his head. "Could be a while. Could be tomorrow."

John stared off into space.

"Come on, Dad. It isn't as if I'm thirteen and running off to join the circus."

"I like having all of you here."

Well, that was a shocker. Nate tilted his head as he gave his dad a sidelong glance.

Yep. It did appear to be his father sitting there, staring at the table.

"Garrett, Seth and you," the old man continued, as if there might be some confusion as to who he was referring to. "I like having you around."

"Yeah," Nathan said. Had the old man had another episode?

"Callie was here."

"She was?" Nathan asked cautiously, not liking his father's odd tone.

"Yeah. I, uh, told her something I don't think she knew."

"How bad of a something?"

John glanced down at the cards. He reached out and put a red ten on a black jack, then settled his hand back in his lap before looking up at his son. Nathan stared at him. What on earth? His heart wasn't beating faster, but it was beating harder. It felt as if it was hitting his rib cage with each slow pulse.

"What did you tell her, Dad?"

"I told her that her father abandoned her in the Elko K-Mart."

For one long moment, Nathan simply stared at his father, not quite able to believe what he'd heard. John stared back in defiance.

"I thought she knew, damn it. I thought she was putting on some stupid act to get information out of me."

"Her father left her in a store?" *This was crazy.*

"They found her sleeping under a clothes rack after hours. She was six years old." His father dropped his chin, slowly shook his head. "Hell, I remember stuff from when I was six years old and that was almost sixty years ago."

Nathan shoved his hands in his pockets and turned to stare blindly out the window. Her father had abandoned her in a store? Some things were falling into place. He muttered a curse.

"You remember stuff when you were six, right?" John asked.

"Yeah." He remembered Callie when she came into Mrs. Milliken's first grade class, with her long blond braids, and baggy tights over her skinny legs.

"Then what the hell?"

"Dad. You're a cop. You know about traumatic memory loss."

"That happens in car wrecks, beatings. Not from falling asleep in a store."

"Who knows how terrifying it might have been to wake up in a store? To be surrounded by strangers. Especially for a kid who didn't have the most stable existence." He took a few paces to the door, then pulled his cell out of his pocket and hit her number. No answer. But he hadn't expected one. "How did she look when she left?"

"Upset," John confessed.

Nathan cursed and paced some more. "What the hell were you thinking?"

"I told you what I was thinking. I was thinking she knew and was pumping me for information."

"What kind of information?"

"I don't know!" his father bellowed. John Marcenek was not accustomed to being wrong, and this time he'd screwed up and he knew it.

"Why didn't you tell me?"

"Why? Grace asked me to keep the facts quiet. She and I were the only ones who knew."

"Why the secrecy?"

John gave him a withering look. "Grace thought it would be easier on Callie."

"Well, she was probably right," Nathan

admitted. People would have been all over a story like that. Instead of being involved with a mystery, Callie would have been the object of pity, and heaven only knew what kids would do with ammo like that if they hadn't liked her. Kids were ruthless creatures.

"You could have told me after she left town that first time. It wouldn't have mattered then."

"Why should I have told you?"

Nathan turned an incredulous gaze toward his dad. "Because it might have helped me understand why she left."

"So you could have gone after her? Tried to fix things?" John demanded.

"Yeah. Maybe," Nathan answered in the same tone. "It was my choice. I was eighteen."

"Oh, yeah. Eighteen-year-olds are known for brains." John shoved the cards into a messy heap in front of him. "That girl had issues. There was no way I wanted you chasing after her."

"I loved her."

"You were better off without her," his dad said bitterly.

"How so?"

"The writing and all that shit. You never wanted to do that until you hooked up with her. You were planning to go into forensics. It was the one thing you were interested in that I understood. And then along came Callie and all that was out the window."

"I always liked to write. Like Mom did. I just never said it out loud. Callie had nothing to do with it."

John snorted.

Nathan didn't give a flying you-know-what what his dad believed. He started for the door.

"Where you going?" his father asked, even though he had to know the answer.

"I'm going to find Callie. It's what I should have done the last time." Although neither of them would have been prepared to fight this battle back then. Now…now there was a chance.

He hoped.

NATHAN DROVE to Callie's house. As he expected, the Neon was gone. He walked past the For Sale sign and went to the door to knock. Just to be sure. The Hobart kids were playing in their yard. He could hear them arguing over a ball, which soon came sailing over the thick honeysuckle bushes and rolled to a stop in the vacant lot. Nathan walked over to it just as the kids came out of the yard. They stopped when they saw him.

"Have you seen the lady who lives here?"

The children looked at each other, then simultaneously shrugged. They had been taught not to talk to strangers. They were also skinny and dusty, and he could understand how Callie, having seen them out after dark, when Grandma had fallen asleep, would have been concerned. Especially since she had a deeply ingrained reason to be sensitive to neglect.

"If you've seen her today, nod your heads."

The girl nodded and the boy shook his head.

"Great. Thanks." Nathan went back to his car and hit Garrett's number on speed dial. "I want to know the name and address of the owner of Callie's Neon. And don't tell me you have no way of knowing, because you ran the plate. If you didn't, then you're some kind of pod person impersonating my brother, the anal cop."

"I'll drop the information by after shift."

"I want it now."

"I'm on patrol. I'll be at your place in ninety minutes. If you can wait that long."

Nathan didn't want to wait that long. He'd waited over a decade to straighten things out with Callie.

THE NEON WAS PARKED in the driveway. His driveway. Nathan was barely aware of getting out of his truck and crossing to the kitchen door through the open garage. Callie was sitting at the table, her laptop in front of her, the lid down. For a moment they just stared at one another. Then Callie spoke.

"Your father is such a jerk."

Nathan stopped, his hand on the back of the chair across the table from Callie's. "I'm sorry he did what he did, Callie."

"He tried to make me think you knew about my dad and didn't tell me. He doesn't understand you at all."

Nathan tilted his head to one side. This was not what he expected. "But I think he likes me," he said slowly, studying her. *Finally.*

"Then I guess you're better off than me," she said.

She stared down at the table. Nathan waited, but when she didn't look up, he finally asked, "Why are you here? At my place?"

She seemed shell-shocked as she raised her eyes and said, "I think I'm in the process of staying."

"Callie." He opened his arms. She rose from the chair and walked around the table and straight into his embrace.

"Oh, man, Nate." She leaned into him and he tightened his embrace. "You had it nailed. I was doing what my dad did. I was abandoning before I got abandoned."

"I kind of figured that."

"I have this dream. I've had it forever, but I could never remember it. It would come when I was stressed or anxious, scare the heck out of me. I've been having it so often while I was here. I thought it was because of you."

"Same dream every time?"

"I shouldn't call it a dream, because it's more like a flashback. A moment of recognition and terror. I had it before I went to stay with Grace, so I was certain it wasn't related to what happened to my dad…"

She rubbed her forehead. "I figured it out. I know what it is now. It's a flash of waking up under all the shirts on the clothes rack when my dad left me in that store, and seeing hands coming at me. I had no idea what was happening, where I was. I didn't know where my dad was. I was supposed to wait for him and they were taking me somewhere…." She stilled, staring sightlessly across the room. Finally she pulled in a deep breath and exhaled. "The first dream wasn't a dream at all. It was real. And the other dreams were flashbacks I wouldn't let myself remember." She sighed against his shirt. "I guess I'm glad I went to talk to your dad, even if it was traumatic."

"He could have gone at it a little more tactfully." Nate hesitated. "I figured after he did that, you'd be long gone by now."

"I started to leave," Callie confessed. "I drove almost twenty miles. It felt wrong. I mean—" she lifted her head so she could look into his eyes "—really wrong. This was a problem I couldn't outrun. This is a problem I'm going to have to face." She bit her lip. "I'm going to break the McCarran cycle."

"I'll help."

She leaned her cheek against his chest and he stroked her hair. "I'm so sorry, Nate."

"Don't be."

"You trusted me with your leg and even then I trusted you with…nothing."

"You had reasons."

"Which were a bunch of made-up crap." She tilted her head back to look into his face.

"Self-protective made-up crap."

She choked out a small laugh. "Yeah. I had this brilliant strategy. I'd make up excuses for my knee-jerk reactions instead of trying to find out why I acted that way."

"Did you have any clue about what your dad had done?"

"Just the dream."

Nate pushed the hair away from her face. "Well, I happen to know a little about self-protection myself. And I know that while it's hard to overcome those impulses, you can. Maybe not with everyone right away, but with certain—" he gently kissed her lips "—special—" he kissed her again "—people. The people you love and trust."

She smiled against his mouth. "What exactly are you saying, Nate?"

"That if you hang around with me, we can whip this together."

She drew back slightly. "And what about your father and your brother? You know…the ones who like me so much?"

Nate touched his forehead to hers, loving that she showed no sign of backing away, putting up the barriers. "You'll get used to them. I did."

"Garrett told me you took the job where you got hurt to prove to me you weren't boring."

Nathan made a mental note to kill his brother. "It may have entered into the equation," he admitted. "I wouldn't have minded becoming a dynamic guy who you regretted dumping."

"I never stopped regretting leaving you. Trust me. But I thought it was the only way things could be, that one of us would have devastated the other if I'd stayed."

"I'm not going to leave you, Callie, and I hope you never leave me. We can go places, we can stay here. I don't care."

"Let's go to where you have a job." She

pushed her hands into his hair as she tilted her lips up to lightly touch his. "Because I can always—"

"Find temp work."

"Except with you," she said just before she kissed him. "I plan on this being a permanent job."

Nathan gathered her closer, pressing her body against his, not caring one bit about scars. "With full benefits," he murmured.

"Exactly."

* * * * *

*Harlequin Intrigue top author
Delores Fossen presents
a brand-new series of breathtaking
romantic suspense!*
TEXAS MATERNITY: HOSTAGES
*The first installment available May 2010:
THE BABY'S GUARDIAN*

Shaw cursed and hooked his arm around Sabrina.

Despite the urgency that the deadly gunfire created, he tried to be careful with her, and he took the brunt of the fall when he pulled her to the ground. His shoulder hit hard, but he held on tight to his gun so that it wouldn't be jarred from his hand.

Shaw didn't stop there. He crawled over Sabrina, sheltering her pregnant belly with his body, and he came up ready to return fire.

This was obviously a situation he'd wanted to avoid at all cost. He didn't want his baby in the middle of a fight with these armed fugitives, but when they fired that shot, they'd left him no choice. Now, the trick was to get Sabrina safely out of there.

"Get down," someone on the SWAT team yelled from the roof of the adjacent building.

Shaw did. He dropped lower, covering Sabrina as best he could.

There was another shot, but this one came from a rifleman on the SWAT team. Shaw didn't look up, but he heard the sound of glass being blown apart.

The shots continued, all coming from his men, which meant it might be time to try to get Sabrina to better cover. Shaw glanced at the front of the building.

So that Sabrina's pregnant belly wouldn't be smashed against the ground, Shaw eased off her and moved her to a sitting position so that her back was against the brick wall. They were close. Too close. And face-to-face.

He found himself staring right into those sea-green eyes.

How will Shaw get Sabrina out?
Follow the daring rescue and the
heartbreaking aftermath in
THE BABY'S GUARDIAN
by Delores Fossen,
available May 2010
from Harlequin Intrigue.

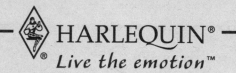

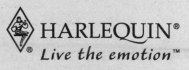

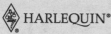

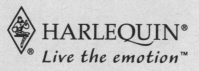

HARLEQUIN®
INTRIGUE®

BREATHTAKING ROMANTIC SUSPENSE

Shared dangers and passions lead to electrifying
romance and heart-stopping suspense!

Every month, you'll meet six new heroes
who are guaranteed to make your spine tingle
and your pulse pound. With them you'll enter
into the exciting world of Harlequin Intrigue—
where your life is on the line
and so is your heart!

THAT'S INTRIGUE—
ROMANTIC SUSPENSE
AT ITS BEST!

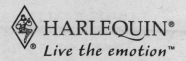

HARLEQUIN®
Live the emotion™

Harlequin® Historical
Historical Romantic Adventure!

Imagine a time of chivalrous knights and unconventional ladies, roguish rakes and impetuous heiresses, rugged cowboys and spirited frontierswomen—these rich and vivid tales will capture your imagination!

*Harlequin Historical...
they're too good to miss!*

HHDIR06

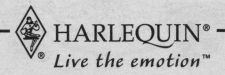

"It's been _____ _____ _____
If you p_____ _____
you must _____

He was pinn_____
husky, whiskey-l_____

Her strength didn't surprise him. After all, everything he had profiled about Marlena Maxwell showed a woman who knew how to take care of herself. What caught him by surprise was how his body responded to her. From his table watching her, he had appreciated her tall, sultry beauty. But up close and personal, the appreciation became a growing private interest.

She pushed an elbow hard against his lower back, forcing him to buckle against the wall. "It would save me time if you introduce yourself," she said, still in that husky drawl. "And I hope you don't mind. I have to make sure you're not armed, sweetheart."

The hard stucco of the building cut into the side of his face. "No problem," Steve assured her. "Look all you want."

She slid a hand into his jacket, checking for secret pockets. Then her hand glided down his chest to his jeans, obviously knowledgeable about the places a man could hide a weapon.

"Lower," Steve suggested, reckless desire spurring him now, "and you might find something loaded."

GENNITA LOW

INTO DANGER

AVON BOOKS
An Imprint of HarperCollinsPublishers

This is a work of fiction. Names, characters, places, and incidents are products of the author's imagination or are used fictitiously and are not to be construed as real. Any resemblance to actual events, locales, organizations, or persons, living or dead, is entirely coincidental.

AVON BOOKS
An Imprint of HarperCollins*Publishers*
10 East 53rd Street
New York, New York 10022-5299

First Avon Books paperback printing: April 2003

Avon Trademark Reg. U.S. Pat. Off. and in Other Countries, Marca Registrada, Hecho en U.S.A.
HarperCollins® is a registered trademark of HarperCollins Publishers Inc.

Printed in the U.S.A.

10 9 8 7 6 5 4 3 2 1

To Mother and Father,
my Stash, and Mike, my Ranger Buddy

———————————————————

Acknowledgments

Special thanks to Patti O'Shea, my writing partner; Melissa Copeland, who kept me sane; the sea mammals, who helped with research; Genitta Pearson, my wonderful editor; and Liz Trupin-Pulli, my agent who believed in me.

And from my heart thanks to the Delphi TDD ladies, my best reading BSHes—Maria Hammon, Miriam Caraway, Karen King, Angela Swanson, Sandy Still, Mo Kearney, Jenn Carr, Theresa Monsey, Rosie Lockhart, Shelly Hawthorne, and Tina Weena Smith.

Chapter One

There were many ways of kissing a woman. And many reasons to taste her. There were kisses that asked permission. And then there were kisses that sought an answer.

Steve McMillan had once assured the amused leader of Black STAR, his elite covert operations team, that there was a difference, at Admiral Jack Madison's bachelor party when things had gotten a bit rowdy, and the topic a bit . . . salty among the men. In real, everyday life, Steve McMillan wouldn't have dared bring up kissing and women, but everyone was having a good time ribbing the admiral about his young bride, and how he was going to kiss her after the ceremony. When someone brought up the subject of kissing . . . well, everyone started hooting his name to give advice to the old man.

It wasn't as if the admiral needed lessons, Steve reflected wryly, as he recalled the festivities from a year ago. If there was a man who didn't have to work at looking good, his leader was the one. In his early fifties, he still rated enough female sighs in the navy grapevine. But the navy grapevine had voted Steve McMillan the Best Kisser of the Millennium during some cornball poll on a website that had somehow became public snicker fodder on the naval bases. So now his buddies teased him mercilessly.

That was okay. Steve McMillan liked kissing women.

Which was not what he should be thinking about right now. He looked across the room at his target. She was a lot taller than he had expected; dressed in black leather, she made a striking figure standing against the bar, calmly sipping a drink. She didn't look like she was waiting for someone. Her stance was relaxed, her smile a little bored. One or two men had approached with interested smiles, but she had sent them away with a few words.

In the dark corner of the bar, he had been watching her for almost an hour now, and her patience seemed endless, because she hadn't glanced once at her watch or looked around at the patrons. She didn't fidget with her dark auburn hair. She didn't make small conversation. She didn't smoke. Once in a while she would turn around and lean back on her elbows to watch the baseball game in progress on a giant television set above the bar.

At exactly an hour later, she finished her drink, picked up the small suitcase by the bar stool, and walked off. She didn't look back, so she didn't see the appreciative glances admiring her long, leather-encased, shapely legs. Steve stood up and followed. It was dark and cool outside. He pulled on his jean jacket as he looked around for the woman. She was nowhere to be seen. He turned the corner, keeping to the shadows.

He was a trained operative. He knew not to show his training. So he allowed her to have the advantage for now.

Movement. Speed.

He was pinned hard against the wall, and a husky voice, whiskey-laced, drawled in his ear, "It's been an hour, sweetheart. If you plan to make a move, you mustn't make a lady wait."

Steve angled his head sideways, and the light out of the windows was just enough for him to make out her face. Her eyes gleamed back, no fear in them. Her lips were temptingly close and perfectly shaped.

There were kisses that stole. And there were kisses that gave away secrets. Steve wondered which kind would persuade a hired assassin to reveal who her target was.

Her strength didn't surprise him. After all, everything he had profiled about Marlena Maxwell showed a woman who knew how to take care of herself. What caught him by surprise was how his body responded to her. From his table watching her, he had appreciated her tall, sultry beauty, but up close and personal, the appreciation became a growing private interest.

"What's the matter?" she asked, when he didn't say a word. "Don't you like it when a woman comes after you?"

"It depends on what she's after," Steve answered.

"Oh? Like what?"

"I don't mind a lady after my body," Steve replied dryly, "but I do draw the line if it's my dead body."

She pushed an elbow hard against his lower back, forcing him to buckle against the wall. "Let's not bicker over details. It would save me time if you introduce yourself," she said, still in that husky drawl, "and I hope you don't mind. I have to make sure you aren't armed, sweetheart."

Damn, but the woman's elbow was sharp. The hard stucco of the building cut into the side of his face. "No problem," Steve assured her. "Look all you want."

She slid a hand into his jean jacket, checking for secret pockets. Then her hand glided down his chest to his jeans, obviously knowledgeable about the places a man could hide a weapon.

"Lower," Steve suggested, reckless desire spurring him now, "and you might find something loaded."

There was a pause. Her eyes looked into his for a moment, then she took up his challenge. And went lower.

Steve didn't blink. Or breathe. The woman, if nothing else, was bold. He supposed there was a first time for everything, even having his zipper down in front of a bar. He vaguely wondered what she would do if someone came out right now, but there was no time to think of such things when a woman's hand was down his pants. She felt cool against his skin, moving left then right. And she certainly was taking her time.

"No small weapons, not even a knife," she murmured. "There is nothing stashed here. This is very unprofessional."

"Sweetheart, now you're hurting my feelings," he murmured back, in the same low tone.

"I'm going to let you go and you may turn around very slowly." Her voice had a tinge of amusement. "Be careful, though, Stash, because unlike you, I'm armed. Do you hear me?"

"Yeah."

Steve did as he was told, letting his arms hang loosely. He looked down at her as she, too, spent a few moments studying him.

"Well," she finally said, "you're not whom I thought they would send."

Of course not. Said subject had been knocked out and was currently under protective custody. That middle man unfortunately knew nothing. He only had instructions to take care of Miss Maxwell. Whoever set this up had been careful, covering his tracks with fake identities. So Steve became his substitute to help Miss Maxwell find a place to stay, get her whatever she needed, give her all the company she wanted, play goon—and wait for her contact to show up. Or contacts. Their info hadn't been clear about that. Only one thing was certain. Marlena Maxwell wasn't in town to visit the Library of Congress.

"Name," she requested, her voice turning a little cooler.

"Steve," he answered. After a moment, he lifted a shoulder, "Just Steve, sweetheart."

She took a step back and folded her arms. "It's Miss Maxwell to you, Stash." She smiled suddenly. "And you'd better zip up those pants before you take me to the apartment."

Marlena Maxwell had specific instructions in all her jobs. A luxury apartment. A foreign-made top-of-the-line automobile rented under someone else's name. Ten thousand dollars in cash spending money, not part of the deal. Finally, a lackey to do her bidding.

Steve zipped up his pants. A lackey, he supposed, had to be obedient.

Marlena watched as the man picked up her small suitcase and headed toward the parking lot. She had to admit she was impressed. Very cool, under the circumstances. No one had ever sat and calmly waited for her first move before.

Of course she had noticed him sitting there. Who wouldn't? He wasn't exactly hard on the eyes. Dark and handsome, with the kind of eyes that asked all kinds of intimate questions. He gave himself away by hiding in a corner like that, but then he wasn't a professional like her.

Steve. She smiled in the dark as she followed him, looking around her once in a while. The view was spectacular, even in the shadows. The man wore his jeans well.

Sometimes Marlena wanted a normal life. But only sometimes. The perks were nice. Like this car, for instance. A Porsche Boxter. She climbed into the passenger seat while he held the door open. Breathing in the new leather smell, she ran an idle finger along the seat. Others like her preferred not to flaunt, but then she wasn't like the others. Flamboyance was her style. She turned to face the man by her side in the car, lifting one leg onto the seat so she could rest her elbow on it. And now for the other perk.

She liked starting with an aggressive stance. It amused her how an aggressive female would affect a male psyche. Leisurely, she ran her eyes over the man sitting next to her as he backed out of the space and drove into the street.

Strong masculine features. She couldn't tell his eye color, but his gaze had been bold. Strong nose. Stubborn chin. She remembered the imprint of his body against hers when she leaned on him, and she hid a smile. No, there was certainly nothing small about him.

She hadn't meant to touch him as she had, but a challenge was a challenge. Most of the others had never been quite this interesting. The last one had been so nervous, she was sure he had peed in his pants when she'd jokingly bared her teeth at him. No, this one . . . well, she could feel that he was different.

He stopped at a traffic light and finally turned to face her. He wasn't unnerved by her scrutiny at all. Instead he smiled, a slow easy curve of his lips that heated her insides.

"I'm new at this," he said. "What do you expect of me?"

Marlena lifted a brow. "Obedience."

"Do you get it?" He cocked his head, a curious glint in his eye.

Yes, she did. She deliberately cultivated fear so she could get it. Fewer questions that way, and fewer missteps. But for once she didn't mind questions. Normally she would ignore these lackeys they sent her, giving them the silent treatment most of the time, but then all the others were shifty-eyed and boring. "The light is green," she said, turning away from him.

He shifted. The powerful car sped forward. "A woman who doesn't want to talk; there is a God," he muttered.

Marlena glanced back at him. "Stash, you're very annoying." She leaned back in the seat. "Speed up. We're being followed."

Steve looked in the rearview mirror. "How do you know? There are four cars behind us?"

The man had to learn to be quiet, she decided. At least he obeyed her and sped up. "That's because I watch out for these things. I obviously can't count on you for my own safety."

He gave her a brief smile. "Wanna bet? I can lose them for you."

She looked at the side mirror at the car steadily keeping up with them. Her arrival in town hadn't exactly been a secret for those who wanted to find out, so she had expected to be followed. But she didn't need to make it easy for them.

And frankly her companion amused her. "Sure," she said. "What's the bet?"

Oh, she had thought him amusing a second ago. Strike that. The smile he gave her sent her insides churning. The man wasn't amusing; he was one sexy devil.

"If I lose the car, I get a kiss," he told her.

Marlena's mind went blank for a second. A kiss? When was the last time she had kissed anybody spontaneously? She narrowed her eyes, considering the wager. "How good are you?"

"The best," Steve assured her gravely. He shifted to a higher gear. "I can kiss in more ways than you can . . . move."

It was her turn to smile. She had yet to meet someone bold enough to challenge her, twice in a night, at that. She laid her head back and closed her eyes. "In that case you're in charge here, Stash." She opened her eyes again as a thought occurred. "What if you lose the bet?"

His eyes never left the road. "I won't," he said and shifted gears.

An arrogant man indeed. Marlena watched as he coolly adjusted and looked at the rearview and side mirrors, as if studying his options. He seemed to know what he was doing as he cut out into the speeding lane. The Porsche's slow hum became a distinct rumble as its engine raced. She peeked at her side of the mirror again. Even though she had told the man beside her that he was in charge, well—there was no such thing.

She didn't know what surprised her more—the wager or the fact that she had relinquished control. Kissing wasn't something she did often. It was an offering, a sharing of intimate time, and she didn't offer or share her time very generously. Agreeing with such an outrageous bet with a stranger was something new.

The pair of headlights behind them moved closer. He might lose, she thought, and glanced sideways at him. Traffic was uneven, with patches of cars interrupting open lanes. He seemed in no hurry to lose them as he kept enough speed to just pass the cars in the right lane.

Marlena analyzed people who interested her. A man who took his time like this intimated more than a deliberate thinker. A man who took charge without hesitation suggested leadership, someone who didn't intend to lose. She sat there quietly, intrigued at the thought, half studying him and half keeping an eye on his actions. The change from cocky sexiness to this self-assured determination was exciting to watch. For the first time she wished she could see his face closely, see exactly what he looked like.

The Porsche caught up with a long line of slow traffic on the right. His driving was very smooth, and there was a certain calmness in his execution that suggested he had done this before. She frowned slightly, but her thoughts were interrupted when he swerved sharply back into the slow lane, in front of several cars. Any vehicle, if it was following them, would have to pull up to settle back into the same lane or stay where it was, with the slower cars in the way. All of them honked as the Porsche surfed sideways right down the exit ramp.

The ramp was dark as the long line of lights roared by. Steve slowed only enough to merge, and then he sped up again. Marlena led out a slow breath. That was beautiful to watch.

"You know," he said conversationally, "fast cars are nice, but easily recognized. If it were daylight, it would be more difficult to lose them."

"With moves like that, I don't have to worry too much, do I?"

He looked at her for a second and smiled, almost wolfishly. "Guess not." Then his expression became serious again. "But who's following us, do you know?"

Marlena smiled wryly. Well, maybe her suspicions were unfounded. Someone used to her kind of life didn't need to ask silly questions like that. No, the man was just some young minion given to her for a few days.

She shrugged. "Does it matter?"

"Hell, yeah."

"Stash, not to you it shouldn't."

He was silent as he drove on. Ten minutes later they were in a secured, well-lit underground parking garage. He cut the engine.

Now Marlena could see him. She already knew he had

dark hair but now she saw that he had dark eyes too. High cheekbones. Vertical slashes on each side of shapely masculine lips. A deep dimple in his chin kept her eyes focused on his mouth. He was also older than she had first thought—in his thirties.

"I suppose you want your kiss," she said, suddenly very aware of the small space in the car.

His dark eyes glinted back at her. "No suppose about it, lady. I've wanted that since you put your hand in my pants."

"A move not intended to excite," she explained in a soft, low voice.

"Want to try that move again?" he asked. Somehow he had moved closer.

"Our bet was a kiss," she reminded him, but allowed her eyes to stray down.

"So it was," he agreed. "I'll have to think of another wager next time."

Did he move closer? She was sure he did. Either that or the car had gotten smaller. She took her eyes off his pants and looked back up. His lips were beautiful. Reaching out, she traced their outline with a finger. They parted slightly.

"I suppose you want it now," she said.

His lips caressed her finger as he said, "Now is good."

Her heart was beating a little quicker. A kiss. She must be going out of her mind. Calmly she said, "Let's see how good you are, then."

His dark head dipped down even before she finished her sentence.

Lightning. That was the only way to describe his kiss. The first touch of his lips seared every nerve with a current of desire that made her gasp. A mistake. His tongue, like a thief, slipped inside her mouth. And stole away reality.

He kissed her as if he were trying some exotic fruit for the first time. A slow, silky dance of tongues as he took that first taste of her. Apparently liking what he found, the lazy exploration deepened into something more than mere tasting. He slanted his head, nudging her back so he could get more of her. She curled one arm around his neck and ran her fingers through thick, soft hair. He bit her lip softly, and the feverish longing to have him pooled hot and needy in her.

She had expected casual desire—he was a desirable man, after all—but not this heady need to be taken. She wanted to say yes to everything he was silently asking her as he pulled her into his mouth and let *her* taste *him*. He was like dark chocolate—the kind that wasn't too sweet, a smooth and bold flavor that was totally masculine. And she wanted more.

It was too much. Losing control over one kiss was not an option. Marlena placed her other hand on his chest and pushed. Not too hard, but just enough to remind herself that she was still in charge. She forced her eyes to remain open.

Steve felt her hand pushing him away. Her mouth was his, but she didn't trust him enough to close her eyes. It maddened him. She had spent the last hour successfully evading his questions; he wasn't going to let her win this round, too. Not when he was going crazy trying to keep himself from pushing her down on the seat and just having her right then.

He took the offending hand in his and slid it down, all the way, and held it firmly where he wanted it, right between his legs. She made a sound, and he didn't care whether it was surprise or outrage, he went in for the kill, tilting her head back even more, and gave in to baser needs. No time for exploration anymore. He just wanted her to give in to him.

She tried to squirm her hand away, and the friction had him groaning in her mouth; then she squeezed, and he almost lost it. To his satisfaction, her eyes finally closed. So did his, as her hand kept in rhythm with his tongue.

Steve had no idea how long they would have gone on kissing if some car hadn't entered the parking garage. They broke apart, instantly alert, breathing heavily. Doors slammed. Footsteps and female chatter faded away.

Her eyes stared back at him, dark blue, like the deepest part of the ocean. Mermaid eyes. The vulnerability in them startled him enough to restore reality. This was Marlena Maxwell, Ste-vo, top-notch assassin. No vulnerable mermaid.

"Can I have my hand back now?" she asked, in that husky voice that had had him thinking of tangled bedsheets all the way from the bar to here.

He released her. He already had what he wanted for now. "I like it there," he told her.

"I can tell." Her voice was whisper-soft, and her hand hadn't moved a damn inch.

"Are you going to do something about it?"

"Demanding, aren't you? Not exactly how a lackey should act."

"Told you I was new at this."

"We have to practice on this obedience thing, Stash."

"You want a pet." He grinned at her. Could be interesting. Besides, he needed to spend as much time with her as possible. He glanced down where her hand still was. The sight of it had him wondering whether a man could die from zipper strain. "I'm . . . game."

Much to his disappointment, she didn't want to pet him anymore, letting go after one last suggestive slide of her hand. Her smile was wicked, knowing. Damn woman was a tease, too, he thought sourly.

"Good boy," she said, and startled him with a girlish chuckle when he growled. "Let's get out of this car, shall we? Let's see whether we can go on up without any more interruptions."

Steve thought of the luxury apartment on the twelfth floor. He hadn't had time to check it out while his team was there setting it up, but that place had enough cameras and bugs to catch a fly buzzing by. He hadn't thought about it till now. There wouldn't be any privacy for them.

He mentally shook himself. What the hell was wrong with him? His job was to secure information from the target. This was a matter of life and death, and its import had flown out of his head with the rest of his brain cells when he kissed her. As they walked to the elevator, he told himself that he had to remember what kind of woman he was dealing with here.

He had started the evening wondering about kissing an assassin and what it would take to get what he wanted. The elevator opened and they stepped in together. He glanced at the tall woman beside him, who was ignoring him again. Auburn lights glinted in her brown hair. Eyes that saw too much. Lips that had him begging for a bed. And the entire package encased in tempting, figure-hugging black leather. He wanted to unwrap the whole thing for himself.

To get what his agency wanted, he would have to lie to Marlena Maxwell and wait for her to miscalculate, but the last hour with her told him that she wasn't going to be an easy person to persuade. She had brains and plenty of moves. Plus she didn't trust anyone. It was, he concluded, going to take a lot of man to persuade her.

The elevator came to a stop at their floor and the doors swished open. Steve picked up the small suitcase and gestured the way to the apartment. Her blue eyes were mocking, as if she found his "obedience" amusing. It didn't take long to think up several interesting ways to persuade. He told himself that he just had to keep his head while he was doing it.

Marlena couldn't remember the last time she had retreated from a challenge. She peered from under her lashes at the man walking beside her. Lord, but he wasn't lying when he'd told her he was the best at kissing. Her lips still tingled from it. Everything was working overtime. Her whole body. Her blood pressure. She made a tiny moue with her lips. Her brain, too. When was the last time she'd kissed like that in public and not cared if it endangered her life? Never.

She leaned a shoulder against the wall as Steve searched for the keys. The dark hair, those almost-black eyes, and that mouth with the dimpled chin—he was too damn good-looking for a lonely woman. If she weren't Marlena Maxwell . . . hell, if she weren't Marlena Maxwell, the point was moot—she wouldn't be there.

Steve opened the door to the apartment and stepped back for her to enter first, servile as a butler. Except for the glint in those midnight eyes. And the knowing lift of those lips. She chose to continue to ignore him, sweeping past nonchalantly.

The apartment was spacious and furnished in a modern but expensive airy style. Not too flowery, like her last assignment. That one had given her a headache every morning when she walked out of the bedroom. She crossed the tiled floor to the middle of the living room, turning around slowly. Steve closed the door behind her.

"The kitchen's smaller than most but it's stocked per your instructions," he told her, setting down her things. "There's the bar. The main bedroom is to the left, and over there are some sort of lounge and . . . a guest bedroom."

At the slight pause, Marlena gave him a mocking glance, but his expression was properly innocent, except, of course, for those bedroom eyes. She casually unbuttoned the small leather jacket she was wearing as she looked around her again.

"Make me a drink, Stash, please? Whiskey on the rocks with a little lemon."

Steve thanked the stars she'd asked for a simple drink. He had no idea how to mix complicated concoctions, but whiskey on the rocks—okay, he could handle that. He kept covert watch as he walked to the well-stocked bar and clanged glasses around. The mirror behind the bar helped. He watched her wander in and out of the lounge area, then into the guest bedroom.

The whole apartment had been gone over, bugged to the teeth, with the best micro eyes on the market. Steve wondered briefly whether Marlena was looking for them. The man loaned by the Directorate of Administration had assured them that it would be impossible to detect anything, short of tearing the place apart. He almost groaned when Marlena reappeared. Her jacket was undone. Damn, he wished she would take it off. He wanted to see more of her.

"Roomy," she commented, and headed for the master bedroom.

Steve thought of the big bed he had seen there earlier.

"That's a big room, too," he said aloud, as he looked at the bottle of whiskey and the lines of different-sized glasses. Which one did they use for whiskey? That bed was king-sized. He looked in the mirror again, catching the back of her just as she disappeared into the bedroom. He looked down at the whiskey bottle and the glasses again. He pulled out the tallest hanging upside down from the rack. He recalled seeing a sunken marble spa tub in the adjoining bath. He sighed, pouring generously into the glass. There were also strategically placed cameras everywhere. No privacy at all.

Marlena turned on all the lights, admiring the cleverly highlighted expensive sculptures and paintings in each room. The apartment was equipped with all kinds of electronic controls and gadgets. The heavy curtains moved back and forth; the closet doors receded into the wall; soft music came on and off; the TV wardrobe rose from the floor. Pretty amazing stuff. The master bath was her favorite place so far—marbled, mirrored, with an inviting tub. Maybe she would try that later. There was even a steam shower big enough for a party.

"Well? Meet with your approval?" Steve asked when she rejoined him. He held out a glass for her.

Marlena took it from him and flopped onto the plush sofa, resting an arm on the back. "It will do," she said, and sniffed the drink. "How many fingers did you measure for this, Stash?"

He shrugged. "Enough to get you drunk, I hope."

She couldn't help but smile at the lie. He couldn't play servile attendant worth a damn, and not for lack of trying. It was just in his demeanor, the way he handled himself. She was getting very curious about this man. She swirled the drink in her hand, still eyeing him. "I'm no fun when I'm drunk," she told him, tilting her head back as he came nearer. Why would his walking toward her make her heart beat a staccato? "I get mean. I pick fights."

"I look forward to it." He stopped in front of her.

She had to tilt further back to look at him. She sipped at her drink and managed not to grimace. He really was a terrible bartender, unless, of course he really was trying to get her drunk. Holding his gaze, she took another sip, then downed the entire glassful.

"Can I sit down? Do I help you unpack? Shall I take off your . . . shoes?" The tone of his voice was lazy. "Want another drink?"

"Oh, sit down, Stash, your questions are making me dizzy," Marlena said. The whiskey settled warmly in her tummy. "One thing for sure, no more mixing drinks for you."

Steve shrugged. His training as a SEAL hadn't encompassed proper liquor recipes, and he had added a little more to test her. He wanted to join her on the sofa, but thought better of it. Sitting next to her wasn't a good idea for conversation. He dropped onto the love seat close by.

Her startlingly blue eyes studied him for a few seconds, her head slanted at an angle. She had this sleepy look that was all too deceptive. He suspected that her mind stayed razor-sharp, even with that alcohol in her.

"Number one, there's nothing to unpack," she said, in that husky voice. "Number two, *you* can take off for the night. Be back here tomorrow morning at nine. Number three, I want another car. The one tonight is obviously a target."

"Don't you want me to stay?" Wasn't that what lackeys did, make themselves constantly available? Steve still had no idea what Marlena Maxwell's plans were, but he had hoped—well, he had hoped for a few things. He looked at the suitcase on the floor. "Surely you brought clothes in there for me to put away for you."

"None."

He gave her outfit an overall review. "You're going to wear that thing all the time?"

Marlena sighed. "Where is my money, Stash?"

"Hmm?" His eyes were still feasting on the small singlet revealed under the unbuttoned leather jacket.

"The ten grand."

"In the safe in the bedroom." Understanding dawned. "Oh, that's clothes money?"

His heart somersaulted at the slow smile she gave him. "Shopping, one of my various vices," she confessed.

That wasn't the kind of info that was going to help, he thought. He tried another tactic. "Where are we going at nine in the morning?" Perhaps that would give him and those listening to this conversation some clues to work on tonight.

"Why, shopping of course."

If there was one thing that could make him lose a hard-on, that was the magic word. Steve looked incredulously at the woman sitting across from him. Please, not shopping.

"For clothes," he reiterated carefully.

"And shoes." She just sat there, watching him, a small smile on her lips. "Whatever I fancy. Ten grand is good shopping money."

"You're going shopping," he repeated. Was his unit going to have some fun with that piece of information! He mentally prepared himself for jibes later. Shopping.

Marlena stood up. "I like a little distraction when I work. Come on, I'll see you tomorrow then. Give me the combination to the safe before you go. And oh, wait." She walked to the suitcase and slid a hand into the side pocket. "This is your pager."

Steve stood up and took it from her, studying the gadget for a moment.

"In case I need you when you're not around," she told him.

Not for just shopping, he hoped. "Okay," he said. His mind was completely blank. The woman had managed to stymie him with this shopping thing. The unit had discussed the money, had speculated that it was probably for her to bribe someone or buy weapons. The darn woman had been thinking of malls and parcels. He almost shuddered.

"I'll get a new vehicle tomorrow," he finally continued as he pocketed the pager. Sarcastically he added, "Any particular instructions on that?"

He regretted it immediately because the glint in her eyes promised mischief. "Hmm, a butter-yellow Boxter sounds pretty. I don't like the current color you picked. I trust you can take care of that better than mixing drinks?"

Steve muttered something under his breath, but nodded. After answering a few more questions, he let himself out and looked thoughtfully at the closed door. Unexpected amusement filled him. He had never met anyone quite like Marlena. Everything she did challenged him. Okay, so she thought she'd won this round. He turned toward the elevators. At least she would be watched and listened to all night long, in case she used the phone. He'd wanted to be with her, had expected to at least be using that guest room, but obviously she didn't trust him yet. Better work on that.

He didn't have far to go. Fifteen minutes later he entered the office where they had set up to watch Marlena's actions. Wolf whistles and howls greeted his entrance.

"Yo, Stash! Love the new nickname!"

"You're losing your touch, man! Shopping!" Male hoots and laughter.

Steve shrugged, smiling. "She . . . wasn't what I thought she'd be," he admitted, and recalled that she'd said the same about him.

"Did you clean her teeth, man? Huh, Mr. Kisser of the Millennium?"

"You two sure was down in the parking garage for a loooong time!"

Steve shrugged again. He wasn't going to share all the details about Marlena Maxwell that weren't relevant.

"But God, what a looker, huh? Look at them mamas!"

All male eyes turned to the multiple screens on the worktables, and Steve saw Marlena in the master bedroom, shrugging out of that jacket. He didn't like it. He had wanted her to do that, all night, but now, for some reason, he felt a tingle of resentment that the others were watching.

She was wearing a black singlet, low cut in the front and back. She started to unbutton her pants.

"This is going to be fun!" Cameron said, cradling the back of his head with his hands.

Steve wanted to turn the screens off. "We don't have to

watch her do this, do we?" he asked. Foolish request, of course. The other four pairs of eyes turned to him, two of them speculatively, the last pair sharply. Harden was in charge of the operation, and Steve knew he would take note of any display of emotion.

"McMillan, our job is to keep an eye on her. You know her file. She's very slippery. No one has ever caught her in the act of any crime."

"Hell, man, the act she's throwing now *is* a crime, if you ask me!"

Steve reluctantly returned his attention to the scene. They showed her entering the bathroom, the one with the marble tub. The other men jostled to the chairs for a better view. He clenched his teeth but kept his expression calm. Harden was watching him. Steve knew he couldn't do a damn thing, and couldn't understand why the hell it was bothering him. Procedure was procedure—this was done all the time. Yet he didn't want to share Marlena Maxwell.

He was half ashamed because he couldn't tear his eyes off the screen, either. She had just stepped out of her black pants, revealing long, luscious legs. Amid the male growls around him, he gripped the back of the chair hard to stop from smashing the screen. *Turn around,* his mind ordered. Yet his eyes remained riveted on her.

She moved across the room to the tub and bent over. There was a collective groan as her T-backed derriere came into view. She turned the water on, then straightened. Opening the small closet, she pulled out a towel. Hidden from view behind the closet doors for a few seconds, she tossed her black singlet at the screen, like a strip show. There was another collective groan.

When she stepped back into view, she was wearing just a black lacy bra and panties. Steve's mouth dried up. Sexy didn't begin to describe her. His head was pounding. Or was that his heart? She affected him as no other woman ever had.

A strap fell loosely off her shoulder. Every man in the room held his breath, waiting for her next move. She turned her head and stared up, and seemed to look straight at Steve. Her lips were parted slightly, and she flicked her head back.

Then she held up a big piece of cardboard. It said, "Good night, boys." And in silence, the group of men watched as Marlena Maxwell turned a gun with a silencer at them.

One by one the screens went black.

Chapter Two

Marlena prowled around the master bedroom, hands on her hips. She was aware of her flaws, her weaknesses. She had a penchant to act rashly. Most of all, she had a temper that could go a bit overboard. And when the temper and rash impulse went hand-in-hand, Marlena knew she sometimes ignored logic and caution. She shrugged.

It took years of training to learn how to turn her weaknesses into strengths, to change her impulses into opportunities. She could turn her temper down now, like the volume of a speaker, and use the power from those emotions to propel her into action.

In this world she was alone and undefended. She had to think for herself and act on cold calculation. Last night was definitely an aberration. She had gone and let them know she was smarter than they were. A very stupid thing to do in this game, when one was trying to be always one step ahead.

She growled at her stupidity, but she had enjoyed it too much to fully regret her actions. It was such a delicious moment, when she wrote that little note with her lipstick while out of sight behind the linen closet doors. "Good night, boys." Laughter bubbled up, in spite of the fact that she knew she had messed up big time. She stopped stalking back and forth, shook her head. The damage was done; time to consider her next course of action.

So what if her little act told them the camera had gotten

under her skin? The idea that they thought they had her where they wanted grated—how dare they? Her reputation as someone who had never been caught had been at stake, that was how she saw it.

Marlena frowned. First thing she had to do was break protocol and make contact with certain people. There was something very unusual with this setup. These things—she looked scornfully at the small pile of electronic gadgetry on her bed—were standard CIA issues, and the schematics of their layout smelled like a CIA oh-so-predictable plan. She sniffed, feeling her temper rising again.

CIA. These days there were too many in that agency willing to line their pockets. Someone had obviously paid off some CIA boys to help them pull this stunt.

Which brought her thoughts back to the delectable Stash. Her gaze narrowed. Was Stash CIA? Somebody sent to distract her? No, to watch her. Or, even more chilling, to eliminate her when she finished her job. All along, she had known he didn't fit. The other companions in various jobs had been soft men, malleable and ultimately boring. Their uses ranged from being witnesses to what she wished people to think they were doing, to being human carrying carts during her shopping sprees. They were eager to please. After all, she tipped well.

Soft. Malleable. Boring. Her smile was lopsidedly mocking. Three words she wouldn't use to describe Stash with-no-last-name. After last night, would he show up in the morning? She stood in front of the full-length mirror.

Was he really attracted to her? She leaned closer and fluffed her hair, then grimaced. She must be getting soft, thinking about such things. If Stash were CIA, this was just a game for him; he was out to bag her. If he were some guy hired to entertain her, then last night was probably nothing to him.

She cocked her head and gazed into her own blue eyes. Even if she admitted that she was interested in him, she couldn't let anyone close enough to know her, anyway. Her job would always be in the way.

"So," she asked aloud, "what are you going to do with Stash, hmm?"

Steve worked the crick out of his neck. It had been a long night. He took a big gulp of coffee as he reread his report. It wasn't his job to do this; it was the operations chief, Harden's, but after Steve's insistence on continuing the assignment last night, it was up to him to give his reasons in black and white to those who mattered. Of course, he was certain Harden had already called up and reported what happened. This was his way of making sure Steve realized that he still hadn't yet earned Harden's complete trust and respect.

As the newest member of Task Force Two of TIARA, a CIA intel team used by Admiral Madison's special operations teams, he was in foreign territory. At least that was what Harden had told him last night.

TIARA, short for Tactical Intelligence and Related Activities, was the intel side that assisted Admiral Madison's secret special operations teams. When he found out he was being transferred, he had known he wouldn't fit. TIARA had a dependence on CIA training and he was a SEAL, an action-oriented operative. Not only that, he was also Black STAR, the highest color code for a top-secret SEAL assault team "Standing and Ready" for any deployment. What he had learned from various STAR operations was to trust his instincts first, not depend on by-the-book training.

After last night they had wanted to just go in and take in Marlena Maxwell, sit her in some cell, and play a waiting cat-and-mouse game with her. That was standard CIA mode—sooner or later the target would talk, and if not, let her rot. Task Force Two was convinced that Marlena would talk rather than rot.

Steve wasn't so sure. His instincts told him that the woman, who had last night given the men in that room a visual spanking, was a master when it came to mind games. A part of him, one that he hoped wasn't obvious, was filled with reluctant admiration. Beauty and brains. What a deadly combination. He had never thought there were women like Marlena.

He finished his coffee, set the cup down, considered for two seconds, then picked up the pen and signed off on the report. This could either make his life hell or . . . make his life hell. He smiled wryly. Either they transferred him back to what he was more suited to do—back to assault teams with black-and-white options—or they would do nothing, and leave him there to prove to them he was right.

He straightened and took a deep breath. He wasn't mistaken. He knew what had gone wrong last night, why the others were so adamant about going after Marlena immediately. Their sexual egos had been deflated, challenged, and they wanted a confrontation. It was difficult to yell back at blank screens.

Steve's mind was still on that scene as he headed for Marlena's apartment. He grinned, recalling the lurid words hurled at the screens as Marlena, with apparent ease, located all the important micro eyes and bugs. There were a few left, but they weren't in prime locations. Hadn't that CIA operative said that these were practically undetectable? His grin widened. He wondered whether the poor operative still had his hearing after receiving a call last night.

He hadn't yelled. He had been trying very hard not to laugh out loud. That last bit wouldn't have gone over too well. Not when he had insisted that he would still show up at the apartment at 0900 hours. Unarmed.

"Do you freaking know what you're doing?" Cameron had asked incredulously. "She will blow your water-clogged brains away."

"I don't think so. I think she doesn't know what's happening and will want to see whether I know or not."

"Oh, so you just walk in there and she's going to ask you nicely, is that right?"

"You like her," Harden clipped in coldly, "too damn much. Is your head in this?"

Steve didn't like the fact that they thought he would let emotions rule his job. So he had, in as polite terms as possible, pointed out that they were the ones red-hot under the collar about the incident. Even if she sang in her cell, how would they know she wasn't lying? And the contact would just as easily hire another to do the job, whatever it was. All they knew from communications interception was that someone wanted the famed Marlena Maxwell to handle a sensitive case in D.C., and with so many VIPs around here, they needed to know all the details. How was it going to sound in debriefing if they had no names or details other than the intercepted information? The look in the others' eyes almost had him laughing again. Oh yeah.

So now he was to make the report. Let the new guy hang himself. Even after a year and a half, he was still the outsider here in D.C. He thought of the admiral, and the copy of the report he had just faxed to him. Maybe he still was.

Steve parked the car, the butter-yellow speedster that Marlena had ordered. Security garage. Security passes. Stationed agents at each corner of the street. Information and files up the wazoo about the woman. And she could slip away like smoke. After getting off on the twelfth floor, he walked down the carpeted corridors. Every nerve in his body was wired, and not from the three cups of caffeine in him. He liked the feeling. Reminded him of old times, even though he wasn't in fatigues. That woman behind those closed doors was a worthy opponent. He intended to find out what he needed from her, one way or another. She wasn't going to slip away, not if he could help it.

He buzzed the intercom.

"Come on in, it isn't locked, Stash."

He placed his hand on the door handle, his lips quirking. The image of her in that black lacy bra and panties floated into his mind. He had gone to sleep last night and awakened this morning with that teasing scene taking a toll on his body. He was going to have a hard time looking at her and not seeing that vision. He turned the knob.

One different approach—today he would improvise. This boy-toy business that the unit had given him was fine as long as Marlena wasn't suspicious. In special operations situations, the best weapon was sneak attack. Do the unexpected.

Steve opened the door, not sure what to expect, but he was used to walking into the unknown, aware that every step ahead might be a land mine. This very civilized setting was just camouflage. The woman in there somewhere was very capable of injuring him.

"Come right in. I'm in the kitchen."

He turned and followed the voice. She didn't sound like she had murder on her mind. He halted at the sight of her in the small kitchen, looking really incongruous in her leather pants and black singlet. She was flipping pancakes like a pro. There was a stackful on the plate by the oven, so she must have been doing this for a while.

"Hungry?" he asked, eyeing the stack.

"Not for pancakes," she said, and flipped the last one expertly high up in the air. "But this is a fun way to pass the time."

Well, what did he expect from the unexpected? She was flipping pancakes. Then he remembered that one of the micro eyes she had left was in the kitchen directly overhead. She had spent the last hour flipping pancakes for the benefit of her audience—her way, he guessed, of flipping them off. He almost looked directly up at the light above where the camera was hidden, just to smirk, but he kept his attention on the exasperating woman by the stove.

"Want some?" she asked.

He shook his head. "I already ate. But I did bring you some muffins." He held up a small lunch bag.

"Muffins?" Marlena arched a brow.

"I think your original instructions asked for muffins in the fridge, but I thought you'd prefer fresh-baked ones." Steve opened the bag and took out one. "Peaches and cream, bet you never had this kind before."

He approached her, keeping his hands in her sight, and when he was close enough, he lifted the muffin to her lips. She never hesitated. Leaning forward, one hand still holding the griddle and the other a spatula, she took a bite. Then another. She put the pan down.

Her eyes were bluer this morning. There was still desire in them. And curiosity. She might be planning to eliminate him but she still wanted him, and for some reason, that pleased him. Of course she wasn't going to mention anything about last night yet. She was waiting for him to slip up.

"You like?" he asked instead.

Her teeth were small and perfect as she smiled back at him, as if something pleased her. "I like." She licked the crumbs from her lips.

"Are we still going shopping?" He stared at her lips.

"Did you think you could get out of it, Stash?" Her smile turned mocking. He knew she was thinking about last night. "You know, some men would do anything to avoid shopping. To me, it's a perfect cure for a headache or a bad mood."

He glanced at the pancakes. "Do you? Have a headache?" He stepped closer and caught a whiff of her perfume. "Cooking's not the cure, you know."

"The headache is from the drink you made me last night," she wryly told him. "As for the pancakes, it was an invitation to breakfast but I don't think it was accepted. So, you think you can cure my headache? Or is it the bad mood?"

"Both."

"Interesting." She handed him the spatula. "But is it better than spending ten grand on clothes and shoes?"

Steve had no idea. Could one spend that much on clothes and shoes in one day? Impossible. He tossed the spatula into the nearby sink. "I guess you'll have to try me some time and make a comparison."

Marlena laughed. She grabbed him by his jacket lapels and jerked his face closer to hers. He went unresisting, putting his hands on the counter on each side of her slim body. Her lips met his softly. Once. Twice. She tasted of peaches and Marlena. He wanted more. She stopped him with a finger when he tried to capture her lips.

"That's got to be worth at least a few hundred dollars there," she murmured, then shook her head reluctantly. "Damn tempting, Stash, but shopping wins today."

It was only nine in the morning. Steve stifled a groan. If his body continued to react like this every time he touched the woman, he would have to be hospitalized by the end of the day for unbearable blood pressure.

Giving him a slight push, Marlena let go of his jacket. There was a note of reluctance in her voice. "Let's go, sweetheart. Lots of shops out there calling my name." She wagged a finger at him before leaving the kitchen.

This time he did emit a groan. Torture had only just begun.

Marlena smiled to herself when she heard the groan behind her. What was it about this man that made her ignore her own rules? She was actually contemplating sleeping with one of these lackeys . . . but he wasn't really one, was he? She had to be certain, of course, and would find out one way or another.

But back to that more interesting topic—the part that would require him to be without a stitch of clothing. Marlena coughed. Maybe she shouldn't be in this business anymore when she allowed a little bit of male flesh to affect her like this. Everything he did seemed to turn her on. His eyes were too damn sexy. His smile and kisses too damn inviting. Too bad she couldn't trust anything he said or did.

The phone rang. She let it ring a few times, then said, "Will you get that, Stash?" Not the right signals. Besides, she wanted to see how Stash would handle the call.

He picked up the phone. "Hello?" There was a pause. "Is that all?" Another pause. "Care to repeat that?"

The caller didn't because Stash put down the receiver right after asking. From the bedroom doorway, Marlena cocked her head inquiringly.

"It's not a really nice message," Steve warned.

She smiled. She wasn't expecting one. "Yes?"

"A man said, 'Tell her we'll get what we want sooner or later.' That's it, no name, nothing."

Marlena turned around and walked into the room. "Is that all? Not very original, are they?" She was used to getting these kinds of calls. The more important her item of sale, the more people were out to get it.

"Who are they?" He followed her into the room. He looked at the pile of electronic gadgets on her bed but didn't say anything.

She shrugged, putting on some lipstick. He came up behind her and asked again, "Who are they, Marlena? Who's threatening you?"

His dark eyes meeting hers in the mirror were intense, as if her answer mattered. If he were CIA, why should it matter? She shrugged. He was just trying to get information. "It doesn't concern you." That was probably the truth, she thought mockingly.

To her surprise, he placed his hands on her shoulders and gently turned her around. "Make it mine."

Marlena studied him carefully. He was good. She almost believed that he was actually angry for her sake. "Let's play questions and answers for a minute. Why do you think anyone is after me at all?"

"Because you have something they want?"

"Smart boy. Why do you think I'm going shopping anyway?"

Steve knew Marlena wasn't just doing this to satisfy his curiosity. She was gauging him from his answers, seeing what he chose to reveal to her. He could retreat, act dumb, but she was suspicious already. "Not just to get rid of your bad mood, then," he said, his hands rubbing her shoulders. "You're passing time because you don't have what they want yet. If you had it, you would be guarding it."

"Ahhh, don't stop there," she ordered. Her smile complimented his soft massage, but her eyes were flat and cool. "And?"

"It must be something big," Steve continued, keeping his voice light, "because so many people want it."

She shrugged, as if it really wasn't that big a deal. "So,

shall we go now? Think you can handle a few more car chases?"

He nodded. "But I think I'd better ask for a raise in my pay. This kind of stuff is extra."

"The car chases? Yes, absolutely. Hazard pay."

"No, that's not what I meant." He waited till she paused in the middle of opening the safe before continuing, "I can take car chases and threats. It's the shopping."

He liked it when she laughed. There was no pretense in her enjoyment of things that amused her. He wondered again why little things like that made him like her. He didn't want to, but he couldn't help it.

He had omitted something from that phone message. He didn't see the need to tell Marlena that the last part of the message was for him. The voice had been electronically altered, but it sounded male. He played it again in his mind.

"Tell her we'll get what we want sooner or later."

"Is that all?" he had asked, trying to prolong the conversation so his unit could track it.

"And if you get in the way, you'll be the first to go."

"Care to repeat that?"

Steve knew the man had cut off before there was enough time elapsed to trace him, but the call and what Marlena had told him revealed some interesting things. Number one—he glanced at the woman—she wasn't here in D.C. for just a hit. Something else was involved. Number two—who else wanted it, too? What was this item that was so important?

"Ummm . . . you aren't bringing all that cash with you, are you?" he asked. He still couldn't believe she was going to spend all that.

She didn't even look up as she counted the money. "Sure am."

"It's not safe, you know, to carry all that cash."

She folded the notes, and finally looked at him. "That's what you're for—you big, macho protector, you." She looked around. "Oh, there it is. Can you get my jacket for me?"

Steve walked over to the bed. The jacket was near the pile of what used to be thousands of dollars of very expensive electronic equipment. Somehow he didn't think she'd sent him over just to get her jacket.

There were too many holes in TIARA's file on Marlena Maxwell. For example, it didn't mention that she had skills that rivaled the best in the CIA. Steve knew there weren't many who could go around an apartment dismantling this stuff in a mere few hours. He bent and picked up the jacket, and turned around to find her right behind him. Despite his training, he hadn't heard a thing. It annoyed him immensely.

It apparently amused her a great deal to see him annoyed. Those blue eyes were dancing with laughter, although she kept her voice serious. "It wasn't nice, what happened last night."

Steve was surprised. Sneak attack. Damn, she had turned the tables on him again. It was a vague enough statement to mean anything. Damn good. "I enjoyed it," he replied. He meant the kiss, but of course she didn't.

"I'm glad," she said, smiling as she donned the jacket after slipping the wad of money in one of the zipper pockets.

As she walked away, Steve called after her softly, "I'll win, you know. I'll have your pretty little ass."

She didn't even turn around. "It'll be tough, Stash. I'm kind of attached to it."

Chapter Three

M is for Murder.

M is for Marlena.

M is for Massacre. Murder. Mastication. Mangle. M is for . . .

"What are you thinking of, Stash?" The voice was sweet and the eyes so innocent.

Murder. Definitely murder. "I believe I now know what M Street stands for," he answered. After all, he had spent about six hours following Miss Maxwell up and down the famed street as she got rid of her bad mood and headache. In fact, she had given them to him.

He would rather go through BUD/S and Hell Week again. He would prefer to be thrown out into a choppy ocean weighted down with ammo. He would choose wading waist-deep in mud for three days straight with hungry swamp gators and snakes. He would take containment training without the use of a gas mask with CS gas swirling around. Well, maybe not the last choice. That one had emptied out his guts the first few times he'd failed to properly hold his breath.

"Yes, that pair of high heels will go with this outfit. Stash! Come look—do you think the colors match?"

Steve swallowed a groan. He didn't care whether the colors matched. He didn't care whether those heels went with that outfit. He just knew they cost too damn much. He'd never known clothing could be so expensive.

"Well?"

He grunted, not even looking up from the magazine he was pretending to read. She had shown him enough shoes to last him a whole lifetime, as far as he was concerned.

"Sweetheart, don't you like this outfit? Do you think these shoes go with it?" There was definitely laughter in her voice now. She knew exactly what she was doing to him.

Steve reluctantly peeped over the magazine, meaning to just agree, and hoping to be left in peace for another ten minutes. His eyes widened. His pulse came alive. Slowly he lowered the magazine as he took in her "outfit."

He had seen a movie star or someone famous modeling a similar dress. A V-front opened to the navel, pinned with a brooch, exposing enough bosom and flesh to cause a riot. The material had to be illegal; he could see she wasn't wearing a thing under that dress. Blood rushed to a strategic part of his body, and it wasn't his brain because he suddenly felt light-headed. Wow. What in the world was holding that dress together? The vision approached him as he sat there.

"Well, what do you think?" She stood oh-so-close, right in front of him.

He was eye level to her bared flesh, and he tried to look under the material that covered the half of her breasts that mattered. How did it stick to them like that?

M is for Making Love. Magic. Mama Mia. M is for . . . "More movement, please," he answered, circling his finger in the air. Maybe if she twirled around a bit, the material would shift, and then he could see . . .

"I meant the shoes, Stash. Aren't they perfect with this dress?"

What shoes? He hadn't looked at her feet once. "Yup," he agreed, his eyes not straying from more important things. "They're perfect."

"I knew you'd agree. I'll take these then."

He heard the mockery in her words but was suddenly in too generous a mood to care. Hell, let her buy more of these thousand-dollar things, if they all looked like that on her. He didn't even mind missing lunch.

"Okay, I'm ready to go now."

He stood up and looked down. Nope, couldn't see a damn thing from this angle, either. "You're . . . uh . . . wearing that back to the apartment?"

"No, I'll be wearing it later. We're going out to a fancy party one of these nights."

"We are?"

"Why do you think I bought you those expensive clothes?"

That was an hour Steve chose not to ever remember again. Never, he vowed. Never would he again be in the vicinity of a woman buying him clothes. What should take ten minutes took over an hour of excruciating humiliation. He scowled at the memory of being poked and prodded, touched and tucked.

"You look like you aren't enjoying your job, Stash," his tormentor commented as she fiddled with the front of her dress.

Well, he was enjoying *that*. But shopping? Letting a man touch him where he shouldn't? Being asked which side he . . . uh . . . He scowled again. Never mind that the man asking the questions was supposedly a tailor. If he had jiggled that measuring tape a few more inches closer, that man wouldn't have lived to know which side he preferred to . . . His scowl deepened.

A cool hand patted his jaw. "A few more days of this and I'll have you all obedient yet."

More shopping? He shook his head. She nodded, clearly trying hard not to laugh. He shook his head again.

"Next time we're doing this, it'll be on a bet," he told her. He ran a nonchalant finger down the seam of the tempting V-opening. He didn't care that the saleslady was avidly watching them. The material was soft, tantalizing him with the way it managed to stay in place. He felt the slight tremor of her body where his finger made contact with her smooth skin. He smiled. Not so in control after all.

"What's the bet?"

Sneak attack. "That I'll find whoever's after your ass." He

had a job to do, after all, and would like to know who all the players here were. One thing was for sure—if Marlena was out of the picture, then there would be no other way to find out who had hired her, and why.

Her eyes narrowed at the change of subject. "Why are you so interested in this, I wonder." It wasn't a question.

"Told you your ass was mine."

"Ha." She turned away, heading back to the changing room. "You won't win."

"I haven't lost yet."

Marlena heard his footsteps behind her but chose to ignore him. She had no intention of telling him more than necessary. Stepping into the changing room, she closed the curtain. It was drawn open before she even turned around. He stood there, blocking the entrance, making the small changing room smaller with the mirror reflecting him on all three sides. She stared up at him challengingly. "There is something awfully familiar with this situation," she remarked as she picked out what to wear next. "I assure you, I don't need help to take this off."

The look in his eyes was heated, full of sensuous promise. She reminded herself that the man had other things on his mind—hadn't his last bet proved that?

"Scared I'll win?" he taunted.

She wasn't scared. She was tempted. And Marlena wasn't sure whether taking this temptation would prove deadly. Every time he looked at her with those dark eyes with their devil-may-care gleam, she wanted to throw caution to the wind and let him come nearer. She would, but not until she was sure who he was, not until she was sure she would be in total control of her emotions.

She couldn't help it, though. She needed to know what he had in mind. "What's the price this time? Another kiss?" She played with the brooch holding the dress together, feeling excited and intrigued. He hadn't made a move for her but she felt caressed—all over. Another new sensation that bothered her. Men had undressed her with their eyes before, but she had never felt her body responding in this way.

Steve shook his head. "If I win, you're going to let me find out how that dress stays on like that." He looked at their reflection on his right, leaned a little into the room, and touched the area on the mirror he was referring to. He traced the outline of one breast with his forefinger, moving with a sensuous wickedness, as if he were imagining sliding the dress off to one side.

Marlena stopped breathing. He hadn't touched her, and her body was tingling all over.

"Excuse me, sir, but you can't be back here so long. The other lady customers will complain," one of the salesladies interrupted from behind Steve.

Steve's smile was raffish and confident as he stepped back and closed the curtain, and Marlena was alone again. She cocked her head, trying to make out his words to the saleslady.

"Sorry, ladies," she heard him say, "but that dress she was wearing made me forget what I was doing." Pleased female laughter followed his male excuse.

Marlena smiled to herself. Liar. He knew exactly what he was doing. She looked at herself in the mirror as she undressed slowly. He made her feel . . . desirable . . . that was the word she'd been trying to find, to explain this odd warm and tingly sensation. Despite the danger, and maybe because of it, she was beginning to like it.

Half an hour later, as Steve stopped at a red light, Marlena took a quick look around and came to a decision. When she chose to, very few could rival her speed. A quick slide to the driver's side, and she had her foot on the gas pedal; before Steve could react with a "What the—" the car ran a red light in front of the police cruiser.

It all went according to plan. Ten minutes getting a ticket. Two minutes of lecture. Marlena spent an extra minute flirting with the policeman. Steve had looked at her enigmatically throughout the whole incident, but hadn't said anything other than "Yes, Officer."

He was probably too mad to say anything at the moment. In fact, he was probably planning revenge. But Marlena didn't care. She had what she wanted. "Steve McMillan," she said the name with satisfied glee. "Now I know who's after my ass."

His sideways glance was very telling. Oh yeah, he was hot. "This is going to cost you, lady," he promised. "This won't be the only moving violation of the day."

Her laughter was pure amusement, drawing Steve's attention. She shook her hair in the breeze as the sportster sped along, looking pleased with herself. Her new outfit was a chic cream-colored blouse with pearl buttons and matching pants. It was a good contrast to her vibrant coloring, and he couldn't help wondering whether she was wearing some of those lingerie items he'd seen her pick out. He gripped the steering wheel a little tighter than normal, willing his imagination to behave.

Stopping at another traffic light, he deliberately revved the engine and gave her a warning glance. Another cruiser was parked close by, and that sent her into another peal of laughter. Her mirth was infectious and he found himself smiling back.

This wasn't good. He was in danger of having his identity discovered by the most dangerous woman he'd ever known, and he found life funny. He zipped into a higher gear, entering the Beltway in a rush of accelerated speed. It was a longer way back to the apartment.

"No traffic lights on the highway," he explained, when Marlena looked at him inquiringly. There was nothing like driving a fast car with a faster woman. Risking another traffic ticket, he stepped on the gas. The woman beside him only laughed more, her hair whipping back in the wind. She looked so carefree, as if she didn't have murder on her mind. Then she placed her hand over his on the gearshift, and it felt   strangely right.

Magnificent.

Machiavellian.

He told himself this was just an exercise to remind himself to be careful, that he wasn't driving himself crazy thinking about her. It wasn't a very convincing excuse. They were both quiet as he drove the car into the secured parking lot. Why did it feel like they had shared a moment that was only theirs, back there on the highway?

"I can play lackcy again, or I can play maid," he offered.

"Hmm, a gentleman," Marlena mocked. Pretending to consider a moment, she then lifted a shoulder. "Well, practice makes perfect, and you still need to get better as a lackey before I can promote you. Make sure no one bothers me while I'm in the bath, okay?"

She was baiting him about last night, of course. Steve would have preferred to be ladies' maid, but kept his expression as bland as hers. "No one will dare bother you," he said, managing to tone down the dry sarcasm in his voice.

There were so many packages, he had to make a couple of trips, but he didn't mind. It gave him time to clear his head, plan his next move. Marlena had said something about a fancy party. Who in D.C. would invite someone like Marlena? Was there any connection with the contact TIARA was trying to find out? He hoped so. He sure didn't want to attend any fancy-schmancy do and stand around like an idiot.

Maybe he ought to just give in to Harden and let him just go after Marlena Maxwell and press her for details. Shopping and partying weren't his way of working for Uncle Sam. More than once he had wondered why he'd allowed himself to be transferred. D.C. was too formal for him, too bland.

Well, last night and today had added some color. This assignment had been the most action he'd seen in a while. It was the sitting around in intel work that had him climbing the walls. More than once he had jerked out of a daydream of hiking in jungles or racing through the desert in his favorite dune buggy, the Desert Patrol Vehicle. And God, of all things, he missed the rubber duck, the amphibious thirty-foot inflatable boat his fire team fondly named Joy, for the great ride home after a recon mission.

Steve grimaced. It wasn't as if he hadn't done info gathering before. He had dealt with similar situations that had required him to sweet-talk a woman into giving him information. He glanced in the direction of the bathroom. The sound of water running and music came from behind the closed doors. What was so different now was that he felt myopic. Whereas, in fatigues, everything was twenty-twenty—black was black; white was white. Now he had to fight himself, his new team, and his instinct. That, as any experienced soldier would tell him, was suicidal in any mission.

He surveyed the group of shopping bags, picturing Marlena emptying them all over the plush carpet. He wanted her. What healthy hot-blooded man wouldn't? What he was fighting was something more than the usual urges. He just wanted to know her. What drove a woman like her to be on the other side of the law? And why didn't her background bother him? He ought to be disgusted, abhorred by her nature, but he wasn't. Was Marlena really so good at manipulating him that he would be blind to what she was? That didn't sit too well.

Sitting down on the big bed, half listening to the water in the background, Steve played with all the stray wires and parts courtesy of the same woman on his mind. Then there was his second problem. His mouth twisted, as he threw one of the micro eyes in the air and caught it, then repeated the motion. Task Force Two was a different kind of team. He was a sudden replacement, and not from the usual ranks. The admiral had told him the transfer would add to his skills for later. He had been trying to fit in since day one. Not that his teammates weren't good operatives, far from that. But they weren't soldiers, and they didn't like his methods. CIA training was very different from SEAL training.

As for his instincts . . . well, his instincts were either still as trustworthy as he believed, or he was going to get the worst dressing-down from the admiral in the history of Black STAR. His restless gaze caught sight of Marlena's small suitcase by the dressing table. His back straightened. And maybe, just maybe, Steve McMillan was still a damn good SEAL operative.

He looked toward the bathroom door briefly. She had

been in there ten minutes. All he needed was another five. Picking up the suitcase, he strode out of the room and headed to the kitchen. He placed it down on the kitchen table, then looked up at the hidden camera eye.

There was a small rocket pocket gun, as they called it, a silver Walther PPK. There was the Bersa from last night, with a silencer. He used the tablecloth to handle them, checking the chambers. Surprisingly, the weapon wasn't loaded. Leather gloves. A jewelry box. There was a small black book. He didn't have time to do more than flip through it. Poetry? Looked like poetry. He frowned. Glancing up at the electronic eye, he shook his head, indicating that he didn't think the book was important. Then he pulled out a laptop. A small Toshiba. There wasn't enough time to turn it on and check it out, so he just took note of the type of laptop. Then he signaled that he would join them later and replaced all the articles back into the suitcase.

Not much progress, but he had something to work on later.

The game of hide-and-seek, Marlena mused, was a game of percentages and probabilities. She understood the risks she took too well. One too many—and she was due for one too many—and Marlena Maxwell's life would be over.

She quietly stepped out of the shower stall, leaving the water running. Noise was also a great mask if there happened to be some listening device she had missed. She pulled a mini cell phone, the size of a compact, from her purse and turned the music down.

"I had hoped your number is still the same," she said softly when she got through. She smiled, then continued, "I heard you were going to be the courier. This will have to be quick—I have company. I'm bringing somebody and I want any files you can find on him." Pause. "Of course he's good-looking, and no, you can't have him, get your own." Pause. "Steve McMillan. Possibly CIA. I have his driver's license number." Marlena gave it. "Can't say. You find out as much as you can and I'll try to find out whether he has any bad

side." She laughed. "You're right. I'll have a good time finding out. Bye."

Marlena wondered what Steve was up to. She was sure
the man wasn't merely sitting out there docilely waiting for
her. She had changed the safe combination, so he couldn't
get into that so quickly. Maybe he was waiting for the right
moment to kill her.

Sobering thought. She cocked her head, looking at her
reflection. Fear was a familiar feeling in her profession, but
she had been trained to see it as a good thing. Fear kept one
alive. Yet nothing Steve McMillan did played with her
fears; rather, it was anticipation he called up. A thrilling,
nervous energy that made her feel slightly more reckless
than usual.

Hide-and-seek. Keep him so close he couldn't see what
she was hiding. That was a good plan for now, she thought.
But how close? Her blue eyes in the mirror mocked her. For
once she had no answer.

She walked barefoot into the bedroom, taking in at a
glance the different boutique bags and the slight crease on
the bed. She stood there for a moment, enjoying the image
of him sitting there on that bed, waiting for her.

It had been a long time since she'd had a man doing that.
She had discovered a long time ago that men didn't like role
reversals. They didn't mind it if they were gone and their
women waited for them, but ask a man to do the same, and
the relationship was doomed. A man, she had found out the
hard way, couldn't wait. Of course he'd then lie to cover up.

"May I come in?" Steve asked from the doorway.

Marlena turned to face him. Tall, broad-shouldered, and
easy on the eye. A mouth that could kiss away any excuses.
Women would snatch him up just like that, CIA or not. And,
she concluded with a touch of irony, he didn't look like a
man who liked to wait.

She turned away. "I had fun today," she said as she picked
up one of the bags and emptied it on the bed.

Steve sensed her withdrawal. It was difficult to read the
woman, but her moods were discernible to him. She ran the

gamut between teasing and calculated. Right now she was neither. She was wearing a large T-shirt with a cartoon of Tweety Bird on it. Without makeup, her hair damp, she looked ridiculously young. The look she'd just given him reminded him of the time after their first kiss. It made him want to pull her in his arms and hold her.

"I didn't," he complained.

Her lips curled slightly. "Your job's to amuse me, not yourself."

"Is that what you were doing, amusing yourself?"

She held up a dress against her body, smoothing away the wrinkles. "Well, somebody has to." Glancing up, she added, "Amusement is much better than boredom."

Well, well, if that wasn't an acknowledgment from the lady of being lonely, he didn't know what was. He stepped a little closer, handing her another bag to dump out. "Is that your secret then? Go through life amusing yourself?" He had the urge to find out what motivated a woman like Marlena. "Take what you want, enjoy it, then leave—no responsibilities, no conscience?"

Marlena paused in the middle of pulling out a long double strand of pearls from a large, flat, golden box. "Oho, judging me, sweetheart?" She climbed up on the bed, so she could reach over his head and loop the long necklace around his neck. One hand twisted around the dangling strands, and using them like a rope, she pulled until his face was close to hers. "Do you know what I do when I'm no longer amused?" she asked ever so softly.

"Kill?" Steve countered, feeling her tightening her hold. In a minute the pearls would be so many little pieces all over the bedroom. But he didn't want to break the necklace, or her hold on him, so he inched closer.

"Is that your final answer?"

"Can I call on a lifeline?" he quipped.

Her eyes were so blue he could drown in them. "Are you in trouble?"

He was sinking fast. "No. I'm not the one with people threatening me." He was so close he smelled the scented soap she used. Deliberately he looped the remaining length of the necklace around her neck, trapping both of them together. Her pupils flared, darkening the blue to that deep underwater darkness that had made him think of mermaids the first time he had looked into them. Not again. No mermaid, he reminded himself. In defense, he added, "I'm not the one in danger."

She made a sound of disbelief and jerked her hand. Steve was surprised the necklace hadn't broken apart from the tension. Or maybe it was just the tension in the air he was feeling.

"I rarely sleep with a man on a first date," she murmured against his lips, nipping softly.

"I don't have sleeping in mind," he assured her, trying to capture her lips more securely. Far from it.

But she resisted, seeming to be satisfied with just exploring his lips with her teeth and tongue. "I rarely do anything with a man on the first date," she said.

"You don't have to do a thing," he promised. Her whispery kisses were driving him crazy. Impatiently he tugged on the necklace so she had to tilt her head up. "I'll do everything."

Her lips were softer this time, and he teased them open the same way she teased him. Again he tried to deepen the kiss, but her hand between them loosened its hold enough so she could pull back from him.

Forget those pearls. He went after her, using his weight to pin her down on the bed, among the clothing, bags, paper, wiring. Her hands mussed his hair as she pushed her tongue into his mouth and boldly met his.

It occurred to him as he became thoroughly immersed in having her tongue explore him that she was the one doing the kissing. It was a novel feeling, being kissed like that. It made him aware of other things about her, how the perfume of her shampoo clung to her skin, how surprisingly soft her body felt beneath his, how one of her thighs was pressing firmly between his legs. He was the one in danger here . . . and he hadn't done a thing yet.

A low, rumbling sound broke the spell. Marlena pulled back, surprised.

"What was that?" It came again, a longer disturbance this time. Realization dawned in her eyes.

"I'm sorry," Steve said. He couldn't be more embarrassed.

Marlena started laughing, that unexpectedly delightful and infectious chuckle bubbling out of her. "Well, I've never made a man that hungry before."

He found himself laughing back. "I'm sorry," he apologized again. He was willing to continue but his body had different ideas. He was a man used to two things—lots of food and hard training. There came another grumble, and the two of them both broke up in hysterics.

"It's my fault," Marlena gasped out. "Really, I should have let you take lunch."

"You're not hungry?" What did the woman take for energy?

"Mmm . . . well, food wasn't on my mind a minute ago," she teased, smiling, "but let's raid the fridge you claimed is full of my favorite things. See what we can come up with."

He remembered the cold cut chicken. The big carton of mint chocolate chip ice cream. And groaned. Surely he was going nuts. He was thinking about food when he had a woman under him, in a bed. Where were his priorities?

She read his mind and chuckled again. "My ego is shot all to hell, Stash honey. To lose to food . . . I guess the tummy complaints weren't the moving violation you had in mind?"

"No." Reluctantly he lifted himself to a sitting position.

They had both forgotten about the necklace tangled around them, and Steve pulled Marlena up with him as well. Laughing aloud, she steadied herself by flattening her palms against his chest.

"Mmm," she murmured, distracted. Her splayed fingers traveled up and down the front of his T-shirt. "Nice and hard. I was quite jealous of that tailor today. He was touching you all over. You must work out a lot. I can feel all your muscles."

Oh-oh. Warning bells rang in his head. His kind of body

was not sculpted in the gym. "I like outdoor sports," he told her, trying to ignore what her hands were doing to him.

"What kind?"

The lady was good with her hands, but he wasn't going to be conned into slipping up. "Jogging, running, swimming, outdoor stuff."

"We'll have to exercise together if we have time," she said.

"Sure." He doubted that she would like the stuff he did. He began to unwind the long necklace, taking it off her first, since it had somehow twisted into a double knot near his neck.

She barely paid attention, seemingly finding the hard ridges of his abs fascinating. She tried to pull his T-shirt out of his pants. Normally Steve wouldn't stop any beautiful woman wanting to explore his chest, but her questions had left him wary. He had learned that she was always after something else.

He looped her hands with a chain of pearls and brought them to his lips, kissing her fingertips softly. Her blue eyes gleamed back at him, but he couldn't tell what she was thinking. "Fair is fair," he told her. "You want to see what's underneath, you have to show me what's underneath that silly Tweety Bird shirt."

"It's not silly. Tweety Bird is my favorite cartoon character." She pulled her hands loose and worked on the knot holding them both prisoners.

"Your favorite cartoon is a bird?" Steve asked incredulously. Somehow he couldn't picture Marlena watching cartoons. And certainly not a bird. At her gesture he lifted his chin up and patiently let her untwist and unwind.

"Yup, even have a tattoo of Tweety."

"Where?"

Her answering smile was small and secretive and instantly made him want to go on search mode. "Where?" he demanded again.

"There, free at last," Marlena said. The long double strand

of pearls swung loose. She eyed it admiringly. "I must say you look good in pearls."

"It doesn't go with my shoes," Steve dryly mocked. "I want to see that Tweety Bird."

"All in good time, Stash, all in good time. Let's go fix you something to eat first, hmm? Are you as good at cooking as kissing?"

Steve reluctantly stood up. "We'll both find out." He didn't want to go but he remembered the tablecloth he had used to handle her things. With her keen eyes, he should really double-check to make sure there were no smudges.

Marlena folded up the clothes on the bed while sounds of dishes and silverware clanging came from the kitchen. She was glad about the interruption. Another minute and she would have forgotten her self-control. She couldn't afford to forget anything, not at this time. She gathered up the wires, walked deliberately to stand a few feet from a portrait placed strategically facing the bed, and dumped the electronics leftovers like trash. Staring straight ahead, she lifted her chin in a silent challenge.

A little over an hour later, Marlena came back into the room and with a small blade dislodged the tiny electronic micro eye hidden in the frame. She had returned that device there on purpose earlier. Disabling it, she dropped the useless chip into the pile on the carpet. It had served its purpose.

She walked out to the mini bar. She shoved aside the bottle of whiskey. She needed something smooth and rich. Cognac. Yes, that might put her in a mellow mood.

It hadn't been easy saying no to a man like Stash. He had left after dinner, given her one of his long looks that almost had her changing her mind. Her attraction for him was stronger than she'd thought. It had been a long time since she had actually lusted after a man from the other side, and she knew how high a price that could be.

Marlena wasn't willing to pay that price again. Except for one thing. She frowned and took a long swallow of the brandy, feeling its fiery heat go straight down her throat into her tummy. The last time the lust she had felt was never like this. She'd never been so aware of a man as she was of Stash McMillan. She felt it down to her toenails whenever he followed her with his dark gaze. He reminded her of a caged animal for some reason. She had tested his depths and knew that he had a mind of his own. It was in the way he stood watching her with those brooding eyes, in the way he demanded her attention by merely quirking his beautiful mouth, in the way he pretended to be just what he claimed to be. And he made her laugh. She couldn't remember a day when she had laughed so much. He was good. Very good.

The phone rang. It still wasn't whom she was expecting. Picking up the receiver in the kitchen, she didn't bother to be polite. "Yes?"

"Marlena Maxwell, your bodyguard is useless against us. We want what you have. Hand it over or we'll come after you from all sides, wherever you are."

Marlena sighed. "Dear me, and if I give it up, you'll just leave me alone." She studied her hand, frowning at a chipped fingernail.

"You don't have an option. Give us what we want, or die."

"Um, sorry, you just gave me two options."

"You think you can joke with us over this?"

"Why not? Only clowns would talk over a bugged phone this long."

The line went dead. Marlena tapped her chin with the receiver as she thoughtfully looked overhead, at the micro eye and bug she knew were above her. No doubt, whoever was on the other end of those stupid things had heard every word exchanged, just as they had this morning, when Stash answered the phone. She also knew that they wouldn't be able to trace those calls.

Probabilities and percentages. That was the tightrope she balanced on. The probability of these two parties working together was low, and the percentage that they might help her cause by getting in each other's way was higher. Thus it didn't hurt to let whoever was monitoring her know that other people were after her, too. She was used to different groups trying to get what she had, thinking they could handle one woman. She smiled mirthlessly.

It was easy to let her gender blind them all. From the moment she had walked into this apartment with Steve, she had been ready for a setup. What she had come to D.C. for was big enough to attract those who couldn't afford to pay its real worth. She was used to shady types coming after her. Apparently it might not even be just the usual kind of crooks.

The special CIA-originated electronic devices betrayed them. They didn't think she'd know the difference, but she had contacts, and there were plenty of CIA boys who were greedy for money, showing off new inventions being tried out by the agency. So the question of the day was—which side was Steve working for? Good CIA or bad CIA? It was going to be a challenge to find out. Her contact had been very careful thus far, doing everything through middlemen. She would have to take a few more risks than usual. And letting those others know her phone was bugged was one of them.

The thought of putting Stash in danger made her heart skip a beat. Marlena frowned. Why would she be concerned about that, if he were just someone hired to keep an eye on her? He shouldn't mean a thing, not a damn thing.

Confusion in the enemy camp was good. Steve's commander from his SEAL team had told him that, quoting some ancient Chinese text called *The Art of War.* He was right. Steve was confused, tired, and frustrated. He had this simple plan. Charm the shoes off a beautiful woman. Get some names. Send her to the Department of Justice. His task force team would then get some action, going after whoever had ordered a contract on . . . on whom? That was the problem. Too many things missing in this assignment.

When he was with his former team, he knew who the enemy was, why they were there, what they were after. Black STAR's objective was to search and destroy paramilitary enemies with an agenda against the U.S. government. The wars were always covert, out of the public eye, but they were real. There was a procedure to each maneuver—his allotment of ammo, location of a target, a timetable, and a clear briefing on the goals of the operation.

Since his transfer he'd been trying very hard to adjust to this new kind of war. Admiral Madison had told him that he was needed here for now, and he had accepted the orders after voicing a few objections. The higher pay was an incentive; he needed the money. From the beginning, the friction between him and his new team had been obvious. It wasn't that they disliked one another—it was just his style didn't suit theirs.

This was the first real test. At least Steve saw it that way. For the first time in months there was something tangible happening. He could feel in his bones that it was big. This operation would show him why he'd been transferred, why Admiral Madison told him his skills were needed here.

His mind skimmed quickly through the important things from the day. There was the early morning call with the threats. No one had followed Marlena and him all day, except for his own task force men who were now outside the apartment building for the night. Then there was the quick search of Marlena's suitcase that hadn't yielded anything of significance.

When he entered the surveillance room, he found Harden there alone. Great. That was all he needed, another clash with the operations chief.

It wasn't that he disliked his O.C. Harden had been nothing but fair to him, but the man had a black hole where his personality should be. In the hallways, Steve heard them whisper his nickname, Hard-On, and the reference wasn't meant to be complimentary.

"Where are the others?" Steve asked as he walked over to the desk where his O.C. sat. As usual he sensed disapproval from the man, even though nothing in his face betrayed it.

"I sent them home. They're on call in case your target does something between now and tomorrow."

"My target?" Steve raised an eyebrow.

"You've made it personal. Once you let your emotions get involved, you crossed the line." Harden looked back at him steadily, challenging him to deny the accusation.

Steve kept his gaze level. "I haven't done anything to suggest that I can't handle this."

It was Harden's turn to lift an eyebrow. "No?" He leaned forward and clicked a button on a console. "Watch this."

One of the many screens showing the few rooms at Marlena's apartment flickered, catching Steve's attention. The couple on the bed. The necklace. The intimacy of shared laughter. There were no sounds, since the mikes had been destroyed, but the evidence was damning. Steve didn't move or say a word, letting the tape run its course.

"She got you, man. How are you going to catch her if you're doing your thinking with your gonads?" Harden asked, his voice laced with acid sarcasm.

Now wasn't the time to think of Marlena's betrayal, Steve told himself. He turned to face his chief. "I know what I'm doing," he said levelly. "She's just trying to cast confusion among her enemies. She knows you're watching her."

"Of course she knows. She placed that eye there herself." Harden smacked his hand on the desk in disgust, showing his anger for the first time since Steve walked in. "She's telling her watchers—me, specifically—that she has got you, that we can't fully trust you anymore."

"Sir," Steve reverted back to formality. There was no way to defend himself by being familiar. "Marlena Maxwell wants you to think a certain way. She's good at this; I know, I've been around the woman long enough to experience her manipulative ways. That"—he pointed to the screen—"was meant to create problems for me. We just have to figure out why she did it."

Of course Steve knew the reason, but he wasn't going to admit it. It had to do with a bet they had made that day. It was just Marlena's way of showing whose ass was being had. Another time he might even have found what she did amusing, but not tonight. He was too frustrated to be amused. And she had so cleverly backed him into a corner with his own men. How could he tell them that he knew her so well, that he understood her message here, without them turning suspicious? His own O.C. was skeptical of his motives, for God's sake.

"You think I don't know what she's up to?" Harden asked in disgust. He leaned back and sank deeply into his chair, his eyes flint-hard as he looked at Steve. "I've been in this kind of stuff a lot longer than you. You're used to playing Superman, McMillan. Don your gear and go out and fight the bad evil dudes. Well, that kind of mentality isn't suited for TIARA. We use intel to fight the enemy, not firepower."

Steve didn't think it appropriate to point out that Superman always won. He might not have the kind of cloak-and-dagger training that Harden had, but he was a SEAL, and he held his team's record in the BUD/S infamous O course, an obstacle course created not just to test mental toughness and confidence, but to teach the trainees there was always a better way. "Each enemy needs a different approach," he said. "I just think there are more things happening here than a quick assassination. Marlena is—"

"Playing hide-and-seek," Harden cut in. "She hides and you seek, except that we don't know what she's hiding, and she's picking things for you to find. That is pretty obvious. What isn't obvious to you is that you're falling for her. What isn't obvious is that every time she manipulates you, over here, on this end, it adds another nail into your coffin. I'm not the only one assessing these videos, and believe me, I'm only voicing the conclusions of those who are going to see this. One wrong misstep and it's free fall, McMillan."

"The order was to get close to the target," Steve reminded. He no longer cared if he was stepping out of formal protocol. "I've been doing that."

"And your emotions weren't involved in your decision-making process?"

Steve straightened. There was more here than his being accused of impropriety, whatever the hell that meant. On some other level, Harden was being personal here, but Steve couldn't figure out why.

"Of course emotions are involved," he answered, frowning slightly. "Every decision always has an underlying emotion. The point is not to let it affect one's better judgment. That is, sir, how I approach my job."

Steve caught the glint of something in the eyes of the man across the desk from him. *Something else going on here,* the line kept repeating in his head.

It was impossible to crack a tough nut like Harden. Steve had tried to be friendly, aloof, distant, formal, conversational, every way he could think of, to connect with his operations chief. He wanted to get along well with the man because he was the main focus in any sensitive operation. In his special operations group, every commander in charge of each team took time to make sure that everyone was on the same page. TIARA Task Force Two's operations chief gave orders without instructions and expected them done his way. For Steve, that meant hit and miss. Obviously he'd missed by a mile in this assignment.

Steve decided to feel around for the missing instructions. "So what do you want me to do, sir? Just let it go and let you have a shot with her?"

"It would be easier to take her in and grill her."

"Like I said before, suppose she says nothing?"

"Suppose we make her? There are ways."

Steve carefully studied Harden. Ruthlessness was part of the job, but for him there had to be a very good reason for it. One just didn't randomly hurt a civilian without proof of intent. This wasn't jungle warfare, after all. Plus the thought of Marlena in a cell . . . He quelled the thought immediately. *Don't even go there.*

He shook his head. "From those threatening calls, someone else thinks she has something valuable. I think she's here for this something, and keeping her locked up could end up with us never knowing what it is. And let's say even if she did tell what it is, how are we going to get it without her? It's important enough that someone else is going after her for it."

Not the most brilliant argument, Steve admitted, but that

was the best he could come up with at the moment. He really, really wanted to go back to Marlena's apartment and . . . and . . . what? He had no idea.

"Relax, McMillan," Harden interrupted his reverie, a corner of his mouth lifted wryly. "It's out of my hands right now. Your report from this morning obviously pushed some right buttons for you because I've got orders to nail Miss Maxwell this time. Seems that no one had ever had concrete evidence of her crimes, not enough to stick to that leather outfit she loves so much, anyway. She's all yours for now. Who knows? If you actually get her what is due to the likes of her, that would be a serious notch in your belt, Superman. That is, if you get her, of course, before she gets you." He jerked his chin toward the screen. "So far, she's winning."

Steve knew he couldn't say a thing to defend Marlena. She already had him twisted up enough to even consider making such a stupid move to his own team, no less. Of course, if he were stupid enough to even voice some sort of defense, she would get her wish—his whole team would never fully trust him. He just had to work his way out of this emotional web she'd weaved around him on his own. Pronto.

"As long as we watch her every move, sir, we'll find out what we're after."

Harden nodded. "Let's hear what happened today from your own mouth. Then you can go home and get some beauty sleep. Seems like your Miss M. likes her men pretty. We'll keep watch while you play."

Steve ignored the insult. He was used to being tested. Besides, he heard the underlying warning. He would be watched as well.

Chapter Four

Wow, if he looked like that when he was pissed off, Marlena couldn't wait till she really pushed him over the edge. This Stash had a brooding look that spelled dangerous with a capital D. He looked as if he had been up most of the night—his hair was wind-tossed and he hadn't shaved. He must have thrown on his oldest things—a dirty old sweatshirt and jeans so faded there were white creases in the most interesting places.

Marlena had never had a wild animal waiting on her doorstep before. She took in his appearance silently, from the top of his messy hair down, down those long Levi's—pausing a moment there—to the scuffed-up shoes. There was a backpack by his feet.

She returned her gaze to his. "Bad night?" she asked lightly, holding the door ajar.

"What makes you think so?" he retorted, picking up the backpack and coming in.

Steve waited till they walked past the surveillance device that he knew she had left out in the hallway (she was a sensible assassin, if there were such a thing), until they were in the living room. Without another word, he pulled her around by the elbow and pushed her against the wall.

Maybe if he kissed her in anger, he would get rid of the constant craving to taste her. Maybe if he was a little rough this time, he would get under her skin and she would push back. Show him that hidden side of her that would repulse him. Then maybe he could get past the idea of actually liking her.

Instead of fighting him, her arms snaked around his neck and she pulled herself up, twining her legs around his waist. Then she opened her mouth invitingly. That maddened him even more. He grabbed her hands and held them prisoner against the wall, grinding his hips against hers as he savaged her mouth. Why did she have to smell so damn good? He tried to ignore its seductive grip, concentrating on conquering the woman instead. He *would* conquer this strange weakness in himself.

She shouldn't be responding to him. She wasn't a submissive woman. Why wasn't she fighting him, damn her? He pushed her hands high up above her head and locked one hand around both wrists, then he roughly pushed up her blouse and cupped her breast. He muttered a curse against her lips—she didn't have a bra on. Why the hell didn't she have a bra on?

And suddenly her scent, her compliant mouth, the taste of her, the yielding softness of her breast engulfed his senses, and with a groan he settled more comfortably between her open legs. She gave a throaty response of her own when he gently played with her nipple, arching up against him. He wanted more. He wanted a response from every part of her.

In the back of her mind, somewhere back where she stored caution and sanity, Marlena reminded herself that she could break out of his grip. The problem was, she didn't want to. He was pissed off as hell, and it excited her. He tasted male and menacing, his lips were hard and punishing. His morning stubble scraped her cheeks, as he silently and insistently took his fill of her. His hold was anything but tender, yet she found herself responding to him, giving in to his demands. It was exhilarating to have this man focused entirely on her—his attention, all his emotions, all thought was zeroed in on her.

This just couldn't be. She never ever let a man take over. Not in this kind of situation. But here she was, hands locked above her head, at her most vulnerable. She would not be dominated like this—should not—and the thought of stopping surfaced for a moment before he slipped his hand inside her blouse and touched her breasts. A moan escaped from deep inside her. The feel of his fingers brushing her nipple gently was a direct contrast to his conquering mouth. She felt weak, breathless. She forgot about stopping him. There was only his scent and the taste of him as his kiss became less urgent, but not less commanding. And always, always, that soft caress of his fingers on her sensitive skin. Back and forth, his thumb rolled and teased.

Steve tried to hang on to his disappearing anger. He didn't want it gone. It was the only excuse he had to kiss her, to want her. He felt a certain charge of power when he was angry, as if he could handle this woman without letting his emotions get involved. To his surprise, instead of fighting him like the control freak she was, the damn woman was giving in to him. That not only dampened the edge of his temper, but now the thought of her weak and yielding only increased his desire. Damn, damn, damn.

He broke off the kiss, fighting himself more than her. Her soft moan of protest didn't help, either, and he sucked in his breath when the strong legs around his waist pulled him even harder against her lower body. She opened her eyes and they were so blue they looked violet. Her expression was so shatteringly open, he forgot to discharge the air in his lungs. Not the usual amused mockery. None of the confident and knowing gaze. Instead she had that startled, vulnerable look in her eyes again. And a hunger in them that caught him by surprise. Beneath his hand, her heart beat as rapidly as his. She blinked. The look disappeared.

Marlena licked her swollen lips slowly, willing that thundering sound in her head to slow down. The heat of his lower body burned through her cotton shorts. She had to say something—anything—to establish control again.

"Are you hungry again?" she asked, trying to clear the huskiness from her voice. She jerked her imprisoned hands a little, testing his strength. His hold remained viselike. Yet she didn't feel at all threatened.

His midnight eyes glittered back with suppressed emotion. There was still anger, but also something else. "I'm very hungry."

His growl shook Marlena's very being. He aroused something primitive in her that made her breathless and eager, like a young schoolgirl. She didn't think she liked it.

"Leftover muffins? Stale pancakes?" She had to cool the situation down right now.

His eyes narrowed. "That's not going to satisfy my hunger. I'm looking for something tastier. Something different." To demonstrate the direction of his thoughts, he bent his head and scraped his teeth along her jaw, adding, in between nibbles, "Something delicious."

The shaking inside her had become tremors. She didn't like it. No, she wasn't liking this one bit. She opened her mouth, intending a smart, distracting observation. "Oh . . ." was all she managed when teeth sank into her pulse point.

"Not so in charge now, are you, Miss Maxwell?" he mocked, his breath hot against her skin as he continued nibbling.

That was it. No man was allowed to think he had the upper hand where she was concerned. She moaned and went limp, allowing her weight to pull her down. Her legs slid down the sides of his body and she rubbed herself sensuously against the front of his jeans. Pleasure exploded in her loins and she used it ruthlessly to further her end, as she pretended to try to hoist herself back, and seemingly unable to muster the strength, she kept shimmying up and down where groin met groin.

Steve couldn't see a thing as all his senses rushed eagerly to converge in one happy place. Oh man. His eyes crossed when Marlena slid in a particular way as she tried to regain her balance. He slid his hand from under her blouse and took a step back so he could fit it under her butt to hoist her back up.

Steve learned a new maxim that day. Never allow Marlena Maxwell a few inches of freedom. The moment his hand came in contact with her nice, firm behind, she slammed backward—hard—trapping his hand against the wall, and at the same time lifted her knees to her chest. She kicked out and he chose to let her hands go, rather than risk an injury where her feet were too close for comfort. Her pointy little toes certainly weren't sliding up and down as she had been doing moments before.

She dropped down on her feet, and one hand shot out to grasp his neck. Steve turned his head slightly and pinched her bottom at the same time. Hard.

"Ow!" She was so startled by the unconventional fighting tactic that she stopped going on the attack. He almost laughed at the reproach in her blue eyes. In fact he did when she complained, in the mildest of voices, "You don't play nice."

The laughter did it. His temper evaporated into nothing. And what was left behind—Steve didn't even know whether he could deal with. He still liked her, damn it.

He especially liked the way she looked now. Her hair had these cute little waves sticking out in different directions. Her lips were rosy and swollen from his kiss. Even now, desire still glowed from those eyes. She had the look of a female about to be claimed. And he had put it there, he thought with a certain male satisfaction.

He rubbed her sore tush. "After what you did to me last night, I don't feel nice." He was used to talking on several levels with this woman by now. Two could play at these kissing games. He was referring to the incident on her bed as well as her betrayal, getting him in trouble on purpose. Undoubtedly she, queen of innuendo, knew that, too.

Marlena leaned back against the wall. Its coolness helped to disperse some of the sexual heat emanating from this man. He had surprised her once again. She had expected anger, had anticipated some sort of retaliation, but certainly not in this fashion. Like a man intent on conquering her. That had never worked before.

Dangerous. That was the description she had come up with at the door. Very dangerous. She frowned when he gave her a crooked, taut smile, as if he'd discovered something she didn't want him to know. He deliberately crowded her, placing two hands on each side of her head, leaning so close she wanted to rub her face into his chest and enjoy that very male scent of heated desire. Instead she looked up.

"Nothing to say?" he taunted softly. "Aren't you going to teach me obedience?"

"You realize I'm definitely going to lodge a complaint to your handler," she said.

"I don't let anyone handle me." Then he added sardonically, "Except you, of course, Marlena Maxwell."

Ah, back to familiar territory. She did so enjoy fencing verbally with him. "Stash," she drawled, lifting her chin in challenge. "I must have missed the part of the label on you that said, 'Handle with care.' I do hate high-maintenance things that need extra attention."

She wished he was still in a rage, because the lazy smile that settled on his sensuous lips now gave her heart strange butterfly flutters. His mouth was a mere breath away from hers.

"Oh yeah? You forgot to read the rest of the label."

"What's that?"

"It also says, 'Made in heaven.' "

She blinked, caught between amusement and desire. It must be the cocky charm, she decided, that kept her off balance. "What do they do in heaven to clean up?" she drawled. "Surely heavenly beings look a lot less . . ." She paused to find a substitution. No need to let him know she thought him dangerous. ". . . disastrous."

Steve sniffed. Smart ass. "I brought my things in the backpack. I figure I can use the spare room here." He canted a brow. "Unless, of course, you want me to use the other bathroom. I can be persuaded."

"I bet." Her answering smile was wry, suspicious. "Why didn't you do it at your own place? All you had to do was call in late."

"I overslept," Steve lied. He hadn't slept at all. He had spent most of the night after debriefing going through Marlena's file, rereading it, trying to fill the holes. "Instead of being late, I just came here as is."

She laughed. "As is," she repeated, wrinkling her nose. "Now you sound like some damaged goods off the rack."

"Want to check for damage?" Steve invited, straightening up. He lifted his arms out voluntarily. "You can hardly see it."

He almost choked at the place she was staring at. Did she think he was damaged *there?* On second thought, the last few days' zipper frustration probably exacted some kind of damage.

"Are you sure I can hardly see it?"

"Nothing you can't easily repair," he assured her. He backed up, giving her some space. Or maybe it was he who needed breathing room. Anger. He needed some kind of negative emotion to keep his mind on her, not on his needs. He added, for good measure, "And it shouldn't take that long."

The speculative gleam in her eyes curled his toes. Raised his blood pressure in the wrong place. She looked at him as if what she had in mind was going to take a long, long time. He felt an answering nudge, nodding in eager agreement. Traitor. More zipper damage in the future.

Marlena looked up at the electronic surveillance device she had left intact in the kitchen. She stuck her tongue out at it. "It's all your fault," she scolded out loud, even though there were no microphones. "I hold you fully responsible for my doing this."

"This" was something Marlena Maxwell hadn't done in a long time. "This" was standing at the kitchen stove with an apron on, cooking a meal for two. It was unfamiliar territory, this domestic intimacy. And the horrible thing was, she was actually enjoying it. Preparing a meal for two was a lot different from opening the fridge and picking out things to eat. It had all the promises that she wasn't able to make to any man. Dedication. Commitment. Compromise. Nor had any man ever been able to make the same promises to her.

So why was she even doing this? Let him make himself a sandwich. Let him serve her. Yet here she was, humming a tune and fixing some omelets. She popped a piece from the frying pan into her mouth and licked her fingers thoughtfully. More salt? Pepper. She frowned at the spice racks. Or maybe a little bit of everything else. She shrugged, then chose paprika, and shook it into the bowl. A dash of this. A dash of that.

"Do you know what you're doing?" Steve asked from the doorway. He had been watching her for a few minutes, feeling more amazed by the second. Maybe he had fallen asleep back at his apartment and this was just a strange dream. He raked a hand through his hair and found it damp from the shower he'd just taken. Nope, he was definitely awake for this.

He could just imagine what the boys were saying on the other side of the electronic eye. Doubtless this domestic scene was going to generate more snickers on his behalf. He, Steve McMillan, had gotten the notorious Marlena Maxwell to don an apron and cook. He was thankful that they couldn't hear her singing softly, in a low contralto, "He said 'either.' I said 'eye-ther.' He said 'neither.' I said 'neye-ther' . . ." He wondered whether she deliberately chose that song to egg him.

Then he saw that she was making omelets. Oh yeah, she was definitely egging him on all right. Did the woman ever do anything without making a point? He had better stop her sudden desire to "spice up" his life.

"What? You don't trust me?" she asked, wide-eyed, in mid-shake of yet another spice.

Steve sighed. "I just thought that was enough of whatever you're adding to the poor omelets. Really, when you mix them up like that, it will taste . . . strange."

"Don't eat it then," Marlena told him and turned back to the stove.

Her shoulders were hunched defensively. Something told him not to make another comment about her cooking. He set the kitchen table and then sat down obediently when she plaintively waved away his silent offer to help. When she finally served him his plate with a little flourish, he warily eyed the weirdly shaped omelet, wondering whether he should be polite and wait for her to eat hers first. It had a strange green tint. He sniffed it and almost sneezed. It smelled spicy.

Marlena put down a tall glass of juice with a loud thud, then went to sit down across the table from him. There was a glittery challenge in her gaze across the few feet separating them, daring him to make a comment.

Steve calmly picked up his fork. So did she. He cut into the greenish substance and was relieved to find some kind of meat inside. Poking around, he slowly lifted a small portion to his mouth. It was kind of gooey, almost falling off his fork. He lifted his gaze. She was watching him intently. Without batting an eye, he put the food in his mouth. Chewed. Swallowed.

Marlena's eyes narrowed. "How is it?"

"Mmm," he said, chewing.

She picked up a forkful. It sure was kind of runny. And the green color looked sickly. She peeked at Steve from beneath her lashes. His eyes never left her face, so she would be damned if she was going to show him any emotion, either. Stone-faced, she ate the greenish, gooey omelet with relish. There were people watching, and one thing she was good at was living a lie. She chewed the omelet slowly and swallowed. Clucked her tongue to make a show of considering the taste. "Just the way I wanted it," she declared.

She plunged her fork into another piece of omelet. She arched her brows in challenge. He met her eyes and did the same, and they both put the food into their mouths simultaneously. She couldn't help but admire the way his freshly showered hair was drying into natural waves over his forehead. She wanted to run her hand over that smooth, newly shaven face. He looked so good across the breakfast table that she wouldn't mind . . . She blinked. She had almost admitted that she wanted to see him across the breakfast table like this every day. Hoping to hide her shock and dismay, she looked down at the sorry-looking excuse for an omelet she had cooked.

The silence that followed was broken intermittently only by the clanking of utensils. Steve noted that they were staring each other down as if they were dueling, which was ridiculous, since he wasn't going to say a word. Not one. Uh-uh. When she stood up to get something from the fridge, the moment her head ducked behind the door, he took a long swallow of his drink, barely keeping down a sigh as the icy liquid put out the flames in his mouth for a few seconds. God, *he* was going to cook next time.

Marlena heard his sigh as she pulled out the dessert. She sniffed. It didn't taste that bad, she told herself, although it didn't taste like any omelet she ever had before. Too much of that bottle of green curry, that's all. Next time she would try another one of those pretty bottles.

"Tiramisu for dessert," she announced.

"Dessert at breakfast? Fine, what's one more unusual thing to eat?"

"You did have that on your list of favorite foods."

"It's not that tough to make. I'll make us some if I have time."

Steve took another long swallow of juice, using it as an excuse not to answer her. She had a mulish look on her face, as if she suspected his evasive tactic, but hey, he had been good. He hadn't said one word. He probably couldn't, anyhow; he felt as if he had a raw fillet of meat for a tongue at the moment.

She stood beside him, waving a small plate of the dark, sweet dessert in front of his face. "Did you like the omelet?" she asked.

Her smile was radiant, and Steve noticed that she had very white little teeth. Sometimes a woman asked very difficult questions. "Am I overweight?" "Do I look good in this dress?" "Did you notice that pretty woman walking by?" "Did you like the omelet?" Same type of double-edged-sword queries. He picked up his glass and found it empty.

Staring at the tiramisu as if it were a life preserver, he nodded. Not a word, he repeated silently. One word and she'd pounce.

"Not too spicy? Not too yucky?" she pushed. She spooned half the tiramisu onto his plate and began to eat the rest herself.

Steve shook his head and attacked the dessert. He needed something sweet to counter the fiery taste in his mouth. The fluffy concoction of chocolate, cream, and brandy was soothing comfort. He finished his plate in two mouthfuls and wished for more.

"Well, I'll just have to remember how you like your omelet next time," she murmured.

Steve grunted some nonverbal reply. He was going to play this safe. Next time he would eat the stale pancakes and day-old peach muffins. Next time he would eat her for breakfast. Damn, why did he have to think of that again? He thought he had taken care of the "problem" in the shower, but all Marlena had to do to prove him wrong was stand close and he wanted to pull her onto his lap and kiss her again. Unfortunately she would taste of green spicy omelet. He grimaced. Better let her down more of that sweet tiramisu first.

She offered him a spoonful of the dessert. He obediently opened his mouth for her.

"Why so silent?" she asked as she licked the spoon clean.

Steve eyed the little tongue at work. "You're so hard to please. I say something, and you complain about my talking too much. I try to be obedient, and now I'm too quiet."

She contemplated this as she ate another mouthful, then started to lick the spoon again, just as before. Steve tried not to imagine her licking somewhere else with such dedication. At this rate he was going to need another shower.

"So it's not because your mouth is on fire and you'd rather have a glass of ice water?" She arched her brows, mischief in her eyes.

He would rather die of pain than admit that. "Now that you mention it, the dessert has made me thirsty." And just to

64 | Gennita Low

annoy her, he added, "Can you fetch me something to drink, please?" Then he sat back, ready to enjoy some fireworks.

Her blue eyes narrowed a fraction. "Fetch?"

"Yeah. You make a good serving wench."

"You're asking for it, Stash." She held up her own filled glass threateningly.

"Do that and you won't like what I'll do." Not trusting that she wouldn't carry out her threat, his hand shot out to grasp the other side of her glass. Her answering smile was so innocuous he had to grin at her. The woman just couldn't leave a challenge alone.

She stared at his lips for a few seconds, then looked up. There was silence again because he didn't have anything else to say. There was an intimacy in the moment he couldn't explain—in the teasing manner she looked at him, in the way her body tilted slightly toward him, in the half-opened lips that seemed to promise a sensual interlude. He knew she felt it, too. There was a softness in her eyes, a warmth that hadn't been there before.

Her voice, whispery soft, sent shivers down his spine. "Sure I won't like what you'll do?"

Steve was about to reply when the sharp ring of the phone on the kitchen counter jerked them apart like guilty teenagers caught by their parents. Water splattered out of the glass Marlena still had in her hand, wetting the tablecloth. She blinked, and the dreamy expression disappeared, as she seemed to count the number of rings. She walked over to the phone after the ringing stopped. Almost immediately, it started again, and she picked it up.

"Yes?" she said, her gaze still on Steve.

There was a different kind of alertness in her eyes and stance now. Steve realized that he had become second fiddle to whatever that phone call meant. He also knew that this was the beginning of his assignment. And the end of a very special interlude.

He had deliberately placed the call then to interrupt those two. That homey scene was disturbing to watch. A sudden thrill shot through him at the sound of her voice. He'd so looked forward to this. His grip on the receiver tightened.

"Miss Maxwell, I believe you've been waiting for my call. Please listen carefully since I don't have a whole lot of time." He paused, glancing up at the television screen. "No, no, of course not. D.C. is a fun city, and I'm sure you found plenty to do."

He pulled a folder from the in box on top of his office desk and opened it. "Plans have changed, Miss Maxwell. I'm sure you'll understand, what with the interest you've been generating lately. I really can't afford being seen with you. Not yet, anyway. People recognize me in this town."

Picking up his pen, he idly drew a big mustache onto the photograph in the folder. The man, he mused, was much too good-looking. No wonder the inimitable Miss Maxwell was distracted into domestic play.

"Oh, we'll meet, not to worry," he continued on the phone, as he added more flourish to the mustache he'd been drawing, curling the tips outward into exaggerated swirls. "It's just too dangerous right now. I'll get what I promised to you, but you have to do things my way."

He glanced up at the screen again and almost laughed out loud. Everything he'd heard about Marlena Maxwell seemed to hold true. The woman was incredibly sexy, with exceptional control over her talents. Without any apparent effort, she was simultaneously able to hold a business conversation and seduce another man, as she was doing now, waggling a come-hither finger to her victim. Poor man, he didn't stand a chance with the wily lady.

"Oh, I'm sure you'll find everything exactly as I promised. Your buyer will be pleased with what I have, and I expect my payment once you sell it. No, no, I understand the terms."

Her sassy reply amused him. He was really enjoying this conversation. Maybe one day they would do more than talk. He felt a little tingle of excitement at the thought of meeting her in person and touching her. "Thanks for the invitation, but I would imagine that apartment has very little privacy."

Her smile became bigger. After all, he was responsible for intercepting the real middleman and putting his boys there now. He wanted a personal viewing of the woman herself. Leaning a hip on the oak desk, he studied the screen again, then punched a few more buttons on the keyboard nearby. Ah, close up, she looked even more appealing. He'd always had a soft spot for auburn hair. And there was the tiniest mole above the right corner of her generous mouth. No, left, he corrected, since the camera reversed everything. "Oh, they won't trace me, but thank you for your concern. This call is directed through several locations in the country."

He frowned. His view was being blocked. He didn't like it when another man interfered with his pleasure, even though he had deliberately allowed this to happen. Right now one wouldn't think that there was even a phone conversation going on, the way those two were touching each other. His frown deepened. Did they think what they were doing didn't have any repercussions? There was a certain disrespect in the way they flaunted their attraction for each other, and he didn't like the way Marlena was treating him so casually.

His voice hardened imperceptibly. Enough of this nonsense. "A package is on the way today, special delivery. If you follow the instructions in it, everything else will fall into place. And oh, Miss Maxwell? I trust no one, not even you. If you double-cross me, I'll kill you."

He smiled again, pleased that he'd regained the upper hand. "Please, don't see this as a threat. When this is over, and if we're both successful, I'll buy you . . . breakfast."

He hung up and laughed. He wondered whether she was smart enough to catch his joke. Breakfast. He laughed again. When he finally shared breakfast with the delectable Marlena, he'd make sure it was after a night in which she'd forget that man she had her arms around now. Standing up, he stretched lazily, checking his watch for the time. Another few hours and the package would be at her door, and then everything should go according to plan.

He thought of having a cigarette, then shrugged off the

temptation. He had quit, but once in a while he enjoyed one, for old time's sake. Addiction was too dangerous for his profession and he really loved cigarettes too much at one time, but right now thinking of Marlena Maxwell in leather—and out of it—was so stimulating, he wanted a good, satisfying smoke.

Maybe he would have an entire pack as a celebratory present. Taking the folder off the desk, he sank down into the leather chair and lifted his legs to rest them on the desk. He flipped through the papers again, reading the classified information with mild curiosity.

It was a smart move, putting someone from outside his circle into TIARA. The admiral must have some suspicion to send one of his precious water cowboys to D.C. to replace Sorvino. Damn Sorvino. He'd thought he had him under control, but the foolish man thought he could outsmart him. From the files, he had been the most ambitious, the most eager to move ahead, but it was all an act. It was easy enough to arrange an accident.

The man gave a disdainful sniff. He hadn't accounted for some unforeseen roadblocks, that was all. He'd taken care of Sorvino. Now he had to deal with this water cowboy.

A nasty little smile settled on his lips. The admiral had also made a smart move, getting his man in. But he was way ahead of the game. The new man he sent didn't stand a chance against him. Already, with a little help, he'd made work life a little uncomfortable for the man. He'd made sure he didn't fit in, made sure to exploit the natural action-oriented nature of a man used to attacking rather than talking, although from the looks of it, he seemed to enjoy talking with Marlena a lot.

He frowned, feeling anger replacing displeasure. Too bad she was so damn good, taking out all those devices that very first night. He couldn't hear what those two said to each other. Of course, he needed very little imagination to fill in the blanks, from the few videos the remaining cameras had captured. However, he was a careful man. Marlena might not have figured out that anything was wrong yet, but he had better be prepared, just in case she did. She was suspicious enough to go looking for a surveillance device.

He watched the two figures leave the kitchen, eyes bright with laughter, and then no more video. What were they doing? He really hoped she was just playing, that she wasn't falling for that replacement. The thought made him sit up, his shoes scraping off the desk. She wouldn't be stupid and fall in love, would she? He thought of Sorvino's betrayal.

He recalled reading about the cold-blooded activities associated with Marlena Maxwell in the files he had, and relaxed. No, no woman like that would sacrifice herself for love. He smiled at the sight of the now-empty kitchen. Marlena Maxwell wasn't meant for a fresh navy SEAL who didn't know he was going down. She would much more appreciate a clever, ambitious man like him.

Chapter Five

Steve plucked at his lips as he went through the files in front of him, blocking out the noise from the rest of the guys around him. He had come straight back here as soon as Marlena had told him he had the rest of the day off till evening, eager to catch the other side of the phone conversation he'd overheard at the apartment.

He didn't really want to leave her, and it wasn't because it was his job to keep tabs on her activities, either. The men stationed outside would report if she stepped out of the building, but with the cameras gone, he was the only link to what she did on her own. Not that he had much to report to Harden. He couldn't just say that he spent half the time with his lips locked on the woman. He could just hear what his O.C. was going to say to that, considering the harsh words he had thrown in his direction last night.

But damn it, why was it that sometimes, for no reason, he thought of her blue eyes on him and something inside just shivered like a tray of Jell-O? He wished he could read what was behind those secretive blue eyes. The woman wasn't what she seemed. She wasn't this funny, wholesome, exasperating, sexy, crazy, mind-blowing creature. She was, but she wasn't. She, he told himself, owned two weapons that he knew of, and from the way she had used one of them the other night, she was very proficient with them. She also happened to be known as a hired assassin, her name bandied around among international criminal circles with a certain reverence, mainly because no one had been able to catch her in any criminal activities.

"You've gone through those files a dozen times, McMillan," Cam said, dropping into a chair nearby. "Anything new in there that you or I, or any of us, have missed?"

Steve looked up. Cam was one of the few with whom he had formed a friendship of sorts since coming to town. The man looked like an ex-hippie, long hair and an earring, most mornings coming in to work looking as if he had been to a wild party, but he had been the first to welcome Steve aboard, taking the trouble to explain how things were done in TIARA. Steve liked him. Cam didn't look it, but he had a keen eye for details that most people didn't catch.

"It's not what is there that I'm looking for, it's what's not there," he explained.

"Oh yeah?" Cam scooted the chair closer. "Tell me."

"These files we have on her account for her whereabouts the last two years. The pictures proved that she was always around certain incidents, but nothing else could be found to tie her with any of the crimes."

"That's her mystique," Cam said. "It's her shtick, actually. She arrives at the scene with a lot of fanfare and lots of people keep an eye on her. She usually has some arm candy on her—um . . . pardon me, Steve—that she takes around to several very public bashes. Then wham! Someone disappears, or gets whacked, and she always has an alibi."

"She's never been caught, not once, in all the years she's been monitored?"

Cam shook his head and pointed at some highlighted paragraphs. "The last two years, she's been tied to several crime organizations as well as big-time arms dealers, but you would never guess from the parties she hangs out at. See that pic? That was at the wedding of Prince Talimar. And that one? That was at a very big to-do at Mad Max Shoggi's. A guest in a royal wedding and at a wealthier-than-royalty arms dealer's shindig. That is the mystique. How does she do it? No one knows."

"No family. No friends. Yet surrounded by people who know her," Steve said.

"Well, hey, you didn't expect an assassin to have a family with kids in tow, did you?" asked Cam, reaching for the bag of stale chips nearby.

"If we have no evidence, why do we call her an assassin?"

Cam crunched the chips loudly, then popped open a can of soda. "Good question," he said, then took a long gulp, followed by a loud burp. "Ahhh, nothing like warm Coke for lunch."

Steve watched him pour the rest of the bag of chips into his open mouth. "That is pretty disgusting, man. That bag was there a couple of days ago."

Cam lifted one dark brow at him. "Hey, I didn't eat green shit for breakfast."

"It wasn't shit." Although it was green.

"It looked like shit from here. We were all yelling at the TV screen, 'No man! Don't eat it! You're gonna die!' But hell, you were some brave soul, putting that into your system," Cam told him with a straight face. "Must be that SEAL training."

Steve scowled and shuffled the papers in front of him. The guys had already given him enough ribbing over that breakfast. They had started calling him Stash, too, making crude remarks about him and Marlena.

"Of course," Cam went on, "if I got that kind of kiss every time I ate green shit, I wouldn't hesitate, either. Hey, hey, hey!" He lifted his arms in surrender, the laughter in his voice and eyes betraying his teasing. "You aren't going to punch me out just because you got a nice-looking chick and an apartment for a while, are you? I mean, from the look of things, she's got the hots for you, Stash baby."

Steve didn't want to talk about Marlena and how hot she was. That subject led to thoughts he wasn't willing to discuss with anyone. "Let's backtrack to my question," he said, ignoring Cam's wicked grin. "I've heard of names given to faceless assassins and criminals who've never been caught, but I haven't ever heard of an assassin with a name and a face whom nobody has ever seen in the act of a crime."

"Well, a good assassin is supposed to never be caught."

"Yeah, but there are usually witnesses or people around who give information we can never use in court. Or there's some kind of criminal record in her background. These files show nothing, not a damn thing."

"Well, I'm sure her older files will show her previous amateur criminal activities. You know how it is. She's so well known, her files are probably a closetful, still not updated into the mainframe. This is the recent information on disk and that's what counts. We want to see whom she'd hung out with recently, why she's here in D.C., and whether we can connect her recent activities to her current contract. Two years is plenty long to try to see what she's up to, Steve." Cam finished his soda and burped loudly again. He noisily crunched the aluminum can, then took aim at the wastepaper basket on the other side of the room. "Don't forget, she's an assassin, a contract agent. Damn, missed by inches. That means what she's asked to do is very current, very up-to-date. No one contracts to kill two years ahead of time, man. Yo, Arms, can you pick that can up for me?"

Steve glanced in the direction of Arms, who gave a crude answer to Cam's request before complying. The two men exchanged basketball banter while he thought about what Marlena was up to. Cam's analysis made sense, of course. This wasn't some war in the jungles against some drug lord that could take months and months and not see any resolution. A contract was something that had a time frame.

Steve looked down at the picture of Marlena dancing with some handsome tall Asian punk, taken at that fancy wedding of some prince last year. She looked glamorous, in a glittery slinky gown, not a hair out of place. Her companion was looking at her like she was some goddess, his attention totally focused on her. Her eyes held the familiar sensual heat, but they were looking at the camera, not her companion, as if she wanted to make sure the world saw her.

Something clicked in his mind. A woman who liked to

act in a certain manner when the camera was around. A woman projecting a certain image.

When there was no camera around, Marlena was totally different with him. During the shopping spree, she had a certain sparkle and fun that were missing in these pictures and in those videos the others saw. But why did she show it to him?

"Tough, isn't it?" Cam interrupted his reverie.

"What?"

"To reconcile that creature with cold-blooded murder. There's something totally different about her when you look at her picture, like she has more than she's willing to show." Cam shrugged, then his gaze on Steve sharpened. "But then aren't all crooks like that? Something to hide. She'll probably slit your throat if you aren't careful, Stash baby. Don't trust her, no matter what you do. Get naked with her if you want to, but don't give her a chance to take you down, man. She's got you all cross-eyed with lust."

"I can handle it." Steve mustn't have sounded convincing enough because Cam gave a snort of disbelief. He stressed again, "I can handle it. I just need to find out what this other thing is, then we at least have a clue what we're after."

"What other thing?"

"The recent recorded conversation. We're tagging him as the seller."

"Yeah."

"What is he selling? Marlena's supposed to play courier between him and the buyer, and then what? What has that got to do with a contract? We thought the seller hired the middleman to get her the apartment, but this call seems to point to another direction. The buyer, perhaps?"

"Don't forget the threatening calls, too. Or that first night, when you were followed."

"Yes, what is this thing they're all after, that they think she has gotten from the seller?"

"Our intel interception had only mentioned a contract out, and that Marlena Maxwell was going to D.C. That's usually the code over the air that means she has a job."

Cam's voice turned thoughtful, as if he was getting intrigued, too. He scratched the back of his neck, pushing his long hair out of the way. "You're right. Knowing what the article is could be the key."

"Can you get the files from before two years? Or some of them."

"Sure. What are you looking for?"

"Don't know yet. Just gut feeling." A thought occurred to Steve. "Do I have to clear it with Harden?"

Cam shrugged. "Don't think so. But if you have to, I don't know why he wouldn't approve it."

Steve could give several reasons, none of them appropriate. "I suppose not," he vaguely agreed. He hoped he didn't have to, anyway.

Cam placed a hand on Steve's shoulder. "Look, Hard-On has been tough on you but that's the way he is, man. He's an SOB but he listens more than you think. He's good at coordinating a sting." He got up from the chair, brushing off tiny crumbs from his rumpled shirt and pants. "He just has this almighty attitude about control, that's all. Doesn't like to have unknowns in the equation, and you're an unknown, Steve. You aren't from around here. He can't tell whether you're reliable or not."

Steve met Cam's eyes steadily. "I'm a SEAL. I can be relied on to carry a team."

"Hey, I ain't saying you aren't. You've been okay in my book since you arrived. Thing is, we haven't had a big case till now, so this is like your test, *capisce*? Not only that," Cam lowered his voice several octaves, "Hard-On has a thing against what you're doing."

Steve frowned, puzzled. "You lost me."

Cam bent down to pick up several of the files on the desk, as if he didn't want to bring attention to what he was saying. "Not good to talk about it here, even though he's somewhere else. Let's just say that rumor has it, Hard-On was an operative for Internal Investigations a long time ago, and some female operative nearly destroyed his career. He was supposed to be going up into the elite tiers of the CIA but was demoted to almost nothing because of one slip-up."

Things were certainly clearer now, Steve thought, recalling certain aspects of the conversation with his operations chief. "So he thinks I might go that way," he murmured.

Cam slipped the folders under his arm and tucked a pen behind his ear. "Maybe. Maybe not. You can't tell with him. Got to go, but will get you the info ASAP. Meanwhile"—his voice turned into a sneer—"make sure you don't splatter any wine on your penguin suit tonight."

That brought another scowl to Steve's face. He wasn't looking forward to a night of playing Marlena's arm candy. "She'd better not make me dance. I don't dance," he warned nobody particular in the room.

Cam chuckled. "Life is good, man. I wouldn't mind twirling that woman in my arms. She's just my type, too: passionate, a little dangerous, and nice, shapely"—gesturing suggestively, he started chuckling even more at the look Steve tossed him before continuing—"ummm . . . shapely legs. Remember, she wants you around as an alibi at all times, and hey, if you ask me, Stash, you've had no cause to complain so far, penguin suit or no penguin suit."

Steve decided to change the subject. Talking about Marlena and him together made him uncomfortable. He didn't like sharing his private moments with her with anybody. "Yeah, well, I'd better go back to my place. You'll get me the info, right?"

"It'll take some time, since it's all hard copy, but that's my job." Cam gave a mock salute. "Just remember I'm the one working hard while you're hardly working."

After Cam went off, Steve rubbed his eyes with the heel of his hands. There were too many screens to stare at around here. Computers, TVs, videos, cameras hooked to videos. Everything focused on that one person who had somehow become mixed up with a mermaid in his mind. And like a mermaid, she had never been caught, never been seen.

Stuff of myths. He frowned. Another M word. Marlena the Myth.

He had a plateful piled high with information. Marlena stuff. His own operations chief stuff. His very own stuff. And somewhere in there was a nugget of truth. All he had to do was figure out how to see what wasn't there, because he didn't trust the cameras like these guys did.

That conversation between her and the seller bothered him somehow. He had a feeling that he was close to getting a big revelation, but so far everything was clouded. One thing was sure, though. Harden didn't think he could do the job because of his attraction to the target. Knowing that only added to his determination to be successful at this assignment.

He, Steve McMillan, had a job. And that was to catch a mermaid. Another M word, he realized with growing despondency. He was much too obsessed with M words.

Marlena put her hand on her heart. Her eyes widened appreciatively. Good Lord.

The object of her attention frowned down at her, obviously unhappy with his situation. The corners of his masculine lips were turned down like those of a sulky child, begging to be kissed. Tempting, very tempting.

"What?" he demanded. The recessed lighting in her bedroom cast intriguing shadows on his handsome face, giving him a mysterious and dangerous air. It just wasn't fair for a man to have cheekbones that perfect, Marlena mourned in silent envy. Most women had to suck in their cheeks and blow out their lips to get that look. It just wasn't fair. His smoothly shaven jaw line was chiseled perfection, ending with that cute dimple in his willful chin. His dark hair was combed back, the first time she had seen it so neat. The crisp dark Valente tuxedo emphasized his broad shoulders. Its clean, simple straight lines gave an illusion of leashed power. From the top of his head to his polished new Guccis, Steve McMillan looked as if he had stepped out of a *GQ* magazine. He would look good in uniform, she thought, and rubbed her poor palpitating heart again.

"Such beauty," Marlena mocked, smiling up at him. "I don't think my heart can take it."

His dark gaze slithered possessively up and down her, resting a few moments on the bare flesh of her bosom. Her heart beat faster. "I think that's my line," he told her, his lips softening into a reluctant smile of admiration.

She wore the new daring gown she'd bought. That day she'd deliberately chosen it because she'd wanted to turn him on, knowing very well how he hated to be there waiting for her to try on yet another set of clothes. For reasons she couldn't explain, she found it amusing to tease him, to make him as aware of her as she was of him. She'd never felt the need to garner any man's attention before.

"You've already seen me in this," she told him, brushing down the soft material with one hand. She adjusted the new brooch holding the gown together under her belly button, arranging the folds of the dress to fan out at the bottom with an artistic flair. It was a delicately designed piece, yet heavy enough to be used for the bold designer outfit. Little diamonds sparkled among fleurs de lis shaped by tiny seed pearls, drawing attention away from the plunging neckline. She had fallen in love with it, even though the fastener behind it had a tricky catch.

"Let me." He came closer. He couldn't reach the brooch standing up, so he went down on his haunches, coming eye level to it. "Is this what's holding the dress together?"

His voice was soft and seductive, and Marlena held her breath as his fingers touched the piece of jewelry, lifting it and the attached material off her body enough so he could properly fasten it. Sheer torture. But it was important to let him take his time.

She closed her eyes, feeling unbelievably aroused at the thought of how gentle his hands were. How could such big hands be so tender? He didn't touch her bare flesh at all but she felt his warm breath caressing her in a slow rhythm. Her plan to distract him, keep his mind occupied with other things, was working far too well.

"Do you have anything underneath this at all?"

Marlena opened her eyes to see Steve's dark gaze contemplating his own question. He leaned closer, as if to find out for himself. "Yes. My Tweety Bird tattoo," she answered very softly. "And we're going to be late if you mess with my dress. The trick in keeping it in place is not to play with it."

Her words had the desired opposite effect. She knew Stash would take it as a challenge. His hands spanned her waist, and her breath caught when he rubbed her lower belly with his thumbs. She closed her eyes again, wondering whether she could afford to be late for the party. His hands slid from her waist to her hips, his thumb scoring down the front of her tummy with erotic slowness. Lower. She felt his hands hugging her thighs, his thumbs exploring the curve where her legs met her hips. They followed a sensuous pattern as his long fingers cupped her buttocks, and desire swamped her senses as those magic thumbs explored the twin geometrical lines that ended at the point of a triangle. God, if she wasn't careful, she would be the one distracted, not him.

Marlena bit down on her lower lip, refusing to allow any sounds to escape. "Stash . . ." she began, trying to sound normal. His thumbs pressed down on the apex of the triangle and a soft involuntary moan rose from her lips.

His voice held a trace of curiosity. "I don't feel any panties, but there's something here . . . what is it?" He pressed down again, tracing the small little bumps.

Marlena laid her hands on his shoulder for support. Why had she come up with such a naughty idea? Part of her understood her own seductive power over him, and she had to use it, so she could conduct business while his mind was on other things. However, right now, she discovered that there was a part of her that was very weak and helplessly under the power of the very same man. Her knees were melting under her from the delicious torture he was putting her through. But she wasn't going to tell him that, or they would never leave this room.

"What is it?" he asked again.

"I already told you," she replied stubbornly and gripped harder as his curious investigation pulled and stretched her sensitive skin. Clearing her throat, she said as firmly as she could, "We have to go."

He finally looked up at her. The heat in his eyes threatened to set her in flames. He slowly stood up, his thumb following the mysterious object under her gown. "All right, if you say so," he said, but his eyes promised other things.

She felt disappointed that he had stopped. *Don't be ridiculous,* she scolded herself. *Keep your mind on your job.*

As if he'd read her thoughts, Steve asked where they were going. "What kind of party is it? What do I have to do?"

He would know sooner or later, so she told him their destination. "Do you know du Scheum?" He should. The name was synonymous with synthetic and plastic products, for both household and scientific uses.

"Not personally, no," he replied facetiously, as he watched her squirt some perfume on her wrists. He frowned slightly. "Hell, we're going to a party given by du Scheum? You run around with some big names, don't you?"

Marlena smiled secretively. She could see that he was already busy going through the possible reasons for her going there. That was why she needed to distract him. Wanting to test him, she said, "I make friends easily. Part of my job."

"Really. You know, you've never elaborated exactly what it is that you do." He opened the apartment door for her and they stepped out into the carpeted hallway. "After all, being chased by cars and getting threatening phone calls sort of eliminated the usual socialite party animal I was told to accompany."

She coughed. "I can hardly believe the man who hired you told you that."

"That's the description he gave me when I asked what you were like," Steve said smugly. "He didn't say anything about car chases. Or shopping."

Marlena smiled again. The last word was said with a great deal more disgust than the car chase. Surely the man had some warped priorities. She would have to teach him the fine art of shopping a whole day away another time. But for now she had to concentrate on tonight's agenda.

He seemed to read her mind again. "What do I do? I don't know anybody. Do I say hi and shake hands vigorously? Do I clap Mr. du Scheum on the back and talk to him about what a wonderful invention the plastic egg beater is?" When she burst out laughing, he shrugged, as if he had the right to ask stupid questions. "It's a tough thing to do well, this obedience thing."

Marlena rolled her eyes. Like he really was trying so hard. "I doubt du Scheum and you will get a chance to sit down and talk. There are more important and wealthier people there who need his attention, Stash. Unless, of course, you have connections to help du Scheum Industries?"

"Do you?"

Ah, a loaded question. If she didn't, why would she be at this exclusive party? Du Scheum didn't invite just anybody. He was a facilitator, a powerful ally between politics and business. Of course, sometimes these two things brought together blurred ethical lines.

"Let's just say that I know people du Scheum knows, and he knows people I know," she told Steve. "And all I require you to do is to stay close by me, but don't interrupt too much with your questions. Would that be too much to hope for?"

He gave her one of those quizzical looks that she was beginning to recognize. He would do as she asked but would exact payment afterward. Warm desire rose at the thought of his hands on her.

"I'll be so good, people will want me for their lackey," Steve promised. Marlena made a rude sound. He studied her as they descended in the lift, then asked, "You know so many people, why can't you get a rich man to take you to one of these parties?"

Marlena sighed. Obviously it was time to distract him again. She ran a hand down the front of her dress, knowing that his eyes would follow as she pretended to smooth away some imaginary wrinkle by the brooch. She fingered the jeweled piece. She ran a suggestive hand down her hip, adjusting the skirt. The elevator door opened to the underground garage and without a word, she stepped out first, making sure she brushed against him as she passed.

She smiled furtively again, pleased to have interrupted his thought process. His footsteps behind her were somehow erotic to her ears, as if he were hot on her heels. Just after she slid into the passenger side of the Porsche, he leaned in, his expression scorching as his eyes traveled down her body. She inhaled the woodsy cologne he wore, mixed with a certain scent of desire. He was fast. He'd already figured it out.

His eyes pierced the dark interior of the car, knowledge and surprise mingled with sensual awareness. "That long pearl necklace," he muttered. "Lady, you aren't just wearing a Tweety Bird tattoo under there."

Marlena scooted a little away and flashed Steve an innocent smile. It was wiser to be quiet, letting his imagination do the work. If she pushed too hard, he could see through her scheme, and where they were going, she needed to constantly be on guard, to be in control of the situation. She was there to be seen and documented, as well as to make sure everything was going according to plan.

Turning the radio on, she chose a station playing light jazz. Steve's silence didn't bother her at all. In fact, it was one thing about him that fascinated her. Most people were usually deep in thought or concentrating on the task at hand when they were quiet, but she always felt that Steve was constantly on alert, even when he lounged lazily on the sofa. He seemed very at ease doing nothing, as if he spent a lot of time sitting alone, yet it wasn't a relaxed, detached easiness caused by a lazy lifestyle. Even sitting in the middle of a women's boutique, he gave the impression of a jungle cat watching his prey.

So the million-dollar question was—was Steve McMillan stalking her? Or was he just a pawn in this game she chose to play? Tonight she would have some answers.

She studied him surreptitiously. This wasn't just sexual attraction. She had dated good-looking men before and had only enjoyed their company. She'd certainly never had the urge to make them breakfast, she thought with a touch of self-mockery. Even during her last attempt at making a relationship work, she'd never played housewife. Of course, that had been the problem. She just couldn't see herself in that role, and compromise was out of the question. She'd put the lives of some friends in jeopardy because she wanted things to work out, and she'd vowed ever since to be alone. It was better not to be emotionally dependent on others in her line of work.

She checked her newly painted nails with distracted interest. It wasn't good to want a man so badly. It would only end up getting her killed.

Chapter Six

Steve made a mental note to one day drive up here in the daylight and check out the neighborhood. They were in one of the more exclusive neighborhoods by the Potomac River, the kind of houses surrounded by walls and electronic gates, with boat docks in their backyards.

Not that he would be shopping for a pad here, he mocked. Du Scheum's pocketbook far exceeded the pay of a navy SEAL. Even with the extra money he was getting for this new transfer, he'd probably never be able to afford land a quarter the size of this—he looked around—place. He looked at the beautifully lit driveway with its swaying trees as they drove on.

Uniformed servants opened the car doors as each limousine and expensive car inched its way to the front steps of the beautiful mansion lit up by dozens of colored globe lights. Steve stepped out of the Porsche and waited for Marlena while a uniformed servant helped her out. He frowned when her smile brought a blush to the young man's face as he tried not to stare too hard at the front of her gown. It didn't help to think about those pearls not far away.

"Thank you, madam," the usher said as he accepted his tip. "Please let me know if you need anything else. Please keep this card so we can know where we parked your car."

Marlena's smile became wicked when she reached Steve's side. "Lackey," she teased, knowing that it would get to him. "I think I'll hire him next time."

Steve glowered down at her. "Better buy a cemetery plot. He'd bore you to death and have to bury you."

"Oh, and would you mourn my demise, Stash darling?" She laughed, slipping her hand into the crook of his arm after adjusting the light wrap folded across her arm. The night air was cool against her bare skin, but she knew it would be warm inside the mansion. "Would you come visit me once in a while? Put some flowers on my headstone?"

She had meant it as a joke but was surprised at how solemnly they regarded each other for a second. He turned and touched her right cheek with the back of his hand. It felt like regret.

"I'll do that," he said, his obsidian dark eyes for once flat and expressionless.

They walked through the grand arches into the hallway, already filling up with arrivals. She smiled to break the tension. "Something to look forward to, then," she said wryly.

Steve looked around him with interest. She wondered whether he recognized anyone there. These people weren't exactly anonymous. She had attended enough of these parties in the last two years to assume the mantle of the elite, where everyone needed only a first-name introduction with her, but the first time was a revelation, a culture shock to those who never understood the thin line between black and white. Here people ordinarily separated by social position rubbed elbows, kissed each other like old friends, and talked of business and politics over drinks and cigar.

That is, she thought, assuming Steve McMillan recognized the presence of the likes of an infamous arms dealer such as Max Shoggi talking ten feet away from a UN ambassador. Or the likes of her, she added with a little irony, smiling with familiar secrecy at the royal prince of the kingdom of Desah, who silently toasted her with his flute of champagne.

"What do lackeys do at these things?" Steve asked, light sarcasm in his voice, looking at the royal prince with a frown. He recognized him from the recent news about Desah's new business contract with U.S. firms amid news of a coup. How well did Marlena know him? "Is there a lackey lounge area for us to sit and exchange notes or something?"

Actually there was, but she wasn't going to let this man stray too far. Not when he looked like that. "What kind of companion did they get for me?" she wondered aloud, with mock exasperation. "Didn't they ask for prior experience? Whatever did you say to get hired?"

"I told them I was good at kissing," he deadpanned.

She sighed, shook her head, and started walking toward the main room. "I suppose you're good at that," she conceded. A waiter appeared from nowhere, offering her a glass of champagne from his tray.

"Suppose? I'll be happy to help you be very sure about it. All doubts removed, I promise. As long as I find out where Tweety Bird is."

The conversational murmur in the huge room somehow enhanced the intimate invitation in his words. His hand moved down the small of her back, tracing her spine suggestively. Stay focused, Marlena reminded herself. She needed things done in an orderly fashion, so that she would be in constant control of the very charged situation they were in.

"I'm beginning to think it's the other way around," she said lightly. "It's me who is good at kissing, and you just can't get enough of me."

His eyes glinted down at her, settling on her lips. "Let's make a bet."

"Another one?"

"You let me kiss you the way I want tonight."

The rush of excitement through her was heady. Like the champagne in her hand. "And?"

"And by the time I'm done, you'll show me your Tweety Bird."

Marlena laughed. He did have a way with words. And he was doing exactly what she wanted, keeping his thoughts focused on her. "That doesn't sound like a bet to me." She took another glass of champagne from another waiter passing by. "What if you lose?"

Steve took the champagne glass from her and drank deeply before handing it back. Not exactly an appropriate lackey thing to do, he admitted, but she didn't say anything. Instead she tossed the rest off, her blue eyes meeting his over the rim of the glass. He knew she would accept his challenge. The glass of champagne sealed the pact. Later. Tonight. Those sultry eyes promised things that were going to cause him discomfort for the next few hours.

She had placed those thoughts in his mind to tease him. He knew Tweety Bird wasn't in a decent place. It couldn't be, because there weren't any tattoos on her exposed body in those outrageous black things the other night. That left very few possible places. A pearl necklace worn nowhere near the neck. The erotic images were going to haunt him all night. He tipped her head back with a forefinger and gave her the merest wisp of a kiss at the corner of her lips. He felt her shiver, and a mocking smile tugged at his lips as he straightened.

However, for now he would watch and learn as much as he could about how Marlena Maxwell got things done. The important thing was to keep a step ahead of her, make sure nothing happened without his knowing it.

Cam said that this was her shtick. She mingled among the wealthy and the infamous, the influential and the notorious, with a familiarity that suggested she knew most of them. What he couldn't understand was how these people ended up together in the same room. Cam had given him a thorough briefing about what to expect, the usual crowd at these functions, but he still couldn't accept it. He had questions for which Cam had no answers at all.

He overheard snatches of conversation—politicking and gossip—among these people who wouldn't normally be seen in public together. It disturbed his sense of ethics. Half these people he worked for, and the other half—he hid a grimace—he wanted to wipe off the face of this earth. The glimmer of jewelry on the throats, wrists, and cuffs everywhere caught his eye. Wealth, the common denominator. This was the world Marlena walked in.

He looked around at the guests again. Everyone seemed very at home in these opulent surroundings—marble and crystal, modern art and fountains, sumptuous feast and plush furnishings. He'd never been inside a place quite like this, but then he'd never had friends this wealthy, he thought wryly. The few rooms he'd seen, if one could call them rooms, had ample square footage to house several families. The main place where everyone gathered looked like a ballroom, arranged in several sections to accommodate those who wanted to sit in a group, those who preferred to have quiet conversation, and those who were in a more swinging mood.

Huge aquariums filled with colorful saltwater fish decorated the walls as well as divided sections of the room. In the middle, the floor tiles gleamed with an intricate sunburst pattern, accented by a huge crystal chandelier hanging from the thirty-foot ceiling that reflected the colors of the aquarium, imported tile, and glittering fashions. The effect was spectacular, like an underwater congregation of colors and movement. His gaze finally rested on one particular woman. A perfect place, he admitted, for a mermaid.

"This is nothing. You should see my place," he told Marlena. Her husky laughter drew attention to them, and especially to what she was wearing. He drew her a little closer, then stopped, surprised at his possessive reaction. He'd never done that with any woman before, even with the few girlfriends he had dated on and off. He glanced quickly at Marlena, but if she'd noticed, she didn't show it, as she made her way slowly around the room.

Steve stayed by Marlena's side as she mingled, and on the surface it appeared like a very superficial gathering. The conversation was general, but once in a while he noticed animated gestures accompanying a discussion of some current hot political topic. He watched the body language. He studied Marlena's every move. She laughed as if she were on top of the world. That part, he knew from experience, was one big façade.

After the superb dinner, he did get to put his foot down on

one thing. So okay, he would play around with ten different forks and spoons. He wouldn't touch the food with his hands. But absolutely no dancing. The host, who seemed to be absent, had a live band playing in the backyard by the Olympic-sized pool, and the music had an international flavor, mostly Latin rhythms. Marlena wanted to dance. Steve gave her one dark look, and she sighed.

"Coward," she complained.

"You want to be brave enough to have two left feet stomping on your little toes?" he challenged. This wasn't even swaying music. It was the kind of music that required him to do things that Steve McMillan didn't do. Not in public anyway.

"Stay here and eat munchies then, and watch me," Marlena ordered, and pulled the young ambassador from some developing country onto the dance floor just outside the patio.

Steve sat down on one of the soft leather sofas by an aquarium, but he didn't take his eyes off Marlena. She was having a good time, laughing softly as she moved sensuously in her partner's arms, her steps matching the music perfectly. He sniffed. He turned to look at the fish in the tank. They were exotic, like the woman on his mind, and they, too, seemed to be swimming to the music. His eyes wandered back to Marlena. She seemed to have forgotten about him, talking animatedly to her partner. He considered cutting in. Rudely.

"Oh, an empty seat with no crowd," a voice murmured. Steve turned to find a tall, attractive woman standing by the sofa. "May I join you?"

He shifted slightly to make room, and she sat down gracefully, crossing her model-length legs as she held a glass of champagne between long, elegant fingers decked with rings. Close up, she was even more beautiful, her short blond hair cut in a blunt pageboy, accentuating classical features. Her eyes were a honey-brown color, and they studied him with warm curiosity.

"I've never seen you before."

"Steve," he said, holding out his hand.

"Tess." She sat back comfortably. "You look out of place here."

"Really?" Steve shrugged. "I didn't know it showed."

"You aren't talking to the right people. Sitting alone tells me you either don't know or don't care."

Steve studied the woman thoughtfully. Here was someone to provide information. She returned his gaze just as frankly. "I'm here as company," he explained, resisting the urge to look at Marlena and her dance partner.

She lifted an eyebrow and sipped her drink. "You aren't here to do business, then."

"I'm not sure what business someone like Max Shoggi would have with du Scheum, or why a prince would need to talk business with some of the questionable characters milling around. Besides, I suspect it's all about politics, anyway." He tried to sound nonchalant, flashing her a smile. If he could just get her to answer a few questions, he might end up with more clues.

"Everything is about politics, darling, don't you know?" Tess shook her head, gold hoops in her ears glinting, reflecting the lights from the fish tank. "I can tell you need a lesson in how big business and politics are done in D.C."

"So give me a lesson," Steve invited. "I'm new around here, as you can tell."

She smiled, and he thought he saw amusement in her eyes. She flicked her hair with her free hand and took another sip of champagne. "Like a fish out of water, hmm?" she asked.

More than she would ever know, Steve silently acknowledged, but he just nodded.

"Hmm, how do I make this sound interesting? Do you like baseball?"

"Yes."

"Okay, suppose you have the best seats to watch the World Series. Let's make it a Subway Series, between the Yankees and the Mets. Suppose you want to sell those tickets."

"I wouldn't. I would want to watch it," Steve said. He wanted to keep this woman amused enough to impart more information than baseball games.

Tess laughed. "Business, remember?" she reminded gently. "We're doing business."

"Okay."

Her eyes glinted, and now he was very sure she was laughing at him. "Let's make it less personal. Some guy has these tickets, and he's going to sell them to the highest bidder," she said. "Now, it's illegal to sell them a dollar above face value. What do you think he'll do to get around this?"

"Different ways. He can sell through an ad in the paper without specifying the price."

"He would still get caught, if a cop called up," Tess pointed out.

The woman was trying to tell him something. "There is another way. He can sell a pencil for two thousand dollars and if you buy it, he'd throw in a free gift—say, two tickets to the World Series."

"Ah, so you do know how to do business." Tess finished her drink and as if by magic, one of the uniformed servants appeared with a tray offering munchies and drinks. She chose some chocolaty thing and another glass of champagne. Steve shook his head, not needing another drink. She licked her fingers and took another sip, closing her eyes as she savored the taste. "Hmm . . . to tell the truth, I come to these things for the champagne. Simply divine."

He wanted to get back on track, but not too obviously. "So, you're here for business, right? And you're hoping to buy a pencil for two thousand dollars."

"Or I might be trying to sell a pencil for two thousand dollars," she countered, a wicked light entering her golden eyes now. She glanced to her right. He followed her gaze. Marlena had finished her dance and was approaching them. Tess murmured softly, "Do you suppose she's buying or selling, darling?"

Marlena reached them, and Steve got up to give her room to sit down. Although she was smiling, Steve felt her anger,

but nothing in her expression betrayed that. "I've been looking for you, T.," she said, without any formal greeting.
"You've been trying out some of those evasive tactics your
new friends taught you."

"I don't know what you mean, I've been here all night,"
Tess drawled lazily, leaning a little back into the sofa. Marlena had, Steve noted, the most expressive eyes. She seemed
to be able to convey many emotions in between sentences.
Right now they held Tess's gaze challengingly. "Sit down,
darling. You look indecently gorgeous, as usual."

"And you look like you need to mud wrestle once in a
while," Marlena retorted, joining the woman on the sofa. She
reached out her hand for Steve's. "You've lost some weight."

"Maybe I've been mud wrestling, you never know." Tess
looked at their clasped hands and took another sip of her
drink.

Perched on the arm of the sofa closer to Marlena, Steve
watched them exchange air kisses. Definitely a woman
thing, he decided. Must be the fear of lipstick. The two
women studied each other for a few seconds, and he wondered whether they were friends. He couldn't tell, from the
way they were dueling with words.

"I knew you would catch sight of me if I chose the right
place to sit." The mockery in Tess's voice was obvious as she
turned to Steve. "So, it's Marlena you're keeping company."

"I'm her lackey," Steve told her dutifully.

Beautifully curved eyebrows lifted a fraction, amusement
gleaming from the eyes that slanted slightly at the corners.
"Lackey?" she drawled out the word, then laughed. "I don't
see anything lacking in him, M. darling."

"T. darling," Marlena drawled back. "You haven't seen
all of him."

"Well, do tell, what does he lack?"

Marlena gave Steve a wicked grin. "Well . . . He definitely lacks manners."

"Maybe you lack finesse. Sometimes it takes a subtle
touch. His manners were fine while you were away, I assure
you."

Steve watched as Marlena leaned back, cocking her head to one side as she looked directly at the other woman. Definitely not friends, he decided.

"I see you still like to play with words," Marlena commented, after a moment. With the nearby soft aquarium lights reflecting the exotic colors of the fish, her eyes looked like glittering jewels as she added softly, "Just don't play your mind games with me."

Tess's smile was indolent, amused. "Don't mind me. You're the control freak." She turned to Steve again, dismissing Marlena with a sweep of her elegant hand. "I was bored till I spotted this interesting man over here. But things are looking better now."

Steve didn't know what the woman was up to, but her words were calculated to rile Marlena. She was also succeeding. "It looks like an interesting party," he said. No harm in digging for more information. Tess, whoever she was, liked to talk. "There are too many important people here for me to find it boring."

"True," Tess said, "but they are such a lackluster bunch."

Steve laughed. The woman obviously loved words, and the way she used them was funny. "Here to buy pencils, of course," he joked.

Tess laughed back, genuine pleasure in her eyes. "And to keep company." When Marlena used a napkin to fan herself, she added, "You should go freshen up, darling. You look a little out of breath."

Marlena's eyes narrowed. She didn't like being left out of the conversation. "A breath of fresh air sounds great." She touched Steve's knee briefly as she got up and brushed his lips with hers, murmuring, "Don't go anywhere, especially with her. She eats lackeys for breakfast."

"I won't," Steve promised. He watched her go off. She was mad as hell. Jealous, too. He felt ridiculously pleased.

"I suppose I'd better go after her before she returns to scratch my eyes out," Tess said thoughtfully. She uncrossed her shapely legs and arched a brow at Steve. "She's a possessive woman."

When she lifted a hand for his help, Steve obliged, pulling her to her feet. "I gather you don't like Marlena. Have you known her long?"

Tess was eye-to-eye with him on her feet, and he was surprised at how direct her gaze was. Cool. Fearless. It reminded him of Marlena. "It was nice talking to you, sailor," she said and smiled when he blinked in surprise. Did she know about him? She nodded her head to their right. "In that far corner, that man in white is du Scheum. He's a powerful man, with many enemies and friends."

Steve looked in that direction. "Who are you? Why are you telling me this?" he demanded quietly.

"Things never look quite the way they ought to, darling. Now I'd better go find Marlena. You know how it is— strange things happen around that girl. She can't keep out of trouble." When Steve tried to stop her from going, she evaded his hand with a speed that stunned him. She was still smiling but her voice was cool. "You may be a fish out of water here, darling, but that doesn't mean you can't adapt. You can still step into danger outside jungles."

Before Steve could say anything, she slipped away. He wasn't quite sure what had happened there, but that woman knew who he was and had given him a warning. She'd cleverly sidestepped his question about knowing Marlena. He frowned, looking at the group of men talking. That was du Scheum, huh? Danger, Tess said. Was she saying something was going to happen tonight? He recalled Cam's words earlier that day.

It's her shtick, actually. She arrives at the scene with a lot of fanfare and lots of people keep an eye on her. She usually has some arm candy on her—um . . . pardon me, Steve—that she takes around to several very public bashes. Then wham! Someone disappears, or gets whacked, and she always has an alibi.

Steve pursed his lips grimly. Well, he wasn't just any arm candy; she couldn't make him her alibi. Task Force Two's intel stated Marlena Maxwell was in D.C. on business. She had been called an assassin, whatever the hell that meant.

However, he understood the dangers of putting a lot of important people in one room, and D.C. had plenty of VIPs. If she truly had been hired to kill someone, he must find proof. And a way to stop her. One thing he knew for certain—no one was going to get whacked under his watch.

Chapter Seven

Marlena read the note from a waiting uniformed servant as she pretended to finish yet another glass of champagne. This was the second bid for the night. Soon she would have to confirm the sale to the highest bidder, and her job would be finished for tonight. She thought of Steve. He hadn't seen her quiet negotiation, thanks to the dancing and to Tess.

It was important to be seen and remembered. She knew there were all kinds of people watching her. Probably CIA. Some enemies. A few friends. Most of them knew why she was there and would be reporting to their respective bosses about the bidders present, and who could be the winning buyer. Her job was to muddy up the water, so they could never be too sure. She didn't want her long-term plans running afoul. No one must die before his time.

There were several rest rooms to choose from, and Marlena made sure she met enough people on her way out to the back patio. She stopped an acquaintance to ask the time, then chatted briefly with someone else before slipping inside. She didn't have to wait long, which was good, since she was about to burst. Seeing Stash and Tess together did horrible things to her temper. She even had to cut short her important conversation with her dance partner, just to get back to Stash. The knowledge that she'd broken her own rules shocked her. Infuriated her.

The door swung open. Tess came in and locked the door

behind her, her golden eyes giving the rest room a quick look around.

"I've already activated a bug sensor. It's clean," Marlena assured her, looking at Tess's reflection in the mirror as she played with her hair.

Tess joined her at the big marble counter and surveyed all the tiny jars of expensive perfumes and lotions laid out for the guests' convenience. She picked one up, pulled off the stopper, and sniffed appreciatively. "My favorite," she declared.

"You look good playing the blond vamp." Marlena couldn't help it. She couldn't forget the sight of them on the sofa, sitting there chatting so intimately.

Tess laughed, a deep-throated sound that echoed through the room. Her eyes caught Marlena's in the mirror. "You're mad at me."

She was, but wasn't going to admit it. "What makes you think so?"

Tess chose another bottle and removed the stopper. "Because you weren't listening to us. You were too busy reacting."

"I didn't bring him along for you to sink your teeth into." Seeing Stash and Tess so cozy together hadn't gone down well at all. She knew what Tess was, and how good she was at what she did. Still, he didn't have to fall so easily under her spell.

"He does have delicious possibilities," Tess said in a musing tone of voice, as if she found the idea very tempting. "But like I just said, you weren't listening."

"So tell me what it is I missed. Did you find anything from the information I gave you over the phone, rather than this probing stuff you're so good at?" Marlena knew she could depend on Tess to discover Steve McMillan's motives, but she would much rather deal with hard facts right now. Tess's methods were too intimate for her liking.

"One thing's for sure. He's not lacking in the brain department."

Marlena sighed. "Still playing word games? Tell me something I don't know."

"He's trained."

"As if I can't tell that from watching the way he sits or the way he works a room. T., darling, you've trained me well enough to get this info without your professional eye."

Tess dabbed some perfume behind her ear, then adjusted a stray golden curl out of the way. Marlena waited patiently. Tess had always been very deliberate, not showing her hand until she deemed it the right moment. It was a very annoying trait, calculated to make the other person react, something Marlena wasn't going to do, not after she had been told she was reacting rather than listening. Well, she was listening now.

"He wants you."

Tess's announcement shouldn't have caused any surprise to Marlena but those three simple words zapped her like an electrical shock. For some reason she hadn't wanted to think about that subject, and having it brought out into the open like that also summed up how confused she was about Stash. She didn't want any of these contradictory feelings. She swallowed, then tried to be nonchalant. She knew more was to come. Tess always had a surprise or two up her sleeve. "And?" She didn't want to admit that part of her was eager for anything about Steve McMillan.

"And he doesn't want what you are." Tess turned slightly, and for the first time gazed directly at Marlena's profile. "A big conflict, don't you think? Especially from a man who tries to follow orders all the time, and right now his orders are in conflict with his emotions. I thought it'd be fun to give him a choice."

Marlena jerked her head up seriously. That was it—the thing up Tess's sleeve. She was a master manipulator, always moving people around like chess pieces. "Choices? What the hell are you talking about? You sound more and more like those guys you hang around with."

Marlena was a loner; she worked alone. All her kind did.

She understood too well how too much trust could endanger one. "My feelings for Stash have nothing to do with my choice to be alone."

"Don't you want him?" Gentle. Probing.

Marlena didn't want to be probed, so she went on the attack. "Sometimes want isn't enough, T. You yourself should know. Sometimes you have to let the man make the choice." Regret flooded her as soon as the words came out. Tess was just doing what she did best. She shouldn't have hit below the belt like that. Marlena touched Tess's elbow apologetically. "I'm sorry. Brought back some bad memories, haven't I? Get over him, T. It's been a while since you left that outfit anyway."

"Four months." Tess washed and dried her hands carefully, her face still devoid of expression, a direct contrast to the amused woman a few moments ago.

Marlena sighed. "Think you'll ever see him again?"

"No, and we're not talking about me. Or him. He has issues with his past that he has to deal with. Which brings us back to you and Mr. Steve McMillan."

Marlena was relieved. She didn't like apologizing, and was only too glad to veer away from the subject that hurt Tess. Now that she looked closely, she noticed the little lines of strain around T.'s mouth. Of all things, Marlena understood the need to control and its toll on one's psyche. She let Tess change the subject. In a milder voice, she continued, "There's nothing you're saying that hadn't crossed my mind. You think I don't see the price you paid? I see it in your eyes, T. Your Alex hurt you. Want isn't enough."

"No, want isn't enough," Tess agreed gravely. She smiled, as if she were about to say something, but changed her mind.

"I won't let Stash hurt me. Besides, he's probably a rogue operative, out to cancel me."

"We'll know soon, won't we?"

Her earlier suspicion was right. Tess was up to something, as usual. She hated it when she was being played with. Her temper flared again. "What do you mean? What have you been planning without my input? You know you aren't supposed to do anything to undermine my negotiations. Give me what you've got about him, T., or I swear—"

"You can't fight in that dangerous-looking dress, darling." Tess leaned a hip against the counter, her earlier demeanor back in place. She thoughtfully inspected her ringed fingers, reaching out to stroke one that was ringless, as if she missed something. Without looking up, she continued, "Steve McMillan is a sea mammal. Specializes in South American extraction tactics. He belongs to a very covert fire squad in the black unit of STAR Force before being transferred to TIARA on orders."

Marlena had been ready for anything but certainly not that. "A SEAL? STAR Force?"

"It's the acronym for Standing and Ready Force," explained Tess. "They are separate from the other SEAL teams, notorious for doing stuff that circumvents conventional rules, and each team has a color code for different tactical emphasis. Your Stash is in Black STAR and is point man in his fire squad. So, as you can see, the man is quite a warrior."

She knew it. She had felt that aura of danger about him. She recalled how calm he was during the car chase. A man of action. "What's he doing in a boring desk job like TIARA?"

"That's the key, isn't it? I accessed his personal files. He has a sick sister out in California. And you know what? Fifty thousand dollars deposited in an offshore account the week after his transfer to D.C. And another fifty grand the day he was assigned you, Miss M."

That man was far too bright to be a mere companion sent to distract her. She'd been proven right, so why was her heart hurting? She glanced away, muttering, "He's a rogue, then."

"Not necessarily."

She flashed Tess a warning glare. "T., don't play your mind games right now, okay?"

Tess's silent appraisal was unnerving, making Marlena

want to yell at her. Again Marlena held her tongue. She didn't remember Tess with this maddening habit before, so she must have gotten it from that group she'd been with again. Which meant she had been testing her all along. Damn, damn, damn. If she weren't wearing this dress, she'd teach that woman a lesson. This was the reason she didn't need a complication like Stash. He'd become a chink in her armor, and a smart opponent like Tess would zero in like a predator.

A slow smile spread across T.'s face, her golden eyes glittering with repressed laughter. She nodded her approval, as if she liked what she saw. "I've gone over his records with a fine-tooth comb. He's the perfect SEAL operative, a straight team player. STAR Force members are handpicked by Admiral Jack Madison, which tells you how trustworthy Steve McMillan is."

Admiral Madison was a decorated war hero, his loyalty to the country without question. "T., how do you know so much about STAR Force?" The idea of Stash being a dangerous man was strangely exciting. What else was hidden under those good looks?

Tess shrugged. "My job. My question is, why was he asked to transfer to replace another operative in TIARA? An operative who, I might add, died under suspicious circumstances? With that in mind, most importantly, can he take care of danger when he's not in fatigues?" She cocked her head, an expectant look on her face. "Listen."

Crash. Screams. Distinct sounds of gunfire. Training took over. Marlena strode over to grab the door handle. To her surprise, Tess beat her to it, planting herself firmly between her and the exit. She was still smiling, but her eyes were flat and cool.

"What are you up to, T.?" Marlena asked through gritted teeth.

"Making a point."

"What point? There weren't supposed to be any incidents here. Did you start this?"

"Of course not. This is your job, entirely under your control. What's happening outside must be someone else's doing." Tess leaned back against the door, still listening. "Sounds like someone is getting things back under control."

"I still don't understand." Marlena frowned. "I know you have people out there to prevent any incidents. Again, what point are you trying to make?"

"Silly girl. You don't think I didn't leave some information to test him while we chatted, do you? I'm trying to see which side your sea mammal is on."

Steve stared after Tess's departing back as she made her way through the crowd. She cut a striking figure, moving with the grace of someone who was in touch with her body. What was this woman's relationship to Marlena? His mind raced through their conversation. Who was she, and how did she know about him?

He scanned the room for Marlena but couldn't find her. He just didn't believe that she would be planning a hit here and now, not in *that* dress. Again, the memory of those strands of pearls under that outfit filled his mind. He cursed softly. Why couldn't he forget about that and concentrate on what was happening?

He'd never had to deal with anything like this. In his old world, the enemy was the enemy. A target. No more. He'd never had to consider the flesh and blood behind the name, nor had he ever felt the need to make excuses for the other side. But then most of his encounters were with drug lords and terrorist groups, and he'd stared at some of them eyeball-to-eyeball and seen the cold ruthlessness of murderers.

He cursed again. They sure didn't wear any strands of pearls or have a Tweety Bird tattoo for underwear. He took a deep breath. Concentrate. On. The. Information.

This isn't the way you'd stop danger when you're in one of your jungles. All of a sudden, Tess's provocative challenge flashed up in his mind like a marquee sign. The rules of the jungle were simple. Let the noise of nature recede, and listen. Be still and wait for movement. The smell of danger was distinctive; his commander had likened it to cigar smoke in a nunnery. Close the mind and use the senses. And above all, watch out for the most mundane, because that was usually where danger hid. Lastly, the target always stood apart.

Steve exhaled. Everything within himself became still as he rescanned the jungle of guests moving about. The room, with its shiny extravagance, receded into the background as he mentally looked for details that a soldier would. He ignored the laughter, the clinking of glasses, and the murmur of conversation, letting the sounds wash across him like white noise. The trees in the jungle hid the danger he sought. Where was the danger hiding among these guests?

Marlena was nowhere in sight. The groups of people moved in slow motion, growing apart and reforming, but what caught his attention was the very group Tess had pointed out to him. The one with du Scheum and some other guests. They never moved from their spot. Nor did anyone seem to go near them, as if they knew they weren't invited into that circle of power. The small circle of men stood out, smoking cigars while discussing intently, barely paying attention to the laughter and music around them.

The target.

Steve slowly made his way within a few feet of the men. His gut instincts were humming like the brush of an electrical current generated by a live wire. Du Scheum, if he were really the man in white, had his back to him, but even from this angle, Steve saw the way the others leaned toward the man, paying attention to what he was saying.

With deliberate care Steve turned his head left, then right, studying the faces that seemed to be floating by. He had done this hundreds of times, shutting out and listening at the same time. It was the exact feeling of swimming under water and trusting his heightened senses when the sound of the deep could overwhelm the careless swimmer. Sometimes a shark would swim too close, coming in from behind, out of sight, but his mental awareness would assess the situation. Not dangerous. Not yet.

And as he had countless other times, Steve turned

around, trusting what his senses were telling him now, even though he couldn't see or tell. He searched the faces for Marlena. Smiling women talking to each other. Someone calling out a name. One of the servants trying to balance a tray with too many glasses. A man standing alone by one of the aquariums.

Steve gave the man a once-over. He stood apart from the crowd. Then he took a step forward toward Steve. One of his hands reached into his trouser pocket.

Steve was about to pivot toward the oncoming man when something else caught his eye. Guests were laughing and trying to save the unbalanced server, who tried desperately not to lose his platter. The tray bobbled in one hand. The other hand holding a towel. It was as if his mind became a zoom lens, his entire attention focused on that one hand.

One hand holding a towel. The most mundane thing in the world. But when one tried to prevent something from falling over, one used *both* hands.

The man lost his fight with the tray, and glasses flew in all directions. The loud crash had guests shrieking. Laughing. Man falling over. And extending the hand with a towel . . .

There wasn't much time. Steve launched into the air.

"Let me out. Now." Marlena held on to her temper. Barely. Stash was out there alone.

"He thinks you're here to cancel someone, Marlena. Give him a few minutes to figure out that you aren't who he thinks you are, darling. He's been sent by Admiral Madison into TIARA to do something. I want to see how good he is."

"There's a hit out there and you let it happen?"

"Don't worry, du Scheum is too important for us to let anything happen to him."

Marlena narrowed her eyes. She hated it when she was on the other side of the information scale. She wanted to force her way out of there. Images of Stash injured and in need of help flooded her mind. "Let me get this straight. You knew

du Scheum was in danger tonight. Then you lured me in here
and left him wide open."

Tess smiled. "Your Stash is out there."

"With no weapons. No backup." Marlena didn't try to
lower her voice.

"He's a SEAL."

"And that's supposed to guarantee du Scheum's safety?"
Marlena asked, incredulous about the whole thing. "T., this
about tops everything I've ever seen you do."

Tess shrugged, then reached out to brush at Marlena's
sleeve. "Hair," she explained.

"T.!" That was enough patience. Marlena had controlled
her temper long enough.

"There are others out there to do their job if your honey
fails, Marlena," Tess told her, her voice soothing. She still
stood in front of the doorway, unyielding. "You need to be in
here. You know that. Even though this isn't a planned incident, per se, let's take advantage of it. With your reputation
you always need a strong alibi. Besides, the more people
seeing you in here with me, the better for your image. Just
do your job."

"Haven't I always?" Marlena countered heatedly. "If he's
with the admiral, why must you play with him? He's useless
to us."

Tess cocked her head. "I'm not so sure. That money in his
account is troublesome, I must say. If he's rogue, we can use
him to lure whoever is trying to set you up at that apartment.
You and I know it's not our darling middleman du Scheum
fitting in micro eyes all over that apartment. It's not the
buyer since you're still in the bidding process. So . . . Stash
could be working for the seller, hmm? But, and I'm saying
this because I have the utmost confidence in Admiral Madison's ability to cull men of honor, if Steve McMillan isn't a
rogue, then he could be in a lot of trouble." She raised an
eyebrow, eyes glinting with mockery. "Don't you want to
save him if his life's in danger, M.? We can't trust him to be
a good alibi yet, so that's what I'm here for, darling. If things
go wrong, and du Scheum happens to be injured out there,

we want your reputation intact. Keep them guessing. Did you? Didn't you? It enhances the enigma."

Marlena hated being bested, especially by T. She wanted to childishly snarl out something rude, but she knew better. Manipulating people was T.'s business, and she deemed it a victory if they reacted according to her bible. She was right. Marlena Maxwell had an image to uphold. Every situation to further her reputation, be it true or false, would attract more clients. And perhaps she would finally lure this anonymous seller to show his face. Above all, she did trust T. Slowly she allowed herself to relax.

"One day," she said, "I hope someone will order you around and you'll be his puppet. Then we'll see whether you like being out of control."

A faraway look entered Tess's eyes. "Somebody already succeeded," she said enigmatically. She blinked. "I'm ready to go out whenever you are."

"I'm sorry," Marlena apologized again. Damn it. Even when she tried to be nasty, she was outmaneuvered into backing away. She sighed. "You bring out the worst in me."

Tess moved away from the door, no longer blocking it. "Darling, don't insult me. I bring out the best in everyone." She flashed Marlena a knowing smile. "Especially men. I'll bet Stash handled the situation exactly the way I prepared him."

That brought on a quick scowl. "He's Steve to you," Marlena said in a fierce voice.

Soft laughter echoed through the restroom. "Possessive, aren't we?" Tess drawled.

Marlena observed quietly as Tess played with one of her rings, turning it a certain way. Turning off her own version of a bug sensor, she guessed. The woman had an arsenal right at her fingertips. Marlena wished she could play with every ring her friend owned. She watched with interest as Tess opened her purse and pulled out a small flat envelope.

"Is that what I need?" Marlena asked, knowing very well that she had been deliberately led on again. Tess was right to want her to focus on her job.

"Yes, the instructions are inside, in case I'm not around later. I suppose you have a place to put it safely in that outfit?"

"Darling, you taught me the best hiding places."

"In that case, darling, I've taught you well." The rest room door swung open and the outside agitation cascaded into the room. "Even with men."

"You just leave Stash alone, or I'll teach you a thing or two."

Laughter. The door swung closed and both of them gave exclamations of shock and concern as the people outside told them what happened.

Chapter Eight

Steve felt isolated from the pandemonium around him. He had been vaguely aware of people diving for cover at the sound of the gunshots, with those closest to the waiter crouching and yelling as confusion broke out. There was a breathless minute as everyone waited for a second gunman after Steve had downed the first one. Then the silence broke and there was a rush for the doors as people started to leave. A few women in hysterics were carried out. Some men carrying walkie-talkies had appeared out of nowhere. Security, probably.

Where was Marlena? Amid the screams and shouts, Steve shrugged off the hands that seemed to be everywhere. He didn't need them touching him. Didn't they know not to get too close to a soldier after a hit? Everyone was talking at once. His ears hurt from all that babble.

"Somebody call a doctor!"

A man's authoritative voice rose above the melee. "Everything is taken care of, my friends. Now, just move to the patio so there's some breathing room for the gentleman. Please, everything's fine. Security is here. No need to panic."

Steve turned to the man in white, seeing his face for the first time. Lean to the point of gauntness, du Scheum had the intelligent face of a negotiator, flinty-eyed and inscrutable. Except for the telltale white ring around his lips, he appeared uncommonly calm for someone who had nearly been killed. As they stood there studying each other, Steve realized that the businessman was trying to place him.

"Thank you," du Scheum said, "but I don't believe we've met."

"Steve McMillan."

"Mr. McMillan. That was a very brave thing you did. I owe you my life." Du Scheum nodded to some men standing close by, and Steve noticed them herding out the few curious guests who hadn't panicked and run out of the ballroom.

One of the men with the walkie-talkies said politely, "Watch for broken glass, ladies and gentlemen. Please be careful as you make your way to the patio. Let us know if you need anything." The small group left dispersed slowly, murmuring about the incident.

Du Scheum spoke quietly to a man close by. Steve recognized him as the one standing by the aquarium before all hell broke loose. "Make sure no one leaves. I want a headcount of every guest. Move the VIPs, the ones with diplomatic immunity, to the secured room so they won't feel hassled by the police when they come." The man nodded and slipped away. Du Scheum returned his attention to Steve, looking him over. "Are you injured, Mr. McMillan? There's blood seeping through your collar."

Steve reached up and then gazed down at his hand. It was blood. He didn't think a bullet had struck him. He remembered sliding across the floor. "Must be a cut." He shrugged. Adrenaline always dulled the pain. He would know soon enough whether he was hurt.

"Stash?"

He turned abruptly at the sound of Marlena's voice. She didn't even look around her as she hurried to his side, her eyes restless. This wasn't the cool and collected woman he was used to. She was worried about him! Stunned at the realization, he didn't say anything as she came to a stop in front of him. A flat and deadly expression slid into her eyes.

"You're bleeding." She didn't wait for an answer, reaching up to investigate for herself.

"Where were you?" he asked quietly.

"With Tess in the rest room," she answered impatiently. "Take off your jacket."

"I'm okay," Steve assured her. "I think the other guy needs more attention than I do." It struck him as weird that du Scheum hadn't once looked at the man crumpled on the floor not too far from his feet. Nor had Marlena. She was too busy tugging at his tux.

"You want me to take off this suit?" she challenged.

"He bled, too."

Marlena sighed, then finally gave him what he wanted. Her blue eyes met his, and he saw the distress lurking in them. He didn't see guilt. Or disappointment. Or anger that she'd failed, if this was part of some plan of hers. Something that felt like relief rushed through his system like a deflating balloon. She cocked her head. He knew she was too smart not to know about what he had been speculating.

"He isn't wearing clothes I bought," she told him. "Look how you've ruined them."

Steve obediently looked down. Torn buttons. Splattered shirt. Blood. "What are you going to do about it, dock my pay?" He could afford to be playful now that he was certain she hadn't had a hand in this attempted murder. "I just did my good deed for the day and you're going to make me pay for a new jacket?"

She patted him on the cheek. "Darling, I'll just have to reward you. Let's go shopping." She stressed the last word, saying it louder.

"Heartless," he chided.

"Dumb hero," she scolded. But her hand busily unbuttoning his shirt was tender.

"Lackey, remember?" he reminded her, his voice a jeer. He was intrigued by her concern. It didn't fit the profile of an assassin.

"Idiot. Fool." Marlena pulled him by the lapels till his face was inches from hers. She obviously had concluded that he wasn't that hurt. "Did I ask you to go around stopping bullets?"

"No." She smelled so nice. Steve wanted to kiss her.

"Then stop acting like Superman."

"Yes, Lois." He goaded her on purpose. He wanted to remove the worry from her eyes.

Whatever she was going to say was cut short by polite coughing. They both turned, startled by the sound. They'd completely forgotten that there were people around them. That there was a dead body nearby. That there'd been any kind of excitement other than their own. Du Scheum and the few bodyguards left, along with a very amused Tess, were eyeing them curiously. Steve didn't blame them. Marlena and he probably appeared to be behaving really oddly. He could only blame the rush of adrenaline making him light-headed.

Marlena wasn't in the mood to talk to du Scheum or anyone else. All she wanted to do was get Steve alone so she could check for herself that he was unharmed. She didn't care that Tess had told her he could take care of himself. All she could see was the blood seeping through the shirt under his tux. Panic filled her when she realized he could have been more seriously injured. Not far behind were the beginning stages of a growing fury, simple and strong, that someone had caused it.

"The authorities will be here soon, Marlena," du Scheum informed them. "It's not going to be easy to keep this quiet with a dead man."

"And they'll want to talk to every one of your guests here." Marlena nodded toward the patio. "Do you know who is behind this?"

Du Scheum shook his head. "They'll probably be more interested in interviewing Mr. McMillan. You do know how to make a party memorable, my dear."

Memorable. Steve picked the word out and scowled. Another M word. How close was this du Scheum guy to Marlena anyway? They seemed to know each other pretty well. Another reason not to think this attack had anything to do with Marlena. He made a note to include this in his report later.

"Me?" Marlena fluttered her hand to her throat. "I was

nowhere near the fun, darling." She glanced at Steve. "I only found out what happened from David and Sylvia Jackson outside the rest room when Tess and I came out. We didn't hear a thing, did we, Tess darling, with the band playing?"

"I thought there were some loud noises but you and I were busy talking. I didn't pay much attention," Tess answered. She looked at the man lying on the floor and shuddered. "I'm glad I wasn't out here. Can you imagine how horrible it'd have been to be so near that . . . creature? You're such a brave man, Steve, to stop him like that!"

"I didn't," Steve said. "I managed to push Mr. du Scheum out of the way and because the man was on the floor, I rolled toward him to try to get the weapon out of his hand. He was about to shoot again when someone else shot him. I believe it was the man you talked to earlier, Mr. du Scheum."

"Yes, my bodyguard," acknowledged their host. "But you're being entirely too modest. That little knife trick hurt him enough to make him drop the gun."

"I thought keeping him alive would help," Steve explained. If not for the bodyguard, they would have someone alive to question. He studied Marlena for a moment. Maybe that wasn't concern in her eyes. It could have been relief.

"You're right," du Scheum said, giving the body a cursory glance. "Too bad he's dead. We'll just have to let the police do their job."

"While we wait, do you have a medical kit, Pierre? And a little privacy?" Marlena tugged at Steve's arm. "I want to look at that cut."

Du Scheum nodded and Marlena didn't wait for anyone to show them the way. Steve looked back and saw no one following. Obviously there was a certain amount of trust between du Scheum and Marlena for him to let her go wherever it was she was taking him. Steve didn't know whether he was happy about the fact that they were friends.

They entered a room with huge double oak doors, the kind that shut with authoritative silence. It was more a library than a study, impressively lined with walls of books. The room smelled of leather and cigar smoke. Standing by a small bar near the fireplace, Steve watched with hooded eyes as Marlena moved to a cabinet, opening and closing closet doors with a familiarity that irritated him. Murmuring a satisfied yes, she pulled out a small white box, snapped it open, and examined the contents.

She looked as if she fit this kind of lifestyle. Elegantly dressed. Not a hair out of place. Comfortable with the splendorous background. Not quite a mermaid, Steve taunted himself.

He was too damn quiet, Marlena thought. "Are you going to let me see that cut now, before you bleed to death?" she asked.

"Did you hear du Scheum just now? It's the assassin who's dead," he told her quietly, "which is too bad, he said. Don't you think it's too bad that the assassin is dead?"

Marlena gazed at him levelly, trying to read his mind. "He's a henchman, not an assassin," she finally said. There was a difference. An assassin had more patience and certainly wasn't this clumsy. A henchman was sent, not hired. "And obviously not a good one."

She helped him out of his tuxedo and said something unladylike at the sight of the blood-sodden shirt underneath. Her eyes widened. This was no mere cut. The top of his shirt near the shoulder had gunpowder streaks. She started unbuttoning impatiently. He just stood there quietly, watching her with those intense eyes. He didn't seem to be in pain.

"Playing at words like your friend Tess, aren't you?"

Not really listening, Marlena told herself to ignore the bare chest until she saw to the wound, whatever it was, but her straying eyes already registered the perfectly sculpted torso with the hard, defined muscles. The light mat of hair that beckoned to be stroked. The sun-kissed chest with the flat male nipples. And blood smeared all over the left side. Swiftly she checked the gash near the collarbone.

"The bullet grazed you." Too close. Too damn close . . . "Damn it, Stash, why didn't you say anything?"

"I'm not worried about it."

"What did you do, jump in front of the bullet to stop it?"

"Must have bounced off my shoulder then."

She stopped dabbing at the wound and glared up at him. "Not funny." She threw away the cotton balls in her hand, took a roll of gauze out of the box, and cut off a strip. "You could have been seriously hurt."

His hand stopped her, pulling her smaller one against his chest. "Then you would be the one to put flowers on *my* headstone."

Marlena looked up sharply. Steve's amusement was barely discernible. His eyes were still watchful, studying her face intently. To admit that she cared would open a can of worms. To disclose that she hadn't even bothered to wonder who was trying to kill du Scheum would mean admitting something significant, something she didn't want to face. It was better to be glib, to keep a distance.

"What kind of flowers?" Under her hand, his skin felt very warm, and his heartbeat was strong and steady.

"What's your favorite?" he countered.

She felt his hot gaze on her lips as she answered softly, "Sunflowers."

"Sunflowers it is, then," he agreed, his voice seductively soft too.

Their conversations were always like this, Marlena thought dazedly, full of promises of some kind of illusive future. "You realize," she said conversationally, tugging at her hand, "tombstones aren't one's regular idea of a sexy date."

He released her so she could resume what she was doing. The iodine must sting, but he didn't flinch. At the sight of the raw wound, her slowly building anger went up another degree.

"I want you," he said.

Exactly the way Tess had phrased it earlier in the rest room. *He wants you.* Marlena carefully bandaged his shoulder, securing the gauze so it wouldn't slip. *But not what you are.* Suddenly his hand was on her back, softly caressing up and down. The urge to take that step closer was strong.

"Now." His voice was low, hypnotic. The pressure of his

hand on her back was insistent, inexorable. She knew if she touched, there would be no going back. The sight of him half naked like this, his shirt hanging open, exposing flesh that tempted her, was too erotic.

"Now, Marlena."

"Not now. Not here."

"I intend to win that bet."

Marlena laughed. That bet seemed like ages ago. Her ruse to distract him hadn't worked very well because he was in deeper than ever. After tonight's incident, he would be delving for more answers. "You're obsessed with Tweety Bird," she said. And because she couldn't help herself, she leaned closer and kissed his chest. Salty. With the taste of his blood on her lips, reminding her of the danger around her. The hand on her back pulled her in harder, but she still resisted. She smiled up at him, shaking her head. "I'm not going to let you destroy two expensive outfits in an hour, Stash sweetheart. Besides, someone will be here soon."

"So?"

"So you should start thinking about what to say to the cops when they ask you questions."

"Am I supposed to have a story ready then?"

Marlena fingered the streaks of drying blood. "I don't know. Do you have anything you're hiding?" Like the fact that he wasn't who he said he was.

"Do you? You will be questioned, too." His hand had resumed its soft caress. He didn't seem overly concerned. "But of course you weren't involved in this one incident, were you? I know Tess told you things in the rest room, Marlena. She couldn't have just gone there after you to apologize. So what did you find out?"

There was a lot more to Steve McMillan than she gave him credit for. He didn't just sit there taking notes. He assessed everything going on around him and connected events to get answers. Now that she knew his background, she suddenly realized that he hadn't been really sitting around, as she'd thought. He had been waiting. Waiting for his target's next move. He was, after all, a man of action. With this new role as her companion, he was just biding his time. The thought of him stalking her was annoying. And definitely intriguing.

She smiled, more to herself than him, and noticed his small frown. A target could easily become the hunter, after all. She could stalk as well as any macho sea mammal. What was it that Tess had accused her of? Oh yeah, that she wasn't listening, only reacting. Now would be her turn to make Steve McMillan react and not listen.

As she licked her lips, the faint taste of his blood continued to remind her of the danger associated with her. Time to distract him from his line of questioning again. His eyes followed her tongue like a fascinated animal. She slowly slid her palm across his chest and down the flat stomach, scraping her nails lightly. She felt each hard muscle under her hand bunch and tighten at her teasing. His nose flared. Ah, the prey sensed danger.

"She didn't tell me anything I wouldn't find out eventually," she told him, admiring the symmetrical perfection of the abdominal muscles on that beautiful chest. She wondered whether the rest of him would look so perfect, too. She reached for the top button of his dark pants.

"I thought you said no a moment ago." His voice had a hard edge to it.

Marlena glanced up quickly. Suspicion gleamed from his eyes, yet he didn't stop her when she unhooked the button from its hole. He continued to stand there, waiting. "A woman has the prerogative to change her mind."

"You're trying to distract me again."

That almost stopped her. She had to remember he was a smart prey. "Am I succeeding?"

"No."

She slid her hand down his pants. Just as she had the first time they met. His sharp intake of breath made her smile as she went after her prey.

"Now you are," he said through gritted teeth.

However, the sound of the huge study door opening penetrated their little world. Marlena sighed and reluctantly took out her hand. Steve sighed and buttoned up his pants.

"I can't help it if we can't find the right moment," she told him.

"Not from lack of trying," he taunted, lips quirking.

Marlena threw up her hands. "That's it. You're forbidden from talking to Tess anymore. Now she's got you playing her word games!"

Seize the moment. As a soldier, Steve knew that an instant could mean a lifetime. And that some moments were meant to be his alone.

The cops took their time, asking him a bunch of questions, but they would find nothing on him that would be suspicious. Besides, Marlena had mentioned that people like du Scheum didn't get negative publicity if they didn't allow it. It'd be a small blurb in the news, since no one of consequence had been injured.

Steve knew better, though. The guest list at this function wasn't something to ignore. He supposed that it was very usual in the political world to see lawmakers, arms dealers, and businessmen making deals in the same room. It went against every code he had been taught in the military, and his SEAL buddies wouldn't take too kindly to the notion of enemies partying with them. Yet here he was, transferred from one world to another, and not liking the new rules.

The cops weren't going to do more than procedural stuff. His own TIARA task force was too damn slow. And Hard-On would be pushing to haul in Marlena soon. The more he tried to untangle this skein of events, the more knotted up the mystery. He glanced over at Marlena, sitting there sipping brandy, calmly answering the last of the questions. Much like the fascinating woman behind them, who was the biggest mystery of all.

They were finishing up. The cop interviewing Marlena was obviously smitten with her outfit, his eyes hardly ever on his notepad. Steve scowled, annoyed. Did every man get the same treatment? Did she put her hand down each one's pants, too?

At one point, sensing his scrutiny, she glanced in his direction and smiled. Then she caught sight of Tess sitting next to him. The smile stayed in place, but he discerned a slight hardening of her expression. Tess must have noticed it, too, because she placed a hand on his arm to get his attention; when he turned to her, there was a merry glint in those honey-gold eyes. Her elegant hand, decked with rings, squeezed him until he took his gaze away from Marlena.

"You're a troublemaker," Steve accused in amusement. "You seem to like riling her."

"It's a rule in my meetings with Marlena. I don't see her often enough."

Steve cocked a brow questioningly. "You mean, since you don't see her that often, you have to make her mad at you?"

Tess nodded. "So to speak."

Curious, he asked, "Why?"

"Darling, Marlena is magnificent when she's mad." Tess squeezed his arm again and leaned closer confidentially. "Besides, you're going to get the brunt of it when she's done with that policeman. That's what lackeys are for, you know. Great to vent frustration at."

Steve didn't know how, but this tall, beautiful woman seemed to be able to read minds. She had somehow seen his inner frustration and was teasing him and Marlena. And helping him by giving Marlena a dose of the same frustration. There was nothing else to do but laugh and shake his head.

"You're something else," he told her. "Won't you tell me exactly who you are, or do I have to go find out myself?"

"Can't, darling. Here comes Marlena. She's giving me evil looks already."

Steve couldn't take his eyes off her. To him, she was the sexiest woman alive, even when she was magnificently angry. As she stood up and spoke some parting words to the officer, her blazing blue gaze torched him for a few seconds, setting his blood on fire, and all he could think about was finally putting his hands on her and just forgetting about principles and codes for a while.

"Are you sure you can afford to?" Tess murmured.

"Damn, are you a mind reader?"

Tess chuckled softly. "Just another one of my talents."

"There will come a time when you'll have to answer my questions, Tess." Steve didn't need to elaborate. He had a feeling that Tess knew a lot about him.

"Au contraire, darling. There will come a time when you'll have to answer more important ones. Remember our conversation about selling and buying?" Tess's ringed fingers drummed lightly on his dark sleeve, the gems catching and reflecting the light. Her voice dropped a notch lower. "Will you sell what you want? Will you buy Marlena enough time? Can trust be bought? If I give you Marlena for information, how much is it worth? Hmm?"

Steve studied the woman beside him. One enigmatic woman on his hands was enough. He didn't think he could deal with two.

"You don't shop, too, do you?" he asked.

"Shop?"

"All this buying and selling," he explained. "It tires me out as much as the shopping Marlena loves."

Tess laughed, her enjoyment of his humor sparking interested glances their way.

"You two are enjoying yourselves," Marlena interrupted. She eyed Tess's hand sliding off Steve's sleeve as he got up to meet her. "I'm ready to go home now, Stash. Found something funny, T.?"

"Yes," Tess replied, still laughing. She got up lazily, totally unperturbed by Marlena's watchful gaze, and gave her a light goodbye hug. "Now I know why we're in the business we're in, M. We both like to shop. Call me if you need help with . . . your packages, darling. I'll see you both later."

Steve smoothed a hand down Marlena's back and was reminded immediately about certain items underneath that dress. "Ready?" he asked.

"Yes, let's get out of here."

That wasn't what he'd meant. He was ready to find things out his way. Recent events might be confusing, but there was one thing about which he was very certain. He wanted Marlena Maxwell more than any woman in his past. Before, he had kept his relationships on a casual level because of his monetary situation as well as his high-risk career. No need to pull anyone into the mire of debt he was trying to pay off. Not to mention the inherent frustration and pain of not knowing where he'd disappeared to most of the time.

He'd had his fair share of frustration but he had learned to deal with it. This time was different. Marlena was a source of frustration as well as challenge. His current job required him to not make a move, but he sure wished he was back in the jungle right now.

There, hidden among trees, away from civilization, he dealt with frustration in various ways. Ultimately it honed a sense of determination in him to find a way around a problem. When pushed to the limit, he couldn't just sit there and wait. He had to vent the frustration before it took away his ability to think things through. He was used to stalking and hunting.

Marlena. She pulled at him like a magnet.

Steve sighed. She had been wrong about the word games. He'd started that obsession all by himself without any help from her friend. *Marlena, my magnet.*

He had told himself for months that his new life didn't have any jungles. That he couldn't vent his frustration the usual way. Violence was a temporary cure, anyway. The adrenaline gave a high that a soldier could get too addicted to. One became seduced into believing that one was unbeatable, indestructible.

Steve watched the policeman come over and take Marlena's extended hand, shaking and holding on to it a moment too long. Her blue eyes shone with sincere friendliness before she freed her hand. He didn't doubt that she had an excellent alibi and had persuaded the poor man that she was an angel.

Angel, his ass. She was his mermaid. And if he chose to live life like he was still in the jungle, who was going to stop him?

He watched them through narrowed eyes.

He had misjudged that sailor. He hadn't thought a mere uncouth man who'd never set foot in surroundings like this would thwart his plans. McMillan was smarter than he'd thought, reacting to that bumbling servant act. Quick with a knife, too. He had wanted du Scheum out of the way. He was getting too close to the truth. Damn it. What had given his man's ruse away?

Now there would be questions about the hit man, something he shouldn't have to deal with. Good thing the man was dead. Not that he couldn't handle the problem, of course. He always had backup plans. He just hadn't thought that Steve McMillan would best him.

Being up close to Marlena Maxwell tonight was strangely exciting. What a fascinating creature, able to live in light and shadow with ease. So much like himself, in fact. Leather and guns one night and drop-dead sophistication the next. A powerful combination.

He wanted her. When she had exchanged greetings with him, the smile she gave seemed to have a personal promise to it. He wondered whether she made love as well as she seemed to kiss. He already knew she liked kissing too much, after watching her with . . . He frowned at being reminded of his problem.

He hadn't thought about how to get her to work with him side-by-side. She was smart, having frustrated those on her tail all these years and gaining the reputation of someone who delivered. He just knew that they would be perfect together. He with his connections and she with hers. As partners they could gain so much power. Or at least he would. And she would shield suspicion from him because he was ready to branch out to bigger things, and needed someone else to handle all the sensitive matters to pass along. Why, with her social skills she would have a grand time negotiating and dancing with all of them.

He smiled. Yes, they were alike in that respect, able to enjoy themselves with their victims and business associates. He thought about his own power and manipulation of his underlings. Yes, they were totally alike.

He remembered the way she swayed to the Latin rhythm, her head thrown back with the passion of a sensual woman. And that smile! It was something special, lighting those deep blue eyes with a secretive promise that had his body responding in a way that had surprised him. It had been years since he'd reacted so freely to a woman to whom he hadn't yet spoken a word.

He looked forward to having her. Maybe he would ask her to dance the next time. Something slow and intricate, like a tango. He was sure she would like partnering him. His smile turned into a sneer. Unlike her date tonight, who wouldn't even dance.

It didn't matter that his plan had gone off course tonight. By the time Marlena finished her errand for him, that interfering fool of a sailor would be in deep enough dung that he would wish he was back in those stupid, thoughtless, gungho operations in South America that didn't need any finesse. The likes of him—blind, obedient, uniformed robots—could never compete with him in this world. He would have to devise a way to separate the two of them soon. As for Marlena, when she finally saw his wonderful plan come to fruition, when she finally met and recognized him for the genius he was, she wouldn't waste another thought on Steve McMillan. There was simply no comparison.

Chapter Nine

Marlena sighed. Well, who was she to say no? There was a tall, dark, and handsome man framed at the doorway of her bedroom. The backlight from the living room made it difficult to see his expression, but the indolent outline of his body, striking the classic masculine pose of a man on the hunt, sped up her heart rate. He leaned one shoulder against the door jamb, with the tuxedo hitched over his other. She imagined his sexy half smile, that hooded watchful gaze. From where she stood, he looked very male, very territorial.

Possibilities and probabilities. Conditions and consequences. All of Marlena's rules flew out the window where Steve was concerned. If she had time to sit down and consider carefully what she was about to do, she might come up with a good argument. She shouldn't be standing in the velvet darkness of her bedroom with this man. Not when she was still reeling from the sudden fear of losing him. Not when she wanted to tell him things best left unsaid.

"I should ask you to go," she murmured.

"And if I don't follow orders?" Steve reached out and clicked on one of the switches in the electronic panel. Muted recessed lighting slowly brightened the room to a soft glow.

Marlena blinked as her eyes adjusted. The dried blood on his torn white shirt only emphasized the danger in getting involved with this man. "With your problem with obedience, how do you work in a team, I wonder?"

She baited him on purpose, trying to give herself a chance to escape from her emotional needs. He came to her silently, eyes daring her to retreat. She didn't. He dropped the tuxedo and placed his hands on her shoulders, slowly sliding them under the front of her dress. Her skin tingled hot and cold where he touched. She caught her lower lip to stop a moan. There was still time. She could still back away, if she chose to. She didn't.

"There's a problem to consider," he said.

"What?" He was so close she had to tilt back to stare into his eyes. Why did his scent make her want to lean forward and kiss him all over? "What problem?"

"We aren't a team," he answered, and with a swift, easy motion, pulled the dress off her shoulders, trapping her arms at her sides. Silence. She couldn't breathe as she watched his eyes travel possessively down the front of her body. He gazed at her breasts for long moments, until her nipples ached from the seductive heat in those dark eyes, and when he finally looked up, the hunger in them propelled the rest of the fight out of her. The corner of his lips lifted slightly, and he whispered, "Unless you're saying we're one?"

But Marlena was no longer in the mood to talk. Desire emanated from his body, drawing her even closer. She wanted to slake her own hunger.

Her eyes were half closed as she lifted her mouth up as a silent offering. "Kiss me."

"You realize I won my bet," he mocked, his hands sliding the dress lower.

"Which one?" As if she cared. She wanted more than his eyes on her. With her hands freed from her sleeves, she pushed off his chest and fell backward onto the bed behind her. When she landed with a soft bounce, she stretched her arms above her head sinuously, lifting her breasts invitingly. "You going to stand there and look all night?"

Steve undid the top button of his pants. Thank God there was no zipper because he didn't think he could free himself without serious injury. He probably had permanent zipper track marks imprinted down there as it was.

The light caught the red fire in her hair, the luminous blue in her eyes. Her skin gleamed like expensive silk against the dark red sheets and with her dress bunched together from her waist down, folds of blue and green and silvery colors concealing her long limbs, she resembled the very mermaid he'd been calling her.

She looked between his legs and blew him a kiss. The happiest part of his body responded instantly, insistently pounding against the confines of his pants, like an overeager puppy seeing its mistress. She licked her lips, then moved a suggestive finger to touch one of those coral-colored nipples that fascinated him. He unbuttoned in record speed. Then fell on top of the mermaid on the bed. His hips surged forward in automatic anticipation, already wanting to claim his prize. All his. All night.

Her laughter was that of a smug woman who knew how desperate she had kept him. He smothered that laugh with a kiss, pushing his tongue inside that delectable mouth. It was as if he'd traveled a long journey to this moment, tasting and not finding what he was looking for, until now. His hand cupped the rounded swell of her breast and he swallowed her gasp of delight, pushing her deeper into the bed as he explored the silken secrets of her mouth.

Marlena was on fire. His kiss was demanding and cajoling at the same time. There wasn't any question who was in charge here. His tongue devastated her mouth with a seductive skill that left her clinging helplessly to his shirt. She arched into his hand, trying to get him to put all his weight on her, but he held off as his hand explored lightly.

She ripped his shirt apart. He softened the kiss, nibbled at her lips. She ran restless hands all over his hard chest, moving insistently lower. His hard need burned through the bunched up material around her hips, and she wanted the barrier gone. Muttering against his lips, she tried to remove her dress with her free hand.

"Relax. I'll do it," he murmured, still kissing her lips lightly. "My way."

He kissed her chin and the hollow in her neck. He bit her

shoulder and slid lower. She moaned when he gently laved her aching nipple, playing with one breast, then the other, as if he couldn't decide which one to feast on. Her head went back and forth as she impatiently pulled his hair. It was surprisingly soft.

Steve punished her with a small bite. Under her right breast. And another. He kissed the sensitive flesh of her ribs and held her down as she squirmed. He licked her belly button and went lower where the jeweled brooch glinted in the light like some guardian to the treasure trove.

He slowly sat up so he could unhook the ornament. Anticipation thrummed through him. He wasn't sure whether he was breathing. His hands were trembling slightly. Absolutely useless if he were to aim right in combat. He paused at the ridiculous thought. Surely he wasn't nervous. This wasn't combat. This wasn't life and death. Yet it felt just as important somehow. He hesitated, trying to grasp some sort of truth.

Her hands covered his, sliding them out of the way. Her hands, elegantly tapered, unhurriedly sought the little button that released the jewelry. It fell away. His whole attention focused on those hands as they parted the dress in a gradual striptease. Soft, silky flesh beckoned. And adorned like an offering, strings of pearls glowed like tiny milky stars nestling in curls that teased him to touch. Slowly, inch by inch, she opened her legs. Another loop of pearls fell between her thighs, as if showing him the way to heaven.

Hooyah! Steve forgot about truths and combat. He leaned forward on his elbows, taken in by the erotic sight of pearls sliding against silky skin blushed with arousal. He caught her scent and growled in satisfaction. This was no combat. He dropped down for a taste, running his tongue along the already glistening wetness where pearls and heated flesh met in the middle. She jerked against his kiss, and he heard her gasp.

"Easy," he murmured, twining one waterfall strand of pearls around his fingers. She tasted different here. He licked again, probing a little harder this time, nudging her legs apart. The length of pearls moved away, hiding between her feminine folds. Determined, like a knight after treasure, he went after it with his tongue. Not combat. Just the lovely, tasty, wonderful, heavenly spoils of victory.

Marlena clung to the sheets by her side as control slipped inexorably away. His tongue, slow and deliberate, branded her as he painted a landscape of sensual need. His brush-strokes were bold, long sweeps that arched upward until she undulated with anticipation, and his descending detail so languorous and feather-light, she vented sighs of frustration.

She felt his fingers moving over her thighs, under the loops of pearls, massaging the sensitive inner sides. "I like these things," she heard him whisper. She bucked when his teeth scraped her lightly, sending ripples of tingling electricity orbiting through her.

"Stash . . ."

"Mmm." He was busy.

Harder. Please. That was what she meant to say. But only soft moans escaped her lips when he continued to assault her with satisfying quick, upward strokes of his tongue, building her desire to a feverish pitch, which he stoked by slowing ever so tortuously as he brought her back down. She gasped at each lightning stroke up, and moaned at each seemingly endless caress.

"I like them," he said again. "I can do things with them." He pulled on the strings of pearls like a master puppeteer, manipulating the beads to slide wetly between his tongue and her budding fiery need.

"Ohhh . . ." Every logical thought drifted away when his tongue played with the pearls, rolling them against her. He pushed each bead into perfect position, so that every movement of his magical mouth was followed by the runaway chain.

The gems tumbled like a waterfall when his fingers loosened and slid sensuously back up when he pulled, all the time maintaining intimate contact with her straining flesh. Her whole body became a slave to his mastery, twitching helplessly as his tongue played its ruthless game, running skillfully with the pearls, then nudging them delicately where it felt so . . . good. She moaned again. She realized now that he was keeping his promise to her. He was giving her the kiss of a lifetime.

Still playing with the strands of pearls, he kissed up her body, until he reached her mouth. "Tighter?" he asked, as he reined in the strands. Her body tightened, about to explode. "Or should I let go, like this?" Her body screamed for the release that wouldn't come.

She couldn't answer. There was only that sensation of being controlled. Each slide of that necklace only made her hotter. She closed her eyes, giving in to the master puppeteer.

Steve liked it. Power over a strong, spirited woman was intoxicating. Her responsiveness excited him, and he wanted to continue holding her there on the edge. Her strong legs curled around his flanks, flexing insistently as little mewls of pleasure escaped her lips every time he pulled at the necklace. He let out a laugh of satisfaction. Her eyes opened for an instant, and he'd never forget the look in them, a deep blue sexual invitation, a gleam of hidden secrets in a depthless ocean. A hot pulse beat in his loins. The urge to follow her won over.

Leaning forward, he kissed her eyes and her half-opened lips as he positioned over her. Her hand came between their bodies all of a sudden and touched him, and he almost lost it, as she tested his whole length with one long stroke.

"I'm ready, don't worry," he told her, half amused and thoroughly aroused.

"Not as ready as I am," she panted. "See how hot I am for you?"

She showed him, moving her hips. He closed his eyes, savoring the feel of her. Slick hot honey. She shifted, and her parted legs tightened around him, holding him still with her hand.

"Marlena . . ." he warned, then gulped for air as she gave a knowing squeeze. He felt the beads of pearls brush against his erection, and then her fingers rubbed the gems down the length of his rock-hard arousal. Holy . . . He looked down through the haze of desire. She'd looped the necklace around him twice, and he found that each time he pulled away, the damn strings were tightening around him, too. Their two bodies were chained together. He looked up into her smug eyes.

"Now you're ready," she purred. She tugged at the link between them, letting the nubbly pearls do their job, until he growled. "Come in me."

"The necklace is going to break," he warned. "This ride isn't going to be nice and slow."

In answer she shifted again, until her core touched him. He jerked forward with a groan, and the chain tightened. "Go ahead," she invited, lifting her legs higher around his waist. "I'll just take it out of your paycheck, Stash baby."

He snarled out some expletive, but his body was already pushing of its own accord. His thought process disappeared as his whole being concentrated on one thing only—possessing a certain mermaid. He forged slowly inside, and the intensity of her welcome checked his breath. The looped chains tightened as he pushed in, effectively collaring him. He pulled out, and the sensation of sliding beads up his entire length had him groaning again.

"Good Lord Almighty," he muttered as it began tightening again when he withdrew. He could feel the blood thickening down there. He couldn't possibly get any harder.

"You said you . . . liked the thing," Marlena reminded him huskily. Her eyes were closed, her teeth biting her lower lip. She was enjoying it as much as he was. "Hmm, Stash, more."

He was going to give her so much more she couldn't give any more orders. He didn't think he could stand any more torture, but his hand went down there to touch her anyway, unerringly seeking her capitulation. She gave a soft shriek and her inner muscles tightened. God. The woman was going to kill him. But he would have her mindless with pleasure, too.

Half blinded by his own throbbing need, he groped for the rest of the pearls that were free and ground them against her own little pleasure pearl, simultaneously plunging in again. Her gasp turned into a half scream. And then he was lost in the sensation of her orgasm as she trembled and jerked under him. Over and around him. Wet. So wet and sexy. Her throaty sighs mingled with his own grunts. At each wave of satisfaction, her aroused body pumped him. And pumped him. And kept pumping him.

He went berserk, taking and pushing, wanting more, needing more of her. She was still coming, and he shuddered as the chain between them rubbed and teased, enhancing each rising sensation like background music. She moaned, and her head shook back and forth, her hands scrunching the bedsheets. She tensed again, arching her back sharply, sending a series of rhythmic desire as she peaked, a hot drenching that consumed his control. He stopped breathing.

"Lena," Steve choked out, holding her face still for a kiss. "Lena." And dived into the deep orgasmic ocean after her, succumbing to the most powerful experience he'd ever felt. All he could say was her name. "Lena . . ." He kept coming, waves upon waves blasting out of him, and he kept on going, unable to stop. The chain tightened and loosened, tightened and loosened. The beads slid endlessly, torturing them both. They were slaves to each other's possession.

He didn't know how long he chanted into her willing mouth. "Lena . . . Lena . . . Lena . . ." as she held on to his shoulders, drowning in sensual delight, gasping his name, then losing control again as she went under one more time.

The expensive strands of pearls linking them together never did break.

She was a dead woman.

Marlena stared up at the apartment's cathedral ceiling in a daze. Her whole body glowed from the aftermath of their incredible lovemaking. He lay half on top of her, so still she thought maybe he was dead, too.

The slight hum of air-conditioning coming on. The quiet clicking of the clock on the wall. The slowly receding heartbeat in her head . . . hers? His? She wasn't sure anymore.

She still throbbed with heat, and little ripples of pleasure intermittently shook her body.

That was some serious orgasm.

He moved slightly, lethargically, and she returned her gaze to the body holding her captive. His weight wasn't uncomfortable at all, and when he shifted to give her some room, she couldn't bear the loss of his body heat. She closed her eyes. Maybe it was okay to die for this.

"One more time," he drawled into her ear, one hand sliding up to cup her breast.

She snickered. And they both laughed, their bodies shaking with mirth. They could barely move as it was.

"Did you come?"

"Nope, did you?"

"Barely. I faked most of it."

"Did you now?" His voice had the lazy tenor of a man who hadn't faked anything. "Which part? The one where you were telling me I was a god or the part where you had your legs around me so tightly I couldn't breathe?"

She turned to give him a narrow-eyed stare. "A god? I wasn't the one worshipping me with his mouth."

"I was counting pearls."

"Prove it."

"Two hundred and forty-six," he told her without a pause.

Marlena pushed at him, and he went on his back, taking her with him. "A very calculating tongue," she murmured, taking a good look at the body that had given her too many fantasies lately. She hummed approvingly to herself.

"So I've been told."

Cockier than ever, he challenged her at every turn. She wasn't used to it, a man who kept her interested this long. She sat up, pushing her hair out of her face. Looking down at him, she realized her raised arms only served to tease him. His gaze was hot again as he regarded her breasts, a small smile touching his lips. She bent forward a little, just to tantalize him some more. She just loved teasing this man.

"You like tormenting me," Steve said as he reached for her. She smacked his hand away.

"It's called foreplay, dummy."

"Another day of your foreplay and I'd be dead."

She frowned down at him. She didn't want to be reminded about the subject of death right now. He had been too close to it tonight, and she wasn't even sure whether the hit had anything to do with her current assignment.

"What's the matter?" he interrupted, eyes watchful again. "You've lost that glow."

Marlena made a quick decision. She had rolled the dice already, so why not enjoy the rest of the night? *Que sera sera*, as the old song went. She jiggled her bottom, rattling the necklace that still linked them together.

"Lost my glow? Are you challenging me?" she demanded. "I was just checking you out, see whether you meet with my approval." She sniffed, gazing downward, and shook her head.

Her words were intended to distract, and the effect was immediate. A macho man couldn't bear to be challenged that way.

"What do you think? Do I pass?" His hands roamed up and down her thighs.

"I have had better lackeys," Marlena lied as she secretly admired the broad expanse of his chest. She pressed her palms on him, sliding them downward, enjoying the hard muscles under her hands. She ran her fingers along his lats, the curve of his waist, till her thumbs met just above his masculine pride. The man *was* built like a god. She pressed down and smiled up knowingly at the low rumble he made as he arched upward. She continued to mock him, "My other lackeys were also a lot more obedient. They didn't move when I ordered them not to."

"It's no fun obeying all the time," he countered, then jerked at her touch. He looked at her hands, fascinated with what they were doing.

"That's not what they say," she drawled, slowly winding the chain, looping his hard length. She unhooked the clasp of the necklace and freed herself, pulling the strands off her seductively. He was straining against her hand by the time she was through. "See, eager for more foreplay." She touched the drop of moisture at the tip and twirled her finger round and round.

"Lena . . ." he muttered. "What are you doing?"

"Counting pearls," she mocked, grinning. "One, two, three . . ." No longer chained together, she slid down till she reached her goal. She flicked her tongue. "Five . . . six . . ." There was a male groan from above. She looked up naughtily. His thighs tensed under her hands. She brought her mouth down again, very close to his source of wicked pleasure. "How many did you say there were? Two hundred and forty-six? Eight . . . mmmmm . . . nine . . . ten . . ." She ignored the grunts of surrender and concentrated on counting. It was important to be accurate. One of his hands tangled with her hair. She bit him lightly. "Careful, I don't want to lose count and have to start all over again."

A while later, Steve interrupted, his voice huskier than normal, "You're going backwards . . ."

"Ninety-nine . . . ninety-eight . . . hmm? Oh, you *were* paying attention!" Marlena was thoroughly enjoying herself. The taste of him was addictive, a tangy sweetness that was wholly male. And seeing him completely helpless heightened her own arousal. "Um . . . where was I? Eighty-five?"

"One hundred . . . and twelve."

"You're choking, darling." He was so big, absolutely gorgeous. She planted a wet kiss on an erogenous spot. Oooh. Look at how he quivered! "Shall I stop and count later?"

"Is that how you reward obedience?" he asked, his eyes closed, his hips surging up.

"Hmm, you're right. I have to reward obedience." She smacked her lips. "Did I tell you I come from Florida? We don't count very well there. One . . . two . . ."

The man she held prisoner with her mouth muttered an expletive. And moaned.

Steve opened an eye. For a second he wondered whether he'd had an all-night wet dream. His hazy, sleep-deprived mind reported that he had spent the last seven hours doing bed gymnastics with Marlena Maxwell. His sated body affirmed the activities.

Her scent woke him up fully, and he became aware of her curled up against him. They had slept with their arms around each other. Her face was half hidden, snuggling into his body. One of her legs was inserted between his, and even in sleep her free hand held on to the mass of tangled loops between them. He smiled in wry amusement. Always needing to be in control, that was his Marlena.

That last conclusion jolted him wide awake. His Marlena. And he didn't have the energy this morning to deny the fact that he saw her that way. The implication of such thoughts brought a tug of anxiety. The assignment, his job, his operation. He wondered what the hell he was going to do about the whole thing.

Her long eyelashes flickered as he watched. What did a person like Marlena dream about? he wondered. He had been so sure of what she was like, how she would be, and instead she had tangled up his insides and his life in all kinds of knots. She seemed to feel his thoughts because her hand tugged on the chain in answer. He smiled again. Oh yeah. She did have him all tangled up last night.

Marlena's eyes fluttered open. Deep, sleepy blue between thick, black lashes. His gut reacted with painful need. What was it about her looking at him that turned him into Class A pudding? And the slow, catlike smile elevated his blood pressure to boiling point.

" 'Morning." She gave a long sigh. She sounded relaxed and sexy.

"Morning, baby." He couldn't help himself. He had to kiss her. Long and sweet. Slow and tender. He wanted to drift endlessly in her arms.

She was the first to break away. Her eyes, passion-filled, searched his, looking for some kind of answer. But he couldn't guess at the question. Didn't dare, maybe. So he gave her a trademark Marlena stare, lifting one brow inquiringly.

She returned the same gesture, that flash of vulnerability gone. "Hungry?" she asked. "Want me to cook breakfast?"

He answered a tad too fast. "Nope, not hungry."

Her smile was filled with mockery. "Not at all hungry?" When he shook his head, she yanked at a certain necklace. "Tired? Poor baby."

He frowned.

Her smile widened. "Last night was a blur . . . I recommend a recount."

Oh God, not that way, he thought. He remembered too well how long she took. "I concede," he offered.

"Coward."

"Never," he objected. "I'm planning my next move."

He discovered how lightning-fast she was, even in the morning. He didn't even bother countering her move. She was on her feet, gloriously naked, and walking away. Nice, shapely ass. He frowned.

Looking back, she tossed out, "Come shower with me and show me your next move."

"Wait," he said. She stopped walking away. "Turn around."

Her brow lifted again at his order, but she didn't say a word. She slowly pirouetted around. Her beautiful breasts beckoned temptingly. Her tummy was that of an athlete— trim and slightly muscled. He loved the way her hips swayed when she walked. Loved those thighs. Especially when they were parted. And of course . . . "Come closer," he commanded softly.

She took a few steps closer, but stayed just out of reach.

Steve looked up. Marlena's expression was bemused, waiting. "Where is it?" he asked.

She frowned. "Where is what?"

"Tweety Bird. It's not on your back, and I don't see it on your front." His eyes roved over her body. "Anywhere."

Marlena's expression froze an instant. Then she looked down slowly. His eyes followed her gaze. "Oh my God!" Her shock had him sitting up.

"What? What?"

"Tweety Bird!" she gasped. She touched herself frantically. "My pussy must have eaten it!"

Shrieks. Screams. The chase to the bathroom left the room in chaos. Naked flesh met naked flesh as laughter turned into more shrieks.

"You set me up! I can't believe I fell for that!" There was a long pause. "Hmm . . . do that again." And after another long pause, "I can't believe you set me up. Not funny! Stop laughing! It's not funny!"

There were many ways to shut up a laughing mermaid.

Later, while she finished whatever women did in front of the mirror after a bath, he thought he'd better cook breakfast before she decided to torture him some more. He grinned. He wouldn't blame her if she did—the spa tub in that master bathroom had amazingly useful jets . . .

Looking in the fridge, he pulled out the different items he needed. Better not be an omelet. That might bring about a comparison. He grinned again, feeling remarkably lighthearted. Ham and eggs. Coffee. Should take about fifteen minutes, tops. She ought to be all dolled up by then.

He was setting the table when the door chimed. Security usually called up first to confirm the arrival of any guests, and he hesitated, wondering whether he should let Marlena know. She was still in the back; he could hear the water running. He went to the intercom.

"Yes?"

"Open up, McMillan. We're coming in."

Shit. That was Arms. And that meant bad news. The shooting last night. Steve knew Task Force Two would get that piece of news and conclude that Marlena was behind it. Harden must have come to a decision. Shit. He was under orders. He unlocked the door.

Chapter Ten

Marlena studied her reflection as she combed out her newly dried hair. Her eyes sparkled back. Her lips kept curling into a smile. She touched her lips. They were a little tender from all the kissing. Shaking her head, she made a face.

What was she doing, acting and feeling like a teenager after her first hot night? This was going to ruin her reputation. She sobered up. A reputation that should never be associated with someone like Stash, whether he was rogue or not.

There was so much she wanted to share with him, and therein lay the danger. She had done this before, knew how terrible the consequences could be. And look at Tess, all mushy over a man who couldn't forget his past. No, no, not for her. When this job was over, and if Stash was still around, she would wave a cheery goodbye and move on. Better that way.

And what if Tess was wrong, and Stash was a rogue operative? After all, everyone knew how infected the CIA was these days, in all levels. Hadn't Tess said that he had large amounts of money deposited in some offshore accounts? That could be payoff money.

Marlena gave herself a final inspection in the mirror, tightening the sash of her bathrobe. Before leaving the room, she let the water out of the spa tub, smiling again as she watched the water gurgle away. She thought about the past hours.

The sea mammal liked water, for sure, she mused. He was absolutely creative in it.

The smile was still on her face when she opened the bathroom door. And came face-to-face with three strangers in her bedroom. Stash had his hand on one of them, apparently in the middle of stopping him from invading her privacy.

Her smile turned acidic sweet, and crossing her arms, she leaned one shoulder against the door. "Guests, Stash darling?" she asked, surveying the three faces. So, for once Tess *was* wrong. But somehow Marlena didn't feel like yipping it up with her mentor this time.

One of the men gave her a look meant to insult. "You look just as good at close quarters."

"If you're here to take her in, do so," Steve cut in. His curt tone made the others stop their leering perusal of her. There was a small silence, as if they were each waiting for someone to speak up. Marlena noted that Steve exchanged different looks with each of the men. Interesting. Two of them didn't like her Stash.

"It's our turn, buddy," the man said defensively, looking at the bed. "Looks like you've taken her in already. Right into bed, that is."

The other two men laughed. Marlena studied each of them, gauging who the leader was. None of them, she decided. "Ah, the peeping Toms," she said, still leaning against the door. "Wondered when you would make an appearance."

"You have to come with us."

"Am I under arrest?" She doubted that. Too much paperwork, and she would be out with a call to a lawyer. No, she knew these people weren't going to follow protocol. Bringing in the law made it tough to hold her for long. Ignoring Steve, she met the first man's eyes squarely.

"How do you know we're the law? We could be just the usual scum you deal with." The man obviously enjoyed the role of intimidator, letting his eyes rove her body again in an insolent manner. Except that he wasn't very good at it.

"Your clothes," Marlena drawled out. He looked down at

his clothing, clearly puzzled. "Most of the scum I deal with dress a lot better, darling."

One of the men—lean-faced, with longer hair—chuckled, and patted the man she addressed on the back. "She's got a point there, Whitney."

"I think Miss Maxwell here doesn't know how much trouble she's in, Cam," Whitney said, pulling at his tie and suit. "Weapons are illegal in D.C. We know you have at least two in this apartment. That's enough to haul your ass in. Then there is attempted murder."

Marlena finally turned to Stash, who didn't waver under her scrutiny. "Well, well," she said softly. What had she expected, that he wouldn't go through her things? "Three peeping Toms and one thief. Do you mind if I get dressed first? Or do you want me to go with you like this?" She dropped her lazy stance and made to turn around.

Whitney shook his head. "Uh-uh, you aren't changing in there."

"In front of you?" She lifted an eyebrow. "Expecting a show?"

"Why not? You were pretty good at giving one the other night," Whitney reminded her. He took a step forward. Marlena didn't back away. She knew the man was just acting out by-the-book tactical training. This kind of manipulation, however, wouldn't work with her.

"No," Steve said quietly. But there was a dark heat in his eyes as they met hers.

Oblivious to the emotions surging under the surface, Whitney sniffed loudly. "Man, you're nuts if you think we're letting her go in there to get dressed. Who knows what else she has in that bathroom?"

"Are you saying she's going to come out guns blazing and none of us can handle her?" Steve countered mildly. Yet his eyes continued to convey an entirely different message.

Whitney hesitated at the logic. "Look, Harden's orders were not to allow her out of our sight." It was apparent that he wasn't going to back off on this.

"I'll go in there with her." Steve glanced at Cam. "Okay?"

"Oh sure," Cam said, shrugging. "You've already eyed her anyway. Hey, can I eat that ham and eggs in the kitchen while you're in there, Marlena?"

Marlena decided she kind of liked the tall, lean one. At least he didn't attempt to play *Dragnet* with her, choosing instead to diffuse the situation by mentioning food. "Sure." She allowed a nicer smile, to show her admiration of a skillful negotiator. "You look like you need some meat on you. There are plenty of pancakes and muffins, if you like. I can even make you an omelet."

The tall, gangly man coughed into his fist. "I'm sure Stash . . . um . . . Steve's ham and eggs will be sufficient for now."

Amused, she let slide the fact that Cam had probably seen the green omelets she was capable of producing. "In that case, I'll be right out as soon as I can."

"You do that," Cam said easily. "Come on, boys. Give the lady some privacy."

"I'm standing right out here," Whitney said stubbornly.

The third man shrugged and followed Cam. "Yeah, okay," Cam said, not even bothering to look behind him. "You can back up Steve if he gets in trouble."

Steve came forward and took Marlena by the arm. His grip was firm, and she was tempted to shake him off. She didn't want him touching her right now. Dirty bastard.

"Let's go in," he said, as if he understood she was contemplating a fight. "You can deal with me in there."

Marlena could think of several ways to deal with men who betrayed her, none of which was quite as pleasurable as last night's odyssey. Images of what they had done several hours ago interrupted the torrent of names she was mentally calling him, dampening her anger. Damn it. Why did she have to like the man so much? She couldn't even get worked up when he betrayed her.

"I'll be right out here, Steve," Whitney called after them. "She makes a move, just yell, and I'll be right there."

"Uh-huh, thanks, man," Steve murmured, as he gently nudged Marlena back into the master bathroom. He closed the door and locked it.

Steve knew he didn't have much choice in what was happening. This was Marlena Maxwell, known assassin. This was an operation to find out whom she had been contracted to kill. He was part of the team, following orders. Last night there had been an attempt on a very prominent businessman's life. That kind of news made it quickly through to headquarters, and of course by morning TIARA HQ would know from police reports that Marlena Maxwell happened to be a guest at the party. These facts pointed to a possible tie between their suspect and the attempted murder. Marlena Maxwell was known for these kinds of things. And here was where it all ended.

Except that last night he had been very sure Marlena hadn't had anything to do with what happened to du Scheum. In fact, du Scheum had trusted her enough to let her wander around his study. But he needed Marlena to tell him that herself.

"It isn't what it looks like," he began, then wished he could retract his words. Not the best way to begin an argument with Marlena, by going on the defensive.

She moved away from him and walked to the closet. Not looking at him, she said, "No? You mean you weren't sent to keep an eye on me and report on my whereabouts at all times? You weren't going to put me into a slammer the moment you found any evidence against me? You weren't planning to sleep with me just to get closer?"

He knew that no matter how he answered, she had him. He couldn't be defensive and do his job. He leaned back on the closed door. "If you knew, why did you let me?"

She paused, then pulled out two pairs of lacy underwear. "Let you what?" she asked, frowning at the panties as if she had to make a very important decision.

"Let me stay with you. Why did you let me make love to you?"

Marlena tossed one pair of panties back into the closet and pulled out another. "Red or black?" she murmured.

He wasn't going to be rated below the importance of ladies' underwear. In one swift stride he was behind her, turning her around to face him. Her hand swung up, aiming for his solar plexus. He blocked it, barely escaping a blow as he ducked from her other hand. There was a loud clatter where his hip hit the dressing counter, scattering makeup and jars.

"Hey, McMillan, you okay in there?" Whitney yelled through the door.

Steve grunted when he was quick enough to avoid the brunt of the second attack. He caught her arm and used her forward momentum to propel her into his arms.

"McMillan?" Whitney said again, banging on the door.

"Yeah, stay out there . . . oomph . . ." The woman had sharp elbows. He curled an arm around her waist and lifted her off the floor. "Lena, please, I don't want to hurt you."

That was another wrong statement, he realized. It only made her madder. Now she wasn't just throwing punches; she was using her training to hurt him.

He cursed loudly when she connected with his kidney, forcing him to release his hold. She dropped to her feet and jammed another elbow into his ribs. He managed to get out of the way this time, slamming the closet doors shut.

"I'm coming in," Whitney yelled, jiggling the doorknob.

"Stay out there," Steve yelled back. Obviously his brain had gone south, not using his skills to subdue her. Grimly he caught one attacking hand and pulled her forward again. This time, knowing about those elbows, he locked both her hands behind her and jerked her back so she would lose her balance. He forced her backward against the counter and with his free hand, pulled her by the hair, tugging her face up.

Her eyes were blue fire as she glared. "Let me guess," she taunted. "Now you're going to kiss me into submission."

"Done," he snarled back, temper edging over. The woman obviously didn't know how to talk. He bent his head and fitted his lips on hers.

Her response was just as savage as his. Wild heat. Molten passion. There was a raging need in him to make her admit that there was more between them than what she accused him of. Her taste—untamed, yet sweet—enveloped his senses. He kissed her till she just held on to him, no longer fighting him. They were both breathless when he came up for air.

"Your gang out there is waiting to interrogate me, and you have a hard-on," she whispered huskily. "Lots of things going on, darling."

She wasn't angry anymore. There was a soft sadness lurking in her eyes, as if she had something to say but wouldn't. Steve shook her by the shoulders. "You can stop this," he said, temper roughening his voice. "Give them what they want and stop this. Then you and I can continue what we started."

Marlena caressed his cheek. Her smile was evocative, resigned. She shook her head. "Do you know the law of inertia?"

Steve frowned. She wanted to talk physics now?

She leaned closer and kissed him lightly on the corner of his lips, her tongue flicking out sensuously. "Law of inertia. A moving object continues to move and will keep moving." She sighed. "I always finish my job. This keeps going, all the way. Hand me my panties, please."

Steve shook her again. "Give me something to work with, damn it!" He couldn't believe she would choose to forget what they had shared, just like that. "I can't do anything if you don't help yourself."

Marlena gazed at him curiously. "Why would you want to help me, hmm?" He didn't know what to say, since he had no answer. She gave a wry grin. "You have to give me a reason to trust you."

Steve picked up the red panties from the counter and handed them to her. He took a step back and let her slide off the counter. She ignored him as she prepared herself.

Chapter Eleven

It had been five hours. Steve had run the gamut of emotions throughout the afternoon. He hated not being able to do anything. For five hours he had felt frustration, anger, admiration even. He hadn't been allowed into the interrogation room, and could only watch through the two-way mirror. He hadn't been allowed to talk to Harden before he went in there, and thus, wasn't able to convince his commander about Marlena's possible innocence.

He had sent a message through Cam, telling Harden that he had information about last night's events. He wanted to give his side of it, about du Scheum's friendliness with Marlena, about the dead man. He wanted to point out that Marlena's weapon was in the apartment at the time of the attempted murder. He wanted to ask why the need for the alternative hit man, when she was usually the one suspected of doing the job herself? Cam had come out of the room shaking his head.

"Not necessary, he said. He had read the police reports. Later, he said." Cam looked at Marlena on the other side of the mirror. "She's one cool customer, boy. Damn if I don't start liking her mind as well as her body. She sure knows how to distract with that leather outfit."

Steve just sat and watched. He wanted to smash a fist through the mirror. It didn't matter how cool she looked in leather, how she didn't bend under Harden's tough grilling. It'd been five hours, and they hadn't given her a break.

Hadn't offered her a phone call. Since she wasn't technically arrested, she didn't even have a lawyer. They were in an underground room, a top-secret entity investigating a sensitive case. They had broad powers to do certain things that wouldn't hold water in a court of law.

He knew in his gut that they had it wrong. Harden's refusal to listen to his conclusions puzzled him. From questioning Cam, he found out the reason Harden had given the orders to haul Marlena in. They figured that since the attempt on du Scheum's life had failed, they should stop Marlena before she tried a second time. But if his O.C. would at least give him a chance to tell him about her and Tess, and his suspicion that she was here to sell or buy something, he could at least show an alternate reason she was at the function. No, Cam said, with a shrug. Harden had said that they had her cornered now. Sooner or later she would break down and tell everything they wanted to know.

Well, it had been five hours, and as far as he could tell, she hadn't told them a damn thing. He could only grit his teeth as he listened, wishing that he could just walk in there without jeopardizing the investigation. His O.C. was obviously isolating her from all that was familiar. That was the first thing to do in an interrogation of this kind. Steve had never seen it firsthand, since his job with his SEAL buddies usually ended at this juncture of an operation. If there were prisoners, they were taken out of their hands. So now he was seeing what happened after the fact, he thought. At any other time he would have been totally immersed in the experience, but this was Marlena. And he found himself torn between duty and . . . and what? He ran weary fingers through his mussed-up hair. It just wasn't possible to care about someone after such a short time, was it?

"You must be getting tired and hungry, Marlena. Don't you want to eat or drink? We'd be happy to get anything you like. This is taking longer than we anticipated." Changing tactics, Harden's voice was deceptively concerned. Listening on the other side of the mirror, not caring if anyone was watching him, Steve snorted.

Marlena sat slightly sprawled on her seat, rocking her chair back and forth. "You must be tired and hungry yourself, Mr. Harden," she said, giving him a crooked smile. "You do know I can beat you at this pissing contest, don't you? Women have bigger bladders, you know. And fewer control problems."

Steve just knew she was going to launch into another ten-minute protracted discussion of bladders and control problems. This had been her routine the whole time in there. Harden had started out tough in the beginning, but couldn't intimidate her. He had then, in turn, been sarcastic and rude, threatening and insolent, and now his demeanor was quieter. Yet his cool green eyes never betrayed any of the frustration Steve felt. He seemed to be perfectly satisfied with whatever answer Marlena gave. Where the hell was he going with this?

"Well, you must admit, I have something you don't have at the moment. Freedom." He leaned forward, his hands on the table. "And freedom is so important to a woman like you, isn't it? Tell us who hired you and why target du Scheum. We know you're connected to arms dealing. All we need is the name of the person who hired you. If you cooperate, I can assure you that your freedom won't be too severely curtailed. The state attorney is a friend of mine."

Marlena stopped rocking her chair and leaned forward so that her face was close to her interrogator's. "Know what? He's a friend of mine, too," she confided in a whisper.

"These friends in high places," Harden said, totally unperturbed by her revelation, "are they willing to help you out of your predicament? Or are they going to throw you to the sharks?"

Elbows on the table, she rested her chin on folded hands. Steve couldn't see her expression, but he knew how she looked anyway. Disdainful. Arrogant. And powerfully sexy in her cool and collected way. This was the Marlena he'd first known, who knew he'd been watching her in the bar, who had been aware someone was following them to the apartment.

"Like you were thrown to the sharks, Mr. Harden, when you dropped the ball a few years back?" Steve saw his operations chief stiffen, for the first time caught by surprise. Marlena had bided her time to attack, that was all. "Do you think, like you, I would lie down and let them bulldoze me?"

There was a pause as the two adversaries in the room stared at each other. Then Harden slowly straightened. Very softly, he said, "Miss Maxwell, I'm going to give you a couple of hours to think this over. If you won't cooperate when I return, we will try again tomorrow. This can go on indefinitely, do you understand?" When Marlena shrugged in answer, Harden studied her a moment longer before adding, "There are people like you rotting in jail without formal charges, Marlena. The state attorney can't help you without appealing to the attorney general. And it takes a long, long time for the process to go through."

Steve's heart plummeted when he heard those threats. He didn't doubt that Harden would keep his word and send Marlena into captivity. He had recently read about the case where a Libyan had been held for more than a year without his attorney ever reading any of the evidence claimed to exist, linking him to a terrorist organization. It took two years before the lawyer managed to put the case in front of the attorney general, who finally freed the man. Steve didn't know whether the Libyan was really a terrorist or not; all he cared about at this instant was that his Marlena might face the same fate. His hands fisted on his lap.

"Think this through very, very carefully, Marlena Maxwell," Harden warned.

"Can I have my purse now that you're going off?" Marlena stretched, seemingly unafraid for her future. "A woman can only do so long without a little lipstick, darling. And I'll have my glass of water now, please."

Harden's expression was shuttered as he examined her, then he nodded and left the room. Breathing in slowly, Steve willed his hands to unclench. It wouldn't do to let his O.C. see him in this state. Marlena, on the other side, accepted her handbag from the newly arrived Cam. There was nothing in it except makeup and some cash. Didn't she understand that she wouldn't even have that stuff if she allowed herself to be confined? Frustration rose again.

"Thank you . . . Cameron, isn't it? For the drink, too."

"No problem. If you need the ladies' room, just yell. Someone will hear you."

"Would they come to let me out or would they just sit there and watch me squirm?" Marlena's query was amused, nodding toward the mirror.

Cam didn't deny that they did that sometimes, but after a pause he said, "Tell you what. I'll check back in myself to make sure you get to the ladies' room, if you want to."

"Thank you," Marlena said.

When Cam left, she turned to the mirror to face Steve, and for the first time in five hours, they met eye-to-eye, even though she couldn't possibly know where to look. But Steve felt her gaze deep into his soul anyhow, whether she knew it or not. She cocked her head slightly, raising one elegant eyebrow. Then she smiled slowly, in that challenging way of hers that reached right in and grabbed his beating heart.

"Hi, Stash baby," she crooned. Then she coolly started to apply some powder and makeup. He didn't know whether to laugh or curse.

The door behind Steve opened. "Thanks, Cam, I owe you one," Steve said as he continued watching Marlena.

"Not a problem."

"Will Harden see me now?"

"In an hour, he said. He wanted you to cool off first, I guess, after sitting in here for five hours yourself." Cam sat next to him and watched Marlena for a few seconds. "He probably wants to give you a chance to think about what you're going to say to him, buddy."

Steve stood up. "He doesn't want to talk to me, does he? Why didn't he say so?"

Cam shrugged. "Can't really guess what's on the chief's mind. He didn't break her in there but he seemed quite satisfied when I talked to him, as if he had a few answers already."

Steve shook his head. "Then the art of interrogation is lost on me. I didn't hear anything she said that was of help to the case."

"That's probably because you weren't listening much, I bet." Cam's voice was wry.

"I heard everything," Steve said quietly. "Harden and you and the rest of the team may think my head is elsewhere, but I can assure you I pay attention to everything. After all, I knocked down that would-be murderer and talked to du Scheum. I was there. What I saw and heard is just as relevant as the police report. If he doesn't want to listen, I'll have to go about it another way."

Cam made a tsking sound, but his grin was lopsided. "That's not teamwork, Stevie. You're supposed to work with us, not against us."

"He's against me for some reason," Steve accused.

"What do you want to do, Steve—stop this? How?" Cam asked, turning his back to Marlena so he could study Steve closely. "The O.C. is doing his job. He gets the order from the deputy director to monitor Marlena because of her presence in this city. You know, we do have many important people congregating in a small area. She's known internationally for certain incidents that left several political and influential deaths, so of course our O.C. is antsy about stopping her. Last night's incident, perhaps not ironclad with evidence, was a good excuse to jolt her timetable, if nothing else. Who knows how long she could take this? Harden is a thorough bureaucrat. He does his job by the book, so unless she tells him something to convince him she's not in town to do anything other than shop, he'll continue doing his job."

Cam's long speech made sense, but Steve's gut was telling him otherwise. He tore his gaze from Marlena, who was fluffing her hair in the mirror. "I know she didn't do this one. And if you help me, it's teamwork, isn't it?"

Cam gave a long dramatic sigh. "I knew it. I knew you would drag me into this."

"I just want to think things through logically. Remember

when I said I wanted to look at her old files? I want to see patterns and her victims, as far back as possible. I want to know how she worked besides what you told me. For example, are there any incidents that echo the one last night? Where are the files you promised me, anyway?"

"They're still on request, probably."

"Can we get there right now, and read them right there? You know those people better than I do. And can we also pull up anything about the dead perp last night?"

Cam sighed again. "You're going to owe me again," he warned. "Come on then, we don't have much time, if you need to find a strategy to talk to Harden."

"I'm ready," Steve said. He badly wanted to go to Marlena, but all he could do was give her a backward glance. The law of inertia, she had said about her job. Something started in motion keeps moving. Steve nodded at her, finally understanding. He said aloud, "Unless stopped."

"Huh?" Cam asked at the door.

Steve joined him. "Something left by itself will remain constant. Something started in motion keeps moving, unless stopped," he repeated. "That is one of the laws of inertia."

"Uh-huh. That is going to carry over real well when you lay that theory on Harden."

But Steve's mind was already on Marlena's past. What if she had meant to tell him that whatever was set in motion was started way before this D.C. foray? That she couldn't stop it herself? That didn't mean an outsider like him couldn't try. One way or another, he would make up his mind whether he was right about this woman.

Marlena balanced the empty glass on her index finger. Isolation. Then boredom. She knew what would come next. Bait.

Unless, of course, the TIARA operations commander had undergone more than basic training in textbook interrogation. If he had, he should already guess that she was testing him as well. He was difficult to read, with his indirect questions that moved back and forth from what he wanted to know to what he suspected. She had deliberately given him certain answers, watching him surreptitiously. Except for that last reaction, he was surprisingly tough to gauge. Which led her to conclude that he had more than the basic training. And maybe, just maybe, her gamble would pay off.

The glass tipped over. The loud clatter when it hit the table echoed thunderously through the carpetless ten-by-ten room. She didn't have much time to waste. She had been in similar situations before and had never lost an assignment because something unexpected cropped up. She didn't intend to mar her record. Unlike a gambler, she had other chips to fall back on. There were a variety of ways to get out of her jam, the easiest of which could also be her death warrant. Admit what she was on record. That would really be the end of her.

Not that she feared the end. In fact she had once contemplated it, thinking that she could just recede into oblivion, like some famed mobster. However, admitting defeat wasn't her way. If she had to go, she would end it on her own terms, not because she was cornered.

And she was far from being cornered yet.

Pushing with experimental fingers, Marlena sent the stationary glass rolling. The desk, she mused, must not be level because the glass glided back to her. She repeated.

She had done this dozens of times. Set things in motion. Used them to her advantage. It was her job. Sometimes she accidentally set things off that she hadn't meant to start. Like this thing between Stash and her. Right from the beginning she had felt that he was different. Her body responded to his like a chain reaction of sensual atoms colliding. And yielding to temptation was a mistake on her part. Making love to him once only made her want more of him; she had caught herself daydreaming about him once too often. She couldn't afford that kind of reaction to anyone, any man.

She couldn't feel him on the other side of the mirror any longer, but during her interview she could have sworn she felt his anger. That touched a raw nerve, knowing he was mad for her sake. She didn't blame him. After all, they both had a job to do, no matter how unpleasant. If only she hadn't been weak last night, giving in to her heart instead of listening to her head. Knowing that he'd had an ulterior motive all along left a flat taste in her mouth.

He was probably being debriefed right now. Something twisted inside her. She wondered whether he would include the more intimate parts of last night's activities, besides his part in saving Pierre du Scheum. She willed away the little nudge of pain. Been there, done that. She had gone through this before. Hadn't she sworn that she wouldn't be used this way again?

Granted, it was an entirely different situation, but the consequences were still the same. The man she'd thought cared about her had given information to others to expose her, with the twisted naivete that once they knew who she was, she would retire from the job and live a quiet life with him. He had bugged their conversations, willingly imparted clues to her whereabouts so that she could be followed and monitored. Not for money, but for love, he had claimed later.

Fortunately for her, he had contacted the wrong person, someone who had, in turn, moved in quietly to save the day. She'd never met him to thank him for saving her life, but he and his group were now working closely with Tess.

Everything had worked out. She hadn't died. Marlena Maxwell was, however, alone again after that. As she ought to be. Tess had even fallen for one of these men, and look at her sorry state now. Like her, back to square one.

She sighed. There were more urgent matters to think about, and here she was behaving like a rejected lovesick teenager. Stash—Steve, she corrected with a sharp grimness—was out of the picture right now. He had probably been taken off the case and reassigned after having done his job. Gotten close to her. Searched her belongings. The weapon charge was just an excuse, she knew, to get her in here to answer questions. There would be no charges. She looked around her. This was no local law enforcement holding facility, after all. Oh yes, he did his job well.

Well, let him move on then. That should make things easier. Out of sight, out of mind. She was getting too lackadaisical as it was. Oh, damn, damn, damn. Her lips twisted in self-derision. Now she was beginning to sound like Tess and her word games, which reminded her . . .

Marlena picked the glass up and balanced it on her finger again. When she was powdering her nose, she had activated the call on her compact cell, a secret code that should have reached Tess by now. She had no idea what her friend would do to help her, but if Rick Harden didn't do something soon to get her out of here, she was sure Tess would.

"Welcome to the Gatekeepers' Place," Cam said as they entered the Records department.

Steve let Cam lead, since he had no idea who was in charge in here. The middle of the room was a long aisle cutting the space effectively in half. On each side of the aisle were narrow tables about eight feet long, with breaks between for walking space. There were envelopes and files, stacks of folders, boxes, all of which Steve noticed had names marked clearly in thick black ink, and arranged in alphabetical order down the tables. At each corner of the room there was a desk and an operative working, all four ignoring the people walking up and down the middle aisle as they looked for their names. Cam cut through one of the spaces between the low tables and headed for a desk.

"Watch this," he whispered to Steve.

A woman sat with her back to them, typing at a furious pace. Her back was ramrod straight. Her ash-brown hair, pulled back neatly in a French twist, was a stark contrast against the crispy white of her silk shirt. She didn't turn around to greet them.

Cam reached down and moved the in box an inch to the right. Then he pushed the out box an inch to the left. He gave Steve a wink, then gave a fake cough.

The woman ignored them, continuing to type. Cam opened the candy jar and picked something out before offering Steve the container. Steve shook his head. Cam unwrapped his candy and popped it into his mouth, scrunching the wrapper loudly and dropping it on the desk.

The woman stopped typing. She looked up at the ceiling for a moment, as if to look for help there. Steve watched her back expand and constrict as she took in what looked like a calming breath before turning around.

Expressive gray eyes behind glasses peered up at both of them. She didn't return Cam's big smile. Gingerly she picked up the candy wrapper with two fingers and threw it into a wastebasket. She moved the in box back an inch to the left. Lastly she rearranged the out box to its original position. She looked up again, clearly not going to say anything as she waited.

Cam didn't seem perturbed by the telling look she directed at him. "Hi, Patty, miss me?"

"No, since I'm not in the mood to shoot." Her voice was frosty and polite.

"Oooh. Ouch. Ouch." Cam patted his chest and turned to Steve. "Do you see any holes, buddy? I think I've been hit."

Steve shook his head. Clearly the woman didn't like Cam at all as she continued looking at them without smiling at his antics.

"Meet Patty, Gatekeeper of Details Nobody Cares to Know Anymore. Old unconverted classified files. Dead people. Missing links. Ask Patty. She will make them magically appear. Patty, this is Steve from Task Force Two, here to beg a little favor from the goddess."

Patty looked annoyed at Cam's introduction, but she gazed at Steve with mild interest. "You're the new guy," she said. "The Kisser of the Millennium."

Damn. The Internet was a gossip line. He was never going to live that name down. "Yes," Steve answered, keeping it simple. He didn't have time for small talk. Not that—he looked at the name plaque on the desk—Miss Patty Ostler looked like the flirting type.

She looked exactly like a woman in charge of details— the carefully drawn-back hair revealed intelligent eyes under a wide forehead, a standoffish expression on a face that had a stubborn square chin, a mouth that she pursed into a straight line. The impeccably clean white of her shirt, with the little buttons all the way to her neck. The way her pencils were arranged by length. The exact spacing of everything on her desk.

"See?" Cam leaned a hip on the desk, pushing the in box out of the way, oblivious to Patty's frown of displeasure. "Told you how good she is."

"You did say Gatekeeper of Details Nobody Cares to Know Anymore," Patty pointed out, looking at Steve wryly. "Judging by the avid postings in the naval grapevine bulletin board, that is one detail everyone cares about."

"Yeah, well. I'll just have to kiss him one of these days to see whether it's true," Cam mocked. "But we're here for other more unimportant things. I'm trying to help Steve out. I put in a request for some older classifieds, and knowing how long it takes to rummage through records, I thought I'd come straight to the goddess herself."

"Agent Candeloro, if your stuff isn't out there on the long table, it's not ready. Everyone wants to bypass the system so they can get their stuff. If I help one out, then everyone will want me to do him the same favor. Now why would I make my life more miserable than it is?"

"Because deep down, you really want to go out with me. And if you get me those files, I'll take you out to dinner next weekend." Cam reached for the candy jar again.

Patty smacked his hand away. "Leave my candy alone."

"Never," Cam said, with a wicked smile.

Patty glared and turned to Steve. "Tell him to leave my stuff alone, and I might help you."

Steve shrugged. He needed Patty's help right now. "Leave her stuff alone, Cam," he said.

"See how soft other men are with you, princess?" Cam said, somehow managing to snag the candy jar. Opening it, he picked out another candy. "Me, I don't fall for your charms so easily."

"You, too, can be trained," Patty warned.

"Next week. Dinner. You can train me all you want."

She shook her head. "You're hopeless."

"Please, Miss Ostler, I need those files as soon as possible," Steve interrupted the tête-à-tête. "It's important."

Patty studied him for a few moments. Steve returned her gaze as Cam crunched on his candy noisily. "Very well," she finally said. "But only because it's for you."

"Ouch. Ouch. Now she's stabbing me," Cam said with his mouth full of candy.

"Thank you," Steve said.

"My break is coming up in five minutes. I'll meet you at the back room then. Ask Agent Candeloro to take you there, if you can stop him before he dies from sugar shock."

Cam got off the desk, moving the name plaque as he did so. As they walked away, Steve watched Cam glance back at Patty Ostler putting everything back in place. A big grin of satisfaction spread on his face.

"That's not the way to get someone to like you," Steve commented.

Cam shrugged. "She never paid me any attention until I found her weakness." He pointed to another door to exit.

Following him, Steve asked, "What's her weakness?"

Cam opened the door, his grin becoming a smirk. "She can't stand me."

"Oh, a good foundation for a relationship," Steve said, walking past Cam.

Cam sniffed as he went in after Steve. "Oh, Kisser of the Millennium, lackey of the century, Dr. Ruth of Task Force Two." He laughed at the rude name Steve called him. "Well, I bet Marlena is calling you exactly that too, buddy. And if you find what you want, both of you owe Patty and me a dinner. Out at someplace fancy. No home cooking please."

Poker-faced, Steve sat quietly as his commander looked at the copies he had gathered quickly to make a file. The other man's expression was remote as he read, occasionally flipping back to review previous pages. He took his time. Finally he looked up. Steve waited.

"And how do you feel about this discovery?"

Steve looked back coolly. He should feel elated. Exhilarated. His instincts had been right after all. Instead, a ball of anger sat heavily in his stomach. He was having a hard time digesting the bitterness of being played for a fool.

He hoped none of what he felt showed on his face. "I guess, as surprised as you are, sir."

Harden's lips quirked up at one corner. "Then you're not surprised at all."

Steve's interest sharpened. "You knew?"

"I spent five hours in intense interrogation with Miss Maxwell, remember?"

"But she didn't answer anything." That was the only thing left in the puzzle. Why hadn't she just cut to the chase? She didn't have to pretend anymore at that point.

"Oh, but she did." Harden looked down at the papers in the file again. "She had extensive lessons in what the CIA calls NOPAIN training. She isn't a probe, but someone taught her this skill well."

"NOPAIN?" Steve queried.

"Nonphysical persuasion and innovative negotiation," Harden explained. "There is a select group of contract agents who specialize in NOPAIN. The CIA pays for their services occasionally, as well as other of Uncle Sam's covert agencies. I'm sure naval intel uses them, too, now and then."

Steve had never heard of them, but then his SEAL team used direct confrontation. However, his cousin dealt with more covert work in his SEAL team. He made a mental note to call Hawk up for information later. A sudden thought struck him.

"If Marlena has this training, that suggests she is a contract agent."

Harden paused a moment, then nodded. "She said as much in her code words to me. She tested me several times before letting me know that she was more than what she appears to be."

The ball of fury inside Steve grew tighter. "Whom does she work for?"

"That I don't know. She refused to give more than the required code words that only a few select operatives understand." It was clear Harden wasn't going to elaborate. He
tapped the small stack of papers lightly. "But here is clear
evidence that it's true, at least."

Steve glanced at the report—his fast and furious handiwork—that he had hurriedly put together into a coherent file
so that he could run it off to his operations chief. And all
along Harden had known. All along that woman continued
playing her stupid game.

Harden pushed the open file across the table. "You didn't
waste your time," he said, reading Steve's mind. "She isn't
ever going to tell anyone about what she is until truly necessary. Even I don't know exactly what's going on. It's good
we didn't arrest her through the legal channels, or there
would have been red tape from hell to deal with. This file
helps to explain things if the top brass wants an answer for
her disappearance and it gets sticky for us."

Steve stopped himself from jerking out of his chair.
Somehow he already knew the answer. "She's gone?"

Harden tented his hands, tapping his fingers as he studied
Steve. "Yes."

"How long ago?"

"About an hour."

He sacrificed considerable pride to ask the next question.
"Did she leave a message?"

Harden's pause was deliberate. Stone-faced, Steve stared
back unblinkingly. "No. Did you think she would? She has
work to do and we were all in her way." The glint in the
older man's eye matched the sarcasm in his voice. "Women
like her work outside the system and think they are above
the law. And they don't last long, McMillan. They are cor-
rupted because they are loners, easily used by and used up in
their short careers. Their ultimate downfall lies in the fact
that they don't understand the concept of teamwork."

"Why are you telling me this?" His commander's assessment of Marlena left Steve cold and even angrier. Harden

portrayed her as a cold-hearted bitch, but Steve didn't defend her. What could he say? After all, hadn't she been as calculating and cunning as described?

"I think you're in over your head, McMillan. Emotions are easily played with, and you've obviously been a victim to Marlena Maxwell's charms. I suggest you watch your back the next time you let one of her kind close. She might not be as generous—she could feed you to the wolves, leave you to pick up the pieces of your career because you stood in her way."

Steve maintained a calm composure. There was a lot more going on here than a dressing-down of a subordinate by a superior. "We're not exactly talking about me being the victim, are we, sir?" he asked quietly, watching the other man closely.

If possible, Harden's expression became even more shuttered. He folded his hands flat on the desk. His mouth was a straight slash on his expressionless face, but Steve noticed the tiny tic on the side of his jaw. "We are," he answered in a flat tone, "talking about teamwork."

"I'm a navy SEAL, sir," Steve pointed out, wondering what it took to get under that immovable distrust of him that his leader barely concealed. He chose his words carefully. "I know what it takes to work within a group, in whichever mode, whether it's mobilized or undercover infiltration. Covert is covert. And while I admit that past experiences play a factor to make one a better operative, I cannot let them color each operation until there is no room to make adjustments. Just my opinion, sir. Are there any other orders, sir?"

If his commander was persuaded by Steve's argument, he didn't show it. "Not for you. There's nothing we can do till we hear from the top, McMillan. We all report to our superiors and wait. Maybe the admiral and TIARA top brass will have an idea where to proceed once they look at our findings."

"Sir, what do you want to do about du Scheum? He's obviously a target."

Harden impassively answered, "My job is to follow orders."

Steve thought so. Cam had hinted as much a few days ago that Harden's past affected his judgment now, that he had paid a high price for some mistake. He just hadn't paid closer attention because his mind was on Marlena. Now it was obvious that Harden no longer trusted any action without first going over it through all sorts of channels. Steve understood. It was the best way to cover one's ass. Harden wasn't going to pay for mistakes again.

Meanwhile, they were just going to sit there and knowingly wait for someone innocent to be killed. This just wasn't done in his combat days. Besides that, no one seemed to care that something else equally big was going down, and it had to do with a certain woman he would like to get his hands on right now. And somehow all this was connected.

"I thought you were dead certain that Marlena Maxwell would try to get to du Scheum again? What about that theory? Wouldn't the cops have questions linking her?" Steve asked.

"No bullets in her weapons. And they were in the apartment, cold. So that closes our file on that incident. As for the cops, that's their business, out of our hands."

"What about the dead man? Any follow-up that may connect him to her?" Steve insisted, knowing that he was stepping out of line again. So much for his teamwork speech, he thought. Might as well continue to self-destruct. "I don't get it. Why aren't we working to find out what is happening?"

"Why don't you? As far as I'm concerned, Marlena Maxwell isn't our business any longer, but you have your own private orders, don't you? Wasn't that your assignment? To come into TIARA and find out what is happening?"

Steve's whole being sprung to life. Mental blinders fell off like big heavy icicles. "I was never part of the team," he breathed out. "You think that—"

"What I think doesn't matter," Harden interrupted. "I know you have an agenda."

"What?" Although surprised, Steve didn't raise his voice.

The implication of Harden's words didn't fit with the revelations on his mind.

Harden's frosty green eyes were direct, challenging. "I don't think a team member reports back to anyone, even if it's to the admiral, unless it's to investigate the team itself. Task Force Two has obviously been under the admiral's suspicion for a while. If Marlena Maxwell fails at her job, I don't care to have her death as another black mark against me. Your work here is done, McMillan."

Chapter Twelve

It had been a long day. Marlena parked the butter-yellow convertible in the hotel parking lot and cut off the engine. She sat in the silence, looking out through the windshield with half-seeing eyes. Returning to the apartment to get her things was harder than she had thought. The sight of the unmade bed had sent a jolt of pain.

Fortunately for her she was racing against time, so she had limited herself to packing a few things, along with certain items she had hidden. There was still some cash left in the safe, and she took that. Walking out of the bedroom, she had glanced at the bed again and almost rushed back when she caught sight of the pearl necklace lying carelessly among the pillows. For a long frozen moment she just stood there, looking at it, fighting the storm inside her. She didn't think she could bear taking the pearls. She had taken a step forward, then abruptly turned and strode out of the room.

Still in the car, Marlena rubbed her heart absentmindedly. Five minutes, she thought. She needed these five minutes to think about him, get over him, wallow about him, do whatever necessary to get rid of his memory. Once that was done, she would go into the crowded hotel lobby, take the elevator to the suite she had reserved, and leave all her feelings down here.

God, but walking away had never been this tough before. She wanted to see him so badly and he was only a phone call away. When Harden had released her, she had toyed with the idea of leaving Steve a message, but what did she have to say?

"I want you. Wait for me." Marlena said it out loud, and laughed cynically.

"Ta, it was fun. Let's do it again." She could just imagine how he would take that line.

"Sorry your assignment wasn't that successful. Better luck next time." Her laughter held a hysterical edge.

"I will miss you." She sobered. "Will you miss me?"

"I want you to miss me. As much as I am missing you." She cursed, then raked careless fingers through her hair. "God, I must be going nuts."

The thing was, she really did miss him. And it hurt that he didn't even care enough to be around when she was freed. Harden almost said as much.

"He's no longer needed for the case," he had informed her. She shouldn't be hurt or surprised. People in Steve's line of work didn't stay to say goodbye. She had met plenty of them in her time.

Harden hadn't said much, but from the little explanation he did give, Marlena had gathered that they'd taken the real lackey into custody. Stash had taken his place to find out her target's identity. She hadn't volunteered any information of her own, and Harden hadn't pressed for any. She was well aware of her profile as a possible assassin, but she wasn't in town for that kind of business this time. As a parting shot, she'd praised Steve for doing a good job. Harden hadn't acknowledged her sarcasm. She supposed he was off to another assignment. Her lips twisted. If it was to bed another woman, she hoped he rotted in hell in the worst way.

She climbed out of the car and slammed the door shut. There, all done. See, it was easier than she realized. He was gone forever. She would walk away just as nonchalantly as he had.

Steve didn't know why he felt compelled to drive back to the apartment. There was nothing left there for him. He ought to just go home and pack, get ready to drive down to

Virginia to meet with the admiral. His call was brief this afternoon, but it was enough to confirm Harden's accusations. The admiral had told him he would inform him of the reasons during their meeting.

He had always been in awe of the admiral, whose service record was a kind of sacred invocation among all SEALs, and after every grueling mission the old guy would show up to commend them. The act was simple but the effect wasn't. Every member of his team always felt taller, better focused, and useful.

Steve had never thought about this much until his short conversation with the admiral earlier that day. A team couldn't function without a leader who understood what kept a group of men together in a challenging situation. His SEAL commander gave the orders, set up the operation, and kept everything under control, but it was the leader of Star Force, the admiral himself, who saw the big picture. The fact that he shared much of the information with his men had earned him undivided loyalty and the highest respect among his elite covert teams.

He missed that kind of team spirit. He wanted the assurance from the admiral that there was a big picture in all this.

Steve opened the door to the apartment. He knew the cameras in the hallway were still being monitored, and wondered what they thought of his being there. Not that he particularly cared. Why monitor a place where the most important element was missing? On the other hand, maybe whoever had threatened Marlena those couple of times would call back.

He hoped so. He was in the mood to blast away some bad guys. The knowledge that they would knock off Marlena for whatever item they believed she had only served to add fuel to his ire. He was off the case, but that didn't mean he couldn't track them down himself and find out who they were.

The bedroom.

Why the hell was he here? She was obviously gone. He

didn't have to look around to see that she had taken some of her things, yet his eyes were drawn to the bed, still unmade. His nose flared slightly as he detected a trace of her perfume in the air, and he scanned the bedsheets with restless eyes. A milky gleam among the dark sheets beckoned. His jaw locked. She had left the pearl necklace.

He went to pick it up, running his fingers along its glossy length. She obviously didn't think it worth keeping. He didn't think she would just simply have forgotten. He ought to leave it there, too, and leave everything else that reminded him of her.

Steve was about to drop the pearl necklace back on the bed when something in his back pocket started vibrating. Frowning, he reached behind him to pull the gadget out. His heart skipped a beat. It was the voice message beeper that Marlena had tossed to him that first night. Could it be . . . ? He didn't waste any time conjecturing. Pressing down, he read the message.

Call me. He memorized the number, pocketed the pearls, and tried not to appear in too much of a hurry as he left the apartment. In the safety of his own car, he dialed the phone number.

"Make a choice. If she's in danger, would you save her? Are you in or out?"

It wasn't Marlena's sultry voice on the other end, but Tess's, whom he was now very certain was connected to Marlena through more than mere friendship. He didn't even stop to think. All he heard was that Marlena could be in danger.

"I'm in," he said. What the heck. He was still in the mood to blow off some steam.

However, first he would enlist the help of Cam and his gatekeeper friend to find out about the mysterious Tess. Then he would talk to the admiral. If he was right that he had been sent to D.C. to be the eyes and ears for the admiral, he might as well use some muscle and brain to get what he wanted. And what he wanted was the big picture. With his mermaid in it.

* * *

He drew long and hard from the newly lit cigarette. The smoke filled his lungs, warmed him from head to foot. He thought he could actually feel each individual cell in his body moving eagerly to meet the nicotine, welcoming it like a long-lost friend.

Exhaling the smoke through his nose, he idly played with the cigarette between his fingers, holding it in various positions. It had been that long since he last had one.

He had been yearning for one lately, thought he could hold it off till he met Marlena Maxwell, but—he flicked ash into a tray—the celebratory gesture was no longer necessary. After all, she no longer would play that all-important role of being his partner.

He looked at the different pages of information scattered on his big desk. No one going through the CIA electronic request sector could escape his knowledge. It was fortunate that Steve McMillan had decided to run a check of Marlena Maxwell. He would never have found these items since they weren't in current computer databases. Yes, he was very fortunate indeed. He could use this to his advantage.

The moment those documents were signed out to be Xeroxed marked the end of Marlena Maxwell. And to have them end up right before him so easily! He was after hard-to-find information, just as everyone going through the databases was. It was just his genius to follow somebody else's paper trail instead of working blind. The most requested files were often the least interesting, so he always looked out for unusual requests, and old documents not yet input in the database were certainly unusual. McMillan had more brains than he had given him credit for. And what a bull's eye he'd hit! Too bad he couldn't use the fellow. The reason for his presence in TIARA was so obvious, those in charge must really think their adversary stupid.

He drew on the cigarette again. Ahhh, the first nicotine buzz was here. He welcomed it like an old lover. Looking at the picture of Marlena, he smiled mirthlessly. He had meant to woo her, slowly show her the glory of a different kind of power—the kind she and he would share together. When they met, he had planned to offer her more than her life as some hireling for the highest price. He had thought her perfect at his side, a beautiful woman who understood the meaning of power and happiness. Instead she turned out to be nothing, nothing at all.

So they were to meet finally, but not as he had intended. The stage was no longer friendly. He might still seduce her; after all, she didn't know that she had been found out. It would be amusing to see how far she would go to get her clever little hands on what he had.

Abruptly he squashed the cigarette in the crystal ashtray. Picking it up, he heaved it violently at the wall across the desk. It smashed into a picture frame, breaking the glass into hundreds of shards. Cigarette ash smeared an ugly gray line down the white wall.

Stupid fucking bitch! He would see to it that she paid for this! He had worked too long to be denied this important sale. He couldn't just broadcast what he had discovered, or the buyers would be wary of any more go-betweens, thinking that he was setting a trap. He couldn't afford to lose their confidence right now. No, he wouldn't allow Marlena Maxwell to destroy any more of his plans.

Maybe he would use her first. Then he would kill her. After all, what difference would it make? The real Marlena Maxwell was probably dead already.

He squinted his eyes thoughtfully. He could allow her to continue with her charade, as long as he kept her under control. He had to admit he was curious about her.

A slow smile formed. He didn't need any Marlena by his side.

He inhaled, then calmly reached for the packet of cigarettes on the desk. And oh yes, he would use her to get rid of that SEAL, too. He laughed. That would be killing two lovebirds with one bullet.

Chapter Thirteen

Steve rubbed his jaw, playing with the couple days' growth of beard as he tried to pick one of a dozen questions jumping around in his mind right at that moment. He was in a crowded café near Connecticut Avenue and obviously picked by the lady across the table for its tourist clientele. He wouldn't have known it was Tess if she hadn't told him the exact location of a booth in the corner. Sitting down, with shopping bags and D.C. and museum maps on the seat and table, she was busy perusing the menu when he stepped inside the cubicle and sat down. He had hesitated, but gone with instinct anyway.

It wasn't because he didn't think he could handle another surprise, but this one was . . . unexpected, to say the least. Tess was nowhere to be seen. Well, it was Tess, but she sure didn't look like the Tess he'd met until she glanced up and greeted him in her sultry voice.

He sat down and picked up the menu, even though he was too busy taking in her appearance to read. Her hair was black and spiky short, accentuating her cheekbones. Her eyes were gray when they glanced up at him, not the liquid honey-gold he remembered. She had done something with her face because her nose looked different somehow, but the smile she gave him was a familiar curve.

"Hello, Steve," she said, in Tess's voice.

"Who the hell are you?" he demanded in a soft growl, for her ears alone. He added, "Who the hell are the two of you?"

Tess handed him a small buttonlike pin with an insignia. "We're GEM. You should be familiar with contract agents."

He sat there waiting for her to continue, but she just sat there, reading the menu.

"Is that all?" he asked, reading the insignia with quick interest. "GEM. Contract agents. I'm supposed to take your word and go on from there?"

She closed her menu. "Yes."

"Not likely."

"We don't have much time. I only called you because I can't do this myself and you're the only person that might be able to save Marlena."

That wiped out most of his questions for now. He pocketed the insignia button. "Where is she? What danger is she in?"

Her gray eyes glinted with what looked like approval. "Still interested? Even though you know nothing?"

Her laugh hadn't changed, either, a husky undertone. Steve couldn't believe the transformation from Tess to . . . to . . . "Is Tess your real name?" he asked. "If I do a search on you, is there a profile, a real person? Or are you like Marlena?"

"Oh, there is a Tess. It's Tess Montgomery, to save your friend Cameron's time." A waiter showed up at the table. Again there was immediate change. Tess gave her order with a softer Southern accent. Even her gestures were different. After the server left, Tess added, back in her normal voice, "I know how intriguing I am, darling, but now is not the time to ask everything. You are a SEAL operative and understand covert activities. Need-to-know basis, and all that."

Steve smiled grimly. "That's when I know whose side I'm working for," he reminded her. "Right now, GEM means nothing to me. All I want is to find out where Marlena is and what she is doing."

"There, common ground," Tess countered. "And don't you think if she weren't kosher to Mr. Harden, she would be running around free?"

"I don't think Harden has a choice," Steve replied. "I think you would have gotten her out some other way if my O.C. hadn't followed through. I get the definite feeling that you're a little higher than TIARA, able to pull muscle where it counts. So why don't we cut through the B.S. and you tell me exactly what you are and how exactly you want to use me? Somehow I don't think you're asking me because you feel sorry for me." He was still mad as hell at Marlena for leaving him without even a goodbye.

"Tactical Intelligence and Related Activities," Tess drawled out the long version for TIARA while playing with the straw in her glass of Coke, "is such a boring place after being in SEAL-related activities, don't you think, Steve? Don't you miss the field action? Taking matters in your own hands without red tape and someone with mental baggage breathing down your neck? Yet the admiral chose you because he saw something beyond the Kisser of the Millennium stuff that told him you could handle tactical intel, that you aren't just a SEAL warrior gunning around in enemy territory. So he sent you to TIARA and you've been stuck there. You like the intel enough but miss the action, don't you, Steve? You think if you could just jump into the fray, be given some leeway in this matter, you could actually feel more . . . complete?"

Steve stared across the table, his gaze narrowing as he weighed Tess's speech. He had enough training to see that the woman was playing with his mind. "NOPAIN, isn't it?" he tartly concluded. "Nonphysical persuasion and innovative negotiation, I think my operations chief said. Is this a taste of it?"

Tess laughed. "I knew you never lacked in the brain department, darling." The food arrived. Back to her accent, she said, "Have lunch and let's go sightseeing afterward, shall we? You never know, we might catch up with our missing friend."

"We aren't going anywhere until you answer a few questions. First, what is Marlena after?"

"Marlena did accept an assignment in D.C., but it wasn't

what Task Force Two thought it was." Tess raised an eyebrow. "Not what you thought she was."

Steve took a bite out of his hamburger and stared at Tess as he chewed. She smiled and continued, "Her job is to find out who hired her because he left a clue that he had something very important to our country's security. Once we find out who it is, everything will fall into place."

"What about this item?" Steve asked, remembering the threatening phone calls. "Don't you want it in your hands, too? Everybody else seems to be after it."

"Definitely," Tess said, "but this person is not your usual criminal looking for a quick sale. He is very good at disguising himself, and so far our contact with him is minimal. He doesn't want money but power, which makes him more dangerous. But Marlena can handle him. She's very good with men of power."

That made Steve scowl. He knew Tess was provoking him on purpose, trying to extract information with her NOPAIN methods, but he couldn't help it. "So why is she in danger?"

"She is always in danger," Tess countered, her expression turning serious. "You've put her in even more danger by giving Harden those files."

Steve jerked up sharply, a ready denial on his lips, but the gray eyes studying him across the table stopped the words. He remained silent, waiting for the rest of the information.

Again she nodded in approval, as if he'd passed another test. "We've always known there are moles in the CIA, and TIARA leaks enough information that makes it very probable that there is an inside as well as an outside entity working. Why do you think the admiral transferred you there? He wanted someone he could trust in TIARA to report back to him. You obviously have his confidence, Steve."

"How do you know all this?" Hell, he'd just found this out himself. How did this woman know so much?

Tess wiped her hands with some napkins. Steve noticed that she had on different rings today. "I called the admiral last night to confirm my findings, of course," she answered, her gray eyes twinkling.

"Oh yeah, right. You just picked up the phone and informed his secretary that you're Tess Montgomery with GEM and you have a few questions to ask him," Steve said dryly.

Tess's lips quirked. "I did, but I also used your name." Leaning closer, she added, "I also have his private line, so no secretary."

Steve met those amused eyes with his own incredulous ones. "Who are you?" He made a mental note to call his cousin Hawk and ask about GEM. Contract operatives just didn't have a direct line to top Pentagon brass.

"You can call the admiral and confirm my conversation with him, if you like," she offered, "and get permission to finish this whole operation."

Steve frowned. "You mean I'm back in the game?"

Tess nodded. "If you want, but this time you'll be on your own, with us. Your main objective is to follow Marlena, make sure she's okay, then let them take her prisoner."

Steve shook his head. "No, I won't let her be taken prisoner without me."

Tess's eyes narrowed. "It's her job, Steve," she reminded, her voice deceptively gentle. "She has to find out who is behind the sale."

"And let's say she does, and she's still a prisoner, what then?"

"Once we find out who the man is, we will decide what to do with him."

"What about Marlena? How does she get out, if she's in danger? If there is a leak, she's probably walking into a trap." The thought of it made his blood run cold.

"It's the risk we all take. She understands the probabilities of the situation."

"No." Steve shook his head again. This time he wouldn't just stand around. "If I'm in, I do it with her. If I'm to follow her, I follow her into danger all the way."

"And how do you propose to do that?"

"Simple. I get caught." He looked straight at Tess, determined to have his plan taken seriously. "The probabilities for keeping Marlena safe just went up."

He had expected protests, but then Tess wasn't exactly a predictable woman. She sipped her drink. It took a second before he realized that she was trying not to smile. Somehow he had been manipulated again, to do exactly what . . . he wanted. He stared stonily back at her.

"A good plan," Tess agreed, "and I'll allow it on two conditions. One, you aren't allowed to report anything back to Harden or your Task Force Two team."

"Why not?"

"Well, first of all you're off this case, as far as Harden is concerned. Then there are the leaks, remember? Besides, Harden will go by the book and storm in to get his man." Tess' expression became harder. "We don't want that yet. Our objective goes a lot further than clogging up a leak temporarily, Agent McMillan. Do you understand?"

Sure he did. They wanted to see the whole mole organization fall apart, which was all right by him. If there was indeed someone betraying the agency from the inside, and if catching him was the admiral's objective in the first place, he wouldn't be working against his team. He realized with sudden clarity that he would be working on Marlena's side, too. Which made it more than all right.

Tess was waiting for his answer, that small smile still playing on her lips. "Unless, of course, you don't want to be . . . um . . . Marlena's partner?"

Steve couldn't help but smile back. "Did I tell you that you don't lack in the brain department, either? What's the second condition?"

Tess laughed. "You're perfect for our kind of work, Agent McMillan. We'll get you some tools to put on, set you up so that Marlena will know you have my approval, and then we're ready to go over the details."

"Please don't say I have to dye my hair," Steve countered in mock horror.

"No, but you're going to be wearing an earring."
"What? No way."

Danger had different smells and sounds. This time it had the scent of plush leather seats in a quietly droning car. Expensive cologne. Very quiet commands.

Marlena let the sounds and smells drift over her, getting ready for the confrontation. She must remain in control no matter what surprises the enemy sprang on her. One little mistake could be her undoing.

Hands led Marlena up some steps. A house, maybe, she thought, listening for clues. It smelled of a house, not a hotel room. The floors were tiled. Her boots clacked as she walked carefully, guided up more steps. Then her heels sank into deep carpet. She caught the scent of fresh flowers. She heard a door closing.

"You may take off the blindfold, Miss Maxwell."

She did. Oh-oh. She was in a bedroom. A familiar-looking place she shouldn't be in. Calmly she looked at the man sitting on the bed.

"I don't see the need to waste my whole day just to bring me here," she said, folding her arms. "You could have just given me the address."

It was, after all, du Scheum's bedroom. The man on his bed, however, wasn't Pierre.

All day, while following the instructions in the special delivery package, she'd had the feeling that she was being watched. The walk down the Vietnam Memorial trail to the Washington Monument. The little tour given by the ATF agent. Walking in and out of the Pentagon. By afternoon her scheduled stop was at the Naval Research Laboratory at the edge of D.C. She walked through the specific areas inside the facility, a vast research base for technological development of maritime applications. All very interesting choices of places.

Then, following the map, she went out the other exit, and two men had approached her and very politely asked for her to follow along sans her yellow sportster. They were armed, too, of course, their weapons protruding threateningly under their jackets.

Why the elaborate, roundabout way to meet? She didn't think it was just to show her D.C.'s historic and tourist sites. She started to go over all the details.

His choice of meeting place was also telling. The man was ego-driven, needing to prove something to her. He looked familiar. Mid-forties, almost nondescript in appearance. Sandy hair, brown eyes, too pale to be an outdoorsman. In fact he was gaunt-looking, with shadows under his deep-set eyes, as if he spent too much time staring at screens. Except for his eyes, he wasn't exactly how she thought a traitor would look.

Despite his deceptively mild looks, his eyes had a malevolent glitter in them. Marlena was sure they had met several times before, but how was it she couldn't remember him, especially with those eyes? Not an important player, she decided. With those looks, he easily receded into the background if he chose. He was waiting for some reaction from her. Everything he had done so far was calculated.

Showing her the city meant something. Blindfolding her. Being here of all places, in du Scheum's bedroom. He wanted to make a point to her. But she didn't have much time to analyze all this.

"You seem to be good friends with Pierre." She eyed her surroundings in reference.

"Ob-obviously n-not as well as you, my dear, since y-you recognize his bedroom." He spoke with a slight stutter, but he didn't seem nervous. "Aren't you going to ask me why I picked this place for our meeting?"

Marlena shrugged. "I'm here. I expect you will tell me before I leave."

His eyes narrowed as he leaned back against the richly embroidered pillows. "And wh-what if I am not allowing you to leave?"

She raised an eyebrow. "You hired me to negotiate a sale for you with my business contacts. Are you saying you don't have anything for me?" She lowered her voice. "I don't take kindly to having my time wasted." She suddenly recalled his name as she continued studying him. His eyes. Every time they had met, he wore tinted glasses. That was why he looked so odd. She added, "Nor do I think Pierre would want to see you in his bedroom, Mr. Cunningham, isn't it?"

"You remembered!" He sounded pleased. "I wasn't sure whether you would. You barely paid attention whenever we shook hands."

"Oh, I wouldn't say that."

"Won't you sit down? Or would you pr-prefer to join me here, on this bed?"

Marlena shook her head. Why did villains always act in such a cliché manner? So she answered with a boring cliché. "I never mix business with pleasure."

"In that case you wouldn't mind if I bring in our prisoner, would you?"

The door opened again, and this time Marlena blinked. There was Stash, with a man standing behind him, prodding him into the room. Her heart skipped a beat, then started to dance a quick staccato. It hadn't been that long, but just the sight of him made her catch her breath.

She hadn't expected to see him again. And certainly hadn't expected the surge of happiness that burst forth from somewhere inside. How could a man make a room smaller by merely standing in it? Her eyes hungrily took in his appearance.

Although his hands appeared tied behind his back, a quick all-over scan reported that he wasn't injured. He looked so good in a black bomber jacket and black jeans. He was even wearing black cowboy boots. She was in the middle of a dangerous assignment and all she wanted to do was run to him and kiss him hard on those sensual lips. His dark eyes met hers across the room, and to her disgust he grinned, a wolfish slash of a smile. She sighed. That was all she needed. Complications.

"Nothing to say?" Cunningham mocked. "Is this man your pl-pleasure or your business, Marlena? You have to decide."

"How did you get him into this?" she asked, putting on a disinterested expression.

"He was following you all day, so I thought I would bring him to you. You're the expert here—didn't you know you were being followed?"

Of course she did, but she had thought it was Tess or the men after her. Certainly not Stash. He grinned devilishly, as if daring her to admit she was happy to see him! "People follow me all the time. That doesn't mean you have to capture them for me, Cunningham."

"Please, call me William."

Marlena wanted to call him something else, but right now she had to think quickly. This man was more dangerous than she had thought. And he had something up his sleeve. She could sense the danger around her. She turned her back to Steve and focused all her attention on William Cunningham.

"Okay, let's deal," she said.

Smiling, Cunningham laced his hands behind his head. "We have time. Your old lover won't be here for a while yet, if you're worried about interruption." His smile widened. "Ahhh, I see your b-boy toy here didn't like to hear about your past with du Scheum."

Marlena chose not to deny anything. She especially didn't want to glance Steve's way. "My past has nothing to do with our agreement."

Stash was a SEAL operative. He couldn't be captured that easily, so he must be there because he wanted to be. But first she needed time to gauge this man who had hired her for an exclusive sale.

She walked away from the bed, heading for the brocade love seats in the corner of the luxurious room. Sinking down into one of them, she sat with booted leg lounging nonchalantly over one arm, giving a picture of lazy indolence. She fingered the tassels on the small pillow by her. "Okay, I'm finally here, and all you have for me is a man. Anything else?"

Cunningham laughed and got off the bed. "You know, I really do like your style, Marlena. It's the first thing that drew me to you when I was looking around for someone to help me." He nodded at his man standing behind Steve. The man gave Steve a slight push toward Marlena. "Do you know why I chose you?"

Marlena answered in a bored rhetorical drawl, "No, why don't you tell me."

"A drink first, perhaps? Whiskey, wasn't it? I assure you I can make it better than your lackey."

The comment made her dart a quick look at Steve, who so far had remained silent. His eyes were alert, so he wasn't drugged or anything. He didn't react to the reference to the first night in her apartment, when he had attempted to make a drink for her. What was he thinking? She had never seen him docile, so she knew he was up to something.

Accepting the glass from William, she calculated the possibility of it being poisoned or drugged. But her dead body in Pierre du Scheum's house wouldn't be any good to William Cunningham at the moment. He still needed her to achieve his ends.

"It's not drugged," Cunningham told her, with a knowing gleam in his eyes. They clinked glasses. "To business, then pl-pleasure."

Marlena sipped, then glanced in Steve's direction again. Better try to find out what was going on with him. She crooked her brow inquiringly. "Can't live without me, can you, Stash?"

Cunningham interrupted before Steve could answer. "He obviously doesn't trust you, my dear."

"Oh?"

"Look at this and decide."

The older man snapped his fingers, and another assistant came in with a briefcase. Cunningham set it on the coffee table.

"First, let me make a formal introduction, my dear. I'm one of Pierre du Scheum's associates in a s-subsidiary within du Scheum Industries. I head the department that does research with the government, some of which is highly sensitive." He pulled out a folder. "In fact, I make sen-sensitive information my business."

A boast. She could use that weakness.

Marlena took the file he proffered and leafed through it. She glanced back up at Steve, careful not to betray any emotions. His expression offered no clues about his feelings, either. How had Cunningham gotten hold of a report that was prepared by Stash?

Better attack before she was cornered, she decided. Carelessly flipping the folder back on the coffee table, she leaned back and took a swallow from her whiskey. "So what if I'm not the real Marlena? I've been doing well the last two years, haven't I?" She smiled challengingly at Cunningham. "Besides, I think I look better than the original Marlena, don't you agree? Those old faded photos the CIA boys took of her from her Berlin days were horrible."

Cunningham studied her with narrowed eyes. His stutter was more pronounced. "Y-you don't s-seem afraid, but of course a woman like y-you can't fear m-much. But you must admit this makes you very s-sus-suspicious to me. You can be someone laying a trap, after all."

Marlena shrugged. "Look, I have two years in the game without you bothering me. You contacted me, remember?" Then she frowned. "Wait a minute. You were the one who hired Stash for me, remember? So you're setting me up! What are you talking about?"

The older man looked at both Marlena and Steve for a few seconds. "I didn't hire him. Mr. McMillan's team of CIA agents got hold of the man who was going to take care of all those details that you favor. As you know, they are very interested in your current activities."

"So why didn't you warn me?" demanded Marlena.

"Why should I? I knew ev-everything that was happening and if I can see everything, the better my control." Cunningham's light eyes gleamed triumphantly. "Which brings us back to the is-issue at hand. You were interrogated. Mr. McMillan found out things that exposed you. How come they let you go? Unless you cut a deal with them or you had been working with them all along."

"You fool!" Marlena stood up and stepped closer to the

man sitting across from her. Something warned her he didn't like being told that he had made a mistake, and she ruthlessly exploited this suspicion. She wagged an accusing finger at him. "*You* allowed these guys in my apartment. *You* didn't warn me of any of this, even at Pierre's function the other night. I have to extricate myself from trouble, and now you dare accuse me of being on their side?"

To stress her point, she boldly stepped one leg on the low table, leaning closer, threateningly enough to have one of his men move forward, a hand going inside his suit for his weapon. Cunningham put up a hand to stop him. Marlena pretended not to notice, carrying on with her tirade. "You even tried to use me as a foil to kill off Pierre, didn't you? They were after me because of the attempt on Pierre's life, you idiot." She tossed a sarcastic glare at Steve. "I suppose I have you to thank for saving his life, since if he were dead now, I would still be in that hole being questioned. Well, say something!"

Oh, but his mermaid was magnificent. Steve stood there admiring the quick way she turned the tables on the enemy with mere words, establishing doubt without an ounce of fear. And she gave him the perfect opening to say something without sounding fake. Tess had told him that Marlena would try to feel out a situation before her next move and to wait for her prompting before giving her any clue. "You're welcome," he said, in the same sarcastic tone. "You can thank me later, *darling*."

She didn't show any sign that she got the hint that T. had sent him. "Harden put you up to it, didn't he? Following me to find proof." Marlena gave Cunningham an angry glare. "And your foolishness led him right to you. You're an idiot!"

"Enough!" Cunningham ordered sharply.

Marlena ignored the warning. "I'm not going to do business with you," she declared. "I only deal with professionals. And you, Mr. Cunningham, are obviously an amateur at this."

"You forget, I have your files here," Cunningham picked up the folder and slapped it against one hand. He was frowning, for the first time looking unsure of himself. "I can use this against you."

"And who's going to believe you? Anything can be faked these days." Marlena straightened up and zipped up her leather jacket. "I don't even believe you have anything to sell."

"Does the Project X Solar Aquabotics 2000 ring a bell? And believe me, my electronic re-resources are beyond your imagination. I can see and copy anything in Mr. McMillan's office."

Steve stopped his sharp intake of breath. Man, she was good. She had that idiot boasting without thinking, which was exactly what Tess said Marlena's main job was. Get information, record it.

Project X-S-BOT. He tried to remember what Hawk had told him. Hawk sometimes worked with a very covert SEAL team that was part of the Naval Warfare Development Group. Steve had thought of joining his cousin there at one time.

Hawk had mentioned a new solar robotics project called Project X-S-BOT when the network news reported that a very important laptop had disappeared during a meeting between top scientists and politicians. Project X-S-BOT had technology that harnessed solar robotics and satellite technology in military espionage. Hawk and Steve had speculated over what was in the missing laptop that had the whole naval scientific community in a big brouhaha.

Must be something big, Hawk, Steve silently mocked. Was this what Tess meant about buying and selling at the party the other night? Was this the kind of deal that everyone was negotiating? Another world from his soldiering one, for sure.

It hadn't taken him very long to realize that every entity of importance in this town was crazy. How could anyone live and work here and differentiate between white and black? From the night at du Scheum's party, he had concluded that both ends of the scale mingled together socially, almost daring the other side to catch them at their own game. No wonder he couldn't tell which side Marlena worked for.

Even now he had no proof, apart from what Tess had told him. Yet he willingly went along with her plans because she had told him Marlena was in danger. He watched her now, in her element, walking the edge of a perilous situation, and understood why this woman was the way she was.

She wasn't someone who played a role; she had to *be* the very person she was now. She had been living and breathing Marlena Maxwell for two years, so it was no wonder her act convinced him. However, he recalled the few instances when something had kindled in the depths of those remarkable blue eyes, something soft and vulnerable that never failed to give him a swift kick in the gut. He promised himself that he would peel past this layer to find that woman somehow. Later. After this "let the guy tell all first" stuff.

He himself preferred some good old-fashioned ass kicking, but as Tess had pointed out to him earlier, one had to find out whose butt to kick first. So he had gone along with her plan. Like the woman in front of him, Tess was more than she seemed, with extensive knowledge of covert activities. Steve didn't think he could be surprised anymore, what with her getup earlier and the smooth way she changed from one person into another. There was no doubt now that he was dealing with a very well-trained entity.

He had even let her dress him up like some Mafia cowboy. Marlena would look closer, she had said. He had scowled at a certain item he had to wear. He hoped she noticed it, all right.

He studied this William Cunningham character, who looked nothing like any of the tough war-worn antagonists he had faced. This guy didn't even look intimidating; he didn't need to, with the two men in the room and the two outside the door.

Being in du Scheum's residence came as a surprise. Why did Cunningham choose to bring Marlena here to meet him? He returned his attention to the conversation, even as he subtly loosened the knots behind his back. An old SEAL trick—a small razor blade was easier to hide than a big knife, and sometimes handier.

"The missing laptop from the Progressive Solar Robotics Technology meeting at the Naval Research Lab," Marlena was saying to Cunningham. "That was in all the papers for a while. *You* have it?"

"It was surprisingly easy to just pick up a laptop and leave. Everyone has a laptop these days. Security is lax at the NRL," Cunningham sneered.

Marlena unzipped her leather jacket and sat back down on the love seat. "Why didn't you tell me sooner? Why make me drive around there—to admire your workplace? That's what that was all about, wasn't it? You were showing me your access, your power." Her voice had turned into a croon. Steve watched, fascinated, as she transformed from furious woman to languid female in two seconds. Her smile was dazzling, inviting. She played with her front zipper with lazy fingers, eyes half closed. "That laptop is worth a lot of money."

"Yes," Cunningham agreed.

"And do you have it here with you?"

"I thought you didn't want to do business with me. An amateur." It was the older man's turn to mock.

Marlena pouted. "I thought you were trying to use me to get at du Scheum. You still are, but let's hear what you have in mind."

"Even at the expense of one of your men's lives?"

Steve tried to ignore the jealousy burning his insides. Marlena and du Scheum an item? That explained their familiarity with each other the other night. His eyes were drawn to the bed. No. He wouldn't think about that right now. But he wasn't going to let her use and discard him. Soon she would know that he was more than a lackey. The razor blade between his fingers gnawed slowly at the rope.

"Well, I prefer not think in terms like that," Marlena told Cunningham. "Lives are expensive. And getting rid of them can mess things up. You have been so careful thus far—why the need to get rid of lives at all, especially du Scheum?"

"If I don't, he'll know who stole the laptop, and I can't have that, can I? You see, when I took it, I didn't know that du Scheum gave parties to facilitate business deals like these. Oh, I knew he had influence, but I thought he just had political pull."

"Instead you discovered Pierre and I were good friends," Marlena guessed.

Cunningham nodded, finishing his drink. "A complication, especially when he knows all the deals out there. So of course once the laptop becomes the object to bid, he would be informed, since part of Project X-S-BOT involved du Scheum's own company."

"Let me guess, you hired that man to kill du Scheum the other night," she said dryly.

"Except for Mr. McMillan's interference, I would have suc-succeeded! Then you would have the item out for sale and negotiation, without any suspicion falling on me." Cunningham used his empty glass to point at Steve. "He had to get in the way. He was responsible for making your identity known, too."

Marlena sighed. "I didn't anticipate knocking off all my current men. My price just went up. They're both important to me." Her smile at Steve was full of mockery.

"I'm flattered," Steve murmured, planning revenge. The bonds tying his hands were already loose. He understood that Marlena was giving him the time he needed by keeping Cunningham talking. After all, he had firsthand knowledge of how crafty she could be, and how aware of unseen things around her. No doubt she already anticipated that Tess would make a move soon. He kept an eye on the other two men. There was something expectant in their stance, as if they were listening for something.

"Tsk. Lovers can be replaced," Cunningham suggested silkily.

Marlena cocked her head. "Do you think I will off these two just like that, for you? And how do you propose to do this, since you already appear to have a plan in mind?"

"It's simple really. When du Scheum returns, you can surprise him. He won't be expecting you in his bedroom." Cunningham looked at his surroundings, then shrugged. "We'll make it look like he surprised sailor boy, who of course will get blamed for his untimely death. He'll be our sc-scapegoat, and no one will question much since he was there when du Scheum was shot, too. They will think he botched that one chance."

"Don't you think the authorities would be suspicious and investigate further?"

"You don't have to worry your pretty little head about the investigation. Du Scheum has many enemies, and I've ensured that if they look deeper into McMillan's past, they will find enough things to make him look bad."

Ah, that explained the overseas account, Marlena thought. She would bet money on it that Stash had no idea about what Cunningham was talking. "What about his bodyguards?"

"My men will take care of them, but I only trust you with du Scheum. You can prove to me once and for all that you are what you say you are, if not exactly who." Cunningham's voice had a darker edge. "Take care of both of them, and the laptop will be out in public without any questions. What do you say, Marlena? You and I can make a good team."

This was it. Steve felt the tension gathering thicker. He watched as Marlena approached him, her blue eyes searching his, making sure he was ready. He willed himself to silently let her know that he was. She clasped her hands behind her back, like someone contemplating a decision. She came closer and slowly lifted a hand to touch him. She reached up and flicked a finger at the little pearl dangling from his ear.

She cocked a brow at it, and her smile turned positively evil. He didn't dare respond in kind. Tess's handiwork—a little pearl earring with a microbug in it. Ostentatious enough to catch Marlena's attention. Pearls, he was beginning to guess, were his mermaid's secret passion. GEM. Pearls. The rings on Tess's fingers. Hmm.

Clasping her hands behind her back again, she pivoted around to face Cunningham, who was watching them carefully. "Do I have a choice? You hold all the cards," she said softly. "But where is this laptop? How do I know you won't renege?"

Cunningham pulled out a laptop from a briefcase. Steve recognized it immediately as a similar brand to the one in Marlena's possession when he searched her belongings.

The older man's smile was triumphant, with a touch of cunning in it. Clicking the laptop open, he turned it on. "Come and see."

It took a few minutes for the program to run its course. Steve wished he could just walk over there, too, like Marlena. There was a look of concentration on her face as she stood there looking at the screen, her arms folded across her chest.

Something else caught his eye. The man guarding Cunningham wasn't looking at either his boss or Marlena. He kept looking at the entrance to the room every few minutes. It made Steve uneasy. He also realized that the bigger man who was supposed to be behind him was no longer there. He was standing closer to Marlena than to him. Granted, he was supposed to be tied, but still, shouldn't he be guarded?

Steve's instincts kicked in again as he brought back his hostage-taking training. It was a trick he had learned from his cousin—he blurred his mind, putting aside what was obvious. There was always a hostage decoy. He wasn't the target here.

Marlena didn't seem aware of anything wrong as she leaned down and tapped a few keyboard keys. "Encrypted," she murmured. "It could be junk."

"This is from the lab in Nevada. And I have the du Scheum files available. We can sell this piece by piece. More negotiation power that way." Cunningham wasn't looking at the screen but at Marlena's breasts. She was too busy reading to notice. Steve wanted to sucker punch the man as he watched him lick his lips.

"Parts of this are encrypted," Marlena said. "I suppose that's their problem, not ours."

"I have the codes for the du Scheum files but not for the

Nevada files. But I know where they are." There was a pause. "Downstairs, in du Scheum's safe."

Marlena swept a sideways glance at Cunningham, then straightened. She patted her hair back into place. "Well, well, my darling Pierre is keeping something from me," she murmured. "You know, William, I might like you after all. Pretty devious. Get rid of Stash and Pierre and you think I know where that safe is, hmm?"

"Not think. I know you know." Cunningham's voice hardened again. "And you'll tell me where it is first, or we torture your boy here finger by finger, limb by limb before we kill him. You f-forget, I've seen you with him. You harbor a certain f-fondness for him, shall we say? Although I must admit it really disappointed me."

Cunningham stood up and looked at the big man who had been guarding Steve, who was now standing closer to Marlena. Steve thought he saw a tinge of surprise in Cunningham's gaze.

"Time, isn't it, Dankin?" Cunningham addressed the bodyguard. He frowned, looking momentarily puzzled, as if things weren't quite going the way he wanted. He jerked his head toward Steve, trying to get his meaning across.

However, Dankin stepped toward Marlena instead, one hand reaching out for her neck.

"Now," Steve barked out, hoping Tess was where she was supposed to be. He shook the loosened bonds free and lunged, determined to push Marlena out of harm's way.

All at once the room plunged into darkness. Someone had killed the master switch.

Chapter Fourteen

The bedroom door smashed open. Shouts. Popping sounds. The fireflash of a weapon being discharged. A flashlight interrupted the darkness, zigzagging its way around the room.

Steve ignored them all. Right now he was after a big bruiser named Dankin, who had gone after Marlena's throat. He had kept his eyes on him, knowing that when the switch was thrown, it would be impossible for a few seconds to locate anyone or anything.

The last thing he saw was Marlena bending over to pick up the laptop at his sudden command, as if she had been waiting for his move. He wasn't sure whether she saw who was coming after her.

Dankin had her by the arm. The beam from the flashlight settled on the blade in his hand. The man had switched to a knife in the dark, a good weapon to make sure he got his target where he wanted. And he was heading for her throat.

Fury like nothing he'd ever felt before imploded inside Steve, lending him the extra speed to block the descending hand. This big bodyguard was faster than he had thought. Faster, and very capable with the knife.

Marlena had somehow freed herself. Through the din in the room, Steve heard her calling.

"Stash, watch out, he has a knife."

Like he didn't know. "Stay out of the way," he yelled back. His eyes were getting used to the junglelike darkness.

He caught the flash of the blade again and jumped out of the way. His opponent's brute strength was evidenced by the swoosh of air somewhere near his belly. He caught a brawny wrist and swung the arm outward, turning himself as he did so and viciously jabbing his elbow against the man's kidney.

With his height advantage, Dankin reached over his shoulder to attack with his other hand, clamping his fingers under Steve's chin, reaching for the throat. Steve ignored the oncoming chokehold, bending forward and efficiently breaking the wrist of the bigger man. To his credit Dankin only grunted, loosening his hold. Steve turned away from the grasping fingers around his neck; twisting the broken wrist, he forced the man around and head-butted him in the chin.

Dankin crumpled to the floor. The lights came back on at that precise moment.

Steve maneuvered the jagged blade against the big man's throat. "Gotcha," he said, his voice grim with satisfaction.

"I must admit, my bedroom has never been this popular with men before."

Steve looked up to see the head of du Scheum Industries at the doorway, surveying his room with a bemused expression. He turned his attention back to Dankin, who lay on his back, blood dripping from nose and mouth, looking back with a blank, obstinate stare. Steve put pressure on the knife just a fraction, enough to pierce the man's skin, then released his hold. Tess said she wanted them alive for information.

He stood up and took in the aftermath. There was du Scheum, and three of his bodyguards. There was Dankin at his feet, and . . . two dead men. William Cunningham had a bullet hole in the middle of his forehead. His lifeless eyes looked straight at du Scheum, an expression of surprise still on his face, a small trickle of blood at the corner of his lips. The other bodyguard had also been shot to death. Steve recalled two more standing outside the door before, and he wondered whether they had experienced a similar fate.

And there was no Marlena in the room. He double-

checked, to make sure. Nope. She had slipped away with the
laptop. He noticed the French door to the balcony was ajar.

"It was important to get Cunningham alive," Steve
pointed out as he tucked away the knife.

"It's difficult to wage a fight in the dark," du Scheum said
as he stepped further into his room. His gaze fell dispassion-
ately on the dead Cunningham. "I didn't think he would be
the one who stole the laptop, but then it's always the quiet
ones."

"He had access to people inside the CIA and also in your
house. Without him, we'll never know who the moles are." It
was stating the obvious, but since Tess was probably listening in, Steve thought he'd better let her know that part of her
plan hadn't worked out. He wasn't going to ask how du
Scheum knew when to arrive. He had a feeling he wouldn't
get a straight answer.

Du Scheum shrugged. "My concern was to stop the leak
on my end. The rest isn't important."

Not important, hell. The man didn't care that highly classified security files were being passed in and out of the CIA
channels like used dollar bills in a bank. Of course not. The
man depended on the buying and selling of secured information at his parties. So the more leaks, as long as they weren't
from his end, the better his power base.

Steve shoved his hands into his pockets, disgusted with
the situation. He wasn't going to bring up the missing Marlena, either. He couldn't help feeling slightly antagonistic
toward du Scheum, knowing that she and the older man had
a history together. "Now what?" he asked.

"We call the police, of course. I don't hide dead bodies,
Mr. McMillan."

"They are going to ask a whole lot more questions this
time, Mr. du Scheum."

"Birman will handle it. He was protecting me, as usual."

Steve recognized Birman, the man who had saved du
Scheum the other night. They nodded at each other. "They
won't buy that. How was he protecting you?" Steve asked. "I
don't think you walked right in here."

"My dear Mr. McMillan, this is my bedroom. Of course I have every right to walk in here expecting some kind of safety. Fortunately for me, my bodyguard is always more careful than I am and spotted these men waiting in my room. He disposed of two of them. And then there is . . . Dankin, whom you overpowered."

"You know him?"

"I know all of them. They are in my employ. Cunningham obviously bought their services."

"That also means that you can't trust your own people, Mr. du Scheum. There were more than two of your employees in his pay. In fact there were two outside the door, and I don't see them now."

Du Scheum nodded, a thoughtful look in his eyes. Steve frowned. The man was like one of his robots. If it were his outfit that had men betraying him, he would be doing more than just standing there looking around thoughtfully. He would be tearing the place apart looking for the bastards. Instead the businessman was unruffled by two attempts on his life and perhaps a whole household of insiders working for the enemy.

Not his problem, Steve told himself.

Du Scheum gestured to Birman, who nodded and left the room. "I'll handle the police," du Scheum addressed Steve. "You should leave now. As for the two men you mentioned, don't worry. With Cunningham dead, I'm sure I'll find plenty of wagging tongues pointing to them." He looked around again in distaste. "For some reason, the comforts of my own bedroom don't hold any more appeal."

"You'll have to be doubly careful from now on," Steve warned, ready to go once Dankin was secured.

"Thank you. Just follow my man. He'll show you downstairs and give you access to a vehicle. Please tell Marlena I said hello, and that I'll be expecting to see her soon."

Not without me there you won't. "I'll make sure she gets the message," Steve replied. Casting one final look at the surly Dankin, he followed one of the bodyguards out of the huge master bathroom.

He was given the keys to a Beamer. He had no idea how he was going to return the car, but didn't waste time asking. One thing he had picked up from this adventure—use the prop at hand and go from there. He drove the powerful car down the long driveway, stopping at the electronic gate, which opened slowly. He put the car in park right between the two brick gateposts, interrupting the gate sensors, and waited. He wasn't leaving without Marlena.

He stuck his head out and whistled. From the left a shadowy figure dropped down from the high wall, landing with catlike grace. The back door of the vehicle opened and the interior light came on. The person had a black hood on.

The door next to him opened then and another figure jumped in. Steve put the car in gear and drove off. He glanced at the woman's profile to his right, then looked at the rearview mirror. Tess had already pulled off her face cover.

"A nice car would get a guy some fine chicks," he mocked, baring a wolfish grin at both ladies. He was having fun, after all.

Marlena was scowling at him, obviously not at all liking his presence near her. Steve felt his temper rising again. Well, too bad. She would just have to get used to it.

What was Stash doing working so closely with Tess? What had she told him? Marlena didn't like the idea of them together at all, not one bit. And why did he have to look so damn hot? She wanted to lean forward, kiss that mouth, and forget about her problems, but since he was one of them, kissing him would definitely not solve it. She focused on the woman in the backseat instead.

She turned to look at Tess, studying for a long moment the woman with the jet-black spiky hairdo in black leather from head to—she peered over the seat—toe. She was even wearing black gloves. Her gray eyes were glinting in amusement as she sat back there, seemingly content to be silent for now. She slanted a glance at Stash's leather jacket, then unzipped her own black one.

"I feel like I've just joined a black leather fashion show," Marlena drawled, choosing mockery over demanding questions. "Nice get-up, T. Joining our rock band?"

"Too many catfights over the sexy male lead," Tess drawled back, taking up the whole backseat with a deceptively relaxed sprawl. "Not that it matters, of course, since I always win."

"Always?" Marlena raised an eyebrow at the challenge. What exactly did Tess mean by that remark? Did she mean Stash?

"Always, darling."

"And since when have you developed a liking for catfights?" Marlena didn't bother to curb the hint of temper in her voice. She was suddenly feeling very territorial.

Tess's smile gleamed in the semidarkness, feral and knowing, like a cat with a bird in mind. "Who said I had?"

"Then why get into one now?" Marlena countered.

"Darling, I'm not the one hissing."

"I want to know what you're up to, T. You know my reasons for working alone. Maybe your working within a group the last couple of years has influenced your decision making, but don't forget, this is still my contract."

Tess shifted position, twisting one of the rings on her finger. Her tone of voice was sleepy, as if she had heard all this before. "Who called me for information? I was perfectly content in New York, darling. Besides, you seem unhappy that I've found someone new to work with."

Marlena felt like baring her teeth and snarling. Instead she stared with narrowed eyes at Tess, trying to read her friend's devious mind. Tess's manipulating techniques were legendary among their peers, and Marlena had spent years fencing with her, but since Tess's stint with that group of men, she had gotten even worse. Or better, depending on where one was standing. It didn't matter. Tess was up to no good. Those half-closed slanted eyes shone with mischief.

"Ladies," Steve interrupted the standoff, his voice rich with male amusement. "Can't we just get along?"

Marlena didn't want to talk to him. He had found out who

she was, then abandoned her. Now he showed up with Tess, obviously having spent some time with *her*. Never mind that she herself had decided she was going to forget about him. That was then; this was now. If he wanted to play kissing games, it had better be with her.

"What were you doing, letting yourself get caught?" she demanded, shifting her anger to the real object of her irritation.

Steve gave her a sideways glance. "Saving your ass."

"Saving my ass? I didn't need you to save my ass!"

"Yeah, right. What about the knife-wielding bodyguard? You think he was just attempting to give you a haircut?"

His voice was a notch lower, but she ignored the danger sign. "I can take care of myself."

"Ha, you weren't looking his way. Your mind was on how to get the laptop out of there."

Her mind had been on several things actually. "I was wondering how to get *you* out of there!" She remembered the moment of panic when she realized that the attacker had a knife and that Steve was going to get slashed. She had hesitated long enough to make sure he was going to be all right, then done her job, which was to secure the laptop.

"I'm here now," Steve pointed out.

"You weren't here yesterday." The words tumbled out. Marlena knew she sounded illogical, but she couldn't stop herself. Where was he when she truly needed him?

"No, *you* weren't *there* yesterday," Steve growled back, his voice another notch lower.

Tess's smoky laugh broke their verbal exchange. "Can't we just get along?" she mimicked.

Marlena jerked around and glared at Tess. A biting retort rose to her lips, something stinging that she knew would shut her friend up. All she had to do was refer to Alex, and she knew Tess would back off a little. But she couldn't. Of all things, she understood the raw pain of walking away from someone one cared about too much. Pursing her lips, she turned back to face the front and hoped her silence would get the message across to Tess.

"Stop messing with my mind," she muttered softly.

"My job," Tess replied calmly. "But that's enough for tonight, I suppose. I'll drop both of you off at Marlena's hotel and take this nice little car home with me. I'll pick both of you up tomorrow morning at 0900 hours. We have a meeting with Admiral Madison."

This was getting to be an overcrowded affair. "May I know why?" Marlena asked, then added sarcastically, "Since this is my contract."

"I'm sure Stash will fill you in later," drawled Tess, obviously forgetting about her previous comment that she wasn't going to mess with Marlena's mind any more for the night, "or maybe you prefer to be alone? If so, Stash and I can drop you off."

Marlena tossed a stormy gaze at Steve. "He can do whatever he wants," she answered stonily, not wanting to admit that she wanted him with her. Who was she to tell him what to do, anyway? He was working with Tess. "Or maybe he's waiting for his next orders."

Steve stopped at a red light. "I'm taking us to the hotel. You and I are getting out. Then I'll follow you to your room. We'll close the door behind us. And then"—he looked her straight in the eye, and she saw, too late, that she'd ignored all the warning signs—"I'll do what I want."

Chapter Fifteen

Among his SEAL teammates, Steve was known to be the patient one, the man everyone wanted on point duty in a scope-out for danger ahead. When he walked point, he relied on his teammates to look out for danger around while he was looking down at the trail, making sure it was safe. His life was in their hands, and theirs were totally dependent on his sight and patience.

He must have been too busy looking down at the trail after Marlena, Steve thought as he got out of the car after parking it at Marlena's hotel. If he had looked up just once, so to speak, he would have been aware of how far off the mark everyone else around him was. Nobody seemed to be following the trail that he had cleared for them.

That was the problem, he mocked, as he stood on the curb waiting for Marlena and Tess. He was too patient. Too reliant on his ability to clear paths. None of these folks had asked for a point man; they all were charging full steam ahead. Harden and Task Force Two. Marlena. Tess. The admiral. Even du Scheum was busy covering for his business deals.

He had a few things to say about the whole damn thing, but he was going to be patient one more time. He would wait for the right moment. Right now the frustration he had left simmering since finding Marlena gone was at boiling point. That kind of patience he didn't have. That woman wasn't going to give him an inch. If he just stood there, she would drive on by pretending she didn't see him. That didn't sit too well with him at all.

"That laptop," he said to both women, who had gotten out of the car. Tess was walking to the driver's side. "There's still some people after it. Marlena had some threatening phone calls at the other place."

"Don't worry about them," Marlena said.

"I say, let's," Steve countered, watching the stubborn tilt of those lips. "Why not find out who they are? Get rid of them once and for all."

"I give up!" Marlena stalked away with the laptop, heading off toward the hotel entrance. She tossed Tess a glare as she passed by, adding, "You started this. You explain it to him. I don't like having someone tell me how to get my job done."

Steve was about to go after her, seething for that overdue confrontation, when Tess's hand on his arm stopped his progress. He turned to her impatiently. "I have to go," he said shortly.

"You can keep for another five minutes," Tess told him calmly.

He reluctantly watched Marlena walk farther away. "What is it?"

"Marlena isn't used to working with someone."

"Too bad."

"She is given an assignment, reports back to either me or someone else, gets enough information to proceed, and gets her job done."

Steve shrugged. "I'm not arguing with her over her job."

"It's a matter of style, hmm?" Tess ran a finger down the front of the leather jacket. "She doesn't communicate like a team member. You've functioned within one, know how to disperse certain information to help the team achieve the task. Marlena is . . . not good with that."

"Why are you telling me this, T.?" Steve asked, frustrated and impatient.

"Darling, I don't tell anything without a reason," Tess

replied, and moved away. "When she asked you not to worry about the people after the laptop, you took umbrage. Why?"

"Because they are a danger to her. What's wrong with being worried about that?" It hurt that Marlena had pushed him away when he was trying to show that he cared about her.

Tess shook her head, then turned to open the car door. "Both blind as bats and obstinate as mules," she muttered as she got in. The streetlight gave her gray eyes a strange glitter as she peered up at Steve. Tilting her head slightly, she added, "It's a matter of semantics, darling. M. meant it another way. She asked you not to worry about them because they're part of her mission. Just keep in mind that she has worked alone for a long time, Steve, okay? She doesn't like to share her thoughts too much."

"Part of . . . I see. She wanted to be found." Steve frowned and leaned down, his hand on the roof of the car. "She knows who they are?"

"Don't look at me for answers. I've none where you two are concerned. Just don't walk away unless you are very sure."

Tess's expression was grave, although her voice still held an amused note. Steve studied her for a moment. Tess, who he knew by now could talk circles around anyone, was directly telling him something from the heart. She might coat on that mockery and laughter thick and fast, but he felt the sincerity in her advice. He nodded. "I won't," he told her quietly. "Thanks."

She flicked her hand, dismissing him. "The first five minutes are free. It's $3.99 a minute from now on, darling."

Steve grinned and took a step back. She fired up the car. "She probably locked me out."

"She won't. She'll give you another five minutes before she comes after you."

Oh, that sounded good. "You think?"

"Here's the elevator key to the top floor. You can't just press the button at this place. You've got the room keycard?"

"Yes." He bent down again to take the key from her, and

to his surprise, with her hand still in his, Tess leaned out and gave him a quick kiss on the lips.

"See you two tomorrow." Tess gave him a sultry smile and a wink and backed the car out.

Steve acknowledged her wave and turned toward the hotel, which sat atop a small hill. He barely paid attention to the grandeur of the hotel lobby as he made his way to the elevators. While waiting, he took note of the exit points and the few people that he could see, but his mind was on Marlena upstairs. She wanted a fight? Well, he would give her one, but this time he was on equal ground.

He got on the elevator and inserted the key before punching the floor number. The red light turned green and the elevator door closed. He wasn't going to play lackey anymore, humoring her orders and wishes. There wasn't any need. She knew who he was and vice versa, and he didn't see why she felt threatened by that.

He stepped out into the huge foyer. He looked for the arrows that would show him where to find her suite. Unlike the usual plastic plaques, these were etched on metal and held up by some Greek statue that pointed in the same direction. Steve's lips quirked. Obviously the rich needed bigger road signs than normal folks.

He reached the suite, carefully considering his options. Should he ring the bell? Or should he just use the keycard and walk in? Why would that make a difference?

The door swung open and a pair of intense blue eyes met his like a laser beam. Marlena's arm reached out and grabbed the collar of his leather jacket and pulled hard. Steve didn't resist, following her into the suite. The heavy door closed quietly behind him.

She pushed him down into some chair by the entrance—he didn't have time to look around yet—and jumped on top of him, squishing the air out of his lungs. Not that he was breathing. Her breath was hot against his face. Her hands were busy, moving all over him. Her lips locked on his and her tongue pushed in, fierce and sweet.

What were his last thoughts? Something about options.

Steve felt her hand grope his pants, and his whole lower body jerked up when her hand invaded, targeting his suddenly wide-awake member. He felt it eagerly rising for its treat, like a well-trained pet. Her hand was too damn efficient, sliding up the whole length of him and squeezing. Manhandling him, in fact.

He grabbed her face with both hands and forced her back. Her hair tumbled all over the place and her expression was defiant as she continued to fondle him, her thighs forcing his legs to part further so she could delve deeper into his pants. Staring into her angry eyes, he demanded, with the little concentration he had left, "What do you think you're doing?" He hadn't expected this kind of attack.

"I'm marking my territory," Marlena said, and ripped the T-shirt under his jacket. "Take these damn things off."

Marlena had doubled back and seen that kiss. The fury that had welled up at the thought of Stash and T. together slammed down like a tidal wave. She had never thought much about the expression "seeing red" till she saw them so intimately close. But she did now.

It took all her control to turn away and go up to her suite. It would not do to be caught spying on them like a jealous wife. She wasn't jealous! She wasn't going to get jealous.

Easier said than done. In the elevator, the red monster had turned green, and it gnawed at her as she stomped into her room. Pacing only added fuel to the furnace inside her.

Did he enjoy that kiss? What was he doing now? Where was he, anyway? Did he think he could just move on to the next woman, right under her nose? Did he think that working with T. meant that he could just breeze by her?

Five minutes. Where the hell was he?

When she jerked open the door, she caught sight of T.'s red lipstick on his mouth. It was just a small smear, but she zeroed in on it like a bull to a waving flag. Marked him, did she? Let her mark him, did he?

Marlena didn't stop to think about what she was doing. All she felt was the need to run her hands all over him, to let him know exactly who turned him on and not let him forget it. If it took more than once to teach him that lesson, well, so be it. She had all night.

"Take the damn things off!" she repeated, and shredded another piece of what was left of the front of his T-shirt.

Steve's reply was equally ferocious. With one hand he ripped her lacy black blouse from collar to sleeve, exposing flesh and bra. "All's fair," he growled.

Marlena lunged forward and bit him on the chest, marking him. He grunted and half pushed, half lifted her off him as he tried to get off the chair. She bit harder, mad as hell that he was fighting her.

She was going to take a chunk out of him! Steve grabbed her by the neck, and using his free arm, finally stood up. Obviously, the woman wasn't in the mood to talk. That was fine by him. If she wanted war, he was willing to oblige. His hand still on her neck, he turned her around and quickly wrapped his arms under hers, but she was a second faster, having anticipated his locking motion. He only managed to grab part of her short jacket and she shrugged out fluidly, like wet soap in his hand. He threw her jacket over his shoulder as he went after her.

She dropped down sideways, tripping him over her. He used his hands to break his fall, and she took the opportunity to land on his back. Steve grunted as she kneed him where it hurt. He felt her hand pull aside his leather jacket. He had stuck Dankin's knife back there earlier.

Shit. He lay perfectly still as the sharp blade swished through the air above him, cutting with proficient ruthlessness. He heard the scrape of leather against metal. Well, it had been a nice leather jacket. She kneed him harder as she cut through belt and pants. He was going to have a bad bruise there. Then her hand was on his naked back, pushing aside whatever was left of his clothes. The moment she stopped brandishing that knife he reared up, toppling her backward, and turning quickly he grabbed her ankle.

Marlena kicked out at him. And left a boot behind when she pulled back. Still on his knees, he tossed it over his shoulder. She rolled several times to avoid his quick counter moves, losing her other boot as he tried to grab that leg. He finally lunged forward and gripped her around the waist, using his weight to pin her.

Marlena knew that she was at a disadvantage as long as she remained on the defensive. Instinct and training made her twist at the same time, and his weight caught behind her thighs, his hands still holding on to her waist. She faked a jab at him with the knife, knowing he would try to block it. Sure enough, he tried to grab her hand, and she immediately dropped the knife and used both her hands to help her twist and scoot forward. Right out of her pants.

Steve growled at the empty pair of pants in his hands and under his body, then pushed them out of the way. His glare was met with an equally determined one as she looked back at him while she scooted on all fours to a safer distance. He wiped the sweat dripping off his chin. That's it. No more Mr. Nice Guy. He stood up. And his shredded pants fell down in a dismal pool around his ankles. He kicked them off impatiently, along with his boots. A low rumble escaped his lips as he stalked his prey.

Slowly standing up, Marlena registered with a vague awareness that she was wrestling in her underwear. Her opponent was more beast than man at the moment, tattered clothing hanging on his magnificently sculpted body, barely hiding his briefs. The muscles on his bare legs were coiled with tension, bringing every line of sinew into relief. His hair stuck out where she had pulled at it, parts of it plastered against his forehead. She met his eyes.

They were midnight-black, glittering back at her, promising punishment. And her heart, which was already beating hard from exertion, roared like a runaway train. The wildness in his eyes called to the wildness in her heart. His nose flared as he stalked closer, as if he were really some wild animal scenting a mate. She bent her knees slightly, ready to counter any attack.

For endless charged seconds they stared at each other. There was fury. And excitement. And white-hot desire.

"War? Or love?" he asked, making both sound like a threat.

War. She hated his guts. Love. She wanted him like no other man. Both. "You're on," she snarled, eyes narrowing.

They both leaped at each other at the same time.

Arms grabbed and pushed. Legs kicked and twined together. And their bodies rolled across the thick soft carpet. A lamp fell over with a crash. A vase tumbled off its stand, barely missing Steve's head. He had pulled off some material from somewhere, and it wrapped itself around the leg of the coffee table as Marlena rolled on top of him. Steve flipped her back, pulling off whatever was left covering her body.

A soft groan, quieted by a conquering mouth. Flesh slid against flesh as hands ruthlessly explored each other, making each other moan, pushing each other higher.

Finally pinning her with his weight, Steve clamped his teeth down on Marlena's neck, sucking on her rapid pulse, tasting her feminine saltiness, holding her down as he forced her legs wide apart. She jerked her hips left and right, avoiding his thrusts; he bit down a little harder, making her gasp. Her nails were sharp where they dug into his back. He put his hand between her legs, palming her ready wetness with a wicked touch. She jerked again and her nails dug harder. And still she refused to let him in, bucking him off the moment he tried to thrust inside.

He would make her stay still yet. Throwing her legs over his shoulders, he started loving her with his mouth instead. With her trussed up and open wide in that position, every attempt she made to escape only served to give him better access to her sweetness, and the advantage was his.

He feasted. He licked. He used his lips and tongue and teeth as she fought off her climax. Her scent drove him crazy and he opened her wider, delving his face against her heat as he kept making love to her with his fingers. Her hands in his hair at first pulled, then roamed, then stopped altogether. Her pants became whimpers. That was when he got to the dessert. He licked around it. He stabbed his tongue softly on its protective cover, repeating until her whimpers became gurgles. He took his wet fingers out of her and slid them along the side of the nub. He blew on it. Her hips swiveled higher, begging him silently. He pinched it with his fingers. He had her now. He could feel every tensed muscle in her legs locked securely over his shoulders. *Mine. Mine.* He parted her with his fingers. Such a tiny little nerve, and all his. He twirled the pink quivering nub delicately with his tongue, then placed his whole lips around it, and sucked. Hard. She screamed his name. And this time, with a violence that almost knocked him over, she came.

That was how he wanted her. Screaming for him. Wanting him. Giving herself to him. His own need was sharp and painful, a heavy throbbing thudding between his legs. *No.* This time he had to be the one in control longer. This was war. He was going to conquer this woman. He took one final taste, burying his tongue in the tangy heat, and slowly dragging it over her clitoris. Her wet release only fed his already burning desire.

Marlena was still lost in a spiraling vortex of pleasure when Steve climbed back on top of her. He dragged her hands high above her head, lacing his fingers through hers, and kneed her legs apart. Spread-eagle and still climaxing, she didn't struggle when she felt him prodding, pushing determinedly into her softness. He squeezed her hands as he entered, making sure she couldn't fight back. Not that she wanted to. He felt too good. The friction of his hard possession against her already sensitized flesh made her moan, and she shivered as she started peaking again.

His groin ground against hers, and as if that wasn't enough for him, he pushed in deeper still, undulating against her clitoris that seemed to send lightning up and down her spine. Marlena went limp, letting her body take over.

He seemed happy to remain buried in her all the way, just flexing inside her. Something vibrated inside whenever he touched a certain place, driving her crazy with lust and need. And always, each flex inside rubbed him against her on the outside, too, until she couldn't tell where one climax ended and another began. Sensation spread like wildfire all the way to some center in her that seemed to have taken over her whole mind. Her head fell back as each wave hit her, and she clenched around his hard invasion, needing more of him.

That's when Steve lost control, and he jack-hammered in and out of her. She was slick from coming, and the silky possession of her body felt incredible. Tight. Hot. Eyes closed, totally lost in this sensual paradise, he pushed, felt the tip of her womb, and he wanted to touch her where no man ever had. He changed his angle and heard her strangled cry. There, she liked it there. His pleasure doubled as he felt her long ripples of ecstasy massage his whole length over and over.

More. He needed her to give him more. He buried in deep again and flexed.

And still Marlena kept climaxing, unable to rise to the surface, hit over and over by the darkest of pleasures, hearing her heartbeat. His heartbeat. Feeling the hard pounding of his body into hers as those waves tossed her around in some magical space. She wasn't sure what he did, but she felt like dying. Every time he flexed, the feeling was akin to dropping down into some deep abyss. He was everywhere— in her, on her, scenting the air she gasped in, totally commanding all her senses. Out of control, her body continued to milk him greedily, even as her thighs trembled from the tension of each climax.

Suddenly he stopped, a rough growl escaping him, as if his body protested what his mind commanded. "Look at me." His order was harsh with emotion, bringing her back to reality.

He rose above her again, making her ache for him to come back. She opened her eyes reluctantly to meet his, dark and heated with lust, his lips sensual as he pleasured himself against her. His expression was triumphant, very male, very satisfied with himself.

"You can't hold me down forever." She meant to sound challenging, but her voice came out weak and breathless.

His little thrusts were torturous. She wanted him to come back into her all the way. Little tremors shook her body. "You can't hold my hands above my head all night."

"You think not?" he taunted softly, his smile mocking her attempt to distract him. He lifted his hips slightly, then plunged into her deep velvet heat again, all the way. Her quick exhalation puffed gently against his face—warm and moist, like the rest of her. All his. He felt like a conquering barbarian. He felt like the wild animal that had won his mate after a fight. He smiled down and adjusted his hold slightly, pulling both her hands to each side of her face. "Honey, this is standard position for me. A Navy SEAL can easily do a hundred push-ups."

"A hundred?" She breathed out faintly. Could she take a hundred strokes?

"Or more," he murmured, and started demonstrating.

His breathing fell into a rhythm while he moved in and out of her as if he did sexual push-ups every day. His eyes were half closed as he gyrated against her sexually every time he impaled her, each slide keeping contact with that part of her that seemed to belong only to him.

For once in a long time, Marlena lost all sense of control, letting the man above her take over. This wasn't sex. This was claim staking, and she recognized it even as she wanted him to continue. He was male to her female, claiming her with his body, stamping her with his scent, searing her with his kiss. And she had never felt more wanted.

"I think I'll do this all night," he muttered to himself. "Keep you wet. Keep you wanting. Keep you coming for me. Yeah, like that."

Her spasms started with a slow shudder, responding to the sexual promises he whispered in her ear. Oh God, she couldn't possibly do it again. What he was telling her shouldn't excite her, shouldn't make her feel like this. She shook her head, trying to clear it.

"Come again, sweetheart." That velvet voice seduced her, even as her body started obeying. She heard her own deep-throated whimpers as she did as she was told.

"Again," he commanded, his tongue exploring her ear, stealing the last vestiges of rational thought. "Once more. Yeah."

She climaxed again. And again. And then he, too, began to shudder as he gave in to his own need. A deep groan rumbled from his chest as his hips moved faster and faster. She was vaguely aware of the passionate kiss he gave her, plundering her mouth. The muscles on his arms corded thickly as his body tensed in mid-plunge.

"Lena . . ."

"Stash . . ."

There wasn't any breath left for words. His hands were still holding her down when he collapsed on top of her. Their bodies were slick against each other. Dazed by the whole experience, Marlena could barely move. He finally rolled onto his back, breathing hard. She curled up on her side and tried to remember the last time she'd fallen asleep on the floor of a hotel room.

She didn't have the luxury to recall anything. An arm scooped under her and she was pulled onto her knees, then onto her feet. "Oh no," Steve whispered in her ear, as he swung her into his arms. "That was war. Now we get in bed and we make love." He looked around. "Where is the bedroom in this place, anyway?"

Marlena opened one eye. The bedroom light was still on, but from her vantage, she couldn't see much. There was an obstacle in her way. On top of her, actually. Approximately one hundred and eighty pounds. Six feet of musculature and testosterone. A sex machine whose switch had been on most of the night.

She didn't dare move. Mr. Happy Down There might still be awake, and she was much too sore to even contemplate going another round.

She should be damn mad. And uncomfortable to have a man sleeping on top of her. Yet, she wasn't. She felt . . . satiated. Happy. Wonderfully at ease. When he'd taken her to bed last night, Stash had made good on his promise. He had made love to her all night. Slow and satisfying. The kind that made a woman feel . . . She jerked her head up the few inches allowed her, shock reverberating through her body. Oh no. She had almost said in love . . . oh no . . .

"Don't move," Steve ordered sleepily. His chest rumbled in her ear, and his masculine scent wafted through her senses as his chest hair tickled her nose.

In love . . . oh no . . . Her denial was automatic, conditioned from years of training herself to keep an emotional distance. *Especially from men like Stash McMillan.* She shook her head, or tried to, and instead tortured herself with his scent again.

"Don't you ever listen, woman?"

"I can't breathe," she lied.

"Not true. You have a healthy pair of lungs. Your screams last night prove that."

He was the only man who had ever made her lose control like that. Pleasure without preliminaries, without thought. Just mindless sexual satiation. It scared her, and she didn't like it. She opened her mouth against his chest and bit him.

He yelped and turned over, pulling her on top of him as he did so. His eyes were sleepy and slightly red. His dark stubble somehow made him even sexier. She wanted to kiss the dimple in his chin.

"My back hurts," he complained. "I think you took chunks of my flesh with your teeth."

She wrinkled her nose. "I can't move my right leg," she told him. She must have wrenched a muscle while tussling with him on the carpet.

His eyes started to twinkle. "That's because you opened your thighs too wide last night."

His raunchiness had her flushing. She couldn't believe it. She felt her face heating at the things he did. He had had her every way he wanted. Just as he told her in the car last night, he had shown her exactly what he wanted to do.

"You're beautiful when you're blushing," Steve said softly.

He caressed her bare back, a sweeping up and down sensual motion that had her body squirming against him. Oh no. She wasn't losing control so soon again. She needed time. Needed space. "All my men tell me that," she quipped, trying to be flippant.

It worked. His smile turned into a scowl. "I don't want to know about your other men."

"Good, I wasn't going to tell," she said. She could take anger. Anger she could control and shape. "Maybe you can go ask around, start another file."

"Maybe I'll ask Tess," he came back.

That wasn't the answer she wanted to hear. She forgot that was what started it all. Tess and her meddling. Stash working with Tess. She tapped him on the chin with a finger.

"I don't share," she said.

He cocked a dark brow at her. There was a strange light in his eyes. "That makes two of us. But where does that leave us?"

Marlena didn't have an answer. At least not an answer that wouldn't leave her vulnerable. No man wanted a woman without an identity, who couldn't give him the care a normal woman would. She had learned the hard way. It was much easier to be the first to walk away.

She bent forward and kissed him, shutting out the questions and the doubts. He didn't protest, gathering her closer, hands splaying on the cheeks of her behind. She glided against his maleness, catching her breath at how quickly he responded to her touch. Just like that, he was ready for her again. His desire was mirrored in his sleepy eyes, a torrid lust in them as he savored her fondling. His lips parted when she took him in her hand and guided him into her.

He had taken her all night. This time she would take him. She knew how he liked it, too. Long and hard and slow, pulling his pleasure at a slow pace. And he loved it when she paused just a fraction of a second before taking him again. His hands on her buttocks tightened, trying to hurry her. He sighed when she complied. He seemed to grow even larger the longer she prolonged his pleasure. She smiled down as she rode him. They didn't need any words for this.

This was more like it. Back in control. For now she would make believe that this was her territory. Her man.

Chapter Sixteen

Steve muttered a soft curse. Jackass. Instead of talking it out, he had gone after Marlena with his dick. Now there was a gulf between them. He knew her body but not her mind, and she was determined to keep him at arm's length. He understood why. She had lost control last night and hadn't liked it.

Now there wasn't time. Hands in her jacket pockets, Tess studied them, amusement gleaming in her gray eyes. He knew she was checking out the scratch on his cheek. She would probably have a good laugh if she knew about the big purple bruise in the middle of his back. Or the scratches there. In fact he had marks all over him. His mermaid hadn't started the night very submissively. His lips quirked as he recalled her declaration. Marking her territory, she had said. Ruefully he had to admit that she had done that very well.

He glanced over at Marlena. She was walking a little gingerly. She wore a white angora top over white leather pants. Pale pink pearl necklace with matching earrings. Very cool, very sophisticated. But she still looked well kissed, he couldn't help noting smugly. And she very well better admit she had been marked, too. To his frustration, she wouldn't meet his eyes.

"I said to talk, not walk all over each other," Tess commented, as she surveyed the living room and them. Other than picking up the leftover material that had been their clothes, they hadn't had time to straighten up the place. She picked up half of a leather belt and wagged it around. "Remind me not to take a suite here. The room service leaves much to be desired."

Actually, room service was amazing. A call to the hotel butler had produced a shirt and a pair of pants within half an hour. No questions asked.

"I've already used the intranet component," Marlena told Tess. "Everything should have been transmitted."

"Good. By the time we finish with Steve's admiral, I should have verification from Command, and the rest of the codes. I suppose Steve did get to fill you in with some details since last night?" Tess's smile echoed the mockery in her voice. She kicked one boot aside as she walked toward the dining table.

"All I need to know is when I can get back to my job. Alone."

Steve curbed the urge to say something sarcastic. Last night was still on his mind, and there was no way to get around the fact that he had fallen in love with Marlena Maxwell. He realized that his attempts to get her to talk to him seriously had been a belly flop, and that if he really wanted to get serious about winning this woman, he had better learn more of her ways and the way her world worked. Right now she wanted her comfort zone back. He would give it to her for a few hours while he sorted things out at his end.

"Too many cooks involved in this soup, darling," Tess said, shaking her head. She pulled out a chair. "We have to straighten out who the players are."

"By exposing me?" Marlena asked, picking up her cup of coffee.

"Putting you in danger was the last thing I wanted to do," Steve said quietly. How could she still think that after last night? "I didn't know then what I know now."

"Obviously there are a lot of layers at work here," Tess chimed in. "I wouldn't be here if it were an easy knot to unravel, M. You know I've stuff to do in New York."

"Oh, I know why you're here. I just don't know why he's

here." Marlena finished her coffee, hiding her expression behind the cup.

If she wanted to squash him like a bug under her pretty
white boots, she was doing a good job of it. Steve shoved his
hands into his pants, fisting them. He caught Tess's warning
glance and pursed his lips grimly.

Tess noisily stirred her coffee, then studied the pattern on
the little silver spoon, rolling it between her fingers. "Anger
is such a powerful emotion. Did you know that was how I
drove away Alex?" she asked conversationally. She got off
the sofa, her sideways glance steady on Marlena. Steve
noted her stilted shoulders as both women exchanged challenging stares.

"Don't mess with my mind," Marlena warned.

"Darling, you're already a mess." Unperturbed, Tess indicated their surroundings.

"You got what you wanted, didn't you? Your Alex did exactly what you wanted."

Steve wasn't sure what was happening or who this Alex
was, but the subject was obviously meant to push Tess away.
He was beginning to understand what Tess told him. Marlena had been goading him on purpose. To drive him away.
She'd been using NOPAIN on him.

"Yes, he did do exactly what I wanted," Tess agreed, then
turned toward the door. "But I didn't get what *I* wanted. It's
time to go or we'll be late."

Thankfully, the trip to the Office of Naval Research in Ar-
lington was more businesslike in tone. Marlena didn't ask
many questions, but Steve could tell she wanted to know
more about why they were involving the navy. Tess wore a
brooding far-off expression, even though she answered the
questions without any appearance of being distracted. Steve
had the feeling that she was thinking of something—or
someone—else.

He had things on his mind too, and more questions than
he would like. When he was first told all those months ago

that he was being transferred to TIARA on an interim basis, he had known that there were reasons for his being suddenly sent to D.C., that the admiral didn't just pick one of his field operatives to go behind a desk. His covert training in STAR Force prepared him to enter into something unfamiliar on a need-to-know basis. Perhaps he was a little uneasy and just a tad disappointed with the way TIARA's Task Force Two worked, compared to his own SEAL team, but he had been willing to learn and integrate, had tried to get along with the others, some of whom didn't seem to appreciate his transfer into their department.

At first Steve had thought it was just the natural competitiveness between different covert fields. He was a soldier, and TIARA members considered the military their footservants, so to speak, doing the dirty work for them while they gathered the necessary intel. However, as the months went by, he became aware of an underlying suspicion of him, of the group split into two, some of whom—like Cam—accepted him, and some—like Harden—who distanced themselves from him. It was exasperating, because he knew he couldn't do a good job without total team trust.

He glanced at Marlena, physically sitting so close, yet mentally miles away. She had started it all. Besides wreaking havoc on his emotional life, she had been the pivotal point that had forced out some of the information being kept from him.

The admiral obviously had another agenda when he had sent Steve to TIARA. It wasn't just a temporary fill-in, as he had told him, and an opportunity to learn how the covert food chain worked. Harden had accused him of being the admiral's eyes and ears. The main question was, what did the admiral want him to see and hear?

It couldn't be mere coincidence that they were meeting at the Office of Naval Research, especially after learning last night that Cunningham worked at the NRL. There had to be a connection because the ONR was the parent organization to maritime labs around the world.

Steve mentally connected the dots. Industrial research led to Project X-S-BOT. The missing laptop led to the meeting at the Naval Research Lab in D.C. Maritime research led to the navy, which led to the admiral. Where did GEM fit in? He looked at Marlena again.

She chose to slant her gaze in his direction at that very instant, and their eyes met. He could drown in those blue depths so easily, so full of secrets and promises. He couldn't forget how dreamy she looked when they made love, how those eyes lost the defensive shields that hid what she thought and felt. In bed she responded without suspicion or fear. She didn't draw away as she was doing now.

He wouldn't let her gaze go, and they continued staring at each other silently. He wanted to know what she was planning. Experience had taught him that it was always better to be one step ahead of Marlena Maxwell.

"Looks like we are expected," announced Tess as they reached their destination. They went through security without any difficulty and followed the officer.

Marlena smiled at the smartly dressed young man holding out the door for her. "Thank you," she said, knowing that Steve was watching.

"What would you like to drink, ma'am?" asked the young man, smiling back appreciatively.

"Something hot," Marlena answered. She turned to Tess with an arching smile. "Men in uniform . . . something about them."

"And for you, ma'am? Sir?" The officer didn't know that Steve was navy, too, since he was in civvies.

"The same thing Marlena is having, please," Tess murmured, amusement in her eyes.

Steve repressed the urge to bark at the young officer. These two women were lethal weapons. Didn't they ever stop playing their games? "Something cold," he said.

As the officer left the room, Tess turned to Marlena, "Stash's on to your little fun."

Marlena chose one of the chairs around the conference table in the spacious office. "Stop teaching him things he isn't supposed to know, then," she said lightly, and gave a playful whirl in her seat.

"Well now, that's *my* fun," Tess teased.

"Seems like there is a lot of fun at my expense lately," Steve remarked, and sat down next to Marlena. "Well, you're in luck. You get fun sitting between the both of you."

Marlena frowned, hearing Tess's soft laughter. Why was she feeling so possessive? She remembered what she'd nearly admitted to that morning and firmly pushed the thought away in some corner of her mind. Love was out of the question. Besides, he didn't look like someone who would fall in love with her anyhow.

The connecting door opened. The admiral came in first. Marlena recognized him immediately, not just from the rows and rows of medals on his uniform, but from the photos of him. Admiral Jack Madison was famous. And very handsome for a man in his fifties. Even her heart fluttered a little in the presence of such authority and magnetism.

"Tess, how are you?" he greeted warmly. Marlena sighed inwardly as she witnessed the friendly buss he gave Tess's cheek. Trust T. to have friends like that.

"Jack, marriage suits you well," Tess observed. "Sorry I couldn't make it to the wedding."

"You have to meet my wife sometime," Admiral Madison said, then turned to Steve, returning his salute. "McMillan."

"Good morning, sir."

Marlena could see Steve's respect for the admiral. She supposed it would be pretty hard not to admire a renowned and decorated Vietnam War hero such as Jack Madison, one of the first SEAL commanders known for his saves as well as his kills. She wondered for the first time about working in a team such as a SEAL unit, as opposed to covert self-reliance.

"This is Marlena Maxwell," Tess introduced her.

His handshake was firm and confident. "Admiral," Marlena acknowledged, skipping the usual niceties. She really didn't want to be there, so what was the point of pretending?

Admiral Jack Madison, in turn, introduced the other two men who came in with him. "This is the commanding officer of NRL, Captain Hector Douglas, and this is the civilian director, Dr. Thomas Cafferty. Please sit down. This is just an informal meeting, but I trust all of you understand that nothing discussed here goes beyond this room."

After they spent a few minutes setting up and getting comfortable, the round conference table looked decidedly smaller with six people occupying it with various folders, laptops, and accessories. Marlena couldn't remember the last time she'd attended a real conference that had to do with her job. Most of her debriefing was quietly done, on a one-on-one basis. She was an outside contractor, an entity that usually meant the fullest possible secrecy. Her role as any agency's shadow asset was too useful to allow group conferences. T. must trust the admiral's outfit a great deal more than she had realized.

"We've been working at cross purposes," Admiral Madison began, looking each of them in the eye. "That's why I thought it necessary to call a meeting between us to clear things up. Tess, I didn't know you were involved or I would have contacted you right at the beginning. Then we would have fewer complications."

Tess shook her head. "You know how government agencies are, Jack. Different agendas and no communication. In a way that's good because of our CIA problem right now, but it can become challenging trying to figure out who is doing what, especially in the rare instances such as this one, when we bump into each other."

"Well, this is a rather big bump, isn't it?"

Tess smiled. "Definitely." She clasped her hands on the table as she considered the admiral and the other two men. "I wonder whether you understand how big it is."

The admiral lifted a hand, a casual gesture of surrender. "No, no verbal challenges with you today, Tess. I need this as clear-cut as possible for my two men here. They're in charge of the projects at NRL, as you can see, and certainly have a great interest in the missing laptop."

"This is not my assignment. I defer to Miss Maxwell."

Marlena looked at Tess with a start. She? Answer questions? No way. "The laptop was stolen. I retrieved it, that's all." And she was sticking to that story.

Admiral Madison studied Marlena for a moment. "My man Steve McMillan isn't after the laptop, Miss Maxwell. In fact we didn't know anything about your assignment until yesterday. When I transferred him to TIARA I wanted him to report its activities back to me because of information leaks that were obviously coming from there. The CIA has a major rat infestation, and since my group depends on TIARA for certain intel, I'm putting a lot of my men's lives in jeopardy every time I rely on that information. Your appearance became one of those leaks, as you can see. Your file seemed to have ended up too easily in the hands of William Cunningham, don't you think?"

"Who happened to work at NRL," Marlena pointed out. "How do you know the main leak isn't from the research lab itself?"

"I, too, thought William Cunningham was the main NRL link," Steve said, looking thoughtfully at the admiral. "Since he's dead, that's a dead end. We need the others working for him. There is at least one at TIARA who somehow got hold of what I gave to Harden."

The admiral nodded. "That's right. Without those names, we'll always have those bad apples working inside, selling our secrets. It's too bad Cunningham got himself killed, although I understand that he meant to have Miss Maxwell get rid of you, McMillan."

"I'm still here, sir."

Marlena saw a tiny lift of the older man's lips, as if he found something that amused him. She couldn't help chiming in, "He was really in the way. I'd have made sure Cunningham stayed alive."

"You were after the laptop," Steve said, "You didn't see Dankin coming after you, so how could you have taken care of Cunningham? I had to prevent him from hurting you."

"You think that big bruiser could have gotten me in the dark? Besides, since you were there, I figured you needed something to do."

"You took a big risk turning your back to Dankin. How did you know my hands were free? I could have been too late."

Marlena was beginning to recognize that low tone in Steve's voice. It signaled the beginning of his temper. She smiled at him a little snidely. "Then you would have had two dead bodies, Cunningham's and mine."

His dark eyes glittered back. "Three. Dankin would be dead." He emphasized each word.

"As you can tell, Jack, these two work really well together, don't you agree?" chimed in Tess, amused.

"Yes," replied the admiral, equally amused.

"We weren't working together," Marlena told them. "This one time just happened."

"Nonetheless, it shows how crossed paths could have deadly results." Admiral Madison's expression turned grave. His direct gaze was compelling. Marlena found herself unable to pull away as he added, "There could have been some deadly mistakes in this comedy of errors. Cunningham saw a file that was supposed to be classified. He had an advantage over you. Whatever you did, he would always have that advantage over you. His mistake was letting you find out that he knew about your background."

He had a point. "There's always a risk in my kind of job," Marlena defended. "In such a situation, I've been trained to find a weakness and try to work with it. Cunningham liked to boast, and it was therefore easy to make him give me the information I needed. I'm aware of the percentages and probabilities of getting out of trouble."

"I'm not questioning your methods or your training, Miss Maxwell," the admiral said. His blue eyes smiled at her, even though his demeanor remained serious. "I'm not here to argue with you over how you would handle any assignment. What I want is to make sure you understand that the leaks coming out of TIARA can hurt both your agency and my own teams. Yesterday I told Tess I needed her help, but she said she isn't the one to ask. I'm now asking you."

Taken by surprise, Marlena leaned back against the hard

leather chair. She never liked working with more than one person, and this team stuff meant having to give up a lot of the favorite things in her job—total control and freedom. But a lot of lives were at stake here, and she didn't want to be responsible for that.

"It isn't going to take long," Admiral Madison continued, pushing his argument in that persuasive voice. "You see, you have the connections, with du Scheum, with lots of people. You also have the laptop and whatever your assignment is. I'm sure there's a way to lure the traitors out that would benefit us both. I need you in a team to get the leaks, Miss Maxwell. Without catching the culprits, I can't trust my own information."

"What about Captain Douglas and Dr. Cafferty?" asked Marlena. "Are they going to be part of this team?"

The admiral nodded. He indicated Captain Douglas sitting on his right. "As commanding officer, the captain works with the director of research, Dr. Cafferty. He takes care of the military aspects, whereas Dr. Cafferty takes care of the civilian side of things. I trust them both implicitly. The three of us have known about certain leaks from TIARA through another project last year, and I sent my man there to find out how TIARA dissects intel."

"You sent Steve," Marlena gave voice to her thought.

"Yes. Then you became part of TIARA's intel assignment because of . . . well, your reputation." She noticed the admiral didn't want to reveal too much about her. That added to her respect for him, how he was aware that not everything needed to be spelled out. Too much information could jeopardize any mission.

"So TIARA sent Steve after me," murmured Marlena, giving Steve a sideways look. He was sitting there listening intently, as if hearing all this for the first time. As she had many times before, she noted the way he seemed to bide his time, weighing everything around him before reacting. Must be why he was chosen for this assignment.

She remembered he had slept with her that first time still suspecting her of being a criminal. Then he had turned her in the next day, just like a good boy, and had gone on to get information about her. After that he had left her. After all, he had completed his assignment. It pissed her off all over again.

"And he's still going to be after you, if you agree with the plan."

"Does he know what this wonderful plan is?" she asked, not bothering to hide the sarcasm in her voice. "Perhaps he's already working on it?"

Steve shot her a look that told her he heard all her quiet accusations, but in the presence of his superior, she supposed he had to curb his language. "Harden took me off the case, so you can stop what you're thinking right now. I wasn't after you then."

"Oh, I can tell what you were after." She wanted him to admit that she was more than an assignment. The only way she knew how to get him to do that was to provoke him.

"I just know you're trying to make an excuse not to work with me," Steve growled back.

"Jack," Tess broke in, leaning forward to pick up her cup of coffee, "did I also mention that they can read each other's minds frequently?"

The admiral broke the tension with a quiet chuckle. Even the other two men were trying not to look too amused. Marlena took a deep breath and picked up her cup. She had no idea why she was so out of control with her emotions. What was wrong with her?

Tess gave a loud sigh. "Maybe I can step in. Marlena can do her assignment, and I'll work another angle with Stash."

Before she could stop herself, Marlena sat up straighter and tossed Tess a warning glare. "You said you have important work in New York," she reminded her tightly.

Tess smiled. "Oh good. I was afraid I'd have to be delayed. I take it you can handle everything without my working with Stash then?"

Marlena could see no way out of it. Of course she wasn't going to let Steve anywhere near T. T. was on the rebound from heartbreak, was probably looking for a man to comfort her, and Steve was . . . well, Steve wasn't going to be available. She nodded briskly, looking around the table at the expectant faces. "Let's hear the plan."

Chapter Seventeen

Steve was glad when the admiral asked to see him alone for a few minutes. He had some unanswered questions still. He got up to follow the older man while the others continued strategizing in the conference room. Before leaving the table, he caught Marlena's hand and gave it a squeeze. She was frowning at Captain Douglas. Steve could see teamwork was going to be hard for his mermaid, who had swum alone for so long.

"Don't kill anyone till I get back," he said, just needing to connect with her. She was still trying to get away from him.

"I'll be waiting," she returned in a sweet voice.

Steve grinned. The admiral was talking on the phone in the smaller office. It was obviously not his because pictures of Hector Douglas and, presumably, his family adorned a whole corner of the oak desk. Jack Madison rang off and sank down into the old leather chair, which creaked a little. Steve stood at attention.

"At ease and sit down, McMillan."

"Yes, sir."

There was a pause as the admiral studied him for a few seconds. Then he canted a brow. "Stash?" he asked.

Damn. He could feel embarrassed heat rising in his cheeks. Damn it. "It's just a nickname, sir," Steve explained stiffly. He certainly wasn't going to divulge the details on how he'd gotten it.

"But that does mean you have cultivated a certain friendship with Miss Maxwell, am I right? And I'm not talking about just as an assignment for Task Force Two, McMillan."

Steve hesitated. To admit that he had become close to an assignment could be bad for his evaluation in the future. On the other hand, the admiral demanded and deserved total honesty. "Yes, sir."

The admiral's blue eyes had that piercing quality that made Steve feel the man could see right through him. Knowing that the admiral was thinking about his reputation with women, he felt the need to explain his "relationship" with Marlena, but it wasn't a topic of conversation he cared to bring up with his superior.

To his relief, the admiral didn't wait for any further details. "You've done well at TIARA this last year, McMillan, although I know you're uncomfortable being civvies for so long. Missing the weight of your weapons, I suppose?"

Back on familiar territory, Steve relaxed a little. "It hasn't been an easy adjustment, sir, but I've found my new job educational."

"But you wish it to be more action-oriented, like on our teams," the admiral observed.

"Yes." Steve didn't see any reason not to admit that he preferred life out in the wild.

"Then let me ask you another personal question, McMillan. If you return to your old station, with your old team, this friendship you have cultivated with Miss Maxwell—do you have plans?"

Steve hadn't been prepared for the sudden change of subject again, and he looked up sharply. Of course he had thought about it. But that had nothing to do with anyone but Marlena and him. Rather than sounding defensive, he decided to go about it another way. "Sir, do you have something in mind that has to do with my present position at TIARA, which has been terminated, by the way, and my friendship with Miss Maxwell?"

Admiral Madison smiled his approval. The leather chair creaked again as he shifted his weight. "Do you know why I chose you for the transfer instead of any of the others?"

"The question has crossed my mind several times, sir. I hope it isn't because I was deficient at my old job."

"If you were, you would know it. I don't beat around the bush when it comes to the business of warfare. McMillan, I needed someone working at TIARA who had your qualities as a point man, able to pick out details usually missed by others. Able to focus on the hidden as well as the obvious. I want to find this rat."

"Sir, if you had told me what your objective was before the transfer, I would have looked for the leak sooner."

"No. I wanted you to start exactly on square one. If you were looking, you would be suspicious of everything being done there and you wouldn't have been comfortable making friends or decisions in any of TIARA's missions. Right now I can ask you questions about individuals working there and you can give me honest evaluations. I can quiz you on the operations of TIARA procedure and your analysis would be fair and correct."

Put that way, it made sense. "Is it correct then, sir, to assume that you want me to profile some of the people I worked with?"

"Yes, and there will be no guilt attached to your analyses now, will there, since you haven't been spying on them for me?"

Steve nodded. The lessons he learned from the admiral were invaluable. This one taught him to understand that one couldn't find a rat by sending in a rat. If he had gone in there behaving and acting like one, he would have failed. As it was, those who had treated him with wary suspicion now stood out—was it just simple antagonism, or was it more than that?

"You're an excellent soldier, McMillan, a true example of a navy SEAL. You excel at sea, in air, on land. You can return to the teams and have a career, or as I see it, you can excel further, learn the intel part of covert warfare and become an expert in all phases. It's your choice."

There was a short silence as Steve digested the admiral's words. He frowned at the implication, not sure what to expect. Admiral Madison tapped on the table with two fingers as he continued, "Every soldier needs that extra dash of gung-ho macho spirit. Every warrior needs that instinct to help him survive between civilized and uncivilized moments. But we also need the steadfast ones who can be trained to use both instinct and intellect at the same time, to dissect information and act on it. I picked you because as a point man in one of my teams, you had the experience to rely on your instincts to pick up what is hidden, and to trust your guts over instructions. Also, your reports of your intel work these last months have proven that you have the capabilities to dissect the kind of information that would have made most SEAL operatives suicidal." The admiral grinned suddenly, looking younger than his fifty-odd years, and added, "And you're certainly very alive, especially around Miss Maxwell."

Steve's backache had become a slow, nagging thud. The scratch on his face itched. His left hand felt as if it was longer than his right hand. He had had a very lively night.

"Yes, sir," Steve agreed ruefully, rubbing his neck and fingering another scratch back there. His superior's blue eyes twinkled back at him. "Thank you for your confidence in my abilities, sir. I don't know what else to say. Actually, I'm not sure exactly what you're saying. You want me to go into intel work for you?"

Admiral Madison nodded. "But not at TIARA. I've learned from our current situation that we need a liaison between different agencies so we don't waste time and manpower hunting each other down. If we are sharing a liaison, there is one open channel."

"You mean, you want me as a liaison between you and GEM?"

"Between you and GEM, and especially GEM's major employer."

"Which is, sir?"

The admiral cocked his head to one side. "Only a liaison would know such classified information, McMillan."

"I see, sir."

"I've discussed this with Tess, and her profile of you for

this position is at eighty-five percent success. That's pretty high, according to her."

Eighty-five percent? They had been talking about him working as a . . . what? Liaison. He'd better brush up his French. He had never quite gone beyond French kissing. "You seemed to be very confident with her analysis, sir."

"But of course. I've used Tess's genius often enough to know."

"And she profiles people." Steve was getting more and more intrigued by all these outside contractors. What exactly did they do?

"Let's just say she messes with their minds."

"Is that a job?"

"For certain agencies, yes. She is also excellent at divulging information, or haven't you noticed?" Admiral Madison arched his eyebrows inquiringly. "GEM operatives have certain talents. Your Miss Maxwell, for example, is very good at calculations."

"Probabilities and possibilities." Steve had heard Marlena use variations of those words when she was discussing work with Tess.

"Yes. Think about this proposal. You have seen what their assignments are like. They retrieve whereas we target our enemies. With a liaison, I would be able to double-check our targets, have my blind spot covered. You will be responsible for eliminating our SEAL team blind spot, Steve."

Steve hadn't expected this from the admiral. He had thought he would get answers this afternoon, not a whole plan for his future. Suddenly he felt he understood all about probabilities and possibilities.

"I will certainly give it some consideration, sir."

"The pay is better than what the military pays you. I know you have a sick sister with enormous medical expenses. This will certainly be a big help." The admiral smiled. "Besides, Stash McMillan has a nice buccaneer ring to it, as Tess says."

* * *

Marlena munched on her fries, barely tasting them. She wasn't used to sharing information. It wasn't done in her profession. The probabilities of betrayal went up with more people involved. Right now she had to worry about her back as well as all sides, and it wasn't a comfortable feeling. Tess being there gave a certain assurance, but she still didn't have to like it.

She knew, however, that the admiral and Tess were right in their assessment. It made sense to share information and manpower in this one operation, to get the traitor in TIARA out of the way, or risk more lives in future operations. Their mutual enemy was in the way of their respective assignments. But it was difficult to have to be accounted for all the time.

"Are you going to brood all day about it?" Tess asked from across the dining table. "I need to get back to New York soon, so if you can't handle it, say so now."

Marlena scowled. "I can handle it." She pushed her fries away. "I'm still puzzled by this liaison stuff, that's all." Tess had outlined to her a position created as a bridge between agencies.

"Why, do you think Stash can't handle it?"

"Steve," Marlena automatically corrected, eyes challenging.

Tess smiled. "He's only yours if you take him." She bit into a custard cupcake. "I can always use a good man like . . . Steve." She finished the name, dragging out the S teasingly.

Marlena sniffed. "You're not going to corner me into another catfight. I'm still trying to figure out why you're doing this. I know it's more than the liaison angle."

"You're too suspicious, darling. Steve is going to be good, if he chooses to take the job. We'll see how it goes with our current operation. Someone will evaluate him and if he takes the job, he will get to meet some of the other boys."

"Not . . . Alex?" Marlena tried to be as delicate as she could.

Tess shrugged. "Perhaps. Or Jed might show up."

"Who do you prefer to show up?"

Tess shrugged again, her newly tinted gray eyes bland. "I don't care. I won't be here."

"Don't you want to see him?"

"I . . ." Tess's mouth curved into an ironic smile. "I see him often enough in my head. No need to reinforce the image. M., better think hard before you walk away. Some are harder to walk away from."

"Why do we always end up talking about Stash?" Marlena demanded.

"I love it. Two lovely ladies talking, and my name comes up," Steve interrupted as he came over to the table with a tray. "I know the guy very well. Can tell you anything about him."

How did he do that? Just came within ten feet of her radar and she became a mass of confused feelings? Why couldn't she just have him and none of the emotional stuff?

"How did your talk with the admiral go?"

"Pretty enlightening. We have a lot to do before the next phase. But first I have a few questions of my own. Tess, what's this about an offshore account in my name?"

"You mean the one with a hundred grand in it?"

Steve choked on his food. "A hundred what?"

"It's all yours, baby, if you want it," Tess invited.

"It's not mine," Steve said fiercely. "Who set that account up and why?"

"Take a guess. If I can trace it, so can the authorities. M. thought you were a rogue operative when I informed her of the account."

Steve chewed his food and swallowed as he studied Marlena. "So you thought I was the bad guy, too," he commented. "Pot calling the kettle black."

Marlena bit her lower lip. He'd effectively turned the tables on her. He was right. She had thought he was a rogue and had slept with him. "It was different," she said with a shrug. "T. had evidence of you on the take."

"But it was false. TIARA had circumstantial evidence of

Marlena Maxwell in the past, too, but it wasn't you, either. So why the anger about me? I thought I was doing my job. Why don't you tell me what it is you're so damn mad about?"

He was probing too close. "I don't have to explain myself to you," she told him.

Steve took another bite, a look in his eyes that she was beginning to recognize as sheer stubborn male persistence. "Well, let me explain myself to you then," he said, after he swallowed his food. "I had no knowledge of that account until Admiral Madison informed me just now. Right now I'm pissed off because someone was using me as a straw man. You might be just looking for a rat in the government, and that's fine, but this is personal now. He's declared war on me, and I intend to dig until I get his name. So if this liaison thing gets me closer to the truth, you won't get rid of me that easily. I'm in this. With you. Whether you like it or not."

Marlena stared at him mutinously. He had a right to be angry, but that didn't mean she had to like this new situation.

"May I include a suggestion, Steve?" Tess interrupted. She hadn't said a word throughout their confrontation. "Make a call and place your sister under protection for a while."

"How the hell did you find out about my sister?"

Tess arched a brow. "It's not that difficult to trace anyone, darling. You were doing your job and I was doing mine. Like you said, someone is using you as a straw man. Either you're being set up for a fall or someone has plans to use you continuously. Usually they know everything there is to know about you, Steve, so they can either blackmail or get rid of you in a way that can't be traced back to them. You had taken responsibility for the hospital bills incurred by your sister, and a man in debt can be seen as a desperate man."

There was a short silence. Marlena watched the emotions fleeting across Steve's face. Anger. Outrage. Determination. Her heart raced a little at the deadly calm that replaced the emotions as he continued eating. She understood that he wasn't angry at his situation, but at the threat to his sister's safety. For the first time she wondered about his family, his private life. She couldn't help herself. She had to ask.

"And your girlfriend, too," she said, "if you have one back home. She might be in danger."

Steve seemed to relax at her unspoken question, his lips quirking as his dark eyes zeroed in on her small pout. "No girlfriend," he said softly.

"Wife, then," she insisted.

"No wife," he said, a smile forming slowly. "Never been married. I do have several old girlfriends, but they were more interested in the uniform than the man. Besides, they weren't happy when they found out they might be marrying a man with a huge debt. What about you? Scared of my bad credit rating?"

His mockery flustered her. She rose to his challenge. "Sweetie," she drawled, "I can pay off your debts, and you can be my boy toy."

Steve grinned. "I'll think about it," he promised.

"Now that we've got your misunderstanding settled," Tess interrupted again, satisfaction gleaming in her eyes, "can we discuss your new job?"

"What about the account?" Steve asked.

"Leave it for now," Tess said. "We'll keep an eye on it, see the activity. It might be of use. That's my job."

Steve shrugged. "Okay. I'll take care of my family business. Then I'll get right on the assignment to find our rats."

"Let's hear your plans," Marlena said sarcastically. It was *her* assignment after all.

Steve glanced at the leftover food in front of Marlena. He didn't need to guess her mood; tension practically emanated from her. His mermaid felt threatened from all directions and was on the defensive. "Well, you can make a list of who you think might be the leak at your end, and I will focus mine on TIARA. It's easier to divide our tasks that way. You take care of your suspects and I look into mine, and we put our heads together later."

He grinned at her because he couldn't help thinking about other things they could put together. Marlena muttered something rude about where he could put his head.

"Is that another bet?" he asked, grinning wider, feeling inexplicably lighthearted. He had a future to consider, and the woman sitting next to him played a big part in it. Or at least he planned to make her do so. His mind felt lighter knowing that he wasn't working against her anymore. He added wickedly, "I'll win again."

"Again? Did you look at your face in the mirror, loser?"

"I'm not the one waddling around in pain."

Marlena choked. "Waddling? Waddling?"

"Face it, you're a sore loser."

It was Tess's turn to choke on her drink. Marlena turned to her. "I suppose it's useless to appeal to your sense of pity after saddling this man on me."

Tess chewed on her straw and said with a straight face, "I enjoy a pithy argument myself."

Marlena groaned and Steve leaned over, patted her on the back, and said softly into her ear, "You liked saddling me. Admit it." He smiled at Tess. "Thanks for your recommendation to the admiral, by the way, although I'm curious about one thing. Eighty-five percent? What did I do to lose fifteen percent?"

Tess's brows lifted. "Percentage questions are Marlena's area, not mine," she told him, "which brings us back to more serious matters. What are the probabilities of leaks in TIARA from our end?"

"You mean du Scheum?" Marlena asked. "That's pretty obvious. The two bodyguards working for Cunningham were du Scheum's men, and the other two outside the door sure disappeared easily, don't you think? That's how Cunningham had access in and out of that house, I assume. There is a high percentage that Pierre's in more danger than he realizes."

Steve wanted to ask more about du Scheum and her, but saw no way to do so without sounding jealous. He swallowed his food and casually asked, "He didn't seem to be terribly alarmed by the attempts on his life. Nor is he afraid for yours. Is he working with you?"

"Pierre knows the risks in the business he's in," Marlena said. "I don't think I've ever seen him alarmed. Or angry. Or any other emotion, in fact. He's a very calculating man."

"That's why he gets along so famously with M.," Tess explained further. "He likes the way our M. calculates her risks in every assignment."

Steve swallowed, this time more than food. "I see. I guess he and M. can calculate the probabilities of which guys working for him are actually against him." He pushed back and stood up, picking up the food tray. "I'll head off now to TIARA and take care of my list. Don't worry, I'll get a lift there. I'll see you back at the hotel, M. Talk to you later, T."

After Steve left, Marlena chewed on another fry. Tess studied her rings, taking one off and putting it on another finger. Marlena picked up another fry. Tess rested her chin on her hand.

"He called me M.," Marlena remarked, food in mouth.

"He's mad," observed Tess lazily.

"He's jealous," Marlena said. And felt ridiculously pleased.

Steve nodded absently, not really agreeing or disagreeing with the driver's comments.

M for Mulling. M for Moderation. He needed all the restraint he could muster right now. He tried not to think about Marlena on the way back to D.C. Fortunately the officer who had given him the ride was a chatty young man.

There was time enough to talk things out when the job was done. Right now he planned to go back to TIARA headquarters. He still technically worked there, so his security clearance should be without problems. He thought of all the possible suspects, playing out various scenarios in his mind on how each particular person fit into this circle of traitors.

Someone with high security clearance was part of the scheme. He or she must be able to retrieve and download information without suspicion, transferring whatever Cunningham needed. With Cunningham dead, there was no reason for this person to panic, unless Steve created one.

The main building was crowded that day, with a large group of students on a visit. He was in line going through security clearance when he spied Birman not too far ahead, following du Scheum, going into one of the limited-access elevators. Now, wasn't that something? *Think of the devil and the devil appears.* What was du Scheum doing there? And who was he meeting? Those elevators didn't lead to public-access floors, so it was a safe bet that du Scheum wasn't there for the usual friendly tour.

Well, at least he knew Marlena wasn't spending time with the man at this moment. Everything about Pierre du Scheum bothered Steve, although, to be honest, the main thing was his past with Marlena. Jealousy ate at him every time he thought of their friendship. What was he to her? He didn't want to think of Marlena carrying on a casual affair with anyone at the moment. She hadn't mentioned it, but he was unsure as hell where he stood with the darn woman. He wanted so much and knew he couldn't push too hard. Not with her jumping away two steps for every one he took.

No, he just had to take his time, get her used to him, give her a reason to see that there was more to their relationship than lust. Be moderate, he repeated. They only ended up in bed, anyhow, whenever he lost his temper with her. That cooled his ire but didn't solve a damn thing.

By the time he reached the same elevators, du Scheum and Birman were gone. He keyed in his access codes, leaning back against the wall as he watched the elevator numbers lighting.

First he had to find Cam. Harden wouldn't see him immediately anyway, if he was around. Cam would give him a brief update of the situation. Nodding at a few colleagues, he headed down the passage that led to the small office he shared with Cam.

Good, there was light under the door, so he didn't have to waste time looking for him. He opened the door and almost walked into Cam. The office was too small for two people, especially when one of them tended to be a packrat. With three people, it was like a standing-room only show, and Steve was in this case the spectator.

Cam lifted his head and muttered softly, "Get out of here, Stevie."

Steve saw Patty Ostler's glazed eyes opening wide in shock when she saw him. She was trapped against a tall file cabinet. "No!" she called over Cam's shoulder, in a furious, husky voice. "Let me go, Cam, or I'm going knee you in the balls."

"You would do that to your future children?" mocked Cam in horror, and took a step away from her. "You just wait. I'll tell them what you did to them when they grow up."

"Oh, you . . . you!" Patty pushed up long tendrils of her hair that had fallen out of their knot. Her eyes were stormy with emotion as she tried to find the words to berate Cam, obviously trying not to swear.

"I know, I know," Cam said soothingly. "The speechlessness disappears after a few more kissing sessions."

"Oh!" Obviously the poor woman was having a tough time with words, and Steve tried his best not to show any emotion. He quickly opened the door wider for her when she pushed Cam out of the way and rushed out of the office.

Cam rubbed his lips and gave a sigh. "You have lousy timing, McMillan. Don't you know how to knock?"

"It's my office, too," Steve dryly pointed out. "What were you trying to do with her, file her for future reference?"

Cam adjusted his rumpled clothes. "I was trying out my rendition of Kisser of the Millennium. Wow, Patty gives some serious lip lock. My brain's still not functioning right."

Steve chuckled. "Looked to me like the lady wasn't willing."

"Pfft. There's how little you know about kissing lessons. You just stick to your games." Cam sauntered to his desk and sat on the edge. "Me, I'm a great teacher. The woman had her tongue down my throat. She was attacking me."

"Yeah, that's why she was pinned against the cabinet."

Cam smiled wickedly. "She was grabbing on to my shirt, so appearances can be deceptive."

"Man, you're going to appear so popular with her now. You're lucky she won't press sexual harassment charges against you."

Cam sighed. "I know. But then I'd get the chance to tell the whole world what a great kisser she is. The case of the lip-lock woman." He licked his lips noisily.

Steve laughed, shaking his head. The man had it bad. "Your ass, not mine," he said as he dropped into his office chair. He pulled open the drawer of the file cabinet next to his desk, then flicked the switch to turn on the desktop computer.

"I think I'll give her fifteen minutes. Then she'll be back up here to give me an earful."

"She'll probably avoid you for a while, Cam," guessed Steve.

Cam grinned. He picked up a brown shoulder bag from his desk. "I have her purse."

Steve wondered how Patty Ostler had found her way into their office in the first place. "Well, make sure you make up with her real good because I'm going to need both your help."

"Another favor? Let me guess, something to do with the divine Marlena?" Cam settled into his chair, his hands behind his head. "Aren't you supposed to be off that case?"

"What's happening at your end about it? Anything?"

Noisily munching on some snack, Cam stared up at the ceiling for a few seconds. "Nope. Nothing I can think of that's important. Harden let the woman walk, so he's basically left with an empty file in hand. In other words, he's not too happy at the moment."

"He's got my file on her. Surely he would use that in his report."

Cam shrugged. "The intel we collected was to stop an assassination. We used valuable manpower to set up an expensive downtown apartment for the bait. We paid for an expensive automobile that the lady hasn't returned yet. The only good thing was the free lackey and the ten grand." He arched a brow at Steve. "You tell me what that kind of report is going to do to Harden! No amount of explaining would make the top guy happy with the end result."

Steve fell silent for a second. The deputy director knew about him? Of course he would, since any SEAL team member transferred here by the admiral would be made known to the department head.

"Hey, Cam, have you ever met the deputy director of the department? What's he like?"

"Are you going to eat that pack of chips on your desk?"

"It's open."

"So?"

Steve reached over to grab the snack he had left there a few days ago and sniffed it before using a paper clip to secure the opening. The stuff had probably lost its taste by now. He tossed it in Cam's direction. "You know," he told his office mate, "you're a human garbage disposal."

Cam threw a fistful of chips into his mouth. "At your service," he said in between munches. "Where were we? Oh, Mr. Gorman. I've met him during my interviews for Task Force Two but we aren't drinking buddies of course. Terribly aloof, but what would you expect if you're one of the DOD directors?"

"You were interviewed by Gorman?" Steve frowned. He had never met Mr. Gorman. That suddenly struck him as strange.

"All of us were approved by him. Weren't you? I mean, you were transferred here with his approval, right?"

Steve wasn't sure. After all, Mr. Gorman hadn't interviewed him. "I thought I was transferred here with Harden's approval, since he is ops chief."

Cam snorted. "Harden doesn't have that power. Everything we do must be approved by the big guy himself. He doesn't get along with Harden, either, but then our O.C. doesn't seem to get along with many people. Anyway, Gorman has stood in Harden's way to a promotion several times now."

"Why?" There was something wrong here. Steve could feel his instinct kicking in again.

Cam shrugged. "Politics, I suppose. It has to do with Harden's past, the one that got him in hot water in the first place. I heard Gorman was promoted over Harden because he reported some intel Harden didn't or couldn't produce. Who knows? It's history. Why the interest?"

Steve looked at Cam across the room. The lanky man and he had gotten along since he had started at TIARA. Cam munched on the rest of the chips with serious dedication, his intelligent eyes looking back at him. Steve took a chance. "I'm making a list of names of possible rats in TIARA," he told Cam calmly. He gave a condensed version of what had happened. "Someone has been leaking information for a long time now. I'm only aware of it now because Marlena's files that you and Patty helped me compile were in Cunningham's hands almost immediately."

Cam finished chewing as he continued staring back at Steve. "Could have been me," he stated in a matter-of-fact voice.

Steve nodded. "Yes."

"So why tell me?"

"You can help me prove it isn't you," Steve offered, "or Patty Ostler."

"You mess with my woman's integrity and I'm going to shit all over you." Cam crushed the empty foil bag in his hands.

Steve studied his friend. There was no anger in his manner. Yet. But he wasn't smiling any longer, he noted. "I'm just making a list, and I'm not Harden, Cam. I know how to do things without twisting everything into a battle of friendship and hatred. If it's nothing, you and Patty and anyone else on my list would never hear a thing about it. If it's treason, then I'll track it down. It's my job."

"But you aren't working for Harden on this."

Steve shook his head. "It's more than that now. I'm taking a chance by letting you know."

"Think I might slit your throat after this?"

"That would save me from buying you that dinner I owe you."

"Ha, you aren't getting out of that so easily, pal. A real meal, man. Like at one of those hundred-dollar restaurants." Cam stood up from his chair and picked up Patty's handbag. "Let me go get Patty. Maybe she'll treat me better when I tell her you think she's a rat."

Steve grinned. "Yes, use me to deflect danger, I don't mind." He turned to the desktop. "I'll be here for a couple of hours. I really need your help to get some info."

"Patty's department." Cam opened the door. "Okay, I'll use you as an excuse to get back into her good graces. She thinks I can't kiss like you. That was a demonstration I was giving when you came in earlier."

Steve glanced up, surprised at the statement. "Well, hell, tell her I'll gladly give her a kiss to compare, if she'll help me out."

"Like hell you will," Cam returned, his tone fiercely possessive. "You do that and you'll kiss your ass goodbye."

"Fine," Steve retorted. "I'll kiss you and you can tell her I'm no good."

Cam made a face. "You're disgusting, you know that? I don't know how I put up with you," he shot back, and closed the door behind him.

"So what did they say?" Marlena asked as she turned on the replica laptop she had brought to D.C. with her.

Tess slipped her cell back into her purse. "The encrypted programs are all original. Command double-checked the codes. It's the right laptop."

Marlena nodded. There had been a possibility that Cunningham had somehow broken the encryption and copied everything on a similar laptop. The only way to detect a fake was checking for special laser codes embedded in the hard drive in all government-issued laptops. Most civilian labs wouldn't know about this, and even if they did, the chances of someone able to copy the exact laser depth and burn mark in a specified location onto an exact laptop was low. Only a few people in the field would have the ability or technology to do that. Like her agency, for instance.

The laptop she had with her was one of a kind. Some entity or country, owning sophisticated encryption devices and the technology capable of detecting the laser codes, would find it an authentic United States specially embossed laptop. Even the codes were sequenced in the exact manner of the missing laptop she had regained.

"So my projected calculations that the seller's secret weapon actually was the missing laptop were right," she said with smug satisfaction. She always liked to be right.

Tess placed the real laptop side-by-side with the other one. "Yes. And of course you were right that the culprit would try to sell it to middle men like Max Shoggi rather than deal with the embassies himself."

"That's an easy calculation," Marlena said. She turned on the real laptop. "The probability of someone without influence getting hold of this baby is very low. It had to be someone at that meeting, able to get very near to the demonstration and discussions."

"And someone who could go in and out of NRL without thorough security checks."

"Someone who works there," agreed Marlena.

"Like Cunningham," continued Tess.

"Yes." Marlena took out the disk Tess had given her at du Scheum's party from a panel under her oval compact powder. Its surface shone like polished silver. "You said this thing would do the necessary work to create the worm?"

"Yes."

"Who wrote this?"

"Someone named Nick Langley. Heard of him?"

Marlena looked up sharply. "The Programmer? I heard he's dead."

"Hmm." Tess smiled. "So he is."

"Does Alex know?" Marlena asked curiously. "They were best friends, weren't they, before the explosion?"

Tess turned away, tapped a few keys on the keyboard.

"No, Alex doesn't know. I didn't get the chance to tell him that before we . . . parted ways."

"So he still thinks they all died except him?" Marlena studied Tess for a few moments. "That's not right. He should be told."

"He's no longer my concern. If Nick wants him to find out, I'm sure he will contact Alex." Tess looked up, her gaze blank. "Ready to start this? I'm sure Pierre will make sure Mad Max Shoggi is the highest bidder and the next phase of our operation can start."

Marlena looked down at the disk in her hand again. "Hard to think this thing will direct all communications back to us, telling us what they are doing with the program."

"That's why it's like a virus program, except this one had our Nick's modification, transmitting back to its originator with the same micro-solarbot technology that they are trying to copy."

Marlena had read up on the subject of solar robotics before going to D.C. It was essential to understand the importance of what was stolen, why it could be a weapon in the wrong hands. For so long it had always been weapons of war that attracted arms dealers, but technology had changed supply and demand. Solarbot, using solar energy and robotics, was getting popular in the scientific community. Experiments were done on solar robotics for low-end as well as military technology. There were deep-sea probes called aquabots being perfected for oceanic mapping. There were equally devastating opportunities to use the new technology for destructive weaponry and international espionage.

"Let's hope Stash can help find our leak," she said, inserting the disk. "One slip that we're offering a modified one for sale, and we're done."

"That's why we haven't told anyone about our laptop. If there is a leak, we can narrow this down." Tess frowned. "Did you show it to anyone?"

"Stash searched my things before I was hauled in," Marlena informed her. "They were looking for weapons, didn't touch the laptop."

"I don't like it, what with a leak in TIARA."

"How do you know it's not Steve?" challenged Marlena.

"He's too new there. There's been a leak in TIARA long before that, and that's why the admiral transferred him there." Tess angled her head. "If you think he's on the other side, why don't you stop taking him to bed and just let me take care of him?"

Marlena paused in the middle of typing and gave Tess her full attention. Her friend returned her gaze with a serenity that didn't hide the small lift at the corners of her mouth. "What are you going to do—cancel him?" asked Marlena.

"What is it to you? Unless you really want him around . . ."

Marlena went back to typing. She couldn't have a man around. It hadn't worked before. She had given everything she had, only to be called all sorts of names for not giving up her job, then betrayed for being too trusting. But the idea of Stash no longer there left an empty feeling inside. Could she walk away when this was over?

"Better think quick before you lose him," Tess advised softly. "Then he's fair game, right?"

"Don't even think of it right now," Marlena countered just as softly. "He's mine."

"For now," agreed Tess calmly. "Now, let's hurry up and do this, shall we, darling, so I can get the laptops separated? Dangerous to have two of a kind together for too long."

Marlena smiled. Tess, as usual, had the last word.

Chapter Eighteen

Whatever Cam did or said must have worked. Patty Ostler came back into the cramped office with him. Her hair was tightly pinned again; her silk blouse returned to its impeccable neatness. Her stormy eyes warned Steve not to mention the earlier incident, and he wisely took heed, trying to sound as businesslike as he could.

It wasn't easy, especially with Cam acting without a shred of regret. In fact he looked damn pleased with himself. Steve took in his friend's smug openness and Patty's cool remoteness. Cam had a small ketchup stain on his unironed shirt. Patty didn't look as if she ever ate with her hands. He needed a haircut, what with that long tied-back mane. She probably never had a hair out of place. He seemed to take great pleasure in annoying her, whereas she took great pains to show nothing but cold disdain. What a pair.

Steve gave an inward sigh. Who was he to say that a relationship between the two wouldn't work? He certainly had enough problems dealing with his feelings about Marlena. And what a pair he and his mermaid would make, too. Hot and sweaty, constantly yelping, never boring, filled with wonderfully, incredibly, mind-blowing . . . *Let's not start with the M words again,* he cut through his daydreaming. He needed to keep his mind on work.

He had just given a short take on what had been going on with TIARA and their current assignment that had started with Marlena. He had followed his gut, trusting Cam. After all, he had worked with the man for a year, long enough to know that Cam was exactly what he looked like and how he behaved—a half-wild party animal who used only half the IQ he had when it came to work, but also someone who saw more than his teammates gave him credit for. Cam never seemed to mind going along for the ride, never taking the initiative. Steve supposed ambition was second to having fun, a code Cam certainly lived by.

Patty Ostler was sitting on the edge of Cam's chair, a serious expression on her face. From Steve's angle, he could see that she was agitated by Cam standing right behind the chair, and every time he moved or shifted position, she nervously tried to see what he was doing back there without showing it.

Steve rubbed the smile off his face. "So can you help me?"

"I prefer that we use the proper channels," she said, "but since you brought up the leak issue, I suppose that's not a wise idea."

"Patty doesn't like to do things that aren't according to the rules," Cam chimed in, leaning his elbows on top of the leather seat.

It didn't seem possible, but the woman managed to edge even further forward in her seat. Steve wondered whether she would fall off it if Cam let go of the chair. "That isn't true," she said, looking at Steve as if he'd spoken. "I don't want to circumvent rules just because some people want to do things their way. There are certain procedures that must be followed. If not, chaos ensues." To make her point, she looked around Cam's half of the office.

Cam snorted. "Coward."

Patty's lips pursed for an instant, then she straightened her shoulders. "Agent McMillan, I cannot work with that man making noises around me."

Leaning on his elbows, Cam leaned further forward and whispered something in her ear. She flushed, then glared stonily at Steve. She looked ready to scream.

Steve tried to play peacemaker. Not too good with computer know-how, he needed their cooperation. "You can use my desk, my laptop, whatever. I just need an hour or two of your time at most. This isn't really breaking any procedural rules, Patty. The only thing I didn't do is make a formal request, so that there is no paper trail. If I access information from my own computer, with your help, then I'm not requesting classified access from your department, right?"

Patty nodded cautiously. "Right."

"And if I catch whoever is leaking information from your department, then you have actually stopped possible chaos in your life. You know what Internal Investigations can be like. They will tear your department inside out if they want."

Patty shuddered. Cam discreetly gave Steve the thumbs up, mouthing "Yeah," showing approval that Steve had brought up the thing Patty hated most—chaos in her surroundings. Steve tried not to grin back at his incorrigible friend.

"All right," she finally said. "I'll do this. It sounds like your girlfriend is in danger."

Steve blinked. Girlfriend? He had been so busy chasing Marlena Maxwell in so many ways, he hadn't really thought of her as his girlfriend. It occurred to him that he had referred to her in the oddest terms. His mermaid. His woman. What he felt for her was more primitive than a bland "girlfriend." He wanted so much more from Marlena than a mere relationship.

He studied Cam and Patty again. Cam was lazily rocking the chair, trying to get his lady interest's attention. And succeeding. She had half turned in her seat, and Steve couldn't see her expression, but Cam was enjoying the view, amusement lighting up his mischievous eyes as he looked down at her upturned face.

That was what he should do with Marlena, Steve thought. Keep her off balance. However, he had to concede that it was much tougher to keep his mermaid in that state.

He shook off his daydreaming. Geez, he had thought Cam had it bad. He couldn't function for an hour without thinking about Marlena and what he wanted to do with her. "So," he said aloud, regaining the other two's attention, "who do you think could access Marlena's files without your knowing it?"

Cam and Patty proved to be a wealth of information. They didn't have much time since Patty had to go back to work, but Steve managed to upload enough files to read. He couldn't print them, of course, so that meant staying at the office a lot longer than he wanted. No matter. Harden hadn't returned his message.

As she was leaving, Patty turned to Steve. "Thanks for the ticket. I've been wanting to see the show, but everything sold out months ago."

From behind her, Cam made a cutthroat gesture to Steve. "No problem," Steve smoothly said, having no idea what she meant. Cam was obviously behind it.

"Should I walk you back to your office, my love?" Cam offered, opening the door.

"When hell freezes over," she returned sweetly, and walked out.

Cam closed the door and sighed. "Isn't she romantic?"

Steve cocked a brow. "Mind telling me about the tickets?"

Cam grinned. "Oh, that. Patty wanted to see this opera thing but couldn't get the tickets. I told her you had an extra one, if she would come back here to talk to you."

Steve shook his head. "Man, I don't know about you. I don't even like opera."

"Me neither. But that's beside the point. My Patty does. It's some show called *Turandot* or something like that. Any idea what it is?"

"How would I know? If it's sold out, how am I supposed to get her a ticket?"

"Not a ticket. At least three. I'm going, too."

"Are you mad? I'm not playing third wheel to you and Patty Hell-Freezes-Over."

"So bring Marlena Killer-Figure." Cam wrapped his arms across his chest. "I help you get your woman, you help me get mine. It's a cool setup, I think."

"How the hell am I going to get four tickets to a sold-out opera I don't want to see?"

"Your problem, man. I merely plan the setup." Cam grinned again, not at all fazed. "I'm only worried about myself. I have to get all knowledgeable about opera and singing, and get all spruced up in a penguin suit."

Steve pinched the bridge of his nose. "Why go to all that trouble? Be yourself."

"Ah, then it wouldn't be a setup, would it? Come on, man, help me out here. Patty will see what she wants to see."

"And what's that? A penguin-suited garbage disposal?"

"Excuse me. I'm going to be the perfect gentleman, you'll see. It would give her an idea that I can change, be someone she likes. Adores. Wants. Needs." Cam went off on a tangent, gesturing like an actor.

"Okay, end it there, man. I get the meaning." Steve sniffed, then went back to his notes. "Geez, an opera. Why couldn't it be a football game or something?"

"An unexpected twist, don't you agree? And I set it all up, smart me. Clever me. Devious me." Cam continued gesturing.

Steve laughed, then plucked his lower lip thoughtfully. A setup.

Marlena heard the click of the suite door opening and shutting. Even though she had been expecting him, it was both disturbing and exciting to know it was Stash without checking. It didn't take long for him to find her.

She glanced up with feigned casualness from the magazine she had been leafing through. It was unsettling, this sudden need for a man's presence. She didn't know what to say, what to do. She could only come up with a parody of herself in an apron, duster in one hand, dinner plate in the other. *You're getting hysterical,* she scolded herself. The only option left was to sit there and wait.

He strolled into the media room without hesitating, as if he'd known she was there all along. He had a familiar-looking knapsack with him, which he tossed onto one of the armchairs. He looked tired, and she fought the urge to jump up and kiss him. It was that apron-wearing image influencing her, she told herself.

She nodded toward the chair with the knapsack. "This is a familiar scene. Moving in?"

Steve sat down across from her, his dark eyes glinting. "Yeah. You want me to make you a martini, sweetheart?"

"You want me to make you breakfast?"

"I ate every green bite, didn't I?" he asked with a slight smile.

Marlena glanced at the magazine on her lap. "You see, I'm not made to be a housewife." Now why did she blurt it out like that?

"I can read upside down, Lena. You're looking at a recipe."

She slammed the magazine shut. It had been a whim when she saw the recipe in the cooking section. A whim, that was all.

Steve watched, fascinated, as Marlena tossed the magazine onto the table and settled back against the sofa. In a flash she became someone he was already quite familiar with—the lazy-voiced, bored woman with the mocking eyes. A defense mechanism, he recognized. Once again he had gotten too close.

"I was just reading," she told him, spreading her arms across the back of the sofa. "After all, I'm in a team now, got to wait for people, can't just go off and do stuff on my own."

It was a dig Steve chose to ignore. "I have information that might be of use," he said.

Her blue eyes narrowed slightly. "Continue," she said.

Steve smiled and shook his head. "First you have to tell me something." When she arched her brows in silent inquiry, he continued, "What is du Scheum to you?"

She was silent for a moment. Then, she drawled, "Personally? Or just in general?"

"Both."

"Why?" she asked, crossing her arms. "What does that have to do with you?"

"Everything, Lena. I don't want to find you in his arms when I sneak into his bedroom to kill him." Steve saw that he had startled her with his threat. The blue of her eyes deepened to almost violet as she stared at him. "Is there something between you and him?"

"Are you going to kill off every man I ever slept with?" she challenged.

"No, just the future ones." He sat up, determined to press home his point. "It's me and no one else, Lena. I'm not going to have you playing pearl necklaces with other men."

"Do you think you can stop me?" Marlena got off the sofa and looked down disdainfully at him. "Do I ask you about your women? Or your past? Do I look like the type you can dictate terms to?"

"Come here," Steve ordered softly.

Marlena stiffened at the quiet command. How dare he play territorial male with her? She should just leave him sitting there. He held out a hand, and after a slight hesitation she took a few steps closer and placed her hand in his. "Don't think this is going to be a habit," she warned, as he pulled her onto his lap. She should resist, but she didn't.

"Tell me about du Scheum," he said in the same tone of voice.

She had never taken the time to study his face before. She wanted to dissect every little thing that made him so different from other men. The way his eyes glinted with a knowing gleam when he looked at her. The way the dimple in his chin deepened when he smiled. How he plucked his lower lip when he was deep in thought. How one dark eyebrow, a little higher than the other, gave him that rakish air that hid the serious side of him. Little things like that.

It was a face she enjoyed looking at, even when it had that stubborn expression that she was beginning to recognize. When Steve McMillan wanted something, he went for it and hung on like a bulldog.

"It was a long time ago," she finally said. She ran her fingers lightly up his chest. "We're just close friends now. I was an orphan trying to get out of the projects and Pierre took care of me. He gave me a future."

His dark brows knitted together with undisguised displeasure. "He was too old for you then." He stroked a possessive hand up her back, digging his fingers into her hair. "And you can wipe that smile off your face."

"Stash darling, it was a long time ago," Marlena repeated, still smiling. She traced the frown on his forehead with a finger. "Besides, without Pierre you would never have met me. He was the one who sent me to GEM."

"What is he? The boss in *Charlie's Angels*?" Steve asked sarcastically. "He goes looking for hot chicks like you and T. and then he gives the thumbs-up to recruit them?"

She laughed at the image, then pulled his ear hard.

"What?" he growled, flicking his head away from her pinch.

"That's for noticing T. and labeling her a hot chick," she scolded. "And no, Pierre isn't part of GEM. He had the connections, and saw that I had the potential for my kind of work."

"What is that?" The scowl remained. "He just thought that you'd make a good assassin?"

"Darling, look at it this way. I had no schooling, no money unless I played mistress to some rich man, no family to help me out. I could have a boring job as a waitress or I could be trained to take care of myself." She shrugged. "I chose the second option and never regretted it. There are advantages to starting a new life. And I was perfect for GEM. The fewer family encumbrances the better. So next time you see Pierre, be nice to him. Without him, I would still be a naive woman with a Southern twang trying to make it."

"But you would still be a smart mouth."

"Oh yes, that, unfortunately, must be in the genes of whoever my parents were." Marlena smoothed away his soft hair from his forehead. "So, satisfied with the little story?"

"Not really. But it's a start. What about a significant other? I told you I wasn't married."

She considered lying, but tried evasion instead. "There's no one now," she said. At his frown, she sighed. "I'm not good at relationships, Stash. They don't work well where I'm concerned. I've always been a loner, probably from being a wild child growing up, and don't trust easily. Men don't find me good girlfriend material."

She snuggled against him, and it felt so good. She hadn't snuggled like this since she was a kid. He hugged her closer, and she felt him kiss her forehead.

"What's good girlfriend material? You mean they don't like your cooking?"

She sniffed. "I can cook very well, thank you very much. Just not traditional stuff. If you think you're getting turkey for Thanksgiving and a white picket fence, et cetera, if you think I'll always run home in time to iron your shirt and dust the kitchen, if you're even planning on a Suburban with summer holidays at Disney, then you don't know me."

Oh, but Steve knew her. He was listening intently. Her last revelations were interesting; she was being defensive again, as if someone had tried to make her do all the things she mentioned. Some poor sot had tried to change his Marlena. Steve had no intention of doing that.

"Hell, Lena, I have been a SEAL all my adult life," he told her. "I can't do half the things normal people do. I have enough trouble trying to remember my mother's birthday in the middle of a gun battle. I understand where you're coming from, believe me."

Marlena sat up and kissed him. It was a slow, satisfying kiss, and for once they weren't fighting about who had the upper hand. It had a different kind of passion, something indefinable that left him wanting so much more.

"So are we okay now with my past?" she asked solemnly. "I can't tell you everything, Stash. You know that's the first rule in covert training."

Steve still felt jealous, but at least he now knew more about Marlena's background and where du Scheum stood with her. He supposed no one could ever truly let go of one's first lover, as du Scheum obviously was to Marlena. He scowled again. Cradle snatcher. He couldn't help it. Marlena made him feel possessive in the worst way.

"You going to tell me about what you found out at your office today?"

He understood she changed the subject on purpose because he was probing too close again, but they had gone a lot further than he had anticipated, so he was willing to let it go for now. "I saw your Pierre going up into the secured floors in our building today."

Marlena cocked her head. "Pierre meets with many different people because he's always trying to curry government contracts. That's how he gets to be so influential."

"Only the top brass give out the contracts, Lena. My department deals with information, not government contracts. The only thing du Scheum can get from TIARA is buying and selling of information."

"You think Pierre knows the leak?"

"He could be the top suspect, don't you think?"

She slowly shook her head. "I don't think so."

"Maybe that's because you're too close," Steve suggested.

She tensed slightly on his lap. "I never get too close to anybody," she said, and this time Steve knew he had said the wrong thing. She was no longer soft and pliant in his arms, and her eyes were smoldering flames of blue. "I've taught myself to weigh every situation—"

"Percentages and probabilities," he interrupted, using her favorite maxim.

"That's right." Her mouth curled derisively. "If we want to talk about emotions in the way, how about your jealousy blinding you to facts?"

"Facts? I've got plenty of facts. I checked out du Scheum, Lena. He gives TIARA freebies all the time."

"So?"

"Look, tell me something. How were you able to dismantle all those electronic eyes and bugs we installed? It's because you recognized the type, didn't you? Du Scheum's company had the contract for the latest micro surveillance and thermal cameras and that's why you could so quickly dispose of all the equipment."

Marlena shrugged. "So?" she asked again.

"So he has access to TIARA. He deals with electronics, so he has to have classified access codes. Then whoever monitors the equipment for TIARA could easily be paid to work for him. At the party I saw him deep in conversation with some very interesting characters, some who might be interested in TIARA intel. So he sells. You tell me that isn't a possibility, Lena. I would say there is a high percentage of him being a leak."

She didn't say anything as she sat there, staring back at him. "Everything in that laptop is a collaboration between his and the government's scientists," she told him. "There was no need to steal it at the conference, then offer it up for bid."

"A setup," Steve said.

"You're saying Cunningham isn't the culprit, that what he said that night was all lies?"

"Well, I haven't thought it out that far yet," Steve conceded, "but it was in du Scheum's house and he didn't seem very surprised or upset."

"Pierre seldom shows that kind of emotion," Marlena said, but she was frowning now. "He wouldn't need to use me, Stash. Those parties and meetings are his. No, I've known him too long. If he had planned to abscond with Project X-S-BOT, he would have done so without the need of this charade."

"You still care about him," Steve accused, temper rising. Why couldn't she see how illogical she was? "You'll try to let him off scot-free while he continues to betray our organizations."

Her temper flared just as quickly. She jumped off his lap and started to walk away.

"Where are you going?" he called after her.

"It's obvious we're going nowhere with this teamwork,"

she said, turning to face him, hands on her hips. "We can't even talk about the operation without you getting uppity about the fact that Pierre du Scheum and I have a past. Well listen, Steve McMillan. Just because we sleep together now doesn't give you the right to question my judgment or my ability to get the job done. If you think Pierre is the leak, bring me the evidence; don't cajole me into accepting your verdict just because you like it that way. I can make similar cases with Harden, with Cam, with everyone in that office, but without evidence, it's nothing."

Steve took in a deep breath. Maybe he did overdo the jealous lover bit. "Come back here, Lena. Let's start over. We'll go through the list of names one by one, and this time I promise I won't interrogate you or your past."

"Later. I want to be alone now." She turned to go, then turned back again. "And you're using the spare bedroom. I want my space back."

Steve watched her stalk away, fighting the urge to get off his seat and go after her. She needed space, so he would give it to her. He didn't think she was going to try out that recipe she was reading for him. He had tons of files to read in his laptop anyway. He had DVDs of the tapes of Marlena in her apartment to review. He needed to get all the facts together and present them like a soldier, not a lover. Once this thing was out of the way, then he stood a better chance with her. He smiled ironically at the thought. She would like that—he was starting to think of them in terms of probabilities and percentages, too.

Marlena remained in her room while he ate alone. Room service wasn't bad, but he wished he didn't have to eat by himself. He looked at the closed door of her bedroom. He wanted to be with her, but hell, a man had his pride. She wanted her space, so be it.

Later he lay in bed, laptop on his lap, files and folders strewn all over. He would much prefer to be doing other things in bed, he thought, tapping the down arrow on the keyboard as he read. He would much prefer to hoist an AK-47 and run through the jungle chasing real enemies than shadows. He would much prefer . . .

The door opened. He glanced up. His room was in semi-darkness as he was using just the bedside lamp. The backlight from the hallway illuminated her figure as she stood in the doorway. His breath hitched while he lay there waiting for her to speak. He could see every womanly curve of her body through her nightie. Hot images of what that body felt like under him invaded his mind, replacing dull facts and file links. He leaned back against the big soft pillow and tried to relax. He couldn't contain a rueful smile when the laptop slid sideways, falling to his side. How could he relax when the sight of her woke up the part of him that had suddenly developed enough Herculean strength to throw aside laptops and files? He didn't attempt to hide the telltale bulge tenting the bedsheets. Hell, he was in his room.

She took a step in. "I can't sleep," she said, her voice very soft.

"Why not?"

"The bed is too big." She took another step into his room.

"You come in here, you're in my space," Steve warned. "And in my space, I rule."

She kicked the door shut with one bare foot.

Eyes closed, Marlena wriggled on top of the pillow as teasing fingers drew patterns on her naked back. The man could drive her wild with his tongue and hands. She could almost forgive herself for giving in to her needs last night and coming into his domain. As he had said, he ruled in his space. Totally. What he did to her had her seriously considering the possibility that he had been trained, like some operatives she knew, to imprint women, making them sexually responsive to his touch.

She was feeling too sated to attempt to analyze the situation anymore. She always preferred to sleep alone, but last night she had swallowed her pride and gone to Steve because, of all things, her bed felt bare without him. If she thought about it really hard, she knew she would start doing something totally uncharacteristic of Marlena Maxwell. She would start panicking.

"What are you writing?" she asked, more to stop the disturbing direction of her thoughts than anything else. His fingers were tracing words on her back. Eyes still closed, she followed the letters, frowning as she mentally formed the words. "My mermaid?"

"Mmm-hmm."

"What does that mean?"

"I had a lot of M words to describe Marlena Maxwell," he explained, "but this stuck."

She couldn't see anything mermaidlike about herself. "Mermaid?" she asked again. She turned her head a little, opening an eye. "You think I'm a fishy woman? Are you insulting me?"

He grinned down at her. His finger drew a straight line down her spine, then gently scraped upward again. "A mythical creature from the deep. A siren that supposedly beguiles and drowns unsuspecting sailors."

"Oh, is that what I'm doing to you?" She laughed, amused at the thought of herself with a fishtail. She asked wickedly, "If I sing, would you come?"

"It depends," he told her.

"On what?"

"On whether I would know your true name."

She rolled over on her back and studied him. His morning stubble made him look like the proverbial pirate. "You're mixing up all your fairy tales," she chided softly. "That one was about a dwarf who would marry the heroine if she didn't come up with his name."

He grinned again. "Damn. That would be scary. The siren mermaid turning into a dwarf." His dark eyes glinted with humor. "I can add another twist. Once I find out your name the dwarf will turn into a frog. Then you will have to beg me to kiss you to turn you back into a mermaid."

Marlena closed her eyes. They were talking nonsense like lovers. This was bad. But underneath it, she saw through his attempt to get her to tell him what he wanted to know. No wonder T. wanted him. He was practicing NOPAIN on her without even knowing it. He wanted the one part of her she would never share with anyone.

"Tell me," he said.

She shook her head.

"Du Scheum knows."

She opened her eyes again. "That's different."

Wrong thing to say to a man playing lord of his domain. He pounced on her, hands on either side of her face, his eyes no longer sleepily sexy. "No, *I* am different."

He positioned her like any dominant male intent on making a statement, his masculine weight trapping her, lacing her fingers through his. Marlena tried nonchalance. "Is that supposed to make me do your bidding? Tell you the magic words?"

"You'll tell me," he said confidently. His thighs were very warm as he settled between her legs. "One day." He slid into her without help, as if he knew her body by heart. "Of your own free will." He crushed down onto her until she could barely breathe. She wasn't afraid. For some reason it excited her to know he had power over her. His breath was hot against her lips as he whispered, "Outside my domain. You will tell me. And then you're mine."

He didn't give her time to respond, or to think, for that matter. His kiss was heatedly sexual, curling her toes. Intense. Possessive. And his body was equally so as he showed her giving him control wasn't a totally bad thing. At least her body agreed. Too many times.

Later. Later she would figure it all out.

Chapter Nineteen

•

"What are you trying to find?" Marlena asked, after hearing Steve mutter soft curses for the last half hour.

They had brought all the folders and documents into the media room, arranging them on the large table in the corner. She discovered that Stash was hopeless with organizing data. He could spot something important, circle it with a big black marker, and that was it. Pages and pages of circled sentences, some with big black underlines and exclamation points. When she asked him what those meant, he had shrugged, saying that it just caught his attention. Something about feeling it in his gut.

She frowned. The man relied on gut feeling while analyzing data? That didn't make any sense. She decided to do the same, to see what his gut was thinking. Engrossed, she didn't actually hear his curses until they grew louder.

Steve glanced up. "Do you know how expensive opera tickets are?"

Puzzled, she asked, "Um . . . is that a trick question?"

He shook his head. "I'm looking at all those websites selling sold-out tickets. Who would pay that much to hear warbling?"

He had totally lost her. "You're looking at websites for warblers?"

Beckoning her to come over, he said, "Check out these prices."

She got up and went to stand beside him. His arm went

behind her, hugging her hips as he caressed the rounded curve from waist to thigh absentmindedly. It was distracting. "*Turandot*?" she questioned again. The prices were astronomical, but this opera was a limited number of command performances by the best international stars. But she was still confused. "Okay, why are you checking out ticket prices for *Turandot*?"

"Do you like opera?" he demanded instead.

"Of course." She looked down at Steve. Somehow he didn't seem an opera-loving kind of guy. "Are we going to see *Turandot*?"

Steve sighed. "That's how I managed to get all the files so quickly without red tape. Cam got hold of Patty Ostler and sweet-talked her. Later she thanked me for the ticket to *Turandot*. I didn't even know how to spell it."

Marlena thought about it for a few seconds before amusement hit her. "I gather you owe Cam a favor and what he wanted was a date with this Patty Ostler, who is the opera fan?"

"Yeah." He grimaced. "Worse, I'm supposed to be going, too, because it would look suspicious to her if Cam just showed up without me."

She started to laugh. "Stash, honey, are you running interference for Cam?"

He flashed her a speaking glare. Hugging her closer, he turned and planted a kiss on the side of her belly. "No, we are."

His lips were soft, his tongue a sensual wet tickle. She ran her fingers through his hair, enjoying the feeling for a moment before saying, "You'll never get tickets at this late date. For *Turandot* it's impossible unless you want to pay those prices."

"That is beyond my budget, but I guess I'll have to, since I owe Cam."

He shifted her, so he could have access to her belly button. Marlena scraped his unshaved jaw with her fingernails as she read the screen. Those prices *were* ridiculous. "Stash?"

"Hmm?"

"Let's go talk with Pierre."

He halted his sensual assault. "Why?" He sounded quite reasonable, despite the fact that his fingers tightened on her hip.

"Because I want to ask him about his activities yesterday."

"Don't you trust me?"

"Darling, stop acting like a jealous boyfriend. I'm only asking you out of team spirit. Do you want to come along, or not?"

He nibbled at the flesh just below her navel, making her suck in her tummy. "I *am* a jealous boyfriend, so of course I'm coming along. No man allows his woman to see her first lover alone."

She frowned. Boyfriend? His woman? It sounded so tempting, coming from his lips. "Okay, let me go make a call," she said, carefully sidestepping that issue.

"Why did you bring du Scheum up anyway? We were talking opera."

"Darling, Pierre owns part of the company producing *Turandot*. It'll give me a good excuse to call up Pierre. With his security problems these days, we need to be careful. And please be nice. Like it or not, you still have to play lackey when we are among certain people.".

"Why?"

"I have an image to maintain, darling Stash." She patted his cheek. "Besides, it'd be good practice for you. If you're going to play liaison, you'll have to learn how to . . . um . . . be more sophisticated." She laughed at her choice of word.

He turned his face and rubbed his day-old stubble against her tummy none too gently. "I dislike sophisticated rich old men," he told her. Then he looked up and added, "And I definitely dislike opera."

Marlena smiled down at him. "It's going to be fun baby-sitting with you," she teased. He growled and pulled her onto his lap.

Sophisticated. Wealthy. Powerful. Pierre du Scheum was everything Steve wasn't. He probably loved opera. Du

Scheum hadn't wanted to meet them at his big mansion. He didn't trust the place to be clean, he had said. Steve didn't blame him. It must be tough to own a house where he couldn't change his underwear without worrying about his safety.

Like it or not, Marlena had made a very valid point during the drive there. Du Scheum's life was in danger. There was at least one attempt that they knew of, and of course, if he wasn't the leak, there were people very close to him who were using his household and personnel.

When they'd arrived at the penthouse complex, Marlena had driven through without any ID checks. The guards greeted her by name. Steve bit back the sarcastic comment on his lips.

"It has to be the penthouse, of course," he remarked in the elevator.

Leaning back against the mirrored wall, Marlena crossed her arms. Her hair was tied back and the high collar of her deep red leather jacket accentuated her cleavage. It was open down the front, and her stance emphasized the low neckline of the black silk blouse underneath.

She was mocking him. Steve shrugged. He couldn't help it if he felt a little antagonistic right now. He took a threatening step toward her, bringing her laughing eyes to meet his. The elevator stopped and the doors opened slowly.

She brushed up against him on the way out and kissed him on the chin. He stared hard at her back as he followed. She was back in Marlena mode—tough and edgy. Bold. And sexy as hell. Another reason to dislike du Scheum. He had also seen the real Marlena underneath.

Steve wasn't jealous of du Scheum. What he didn't like was the older man's link to Marlena. There was a fond tenderness in the way his eyes lingered over her. Steve especially didn't like the way he held on to her hand a little too long. The hint of intimacy really, really pissed him off. But he made an effort not to let it show. For now.

"Marlena, *chérie*, so wonderful to see you." Pierre du Scheum's cultured voice greeted them. He was immaculate in white, very much at home with the European decor of the room.

Steve followed the butler to the seating area by the large fireplace. The ceiling was high, with whitewashed oak paneling as relief. A portrait of two cherubic angels peered down from heaven above the fireplace. The silk wallpaper glimmered in the natural lighting from a large glass sliding door leading to the balcony. He was sure the view would be superb.

"And Mr. McMillan, how are you?"

"Fine, Mr. du Scheum," he replied. Out of the corner of his eye, he noticed Birman standing just by a connecting door between where they were and another room.

"Please call me Pierre. Make yourselves comfortable."

Steve had to smile. It was difficult not to. His idea of "comfortable" was kicking his shoes off and going shirtless, with a beer and a remote for television. He looked around. Nope. Couldn't see any TV set. He chose the small couch across from du Scheum and was glad when Marlena joined him there. She could have sat by the older man but she didn't.

Du Scheum's pale blue eyes gazed intently at them out of his lined face. He had the sharp bone structure of his Gaul ancestors, a long aristocratic nose, and thinnish lips that were smiling at the moment. The creases in his cheeks deepened, softening the harsh lines of his face. Sitting back, he pulled out a cigarette case from his white suit and opened it.

"Do you smoke, Mr. McMillan?" When Steve shook his head, du Scheum selected a cigarette and snapped the case shut. "A bad habit. Everyone should have one, don't you agree?"

"I suppose," Steve answered.

"Marlena can be one, Mr. McMillan."

The voice still held warmth, but Steve sensed a question behind the comment. Beside him he sensed Marlena turning to look at him, waiting for his reply. He glanced sideways, expecting to see amusement, but her blue eyes held only curiosity. Very softly he said, "A habit, but not a bad one."

Pierre du Scheum laughed. He lit his cigarette with a gold Cupid lighter from the coffee table. The little arrow shot out a flame. "*Chérie*, you finally found someone who can actually talk back."

"*Oui*, Pierre."

"And now you want to take him to see *Turandot*?"

"Steve is taking me, darling. The tickets are sold out, but of course you know that."

"*Oui*, and that's why you come to me." Du Scheum exhaled smoke through his mouth. "It's been a long time since you've asked anything from me, *chérie*."

Marlena uncrossed her legs and moved a little closer to Steve. "Not true, Pierre. I always ask favors from you."

"Not personal favors, not this kind. This is for pleasure, no? The others always involved business." Du Scheum turned to Steve again. "Do you know how difficult it is to have a woman who thinks of business before pleasure all the time? I gather you like opera, then?"

Steve could tell by the amusement in those light blue eyes that Pierre du Scheum knew very well that he had never been to a live opera before. "A friend of mine recommended it," he fabricated. "I thought Marlena might like it."

"Oh, *oui*, our Marlena loves opera. I took her to her first one. Do you remember what it was, *chérie*?"

Our Marlena? Steve could feel a burning sensation at the back of his throat. One more minute of this and he would pull Marlena out of there and buy those tickets from the Internet.

"Of course. A tragedy." Marlena's voice was calm and soft. "There is nothing more tragic than a pair of dead lovers in opera."

A servant brought refreshments, and Steve quietly took a long sip of his Coke. Was that a subtle warning?

"*Turandot* has a happy ending, Pierre," Marlena pointed out.

"But at a price, *chérie*." Pierre du Scheum tapped his cigarette against a crystal ashtray. "I'll see what I can do. Is that all?"

Steve felt Marlena's fingers playing lightly against his palm. He understood what she was trying to say, that she wasn't ignoring him.

"I didn't want to talk about business on the phone, Pierre."

"Of course."

"When will you entertain again?"

"Are you really going to sell something that belongs to me?" Pierre's tone of voice was the same, but Steve felt an undercurrent in the conversation. And still Marlena's fingers caressed him gently.

"It's information." Marlena gave a careless shrug. "And all information is for sale. I'll finish the sale and keep the money for myself. Mr. Cunningham went through a lot of trouble to get it."

"What if I want it back? It was on my property the other night."

"So it was, Pierre darling. I'm sorry you arrived a little too late." Marlena freed her hand from Steve's and leaned forward to pick up her glass of chilled Chardonnay. "Besides, it's going to look strange if you're out there hawking your own secrets. This way you can negotiate as many favors as you want before letting any buyers know that I have it. See, we both win."

Pierre du Scheum laughed. Amusement lit his features, and he regarded Marlena for a moment. Steve couldn't understand why he heard threats and yet the expression on the older man's face was tender, like a lover's. Ex-lover, he corrected grimly.

"You never fail to impress me with your business acumen, *chérie*," du Scheum said. "Of course your plan makes sense."

"Mine does, but yours doesn't."

"What do you mean?"

Marlena sipped on her wine. "Why the need to set up Cunningham in your place? All you have to do is come to me."

Steve thought about it for a moment, and agreed with her. Pierre du Scheum didn't need to hide behind a William Cunningham to talk to Marlena. He also remembered the second recorded phone call Marlena had received. That person had mentioned looking forward to meeting her, so it couldn't be du Scheum. But was that Cunningham?

Pierre du Scheum didn't answer, just sat there quietly finishing his cigarette. Marlena finished her drink and picked up her purse beside her.

"Go home, *chérie*. Just take care of what you have. It is a wanted item."

"It appears to be. Speaking of that, did you get what *you* wanted at the meeting today?"

Du Scheum's eyes narrowed a little, and he glanced at Steve without any change of expression. "Not yet," he replied.

"I take it that, as usual, you won't want your name in this little matter?"

"I would appreciate it, Marlena. It would be awkward."

"Okay. Hopefully you can get us the tickets, Pierre. Will you be at the show?"

"Of course."

"I'll look forward to seeing you there."

They got up to leave, and du Scheum shook Steve's hand at the door. "Be careful," he murmured in that quiet voice.

Steve didn't say anything. He looked behind the older man. Birman stood far enough away not to be intrusive. They made eye contact, and he nodded at the bodyguard, who nodded back. Sophisticated and powerful, but no privacy, Steve thought. Not when one's life was being targeted at every turn. Pierre du Scheum couldn't go anywhere without a bodyguard. He, Steve McMillan, could come and go as he pleased.

"What was that all about?" he asked Marlena as they pulled out of the complex.

"Process of elimination, Stash."

"How so?"

"Pierre never calls me *chérie*. Our first opera wasn't a tragedy. And Pierre doesn't smoke in the penthouse."

Steve pulled the car over to the side of the road and

turned to look at Marlena. He pulled the sunglasses off her nose so he could see her eyes. They stared back calmly at him, without the usual laughter. "Damn it, Lena," he said. "What are you up to now? Warning du Scheum won't save him."

"Warn him?" Marlena frowned, then realization dawned. She couldn't believe Steve would actually think that, but his eyes were accusing and angry. "You think I was warning Pierre just now?"

"You told me earlier you didn't believe that he could be the informant."

"That's right." She frowned again. "And I still believe that."

"Yeah, so you ran straight to him to tell him he's in trouble, didn't you? Do you really care for him that much?"

She was this close to losing her temper, but managed to speak levelly. "How did I give him this warning, then, Mr. Know-It-All? Did I wink at him or pass him a piece of paper?"

Steve shrugged. "I don't know. I just know you both were speaking between the lines. You just admitted it yourself. He was telling things that weren't true and you went along, so of course he had to know that something was up. You even brought up his meeting yesterday. That is enough to alert him that he's being watched."

Marlena shook her head. He was reading everything wrong. "Stash, someone is after Pierre. I needed to know how deep he is in, and going to him about the tickets was one way to find out. He acted totally in character of how he would act publicly but that's not him in private, so I know he's in deep enough that he doesn't trust talking directly with me. That means he thinks there are bugs and micro eyes at his place, just as at my first apartment."

"So how is he in private? How would he act?"

She gave him a hard stare. "Are you listening at all?"

"Yes, I'm listening. Your Pierre is in danger, and you want to save him."

"Yes, I do, but that's not what I mean." His anger was like palpable waves of heat against her and she wasn't sure why he was acting as he did. She had wanted to confirm that Pierre was in trouble and she had. What was wrong with that? "Look, only a few people know about the missing laptop in my possession. You, me, and Pierre. He didn't answer my question when I asked about the next function. He's trying to warn me about something."

"So you're both warning each other and you leave me standing around like his bodyguard. You could have discussed this with me first."

"Is that what's causing this?" Marlena demanded, sitting upright. "You're mad because I didn't tell you something I didn't know anything about until the meeting?"

"You knew enough to decide to meet with him. This isn't how a team works, Lena. You tell me what's on your mind before you do anything."

If she wasn't so mad, she would scream at him. Coldly she said, "A team? All I've been hearing so far is you, you, you. I think you've forgotten it takes a 'we' to make a team." She slapped away his hand that was reaching out for her and added, "Didn't I take you along? I wasn't hiding anything from you. There was nothing to conclude until after the meeting with Pierre, that's all. I can't just tell you things that I'm not sure of, Stash. The only way to prove to myself that Pierre isn't our informant was to talk to him, can't you see that?"

"No, I don't see that," he told her, still in that grim voice. "All I see is what I saw. You went to your ex-lover, and it sounded like you were warning him about the laptop. He said he wanted it back and you told him how you could both profit from the deal without him being involved. What do you think that looked like? I saw a conspiracy."

Marlena shook her head, trying to clear it. His disbelief hurt more than she cared to admit, and she lashed out, "How can you be so stupid? You can't do this job if you let emotions get in the way like this. Pierre does a better job than you can."

The power to hurt back was a frightening thing sometimes. His face, flushed with anger before, turned into a chilling mask. "Then I had better find a job more suitable for me," he told her, "one that lets me talk to real people with real identities, who can trust me enough to tell me the truth, who can at least make a commitment with some things."

Marlena flinched at his cutting words, and she scooted back against the door. Steve's expression changed as soon as he finished his accusations, and he leaned forward to touch her. She didn't want to hear any more. His words hurt because he was right. She had no identity and couldn't tell the truth about herself. And she couldn't make any commitments; she feared them.

"Lena, I'm—"

"Don't touch—"

Screech of tires. Marlena turned to look back, startled. A mere breath of a moment later, the whole car rattled like coins in a tin can as another larger vehicle slammed against Steve's side. He had been moving toward her at that very instant, and the momentum threw him against the dashboard. His head smacked into the windshield. Her own head hit the car window on her side, hard enough to make her wince. In that split second her mind understood that this was no accident. The vehicle that hit them had done so at a high speed and hadn't tried to brake.

She groped around and pulled at her purse. "Stash! Are you all right?"

There was blood on his forehead. His eyes were closed. She tore open her purse. Too late. She had allowed herself to be distracted from her job. Something smashed the back windshield and she slumped down to avoid all the glass. She turned, hand in her purse, pulling out her weapon.

Too late. She felt a sting in her neck and touching it, pulled out some kind of dart. And the world went black.

Chapter Twenty

Someone was pounding on what sounded like a hollow drum, over and over, determined to get his attention. The beat was insistent, becoming louder and louder until it was impossible to ignore. Steve pushed out of the darkness, grappling with the invisible tormentor, jerking up in one swift motion. "What the—" The rest of the sentence was lost as his whole brain exploded into red and white dots and stars. He cursed, grabbed his head with both hands and found it bandaged.

A man's voice drifted from somewhere to his right. "Man, I love the way you talk when you wake up."

Steve turned his head very slowly. Cam was sitting on a chair, reading. At least he looked like Cam. "Are you related to Cameron Candeloro?" he asked politely. "I seem to be hallucinating him in color-coordinated designer clothes."

"You keep that up and I'll tell doc to give you a couple of shots, pal."

Steve blinked, studying Cam. It was he, all right, except his friend's hair was neatly combed back and he looked too spruced up to be true. Even his tie was straight. "What happened?" he asked, then remembered in a flash. He jerked up again, and ignored the spinning room as he tossed aside the white sheet over him. "Lena! Where's Lena?"

"Whoa, easy, boy." Cam was suddenly by the side of the bed, helping him to sit up. "You have a nasty bump on the head there."

"Where's Lena?"

"Marlena?" Cam shook his head. "There wasn't anyone with you. Someone shot you with a tranq dart while you were driving and then hit your vehicle. You're lucky to be alive. The whole driver's side is crushed."

Steve grabbed Cam's arm. "No, the car wasn't running and Lena was with me. Where is Lena? And what do you mean, a dart?"

He tried to get out of the bed but Cam pushed him back. "Let's get the doc in here first, then you can tell us what happened, Steve. It's not going to help if you fall down and get a worse bump than the one you've got right now."

That calmed him down for a moment. "Get the doctor now, then," he said.

"Okay, but I need to get hold of the O.C., too. His order was to call him as soon as you opened your eyes."

"Sounds ominous."

Cam nodded. "Be prepared for trouble, Steve," he warned as he went out of the room.

Steve gingerly touched the throbbing bump on his head, counting each painful beat. He must have hit the windshield. He remembered turning and seeing a Hummer just before it crashed into them, then . . . nothing . . . They were arguing about something and weren't paying attention. He gripped the sheet as pieces of their heated conversation crept back to him.

It was all his fault. He had allowed his jealousy to get in the line of fire. If he hadn't stopped the car or become so engrossed with their argument, they might have seen the vehicle coming for them. A cold panic swelled up inside him. He needed to get out of this place.

He refused to think about what was happening to Marlena right then. No more emotions in the way. She had been right; his emotions were not helping him do his job. Impatiently he waited for the doctor and Cam.

Half an hour later the doctor was done examining him. No concussion. Just a big bruise and cut where he had hit the rearview mirror. That probably saved him from crashing through the windshield, the doctor said. But all Steve could think about was Marlena. He wanted to be released from the hospital immediately. That was when he found out that there was a guard outside the room, and he wasn't there to ensure his safety.

He turned to Cam. "Care to explain?"

Cam rubbed his nose. "Only if you promise you aren't going to deck me and then try to make a run for it."

Steve frowned as he looked around for something to wear. "I don't think I can run far without a pair of jeans. I'm not going to walk out of this room with my ass hanging out."

Cam grinned. "That isn't a pretty image, buddy." He sighed. "The thing is, they contacted the rental car company to find out who you were, and of course they contacted us. When we got to you, you were already in the hospital, out of it. The cops gave us the details and said they also found fifty thousand dollars in a briefcase by you."

Steve raised a brow. "Fifty thou? And no one took this briefcase?"

Cam shrugged. "Hard-On wants to ask you about that, I'm sure." When Steve opened his mouth, he interrupted quickly, "No, don't tell me anything, man. Don't want to know about the fifty thou. Don't want to get you in any more trouble than you're in. I'm sure you have a great explanation, what with you working with our assassin lady, but if you tell me anything I'm going to have to write a long report. And I hate writing those things, okay?"

Steve quirked his lips. "So now I am enemy number one at TIARA?"

Cam shook his head. "Not to me, but I know what you're doing. Hard-On has told us all that there's a rat in our system and he doesn't want any more leakage, especially to you, so everyone is thinking—"

"—that I'm the rat," Steve finished for him.

"Yeah, something like that. I can't say a thing, or they will know Patty helped you."

"I know."

"They even asked me where you're staying now, so thank God you didn't tell me, or they would be searching your and Marlena's little nest."

That brought on some alarm bells. Steve cocked his head. "They searched my apartment, didn't they?"

Cam nodded. "Yeah, but I don't know what they found there. No, no, don't tell me anything, damn it! I don't want to write that damn report."

Steve sniffed. He understood Cam's motive in trying to distance himself. "You mean you don't want to put Patty's name in it, if possible. You're protecting Miss Ostler, just in case this is going to hit the fan."

Cam's smile was rueful. "That obvious, huh?"

"Cam, bud. You're wearing ironed clothes, for God's sake. There is not a smudge on those light brown pants. Your shoelaces are tied. And you don't have food in your mouth."

Steve almost laughed at the forlorn look Cam gave him. "I know," Cam said mournfully. "And she doesn't even notice."

"I'm sure she did," Steve assured him, then winced. "What the hell am I doing talking to you about your love life? I need to get out of here."

"That's not likely, man. Hard-On looked like he's holding your balls."

The image wasn't very funny. "Do me just one favor, Cam? It won't get you to make a report, promise."

"Okay."

"I'm going to give you a number, and I want you to call a woman named Tess Montgomery for me. Tell her what happened."

"Okay. Give me the number. And don't tell me what or who she is, please."

Steve took the pen from Cam and jotted down the number. He passed back the pen and paper. "Just call her ASAP, okay?"

"Yup."

"I need to get out of here now. Where the hell is Harden?"

As if on cue, the door opened.

* * *

Marlena focused on the swinging light in the ceiling, then at the furnishings within sight. She had been quietly lying on her back the last fifteen minutes, remembering and listening. There was no one around her, so she had opened her eyes. Her head swam and her mind was not very alert, but surprisingly she was free to move around.

After a few more minutes, she decided that it wasn't drugs that were making everything sway back and forth. A boat. She must be aboard some kind of boat. That low humming must be the engine.

Slowly she sat up. A quick look around told her she was indeed alone. No Stash. Her heart lurched as she recalled the sight of him against the dashboard, blood trickling down his forehead. Where was he? Was he very injured?

Except for the cobwebs in her head, she didn't feel she was physically hurt. She touched her neck cautiously, at the spot where she remembered she'd pulled out a dart. It was slightly sore, but no swelling. She studied her hands—no trembling. She wished she had a mirror to check her eyes, to see whether they were dilated. She didn't think anyone had interrogated her while she was out like a light; her training could block quite a lot of drugs, but it had been a while since it had been tested. She sighed. Part of the disadvantage of not working in a group—very few challenges except in real situations.

Her leather jacket had been taken off, but otherwise her clothes were intact. She tried to stand up and fell back on her backside again. She frowned. How long had she been out that the drug still had this effect on her? Was Stash drugged somewhere, too? She had to get up, find out where he was.

The cabin was small but very tastefully furnished. This wasn't any commercial fishing boat, but someone's vacation toy. The wood was real oak. There was a mini bar in the corner of the cabin. The bed she was sitting on was the size of three bunk beds.

The door across the cabin opened with a click. She recognized the man entering as one of Pierre's bodyguards.

She frowned. "Where am I going?" she asked. Couldn't hurt to ask.

The man, as all bodyguards tend to be, was tall and burly. His eyes told her that he wouldn't hesitate to hurt her if she tried anything. Ignoring her question, he pointed to a large mirror and said expressionlessly, "The bathroom is behind the sliding mirror. Your purse is on the night table. We've taken your weapon, of course."

"Well, nothing like makeup to make a girl feel better," Marlena quipped. He had said "weapon." Good. "When do I get to see the big fish?"

The man kept silent, clearly waiting for her to get up. Marlena slowly did so, and was glad she was able to keep her balance this time. She hoped that meant she was feeling better. Catching sight of her purse, she reached for it, aware that the burly bodyguard was watching closely. She slung it over one shoulder and walked toward the sliding door.

She raised her eyebrows inquiringly when he opened it for her. "I hope you aren't thinking of playing watchdog in the bathroom."

"There isn't any need. There's nothing on you."

Ugh. She looked down at his hands. At least she hadn't been awake when those hands were patting her down. She walked through the door and he slid it shut.

She stood in front of the mirror and studied the small room. She had already seen one electronic eye when she first entered. She found another. They were the same kind that Pierre's company produced, the same that were in her apartment that first night. Was it Harden again? Was he the mole? No wonder there was no need for Burly Man to come in with her. Someone was watching her, and if it were the same person from the first night, he knew that she would know. He was daring her to be squeamish.

She stared at her reflection. Her eyes were clear. No dilation. Her confidence level grew. She could play the bastard's mind games without fear that she might not be alert enough. She took in a deep breath. Another challenge about working alone all the time—she didn't get tested enough, to see how far she would go to protect herself. She wondered what T. would do in this situation. However, T. had worked for two years with a tough group that probably challenged her being there all the time. This would be child's play for her.

There were white towels hanging on the rack. She stared directly at the electronic eye as she flapped them open, then deliberately smiled. She was Marlena Maxwell. They would see what she wanted them to see and nothing else.

When she was finished, she went back to the sink to wash her hands. Emptying her purse, she only found her makeup and some accessories. Missing were her small .38 and the electronic key to her hotel room. If someone tried to use that key, T. would be alerted. She still had her makeup, but would T. be in time to save her?

Marlena knew that her bargaining chip was that laptop. Now she wondered whether she would have that to bargain with at all.

If not, then what? If they had killed Stash, would she want to live? Something squeezed her heart painfully, and it was an effort to pretend to put on lipstick. She wasn't totally unarmed; she owned things specifically created to be used in situations like this. She would fight until she found out where they had put Stash. The tight fist around her heart didn't relax as she rubbed her lips together to smudge the lipstick. She would kill them first if they had done anything to him.

"You're going to be charged, McMillan. Fifty thousand dollars in cash in the car and an offshore account book detailing financial transactions in your apartment."

"I'm not going to be your scapegoat."

Steve looked calmly at his chief. They were alone in the hospital room after he had dismissed Cam, who was glad to be out of hearing distance. The situation looked bleak but he certainly wasn't going to let them read him his rights in a hospital gown without a fight.

He had been thinking of a setup for a couple days now and should have followed his instincts and thought things out instead of arguing with Marlena. Now she had disappeared. There was a briefcase full of cash in the car. They'd found some kind of account book in his apartment, with the kind of money he had only dreamed about. Smelled like a setup to him.

Harden was as hard to read as ever. There was something very dead about him, as if he didn't give a damn as long as he was doing his job. And it suddenly struck Steve that when it came to his job, Rick Harden followed instructions to a T, and wouldn't go beyond that.

"You want a scapegoat," Steve continued, choosing his words carefully so as not to betray the fact that he had been doing research on TIARA members, "because you don't want another bungle like what happened in your past."

Harden's brow lifted. "You've been talking to people," he guessed wrongly.

Steve shrugged, willing to let that assumption remain. "People talk," he agreed.

"Don't let a little bit of gossip make you think you know me," Harden warned.

"Permission to speak, sir."

"I think we've gone beyond that point, McMillan. Nothing you say will stop the charges. Not with the evidence against you."

There was a satisfied note to Harden's voice. Steve wished he had some clothes on. It was tough to defend oneself with his bare ass hanging out. He wasn't afraid of what would happen to him. He was afraid for Marlena. He needed to think fast, to find a way out of this.

"Questions to consider, sir. Who crashed into me? And why search my apartment?"

"It doesn't matter to me who crashed into you, or why. The fact remains that you had a lot of suspicious cash on you at that point. Orders were then given to search your apartment."

"By whom?"

Harden's gaze was steel cold. "You're overstepping your bounds," he said softly.

"I'm being accused of certain crimes, sir. I think I've a

right to ask some questions. Since I'm not yet charged, I can't get a lawyer, and since I'm being guarded without charges, it would seem fair to let me ask a few questions."

Harden's brow went higher. "You've been hanging around them too much; you sound like them, trying to mess with my mind."

And his O.C. had a grudge against contract agents. Some past experience had cost him, not just a promotion, but something that had cut powerfully deep. Steve could only guess it had to do with a woman. The information in the files had been vague.

"The people behind this setup knew you would keep me in custody, sir."

Harden pulled up a chair and sat down. "And you think that I would let myself be manipulated by you or anyone else," he suggested sarcastically.

Time to be frank. "You dislike me, sir, and have ever since day one. I was someone who didn't work his way up, some grunt that the top brass had transferred to do a job that you have been trained to do. Worse, you dislike me because I was sent to keep an eye on the task force. Would it make any difference if I told you I didn't know that was why I was transferred?"

Harden blinked but didn't betray any other emotion. "No."

"There has been an informant among us, sir, a long time before I appeared."

"So you say. So the big bad SEAL is supposed to check out the operatives in TIARA, especially Task Force Two, and then you get this big promotion, right? Whether you've been on the take or not doesn't change a thing for me, because you're foolhardy enough to trust those gray-colored operatives to be on your side.

"Well, let me tell you something, they aren't on your side. They have an agenda, and they will use you up until you have nothing to give, then they will discard you with enough evidence lying around to kill your career. Even if the department sees the setup the way you explained it, the black mark in your file remains, do you know that? And you end up mopping your own blood off the floor for what? For not following the rules, not doing it the way the department wanted it done. Why? Because you thought the end justifies the means. That justice is better served if you get the bad guys with a little outside help. And yeah, they make sure you're well paid, that the money is there as some consolation prize, but here you are, alone with none of their backup. How does it feel?"

Harden stopped abruptly, as if he'd startled himself with the long speech. Steve was no less surprised. That was the most he had ever heard his operations chief speak.

"Sir, are you talking about me or you?" Steve asked quietly.

Harden stood up, noisily pushing the chair back. "You or me, does it matter?" he countered coldly. "I've tried to warn you the path you were taking led nowhere but down. The department protocol is very clear about any smear of suspicious behavior, McMillan. It goes straight into your file and remains there. You had better call a lawyer or the admiral. Things don't look too good."

Steve forgot about not wearing any underwear. It was more important at this moment to stand face-to-face with Harden. He wasn't going to have a pissing contest lying down. He pushed off the bed in one quick move and stood in front of the other man.

Harden didn't back off or call the guard as he regarded Steve with narrowed eyes. "You want some advice? Don't fight the system. You will lose."

Steve was taller and used his height to his advantage. Let the man look up at him instead of sneering down while he lay there on a bed. "I'm a SEAL first, sir. Losing is not an option."

Harden's smile was arrogant. "Don't tell me you think your Marlena Maxwell will ride to your rescue?"

"She can't, because she was with me during the accident and no one seems to care. If you think I'm going to sit around in here while her life is in danger, you have got me all wrong, sir. I'm out of here whether I have to fight everyone in the hospital and in the system. Right now her life comes first. Put all the black marks you want in my file. I don't give a fuck."

Harden nodded. "You're the one-man army against all of them. Face it, no one will come to help you in this."

"That's your experience," Steve challenged. He didn't care about Harden's past misfortune right now. The man needed to come to terms with that all on his own, but he wasn't going to let someone's bad experience get in the way of his saving Marlena.

A knock on the door interrupted them. Cam popped his head in and waited a moment as he studied them standing face-to-face.

"What is it?" Harden asked. "Are the cuffs here?"

"No, sir. It's a Tess Montgomery. And she wants to speak to you about Steve, sir. Something to do with the case."

Harden pursed his lips into a grim line. He looked at Steve. "Who the hell is Tess Montgomery?" he demanded. "I don't have to answer any calls from her."

"Sir, she mentioned Admiral Madison's name."

Harden's gaze narrowed as he continued to stare at Steve. "Part of my army," Steve explained. "You see, sir. My side takes care of me."

There was a short silence and Harden turned to leave. "We'll see about that, McMillan," he said over his shoulder.

Steve paced the floor, trying to calm down. Losing his temper wasn't going to solve anything, especially with Harden. He was very confident T. would get him out of there. If anyone could, she would be the one. He pulled at his hospital gown impatiently. Where the hell had they put his clothes? The sooner he had them on, the faster he was out of there.

It seemed to take forever, but Cam finally came back in, a wry grin on his face. He pulled on the lapels of his new suit, as if he wasn't totally comfortable with its fit. "Bet that was fun," he commented, "that heart-to-heart with good old Hard-On."

Steve cocked a brow. "You here to gossip or to tell me some good news?"

"Harden didn't want to deliver the good news himself, so you have to call Miss Montgomery yourself." Cam handed him the cell phone. "By the way, I like these chicks you're working with. Whatever she said sure made Harden's face change colors, and the more murderous he looked, the more I knew she was going to get you out."

"Will you get my clothes, please, while I call her?"

"Pretty please, sweet buns." Cam hooted as he went off.

Steve dialed, and Tess picked up on the first ring. "Are you injured badly?" she asked, without preliminaries.

"No. Thanks for helping me out."

"I need you out of there. You have forty-eight hours before that chief of yours gets a warrant out for you. He said that's the longest he could hold off for your sake."

Steve choked back an incredulous laugh. "For my sake?" That was a little too difficult to believe, especially after their conversation. "How did you arrange this, T.?"

"Darling, I do my job and you do yours, hmm?" Amusement filled Tess's voice. "He didn't sound too happy but it's always easy to pull the strings of someone with a lot of baggage."

So T. had done some research on Harden, too. Steve wondered how much she knew about everyone. "T., do you know what they have on me? Did Cam fill you in?"

"Yes. Something about cash in the car."

"That, and they searched my apartment and found an account book with deposited money. It's meant to make me look like someone bought me off to work with the mole."

"Is it the same overseas account we were talking about earlier?"

"I'd assume so. I have no idea, T., since I wasn't there when they searched it."

"I'll look into it. It's probably an electronic transfer. Tracing it should be easy." She paused, then added, "Aren't you at all tempted to use any of those funds to pay off your sister's medical bills, Stash? It'd take a load off you."

"Dirty money," Steve countered, "is dirty money. It'll come back to bite my ass."

Tess laughed. "Darling, you have to trust me. If there are electronic money transfers involved, everything can be redirected, manipulated as I please. You haven't asked much about your new pay, have you? Contract pay doesn't look anything like your standard paycheck."

Steve frowned. "What do you know about it? In fact, what else do you know about me?"

He could see her shrugging, that slight smile on her face as she answered, "More than you want, and less than you think. All this will be explained to you during your training sessions. Now, we are losing time, darling. There is a problem. I'm in New York and can't join you quickly enough. I do know that whoever took Marlena has gone through her purse and used her hotel key. My men told me there was one visitor, and I assume he wasn't there for a social visit since he had the key."

Marlena's purse. Oh God. If anything had happened to her—"Stash!" T.'s voice was sharp this time. "I need you to stay focused!"

"Can you read minds too?" Steve asked, and determinedly pushed away the dark thoughts. He mustn't think like that or he wouldn't be able to function.

"Let's just say I have my talents. Now listen. Marlena will try to contact me. They have her purse, so if she could access her makeup she would let me know her location."

"Her makeup?"

"There is a laser beacon in her lipstick, virtually undetectable unless activated. And even then one must use the right equipment. It's similar to the signal that military pilots use if they eject from their planes."

"Okay." For the first time there was a glimmer of hope as to where to begin his search.

"I'll contact you the moment I get the information. Meanwhile you have to get someone to help you out. Wherever she is, she will be well guarded and you might need backup."

"Don't worry about me," Steve assured her.

"I want full updates of what your plans are, no going off on your own."

"No, ma'am."

"And Mr. Candeloro goes with you."

"What?"

"He's your insurance. Your commander said he couldn't trust you to just run off and needed more than your word. I told him to have Cameron Candeloro by your side, so he can make sure you return within forty-eight hours."

"Fine." Steve turned to see Cam coming with clothes in his arms. "Thanks for getting me out. I'll get Lena, I promise."

"I never doubted that, Steve. Keep that beeper close at hand."

"Yeah." Steve rang off and caught the clothes Cam tossed into his arms. "So I heard you're my baby-sitter."

Cam shrugged. "It was that or you stay in custody. I know you want out."

Steve grinned. "You realize you're going to have to write a report?"

Cam's lip curled up derisively. "Yeah, now you owe me two!"

Pulling on his pants, Steve looked up. "Hey, two tickets to *Turandot*, two favors."

"You got the tickets?"

"Not yet. But if we get Marlena back, it's a sure bet." *In one piece, please*, Steve prayed silently. *Safe and alive. Please.*

Cam sobered up and nodded. "We'll find her, buddy. I'll gladly do the report if we find her as soon as possible."

Steve nodded, tucking in his shirt. He didn't want to think of the possibility of not finding Marlena in time. He inhaled and released a cleansing breath. "Let's go."

Chapter Twenty-one

He watched Marlena walk into the cabin with the silent bodyguard behind her. He put down the glass of wine he had been sipping. His wait was over.

Those remarkable blue eyes swept the cabin once, and although it looked as if she didn't bother examining the place too closely, he knew that she had taken in all the necessary details already. She had impressed him with her ability to see through her enemies' schemes.

Too bad he was now her enemy. He knew she would try to defeat him. He looked forward to breaking her, and winning, although there was a slight twinge of regret. He could have enjoyed her, very easily. Marlena Maxwell was like the fine wine he loved.

"Ah, hungry, Miss Maxwell? Please join us."

She walked slowly to the seat he indicated, her eyes absorbing his features. He nodded, and one of the bodyguards pulled out the chair for her. Once again he admired her composure as she bestowed a dazzling smile at his companion at the table. A normal person would react with shock. Displeasure. Anger. But not his Marlena. Her voice was low and sultry, sending a soft shiver through him. "Pierre, darling, drugging and kidnapping isn't exactly your style."

Pierre du Scheum didn't smile back. He didn't blame the businessman. He'd had a tough hour negotiating and didn't like to be on the disadvantage end of the discussion. It was very interesting to see a proud man beg. Marlena Maxwell had obviously bewitched this man, too.

"It wasn't my idea, *chérie*," Pierre said.

"No, it was mine," he chimed in, getting her attention back to him, where it belonged. "Your being on this nice boat is Pierre's idea, though. Somehow your comfort matters to him. Some wine? It's from an excellent vintage year. Chateau Margaux '94."

Marlena didn't demur as he poured the rich red wine into her glass. She hadn't expected a sumptuous dinner. But then she hadn't expected Pierre, either. She studied the man treating her with such deceptive politeness. She had met him before. He was in his late forties, with graying hair. It was a striking face, with strong features. A broad forehead. A hooked nose. Now that she took the time, he looked very familiar. It struck her that he also looked a bit like William Cunningham, but with more character. "All he had to do was invite me," she commented, keeping her voice casual. "You didn't have to go to such extreme measures."

"Ah, but then you would have come to me prepared, and with that boy of yours. I like the element of surprise. That is part of our business, isn't it? To keep the other side guessing? Didn't I have you fooled?"

She detected the hint of smugness behind his questions. "You did a good job," she admitted. She reached for her glass of wine. Before she took a sip, she arched a brow, and added, "I'd never have guessed that the deputy director of TIARA would be the mole everyone was looking for. My congratulations."

"Yet you aren't totally surprised?"

She savored the rich smoothness of the flavor for a moment. She could see the interest in his eyes and understood that power was this man's high. He wanted power over her right now. "My . . . Steve saw Pierre going up to see you the other day, and it occurred to me that only one person could have known so many things so quickly. He must have easy access to certain videos and information, and he must also

284 | Gennita Low

have enough authority to counter any moves that are in his way. And everything pointed at you, Mr. Gorman." She turned once again to Pierre, not because she needed him for explanations, but because she knew it would irritate her captor. There was danger in the air. She sensed it in the way Pierre sat. She had never seen him worried, but anxiety was in his eyes as he looked back at her. She chided, "I hope you're not here because of me, *chérie*."

"I don't think I've helped you much," Pierre said. "Believe me, I'd never let you walk into danger."

Marlena heard the hidden warning. "But, *chérie*, danger is a necessary ingredient of my job, no? The very fact that TIARA uses your electronic surveillance technology was a giveaway." She continued to ignore the other man on the other side of her, and reached out to pat Pierre's hand. "Your presence suggests that Mr. Gorman needs you and me here for some reason. What does he want?"

"He was negotiating for your life, my dear," Gorman interrupted abruptly. He didn't like her looking to du Scheum for answers. Pierre du Scheum was helpless against him. "He didn't believe me, though, when I informed him that you aren't who you claimed to be."

He frowned slightly when Marlena and du Scheum exchanged a smile. She was still deliberately turned away from him, and he wanted to make her give him that same smile.

Damn du Scheum. His calm demeanor was irritating. And now he, too, was paying too much attention to the woman.

"I merely pointed out that my dealings with you have always profited me, that I can't believe everything without proof. He showed me files of you, said Mr. McMillan worked under him, that he knew everything you did all along."

Marlena's heart jumped at the mention of Stash, but she kept her composure. Right now ignoring Gorman was the only way to rattle him. She allowed a mocking glance to the man at her other side. Yes, she could see that he wasn't pleased at the moment. "Pierre, those details shouldn't be of any importance. We've done business with each other for a long time now. Have I ever disappointed you?"

"That was what I told Mr. Gorman. He had, at least, conceded to my wishes not to treat you disrespectfully."

"I'm grateful for that, Pierre," Marlena told him softly. She wasn't surprised that he was involved in shady dealings. Pierre always had ulterior motives, few of which he divulged, but she also knew that he could keep her safe for only so long. Gorman wasn't just some mole that would be easily caught and discarded. He was at the top of the CIA's TIARA department; his fingerprints were everywhere. It meant he had a network of men working under him.

"So touching," Gorman remarked, a touch too pleasantly now. "Why don't we eat first? I personally don't like conducting business on an empty stomach."

Marlena looked down at the gourmet meal placed before her. Lobster and scallops, with some spice. She picked up a fork. "I take it then that you want to talk business with me?" she asked as she plunged the utensil into the lobster.

Gorman picked up his wineglass. "Of course. There is the business of the laptop, which is in my possession again, by the way. And . . . your current man, the SEAL."

He had the satisfaction of finally seeing a reaction from her. Her fork halted for a split second on the way to that luscious mouth. It was sad. He hated to see such weakness in a strong woman. That SEAL could never give her what he could, didn't she see that?

He watched, fascinated, as she delicately bit into the meat, watched the food disappear between those sensuous lips. She chewed slowly as her deep blue eyes stared back at him. He wondered whether she was afraid for her boyfriend, and how he would use that to his advantage.

"What do you want me to do?" she finally asked.

Triumph bloomed through him. He could crush her if he cared to. But not yet. She still had some use. "Eat," he ordered, "then we will see how you can please me."

* * *

Steve sifted through the folders. The intruder knew exactly what he was looking for. He wanted a certain laptop and had gone straight into the master bedroom instead of the one where Steve resided. T.'s men had taken photographs of the man. They showed a well-dressed man in his thirties, with a briefcase in which to put the laptop. He looked like any other hotel guest, going up to his room. T.'s men said they were still working on who he might be.

Steve looked through the documents that he had been studying the day before. With a gentle finger, he traced the circles Marlena had drawn using a black marker. Circles and arrows and bold underlines. The woman sure had a way with words. His small smile turned into a sober grimace. Lena. He mentally called out to her, as if that soundless yell would get her to answer back. Where was she? Was she all right?

If he hadn't been yelling at her, they wouldn't have been in the car like sitting ducks. If he hadn't been consumed by jealousy, maybe Lena would still be here, teasing him. The anger directed at himself had been simmering since he woke up at the hospital. He refused to let it cross the barrier; it would impair his judgment again. Right now he needed to concentrate on finding out where Lena had been taken.

If they hurt a single hair on her, he would take them out one by one. The images of her tied up and injured tortured him every time he took a mental break. He slammed a hand on the table to break the tension. The violent sound was welcome in the air-conditioned stillness of the luxurious suite; he wanted to do violence. But not now. The documents with her bold lines caught his eyes again.

She had circled certain names, underlined other things, and her arrows appeared to cross-reference between names and information. What had his mermaid been thinking when she was doing this? He read the circled names. They were Task Force Two, including Harden and Cam. He grinned at the caricature drawn above Harden's name, fingering it gently. Another secret his mermaid had hidden from him. She could draw very well.

There was the police report made out at Pierre du

Scheum's party, detailing what had happened and how the attacker was shot dead by the bodyguard. Here Marlena had underlined Birman's name and cross-referenced it to a big black X. Steve started shuffling all the papers around, looking for a black X. He couldn't find it.

Harden's circled name was on three documents—the task force members, the police report Harden had somehow received, and Steve's own profile called up by Harden through Patty's department. Above the pages Marlena had written the word "Source" with a big bold question mark following it.

Source of what? Steve pondered, trying to decipher what Marlena was thinking when she read the data. He drummed his fingers on the table impatiently, willing some kind of pattern to appear. It dawned on him that he was doing Marlena's job, that this was how her mind worked.

When he had been looking at the same papers, he had been mapping out the action, like any military man would. He had tried to figure out the mole by looking for action. With his way, he had concluded that the inside job dealt with certain security lapses—the ease of information transfer from certain hands suggested unquestioned authority, a person such as Harden. But he couldn't trace a tie-in between Harden and du Scheum and why Harden would want him dead. What did Harden have to do with the missing laptop?

However, now, looking at Marlena's circles and arrows, he saw a different pattern. She thought like a mathematician, circling names and seeing how many times they came up, upping the probability of involvement. For the first time Steve felt a connection with his woman that wasn't just sexual in nature. It was cool to actually see how her mind worked! He grinned again, then sobered just as quickly. Understanding her wouldn't save her, damn it. Where was she? Why hadn't she clicked on her beacon, or whatever it was she had in that purse?

Grimly he went back to his task, knowing that this was all he had at the moment, and Harden was just waiting around the corner. He hoped it was Harden who was the mole so he could fry his ass, but after that long speech his commander had given, he wasn't too sure himself. That man was messed up but he didn't sound like he was selling information. In fact, what he said only emphasized that he had spent the last few years rigidly following the code book and blindly ignoring anything that wasn't under his jurisdiction.

Okay, where was he? Source. Source. Source of what? Who or what was Harden's source? The word was on top of the members listing, the police report, and his profile. Who or what was Harden's source for these pages? Okay. That made sense. Well, as operations chief of Task Force Two, he could call up this data with no problem, but why?

Steve frowned again at the underlined date and information on the top right-hand corner, printed by the computer to indicate day of request. "Info-request sent from office of the deputy director." "Info-request sent to the office of the director." That was a normal enough procedure. Of course the task force operations chief would send communications to his boss at TIARA, but . . . would the deputy director of TIARA send a profile of Steve to the O.C.? Why? If Harden wanted to, he could call up that information himself. Besides, Steve remembered, Cam had told him that Gorman had interviewed all the members himself. Except for him. Was it a coincidence, then, that the deputy director read his profile and forwarded it to Harden?

Steve picked up the black marker lying on the table, and uncapped it slowly. Then, with care, he drew an arrow from Harden's name to Marlena's "Source" to the info-request data on the top right corner of the page. He paused, then added a large X above the word "Source."

His profile. What was so important about his profile that the deputy director would send it to his O.C.? Steve had glanced through it before but since it was about himself, he had given it cursory attention. After all, he was chasing a mole, and he didn't count.

However, his mermaid's method counted him in. He could see it now, how she was weighing his name just like any other, as she underlined aspects of his profile. She had circled his name. Disbelief knifed through him that she had done it. It was logical, but it still didn't feel good. He glared down at the information about his age and height, all the bare facts of Steve McMillan. Did she see anything that would make her think him the traitor? Then he noticed how she had circled the word "SEAL," his military record. The minx had drawn a picture of a seal above that. He relaxed. Her mind might have been working, but her little cartoon here told him she wasn't totally being cold about all this.

"Okay, sweetheart, tell me what is it about this SEAL operative you find suspicious," he murmured as he ran a finger down each page. A fast reader, he had skipped most of the things about himself that he had thought pretty obvious. But not to Marlena. She would be curious and interested, wanting to know more about him, so she had read closely. Here she had underlined his transfer from his SEAL team. Then she had arrowed to the date of transfer and then to the admiral. There it was—something he had missed: he reported to the admiral.

Steve frowned. If he were Harden reading this, of course he would assume that Steve McMillan was there to report to the admiral about Task Force Two. This ought to be the private profile that the deputy director kept for himself, especially if he was working with the admiral. Why would he send this to his task force operations chief?

He remembered Harden's accusations that day during the meeting when he was taken off the case, after Marlena had been freed. It was Harden who had clued him in regarding the reason the admiral had transferred him. If Harden had just gotten this from Gorman, no wonder he was angry enough to remove Steve from the current operation. Knowing his O.C. by now, he wouldn't want Steve to report about the failure and foul-ups of the Marlena-who-wasn't to the admiral. Harden had made up his mind not to secure another black mark in his file. Which also meant that he didn't care if the deputy director knew about the snafu, only Admiral Madison. Slowly and deliberately, Steve wrote down "Source" and an X above it with the black marker.

There weren't any more marks that caught his attention

after that. Steve stretched and cracked his neck. His headache from the lump on his head had returned. Thinking would make that happen, he concluded wryly, as he gathered the pages that were the most important. He set them on the table, straightening the edges, as he tried to make sense of what he had been doing. What Marlena and he had been doing.

They were both heading somewhere but he wasn't sure exactly where. Source. Movement of data. Harden. Maybe he ought to draw a diagram.

Steve turned the pages over to the back and wrote down "Source (director)," then drew an arrow down, then wrote "Data/Info," then drew an arrow down, then wrote Harden's name. He plucked his lip for a moment, then wrote down his own name below Harden's. Then he drew an arrow sideways to show a side note, and wrote in "Admiral." So where would he write the word "Mole"? How was the information leaking out through Harden?

He shook his head. The diagram was wrong, but he didn't know exactly where the mistake was. Deciding to try again, he flipped to the next back page, and froze.

There, bold as could be, his mermaid had drawn a diagram with the X on top.

Marlena ate but didn't taste anything. Training had taken over, and she took the opportunity to dissect and assess the situation. Her being in danger was irrelevant. Her main concern was Stash, whether he was a prisoner somewhere. He was useful as bait to get her to do things for Gorman, and she hung on to that fact like a lifeline. She couldn't bear the thought that he was injured or . . . dead.

She smiled at Pierre when he refilled her glass with wine, and shook her head when he offered her some dish. There was a calmness to him that was very solid, as if he had full confidence that things would work out the way he wanted, and she used his quiet self-assurance for support. She would not dwell on Stash being out of reach; she would instead plan on defeating the deputy director of TIARA, who, she noted with satisfaction, didn't like her friendship with Pierre.

As long as she could nurse that sore spot, she had some control of the situation. Time was of the essence. The boat had stopped, which meant that T. would be able to locate her signal. She sipped her wine and turned to Gorman, who had been watching Pierre and her with hooded eyes. "May I talk about you instead? Or would that be business, too?"

Gorman's features relaxed a little at her attention. "At one time I had planned it to be a combination of business and pleasure," he told her, with the arrogance of someone who was used to people falling in step with his plans. "However, I don't think it too wise now. You aren't strong enough for me, my dear. You let yourself fall in love with someone who would betray you at the drop of his sailor hat."

Marlena stopped herself from stiffening. She had to find out now. "Tell me what you did with Steve McMillan," she said in a level tone, not lowering her gaze from his face.

"Ahhh, the meat of the matter," Gorman said with a cynical smile, "but I thought you wanted to talk about me. Or maybe your mind really isn't into this conversation?"

His enjoyment at having bested her was meant to diminish her own confidence. Marlena allowed a small smile. "Well, well, well. Who would have thought the great boss man of TIARA would compare himself to a mere sailor? Surely you're not jealous?"

She heard Pierre coughing, probably choking back a laugh, but her gaze remained pinned on her opponent's face. Gorman certainly didn't find anything funny about her remark at all. Obviously he hadn't considered that she would see through his hatred of Stash as jealousy.

A man like Gorman didn't like his weakness made public. Nor did he like it to be made fun of. Marlena ruthlessly pursued this theory, using information she had curried from Steve's pile of folders. "Surely you didn't sit alone in that big office up in that building, pondering how to stop a mere SEAL transfer from finding out what is happening in TIARA! You didn't think the inexperienced SEAL would actually be able to unearth anything to report back to the admiral!"

Her amused remarks scored, because a telltale flush climbed Gorman's neck to his face. She was sure it wasn't from too much wine. Softly she continued, in the same amused, mocking voice, "I can just see it. You used your influence with Pierre to hook up the apartment with his electronic equipment. You used one of your CIA underlings to do it, so no one would know about your own camera access to my privacy. You had thought to see me alone, for yourself, and horrors, that awful Harden sent in that SEAL boy after me and you found yourself comparing yourself with him!" Marlena laughed softly. Bingo. She had made a direct hit. "I'm flattered."

Gorman slammed his hand on the table, causing the wineglasses and plates to clatter noisily. Some food splattered, staining the white tablecloth with orange and red spots. "The admiral thought he could catch me by sending in someone as green as Steve McMillan," he sneered. "He assumed that his SEAL operative would be able to see things that other CIA operatives couldn't, just because he was a point man in his little outfit. Funny, that point man couldn't see past his erection, running around with you when he should be wondering who was behind everything. Please don't insult me by saying that you think he could have caught me. I don't even exist in his thoughts. I made damn sure he never met me, and I also gave enough hints to Harden and some of the other men to stop them from bonding as teammates. Your Steve McMillan's career in this kind of work, Marlena, is going down the tubes. My man Harden will help me destroy him."

Marlena shrugged nonchalantly. Gorman didn't know that Steve had a new gig. She was, however, very interested in this thing with Harden. "So that's your secret," she said as she dabbed the napkin to her lips. "Rick Harden, damaged wing candidate. He knows you have power over his career, and so he's willing to tiptoe around your orders."

Damaged wings were operatives the agency no longer wanted because they weren't of use anymore. Too much exposure. Psychological problems. Too much knowledge. These operatives were often put aside. Marlena knew that the CIA and other high-profile agencies regularly culled these men from their rosters, some without any preliminary testing. Damaged wings were left to fend for themselves as prisoners in foreign nations or in public life, depending on the situation. Gray groups such as hers took in some of the luckier ones. Some turned into mercenaries. A man like Harden, though, she understood, would view that as failure, so he stuck to the rules in the belief that it would redeem him. Unless, of course, he had the misfortune to be stuck under a man like Gorman, who would use Harden's weaknesses against him.

Gorman's smile was malicious and self-satisfied. "Why not? Men like Harden and a few well-chosen ones are easy to control. I have a whole special task force chosen specifically to maintain my kind of order. I didn't appreciate the admiral's transfer. He was pretty smart, though, because he somehow linked Task Force Two, and not any other of the other teams, to the leaks. I respect his instincts, but of course that only gave me more incentive to use my robot crew, as I fondly call men like Harden and Candeloro, and the rest of that task force. I interviewed them myself, you know—every one of them is without a backbone. Especially Harden, waiting for me to pat him on the back," Gorman finished with amused laughter.

That was the very moment Marlena decided that if she wasn't rescued in time, she would take Gorman's life with hers. Of all the things she detested most, the worst was a man playing with another's life like a puppet. That came from personal experience, and she wouldn't wish it on Harden, a pain in the ass though he was.

"You have profited on your own," she pointed out, "so I don't understand why the sudden need to get a middleman into your little world. I, as you know, eat up a lot of that profit."

A server brought coffee, and Gorman contemplated the woman sitting there stirring cubes of sugar into her cup. Her

blue eyes were mesmerizing, so deeply blue that he sometimes forgot to be careful while talking to her. Indeed, she
was a very dangerous woman. Men not only found her attractive, but for some reason they developed this urge to protect her, too. Even an old hand like du Scheum. He himself
would have preferred a little less luxury. Perhaps instilling
some fear into those pretty blue eyes would take away that
female confidence of hers that bordered on arrogance.

The old fox had a point, though. "Why do that," Pierre
had pointed out earlier, in that cool and collected demeanor,
"when you can use her still? She's the best at what she does,
no matter what you say, and the people you want to contact,
for some reason, trust her. You already have the item you
wanted, and I cannot help you get rid of it. It belongs to me,
after all, and if it gets out that I handled the sale . . . well,
you know the consequences."

So Gorman had allowed the European businessman to
persuade him. He already had seen the advantages, of
course, but it was always good to let the other side think they
were smarter. Of course he hadn't expected the way the
other man had fawned over Marlena when she appeared.

He wished he could change his mind and keep her alive,
but she was too dangerous. Something in her eyes, those
twin blue flames, told him that she was planning against
him. Whoever she was, whatever she was, Marlena Maxwell
meant to destroy him.

He drank his coffee, tasting its rich texture as the hot liquid slid down his throat. Regret added a bitter tinge to the
flavor. He had nearly made the major mistake of taking a po-
tent woman as a partner. As he continued studying her
beauty, she raised one of those graceful brows in mockery. It
made him think of how she would look at him in his bed. She
took another sip of her coffee, obviously waiting for a reply.

"Why did I hire you?" Gorman said, still contemplating
the waste of such beauty. "Well, you have garnered a very
deserved reputation as someone who can take care of certain
business. One of my men died unexpectedly, and I grew suspicious about certain . . . investigations. My drop-offs to

other agencies were obviously getting some attention, what with the arrival of a transfer I didn't request. I decided it was time to play the game a little differently.

"Besides, I suddenly have in my possession a laptop that contains something bigger than mere information. It is technological advancement, and I have found certain countries will pay a high price for this, more so than mere information."

"Let me guess," Marlena drawled. Her elbow rested on the table, and with her chin nestled in her hand, she looked absurdly like a child raptly listening to a fairy tale. "China. Certain Middle Eastern countries. I think I understand now. You needed somebody who had contacts with arms dealers. Pierre couldn't do it because the laptop came from the Naval Research Lab, where his association would be made known. You couldn't do it because arms dealers just didn't trust any director for the DOD, unlike a foreign embassy. So you found me."

Gorman felt his heart beating faster as she gave him a slow, dazzling smile. She was so quick-minded. He wanted to have her as much as he wanted to break her. "You were doing fine until you became involved with someone you shouldn't. Now you have to do this the hard way, Marlena, dear. If you care for this Steve McMillan, you'll still broker this deal for me, on my own terms, out of sight of anyone for whom you might work, out of reach of anyone set up by the admiral. I no longer trust you, you see, and must therefore treat you like the rest of them."

"Like you treated Cunningham?" Marlena asked boldly. "I'm curious. William Cunningham must have been a relative—you both look similar, same speech patterns, in fact."

Gorman waved his hand dismissively. "He isn't important."

"He was important enough for you to kill," she pointed out, leaning forward confidentially. "That night at Pierre's house. It was set up in such a way to cause a lot of problems for many people, wasn't it? First you wanted to get me to open Pierre's safe, but after you rid yourself of Cunningham.

You want Pierre to find him dead in his room for some reason. Why?"

He didn't answer immediately as he lit a cigarette. His eyes were sharp and amused as he sucked in a breath and exhaled. "No need to bother your beautiful head with so much," he said softly. "The less you know, the more reasons not to kill your Steve, don't you agree? But I'll tell you one little thing because I know what a curious and smart woman you are, my dear. I like to hold things over people's heads. Like now, for instance. Your obedience is predicated on my goodwill because I have something over you—someone you care about."

Ahhh yes, he was a lot more like Cunningham than he cared to admit. He, too, liked to boast. Marlena wondered what he held over Harden's head. She understood Cunningham's death placed Pierre in a difficult position since he was affiliated with the research of X-S-BOT. If word got out, there might be too many inconvenient investigations into his activities. Thus his cooperation was ensured.

She was tempted to retort not to be so sure of her "obedience" yet, but of course that wouldn't be prudent. Stash's safety came first, no matter what. No matter how. She shrugged, allowing boredom to seep into her expression. Sliding back into her chair, she exhaled slowly, deliberately relaxing her shoulders visibly. "I don't digest threats well for dessert. I asked you earlier what you wanted and I think I just heard the answer. But first—" She turned to Pierre. "Pierre, I don't trust him, either. Is he lying about Steve? Do you know where Steve is?"

Pierre, who had kept silent during the exchange, also appeared slightly bored. Marlena knew he heard every word because that was how he was. He was always the third party in any negotiation, and was used to playing the part of disinterested observer, one who just made sure things went smoothly. She hoped he would be able to reassure her that Stash wasn't hurt. That he was safe. At the moment she had no idea how to rescue him, and it took a lot of willpower to quell the panic that surged into her consciousness now and then.

"Mr. McMillan is fine," Pierre replied serenely. "I wouldn't worry about him at all. His injury isn't serious, and I'm sure he's now wondering the same things you are. You should focus on getting this deal done, *chérie*."

His endearment tipped her off that he was warning her about something, but it was difficult to read between the lines. He was being very careful because Gorman was looking to see whether he could use Marlena as a way to get to him. She realized how much he was at risk here. Gorman could make Pierre do a number of things, if he suspected Pierre cared for her.

"Now that we have some sort of understanding," her captor interrupted her thoughts, "you will have to return to your cabin for a while. I have a few phone calls to make. I'm sure by now Harden would be after your Steve with a warrant, and I want to hear all about it."

Marlena frowned. "A warrant?"

"Yes. I forgot to mention—Steve McMillan will be facing charges of being a traitor to this country, and even if the charges are never brought up, I'll make damn sure they remain on his file. He would end up like Harden, always fighting against his past mistake."

"The admiral will never allow it," Marlena quickly countered.

"Oh, if the charges are brought up, it's out of his hands. I've had all the evidence nicely arranged for months—offshore bank accounts, not to mention his connection to you. A court-martial can be downright nasty. Take your pick, Marlena Maxwell. Do you want your lover's career destroyed, or would you rather have him dead? A shot above the ear. A clean suicide, let's say. I can arrange either way."

Marlena looked across the table at the man threatening her. Once upon a time, she had allowed love to get in the way of her job. It was happening all over again, except this time she could get the man she loved killed, or at the very least, everything he valued could be destroyed. She wasn't going to let this happen.

She didn't have the time to work this through. First, she was going to make sure Gorman got his comeuppance. Second, she would have to find the courage to walk away from Stash.

"You got to eat, man. I know you think pacing in and out of your room and consuming pages of print would sustain you, being a warrior and all, but you're making me hungry."

Steve turned and studied Cam, sitting at the dining table. He had been there for quite some time, since Steve couldn't remember when he saw him anywhere else but at said table. "Looks like you're eating my share," he pointed out. "Filet mignon, French pizza, Mexican tacos, cheese sticks, Chinese food, Italian ice cream, Irish coffee, apple pie . . . What is this, the United Nations food convention?"

Cam put down a piece of pizza, swayed his fingers over the different dishes, then went for the chopsticks. "Free food," he answered with a full mouth, "excellent free food, is hard to come by, my friend. You should really try this stuff. Man, I'm totally pissed off by your good luck."

"Good luck?" Steve approached the table and pulled out a chair.

"You know, slinky, gorgeous, James Bond lady, a big bed with a real down blanket, and room service like this. And this place has a freaking butler, for God's sake." Cam dug into his food and munched enthusiastically. "Life is good."

"I gather you like being my insurance," Steve commented dryly. He didn't feel like eating. Worry gnawed at his insides, and he felt listless from his headache and impatience.

"Only bad thing," Cam said, chewing and waving a bread stick, "is I have to look at your mug. Now if I can just get you to stay in your room, yeah, and then call the love goddess Patty to spend an evening here with me and all this . . . wow, paradise, man, pa-ra-dise."

Steve shook his head, smiling at his friend's enthusiasm.

How come he and Marlena were always fighting over who controlled what, when Cam would just willingly let his Patty be queen and that was fine by him? Maybe he ought to steal a page or two from Cam's book.

The cell phone rang and he pounced on it. "Yeah?" he barked. "Oh, okay, no, it's fine. Let her come up." He put down the phone and looked at Cam, "Your love goddess has arrived."

It was comical to watch Cam choking on the bread stick. "What? When? How? Why is she here?" he sputtered as he started pushing away the dishes and stood up. He brushed his pants and looked around frantically.

"You forgot where," Steve added with a grin as he sat back and watched the pandemonium. "Journalism 101, wasn't it? Who, what, where, when, why?"

"Come on, man, help me find my jacket!"

"It's on the floor by the TV."

"Oh yeah." Cam walked quickly to where the new suit was lying, picked it up, and started flapping it out wildly. "Man, shit, damn, and fuck."

"In that order?" Steve started laughing, welcoming the break from tension.

Cam gave him a dark glare. "I suppose I don't have time to iron out the wrinkles." He shrugged into the suit, trying to smooth out the telltale creases.

"You're supposed to hang the thing in the closet immediately after taking it off," suggested Steve, tongue-in-cheek. "Lena taught me that." His amusement decreased somewhat as he recalled a particular night not too long ago, when Marlena had dressed him up in some fancy suit. As a matter of fact he hadn't hung up that particular item of clothing that night.

"Oh shut up. Now, that food on the table? It's not mine, you hear? All yours, all yours. You're eating because you're worried and miserable."

The hotel suite bell rang solemnly. Cam rushed toward the door and tripped. Steve looked downward and laughed again. The man had tripped over his discarded shoes. Indeed, he had made himself very comfortable the last few hours. He took pity on his friend as he struggled to put his shoes on while hopping on one foot toward the door, and got out of his chair.

He signaled for Cam to sit down and went to open the door for Patty Ostler. She stood outside, her eyes big as saucers behind her glasses as she studied the lavish surroundings. Steve didn't blame her. He had done the same thing the first time, too, and that was before he saw the inside. Again he felt a sharp punch to the gut as he was reminded that he didn't actually "see" all the luxury till the day after that; he had been too busy getting rug burns on his back and ass. He forced a smile to his face and stepped back.

"Hey, Patty."

Patty peered up at him, clutching some kind of vinyl zip folder to her chest. "That cut looks painful," she said as she walked through the entrance. "Bet you have a headache. Did the doctors give you any medication? I heard you bashed through the windshield . . . oh!"

She stopped mid-step, taking in every detail of what she could see, her head swiveling from left to right. It had to be designed by a woman, Steve decided, because all those flowery panels and dainty china just didn't do a thing for him. Now the media room was pretty cool, with that remote screen that could control all the things in the suite—that made him feel like a king, when he was zapping on the electronic equipment, calling up channels on the giant video screen, opening and closing the doors to the liquor closet. He could even adjust every light in the room that way.

"I'm okay," he said, making his way to the dining table. She followed, eyes still wide, mouth still agape. "I hit the rearview mirror, so it could have been worse. And I'm not taking the meds because I want to stay alert in case a call comes through about Marlena."

Patty looked at the table, decked with all the dishes, then cast a knowing eye at Cam, who smiled and waved nonchalantly. "Been busy, I see, Agent Candeloro."

Cam's eyes rounded with innocence. "Not me, my love. That's Stevie boy. He won't eat so I've been trying to tempt him with all sorts of stuff from the menu."

"Uh-huh. You need to wipe that red stuff off your lips, unless you're now wearing lipstick," she said caustically. "And stop calling me that."

"Call you what, my love?"

"That! Call me that!" She gestured at nothing in particular.

"I would never call you such a thing!" Cam said, hand on his heart.

Patty swirled to meet Steve's eyes, and he fought to keep the grin off his face. "How can you stand him doing that to you all day? He's . . . impossible!"

Steve pulled out a chair for her, trying to think of a diplomatic answer. He couldn't tell her that she was Cam's object of lust and devotion. Besides, from the kiss he had witnessed, she really didn't harbor as intense a dislike as she was affecting. "Cam needs help," he finally agreed, a small smile forming. "Maybe you can give him some hints."

Patty muttered something under her breath and sat down. She looked at the food again and shook her head. "I can't believe the two of you can eat all of this."

"Three, my love, three. You, me, and unfortunately Scarface." Cam looked at Steve and then at the door to his bedroom meaningfully.

Steve sighed inwardly. That was all he needed, these two playing lovey-dovey while he paced up and down the floor.

"Well, eat, then." Patty surprised them both as she carefully unfolded one of the fan-shaped napkins and delicately arranged it on her lap, pulling the corners here and there, as if the napkin needed to be centered just so, or the food would taste bad.

Cam was on his feet within seconds. Food and his

woman, Steve thought with wry amusement. The man was indeed in heaven. He watched him sit next to Patty, and watched her blush at the heated look in his friend's eyes. Oh man. Did he really need to see this?

He coughed. "I think I'll eat in my room. I have stuff to look through."

Cam's face brightened at the suggestion. "Yes, um . . . I'll stay out here, out of your way."

Patty frowned, laying down her fork. "Are you sure?" When Steve nodded, she picked up the vinyl folio she had brought and handed it to him. "Okay. I've got what you asked for here. I pulled it out manually so there wouldn't be any electronic records."

"Thanks, Patty." Steve took the folio and a plate of food that Cam had helpfully piled on for him. "Enjoy the meal," he added, tongue-in-cheek.

He went into his room, shutting out the sight of Cam leaning toward Patty, and rolling his eyes when he caught the words, "You look good enough to eat . . ."

Steve shook his head. That woman didn't stand a chance. He sat down where he had been all day, among the files and sheaves of papers, and started reading what Patty had put together. He picked up the black marker and chewed the cap off it. With the other hand he groped for and picked up something from the plate he'd brought in. Patty had a point. He did need to eat.

After a while he was surprised that his plate was empty when he reached out and found nothing. He hadn't even tasted anything while reading and diagramming. Damn it, why hadn't T. called yet? As if on cue, the cell phone by his side started ringing.

Steve grabbed it, knocking the folders over. "Yeah? What took you so long?"

"She's being moved away from here. We couldn't pinpoint the exact location till the motion stopped."

"Where is she?"

"Got a pen?"

"Yeah."

He asked several terse questions for the next minute or two. Tess for once didn't mess around with his mind. She was, he discovered, very knowledgeable about tactical coordination, as if she'd run a team before. Which brought up a problem.

"You're in New York," he said. "It's going to take too long for you to get down here and gather men for me."

"I called you immediately, Steve; give me more time."

He couldn't. Not with Marlena's life at stake. "T., you come after me, okay? I'm going to get her now."

"How are you getting to the ocean by yourself?" Tess paused, then answered herself, "A sea mammal will find a way, I suppose. Okay, do what you have to do, but make sure they are still on international waters when you strike."

"Why?"

"Fewer questions, darling."

"Okay."

"Good luck. And bring M. back safely, hmm?"

When she rang off, Steve punched the buttons and dialed another number. A sleepy, raspy voice answered on the fifth ring, "This better be worth your life."

"Hawk. It's Steve."

"I repeat, this better be worth your life."

"I need you here with some gear and a few men you can trust."

"I see." Hawk sounded more alert now. "Is this kosher stuff?"

"No, it's on international waters."

"Tell me what you need."

When Steve finished, he jumped up from his seat and strode to the door. Cam better not be having Patty for dinner, because he didn't have time to wait. He knocked and yelled, "I'm coming in now," and counting to three, he opened the door.

Cam was adjusting his tie. Patty was nowhere to be seen. He had the most satisfied look on his face, though. "Um,

Patty is in the master bathroom," he told Steve, his eyes overly bright. "Was that who I think it was?"

Steve nodded. "I'm ready to kick some butt. My way." Boy, did it feel good to finally say those words.

Chapter Twenty-two

The ocean breeze was wet and cold. Marlena zipped up the light jacket she'd found in her cabin, wishing for her own leather one. They had been standing out on deck for ten minutes, and already her hair was damp from the sea spray. The first crack of dawn streaked the horizon, and soon there should be noise signaling the arrival of a boat with Maximilian Shoggi, known in the arms dealing world as Mad Max, on board. Dawn on international waters, Pierre had whispered to her earlier. She never did like conducting business off land. Less control.

It was just she and Pierre on deck, guarded by two of the bodyguards. She had found out that they worked for Gorman, not Pierre, which told her how much the TIARA director had infiltrated Pierre's network. That reinforced the fact that the director was a very dangerous enemy.

Gorman was keeping out of sight, standing somewhere above with his captain at the helm, where he could view the proceedings. A bright spotlight shone on them, blinding those in its glare to the observers. Very smart, she thought. No one during this meeting could turn and shoot at Gorman.

In every operation there was an apex, in which the goal of the mission was achieved. Hands in pockets, collar turned up, Marlena peered stoically toward the east, pondering this operation that had brought her here. In her job they always said the end justified the means. Her cancellation. The loss of a valuable contact like Pierre. Nameless lives affected by a traitor. Operation Foxhole would be considered a failure if the apex wasn't fulfilled, and in the eyes of those who ran covert wars, her death would have been a waste of an asset. She wrinkled her nose. She didn't think she wanted to be footnoted as a waste, which was possible since her capture. Yet here she was, unexpectedly at the apex of her mission.

It had taken many twists and turns to steal back a laptop holding a devastating formula that could change the weaponry of the world, only to discover the man behind the sale was one supposedly working on her side. She had used her smokescreen to deceive all her opponents, to make them believe that the laptop hadn't been exchanged, and in so doing she had gambled that the people to whom she needed to pass the laptop would come after her. She thought she had lost that gamble when she ended up back in the hands of the very man from whom she had retrieved the computer.

All seemed quite lost, until now. Wasn't fate an odd thing, she mused. She was being coerced to "sell" the laptop to her target from the very beginning, Mad Max Shoggi, arms dealer to a few of the shadier international leaders. She had Pierre to thank for those functions that secured bids. It took a long time to work her way into the inner circle, gaining the trust of men who dealt and bought influence and information as if they were business stocks.

So, after over two years, here was the apex of her operation, and success was very near. After that, she decided, with the laptop out of her hands, she would deal with a very personal mission, Mr. Gorman himself. Taking a deep breath, she gazed expectantly into the darkness, listening for the arrival.

Small swells bobbed the black rubber craft hovering in the darkness. The swells came in timed intervals, and Steve hunched in silence, one hand up. Like the anchored boat ahead, they, too, were waiting, drifting slowly, so as not to disturb the telltale surge of the waves. He could tell by the different wakes and directions of the waves that another boat was coming this way, and would be there not too long from now. He didn't want to strike before he could see who was on the second craft. If they moved in too fast, the ocean's movement would also betray them. Steve didn't want to strike too soon.

It was imperative not to get too close until the other boat arrived. He was very aware that timing would play a crucial role in this operation. He turned to look behind at the men who had come with him. Hawk had brought three men— what they called a fire team—each hauling his own cache of weaponry. One of them was left in charge of the boat they had rented, while he and the others approached the target in their smaller and less conspicuous inflatable.

Earlier he had his pick of heat from Hawk's backpack, whistling at some of the toys his cousin had brought along. It felt good now to have the familiar weight in his hands. They were the kinds of things a soldier's life depended on. Of course it helped, too, that Hawk and his men were his backup; they were all SEALs and they understood what it took. On the other hand, sitting in the rear, his baby-sitter, Cam, crouched quietly—face blackened, betraying his position every time his teeth glimmered as he chewed his gum. For a brief instant Steve wondered who would be baby-sitting whom, since Cam admitted to never having been on an amphibious assault reconnaissance mission before.

"Relax, man," Cam had assured with his usual cocky confidence while Hawk and his men looked on dubiously. Steve didn't blame their hesitancy, since Cam's fashionable attire at that time didn't really add any measure of assurance. "I'll stay out of your way and set up target practice."

"Target practice?" Hawk wasn't the kind who liked to joke around when it came to a mission. His brooding eyes took Cam in from head to toe—the ponytail, the silk necktie, the tailor-made suit and pants. "This isn't the time to practice your aim. We are mounting a direct strike. To storm a room, we have barely ten seconds to conduct business with our enemies. Ten seconds to sort out the good from the bad guys, to execute the rescue, and take down the bad guys. In this one we're going in at night, in unfamiliar territory.

Steve, you better tell him what he has to do or I'll shoot him before he gets us shot."

Before Steve could reply, Cam had picked up the Mossberg twelve-gauge Cruiser, a non-civilian issue lying on top of the table. He disengaged the silencer and took the weapon apart in record time. There was silence as he put it back together just as efficiently and snapped on the heavy cartridge. Steve smiled in the dark at the memory. Cam did what he knew would convince Hawk and his men. Privately, that had surprised the hell out of him. Cam had never seemed the tough and silent type.

Hawk had given Steve's TIARA teammate a close look, then turned back to the maps in front of him. "He'll do," was all he said.

After that, they spent an hour preparing. A basic hostage rescue drill had four components. Rapid insertion. Extraction. Close-quarters target identification. Precision shooting. Steve had done similar operations countless times, but this was different. This time there were emotions involved—worry and anger, two things that could get in the way. Hawk had already questioned whether it was wise for him to be part of the rescue team. Steve understood his cousin was trying to make sure the operation would go smoothly. He didn't bother to answer, though. An exchange of looks was enough.

The sound of an engine becoming louder cut off his thoughts. Dim lights became brighter. The shadowy waves reflected the meeting boats. The engine cut off.

Steve dropped his hand, signaling the others. When the inflatable was close enough, he gave the hand signals to stop. He put on his night vision glasses and looked across the dark expanse at the target point, the first boat. With the infrared thermal imager, they counted the number of humans, memorizing their locations. One of them, he told himself, was Marlena. Then he turned his attention to the second craft.

Hawk passed him a waterproof bag, and both of them readied themselves in silence. They had earlier decided that they would be the go-ahead swim pair, while Hawk's other two men, Dirk and the one they called Cucumber—Cumber for short—were to stay put until the first part of the operation was completed. Once that was accomplished, Steve and Hawk would climb up the side of the target, the signal for the others on the inflatable to get closer.

There wasn't going to be anything subtle about this mission. The first part of the operation was surgical. While the attention of target point was diverted, they planned to secure C-4 explosives to blow the propellers off the boat for effective immobilization. Then they would sneak on board.

His main goal was to get Marlena off the boat before all hell broke loose. He hoped T. and her men would be there for clean-up service not too long afterward. Easier outlined than done. He didn't like the spotlight that had been turned on. He especially didn't like the knowledge that he had caught thermal images of people on deck within that spotlight. That made it very difficult for a covert extraction, more so than close combat in the confined space of a boat's cabin. When he found out from T. that Marlena was at sea, he had already concluded that the missing laptop would be on the same ship. Marlena. Sale item. International waters. Oncoming craft. That could only mean she was needed to broker a deal.

He had called T. back just before they left on their mission to check on coordinates. T. confirmed his theory, adding that Marlena was definitely still alive because she had signaled a second time, with an added coded communication that was their indicator of Operation Foxhole under way. T. had told him not to interfere if he saw any kind of business transactions going on, that this was Marlena's assignment. Steve didn't care about any brokering. What would happen to Marlena after that was of more importance to him right now than who was on the second boat, so he opted to give a chance for the latter to leave. Less risk to Marlena's life.

They double-checked everything silently. They weren't swimming too deep, so they were using Draeger rebreathing systems that recycled expelled air, thus no betraying bubbles would reach the surface. Water-resistant explosives zipped in their haversack. Luminous compasses. They were going to measure distance the old-fashioned way, by the number of kicks. They nodded to each other.

Cam leaned forward, thumped Steve on the shoulder, and gave him a thumbs-up. Hawk just shook his head and climbed overboard. Steve did the same, dropping without a splash into the white-crested sea.

Marlena thought she heard something, but as in a bad-movie FBI interrogation, she was blinded by the glare of the spotlight. The only way to escape was to kill the bright beam, but without any weapon on her, that seemed an impossible quest.

"I never intended things to go this far, Marlena," Pierre interrupted her reverie. "I didn't know he would be spying on you and setting your friend up. To me it seemed an interesting idea at that time to see how this man was going to use the system to make a profit."

He wasn't calling her *chérie,* and she understood the underlying apology behind the explanation. Pierre never needed any excuses for what he was, and she knew these words were difficult for the proud man. "It amused you to watch this game," she explained for him, as much as for herself, "because you wanted to catch the thief as well as make a profit from his scam. And knowing they would look for a middleman, you gambled that it would be me."

He nodded. "The only way to get to the bottom of this was to see it through, so I allowed them to gain closer access to me. Besides, I knew you would want this laptop for Max Shoggi."

She understood the unspoken words. Play with the devil's minions to get to the devil himself. Pierre used the strategy so he could find out who was secretly infiltrating his network. Her organization had employed the same tactic, going after Max Shoggi the past couple of years, slowly squeezing off his well of weapons. Working with a special operations group, T. had spent time underground for two years, and had finally canceled Mad Max's main man, Cash Ibrahim, a few months ago. Then, within her special position in New York, she had frozen the arms dealer's bank accounts, effectively cornering Maximilian Shoggi into desperately looking for something big to replenish his depleted cash flow.

Something like a laptop with a secret high-tech formula would attract his foreign clients. T.'s role in that operation completed, it was Marlena's turn to enter the picture. She would obtain the missing laptop and dangle it as bait to Mad Max. Everything was going smoothly, what with her letting him trail her all the way to D.C. He was even at Pierre's function, making sure he was in line to buy what Marlena Maxwell had to offer. Everything was just fine and dandy, until—she sighed—until she had unwittingly made Gorman jealous of Stash. And because of her, she didn't know where Stash was, or what had happened to him.

She wondered when T. was going to show up. Knowing her, she would send a crew ahead to scout the situation, perhaps disguised as a passing fishing boat. Gorman's boat had been anchored there long enough for her location to be pinpointed, so it shouldn't be too long now. She weighed the probabilities of when things might start to happen—before Max Shoggi's arrival, or after. She hoped for the latter. She had conveyed to T. a coded message that she hoped made it clear that the operation was still in progress. If the scouts appeared too soon, they might frighten the arms dealer away.

No time to worry. In the distance the lights of an approaching boat twinkled. One of the men spoke into his walkie-talkie. The grinding stop of an engine. A flurry of activity. She took in a deep breath.

Lena. Steve silently called to the figure standing in the spotlight. From his position, she looked unharmed. He frowned. She and du Scheum were speaking quietly, no sign of antagonism between them as they watched the other vessel. Once in a while, one of those burly guards communicated with a walkie-talkie. How was du Scheum part of this? Steve checked out the guards through a mini scope, taking in their weapons. When one of the men again said something into his walkie-talkie, he noticed this time that the guy glanced upward toward the spotlight, an unconscious response to the person on the other side.

Steve pointed in that direction, and Hawk nodded his understanding, that someone over there was watching the people illuminated by the beam. Hawk crawled closer to him and indicated three fingers, telling him that the thermal imager showed three observers. He signaled for Steve's decision—pointing at the different options. Upward at the observers. Back toward Marlena and du Scheum, with their guards. Ambush. Or hold.

Steve's gut reaction was to immediately save Marlena, get her out of the way. His instinct told him that the person in charge was one of the three hidden observers, but if he went for Marlena's kidnapper, she was in danger of being surrounded by the guards and whoever was coming over from the other boat, effectively stopping his plans. On the other hand, if he took down her guards where she was now, someone up there would just use them as target practice.

Looming up silently behind them, Dirk and Cucumber slithered next to them. They communicated silently, making sure everything was in order. Reaching a decision, Steve consulted Hawk with finger and hand signals. His cousin nodded in agreement, and the team set their watches. Parting ways, they merged with the shadows of the boat.

One target down. Up the stairwell. Two down. Steve reached the top. He sheathed away his bloodied Bowie, adjusted the safety on his weapon. Voices drifted toward him.

"Don't let her out of your sight. She's very good at what she does, and I don't want anything to go wrong. Make sure the deal is done. The moment Maximilian Shoggi gets off, out of sight, I want her and du Scheum eliminated. Her first. Don't give her a chance to move, do you hear?"

Steve heard the soft acknowledgment from a walkie-talkie. He backed off, then turned away from the doorway. No time. His heart was thumping somewhere in his belly.

Someone out there had just received orders to kill Lena. And he wasn't out there. He wasn't anywhere close to her. Suddenly the same stairs he had just climbed seemed to have too many steps.

Chapter Twenty-three

Marlena smiled at Mad Max Shoggi. She let him kiss her hand. She told him she forgave him for trying to scare her with those threatening phone calls, and that she was glad he'd won the bidding war for the item in the end. After all, he was missing his suave right-hand man, Cash Ibrahim, and he wasn't used to dealing with such minor details as middlemen. She omitted the fact that he had T. to thank for the loss of his man Ibrahim a few months ago; that was another story.

Gorman had promised to release Stash after she had finished transacting this piece of business for him. Of course, she didn't believe he would actually keep his word, but she did know that he wanted the transfer of the laptop to be successful. Someone like Gorman didn't like being duped because he prided himself on being the master of double-cross.

She had intrigued him because of her own deceptive exploits. She felt his desire that had now changed into a perverse delight in pitting himself against her skill. There was nothing funny about having her life snuffed out while her opponent played cat-and-mouse with her, and Marlena didn't intend to walk around in this maze waiting to be rescued.

Once upon a time she had stood beside Pierre du Scheum and watched him negotiate deals with tough opponents, who had gone away trying to figure out how a man who talked with poetic softness defeated them. Relatively speaking, she had learned at the knee of a master, and it was surreal to have him return the favor tonight. He stood by and observed. With his international background, he was the assurance to people like Max Shoggi that there was nothing nefarious with the deal at hand.

Gorman understood this, and that was why Pierre was there with her. But he didn't know that she and Pierre had a history that went way back, that they had their own body language and signals. So she had the advantage there. But would she have time? The moment Max Shoggi returned to his boat, Gorman had no further use for her.

She handed the suitcase full of money to one of the guards. At the last moment, she let go before he could reach for it. His body came in front of hers as he reflexively bent to pick it up.

In those few seconds Marlena's mind barely registered the unmistakable blossoming red on the taller man's chest, as he fell forward, before her trained body jumped into action. That bullet had been meant for her. Instantaneously she turned and shoved Pierre into the other guard. Pierre didn't even make a sound, just tangled with the bigger man.

Diving onto the deck next to the downed guard, she reached for the automatic weapon he had dropped when he was shot. There was no sound as her executioner fired another shot at her, hitting the dead guard next to her again. It went in with a sickening implosive thud; the body jerked violently, pushing the weapon farther away. Marlena went after it again. Another bullet thumped into the body. Her fingers curled around the handle. Pain shot up her arm. She cursed.

The air exploded in a roar of showering glass. Someone had shot at the spotlight, plunging everything into semidarkness. Still half lying on the deck, Marlena blinked, trying to adjust her eyes to the sudden change. She found her fingers curled around the trigger of the weapon, but she hadn't fired off a shot.

Whoever was shooting at her must also adjust to the sudden darkness. This was her chance to get cover. Using one arm to push up, she rose to her knees. Out of the corner of her eye, she caught the glint of metal. Pierre. She swerved and pulled the trigger.

"Run for cover!" she yelled to Pierre as dark figures suddenly materialized from several different directions. Running herself, she reached into her right pocket. A figure jumped out in front. Before she could shoot, someone leaped into her from the right, and she fell down again. To her disgust, she couldn't keep her assailant from using the momentum to roll them like bowling balls across the deck. Whoever it was knew exactly where to stop, because they ended up behind a pillar, with her trapped under a muscular body.

Her breath knocked out of her, Marlena looked up at the man still on top of her, and saw the glint of familiar dark eyes in the camouflaged face. She forgot to breathe. Stash!

She grabbed him by the hair, pulled his face down. His mouth was hard and warm. Salty. And he dared to put his tongue into her mouth. Only when she went for his throat did he release her. "You're not Stash," she accused.

"No, ma'am," the stranger said, and rolled over, out of her grasp.

"'Cumber! Take out anyone who comes down. We have a sniper out there." Steve didn't wait for Cucumber's response as he ran past the large man toward the stern.

"Not easy with that beam on, Steve," Cucumber called after him.

Steve didn't reply. He remembered all the positions of those on board the boat shown by the thermal imager. He would bet anything that the sniper was the figure at the top to the right, on the leeward side of the boat.

From his angle he saw Marlena fall down with the guard, and fear lent him even more speed. "Cover me!" he said to Dirk.

"I'm covering Hawk. Leave the girl to him, Steve. Get the sniper. The spotlight's going to kill them out there."

Steve glanced up toward the high beam and watched it explode like mini fireworks, blinding him for a second.

There was a momentary silence as everyone seemed frozen by the unexpected darkness. Blinking and adjusting his eyes to the deck lights, Steve turned and started to climb the steel ladder, heading for the sniper from behind.

Hell was breaking loose below him, the loud popping echoing upward from the live exchange of weapons. The sniper had used a silencer, but Hawk and the others were now involved in their own battle. Steve kept looking up, even as his mind kept seeing Marlena stumbling down over and over. He knew that Hawk would get to her, no matter what.

His target had his back to him, hunched over the railings on the protective side of the boat, away from the light wind, motionless as he followed the action below him. Steve silently thanked whoever had shot out the spotlight. From up there, Hawk and everyone else would have been easy pickings for the sniper. The man lifted the weapon, sighting someone below.

Cutting loose one of the ropes that were part of the brails, Steve swung onto the landing with a soft thud and rolled, weapon ready. The man turned with one practiced move and had his semiautomatic pointing at Steve. Steve stared at the man, who unblinkingly returned his glare. They were dead-locked, weapons pointing at each other.

"You're not surprised," the man said.

"You gave yourself away with those kills," Steve told him. "Both dead with the same precise shot in the middle of the forehead. Both just before they were caught. I knew you would have a military background. A simple Triple I background check confirmed my suspicions."

"He always did underestimate you," the man said quietly, the shadows hiding his expression, "but it's not my job to tell the boss what to think and how to do his business."

"I know you and Gorman went way back, but why did you agree to kill for him?"

"He saved my daughter's life, and I owed him. He called in the favor."

"Don't do this," Steve warned as he flexed his finger on the trigger. "You've already killed two other people for him.

Isn't that enough payback?" There was a pause as he pressed on, "I know about his saving your life in a war. This isn't a life-and-death situation, and you aren't saving his life now. Come on, man. I don't know about his helping your daughter, but he even had you kill his half brother. Is that the kind of favor you thought you were paying back?"

"His half brother?"

Steve knew he had a chance now. "Yes. Cunningham is Gorman's half brother. That's how he had so much influence in and out of NRL, how he knew about the laptop, how he planned with his half brother until Gorman decided that he was expendable. I don't have time to talk about this, Birman. Put down the damn weapon!"

"I can kill you," Birman said matter-of-factly.

"Yeah, but you won't live to jump for joy," Steve replied coldly. "And, by the way, I have backup just behind you."

"You're bluffing." Birman's voice was taut with confidence. "I turn around and what? You're going to shoot me in the back?"

"One of us is," agreed Steve, "if you want to really test the theory. Right, Cam?"

"Shit, how did you see me, man?" Cam's voice rose from the narrow catwalk about six feet below.

Steve gave a grim smile, but his eyes never left his target. A weapon was still aimed at him, after all. "Your teeth, man. Every time you chew that gum of yours, your teeth show. What do you say, Birman? Weapons down, and let this finish between Gorman and me."

"He'll never let you take him alive," Birman said.

"Then you needn't worry about dying for him," countered Steve. "Either way, I'm not going to let you take out Marlena."

"You'll die for her," Birman stated rhetorically, lowering his weapon a few inches.

Steve kept his weapon up. A marksman was a marksman, after all. "Yes."

"Funny how many men would die for that woman. Pierre du Scheum stood to her left throughout the whole evening, blocking my view most of the time. I thought it was coincidence but now I'm not so sure. Funny what you'd do for people you love."

"Drop the weapon," Steve ordered softly.

His heart thudded as he waited for Birman's decision. It had been a while since he had faced danger head-on, but his grip on his weapon was still steady, his mind in that special place, separated from emotions. He understood that the other man was weighing the same thing. Over a year out of combat action. Long enough to lose the reflex and state of mind of a soldier.

He didn't think. Just reacted. The glint of Birman's ring caught the light as his fingers moved. Steve fired his weapon without any hesitation, and the other man crumpled.

"Not a SEAL, man, never a SEAL," Steve told the injured man as he stood over him. "Not a STAR Force SEAL. We're a standing and ready force, and we're always prepared."

He crouched down. It was never easy to fire a weapon at a fellow human being, but Birman had made the choice when he could have surrendered. Steve felt regret, but no pity. The man had murdered two people for money and would have killed Marlena, too.

"He's all yours, Cam. I'm heading down."

"Ten-four." Cam climbed up from the catwalk. "I'll take care of things up here now. Is he dead?"

"Not yet."

"How did you know he was going to fire at you?"

"You don't wear a wedding ring when you're in the sniper business. In this case, it's you who's gone rusty, Birman."

Before Steve stood up, the sniper pulled at his arm, groaning as he did so. Their eyes met. He gave the same nod he always did, then closed his eyes. Steve studied him grimly for one more second. Then, he got up and pulled on the metal hook that extended a retractable wire from his nylon belt. He nodded at Cam before strapping it to the rope to rappel down to the deck.

Damn du Scheum! If he hadn't listened to du Scheum's plan to use Marlena, he wouldn't be here now, without his

ability to see everything around him. But that damn French-
man had convinced him that he needed Marlena to negotiate
the item since she had already made it known at that function that she had it. Without her the authenticity of the laptop
would be questioned. That made sense then, and he had followed du Scheum's advice. He had known that the man was
trying to negotiate Marlena's freedom, but he had thought he
was in control, that he would show them who finally needed
whom.

Now he was standing there like Napoleon watching his
Waterloo, hearing the reverberations of gunshots down on
the deck. He had an idea who was out there. How did that
sailor locate his boat? He clenched one hand, crushing the
cigarette he was smoking, barely noticing the sting as the tip
of it burned his palm.

He watched as the man responsible for his downfall fell
out of nowhere like a spider dropping from the ceiling,
hanging by a seemingly invisible thread, shooting and not
missing. How could his men miss him? He could see him as
clear as the dawn breaking, and his stupid crew seemed to be
shooting at nothing. There couldn't be that many intruders
on board, could there? From the amount of firepower being
used, it sounded like a dozen men. Surely his own well-
trained crew could contain a dozen men.

With sudden fury, he turned on his captain and first mate.
"We are in the middle of the ocean. How could twelve men
get on board and you two not know about it?"

As expected, they didn't have any answer. He struck the
first mate, then flexed his arm. He hadn't used violence in a
long time. He left that to his minions.

"We have another boat approaching, sir. What are your
orders?" The captain was nervous, sweat popping out on his
forehead. He looked as if he'd rather be somewhere else.

Drawing out his 9mm from inside his jacket, he pointed it
at the captain. "Start the engine and head toward that boat at
high speed." When the man hesitated, he cocked the
weapon. "Ram it. Or you die."

He backed up, kicked the cabin door shut, and locked it.

When the captain still didn't make a move, he pointed the weapon at the first mate and pulled the trigger. The man screamed. The captain went pale and started the boat.

"Speed it up!" he ordered, looking at the horizon, at the oncoming boat. Here was something he could see. "Napoleon never backed down." He lit his last cigarette.

Whoever this man was, he'd chosen the perfect spot for cover. They were just inside the doghouse, the protective construction over the entrance from deck level to below decks. This way they could see whether anyone was coming up from behind them. The shooting was sporadic, as if Gorman's crew was confused. She wondered how many there were on board.

"Where's Stash?" Marlena demanded, between bursts of gunfire. She kept glancing at the man a few feet from her. He had Stash's build, maybe a bit stockier, but with the camouflaged streaks on his face, he could easily have been Stash. "And who are you?"

The man emptied his cartridge in one direction, then turned around, his back against the thick canvas on the side of the doghouse. "Your turn," he said, pulling out a cartridge to reload. His eyes gleamed at her in the dark. "Unless all you want to do is kiss."

The guy even talked like him! Marlena took position, firing in the direction where bullets were coming at them. "Where's Stash?" she yelled again, getting impatient. She needed to know that he was safe, before she went after Gorman. "Is he all right?"

He peered to the left and fired his reloaded weapon. There was a howl of pain. "Right now, we have a more immediate problem, lady. Like an unknown number of shooters after us."

"Seven," Marlena informed him. "Five, actually, now that you got one. I took out one before that."

He slanted her a glance again. "Wait here while I get rid of them." When she glared at him, he shrugged and tossed her his weapon. He pulled out two others from behind him.

The man obviously thought he was Rambo. He asked, "How fast can you run? Are you as good at dodging bullets as I am at kissing?"

He was trying to scare her. Marlena gave the stranger a mocking grin. "Kissing isn't my only talent," she assured him, then moved to his side. "There are two behind that stanchion, the other three are to your right. I'll take them out first. They're using semis and we can count the reload patterns, whatever-your-name-is."

This close to him, she could see the corner of his lips quirking. He nodded and said, "Besides kissing, Steve must be giving you sailing lessons, too."

Did he say lessons? Marlena emptied her cartridge, blasting one of the decorative railings to pieces. "Before I kill you, you had better tell me where Stash is and who you are."

The man cocked his head. Their counterpart in this shootout was returning fire, so Marlena waited as she watched him mentally count the number of shots coming from each weapon. He lifted his heavier weapon to his shoulder and said to her, "On the count of thirteen, those two will reload and we go after them. Ready?" When she nodded, he said, "I'm Steve McMillan, too, by the way. So you kissed the right guy."

Marlena frowned. Two Steves? She didn't have time to deal with this right now; he had started counting. She yelled at him before they headed out of the doghouse, "But you aren't Kisser of the Millennium Steve, SEAL boy."

Gunshots and the cranking sound of chains and cables drowned out his answer. She didn't wait for him as she disposed of the two men behind the stanchion. Mr. Other Steve had better be taking care of the other three because he was on his own. The boat was moving, so that cranking sound must be the anchor cable being hoisted, and she knew exactly where Gorman was.

There were rubber-suited men everywhere! Or at least it seemed like it, because every time she turned at the sound of gunfire, there were Gorman's crewmen being rounded up like cattle. She was pretty sure they were SEAL commandos now. Only they would look this good in rubber. That big one over there looked like he could take down the whole crew himself. Well, let them handle these guys. She wanted Gorman for herself.

To her relief, the big intimidating guy seemed to know her and stepped aside, allowing her to pass. She was afraid that he would shoot her. Well, T. must have briefed these guys.

That imposing cabin door was nothing against the firepower that Mr. Other Steve had given her. It took only one shot. The kickback almost had her on her ass. She didn't have time to admire the destructive beauty of her handiwork, but instead peered in, expecting return fire. Sure enough, she quickly retreated when she saw Gorman. The bullet whizzed past her, hitting the wall harmlessly.

"Give it up, Gorman," she called, putting one hand in her jacket pocket. "It's just you and me now. Isn't that what you want?"

There was a loud spray of bullets and a crash from inside. She muttered a short curse and peered in again. Someone had smashed through one of the windows and landed on top of the other occupant. Gorman wasn't paying any attention to her as he seemed determined to jam the steering wheel a certain way. Here was her chance. She ran at her captor. He turned, gun in hand. She raised hers. Someone pulled her by the ankle, tripping her, and Gorman's shot missed by a couple of feet. She pounded a fist on the floor in frustration. Damn it. She would have gotten Gorman first, the idiot.

She clenched her hand around the special ballpoint pen in her hand and yelled, "I don't want him dead, you idiot. He has one of my men."

She looked up to see Mr. Other Steve wrestling with Gorman, who was no match for this kind of tussle. She had the satisfaction of seeing her enemy getting the daylights punched out of him. There was a painful-sounding crack to the jaw. Gorman passed out.

"Hey!" she yelled as she was unceremoniously pulled up on her feet.

The man had no manners! He grabbed her by the hair,

and she kicked his shin. "Look, you tongue me again, SEAL boy, and I'll make you into shark bait."

He tongued her anyway.

"Stash," she murmured against his lips. Stepping on tiptoes, she palmed his face, pulling him closer. She couldn't get enough of him. How she had missed him!

His mouth moved over hers possessively and she responded fiercely, forgetting everything for the moment except the fact that he was alive. She had been so afraid for him, had never been so fearful of losing anyone. He was her Steve, all familiar sexy masculine musk and heat and . . . the boat was still moving! Shaking off her protesting mind, she released his face and tried to talk to him while she pushed at the hard wall of his chest.

Steve reluctantly lifted his head. God, the woman drove him nuts. He wanted to shake her and make love to her at the same time. What was she thinking, running at Gorman like that? And what did she mean, he had one of her men?

Hawk had been right behind her, so Steve knew she hadn't been in any danger, but damn it, hadn't he told him to get her out of the way? So why was she running ahead of him?

He looked over Marlena's head to ask his cousin, who was standing there eyeing them silently. Steve wasn't worried about Gorman. Hawk would take care of him if he so much as opened an eye. He narrowed his eyes as he zeroed in on a smear of red on Hawk's lips. He knew his cousin's bad habits like the back of his hand. "That'd better be a new line of camouflage makeup and not what I think it is," he warned.

Marlena twisted around to see what he meant. She didn't see anything important about Hawk's makeup, so she turned back to Steve. "Let go. We have to stop the boat." She was facing the water and could see exactly where they were heading. "Stash! Stop the boat! Look over there!"

Steve didn't turn around to see the disaster ahead. He had what he wanted—Gorman out and Lena in his arms. "Why did you kiss my woman?" he demanded.

"She kissed me. She preferred me to shark bait."

"You didn't kiss him, did you, Lena?"

Marlena stared up at Steve. Had they both gone crazy? This wasn't the time to play kissing games! "Stop the damn boat or we're all going to kiss something goodbye!"

"Okay," Steve said and snapped his fingers. He did that to annoy Marlena; she didn't know he had wired the propellers. A rolling rumble shook the boat under them, rocking it sideways. He opened his arms as Marlena fell against him, then closed them possessively around her as he braced himself against a wall. It felt so good to have her in his arms again. He didn't want to let go. The past forty-some hours were some of the worst of his life.

The way the boat came to a stop in time seemed like magic, but of course it was the timing device that had taken care of everything, and he had the operation clocked to perfection. That was why he had chosen that moment to crash through the window, but Marlena's appearance had distracted him a little bit. Just a little. He placed a kiss on her forehead and met Hawk's mocking eyes. He glared at the smear of red again.

"What did she mean about tonguing her?" he demanded, resuming the conversation before the explosion. It was just as if he were back with his team, using adrenaline and banter after a bloody battle. Mundane conversation and sarcastic jokes were the norm to counter the chaos that usually surrounded them.

Hawk shrugged nonchalantly, licking one corner of his mouth. "We sort of tongued each other," he replied. "I was on top and she had her hands in my hair. Accidents happen that way."

Steve growled. Marlena shook her head in disbelief. She tried to get free but his arms were locked tightly around her. "Are you listening to me?" she demanded, about ready to explode herself.

"I stopped the boat like you ordered, didn't I?"

How had he done that? But she wasn't going to let that distract her from her job again. "Take your arms off me right now! I have things to do."

Steve shook his head. "I think the to-do list is finished, babe. You did your thing with the laptop. I did my thing as rat catcher. I rescued you. You're safe and sound. I stopped a runaway boat." His green and black streaked face broke into a macho satisfied grin that made her heart do somersaults. "M for Mission Completed."

"I think we have visitors . . . Stash." Hawk's voice had a mocking lilt to it. One corner of his mouth curled up in an amused sneer. "She did call me Stash before she tongued me. What the hell is a 'Stash,' anyway?"

Steve scowled down at Marlena. "You mistook him for me? He looks nothing like me!"

Actually, he did. Especially since she still couldn't see their faces without the camouflage. It was evident that the two men were related. Not only was their build similar, but she could make out the same strong jaw and dimpled chin.

Now that it was clear that imminent danger was over, Marlena relaxed. Relief bubbled up from nowhere. She peered up at Steve and cocked an eyebrow. "Well, you all look alike with that makeup and getup. But of course I knew it wasn't you when I unzipped . . ." She cast a suggestive look downward, then peeked up, and almost laughed out loud at the rage in his expression. He was remembering the first time they met and how she had greeted him.

Steve sucked in his breath when she pressed one knowing hand on his stomach. Her blue eyes twinkled suggestively. She didn't try that on Hawk! She had better not! From the floor, Gorman emitted a groan and stirred, interrupting his rampant jealousy. Releasing Marlena, he took a few steps toward the deputy director of Task Force Two, lying at his feet.

"I suppose it's too late to request an interview, Mr. Gorman," he said to him.

Chapter Twenty-four

The morning light felt strange, bringing normalcy to the chaotic predawn hours. Marlena watched as two boats reached them. Stash told her one of them was the one his cousin and his men came on, so the other probably was from T.

"He said his name is Steve too," she told Stash, after a belated introduction.

"It's a long story," Steve said, giving his cousin a wry look. "Call him Hawk, Lena."

"Hawk," she murmured, eyeing the other man standing a few feet away. His brooding calmness belied a coiled tension as he quietly gave instructions to his men. He must have heard her, because he turned slightly. In the daylight his eyes were a deep brilliant gold; they stood out against the war paint. Predator eyes. She studied the differences between Stash and his cousin. A slow, knowing smile revealed straight white teeth. She couldn't help but smile back.

"Is there a reason why you're staring at him?" Steve demanded, putting an arm around her shoulders. "It's bad enough that you kissed him in the middle of a dangerous operation."

Marlena shrugged off the possessive gesture. She couldn't understand why he was so mad about that harmless kiss. It was meant for him, after all. "He doesn't look like you after all," she declared. It was just a little lie, but hey, male ego was a fragile thing. "Besides, he doesn't kiss that well."

Hawk laughed out loud for the first time, a warm chuckle that crinkled the corners of his eyes. "I think it was Kisser of the Millennium, wasn't it, that I was compared to?"

"Wait a minute," Steve cut in, eyes narrowing, "let me get this straight. While under siege, you two kissed and had this conversation?"

"It's called multitasking, Stash," Hawk replied solemnly. "Miss Maxwell was really good at it, too."

Steve took a step toward his cousin. Much as Marlena was fascinated by this new, aggressive side of Steve, she didn't want to have two males fresh from a battle, adrenaline still pumping, pushing each other too far. She understood that part of it was ego, but most of it was the rush of excitement still fresh in their system. Her normally steadfast, logical-thinking Stash was in one-hundred-percent warrior-commando, king-of-the-hill mode at the moment. In fact, all these sea mammals around her probably were on a high. She just had to handle everyone on board very carefully.

To take his attention off the unrepentant Hawk, she jabbed Steve in the ribs, then turned away from the arriving boats and looked around at the carnage in awe. As far as she could tell, there were four other men who had stolen on board with Stash. Five men did all—this. "This" was total damage to everything on deck of a six-figure luxury boat, from starboard to portside. Bullet holes marred the once pristine whitewashed deck and walls. Pilings and railings were ruined. Decor was unrecognizable. Big holes. Broken glass. Not to mention the injured.

Her gaze rested on Cameron, Stash's friend at TIARA, who was standing guard over the surviving prisoners. Well. Maybe there was more to the man than the mere charmer she had judged him to be. Pierre was talking to him, probably identifying some of the culprits. She frowned at the tarp covering what could only be those who didn't make it through the firefight. That could easily have been her under there, she thought. Her gaze swung up and caught Gorman's. He stood aloofly, a little away from the rest, with that big commando nearby keeping an eye on him. His face didn't look too good after Stash's handiwork, but even from here, she could see the quiet rage in his eyes.

"Did he hurt you?" Steve lightly massaged her neck.

Although his touch was soft, Marlena felt the taut anger emanating from him. She shook her head. "No."

"But he was going to kill you after this was over," he stated in a low, tense voice.

"It is over," Marlena told him quietly, still aware of the adrenaline rush behind his words, "and I'm fine."

"What if I hadn't made it in time? What if you hadn't been able to send T. the signal?"

She felt a surge of tenderness at the rough emotion in his voice. She wasn't used to anyone taking care of her and couldn't find the right words to explain her feelings. Trying to reassure him somehow, she leaned back into him and reverted to her usual mockery. "I'm trained for these situations, darling. Really, have some confidence, hmm? Besides, Pierre would have thought of something."

"He was trying to protect you. He must have known something, because Birman said he kept standing between you and him."

"Birman is the sniper?" she asked in surprise. She looked for the bodyguard. When she couldn't find him, there was only one other place. She glanced back down at the tarp. Steve squeezed her shoulder. "How did you find out about him?"

"When we were waiting for your signal, I thought about the two men he'd killed, the first assassin and Cunningham. He shot them dead in the most convincing manner. I had Patty do a Triple I check on him, and I found out his past connection with Gorman, so it only makes sense to suspect he must also work for him. That also explained why du Scheum was so careful with his speech the other day before you were abducted."

Marlena smiled to herself. He sounded like Stash again, all analytical, all detail. "What's Triple I?" she queried.

"Interstate Identification Index."

People were boarding the boat, cutting his explanation short. Marlena was surprised to see Rick Harden among them. So far, no T.

Stash muttered under his breath, "What's he doing here?"

Balancing his automatic over one broad shoulder, Hawk looked back at Steve. He didn't seem interested in the newcomers, since he didn't know any of them. Marlena suspected that Hawk McMillan was a loner and not a team player, a characteristic trait she recognized all too well. "Your mess now, Steve," he said. "I'm outta here."

Steve nodded, and said, "Stay in D.C. I have things to tell you. Family stuff."

Hawk nodded back. "I'll make sure they secure the prisoners before I leave. I don't want any introductions."

Just as she had thought, Hawk didn't want to be known. "Don't leave till I see what you look like, Hawk," she baited. "I don't like not knowing what I kissed."

Hawk flashed her that lazy, lopsided, white-toothed smile. His gold-brown eyes were challenging as he told her, "Not shark bait."

He sauntered off to relieve his men. Other operatives were taking over, most of whom seemed to be under Harden. Marlena frowned, not sure why this was so.

"Stash, why is Harden in charge? Only T. gets my signal."

"I don't know," Steve replied. "Come on. We'll find out soon enough."

Harden's expression was inscrutable, as usual. His eyes were glass-bright as he studied the prisoners, ending with a certain figure. Marlena had a feeling that Steve's chief had waited for this moment for a long, long time, but instead of striding there to take charge of his men, he went to meet them. Another man came with him, very noticeable in his stark white top and trousers. His stride was purposeful; his eyes searched the deck as they approached. He stepped over weaponry and splattered blood without a second glance, as if he was used to the sight of gore. Then his gaze fixed on Stash and her.

Marlena raised an eyebrow at the sight of the newcomer. My goodness. Wasn't this a surprise? There were no smiles or greetings from either side.

A muscle worked in Harden's jaw, but he met Stash's eyes squarely. "I owe you an apology, McMillan. You did good here, despite my trying to detain you at the hospital and not giving you any help."

What? Stash in the hospital? And Harden didn't help him? Marlena wanted to pound the man into pulp. Seeing Stash had made her forget that the last time she'd seen him, he was out like a light, with a head wound. She wanted to demand to know more about his injury, but this was Stash's moment, so she just glared at Rick Harden, which seemed to amuse the other man.

Steve didn't let the awkwardness stay in the air too long, though. "Apology accepted, sir. How did you get to be here?"

"I made a deal, remember? She said if I let you out, I would find a way out from under someone's thumb. I took her up on the deal." He looked over at Gorman. "It paid off."

"So she left you in charge? Where is T.?"

"That's what this gentleman wants to know," Harden answered.

Marlena finally shifted her gaze to the man standing there silently. Interesting. Didn't T. get a transfer because he couldn't stand the sight of her? She had seen his photos in T.'s files a couple of times, but they didn't do him justice. The computer pictures didn't show the hard glitter of the lightest blue eyes she had ever seen. When he looked at her, those eyes were laser-sharp, piercing, and shockingly thorough. She blinked at his scrutiny.

There was something very different about him, and it wasn't just his street clothes. Maybe it was the way he stood so still, how he kept movement to a minimum. He was there, but like a shadow, he seemed to be observing and waiting. The mix of arrogance and confidence was a very lethal combination. One couldn't help but acknowledge his presence.

Marlena also recognized a cover when she saw one. With his sun-streaked blond hair and tanned, lean, athletic build, he looked younger than his purported thirty-eight years, and every inch the image he always projected, a globetrotter in pursuit of extreme sports. But Marlena knew his history. Not as intimately as T., of course, who studied him for two years before they'd clashed. Marlena understood now why her friend was so drawn to this man. He was exactly the kind of man that women sought to tame—enigmatic, secretive, uncompromising. Hard as diamonds.

And he had treated T. like crap. Her gaze hardened.

"Hello, Alex," she greeted, ignoring protocol.

"He was in charge of Operation Outfox, and since your assignment followed his, he wanted an update on Maximilian Shoggi," Harden continued. He shrugged. "Since I'm not familiar with your operation, Miss Maxwell, I couldn't give him any information. My part here deals with the prisoners, that's it. I will handle taking in Gorman and the crimes that are connected with his outfit, but the other things, I hope you will get the admiral and T. to straighten out for me."

"No problem," Marlena told him, her gaze not leaving Alex. "We're on international waters. I don't know exactly how to get you what T. promised you, though. We only have Gorman here, but no proof of how much damage he did to TIARA."

"T. wired Cam. He then was told by T. to attach a bug on McMillan," Harden said, and he gave a wry grin when Stash stabbed his shoulder briefly, feeling around. "We recorded everything, from Gorman's order to Birman and Birman's talk with McMillan. That was very revealing, especially about his half brother. It should be enough to get a warrant to look into his home and computers. And I hope Mr. du Scheum will cooperate."

Marlena smiled as she watched Stash frown at Cam. T. always was one step ahead. "Well, then. All things wrapped up."

"Except for T." Alex finally spoke up. His voice was softly commanding. "Where is she?"

Stash didn't seem to like the touch of menace in Alex Diamond's tone because he stepped out slightly in front of Marlena. She wanted to nudge him out of the way; she knew this man posed no danger to her. He was, after all, part of the group T. worked with. But Stash was still playing commando. Better let him get it out of his system. She sighed inwardly.

"She's not here," she said, shrugging. "T. is underground, so I don't know where she is, exactly. You're her chief of operations, so I would think you would know. Can't you ask Jed?"

He didn't take her bait. "Tell me where to find her. You're GEM. I want the information about her ID du jour before we get off this boat."

"Or what?" Steve interrupted, looking annoyed. "My men and I outlined this part of the operation, and you just barge in demanding things. Our main goal was to extract Marlena and has nothing to do with your operation."

"Steve, I told him you were the last to talk to her," Harden said, "and Alex is part of her team, since she sent these men."

Steve shrugged. Alex Diamond remained calm, but there was raw tension in his deceptive stillness. "You're the liaison, right? Shouldn't you be doing your job, telling me what I want to know?" He turned to Marlena. "You studied NOPAIN under her. Tell me where she is."

Marlena raised a brow. She wondered how T. dealt with all that assured arrogance. Folding her arms, she drawled, "I'll think about it. Of course, that doesn't mean you'll find her."

To her surprise, the man smiled. She had meant to bait him, to see whether she could get under his skin. Instead his eyes gleamed with humor, and the tough angles on his face softened. She breathed in. Now she understood exactly why T. was so besotted.

"You can't play her mind games with me, M." The lazy drawl of his voice returned her mockery. He cocked his head, studying her, his blue eyes lighting up with a mesmerizing intensity. Then he added, softly, "Please *find* a way to tell me." Turning to Stash, he said, "Your commander and I will handle things from here, McMillan. We'll talk later. And oh, by agreeing to be liaison, you'll find that we'll be working together a lot."

Steve scowled at the departing figures. "You get the feeling he's done more than talk a lot with T.? He speaks in circles, just like her. And he acts like he owns her."

"Hmm," Marlena agreed, but right now she wasn't particularly interested in Alex and T. She grabbed Stash by the arm, pulling on his swim gear impatiently. "I want this thing off, and I want that stuff off your face. I want to see where you've been hurt."

"Here?" Steve countered, raising his brows.

Marlena started to head below deck. "Are you coming or not?"

"Definitely coming."

Steve looked around him. He was getting mighty sick of these luxury surroundings. What he really wanted was to take his woman back to his own place, where he could pound into her in his own bed. Yeah, that was what he wanted. He could take only so much soft carpet and bedroom sets too expensive to rip apart.

Granted, a big bed to roll around in was nice, but his smaller bed would keep Marlena where she belonged, in his arms, under him, on top—he didn't care, as long as she had no space to scoot away. He wanted home cooking. He looked at Marlena and couldn't help grinning. Well, okay. Maybe not. But he was very sure of one thing. He wanted a place they could call their own, where they could escape the games they had to play outside.

All this grandeur—the parties, clothes, people, suites—they reminded him of how close he had been to losing her. But he was also reminded of how comfortable Marlena was around these trappings. Could he convince Marlena to be with him? He honestly didn't know.

"Why are you looking at me like that?" Marlena demanded.

"Like what?"

"I know that smile by now. You're planning something." She started tugging on him. "How do you get this thing off, anyhow?"

This was a chance to talk to her about the future. They were alone and—he frowned. There was blood on her arm. He hadn't noticed that before. "Why are you bleeding?"

Marlena paid scarce attention to her bloodied sleeve. She was childlike in her enthusiasm to find a way into his suit, exploring places that brought a lot of discomfort to its wearer. "It's nothing. Just some scrape," she dismissed. "It'll wash off in the shower."

The thought of her being shot at curdled all the warm and fuzzy plans he had in mind. He captured her busy hands in his, his heart beating loudly in his head. "I don't want to lose you," he ground out. "I don't want you to take everything so lightly, damn it! Do you know what I've been through the last couple of days, worrying about you, wondering about you?"

Did she know how her blue eyes blazed when she was provoked? That she chewed the inside of her lower lip when she tried to hide her emotions? That the next thing she would do was erect that wall of hers and utter some mocking words?

Sure enough, her smile was brilliant, filled with sexual promise. "I'll make it up to you," she crooned, loosening her hands from his hold. She pushed him gently backward, toward the shower. "You saved me, my big bad knight in a rubber suit. Now you're worried about some silly little cut on me, when you should be enjoying the spoils of victory. Me, naked, wet. You, naked, wet, horny." She had him in the bathroom before he knew it, her hands once again busy. She took his hand and slid it between her legs. "Let me show you where I'm hurting."

A man couldn't stay mad when he had his hand between

a woman's legs and she was climbing all over him. At least that was what Steve discovered.

Steam soon covered the glass of the little shower stall, as the hot water ran green, black, and a little red down the drain. Steve liked her soapy hands on him. A lot.

"Close your eyes so you don't get soap in them," Marlena ordered.

Always obey the woman with a soap bar in her hands. He hoped that luxury cabins also meant ample gallons of hot water because he wanted to stay in there for a while.

Her hands glided over him, slick and heated. Her nails sent a rush of pleasure right down to his . . . toes. "Ummm . . . I thought you wanted my eyes closed to wash my face," he said huskily. Not that he was complaining.

Wicked. She had the wickedest, soapiest hands in the world. And she wasn't washing his face at all. His closed eyes only enhanced what she was doing to him. He felt her holding him firmly, and one silky thumb drove him crazy as it rubbed the underside of his rapidly growing erection. It moved from the tip of his sensitive penis all the way down to the base, where she pressed in, as if he had some secret button he didn't know about. Whoa!

His eyes shot open. "Good God, woman," he muttered as he braced both hands on the wet wall opposite him. His knees almost buckled from the fiery sensation that threatened to erupt too soon. "What are you doing to me?"

"Getting soap in your eye," she told him with the smuggest of smiles.

Steve stared down at himself. Both her hands were wrapped around his erection, one tormenting thumb still stroking a certain spot. The swollen head strained upward as she massaged him harder. He shook the water out of his eyes. There was no way she had both hands spanning his length and he had that much to spare. Unless he had grown several inches, he wasn't that . . . big.

Her thumb moved sensuously, seeming to control his very blood flow. His back arched toward her spontaneously when she pressed down again, and his whole world zeroed in on the liquid pleasure shooting up the length of him to the point of bursting. He tried to focus but only saw her smiling face fade in and out. Every nerve ending that mattered seemed to be zooming warp-speed. His heart beat thunderously.

"What . . . what did you do?" he finally managed, once she moved that thumb away.

"It's called the Venus Butterflytrap technique," she said, but her voice seemed to be coming to him in slow motion as he tried to ignore the long, slow, up and down strokes of her hand. "It's the male G-spot. Makes him all weak in the knees."

Normally a real man didn't like to be weak in the knees, but he would make an exception this one time. He admitted it. He was putty; that was, putty everywhere but in her hands. That part was granite hard, with a heated core that was building higher by the stroke. He closed his eyes again. He would ask about this Venus Flything later. Right now, right at this moment, he had a bigger and harder situation to deal with.

"Grow big and hard for me, Sir Rubber Suit," he heard Marlena croon with the splattering water in the background. "Just like that."

Releasing him, her hands roamed up his stomach, his chest, his shoulders, and he opened his eyes again in protest. He didn't need any soap *there*. The heat in his groin grew as she soaped every part of him but where he wanted, but it also allowed him some measure of control, so that he, too, could do his own soapy torture.

He smoothed the slippery bubbles over her breasts, cupping and weighing them, went lower, where she had a magic button of her own. She moaned as he glided the bar of soap slowly between her thighs, then inserted a finger into her. It was now her turn to lean onto him, as she parted her legs. He slid in another finger and moved his thumb in a circling motion.

He blocked the water from the showerhead, the needles adding a simple pleasure, shuddering when she nibbled her way down his chest and sucked on his nipple. Her hand reached down again and he sucked in his breath in anticipation, not sure whether he could take another one of those . . . oh man. Oh man!

His whole body jerked forward at her knowing touch, and he almost slammed her into the wall. He was on fire. His hard-on was tortuously filled to the brim, growing in spurts as she kept pressing him there. Thoughts burst like the forgotten soap bubbles as a tidal wave of sexual need threatened to engulf his senses.

Mindlessly, he half lifted her as he slid his penis into the crevice between her legs, trying to get inside. It wasn't easy, since they were both slick with soap. Unable to control himself, he moved his hips anyway. In. He wanted in.

"We're going to get killed in here, baby," he muttered, "and I don't want to die before I come in you. I need you. I have to have you."

"The water's turning lukewarm anyway," Marlena said, kissing the side of his neck.

Steve reached back and turned the water off while she pushed the shower door open. They tumbled out of the stall, all tangled limbs and wet hair, panting lips and eager tongues. He wanted her so badly, he couldn't even wait to reach the bed. There was the tiny sink, and whatever was left of his sanity registered the perfect height. He lifted her onto it, spread her legs wide, threw them over his arms, and plunged in, eyes closed. He felt so huge, he had to adjust her position, pulling her legs higher. He pushed in slowly, trying to curb his impatience. She gasped as he ruthlessly forced inward, all the way. He wanted to feel her around his entire length. She was slick and hot, and tight. So tight. When he pushed in the final inch, Marlena gave a deep-throated cry. And he reached heaven. A sound like a growl turned into a groan escaped from his lips.

He had never felt lust like this. He took her in the bathroom. He took her on that thick carpet. He took her again in that big bed.

"Baby, we need to get dressed. Do you realize they know

exactly what we're up to down here?" Marlena asked at some point. Her voice was soft and husky from sex.

But he hadn't had enough of her yet. Steve shook his head and didn't bother to answer since his tongue was busy. When she moaned softly, he shook his head again, just to make sure she understood that he didn't care that there were people outside that cabin who could smash in at any moment. And he kept shaking his head to show her that he didn't really care if a dozen of them entered and stood around the bed at that instant.

"Oh, Stash—you have to—oh, stop that—" Marlena gasped, her hands mussing his damp hair as she tried to slow him down.

The rest of her sentence was unintelligible as her hips bucked and her thighs muffled his hearing. Steve held, forcing her body down on the bed as he kept telling her no in the sweetest way he knew how. He refused to stop loving her.

She went limp, and he buried his head in her musky essence, enjoying the moment when he knew he had her oblivious to time or space. He savored her silent trembling that started slow and became ferocious as he pushed her higher. She gasped his name over and over. Finally relenting, he slid upward, fitting into her easily now. Her wetness eagerly welcomed him, and she was so sensitized she was already gone again.

"Hang on, baby," he whispered, kissing her half-open lips and mingling all her tastes together. "They can come in just in time to see you moan for me."

And she did moan as he moved slowly, taking his time, rocking the already wet bed as his rhythm built to a crescendo. Like an overflowing river, heat rushed forth, uncontrollable, charged with the kind of energy that threatened to crush anything in its way. Steve followed along, his orgasm crashing down like a burst dam, and everything, everything that was him, he gave to Marlena. Her arms wrapped around him tightly.

*   *   *

It was only much, much later, when they were waiting to make that report to Alex that it occurred to Steve that Marlena had done it to him again. She had evaded his attempt to talk about their future. And with some sneaky Venus whatever trick. Light sweat popped up at the memory of how she had affected him.

He scowled as he studied her profile, sitting there so nonchalantly leafing through a report. He wanted time to talk to her, and yet he had allowed her to literally lead him around by his dick. Okay, so that trick was awesome. M for Mind-blowing, he added. Mucho Mojo Mambo, as sailors were apt to say after a wild night. He sniffed impatiently. There he went again. He had to stop obsessing about her and start a plan to corner her. Venus Butterflytrap, indeed. His forehead smoothed as he considered her through narrowed eyes. He had a trap of his own to set.

Harden came out of the office, interrupting his line of thought. Marlena crossed her arms across her chest, obviously still mad at his commander. Steve hid a smile. She had already opined about Rick Harden in the most uncomplimentary way earlier when she had seen the small gash on Steve's head and demanded details about his hospital stay. He told her what happened and how he'd gotten T. to help him out.

"That man walks around with a stick in the ass, you know that? I'm going to find a way to get back at him for treating you like you're the traitor."

"No one likes the idea of being viewed incompetent, or worse, a traitor, Lena."

"Then you work to prove otherwise! And work harder to find out what the problem is! Not sit there pointing fingers, and then, after it's all over, take the credit. If T. hadn't intervened, I wouldn't have given him Gorman so he could get back his badge of honor."

"If not for T. intervening, you wouldn't have me to rescue your sweet ass."

"Hah, like I can't handle a little bit of danger."

Little was not the way he would describe the danger Marlena had been in, but discussing descriptive words became very unimportant when she had distracted him again.

Harden's smile wasn't its usual chilling grimace. A little warmth actually lurked in those eyes. "I have been told that you're working in some special position between agencies now," he said. "It's a good move. There needs to be more communication, and it will help that I can reach you to ask questions."

It was another concession from the hard man. He was telling Steve that he trusted him now to go to him if he needed to get or pass information. Even Marlena got the point; she noticeably relaxed and unfolded her arms.

"If it works out," Steve said. "I don't know yet. I'm still feeling the ropes."

Harden nodded. "You'll do well. The job needs someone who can take an active part in an operation and then disperse both military and intel matters to relevant contacts. These past months, you've shown that you can handle intel work, and with your SEAL training you will be perfect for this, making good use of both your skills. Not every military man can handle intel, and not every intel operative can do fieldwork."

It was ironic to get a compliment from the man now. "Thanks, Harden," Steve said.

"We'll talk later. I have to start gathering evidence on a number of people connected with Gorman, maybe find a couple who will supply more on him."

"Check out the operative that I replaced when I first came," Steve suggested. "Something tells me his death wasn't an accident."

Harden frowned. "Sorvino? Maybe so. I'll look into it. If you need to know what we find, just give me a call." He jerked his chin toward where he'd just come from. "Good luck in there. Diamond asks some tough questions. Just a warning. Nice seeing you again, Miss Maxwell."

"Thanks," Steve said, and Marlena murmured something polite. He gave her a warning glance as she stood up. From the little he had managed to get out of her, Alex and T. were an item, just as he suspected, and she thought Alex needed a lesson because of something that had nothing to do with her. Blue eyes glinting, lips set in a stubborn line, she looked ready for battle.

Steve opened the door and she brushed past, giving him a wink. He quirked his lips. Something told him he was going to be liaising his ass off.

Chapter Twenty-five

Arrogant bastard. Cold-hearted SOB. Relentless devil.
The man at whom she was silently hurling those insults looked at her with those piercing eyes, a glimmer of impatient humor in them as she dodged and evaded his questions. She knew what kind of operative he was and that his training would get through her act of resistance without any problems, but he appeared quite willing to wait it out. He didn't demand what he wanted to know. He didn't ask nicely, either. He just made it clear that they weren't leaving his sight till he got what he wanted. And what he wanted was T.

The overhead light glinted off his sun-kissed hair, but that was the only thing about him that was fair. "She came to D.C. at your request," he said in that silky voice that emanated danger, "so I know you can communicate with her easily. According to your own words, she showed up and rescued you twice, once at the function and this last time, when you were kidnapped. Don't you think that as chief of operations of her last mission, I should track her down and debrief her on this follow-up operation? And if so, are you willing to follow me back to Center and report to Jed yourself about your conclusions of what I need or don't need to do?"

Marlena tried not to glare at Alex. As she had just been thinking, he didn't fight fair at all. She knew without asking that he was very aware that she hated team stuff, that going back to Center would mean playing by the rules there. And knowing Jed and his reputation, he would leave her playing footsy at Center for months before he let her meet with him. Because that was what the Center was. They subjected their operatives to tests there.

Alex was Number One to Jed's Number Nine in their core group. One couldn't go higher than Jed. She was being subtly told that she could fight the whole group of men that T. had been with for two years, or she could give up the information now. Or later. It didn't matter.

What bothered her was why Jed wouldn't just tell Alex where T. was. So she made one final attempt to escape. "Protocol says you should refer to the personnel files and see who signed and approved T.'s request for transfer. That kind of approval comes from way up, and I can't just override them," she pointed out, somewhat smugly. "It must be Jed who gave the final say-so."

Marlena noticed a muscle ticking along Alex's jaw line, but his light blue eyes were hard and fathomless. His lips barely moved as he replied, "I gave the final approval."

She raised a brow in surprise. "What's the matter? Changed your mind?"

He had been sitting there so still that when he leaned back in his chair, she actually caught her breath, because her first impulse was to step back from a possible attack. That was how much animal magnetism the man had. And she wasn't the one he was after, either; she couldn't help wondering how T. ever escaped him.

He subjected her to the kind of scrutiny that would make most people talk just to break the tension, but she wasn't T.'s student for nothing. She kept her expression blank.

Throughout their exchange, Stash had been quietly taking it all in. That didn't surprise Marlena at all. That was how he approached any new situation—watch first, attack later. He was probably enjoying watching her squirm.

"Let's talk about the laptop. Who has it?"

"T.," she replied truthfully.

"And the initial merger of Steve McMillan's assignment under the admiral with ours. Who was the mediating operative?"

Marlena paused. She had a bad feeling about this new tactic. "T.," she acknowledged reluctantly.

"I see. How about your backup, if there was any chance of danger? Who would take over the sale to Maximilian Shoggi?"

She paused. Glared. "T."

"Lastly, with your record of not making reports to Center, who in GEM debriefs you first before making the reports to Jed personally?"

She gritted her teeth. "T." She heard Stash shifting in his seat and didn't turn his way to see what he was up to. She just knew he was trying not to smile. She could feel his amusement.

Alex continued gazing at her in that calm, expectant manner. "Since T. is deep underground, and you know so much about T.'s activities and you are GEM, I think it would be useful to have you assist me in the coming months. I need a report of the big picture of all the operations from the last two years that focused on Maximilian Shoggi. Your expertise in arms dealing, especially in the diplomatic and social circles, is what T. was really good at, and we can use you to gain insight on how to get at them from GEM's angle. When can you be ready?"

No way. She wouldn't go near that group of commandos if they all looked like walking advertisements for outdoor life. Their reputation was legendary. She would never escape their team analysis stuff. She wasn't like T., couldn't function in a team. She was having problems trying to think of Stash and her together, let alone nine of these guys hovering over her shoulder, watching every little thing she did. Ugh.

"On the other hand," Alex continued when she didn't reply, "you can't speak Russian, which is a bit difficult, since part of T.'s job was to go on assignment with me when I travel as Sasha Barinsky. Perhaps we can enroll you in a course at Center, but I don't know whether you're a quick study or not."

"We are GEM, contract agents," Marlena countered, using sarcasm to cover the panic growing in her.

Alex arched his brows. His eyes were calmly assessing. "GEM will send its best available operative to us. You're T.'s special student. Are you saying you aren't the next best?"

She was cornered and knew it. The man was one hundred times better than Harden when it came to information extraction, but then Harden wasn't one of the nine from—

She blinked in surprise when Steve interrupted. "This traveling to Russia, is it with this other team T. worked for, or just with you?"

Marlena finally darted a sideways glance at Stash. She couldn't tell what he was thinking, but he looked relaxed.

Alex's attention diverted to Steve. "With me alone, of course. You don't go around brokering arms sales with a whole team of operatives, Agent McMillan. Just as it didn't take a whole task force to go after Marlena Maxwell. They sent you in alone."

His words were loaded with meaning, suggesting things Marlena knew were meant to unsettle Stash. Yet she could only admire that smooth façade Alex presented, as if he were just making polite conversation of very little consequence to him. Ha. Just like T.

"Maximilian Shoggi will recognize Marlena," Steve pointed out.

"Yes, we'll have to restrategize some plans. There is plastic surgery, of course."

"And T. would go under the knife for this team of yours?" Steve asked curiously.

Alex's lips lifted into a ghost of a smile. "You've met my T., McMillan. She's a woman of many faces, as you know. The face she showed you is probably not even the one I know."

There was a short pause, then Steve said, "I don't think I would want Marlena to have to make such a difficult decision when I can offer some information."

"Steve—" Marlena tried to cut in, but he gave her a warning glance.

"I'm listening, McMillan," Alex said.

"As liaison to all the parties involved, I have the power to broker deals that protocol prevents each side from sharing, isn't that so?"

"Yes."

"I will hand over a beeper that T. has used to contact Marlena and me. You can use it any way you like technologically to find out where she called me from. This way Marlena didn't betray her GEM protocol, and you don't have to waste any more time with us."

"Agent McMillan, I think you will make an excellent liaison."

Marlena pursed her lips. She hated men.

"What are you mad about now? I saved your cute little ass again. I'm losing count."

Stash reached out to tuck a stray lock of hair behind Marlena's ear. He couldn't help it. He loved touching her. Loved teasing her. And she was prime for teasing right now. The woman obviously didn't like the way she was being handled at the moment.

He had to admire that man, though. Smooth and tough at the same time. And totally focused on the kill. He had a feeling that Alex Diamond fought that way physically, too. His whole body language betrayed training and a mental alertness that he recognized in his SEAL brothers. It was that trait that made him decide that if he didn't interrupt soon his darling mermaid was going to be spending a lot of time with Diamond. Right now he wasn't getting the gratitude he deserved, that was for sure, since Marlena was glaring back at him.

"You just gave him what he wanted! And you didn't consult me."

"Sweetheart, you were digging yourself deeper every time you opened your mouth. I've never seen you lose so badly. He's damn good. What's this group he's in?"

Marlena waved away his question impatiently. "I wouldn't have told him anything."

"That's right," Steve agreed with resigned tolerance. He was hoping for more Venus whatever time, but that appeared unlikely in the near future. "That's why I did what I did."

"T. doesn't want to see him!"

"How do you know?"

"Because she told me he dumped her!"

"Lena, if he dumped her, why is he looking for her?"

"Because she doesn't want to see him!"

Steve sighed. He really couldn't understand female logic. "Let's start again," he said. "You said Alex dumped her. Since he's looking for her, maybe he wants to undump her. Maybe that's what T. wants."

Marlena snorted. "T. obviously didn't want anything to do with him again or she wouldn't have snuck in a transfer on him."

"So she dumped him?"

Marlena frowned. "No, he dumped her. I'm pretty sure he dumped her."

"Before or after she dumped him with a sneak transfer?" Marlena punched his arm. Steve shrugged. "I was just trying to help."

"Well, Mr. Helpful, what am I going to say to T. when I call her for debriefing? She helped you out and what did you do? Tell the guy who dumped her where to find her."

"I didn't tell him a damn thing and you and she know it." Steve felt his own impatience rising. "Lena, I didn't want you leaving with him to God knows where. I didn't want you with him in some hotel room pretending to be Mrs. Barinsky, or whatever fake name he uses, okay? I know you and hotel rooms, and I don't want you sharing room service with him."

Marlena studied him for a few seconds, then sighed and drawled, "You're right. If I see him naked, T. will kill me."

Just like that, jealousy swarmed him. The gleam in her eyes told him that she was just exacting punishment, but it still unsettled him how possessive he was with her, and hell, he had never been possessive about anything or anybody in his life. Man, he sounded like Alex with his T. "Then I'll have to kill him," he told her half seriously.

She shook her head, a smile curving that sexy mouth. "A vicious cycle, darling. Then T. will come after you, and then I'll have to kill T." She stood on her toes and gave him a soft kiss, the tip of her tongue teasing the corner of his lips. It sent a jolt through him, and he leaned down for a more satisfying one, but she eluded him. "Think about that till later."

"Where are you going?"

"Shopping."

"Shopping?" Dread replaced lust like a snap of the fingers. "What for?"

She laughed. "Darling, remember your payoff to Cam? We need new clothes to go to the opera. You, me, and all your sea mammal buddies. Pierre sent comp tickets to cover us all."

Oh no. No, no, no. He wasn't going to go and tell Hawk and his men that they had to go shopping. He opened his mouth. She gave him a sultry look that promised him all kinds of things Hawk and his men couldn't do. They might just kill him, but they couldn't do what she could. He shut his mouth.

As he watched her saunter off, her hips swaying suggestively, he thought about Alex and his single-minded pursuit of T. His T., he had called her.

Steve plucked his lower lip. *My M. Mine.* He kind of liked the way that sounded.

Marlena decided to let T. handle her own problem. She was sure if T. wanted to, she could disappear from Alex again. So she gave her report, omitting Alex's name, and told her mentor that Stash was shaping up as an excellent liaison. T. had immediately assumed it was Jed who had interviewed Stash and her, and had replied with her usual tart humor.

"I knew Stash would find this new job won't lack adventure."

Marlena smiled wryly. "Oh, I think Stash found his niche."

"So have you decided to keep him, then, darling? You

know I wouldn't mind having him work in New York. I'll welcome him with open arms."

That sealed T.'s fate, as far as Marlena was concerned. She hoped Alex would tie her up and keep her away from . . . She smiled again. Suddenly she didn't feel so bad about betraying her friend. T. was lonely. She loved Alex. For more than two years she had dreamed of and loved that man, so there was nothing wrong in sending her another chance to work things out.

Skipping their usual sarcastic exchange, she softly said, "I'll see you real soon."

Marlena hung up and thoughtfully considered her next problem . . . dressing five very reluctant men with great bodies in Valentino. Or Armani. Hmm. Not every woman had such a delicious task at hand. Maybe she didn't hate men that much after all.

Chapter Twenty-six

It was a not-for-documentary of navy SEALs being tortured. That was Marlena's description, not his. Steve squeezed the bridge of his nose and tried to stop a laugh. The scene in front of him was far more chaotic than the rescue operation a day ago.

It had taken a bit of quiet negotiation on his part, out of Lena's hearing, to get all the men's cooperation. He had called on all the favors he had ever done for Hawk for this one-time deal, and that was because he wanted the night to be perfect for Lena and him.

"You'd better get what you're after," Hawk had warned, eyes narrowed into slits, "because my men and I will bust your ass if you fail."

So today Steve could say he had seen it all. It was quite a sight, five reluctant commandos dragging their feet and following the leather-clad Miss M. around a men's store. The few people in the exclusive boutique stopped and stared at their entourage. Who could help it? The rambunctious crew looked as in place in D.C. as aliens pretending to blend in with humans. He smirked again. A team of SEAL commandos in a men's boutique. Hoo-yah.

Marlena was enjoying herself immensely, and Steve got a kick out of witnessing the pained looks on his cousin's and his men's faces. Hell, they had it easy. She had only made them suffer for a couple of hours before deciding on this one store.

Dirk and Mink were donning all the name-brand shades as they circled the place, pretending they were from the Mafia. Hawk had the biggest scowl on his face, but of all people, his cousin was the last person Steve had expected to allow a woman to groom him. Of course, one should never underestimate the power of persuasion from any GEM operative, and Steve was smart enough not to mention to the guys the fitting business coming up.

That was where Cucumber drew the line. He was so tall that they couldn't find pants the right length that fit, and the store tailor approached him, tape in hand. Steve watched in anticipated amusement as the man patted on the long-suffering Cucumber without explaining what he was about to do. Within seconds Cucumber roared and pulled the tailor off his feet by the collar, looking like he was going to murder the guy.

"Mr. . . . Mr. . . ." The poor man's gasps were shrill with panic.

No one went to his aid. Steve leaned his hip against a counter as he watched Marlena sigh, roll her eyes, and tap the big commando on the arm. "Let him down, you big bully."

"He had his tape measure between my legs." Cucumber glared at the culprit as he lifted him a few inches higher.

"He was just measuring your inseam. You know, you guys have got to cool it, or I'm going to have to go to another store. You don't want to do that now, do you, boys?"

There was a collective groan from the others. Steve understood their pain. Dirk said from behind his sunglasses, in a pseudo Sicilian accent. "Cumber, put him down, man. Let him measure you. I promise we'll kill him if he shorts you of an inch." He leaned closer to the man whose feet were still dangling off the ground. "You'll measure him right, won't you?"

"Yes! Yes, Mr. . . . Mr. . . ."

Cucumber lowered him back on his feet. "It's Mr. Cucumber."

Marlena laughed and pressed a tip into the poor tailor's trembling hand. "Don't mind them. I'll protect you if they misbehave again." She sidled a little closer to Cucumber. "See, I'll hold his hand so he won't grab you again."

Steve couldn't keep his eyes off her as she soothed the men around her, from the enraged and nervous store tailor to the equally enraged and nervous Cucumber. He liked watching her when she was relaxed like this, having her little fun. He didn't mind this side of her at all. He had a feeling that she didn't often tease people she didn't like. Beside him, Hawk turned and asked softly, "You're thoroughly head-over-heels, aren't you?"

Steve didn't hesitate. "Head-over-heels and under deep water."

"No hope?"

"None whatsoever."

"You're gonna keep her?"

He darted a sharp glance at his cousin. He remembered that kiss. "What do you think?"

Hawk's light brown eyes were amused at his quick anger. "I think I like it, although Stash is still a wuss name. So, have you told her about Kat? What about your mom?"

"Lena knows about Kat. Her health problems don't seem to bother her. She hardly reacted at the hospital bills. As for Mom, you know how she is. She'd want to talk to Lena for hours over the phone. No way. She'll scare her off."

Hawk glanced at Marlena. "She doesn't seem to be afraid of anything to me."

Steve sniffed. "Yeah, well, that woman is more commitment-shy than you, cousin Hawk. I've had to practically force myself on her." He grinned. "But she's worth every minute of it. I've been looking for someone like her for a long time."

"Looks like you lucked out, then," Hawk said. "I think she's a fine woman."

Their little talk was interrupted by Marlena calling Hawk over for his turn to be fitted. Steve smirked as Hawk shook his head.

"I know my measurements, thank you," he said.

"But I don't. Come here, Steve, and let me see. Bet

Stash's inseam is bigger." Marlena pointedly never called
Hawk anything but Steve to his face. Her smile was openly
devious.

Steve's grin became wider. Hawk could never resist a
challenge. Ever. His cousin bared his teeth for a moment,
then he strode toward Marlena. "See whether I'm ever going
to answer one of your calls again, Stash."

Marlena met his eyes over Hawk's shoulder and winked.
And the rest of the day, he thought of the future.

The next night, Steve scanned around discreetly in the
middle of act one of the sold-out *Turandot*. They were in
some of the most expensive seats in the house, and after
Marlena's efforts, everyone looked like fashion plates. He
grinned. He supposed there were things worse than having
five reluctant SEALs in an opera. Actually, they had been
behaving themselves. His promise of a five-star dinner afterward helped.

He slid a quick glance down the row just to see how they
were doing. Cucumber was wearing Dirk's new shades. He
was sitting upright, looking straight at the singers on stage,
but Steve knew a sleeping soldier when he saw one. Not that
he feared the big man would clap at the wrong time or start
to snore. A trained commando could catch a nap and yet stay
alert.

At the other end, Hawk was listening attentively. He had
somehow made friends with the two women next to him,
and of course the one sitting closer already had one elegant
hand curled in his. Steve settled back into his seat with a
smile. He should have known Hawk would find a way to entertain himself.

He himself was surprised to find that he was enjoying the
show, very much so. Marlena sat to his right, holding his
hand. She was running her nails lightly against his palm in
rhythm to the beat of the orchestra, and he wanted to pull her
closer and kiss her. But then, if he did that, he would forget
to watch the stage. Kissing Lena was far more absorbing
than a princess who executed all her suitors. He remembered
that opera stories were mostly tragic, with the lovers dying.

He tightened his hold on Lena's hand. Not what he was planning on.

To her right were Cam and Patty Ostler. They were in a world of their own. Cam had arrived in his new penguin suit with a breathtaking and breathless Patty by his side. Breathtaking because of the daring dress she and Marlena picked out when they had gone shopping by themselves. Breathless from how that dress had probably driven poor Cam to forget what time it was. He had apologized charmingly for their tardiness while she blushed and squeezed her velvet red handbag into a wad. It was obvious Patty Ostler hated to be late and wasn't comfortable being the center of attention. She still brushed off Cam's attentions with a cold shoulder in public, but Steve now understood that she was, in fact, more shy than aloof, and therein lay Cam's fascination with her.

Steve returned his attention to the action on stage. Everything, unlike the poor prince on stage who was getting the thumbs-down from the ice-cold princess, was simply perfect.

"I have to thank Marlena for this and for the shopping trip, man," Cam said later, in the men's room. He pressed the soap dispenser. "Doesn't Patty look gorgeous in that dress? It doesn't have any back! You know what that means, don't you?"

"Nope." Steve zipped up his pants and went to join Cam at the washbasin.

Cam waggled his eyebrows at him in the mirror, a devilish smile forming. "No bra," he said, voice laden with male meaning. He toyed around with the paper towels.

"Did I hear something about a bra?" Cucumber asked, looming up from behind. He took off his shades and studied their reflection sleepily. He raked a hand through his dark wavy hair. "Is that part of the next act? I might stay up for that."

"Yeah, the princess is going to parade up and down the stage on six-inch stilettos in some hot girlie outfit, Cumber," Hawk chipped in from the other side of the wall. He tucked in his shirt before buttoning the front of his pants.

Cucumber eyed the whole counter of men's toiletries, shook his head in disbelief, and gave a big yawn. "Wake me up when that scene comes up," he told them as he tried to stretch. He looked disgusted when his brand-new jacket impeded his long arms.

"It's not that bad a show," Hawk said.

"How do you know?" challenged Dirk. "Everyone who's wide awake got a girl with him. Steve's got Marlena. Cam has his girlfriend. You've got that blond chick hanging all over you. Us three here are playing third wheels to you all."

"Yeah," Mink agreed, coming up to stand by Dirk and Cucumber. The three of them donned their new sunglasses in one fluid, practiced motion, then turned to face the urinals.

Steve laughed as Cucumber, Dirk, and Mink made a big show of their lack of female companionship, making leering remarks as they lined up side-by-side to do their business, and then giving hangdog looks. They went into an impromptu satire of the three court jesters who provided the comic relief in the opera.

"Can't be the size."

"What, are you crazy? We've got Cumber on our side. We can beat those three with just his alone."

"Can't be the nuts, either. We have equal proportion in that category."

"You must be blind behind those shades. Or wishful. One of mine's equal to all of yours." That one came from Cucumber.

"Can't be the looks," Dirk jibed. "We're all dressed up like penguins. They look just as bad as we do."

"So what do they have that we don't?" Mink asked in a mock-forlorn voice.

Steve and Cam were laughing too hard to answer. Some of the other men in there were just as amused by the whole routine.

Dirk and Mink looked at each other, then said loudly, "It's got to be the shoes." And all three of them looked down at the same time.

"If you clowns are done bleeding your lizards," Hawk interrupted dryly, "the rest of us have to get back to our ladies. You three better behave when we have dinner. We don't want Steve to blame us if Marlena refuses to marry him."

"Yes, sir," the trio answered dejectedly in unison, as Steve and Cam left the men's room, still chuckling hard.

Steve reached into his pocket and touched the box. He didn't know what he'd do if she refused him. A hand clapped his shoulder, and he turned to see Hawk on his side.

"Relax. She won't chop your head off like Princess Turandot would."

"Yeah," Cam chimed in. "It's not like she's been ignoring you. Down on your knees, say the words, and she'd melt like that cold Chinese princess."

Steve swallowed hard. It wasn't every day a SEAL felt this nervous.

"Man, you wouldn't have known they were that funny after seeing them mowing down an entire crew of bad guys the other night," Cam said, changing the subject, probably for his sake. "Patty wouldn't appreciate them mocking the opera. I'm glad I read the story from the library, man; otherwise, I wouldn't have any freaking idea why she is so damn bloodthirsty. She's kind of mean, if you ask me, ignoring the poor dude like that when he gave her everything! And then still wouldn't marry him when he got the answers right! Man, talk about cold!"

Steve looked at Cam closely to see whether he was catching the irony of his words, but his friend was oblivious to the fact that he was talking more of himself than the opera. When Cam pulled out a stick of chewing gum and looked longingly at it, Steve couldn't help it. He said, "It's okay to chew gum inside, you know."

Cam shook his head. "Wouldn't go with the penguin suit, man. Besides, opera and gum just don't go together, you know?"

That was what made Cam, Cam, Steve wanted to tell him, but changed his mind. His friend wanted his princess's approval and attention, and was doing what it took. He understood frustration. He felt plenty of it these days himself.

"So tell me what's going to happen next so I don't have to read the program."

"It's kind of cool. He guessed her name as the answer to the third riddle and she got pissed off because she didn't think he would win her, right? So the dude-prince turns the tables on her in the next act. He tells her she can chop off his head if she can answer his riddle, which is what his name is."

"Did she find out?"

"Nope. But she gave the right answer anyway. You'll see." Cam looked around for the girls and shrugged. "Women. What do they do in the ladies' rest room, anyway?"

"I don't think they're giving an impromptu Blues Brothers act," Steve replied wryly, and watched as Hawk caught up with them. "Are they still in there?"

Hawk shrugged. "They're always like that. They are called The Three Stooges."

"Hard to figure out why," Steve said. "Cam, you really did read up on the whole opera! What for? Thought you didn't like opera."

"Well, Patty does," Cam said simply, as if that was explanation enough.

"Conversation with the girl," Hawk gave his take on Cam's actions.

"You surprised me, too," Steve said to his cousin. "You looked like you enjoyed it."

Hawk shrugged again. "I don't get to enjoy civilized culture enough. It's a good reminder that we're all human beings."

Cam snorted. "Yeah, right. That Princess Turandot says 'Off with his head,' if any suitors can't come up with the right answer to her riddles. Very civilized."

Steve understood what Hawk was saying, but opted to make light conversation. This wasn't the time to wax philosophical about their real jobs. "Hey, those were tough riddles. And the main man answered all three correctly, so there. A civilized ending."

"Be still my heart," Marlena's low sultry voice cut into

the conversation. "Three men talking about the opera in analytic terms. What happened to the other three?"

"You don't want to know," Steve said with a grin, admiring the way the dark blue of her calf-length dress darkened the blue of her eyes. She was so beautiful, standing there with a glass of champagne, her head tilted to one side mockingly. The pearl and diamond choker around her neck caught the lobby lights and made her eyes sparkle even brighter.

He stepped closer and ran a caressing hand down her back, which was bare, except for two spaghetti straps crisscrossing it. No bra, he told himself, and immediately felt a familiar heat rising. He slid his hand to her lower back and felt her slight tremble. Pulling her closer, he murmured, "Are you ready to go see the final act? I heard the prince kicks some ass and wins the princess's hand."

On cue, the lights in the lobby dimmed and brightened several times in warning. Steve held on to Marlena's hand as they made their way back inside.

Marlena pressed a hand over her fluttering stomach. She couldn't believe it. She was nervous. She was an operative trained to be casual in life-and-death situations, to acknowledge fear as a survival tool to keep on her toes at all times. She was very seldom nervous.

She wondered whether Stash sensed her tension. Watching him made her catch her breath. The midnight-gray of his superbly cut Valentino fit his tall, well-toned body, emphasizing broad shoulders, and the longer back of the suit gave her fantasies about the narrow male hips. He had on a light gray waistcoat with pearl buttons, and she had fastened a little gold chain into his breast pocket. He looked every inch the refined gentleman. Except for the predatory air he exuded whenever he cast those eyes around watchfully. And the way he touched her when no one else was watching. They weren't the touches of a refined gentlemen at all.

He was actually making an effort to enjoy himself. She

knew how uncomfortable he was in this setting, and even though she enjoyed teasing him, she had only to remember how he looked and acted aboard the ship the other night to know that the veneer over the hunter was very thin. That night he had acted thoroughly in charge of the situation, and so masterful and male afterward, it made her think about what he really was like outside his life in D.C.

But she couldn't bear to lose him, not yet anyway. She had thought long and hard about it for a few days now, and had decided that she couldn't just end it with him, just like that. He wanted her, didn't he? As much as she wanted him.

So. She would devise a plan to make them both happy. It would give him time to adjust in his new job as liaison and work with his new team. And it would give her back some measure of control. She wasn't at all sure where everything fit, but that could wait. As soon as she told him her new assignment, everything would fall into its slot. And she would be in charge again.

The hotel suite was blessedly quiet when they returned. She wasn't used to being with so many people who were friends. It seemed more . . . work, somehow. She unbuttoned her long jacket, a faux fur ensemble that matched her outfit.

"What are you smiling about?" Stash broke into her thoughts. He, too, had taken off his jacket, wearing only his suit, and was already busy pulling at his tie.

Marlena sat on the edge of the bed to take off her heels. "I was laughing at myself because I was thinking it was more work to be among friends than at my usual functions."

"What do you mean?"

He came to join her on the bed, and his cologne, mingled with his scent, gently tantalized her senses. He picked up her foot and idly pulled the strap loose. The feel of his fingers was erotic as he traced them along the arch of her hosed heel.

"I guess I'm not used to just going out and having a good time," admitted Marlena. "If I'm dressed up and out socially, it's always been during an assignment, and I'd be on cruise-control."

"Because the people you bumped into were meant to bump into you, and you would just be Marlena Maxwell," Steve finished for her. He picked up her other foot.

"Hmm . . ." Marlena agreed, half closing her eyes.

"You aren't vulnerable when you aren't with friends, since they don't know the real you."

Opening her eyes, Marlena looked at Steve. She had never seen that expression on his face before. Again her stomach started fluttering. "I don't like being vulnerable," she said.

"That's why you like to be alone, in control. It makes you less vulnerable. I don't know what happened in your past that made you decide this is the way to go, and it probably works for you, but it's not working for me, Lena."

"What are you talking about?"

"You know, you're like that Princess Turandot. You don't like to share yourself."

Marlena struggled to balance herself as she tried to sit up with her feet still in his lap. This was not a good bargaining position. "You're saying that I chop up all my suitors?" she asked, injecting humor in her voice though the gathering tension was like oxygen being sucked slowly out of a room.

"You keep asking the riddles, Lena, and I keep giving. I want to be with you, you know that. I want to be more than one of your suitors who look at you adoringly."

"What are you talking about?" She repeated the question, enunciating each word carefully. She hadn't expected this much antagonism. Why was he so mad?

"Du Scheum was looking at you tonight. So were other men connected to you in the past."

"Stash, that was part of my job. They meant nothing to me."

"And me?"

Marlena stared up into those eyes, still not sure what was going on. "What does this have to do with the opera?" she demanded. "I thought we had a good time."

"We did, didn't we." He made the sentence rhetorical. "And what are we going to do next, more operas? More functions? Who will be your next lackey?"

He had her trapped, his hand holding her ankle and his eyes challenging hers. Marlena licked her lips. "We'll have time for ourselves," she began.

"When?"

"I mean, we can spend a few days together after I return from Tibet. And we have some time before that as I prepare for the assignment."

There was a heavy pause. "Tibet," Steve said silkily.

"Yes, it's the perfect assignment after this unusually high-profile one. The deal I made with Mad Max will be known all over soon, and every step I take now will be scrutinized by all sides. Tibet will cut down on the media and spies."

"And I'm supposed to sit around waiting for your call? When were you going to tell me?"

She searched his eyes, saw the anger. She tried to sound reasonable, use logic, the way he always did with her. "Stash, you'll be busy starting your new position. And you will have to meet with many new people. What did you want me to do? We have the next week and then—"

"No."

It was a quiet sort of explosion, but just as deadly. It stopped Marlena cold. "No, what?"

"No. I want you to marry me."

She straightened up then, eyes wide. The fluttering in her stomach felt like wings struggling against a hurricane. "M-marry? Marry you?" she squeaked out. Panic filled her. Marriage?

"Yes. I want to be more than a lover. I want our lives together to be more than a mere schedule to you. I talked a bit to Alex when I handed over the pager, and there are ways, Lena, ways in this outfit where couples work together. I don't want you going off to Tibet without me. There are ways I can contribute to the assignments. And if you go to another of your functions, I want you to be married to me then, to know that you're only mine."

"Married?" she could only repeat the word, dumbfounded. She hadn't expected this. She needed time to think about this. "I had thought . . . we . . . can't we just take this slowly? I . . . I . . . marriage is permanent!"

Steve stared at her a moment, and then let her feet go. He leaned over her, forcing her flat on her back. "Yes, it is," he agreed.

She licked lips that had gone suddenly dry. "But marriage needs . . ." She couldn't end the sentence because it was one word she didn't want to say. Marriage needed love. She dared not say it. Love meant commitment, and giving in, and compromise. Love meant the old fear of being told she wasn't giving back enough. Love turned things upsidedown, inside-out, made people strike out to hurt. Love ended as an option a long time ago, when someone she'd loved betrayed her because he'd thought one failed mission would put her behind a desk. "Stash . . ."

He shook his head. "Lena, I've given you everything so far. You give now."

"Tell me what you want," she asked. Anything but marriage. Anything.

"You. Your name. Hell, I don't even know what GEM stands for! You know so much about me and you don't give me a thing."

"You have me now," she protested. Didn't he see how hard this was for her? "I want you, too, and what we have now is good, isn't it?"

He leaned down closer, his lips inches from her own. "Marry me. Take the step."

She opened her mouth. She lifted her head to kiss him, but he rose a little higher, out of reach. She shook her head, trying to clear away all the panicky thoughts.

His face turned hard and he slowly sat back up. "You want time to do all your probabilities and percentages bullshit, just in case you need to walk away. Fine, Lena." He stood up, stepped away from the bed. "You do that."

Marlena felt suddenly cold. She wanted him on the bed with her. From where she lay, he looked so distant, like . . .

like . . . "What are you doing?" She sat up, true panic invading her voice.

"I'm making it easy for you, Lena. You see, you don't have to do it. *I'm* walking away."

This wasn't supposed to be happening! Why was it happening? She rolled off the bed to go after him. "Stash! Damn it, quit being so melodramatic!"

She made a grab for his arm, but he turned and caught her hand first, jerking her body against his hard muscular chest. His other hand curved behind her neck, and his lips crushed hers. His anger lashed at her but she opened her mouth anyway, trying to communicate the only way she knew how at the moment, but his tongue and mouth remained punishing, demanding something. And because she yielded, molding her body to his, he grew angrier still, tilting her head back until she had to grab his shirt to stay on her feet.

When he let her go, she tasted blood. His eyes were so dark with emotion she couldn't even make out the pupils. His voice was as ragged as her breathing. "It's Steve," he said and shook her. "My name is *Steve*. I'll give you your precious freedom, *M*. I'm not going to come to you anymore. You can ask someone else to play your kissing games with you."

He gave her a hard enough shove that she stumbled backward. Normally she would have caught her balance with no problem, but she felt gutted by the expression in his face as he turned away. He was walking away! Leaving her!

All she had to do was say the right words. Make the right moves. Shock tingled through her system as she realized that she couldn't bear a future without him. But she still couldn't utter those words when he closed the door quietly behind him.

"Don't," she managed to whisper, all too late, "leave me."

But those weren't the words that really mattered, and she knew it.

Chapter Twenty-seven

He'd lied. He couldn't give her the freedom she craved. Two weeks. He had sworn to give her two weeks to make up her mind, and then he would go after her. Well, it had been three long weeks now, and it was pretty clear that she wasn't coming for him.

He knew what he did was a gamble, but he had been too pissed to care that night. He had a ring and a dream in his pocket, and she had told him to keep them there while she weighed all her options. He took a last swallow of beer and crushed the can in his hand.

Well, he was glad he decided not to sit around and wait for her to chop him to pieces. He had known she would run. That pissed him off to no end, no matter that he'd known she would react that way. He had hoped that she might take a chance with the future.

He was glad the past weeks had been so busy that he didn't have time to sit and brood, but he'd finished the first phase of training two days ago, and was given a week off before the second phase began. And through all this time, he had kept hoping to hear from her.

Not even a call. Let's face it—she'd dumped him. He dropped the flattened aluminum can into the nearby basket, then opened the cooler to get another.

"If you plan to drink yourself into oblivion the remaining days off, why the hell did you need to come bother me here?" Hawk asked from a few feet away. He didn't even glance at Steve as he sat on a stool working on some ropes.

Steve didn't tell him that he had nowhere else to go. He certainly didn't feel like going back to D.C. to an empty apartment. Eventually he would have to. But not yet, not so soon. He couldn't bear to walk around and think about Marlena.

So he had dropped in at Hawk's island off the coast of Florida. It was perfect. Hawk called it his sanctuary, and he understood why. It was just the place for someone like Hawk who needed downtime when he returned from some not-so-civilized corner of the world, and wasn't ready to face the neat and tidy lawns of their orderly society yet. The island was private, small enough that the hotels didn't bother with it, and wild enough for a man like his cousin.

But he wasn't Hawk. He didn't want to be alone on some freaking island. He wanted to be with the woman who was driving him slowly out of his mind. He had never felt this vulnerable before, as if someone had ripped him open and left him exposed to the elements. Why the hell did he pour his heart out to her when he had known she would run away?

He finished the can of beer. Crushed it.

"You know," Hawk interrupted his thoughts again, cutting the rope in his hand with his Bowie knife, "having my soft-bellied cousin around in perfect eighty-degree sailing weather, growing fatter and drunker by the second, just isn't my idea of fun."

"If you're trying to tick me off by insulting my conditioning, it isn't going to happen," Steve told him. "Next week they're going to test my physical skills, so why shouldn't I sit back and relax while I can?"

"Relaxation before their kind of tests will kill you," Hawk countered, still not looking at him. His knife cut another splay of rope in half. "This isn't your usual outfit with minimal passing grades, Steve. They're going to find out what you're made of."

"I'm a SEAL operative," Steve said, and he cocked his head arrogantly, "trained under Admiral Madison, who is the head of the STAR Force, one of the best in covert activities. You think I can't handle what they're going to put in front of me?"

Hawk's hand blurred with sudden speed. The Bowie knife snapped through the air and punctured the aluminum can in Steve's hand. If Steve had reacted in surprise, it would have cut his arm, but he just sat there, woodenly looking at Hawk through narrowed slits, beer dribbling down the can onto his T-shirt and into his pants.

His cousin finally looked up, the sunlight and shade making his light brown eyes a peculiar golden yellow. One corner of his mouth lifted. "One more beer and your timing may be off. If they asked you to do what I just did, you would have missed."

Steve knew Hawk was right. Any foreign substance would stay in the system long enough to affect more than the physical state. "I hadn't planned on drinking all week," he said, ignoring his cousin's lifted brows. Okay, maybe he might have. "I'm fine."

The other corner of Hawk's mouth lifted up, and the smile he gave Steve was full of mockery. Steve returned the gaze levelly, spoiling for a fight.

"You look like a lovesick pup, drowning in beer, and coming up for air long enough to yip," Hawk told him.

"This pup is going to kick your ass from one end of the island to the other."

"D.C. has softened you up. I think you need to get back to the basics of being a SEAL."

"What do you have in mind?" Steve rose to the unvoiced challenge. Oh, yeah, let's draw blood.

Hawk dropped the rope by the stool and stretched out his legs. "Let's check out whether those crybaby lungs can still take in air, shall we? We sail to the old lagoon and swim to shore and back on the boat."

"And if I get back on the boat before you do?"

Hawk shrugged. "You get to drink all the beer you want, and I won't say a damn thing."

"Done."

"Don't you think you should first put down that beer?"

Steve pulled out the big Bowie knife and poured out the rest of the alcohol into the sand. He weighed it in his hand for a moment and hurled it back at his cousin in one fluid move. Hawk picked it out of the air with the ease of someone used to knife combat. He raised his brows again. "Ready?"

The lagoon was on the other side of the island, surrounded by a chain of rocks that made it tough for boats to sail in. Again, this was ideal for Hawk, since it discouraged interested visitors. To get to the lagoon, one either had to drive across the island or anchor in the ocean before using a smaller craft to row through the rocks. And even then, one had better be a damn good sailor.

One other way was more direct. Swim. That was no problem for Hawk and Steve. They had done this race numerous times, had memorized which rocks would lead them into the small channel that fed the lagoon. Once inside, Hawk had a dock built there.

Hawk killed the engine and anchored. He was already shirtless, so it was just a matter of throwing off his shades. "Are you sure you can make it there and back, shark bait?"

Steve pulled off his T-shirt. "You're not going to rile me into doing something stupid like waste my breath."

"Good, you're going to need it, beer belly," Hawk said and dove off the boat without warning.

Steve cursed and followed. Hawk never waited. Never played fair.

The water was cold at first, but Steve knew he wouldn't notice the temperature soon. He concentrated on catching up with Hawk, pacing himself till he could count his cousin's strokes. Then he started speeding up. He was alongside in a matter of minutes. He thought of how stupid it was that he was racing his cousin when he should be in D.C. chasing Marlena instead. Anger gave him the strength he needed, and he kicked harder. He began to put space between Hawk and himself.

The ocean felt good, like a cleansing breath after a long

day in traffic. The energy of the waves rolling over and under him fed his will to kick harder. He followed the familiar chain of rocks, ducking under water once he was in the channel to have a better advantage.

He held his breath as long as he could, then burst out into the lagoon and made the final dash for the dock ahead. He reached it and somersaulted under water so he could kick off to return to the boat. If he timed it right, he would come face-to-face with Hawk as he passed him on the way back. His mind and body concentrated on winning.

He surfaced, and Hawk grabbed him from behind. They thrashed under water for a few seconds and Steve kicked and resurfaced, his attacker still hanging on his shoulder.

"Hello there, sailor, are you here to save this poor mermaid?"

It didn't sound anything like Hawk. Steve grabbed and unhooked the arms around his neck. The sudden stop from high-speed swimming caused him to down a mouthful of salt water as he sank under again. But he held on to the culprit who had cost him the race.

Not that he cared. When they surfaced again, before he could breathe or say anything, lips met his and arms circled his neck. He kept both of them afloat as a familiar wicked tongue, salty from the ocean, stole into his mouth.

She kissed him with a mindless hunger that had him hugging her to him as she imprinted her body against his, oblivious to the fact that most swimmers would not be able to stand in water when their legs and hands were tangled. He didn't stop her, even as he automatically adjusted to the new weight. Devouring him still, she forced his head back with her hands, moving with the churning water as they sank in and out of the waves.

Half floating and half standing in water, he allowed her to take his breath to the point of drowning. He could push her off any time, even as she fiercely held on to his hair, but that was the last thing on his mind as he ran possessive hands down the slim back, hips, legs. No, no, this was a fine way to drown.

Suddenly her legs locked around his waist and she released his lips, gasping for air. He saw the deep, deep blue of her eyes shining in the sunlight before she laid her head on his shoulder, holding on to him and letting him do the work of taking them back toward the dock.

He climbed up the steps, carrying his precious cargo easily. He welcomed the reality of gravity. It made everything real. She was really there. In his arms.

"You've gained weight," he remarked, barely able to contain his smile. At the moment she could weigh two hundred pounds and he would still have carried her.

Her face was still buried in his neck and her teeth nibbled the tender flesh under his ear. "I've been eating and waiting here for three days. Where the hell were you?"

She unlocked her legs and slid off his body, but Steve kept her close. It felt too wonderful to be holding her again. "Hawk didn't say anything," he murmured, probing her face for signs.

She looked surprised, then enraged, then turned to face the ocean. Hawk's boat was clearly in view, anchored out there, its bright red flag waving jauntily in the wind. She took a step toward it and yelled, "You bastard! You made me wait three days!"

Steve could see Hawk standing on deck and wondered when his cousin had made his way back to the boat. He hadn't even realized Hawk wasn't behind him. A tiny figure in the distance, he couldn't hear them, of course, but he waved back, sunlight reflecting off his shades.

"I'm going to get back at you, you son of a bitch!" Marlena yelled again, shaking a fist.

Steve snatched at the hand and brought her attention back to him. "You were here the last three days?" he asked, unable to believe that Hawk had pulled such a trick on him.

"Yes, Hawk told me you were coming here after your training session and brought me to this side of the island himself. He said he would bring you to me when you arrived. He left me here for three days! Three days! Do you know I had no change of clothing for three days? Just wait till I get my hands on him . . ."

Steve was too busy looking at her to listen to her tirade. Clad only in a white bikini that was all but see-through, her hair curling wet, falling in tiny ringlets down her back, stormy eyes and pouting mouth, she looked like one of those sirens that called out to sailors, and then drowned them. He ran both his hands through her hair, combing through the whole length.

"What have you done with your hair?" he asked. She was Marlena, but she looked different . . . exotic. There was a mole in the left corner of her mouth that hadn't been there before. Even her lips seemed more lush. He frowned.

Her face softened. "Do you like me?" she asked, shaking her hair out. "I had hair extensions done and then had a perm."

"This is for Tibet, isn't it?" Steve demanded, and he shook her. "Damn it, Lena. Don't you dare show up here just for a rendezvous before you take off!"

He shook her hard enough that she had to hold on to him, but she didn't defend herself or fight back. He stopped, then gathered her into his arms. Swallowing hard, he tried to regain some measure of self-control, but he couldn't for the life of him think of anything to say.

Marlena felt the urgent tension in Steve's hard body and, looking up, caught the flash of pain in his eyes. She bit down on her lip. She had never felt more humble than at that moment, to know that this man felt so much for her and still was strong enough to let her go.

She took a deep breath, swallowed down the old fears and doubts. He didn't deserve her cowardice. This time she would take a chance, and not look at the probabilities. Her smile came out a little tremulously.

"Stash . . . Steve," she corrected, fighting down the butterflies in her stomach again. "I spent the last two weeks in hell, wondering how I was going to live without you. I had my next assignment to prep for and my heart wasn't in it. I spent hours telling myself that it would get better, but it didn't. Do you know why?"

His dark eyes were devouring her with their banked heat. "Why?"

"Because I can't live without you. Because I've fallen in love with you. And I suddenly realized that I didn't have to be without you."

"It's got to be everything or nothing, Lena," he told her softly, still waiting.

She traced his lips with his fingers. So masculine. So sensuous. And she was suddenly unafraid. "M for Marry Me," she said, and with that the quivering nerves inside her dissipated. She felt free. Lighter than the breeze blowing inland. Laughter bubbled from her lips.

"Marry me," she repeated, this time with confidence, "in Tibet. That way, all of our private friends can attend. I might even let you invite Hawk."

The banked heat in Steve's eyes flared with love and desire, and he swung her off her feet, carrying her. "Say it again," he demanded fiercely, as he started down the dock toward the beach. "Tell me you love me. Because I love you, Lena."

"I love you, Stash," Marlena said, holding his face with her hands.

He kicked the door of the tiny cabin open and strode in. "Again," he ordered.

She smiled, happiness swelling inside like warm wine. He was her Stash again, arrogant, demanding, and already untying her bikini strings. He touched her as if she was something cherished, moving his hands over her naked skin slowly.

"I love you, Stash."

"More," he demanded again, just to make sure. "Tell me more because I can't believe this is real."

She did better than that. She slipped her hands into his swimming trunks, hands that he would know anywhere. Then she lowered her incredible body over his and leaned in. She whispered in his ear and entrusted him with her name.

Steve closed his eyes and sighed. Trust. Love. And a woman's hands in his pants. He felt something around him. Opened his eyes. Saw flashing blue eyes full of mischief. A long, long chain of pearls. He closed his eyes again. Oh yeah. It couldn't get more real than this.

From his boat Hawk watched the couple on the beach. His lips quirked slightly as Steve shook Marlena and then a few minutes later strode off with her in his arms. Looked like they were going to leave him waiting out there for a while.

He settled back comfortably on his deck chair, staring up into the sky, lazily following the seagulls circling. And he noticed a larger predator bird flying higher still, alone and wild, surveying its kingdom way above everything else. Probably hunting for prey, he mused. On the other hand, it could be hunting for a mate.

Prepare to be swept away by these unforgettable romances from Avon Books

LONDON'S PERFECT SCOUNDREL by Suzanne Enoch
An Avon Romantic Treasure

Evelyn Ruddick knows she should avoid the Marquis of St. Aubyn at all costs, but she is determined to teach the charming, arrogant rake a lesson in compassion. It won't be so easy—especially since his touch is setting her desires aflame, making Evie yearn to submit to *his* passionate instruction . . .

cummummum

IF THE SLIPPER FITS by Elaine Fox
An Avon Contemporary Romance

Anne Sayer learned long ago that fairy tales don't come true and evil stepmothers do exist. Now dashing and successful, Connor Emory has returned, and this "Cinderella" intends to win back her prince. Because the glass slipper that would never have fit a decade ago, is the perfect size now.

cummummum

KISS ME QUICK by Margaret Moore
An Avon Romance

The instant Lady Diana Westover spies Edmond Terrington across a crowded room, the lovely, sheltered miss believes she's found the man she's been searching for. Though she knows nothing of men, Diana longs to pen a romantic novel. So she resolves to study the handsome, seductive lord's every move, and to experience the pleasures of his kisses . . .

cummummum

CHEROKEE WARRIORS: THE LONER by Genell Dellin
An Avon Romance

Black Fox is determined to hunt down the notorious Cat—a thief who robs from the wealthy to give to the poor. But his satisfaction at finally capturing the outlaw turns to shock when he discovers The Cat is a woman! This breathtaking hellion stirs his sympathy and his desire, yet surrendering to a fiery passion could be disaster for them both.

REL 0403

LONGAR

Longarm did not gi improve his aim. Shooting from his hip, his Colt bucked twice and stitched two messy bullet holes in the man's shirtfront. The man was dead before he pitched over a bench, but Longarm didn't see him because he was twisting around and his six-gun roared twice more. . . .

TABOR EVANS

LONGARM

AND THE
NEVADA SWINDLE

JOVE BOOKS, NEW YORK

LONGARM AND THE NEVADA SWINDLE

A Jove Book / published by arrangement with
the author

PRINTING HISTORY
Jove edition / March 1993

ISBN: 0-515-11061-2

Jove Books are published by The Berkley Publishing Group,
200 Madison Avenue, New York, New York 10016.
The name "JOVE" and the "J" logo
are trademarks belonging to Jove Publications, Inc.

PRINTED IN THE UNITED STATES OF AMERICA

10 9 8 7 6 5 4 3 2 1

Chapter 1

"Custis," Chief Marshal Billy Vail said, working hard to keep up with his tall deputy marshal, "I want you to remember that you are going on vacation. So I trust you've left your badge at your rooming house."

"Oh, I did that," Custis Long said with a smile as they hurried toward Denver's Union Station. "I left it hid under my mattress. Even thought about leaving my six-gun behind and wearing a cleric's collar just so folks would know my peaceable intentions."

Vail snorted with derision. "Don't try to bullshit me, Longarm. You'd rather go naked than unarmed."

The tall, broad-shouldered deputy marshal chuckled. Longarm was in fine spirits this day because he had not had a real vacation in almost four years. And since Longarm had more than his share of enemies in Denver, he and Vail had both agreed that distance would be necessary for relaxation.

"What's that friend of yours named?" Vail asked.

"Which one?"

"The fella you're looking to hook up with on the Comstock Lode," Vail said.

1

"Jim Zack. Like I told you, I haven't heard from him in ten, maybe twelve years. We both started out mean and hungry, taking odd jobs where we could and taking our pleasures where we could find them. I wound up a poor, overworked lawman, and I'm betting Jim Zack got rich."

Vail was puffing just to keep up with his deputy. "Hell, Longarm, everyone *wants* to get rich."

"Yeah," Longarm agreed, "but Jim Zack just might have gone and done it. He was good with money, unlike me. I'd spend what I had on whiskey, poker, and women. Jim would always be looking to invest in one thing or the other."

"And he never hit the jackpot in the years you knew him?"

Longarm shook his head as they hurried along hearing the train's whistle blast its departure warning. Longarm yanked out his pocket watch. "We'd better shake a leg," he said, lengthening his already considerable stride.

"Hell," his shorter, stockier boss complained, "I'm dogtrotting now to keep up with you!"

"Billy, it won't be you that will miss an overdue vacation if that train pulls out before I get to the depot on time."

"It always leaves a few minutes after five," Vail argued breathlessly. "No reason to expect that will change just because it's got you for a passenger."

Longarm supposed his boss was right. And he knew that the train was usually a few minutes late both arriving and departing. The Denver and Pacific Railroad would make up the time on the way up to Cheyenne, where it would hook up with the Union Pacific traveling both east and west.

"Longarm, I do have one little favor to ask of you," Vail panted.

2

"It's a little late to be asking for favors," Longarm growled. "Besides, I'm officially on vacation and that means that the only favor that I have to do is for myself."

"Aw, come on!" Vail complained. "All I want you to do is to look up my Aunt Rebecca Brown who lives in Reno. Just look her up and spend a few minutes visiting her."

"Billy!"

In reply, Chief Marshal Vail yanked an envelope from his inside coat pocket and shoved it at Longarm. "Here! There's a letter for her."

"Why don't you *mail* the damned thing?"

"Because I lost her address!" Vail gasped. "And besides, I stuck ten dollars in the envelope for you to take Aunt Rebecca out on a nice dinner. Tell her that I still think of her almost every day."

"Bull!" Longarm snapped. "If you do, then I'd bet anything that it's because she's an old lady with a trunkful of money and no one in mind to leave it to."

"Jesus, but you're a cynic!"

"Well, is she rich, or isn't she?"

"All right, she does have some money and no children of her own."

"I rest my case," Longarm said with a look of triumph. "So how am I supposed to find this Aunt Rebecca Brown?"

"You're a lawman," Vail said as they rounded a corner and saw the tracks by the depot up ahead. The conductor had jumped on board and the train was beginning to belch steam and lurch into motion. "Figure out how to find her!"

"Dammit, Billy, I'm on vacation!" Longarm shouted as he burst into a trot, his right hand gripping his Winchester rifle and his left a pair of saddlebags packed with a few fresh

3

changes of socks and underwear.

"Here!" Billy cried, panting heavily as he sprinted alongside Longarm shoving bills into his pants pocket. "Twenty dollars for your damned trouble! Twenty dollars, a night on the town with Aunt Rebecca, and that's the best hourly pay you'll ever earn!"

Longarm accepted the twenty dollars even though he knew it was a mistake. He took the money because he had lost a good part of his vacation savings in a last-minute poker game and was now short of funds. But even as he took the money, Longarm knew that he was selling his soul. If Billy Vail was paying a man twenty dollars for something, then that man was going to go through hoops to earn it—one way or the other.

"Do I get part of the old gal's inheritance!" Longarm shouted as he began to sprint after the departing train, which was gathering speed much faster than expected.

"Hell, no!"

Longarm sprinted faster.

"Dammit, you find her and tell her what a great fella I am now!" Vail cried, badly winded and falling behind. "Do you hear me, Deputy Marshal!"

Longarm was running at full speed now, but he still had enough breath in his lungs to bark a laugh, and he would have easily overtaken the train except that a dance-hall girl shot out of the Bulldog Saloon just ahead, jumped off the boardwalk, and also started to race for the departing train. Skirts flying, painted face streaked with tears, she didn't see Longarm as she veered into his path.

A bartender exploded out of the saloon. "Milly, you come back here with that money right now!"

"Go to hell, Harold, it's due me!" she cried an instant before she collided with Longarm.

They both crashed and tumbled in the street. Longarm was up first, grabbing his saddlebags and cussing a blue streak. He would have charged off after the departing train again, but the young woman wrapped her arms around his leg.

"Let go of me or I'll miss my damned train!" he shouted, shaking his leg furiously.

"Not unless you help me catch it too!"

"No!"

"Then I'm hanging on and neither of us will make it," she vowed.

Longarm wanted to strangle the woman. She had a wild mass of auburn-colored hair and big brown eyes, and when Longarm could pull his eyes away from her bulging bosom and deep cleavage, he saw both desperation as well as determination on her pretty face.

"Take the next one," Longarm pleaded.

"No, that's *my* train same as it is yours, Marshal Long!" she cried, hanging on for all she was worth.

"Let go of me!" he shouted, wishing it was a man so he could have simply drawn his six-gun and clouted the fool in the head and freed himself. There was still a slim chance of catching the train, but it was fast disappearing.

"Help me!" the woman begged.

"Milly, come back here right now!" the bartender shouted, waving his fists.

"Did you really steal his money?" Longarm demanded.

"Hell, no! It's my overdue wages!"

Longarm wanted to believe Milly, and since there wasn't time to find out the truth and still catch his train, he gave the girl the benefit of the doubt.

"Come on!" he shouted, yanking Milly erect and propelling her after the train. "And I hope you can run!"

5

"Damn right I can!" she yelled, proving it with an amazing burst of speed.

Milly was short and voluptuous, but when she picked up her skirts, she could fly. It was all that Longarm could do to keep up with the girl as they closed the distance on the departing train.

"Custis!" Vail shouted from back in town. "Arrest that girl!"

"I'm on vacation! No badge, remember?" he bellowed over his shoulder as he overtook the girl and they ran neck and neck down the railroad tracks with about a hundred Denverites watching and starting to cheer.

Longarm was losing steam even as the train was gathering steam. Maybe if he hadn't have been carrying his rifle and his saddlebags he'd have had enough energy to run down the train, but as it was, he saw that he would not be able to catch the damn thing. When he glanced to the side, Longarm realized that Milly was also starting to fade. Her pretty face was flushed with exertion and she was gasping for wind. Milly was a sprinter, not a long-haul runner.

"Come on! Come on!" a pair of cowboys yelled as they came galloping up. "Don't give up, stranger! You neither, Milly darlin'!"

In reply, Milly twisted around and cried, "Give us a damn ride, Walt!"

Walt was riding a big sorrel and his friend was riding a skinny roan. Both of them were galloping easy.

"What you gonna give me fer helpin' you out!" Walt crowed, plainly enjoying himself at their expense. "You gonna give it to me fer free if you come back to Denver Town!"

"Ye . . . yes!" she gasped. "Free!"

6

"But you ain't comin' back," Walt said, spurring his sorrel ahead of them as he galloped between the tracks.

Longarm had had enough of this nonsense. Walt was staring at Milly's heaving breasts, one of which had slipped out from under the top of her dress and was wildly flopping. Longarm had to admit that it was enough to mesmerize any man, but it also gave Longarm the chance to throw himself forward, close on the rider, and grab onto his arm.

"Hey!" Walt screamed.

Longarm tore the rider from the sorrel, dropped his saddlebags, and made a desperate grab for the saddlehorn. He just did manage to latch his fingers around it, and that was good enough. With his Winchester in his right fist and horn in his left, he let the running horse's momentum catapault him skyward. He landed on the rump of the sorrel. It bucked and threw him forward into the saddle.

"Don't leave me!" Milly cried.

Longarm *would* have left her, but the half the town was watching and it would have been a callous act on his part given what they'd gone through in the last few moments. So he drew the horse to a sliding stop, wheeled it around, and raced back to the girl.

"Grab up my saddlebags and give me your hand!" Longarm ordered.

Milly's face brightened. She retrieved Longarm's saddlebags, then threw up her hand. Longarm's fist closed over hers and he swung her up onto the sorrel.

The frightened animal was obviously not used to carrying double. It bucked about four times, and Milly squealed and hugged Longarm like a leech sucking blood. He lost his right stirrup and almost his balance. Somehow, though,

7

Longarm managed to get his boot back into the stirrup, and then he booted the sorrel in the flanks so hard it grunted.

"Come on, damn you!" he yelled at the horse, driving it after the train.

"Can we catch it?" Milly shouted in his ear. "Marshal, I've *got* to get on that train!"

"We'll catch her!" Longarm vowed. "We'll catch her if we have to run this poor damned horse all the way up to Cheyenne."

Milly hugged him even tighter. She twisted her head around to see Walt pop to his feet and scream terrible obscenities at them.

"Goddamn, but I like your style, Marshal Long," she declared, laying her head against his back. "You're a man after my own heart!"

"How do you know my name!" he shouted, booting the sorrel forward for all he was worth.

"You arrested me once."

"I did?"

"Sure! Don't you remember?"

"No."

"Then I ain't going to remind you," she told him.

Longarm glanced back over his shoulder at Denver. He just made out Billy Vail standing by the depot, and he'd bet his boots that the lawman would be fuming. It wasn't every day that the chief marshal watched one of his best men steal a horse.

"Come on!" Longarm cried, whipping the horse as it closed the gap to the train.

It was going to be close. Already, the sorrel was starting to wheeze and falter as it hurled cinders into the air and chased the train. Longarm knew the animal wouldn't be able to carry double more than another mile.

"Here we go," Longarm shouted. "Milly, when I pull up even with the train, you jump for that rail back of the last coach. Hear me?"

"Yes, sir!"

Longarm skillfully reined the sorrel in close to the train. It was moving very fast now and his horse was starting to lose its stride.

"Jump, Milly!"

Milly jumped. She jumped so hard that she flew over the back rail of the coach and crashed headfirst into the door. Longarm tossed his saddlebags and rifle, and Milly cried out in pain when they struck her in the side.

"Dammit, Longarm, now *you* jump!"

Longarm kicked out of his stirrup, and when he threw himself forward, the poor sorrel lost its footing and began to cartwheel over the rails. But by the time the horse hit the cinders, Longarm was already grabbing the railing and dragging himself to safety.

"We did it!" Milly cried. "We did it!"

Longarm laughed. He could still see the Union Depot, but Billy Vail was just a dot on the Denver horizon.

The sorrel came to its feet and, to Longarm's relief, it trotted back down the train tracks toward its master and the town.

"At least there won't be a warrant out on me for horse-stealing now," he said. "But if you ever come back, I'd say you will owe poor Walt a free ride."

"Walt's a pig," Milly said, raising her chin defiantly. "And besides, I'm turning respectable. I got a man waiting for me in Reno and he's bringing a wedding ring and a preacher man."

Longarm looked down at the girl. Her lovely breast was still hanging out, and that made thinking of her becoming

9

"respectable" a near impossibility.

"Here," he said, pulling out the elastic top of her blouse and allowing the breast to slip out of sight. "If you're going to become a respectable woman, you'd better buy some respectable clothes in Cheyenne. I'm afraid that what you have on now sort of advertises your past profession."

Milly frowned. She was a mess. Streaked with sweat, hair wild and mussed, face flushed. Longarm thought she smelled like a whore drenched with enough cheap perfume to take a bath in in the hope of suffocating her own unwashed and heavy sexual odors.

"I've never been a respectable woman," Milly allowed, slipping her arm around her tall savior. "So it might take me some practice. Maybe you'd help give me some pointers, Marshal."

Longarm barked a laugh. "Not me! I make it a point to stay away from respectable women."

She looked up at him, eyes wide. "Oh. Well, I'm sorry to hear that, Marshal. Because respectable I mean to be."

Longarm was about to say something about that when the back door of the coach opened and the conductor stepped out to join them.

He took one look at Milly and frowned. "Young lady, you'd better have a ticket."

Milly gulped. "Sir, I confess that I do not."

"Then you'd better have the money to buy one."

"Sir, I confess I do not have that either."

"Then you'll have to get off this train at its first stop."

"Which is?"

"Darkwater. That's where we take on coal and water."

"Hell," Longarm blurted out, "that's no more than a telegraph office! There's not even any place for Miss . . ."

10

"Taylor," she said. "Miss Milly Taylor."

Longarm frowned. "Conductor, there's not even any place for Miss Taylor to eat or sleep in Darkwater."

"I'm sorry," the conductor replied. "Just like you, I don't make the rules. I just carry 'em out. Now, if I may have your ticket, please."

"Didn't have time to buy one," he growled, not at all pleased at how things were shaping up for poor Milly.

"How far are you going, Marshal?"

"Reno."

"Twenty-five dollars third class, thirty-five dollars second class, and fifty dollars first class."

Longarm was not an extravagant man, but he did enjoy his creature comforts and he'd traveled enough by train enough to know that he wanted first class. So he forked over fifty dollars thanks to his boss and what scarce money he had of his own. If Aunt Rebecca was as well off as Longarm suspected, she could take *him* to dinner.

"Still comes with meals in the sleeper, right?" Longarm asked.

"That's right."

The conductor took Longarm's cash and gave him a first-class ticket. Then, he turned back to Milly and said, "You can stay in the third-class coach until we reach Darkwater, Miss Taylor. After that, you'll have to get off the train."

"Well what am I supposed to do in Darkwater?" she cried.

The conductor was a man in his late fifties, gray-haired and gray-skinned. Even so, he could not help but stare at Milly's bulging bosom and say, "A girl like you, Miss Taylor, isn't going to get lonesome or starve, even in a place like Darkwater."

Milly flushed, and she surprised Longarm when she slapped the conductor and hissed, "I turned respectable!"

The conductor became so angry that, when he spoke, spittle flew. "Is that right! Well, be respectable in Darkwater!"

Tears welled up in Milly's eyes, and she was so mad she was shaking. "No one ever gives a girl a chance anymore, do they! They get her down and they just grind her into the dirt and keep her there for their own pleasure."

Longarm was moved by the hard truth of Milly's words. It didn't help that he was about to head for a first-class sleeper and leave Milly behind to be dumped at Darkwater. Guilt welled up unbidden and Longarm felt rotten.

"Here," he said, digging out the last few dollars he could find and shoving them at the conductor. "Give her a third-class ticket. It's the best I can do."

"Thank you," Milly said, her voice charged with emotion.

But when the conductor counted out the money, he said with undisguised pleasure, "Marshal, you're two dollars short of a third-class ticket."

The man's cruel and uncompromising attitude galled Longarm. He felt his blood boil as he reached out and grabbed the conductor by the shirtfront. "We'll just let the Denver and Pacific absorb the loss. Right?"

The conductor winced with pain. He stared into Longarm's hard blue eyes and discovered that he was nodding rapidly in agreement. "Yes, sir, Marshal Long!"

Longarm released his grip. "Give Miss Taylor her own ticket."

12

The conductor whipped one out of his pocket in no time flat. He even bowed when he gave it to Milly. "Have a nice trip, Miss Taylor."

"Thank you," she said, looking deep into Longarm's eyes. "Thank you very, very much."

Her eyes warmed Longarm's innards and he grinned. In fact, he kept grinning until the conductor left them alone. Then he said, "I don't suppose you brought any food or even any blankets. It gets cold at night traveling third-class."

"I'll survive."

"I'll bring you some food from my sleeper and an extra blanket or two before nightfall," he heard himself say.

"Why?"

Her question caught Longarm off guard. "Well," he stammered, "it just seems like the gentlemanly thing to do for a girl who intends to turn respectable."

She blushed with pleasure. Her hands smoothed her wild auburn hair. "I'm a mess and I know I don't look very presentable. Somehow, I intend to get a bath and fix myself up some before we get to Reno. We stop in Cheyenne for a few hours, don't we?"

"Yes."

"Then I'll fix and clean myself up there. I intend to look a lot better by then."

"I'm sure you will," Longarm said. "Even messed up a little, you're still mighty pretty."

She preened. "You really think so? I mean, you're not just saying that to make me feel good or to get into me tonight in your berth, are you?"

He couldn't shake the vision of that errant left breast. Longarm put his hands behind his back and crossed his

13

fingers. "Naw, I'm just telling you the God's honest truth. That's all."

She threw herself at him so hard they both almost flipped over the rail onto the track.

"Longarm, if I wasn't fixing to get married, I swear I'd get to steaming between the legs."

Longarm guffawed heartily. "Milly, if you're going to become respectable, maybe you're also going to need to think a little more about what you say before you open your mouth."

Her happy expression melted. "Oh, yeah, I see what you mean. I shouldn't have said what I just did about . . . well, you know."

"We'll work on that some," he promised. "Now let's go inside and find you a good seat to Cheyenne."

She linked her arm through his and squeezed tight. "I'm glad we're riding the same trains to Reno, even if we won't be sleeping together."

Longarm looked down at her and that cleavage. "Oh," he drawled as they passed into the coach, "you never know what will happen on a long train ride, Milly."

She cocked up one eyebrow and her eyelids shuttered seductively. "What is that supposed to mean?"

"Nothing," he said. "Only that I'll enjoy your company too."

"Oh," she said, relaxing. "Well, just remember that I'm getting married and I'm in love with a fine man."

"I'll do my best to remember," Longarm promised with a pair of his fingers crossed.

Chapter 2

Longarm smoked a cheroot and sipped a glass of the railroad's complimentary whiskey given to first-class passengers. His little sleeper was cramped, especially for a man of his size, but Longarm was not complaining. He had his own berth and privacy as well as a view out a clean window to watch as the rolling grasslands of northern Colorado sailed passed.

When the train stopped late that afternoon at Darkwater for coal and water, it brought Longarm's thoughts back to Milly Taylor. Even thinking about her was arousing. That was one pretty as well as determined gal, all right. Most dance-hall women and prostitutes, no matter how successful, were all talk. They all constantly talked about escaping their sordid professions and getting respectable, but few had the grit to actually carry out their romantic dreams.

Milly Taylor, and Longarm doubted that was her real name, was the rare exception. As Longarm smoked and sipped at his good whiskey, he could not help but wonder what kind of a man Milly was going to marry in Reno. Milly hadn't said much about him, and perhaps that was just as well. There was also the real possibility that she was lying about a man waiting to marry her. Some girls like Milly wanted respectability so badly that they began to believe their own daydreams.

Longarm, despite his own lusty designs, hoped that there really was a man with a diamond wedding ring waiting for Milly's finger. She was pretty, smart, and determined. If a man could get past the body odor and the heavy paint and rough edges, he'd know that Milly had the makings of a hell of a good wife and mother.

"Here's to you, Milly," Longarm said, raising his glass to his own reflection in the window.

The train remained only a quarter hour at Darkwater, and during that time Longarm saw only one old water tender and his decrepit dog. Hell, Milly would have starved there waiting for anyone to engage her professional services. The old man and his sorry dog sure wouldn't have been up to the mark.

When the train pulled out of Darkwater, Longarm watched the sunset burn a filigree of gold across the peaks of the towering Rocky Mountains. It was a majestic sight and one which Longarm had enjoyed for many years and never tired of witnessing. He finished his glass of whiskey and cheroot, ground the latter under his boot heel, and came to his feet.

He was just about to inquire about the free food he was entitled to from the dining car when a black waiter in a white coat and pants knocked on his door.

"Food, suh?"

"Damn right," Longarm said, opening the door to see a huge platter of beefsteak and potatoes, coffee, rolls, creamed carrots, and apple pie for dessert. "Bring it on in."

"Yes, suh!"

When the waiter had set the platter on a small fold-out table complete with linen, crystal, and silver, Longarm said, "I'll have company for dinner and will need another plate for food and service."

The waiter didn't bat an eye. "Yes, suh, Marshal Long!" he said. "De conductor said you to have whatever you want."

"Very good!" Longarm replied. He realized now that he'd made an indelible impression on the old conductor, and perhaps even instilled some charity in his cold heart.

In ten minutes, another plate was in his cabin and he was on his way back through the passenger coaches to the third-class, where the poorest travelers resided on hard wooden benches without any furnace for heat in winter. Their coach's windows were never cleaned from the soot of the locomotive engine, so that they rode in a perpetual corridor of shadow.

When Longarm entered the third-class coach, he stopped abruptly to see three men wrestling with Milly, trying to pin her down on the bench and get her dress pushed up to her waist.

"Hey!" Longarm bellowed. "Stop that!"

The three men twisted around, and their lust was so naked that it made his flesh crawl. One of the men had the fly of his pants open and his manhood was protruding like a stiff pink snake. The other passengers bore expressions ranging from fear to desire. It was only then that Longarm realized that Milly was the only female passenger traveling third-class.

"Who the hell are you!" one of the three demanded as he saw Longarm's hand push back his coat and rest near the butt of a well-worn Colt .44.

"Marshal Custis Long. Back off from that young lady."

17

"She ain't no damned lady! She's just a broke whore! We was gonna pay her!"

"Back off!"

The three exchanged nervous glances, and one of the other passengers said, "You boys best do as Marshal Long says or he'll shoot holes in your dirty hides."

The three pushed away from Milly. Longarm's hand remained near the butt of his six-gun, but he was familiar enough with this kind of scum to know that they would not openly brace him in close quarters. No, these kind of men would gun you down from behind or in ambush, but they'd never risk a fair fight.

Milly sprang up from the bench, her pretty face bruised. She broke through the trio and ran to Longarm, then hugged him tightly. He could feel her entire body tremble.

"You boys weren't going to pay her for it," Longarm said, voice hard with anger. "You were going to rape her!"

"No we weren't, Marshal!" one of them wheedled. "Honest."

"You don't know how to spell the word 'honest,'" Longarm spat. "If I wasn't on vacation, I'd arrest the three of you and have you locked up in Cheyenne and bound for prison!"

"You're on vacation?" one asked, face relaxing.

"That's right," Longarm sighed. He looked down at Milly. "Get your stuff and let's get out of this stinking coach."

One of the three tittered. "You're gonna poke her yourself for free, ain't you, Marshal! That's why you really stepped into our business."

"Shut up!"

18

"It's true! You're on vacation and you want some tail!" The man laughed until Longarm stepped forward and smashed him in his leering mouth so hard with his fist that he broke teeth and skinned knuckles.

With a roar, one of the men jumped on Longarm and wrapped his forearm around his throat while riding him to the floor. Longarm tried to twist around and fight, but he was wedged in between the wooden benches so tightly that he could not move. He looked up and saw one of the men aim a boot at his face. Longarm managed to jerk his head aside an instant before the man's boot slammed into the bench. Then he threw out a hand and tripped the man down.

Milly screeched like a female cat in heat. Her fingernails raked a cheek, drawing four long streaks of blood and a cry of pain. She drove a knee into a groin while Longarm struggled to his feet with the man still strangling him. Longarm slammed his elbow once, then once more into the strangler's gut.

"Ohhh!" the man grunted as he finally released his hold.

Longarm whirled and his big fists were a blur as he lashed out with a right that connected solidly against the man's jaw and caromed him off the wall. Two more blows to the gut and one to the point of the chin put the man down for the count.

Longarm whirled around in time to see Milly bent over a bench with a man trying to throttle her. Longarm stepped forward and sledged the man just behind the ear. His blow was measured not to kill, but the man was not going to wake up before Cheyenne.

"Are you all right?" Longarm asked, pulling Milly to her feet.

19

She looked dazed and pale. "Yes," she whispered. But then she fainted.

Longarm scooped her up in his arms and spun on his heel. Just before leaving the coach, he turned to survey the damages. All three men that had been trying to rape Milly were bleeding and in bad shape. The other passengers seemed to wilt under Longarm's hard staring.

"What kind of men are you that would allow those three miserable sonofabitches to rape this girl?" he shouted. "Isn't there one decent man among you?"

The passengers would not answer, and neither could they meet Longarm's accusing eyes.

"You're a bunch of weaklings and degenerates," Longarm told them. "There's not a good man among you or he'd have tried to stop what they were doing to this girl."

One man did look up and say, "She is just a damned dance-hall girl."

The man's comment made Longarm even angrier.

"She's a human being who's trying to start a new life in Reno! She's trying to grab the golden ring, only men like you want to pull her down to your own scummy levels."

When no one chose to argue, Longarm turned his back on them and carried Milly up through the passenger cars. Maybe he'd been too hard on the third-class passengers who'd done nothing to help Milly. Maybe, but he thought they more than deserved his tongue-lashing. Maybe he'd stirred their conscience enough that, if they were ever in the same position, they'd stand up for honor and decency.

As Longarm trudged up through the second-class car and then into the first-class where he was staying, he was aware that people were staring at him with curiosity and open disapproval. To hell with it, he thought. There was

20

no hiding the fact that Milly was a working girl and her appearance less than respectable. But Longarm meant to change that in Cheyenne. He'd found he still had a few dollars left and, with a little overdue luck at cards, he was hoping he could recoup his Denver losses and buy Milly a bath and some new clothes. Clothes that would give her a whole new look.

Back in his sleeping car, Longarm poured another glass of whiskey from the complimentary bottle and raised Milly's head. "Here. Drink a little of this."

Milly's eyes fluttered open. She started in fear, but then recognition allowed her to relax. "Did we whup them good, Marshal?"

"We sure did," he said, pouring the whiskey into her mouth.

Milly took two gulps and indicated that she wanted more. She drank whiskey like it was milk, and it brought pink to her cheeks.

Longarm poured himself another glass and lit a cheroot before massaging his bruised knuckles. "We'll be in Cheyenne in a little while and stay until about ten o'clock tonight. I'm going to play a few hands of cards at a saloon that I know and have been lucky in before. Want to come along and give the boys a treat?"

"I don't think so," she whispered. "I've seen the inside of a saloon for the last time, remember?"

"Yeah," he said, "I do. All right, then you can stay here. It wouldn't be safe to leave you alone back in third class."

"Thank you," she breathed. "But I still want to get a bath and a new respectable dress."

"You've got some money?"

"About fifteen dollars that I had been owed from the Bulldog Saloon."

"You ought to be able to get a bath and a new dress for that," he said. "But I ain't sure if the ladies' stores will still be open by the time we arrive in Cheyenne."

"But they have to be!"

Longarm could see how very important it was for the girl to get fixed up with new clothes. "Listen," he said, "I do know a few of the merchants and shop owners in Cheyenne. I'm sure we can come up with something."

"You're wonderful, Marshal," she said, throwing her arms around his neck and planting a big kiss on his lips.

Longarm felt his loins stir powerfully, and the heat from her young body made the hair on the back of his neck as well as his manhood stand on end.

He pushed her back down on his narrow little bed and his practiced fingers began to unbutton her bodice. He looked down at her face and said, "If you want to stop me, Miss Taylor, just say whoa and she's done."

Milly gulped. "I should say whoa, but I feel like saying yes."

"Then say yes," he said thickly as he stared at her melon-sized breasts and bent to lave them with his tongue.

When his tongue worked its way around a nipple, she panted, "Yes!"

It was all that Longarm could do to keep from whooping with anticipation. It was true that Milly smelled of sweat and things best not considered, but she was hot and eager and pretty as hell in a messy, musky sort of way.

As soon as Longarm's tongue started to work around her nipples, Milly began to grab and growl like a feral wildcat fixing to mate. Her hands were all over Longarm and if they'd had some decent space to frolic in, Longarm

22

had no doubt they could and would have gotten into some exciting postions.

But the space was ridiculously cramped and Longarm had one hell of a time just getting his boots and pants off. By that time, Milly's dress was bunched up around her waist and she was ready.

"Don't tease me, Marshal," she breathed. "I'm guilty of sin and I want the full measure of your law."

Longarm growled low in his throat. He squeezed between her muscular thighs and drove his thick manhood into her little hole.

She moaned and her legs came up to lock around his hips. Because Longarm could not stretch out fully on the berth, his feet were wedged up against one wall and the top of his head against the other as he began to bang off the thin metal walls.

Milly was just the right size for the berth. With her legs locked around his middle and her bottom rocking wildly to the sway of the railroad car, she was in bliss.

"This is wonderful," she panted. "Just do me all the way to Cheyenne, Marshal."

"I don't know that I can last that long," Longarm grunted, his back feeling as if it would break between being gripped by Milly's legs and trying to bend to the confines of the berth.

"Sure you can!" Milly nibbled on Longarm's ear, then stuck her tongue into it and breathed fire.

It fed Longarm's already considerable desire. He tried to bend his mouth to her breasts again, but physically could not. Instead, he concentrated on their union, his big rod stirring Milly's stinkpot to the boiling point.

"We're *both* going to get baths in Cheyenne," he grunted, his body driving faster and faster as Milly's

23

fingernails began to dig into his pistoning buttocks.

"Whatever you want," she groaned, eyes glazing with desire, breath coming faster and faster.

Longarm tried to keep Milly's pot stirring all the way to Cheyenne, but somewhere up near the Colorado border he lost control. One moment he was whipping his distended rod around around like the driving wheels of the huge locomotive pulling them north; the next minute it was as if the brakes were thrown and he was jetting steam. His body froze for an instant, his lips pulled back from his teeth, and then he slammed into Milly, spewing his seed as he muffled her scream of ecstasy with his mouth.

Later, he rolled off of her sweaty body and felt the train rolling into Cheyenne.

"Oh," she purred, "do you know how long we did it together?"

"You don't count time in heaven," he advised with a wink.

"It *was* heaven, wasn't it. I can't wait to get you in a full-sized bed."

"And I can't wait to get *us* in a bath," he said, their smell so rank that it filled his little cabin and burned his nostrils.

Longarm lit a cheroot and puffed rapidly until the smoke obscured their scent. He dressed while she watched, making no effort to pull her dress either up or down.

"I guess I didn't do too well on my first test at becoming respectable, did I, Marshal Long."

He buckled on his gunbelt. "Well," he said, "persistence is generally the key to all worthy successes. We've got three states to cross before we get to Reno, and maybe by then we'll be full of each other and can learn to control and behave ourselves."

"Maybe," she said, not sounding very hopeful. "If you weren't such a good lover, I'd feel a lot more confident."

"And if you weren't such a sexy vixen that made me stiff at the mere sight of you, *I'd* feel more confident."

They both laughed. Finally Milly said, "Let's be honest about us."

"Why not?"

"We're going to screw each other half blind before we get to Reno."

"I certainly hope so," he said with a wide grin.

"But when I step off the train and meet my husband, it's over. You're not the marrying kind. Are you?"

"Nope."

"I knew it from the minute I saw you," she said, her voice heavy with disappointment. "But just a few minutes ago, I forgot."

"Don't forget," he told her. "I'm a lawman and I like what I do. However, I am on vacation right now and . . ."

Longarm didn't finish.

"And what?"

"Well, since I'm on vacation, if you weren't engaged and fixed to marry, I'd have liked to have spent some more time with you, Milly Taylor."

Her eyes took on a sadness. "You want just good times," she said. "Gus wants a wife to grow old with."

"Well then you should stick to Gus."

"I mean to," she said defensively, pulling her dress both up and down. "But not until Reno. I couldn't stay away from you, Longarm. Not after you paid my way on this train and saved me from those three animals in the third-class coach."

"If you owed me anything before, the debt has been paid just now," he said, reaching for his hat. "We're even."

"No, we're not," she said, bouncing off the bed into his arms. "And we won't be until you've had me about a hundred times between now and Reno."

He chuckled and feigned shock. "A hundred times?"

"Yep."

Longarm stared down into her face. She could not have been more than eighteen, but she was very wise and experienced. She knew how to make a man feel all man, and even now her hand was stroking the bulge in his pants, bringing it back to new life.

"Train will be stopping in just a few minutes. The conductor or the porter will come by and . . ."

"Let them," Milly breathed, unbuttoning Longhorn's fly again and fondling his stiffening manhood. "We're going to board the Union Pacific Railroad and get another first-class car, remember?"

"You're right," he croaked, pulling up her dress and pinning her against the edge of his berth.

This time, when he entered Milly, she hopped up on the berth and he took her where she hung impaled on his thrusting manhood. Longhorn took her hard and fast and when he came, it was like a stream of fire pouring out of him. It felt so good it shook Longarm to his foundations.

"Cheyenne station," the black waiter said, coming to collect his plates and silverware as he opened the cabin door and stared.

"We're coming," Longarm groaned as the man's eyes grew round and he smiled. "We're coming!"

Milly cried out with pleasure and when she was finished, the waiter was gone.

"I *told* him we were coming," Longarm said, stepping back and cramming his throbbing staff back into his pants.

He scooped up his rifle and, at the door, he turned and looked back at Milly. An easy smile touched his face and made the tips of his mustache twitch. "Come along, my girl. We're going to find us a bath, me a shave, and then you a dress."

"And new underclothes," she said. "A respectable woman ought to wear underclothes, shouldn't she?"

Longarm couldn't help but laugh. "Yeah, she should. We'll find them too, but only if you let me help you put them on and take them off."

She giggled almost shyly as she took his hand. "Let's go, Longarm. I just wish that we had some real money."

"We'll do all right," he said, guiding her down the aisle.

When they stepped off the train, the black waiter called out, "Ya'all have a good time, suh!"

"We will," Longarm said, reaching into his pants pocket and flipping the man a silver dollar.

Milly frowned. "Given how broke we are, weren't you being a little extravagant?"

"Nope," Longarm said, pitching his saddlebags over one shoulder and clenching his Winchester.

Milly just shrugged. "You buy me a ticket to Reno and you give that man a dollar for almost nothing. You're not a very thrifty man, are you, Longarm."

"Nope." He looked down at her. "Some folks that know me well think I'm generous to a fault."

Milly snorted. "Boy, I like a generous man! Only I wish you was rich. But then, if you were rich, you'd spend or give it all away, wouldn't you."

"Come on," he said, grabbing her hand and pulling her across the train station platform. "Here you are trying to analyze me in front of all these strangers and all I want is a bath and a couple hands of poker."

27

"And me," she reminded him firmly. "You want me."

"Yeah," he replied. "All the way to Reno."

She reached up and looped an arm around his neck, then twisted his head down and kissed his cheek. "You're my kind of man, Marshal Long. And if I'm not careful, I'll throw Gus over and come after you full bore."

Longarm's smile faded. He stopped dead in his tracks and looked down at Milly. "Don't do that," he said solemnly. "Don't fall in love with me, Milly. That'd take all the fun out of this adventure. *Comprende?*"

Her smiled died and she nodded her head. "All right," she promised.

Longarm looked up to see the three men he and Milly had whipped watching them with hard, battered faces. He met their eyes and quickly looked away. But when he led Milly on toward town, he suddenly glanced back and saw they were doing their damnedest not to appear as if they were following.

"We've got a little problem behind us," Longarm whispered as he led Milly along. "But don't look back."

"What is it?"

"The same three men that tried to rape you in third class."

"We should have killed them when we had the chance," she told him. "Now, we've got to worry about them killing us. Can't you arrest them or something and put them in jail until we leave Cheyenne?"

"Nope. I left my badge in Denver."

"Why'd you do such a fool thing?"

"Cause I'm on vacation," he growled.

"But . . . oh, never mind."

Longarm knew that Milly wasn't too impressed with his decision to leave his badge behind. Of course, he didn't

28

actually have to have a badge to make an arrest. He could make a citizen's arrest, or even make the arrest as a United States deputy marshal despite having no badge.

But that would require a lot of explaining, and some local lawman would probably not be any more impressed than Milly.

Longarm's hand brushed his holster. He knew where there was a good, private, and not very expensive bathhouse. If the three men trailing him wanted trouble, they'd wind up shot or drowned.

Badge or no badge, a man had a right to defend himself and his hot-lovin' lady friend.

Chapter 3

"Longarm!" the heavyset blond woman cried, grabbing the deputy marshal and giving him a tremendous bear hug. "What a sight you are for sore eyes! Come on in!"

He removed his hat. "Ruby, I have a friend with me and we need to take a bath. Be willin' to pay double for the pleasure and you'll have only half the work."

Ruby leaned sideways and peered around Longarm at Milly. "My, my! Ain't she a mess, though!"

"We've had some troubles, Ruby," Longarm said quickly. "We could use a bath and a little gussyin' up."

"You mean a shave and a haircut?"

Longarm nodded. "And maybe my friend could use a few pointers on how to look respectable."

Ruby was in her fifties, a large woman not known for her diplomacy. "She sure could. She looks like a wildcat that just came flyin' out of the underbrush."

Milly flushed with humiliation. She grabbed Longarm and said, "I don't need to put up with this old bag's insults. Come on!"

"Old bag!" Ruby cried, doubling up her big fists.

"Ladies!" Longarm roared as he stepped between the pair. "For heaven's sakes! There's enough trouble for us out there without going out of our way to create our own."

Longarm's eyes were steely when he looked at Ruby. "Now, we need a bath and maybe even a little help because we've got some men trailin' us with all the wrong intentions. Are you going to help, or not?"

"Have I ever refused you?"

"No."

"Then how can you even think that I might right now?"

Longarm was in no mood for jawing with this woman. "Why don't you just let us inside and start the bathwater to heating."

"All right," Ruby said, casting a hard glance at Milly. "But I don't like that little hellcat and I'd rather you have come by yourself."

"I'll just bet you would," Milly snipped.

"What is *that* supposed to mean!" Ruby shouted.

"Oh, the hell with you both," Longarm sighed as he started to turn and leave. "I'm not going to tolerate a couple of bitchin' women."

Both women caught him by each of his arms and turned him around. "All right," Ruby said, "we'll behave."

"You mean it?"

"Yes."

Longarm looked to Milly. "And you'll be nice?"

Milly nodded and they went inside the house. Just before closing the door, Longarm looked back outside into the fading light. The three men were across the street, lurking in the shadows. I'm going to have to do something about them, Longarm thought to himself.

The bath was made ready within a half hour, and when Milly and Longarm undressed and climbed into the oversized tin tub, Ruby made it a point to pour the near-scalding water across Milly's legs rather than his.

"Damn you, old lady!" Milly cried.

"Hush!" Ruby ordered. "There will be no profanity in my house. Now take that brush and start grinding off the drink, man-sweat, and whatever else you are coated with."

Longarm felt sorry for Milly. Ruby's condemnation was hurting. "Pay her no mind," he whispered when Ruby went out for more hot water.

"Why has she got such a rod up her fat ass?"

"She lost her husband and only son about a year ago. They were the driver and the shotgun on a stage that was robbed over to a small mining town about fifty miles northeast. They were both killed."

Milly sighed. "Oh. Well, that makes her a little more tolerable, I guess."

"She's got a good heart," Longarm said. "Used to be a dance-hall girl like you, darlin'."

"And she found a man and married him and this is how she ended up?"

Then Milly surveyed their humble surroundings. It was a four-room clapboard house, but at least it was neat and tidy. "This is no mansion, but all I ever had was a little room or crib."

"Ruby earned her own respect in Cheyenne," Longarm said. "She's always worked like a mule taking in laundry, putting up a few guests in the extra bedroom, making extra meals and offering baths, haircuts, and whatever."

"Whatever?" Milly raised her eyebrows in question, and her meaning was clear.

"Whatever a respectable woman can do to help her family," Longarm said shortly.

"I'm sorry," Milly said. "And I'll try to swallow her insults. But she damned near scalded me with that hot water."

33

"Here," Longarm said, picking up a bar of soap and leaning forward to scrub Milly's wonderful chest.

"Ummmm," she sighed, "I think, if you keep doing that, I'm going to rape you right here in the tub."

Longarm pulled back with reluctance. He could feel his own manhood stiffening, and Milly was starting to get a predatory look in her eyes.

"All right, let's just agree to wash and scrub our ownselves so nothing happens. I don't think Ruby would be too pleased if she came in here and found us fornicating like a couple of crazed beaver."

Milly giggled. She took the soap from Longarm's hands and began to apply it vigorously to her skin. She soaped herself to a high lather and then scrubbed it off hard with the brush. She washed her full head of hair, and Longarm convinced her that they should scrub each other's backs.

It took some restraint, but with Ruby constantly coming in to add more hot water and to keep them from losing their minds to passion, they both managed to get the bathing done in about an hour.

"Ruby," Longarm said, drying himself off with a towel and reaching for his clothes. "Have you got any dresses that would fit Milly?"

"Maybe."

"I don't want her dresses!"

"They aren't mine, you little squat!" Ruby snapped. "They belonged to my daughter."

Milly blinked. "Your daughter?"

Longarm sighed. "I forgot to tell you. Ruby had a daughter that died last year after a fall from a horse."

"Oh." Milly swallowed, and there was an awkward silence. Milly dried herself off and stared at her own

34

soiled gaudy dance-hall dress.

"Well," Ruby said, "do you want to see my daughter's dresses or not? She was about your size and she at least had some taste in respectable clothes."

Milly blushed, and Longarm thought she was going to explode with anger, but instead, Milly bit her tongue and nodded. "I would."

That pleased Longarm, and when he was dressed and armed, he moved over to the front window and peeked throught the curtains. He could not see the three men, and he wondered if they'd just decided to go on about their own business.

"Hey, Ruby," he called, "you got a back door in this house, don't you?"

"Through my bedroom," she called.

"Interesting place to have a back door," Longarm muttered to himself as he screwed his Stetson down and went through Ruby's bedroom, then slipped outside with his hand near the butt of his six-gun.

It was darker than the inside of a beer barrel in Ruby's backyard, and when he took a few tentative steps, Longarm froze to hear a deep growl coming from the bushes.

"Shit!" he whispered. "Ruby didn't tell me she had a new guard dog!"

The dog continued to growl and it sounded big. Longarm had been bitten once before on the butt. He'd ducked out of a bedroom window just a moment before what would have been a very unhappy meeting with a young woman's irate father.

"Dog, leave me alone, damn you," he told the beast as he tiptoed forward, hoping to circle around the house and watch for his three enemies undetected.

But the dog had other plans. With a roar it shot out from under the bushes and rushed Longarm. He just had a glimpse of the wolf-sized beast as he threw the door back open and lunged back inside. The dog's fangs clamped onto the heel of Longarm's boot and, for a terrifying instant, Longarm actually feared the powerful beast was going to pull him back out and eat him in the yard.

"Let go of me!" he shouted, kicking free and banging the door shut. "Jezus, Ruby! Why'd you go and get a mean sonofabitchin' man-eater like that!"

Ruby rushed into the room. When she saw Longarm on the floor and heard the dog growling and snapping outside, she gave a deep, lusty laugh.

"I got him so no sneaky bastards come in through my back door and take advantage of me all alone."

Longarm stood up. He was not happy and said so. "If I could have seen that vicious bastard, I'd have shot him."

"Well," Ruby said, "Buster likes to hide in the bushes for just that reason. He's mean and he's fast."

Milly stepped in between them. She was wearing a new dress and, with her hair all washed and towel-dried clean, she had a girlish innocence that was most appealing to Longarm.

"Do you like it?" she asked, pirouetting around in a full circle.

"Hell, yes, I do!" Longarm took a step forward. "You look tastier than an all-day sucker."

"Longarm!" Ruby scolded. "I been talking to Milly and she said that she's going to try and become respectable for her fiancé over in Reno. Now it don't help things even a little if you keep talking to her using foul goddamn language."

Chagrined, Longarm had to agree. He nodded his head. "All right, I'll start watching my language."

"And maybe it isn't right that she should sleep with you anymore," Ruby said.

"Now wait a minute! I don't guess that's any of your business, Ruby."

Milly spoke up. "It wasn't her idea, Longarm," she said quietly.

"It was yours?"

Milly stared down at her feet, which were in a new pair of shoes. "Well, sorta."

"Damn," Longarm said. "Well, if that's the case, then I reckon I'll just go find myself a poker game and try to make good use of the few remaining hours that we have left in Cheyenne."

"What about that shave and haircut?" Ruby asked.

"The hell with it," he snapped. "What's the use now if Milly has gone totally respectable after just one bath?"

Milly suddenly looked crushed, and Longarm headed for the front door. He slammed outside, and was starting for the street when a shot rang out. Longarm felt a searing flame burn across his forearm and he dove for the ground, rolling as two more shots plucked at the dirt in Ruby's front yard.

Longarm's gun came up, and he cursed himself for being so foolish as to forget about the trio of would-be rapists. He saw the flash of gunfire and fired an instant later. He was rewarded to hear a cry of pain. Then, all fell silent and Longarm knew that his enemies were gone.

Milly came flying down off the porch, and she threw herself down beside him. "Are you all right!"

"Yeah," he said, climbing to his feet. "I just got grazed a little is all."

"You're shot!"

"Naw, just grazed."

Milly dragged Longarm into the house and they slammed the door shut behind. Ruby yanked up his sleeve and saw that the wound was superficial.

"I'll get some linen strips for bandaging this up," the older woman said, hurrying out of the room.

Milly held Longarm's hand. "Was it them?"

"I expect," he said. "But I couldn't prove it because it was so dark. However, I think I shot one of them."

"I hope you killed the damned ambusher," Milly grated.

"Me too."

Ten minutes later, with his arm bandaged and the bleeding stopped, Longarm said, "I guess I'll go find that card game now."

"No!" Milly cried, grabbing his belt. "They might still be out there waiting."

"Not very damned likely," he said. "And I won't have another good chance to win at cards until we get to Reno."

"Please don't go," she begged. "I don't want you to leave us."

"Me and Buster can take care of things," Ruby said.

Longarm frowned. Maybe Milly was right about it not being such a good idea to leave them alone. Besides, the arm was starting to throb and that would kill off his concentration at the poker table.

"You look in need of rest," Milly said. "You look like you ought to lie down a little while before it's time to go board our train."

"I do?"

"Yes."

Longarm shrugged. "Ruby, got any whiskey in the house?"

"Always do. You know that."

"I could use a drop."

"I think we all could," Ruby said. She went and poured three water glasses full.

"To Milly and her husband-to-be," Ruby said, raising her glass in toast.

They drank to that. Milly raised her glass and said, "To friends."

They drank to that too. Then the two women looked at Longarm for his toast. He cleared his throat. "To . . . to Buster."

"What!" both women exclaimed.

Longarm grinned. "A damn good protector and watchdog."

"I'll drink to that," Ruby said with a smile, and so they all toasted the damned dog.

Longarm went into the extra bedroom and stretched out on the bed watching Ruby and Milly go through dresses. It was obvious that the pair had reached some kind of understanding and, unless Longarm was mistaken, even respect and friendship.

That was good. Longarm liked both women. They had a lot in common for they came from similar hard backgrounds of prostitution and dance halls. They both had had the same dream, of marrying and raising children. Ruby had achieved her dream, but it had brought her a lot of sadness along with respect.

Longarm hoped that Milly Taylor would have an easier time of it after she married and that she and her future children would live well and long.

Chapter 4

Ruby touched Milly's arm at the door as she was leaving and said, "You look real pretty in my daughter's dress and with your hair all washed and brushed up shiny."

"Thank you," Milly said self-consciously. "But I'm so sorry about your daughter. I wish it were her standing here wearing this dress instead of me."

Ruby was visibly moved. Her mouth worked silently, and Longarm thought she was probably fighting back tears as she hugged Milly.

He heard the widow say, "If this Gus fella don't take good care of you out in Nevada, I want you to come back here and stay with me until we find you a good husband. Hear me?"

Milly nodded. "I will. I promise."

Ruby pushed back and turned her attention to Longarm. "You take good care of this girl. And if this Gus turns out to be a louse like most men, then you see she gets a first-class ticket back to Cheyenne."

"I'll do it." Longarm gave Ruby a hug of his own, and then he took Milly's hand and started to walk away.

Ruby called, "You're gonna be fine, honey! Pretend you're good and clean. Just pretend that bath washed away all of your sins. Do that, and pretty soon, you won't even have to pretend!"

As they walked back toward the Cheyenne train station, Milly was lost in thought.

"You all right?" Longarm asked.

"Sure. I was just thinking as how that Ruby is real special, isn't she."

"Yeah," Longarm said, "Ruby has a rough bark but unlike her damned dog, she's a pussycat. She's been real nice to me over the years when I've come through town."

"How'd you come to know her?"

"I gave her husband a break one time," Longarm said quietly.

"A break?"

"I didn't haul him off to prison for trying to rob a train. It's a long story, but the short of it is that the man was drunk, hungry, and trying to take care of his family. I helped him, and he stayed straight up until he was shot to death trying to deliver a coach and passengers back to Cheyenne."

Milly didn't ask any more questions all the rest of the way to the train station.

"Good evening, Marshal Long!" the conductor said as he took their tickets. "I see you are traveling first-class. Things must be good in the law business."

"I'm as poor as ever," Longarm said, "but I'm on vacation and not about to scrimp."

The conductor glanced at Milly and then her third-class transfer ticket. When he looked up at Longarm, there was a question in his eyes.

"She'll be traveling with me," Longarm said.

The conductor nodded quite formally. "Very good, Marshal. And anyone tries to rob this train, we can expect your continued support, even though you are on vacation?"

"If anyone tried to rob this train, they'd have to come through me, Arthur. You can be sure of that."

"Excellent!" the conductor said, giving them both a wide smile. "The Union Pacific has never forgotten what you did for us near Rock Springs."

When they were situated in Longarm's sleeping berth, Milly said, "What happened in Rock Springs?"

"A gang tried to rob the train."

When Longarm did not elaborate, Milly persisted. "And?"

"And I sort of discouraged them. Actually, I shot them all. They were too stupid to break away and ride off. They just kept trying to jump into the mail car and I just kept plugging holes in them until they were all gone."

Milly shook her head. "You make it sound so ... so easy."

"Easy?" Longarm frowned. "I never think of killing men as easy. It's hard to pull the trigger knowing each of them once was as innocent as a babe and had a loving mother and father. Maybe some brothers and sisters that will grieve for 'em as well."

"But you do it all the same."

"That's right," he said. "Just like you've had to do things you'd rather not dwell upon. Eh?"

Milly flushed a little. "Yes."

Longarm studied her. She looked wonderful all dressed and cleaned up. She looked as fresh, innocent, and happy as a virgin on her way to her own church wedding.

"Why are you staring at me?" she asked, cocking her head a little to one side. "What are you thinking?"

"I was thinking that you are a very lucky girl to have

43

such a fine chance at a good life. I'm sure that there are a lot of others who never have the chance at respectability."

Milly gave that a long thoughtful pause before she answered. "That's true. But some actually receive marriage proposals and turn them down flat."

That surprised Longarm. "Why?"

Milly shrugged. "Maybe the fella that asks them to marry is ugly or not so nice. Maybe he gets drunk and beats them or wants to cart a girl off to some miserable soddie or line shack where she'd go crazy all alone. Lots of reasons."

When the westbound Union Pacific train began to roll, Longarm felt a powerful urge to take Milly in his arms and kiss her mouth, then peel off that new dress and . . .

"I'm going to see if those three ambushers got back on the train," he said, "or if they were smart enough to stay in hiding until we pulled out of town."

"I want to go with you."

"Don't be ridiculous."

Milly flushed. "I can handle a gun! Have you got a derringer?"

Longarm patted his pocket watch connected by a gold chain to a pocket derringer. "Yes, but . . ."

"Then let me trail along behind, just in case they're waiting to ambush you."

"I can't."

Milly opened her mouth to argue, but Longarm sealed it with a kiss. "I'll be back in a few minutes," he said. "Don't worry. They'd have to be the worst kinds of fools to have boarded."

Outside in the corridor, Longarm checked his Colt, and then he started through the train's passenger coaches, working his way slowly toward the back and the third-class passengers. When he entered their coach, he halted in the aisle and surveyed the rows of benches until his eyes came to rest on two of the three men he'd already whipped and who had undoubtedly tried to ambush him outside Ruby's house.

Gripping his walnut gun butt, Longarm advanced on the men, who were slouched down on their benches with their eyes closed.

"Wake up, damn you!" he ordered, kicking their boots hard.

The two men started into wakefulness. The other passengers stopped talking and stared as Longarm pulled his Colt and said, "Where's the other man?"

"Huh?"

"The third bastard that was with you. Where is he?"

"I don't know," one said, raising his hands. "I guess he stayed in Cheyenne."

Longarm looked all around. "You bastards tried to ambush me, didn't you?"

"No, sir!" the second man protested.

Longarm reached out with his left hand and grabbed the man's shirtfront and jerked him to his feet. "Don't lie to me!"

The man quaked. He began shaking his head back and forth. "We don't know what you're talking about!"

Longarm was just about to say something when, from the front of the coach, he heard Milly cry, "Longarm, behind you! Look out!"

The third man had been hiding under the bench. He had a hole in his shoulder that was still leaking badly. Maybe that was why the gun in his fist was shaking and his first bullet missed Longarm even though he was less than ten feet from the marshal.

Longarm did not give the wounded ambusher a chance to improve his aim. Shooting from his hip, his Colt bucked twice and stitched two messy bullet holes in the man's shirtfront. The man was dead before he pitched over a bench, but Longarm didn't see him because he was twisting around and his six-gun roared twice more.

Both of the remaining would-be rapists and ambushers took slugs in the gut. Both of them men scooted back on their benches and their mouths flew open as they grabbed at their bellies.

"You bastards should have known when to quit back in Cheyenne," Longarm gritted.

The pair gaped at Longarm. One of them tried to speak but failed. The other stared down at the blood pouring out like a funnel between his fingers.

Longarm watched as their eyes glazed. He would have liked to have put them out of their misery with a bullet between the eyes. You could do a kindness like that for animals—but not men. Not in public, at least. It didn't make sense, but that was the way it was.

So Longarm turned away from the dying pair and holstered his gun.

"Who the hell are you!" a cowboy cried. "You can't just come in here and gun down three men and waltz out!"

"I'm a United States deputy marshal."

"Then let's see your badge."

Longarm stopped and looked down at the young cowboy. He was pretty drunk and kind of scared. The damned whiskey had given him courage and he was going to demand an answer rather than be dismissed and humiliated.

"I left my badge under my . . . my mattress back in Denver," Longarm explained patiently.

46

"Under your mattress?"

"Yeah. But you can ask the conductor. He'll tell you that I'm Marshal Custis Long. And he'll tell you that you had better not challenge me again, boy."

Longarm emphasized his point by tapping the cowboy on the crown of his battered Stetson with the barrel of his six-gun. "*Comprende?*"

The kid stared into Longarm's blue eyes and found himself nodding vigorously. "Yes, sir, Marshal!"

Longarm reloaded his six-gun and as he did, the gut-shot pair on the bench each toppled over like dolls in a carnival shooting gallery.

"What should we do with 'em?" the cowboy asked.

"Leave 'em for the conductor, or pitch 'em out into prairie. Don't matter to me," Longarm said, finishing reloading.

He went back and took Milly by the arm and turned her around. "I thought I told you to stay in your cabin."

"You did. But if I had, you'd be as dead as them three by now."

Longarm looked down into her pretty, scrubbed face. "Yeah," he finally said. "You might just have something there."

"What are we going to do now?"

"We're going to make love all the way to Reno, like we planned before, remember?"

"I remember."

He took her into his arms and kissed her then. Kissed her in front of the whole coach of staring third-class passengers. And then he escorted Milly back to his sleeper.

The moment the door was closed and they were alone, it was as if a dam broke inside them both. Off came the respectable dress and the gun and holster. Pants, shirt, bodice, clean women's underclothes. It all came off mighty sudden, and Longarm's hunger was so immense that he drove himself into Milly while she still was standing, impaling her against their little bed.

"Oh, this isn't going to be at all respectable, is it?" she moaned as the big man's thrusting lifted her off the floor.

Longarm grunted as his hips pistoned in and out. His chin dropped as he sought to suckle her big, clean breasts. "You got that right, lady," he panted.

Milly hopped up and wrapped her legs around Longarm's narrow hips. She leaned back and gave him her breasts and everything else she had. And out in the starlit Wyoming night, their thundering Union Pacific locomotive wailed like a banshee.

Chapter 5

Reno, Nevada, was one of Longarm's favorite frontier settlements. He'd been through it any number of times and he liked the way the towering Sierra Nevada Mountains butted up against the sky and served as a majestic background. He also admired how the Truckee River tumbled down from Lake Tahoe. The river's water was clean and clear. It tasted and sparkled like champagne, and this high-desert air was sharp and dry.

Longarm and Milly had made so much wild and wanton love on the rocking train that the deputy marshal actually felt a little light in the bottom and goosey in the knees when he stepped down from the train. But he was wearing a wide, satisfied smile, and when he took in a deep lungful of air, Longarm felt braced and ready to plunge into a long, relaxing vacation.

"I expect Gus is here waiting," he said.

"No reason that he should be."

Longarm frowned. "What is that supposed to mean?"

"I forgot to sent him a telegram when we were in Cheyenne telling him to meet me."

"Oh, great," Longarm said. "I'm sure that he'll be real pleased about that."

Milly touched Longarm's cheek. "Are you sure that you're not a marrying man? As you found out, I know how to give you satisfaction."

"That you do," Longarm said wearily. "You about screwed me to death."

"Is it wrong for a lady to enjoy making love as much as her man?"

Longarm bit the tip off a cheroot and considered the question while he lit the cigar. "No," he said, "I don't guess it is. Sometimes she doesn't, though."

"Not the women that you've had, I'll bet. Most men don't have the slightest idea of how to do anything but satisfy themselves."

Longarm tipped his hat to a stern-looking matron who passed by looking at them with a hint of disapproval. It reminded Longarm that it was time to say good-bye and let Milly get on with a life of married respectability.

"I don't guess this conversation can take us anywhere but in the wrong direction, Milly. And if anyone happened to overhear us, it would sure wreck your plans for gaining respectability in Reno."

"I suppose that's true," she said, unable to hide the disappointment in her voice. "Then I guess this is where we say good-bye to each other."

"I guess," he said.

"Where are you going now?"

"I could walk you to a hotel or ..."

"No," she said quickly. "If Gus saw us ... well, it wouldn't do."

"Sure."

"Are you going to look up Aunt Rebecca Brown?"

"Yeah. But I'm not looking forward to it."

She reached up and pecked him on the chin. "I hope she's nice. And I hope you find your old friend Jim Zack up on the Comstock Lode."

"I'll find him."

Milly nodded. She looked around at husbands and wives embracing, children and families exchanging greetings. "I better go find Gus."

"Do know where he is?"

"He's a mining engineer," she said.

This was news to Longarm.

Milly continued. "He works at a mine out by a place called Paiute Pass. From what I can gather, Gus is the owner and he spends about as much time here in Reno as he does at Paiute Pass."

"Well, what if he's out there right now?"

"I'll figure out a way to get to him," Milly said, trying to force some lightness into her voice. "I'll be fine."

"Damn," Longarm muttered. "If I had some money, I'd loan it to you just in case."

"I'll be okay," she said, her voice taking on a slight edge as she forced herself to extend her hand the way a lady might do.

Longarm looked at the hand. "Aw, hell, Milly! If Gus ain't even here, I reckon we can at least hug each other good-bye."

"No!"

Milly lowered her voice and stepped back. "Mr. Long," she breathed, "it has been a singular pleasure to share your company. Now . . . good day."

Milly whirled and ran in a most unladylike way across the platform and then up the street. She caused a lot of heads to turn, and watching her go left a hollow place in Longarm's heart. Standing alone on the train platform with so many happy reunions taking place all around made him realize how lonesome it was to be a traveling lawman.

And for one single, searing moment, the thought blazed across Longarm's troubled mind that maybe he'd lost someone who really could have made him content and happy. Could have given him kids and a little more of a purpose than just bringing another outlaw to justice.

"Aw, stop it," he muttered angrily to himself as he forced himself to turn away from the vanishing girl he'd come to almost love.

Longarm picked up his saddlebags and hefted his Winchester. "All right, Aunt Rebecca, where the hell are you?"

Finding Rebecca Brown was as easy as walking into the residential part of Reno and asking people until one of them happened to know of the widow. Reno was still a fairly small settlement. It had originally been called Lake's Crossing, but the name had been changed to honor General Jesse Reno, a Union officer killed at the nearby Battle of South Mountain. Once the Union Pacific Railroad had been completed, Reno had begun to prosper as the jumping-off place for the fabulously rich Comstock Lode.

Now, even though the Comstock had fallen on somewhat hard times, Reno was well established as a ranching and mining town dependent upon the transcontinental railroad for a steady stream of new emigrants and commerce. The town boasted a half-dozen major Nevada banks and as many big department and supply stores.

The widow Rebecca Brown lived just two blocks off Virginia Street, quite near the Truckee River Bridge. Her house was what Longarm considered to be a mansion. It was two-storied and constructed of red brick. The front yard was blooming with roses. The front door was beautifully carved, and embellished with a small, oval crystal of glass. The door's shiny fittings were all of polished brass, and the door-knocker was so heavy that Longarm was sure that it was made of solid silver.

It was late in the afternoon when Longarm used that silver door-knocker.

"Who is it?" a voice soon called from inside the mansion.

"I'm a friend of your nephew, William Vail. He asked me to drop by and say hello."

"William who?"

Longarm frowned. "William Vail."

There was a long silence, and then the door opened a crack. Longarm peered at a suspicious gray face. "Chief Marshal William Vail?" he repeated, wondering if the old bird was senile.

"You mean Billy?"

"Yeah," he said, taking heart. "Chief Marshal Billy Vail. He's my boss, ma'am."

"He's a lawman?"

"You didn't even know that?"

The lady opened the door a little more and shook her head. "I haven't heard from Billy in years. In fact, at least thirty years. Where is he?"

"Denver."

"And you're a lawman too?"

"Yes, ma'am. His deputy."

"May I see your badge, please?"

Longarm groaned. "Well, you see, I'm on vacation so I left it under my mattress in Denver."

"Your mattress?"

"Yeah," Longarm sighed. "I know, it was a dumb thing to do, but I thought that, if I didn't have the thing, I wouldn't be tempted to act like a lawman. It didn't work, though."

The woman opened the door wide. She was short, thin, and birdlike. She was actually kind of cute in an ancient way. She had undoubtedly once been a very pretty woman, and she still had lovely blue-green eyes though she must have been in her eighties. Her hair was more silver than just white. She wore three rings on each finger and every one of the darned things was worth a year's pay.

"It's a nice house you have here," he said.

"I helped design it," the woman said, looking around past Longarm to make sure that no outsiders were lurking nearby. "It's comfortable for me and my babies."

"Babies?"

"My kitty-cats," she said as if he should have figured that out all by himself.

Right about then three or four cats came slinking into sight. Several of them began to rub against the old lady's legs, the door, and then even Longarm's boots and pants legs.

He was not a cat-lover. Longarm didn't exactly hate them, but he preferred horses and then dogs. Cats were far down the list after coyotes, skunks, and centipedes. And the longer he stood on the doorstep, the more cats came out to rub themselves against him and the old woman.

"Sweethearts every last one," she said, bending to pet three or four.

This set them all to meowing and rubbing themselves into a frenzy. That sort of put Longarm on edge. "How many of the things do you own?"

"Oh, why keep count!" she exclaimed, clapping her old hands together.

"Yeah," Longarm said. "Why?"

He waited for the old lady to invite him into her cat-castle, but she didn't. The Widow Brown just kept petting the cats and more of them kept coming.

At last, she picked up an armful and said, "What is porky little Billy doing as a lawman?"

"He's not so 'porky' anymore," Longarm said defensively. "He's become a fine marshal and done right well for himself."

"He was always a porky, grubby little savage when I knew him as a child. I thought sure he'd wind up owning a candy store or becoming a piggy little baker or cook."

"Well, he didn't." Longarm shoved his hands in his Levi's. "And he wanted me to give you his best regards. And this letter." He pulled the letter out of his shirt pocket and held it out to her.

She ignored it. "I can see that you don't much care for cats. Does Billy?"

"Why . . . I don't know," Longarm blurted out. "The subject never once came up between us."

"Well does he *own* any cats?"

"No."

"And I'll bet my mansion that you don't either."

"As a matter of fact, I don't," Longarm said, not pleased with the way this conversation was heading.

"You probably prefer *dogs*."

The way she said "dogs" sounded as if she'd just stepped in a pile of dog shit. It didn't take any genius to figure out that rich old Aunt Rebecca hated dogs as much as she loved cats.

Longarm gave this conversation one last try. "Billy, uh, he said you might like to go out to dinner."

"With you? A down-at-the-heels deputy?"

Longarm felt his cheeks warm. "Well, I thought we might. I'm a little short of money right now, but . . ."

"And you expected *me* to buy the meal?" She snorted with derision. "You big deadbeat! No wonder you are in cahoots with that beastly little Billy."

Longarm had taken about all the insults he could stomach. "Well, then," he said, screwing his hat down tight, "I guess that we won't be going out to dinner after all, huh?"

"You got that dead right, you big idiot."

"Then I'll be on my way." Longarm started to turn, but then he said, "Billy turned out pretty good, you know. If you wanted to write him or anything, you could do it care of the federal marshal's office in Denver, Colorado."

"Now why would I ever do a thing like that after thirty years?"

"I dunno."

"Well, neither do I," the old lady snapped. "I guess Billy knows I'm rich and alone now. He probably worked it out in his greedy little noggin that I'm also a widow without heirs."

"I wouldn't know about any of that."

"Sure you would! I haven't the slightest doubt that he asked you to squire me around and make a pitch for my inheritance and you would get a filthy little percentage. Isn't that right?"

"No, ma'am," Longarm snapped in anger as he booted the cats away from his pants legs and whirled to leave. He accidently stepped on one of the tabbies, and it let out a terrible shriek and clawed at his boots. Fortunately, the leather uppers saved him from some nasty scratches.

"You tell porky Billy that I *do* have heirs! About a hundred of them, and I'm leaving everything to them so that they'll be cared for until they all die!"

Longarm stopped dead in his tracks. He turned. He stared at the old woman, about fifty meowing damned cats, and the mansion. "You're leaving it all to *them* squealing things?"

"Yes!"

Longarm shook his head. "Ma'am, Billy Vail may have had a little greed in his heart when he asked me to stop by for a visit, but he sure ain't stupid enough to leave all his worldly belongings to a bunch of damned cats!"

"I *knew* you hated these beauties!"

Longarm cursed under his breath. Billy Vail was his boss and many was the time he'd sent Longarm on some dangerous manhunts. But sending him to try and milk an inheritance out of that crazy old cat lady was one of the lowest things he'd ever done to Longarm, and the man was going to get an earful when vacation time was over.

Longarm stopped on the Tuckee River Bridge fully intending to try one of the casinos. He'd already spent the ten dollars that came with the letter, so he tore the letter into pieces and let them flutter down into the water below. He dug the last few greenbacks and coins out of his pockets and counted his money down to the last cent.

"Four dollars and fifty-seven cents."

It was a pitiful amount. Hardly enough to stake himself to the lowest form of penny-ante poker.

Longarm expelled a deep sigh of dejection. Every man had his low points, and it was hell to go on vacation being so broke. Maybe his old friend Jim Zack really was rich, and would stake him to a few dollars so Longarm could have a good time both on the Comstock and up at Lake

Tahoe before he returned to Colorado.

Maybe. But until he hooked up with Jim, Longarm knew that he had to rely on his own ingenuity and card-playing ability. And his luck. Luck first, last, and always.

Chapter 6

Milly was trembling nervously the next morning as she stood across from the street from the Bonanza Mining Company, where she had been told she could find Gustav Luther. Milly wondered if Gus even remembered her from the week they had spent together in Denver. It had been a wild, exciting time for them and Gus really had proposed marriage, though he'd been drunk at the time.

Gustav Luther was the tall, boisterous son of a wealthy German industrialist living in Boston. Gus had been educated in a prestigious college in engineering, and had been expected to one day assume command of his father's financial empire, but instead he'd chosen to see the Wild West. Bitten by gold fever, he'd become a mining engineer, supporting himself on a monthy allowance sent by his rich parents, who were sure that their wayward Gustav would give up his folly and come home to Boston.

"Good morning, miss," a man in his sixties said, coming up to Milly.

She had been staring so intently at the mining company that she had not seen him approach. "Oh, good morning, sir."

"Is something wrong?" he asked with genuine concern.

59

"No," she said quickly. "Why do you ask?"

He relaxed. "Oh, it's just that you've been standing here about twenty minutes staring at that mining company office, and I got so curious I had to ask."

Milly took a deep breath. "I am engaged to be married to the man who owns that company," she said proudly.

"Is that right?"

"Yes. His name is Mr. Gustav Luther. Perhaps you know him."

The man's eyebrows shot up. "Everyone knows Gustav. He's quite . . . quite a character."

Milly was not sure that was how she would have described Gustav, but she nodded anyway. "I'm hoping that he is in town right now. I've come all the way from . . ."

Milly hesitated. It hit her quite suddenly that the very last thing she wanted was to give people information about her past. "From back East."

"Is that right?" the man said. "Well, then, I'm sure that Gus will be very happy to see you. And you said you were his 'fiancée'?"

"Yes." Milly could read the man's skepticism. "Why, does that surprise you?"

The man flushed. "Well, I think it might surprise a lot of people in Reno. You see, Gus is not exactly a retiring man and he is known as, well . . . never mind. Why don't I escort you across the street."

"That's not necessary."

"Oh, but I insist! Reno is a rough and wild town, Miss . . ."

"Taylor." Milly could see no harm in telling this man her true name. "Mildred Taylor."

"And what city did you say you were from?"

"Boston. The same as Gustav."

"Well, well! I can tell you this much, Miss Taylor. When the news of this betrothal hits town, there are going to be a lot of broken-hearted ladies. Gus is quite the ladies' man."

When Milly's face paled, the man added quickly, "But like they always say, the best husbands are the ones that have sowed their oats in many a field."

"I never heard that before," Milly said, deciding that this man was an insensitive fool and a bother. She was also quite sure that he was nosy and would recount her meeting with Gus in great detail in every saloon in Reno.

"By the way," he said, "my name is Ed Wheat. I'm a retired assayer."

"How nice."

"I used to do a lot of work for the Bonanza Mining Company in its better years."

Milly looked up at the man. "Better years?"

"Well," the man said, "like all mining companies and related businesses, when the Comstock Lode's production began to fall off a few years ago, things got tight at Bonanza. A lot of the big mines laid off miners and mill workers. Businesses in Virginia City, Gold Hill, and Silver City closed and Reno also suffered."

"Perhaps my fiancé and other bold entrepreneurs will make new discoveries. Perhaps even at Paiute Pass."

"Oh, you've heard of that, have you?"

To Milly, it was just a name, but she did not want to sound ignorant so she said, "Of course. Who hasn't?"

"A lot of people haven't," the man said. "Bonanza offered stock on their Paiute Pass mine, and no one even bothered to buy it although they were practically willing to give the stock away. Good thing Gus has a rich daddy or the whole operation would have closed long before now."

Milly had heard just about enough. This man's discouraging talk was starting to upset her and she wanted no more of his company.

"Mr. Wheat," she said, "you have a loose and unkind tongue and I've heard just about enough of it. Good day!"

Wheat stopped. His false genial manner turned hard. "You're no lady and you've no Boston accent. You're just another whore hoping to marry a rich fool."

Milly slapped the man. Slapped him so hard that Wheat rocked back on his heels. He balled his fists and Milly did the same.

"You just proved you're a fraud!" Wheat sneered, rubbing the sting from his cheeks. "A lady would have burst into tears or hurried away. You acted like the frontier whore I pegged you for right from the start."

Milly took an advancing step forward, her heart slamming against her ribs, her eyes burning with tears. "Goddamn you!" she hissed. "Leave me alone!"

Wheat placed his hands on his skinny hips and guffawed. And then, he turned and hurried off, undoubtedly to tell everyone in Reno what he had discovered.

Milly felt weak and sick to her stomach. She very nearly turned around and went back to the crummy little rooming house where she'd spent the previous night heartbroken over the departure of Longarm. But he was gone, and she had this game to play out even if her bluff had already been exposed by a mean-spirited busybody with nothing better to do than to spread vile gossip.

Milly raised her chin, pointed herself in the direction of the Bonanaza Mining Company, and went marching toward it as if she owned the place. Over and over she kept reminding herself of Ruby's advice to pretend she was a good, decent, and respectable lady, even if she was trash. Remembering and practicing that bit of kind advice was the only way that Milly could get through the mining company's front door.

When she walked inside, there were three men seated at desks, all of them with their feet up on their desktops drinking coffee. Milly's entrance froze them for a moment, and then they stood up to gawk.

One of them, a heavyset man in his late thirties, came forward with a grin and said, "Good morning, miss! Is there something that I can do to help you?"

"I'm looking for Mr. Gustav Luther," she said. "I've come a long way to see him again."

The man appeared to be having trouble keeping his eyes from looking at Milly's prominent bosom. Milly flushed with anger and embarrassment. This man had no manners, and she would speak to Gustav about that after they became husband and wife.

"Is Mr. Luther expecting you, Miss . . ."

"Taylor."

"Is he, Miss Taylor?"

Milly realized she was caught. If she said yes and Gustav was out of town, she'd look the fool. If she said no, how was that going to look when she said she was

Gustav's fiancée? Either way, Milly realized she would appear foolish.

"I told him I was coming, but I had the opportunity to arrive in town a little early." There were two large, glass-enclosed private offices in the rear of the room. She could see Gustav's name painted on one of them, but the office was empty. "Is he out today?"

"I'm afraid so," the man said. "Mr. Luther is down at our mine in Paiute Pass. Has been there for the last two weeks."

"Oh," Milly said, trying to force a smile. "Well, of course, I should have expected that. I know that my Gustav is a very hard-working man. When do you expect he will return?"

The man looked over his shoulder at his two gawking companions. When they merely shrugged, he turned back to Milly and said, "I can't say for sure. Maybe in a few days. He usually comes back after two or three weeks."

"I see." Milly's mind was whirling. "How far is Paiute Pass?"

"About eighty miles to the south."

"And I assume there is a stage that services it?"

"Oh, yes!"

"How often does it depart from Reno?"

"About once a week." The man frowned. "But it's a hard, dusty road, Miss Taylor. I'm sure that you'd be better off to rest and wait for Mr. Luther's return."

Milly needed some time to think. "Perhaps so," she said quickly. She started to turn away and leave.

"Uh, Miss Taylor?"

She stopped at the door. All three men were devouring her with their eyes. Hell, she thought, they acted as if she were naked instead of dressed respectably. "What?"

"Where are you staying?" the older man asked. "In case Mr. Luther returns unexpectedly, I'm sure he'll want to look you up."

At that, one of the other men winked at his companion and they tittered meanly. Milly flushed. She knew what they were thinking. And maybe too, they were hoping to "look her up" themselves.

"I haven't really settled in yet," she hedged, "but I'll let you know when I do."

"The Roark House for Ladies is one of the few boardinghouses in town you can try. It's pretty expensive, but that's where unescorted ladies stay."

She nodded formally even though she thought that they were already onto her game. Milly did not even pretend to understand how they could see through her so completely even though she was dressed like a lady. It was something that Ed Wheat had also done in an instant.

"I'll . . . I'll try that establishment," she managed to say as she left the three gawking men and closed the door behind her.

Milly walked an entire block before the tears began to cascade down her cheeks. She stumbled between a general store and a millinery and sobbed like a fool until she could cry no more.

"What is wrong with me?" she whispered over and over. "What am I doing wrong?"

"Miss?"

Milly whirled to look back toward the street. A young man was standing there watching her. He had sandy hair and he was tall and a little gangly, but he was wearing a smile instead of the knowing leers that she'd already become so accustomed to here in Reno.

65

"What do you want?" she sniffled, drying her eyes and trying to gather her shattered composure.

"I heard you crying and then I recognized you from the train. You're the lady that was with Marshal Long."

It wasn't a question and Milly knew it was useless to deny the fact. "Yes, so what!" she snapped.

The young man took a step forward into the shadows. "Well, miss, I sort of owe you an apology because I was on the Denver and Pacific Railroad when those three men, well, they got rough with you. I was rustling around in my carpetbag looking for my daddy's old six-shooter when Marshal Long came busting in to help."

"Is that right," Milly said coldly. The last thing she needed was a witness in this town to tell everyone about that awful incident.

"Yes. I'm sorry that I never did anything to help you. I've felt awful ever since. I felt so awful I changed my ticket to second class after that fight. I couldn't face looking at you again."

"Well," she said angrily, "you're sure getting a look now. What do you want?"

"To apologize for not helping you out quicker," he said. "And I heard the gunfight and saw the bodies when they laid 'em out in the Union Pacific train."

Milly shook her head. "I don't want to hear about any of this. Leave me alone. Don't . . . just don't bother me."

The man took a step back. "I understand that," he said. "You can't stand the sight of me because I didn't act fast enough to help you defend yourself against those three men. You got the right to think small of me. You got every right."

Milly finished drying her eyes. The young man tried not to look at her. She felt guilty for being so short with

66

him. He'd apologized, and maybe he really had been trying to get his gun and help her back in that awful third-class coach.

"Look, what's your name?"

"Henry. Henry Fry."

"Well, Henry, things are not going real well for me right now, so you'll have to excuse me. I'll be just fine, so thanks for your concern but leave me alone."

"All right," he said, but he didn't move.

"Henry, did you understand what I said just now?"

"To leave you alone."

"That's right. It means—go away."

"Are you fixed with some money?" he said quickly. "'Cause if you aren't, you can have some of mine."

Milly blinked. "How much do you have?"

"A hundred dollars and change. Can I give you some?"

Milly was desperate. If she was to maintain her facade of being a lady until Gustav arrived to marry her, she *had* to stay at that respectable ladies' boardinghouse.

"I guess I could use a loan until my fiancé returns from Paiute Pass," she said. "But only a loan."

"Sure!" He seemed almost thrilled, and reached into his pocket and yanked out a wad of cash. Without even bothering to count it, he said, "Take what you need."

Milly couldn't believe it. She snatched the money from his hand before he changed his mind. She peeled off twenty dollars, gave that back to Henry, and kept the rest. "I'll owe you eighty dollars, Henry."

"No problem, Miss Taylor."

"How do you know my name?"

He shuffled his toe in the dirt. "Everyone on the Union Pacific train knew your name because you were so pretty and you were sleeping with the Marshal. Who's this fiancé

67

you're talking about, Miss Taylor?"

"I'm going to marry a gentleman named Gustav Luther."

The young man's face dropped. "I'm real sorry to hear that. I bet the marshal was sorry too."

"He didn't care enough to marry me himself."

"I would have. You're beautiful."

Milly's anger evaporated. She stepped forward and touched the young man's cheek. "And you're very kind, generous, and I think innocent, Henry. Thanks for the money."

"I'll get more," he said. "As soon as I get work, I'll get more."

She had started to move past him out of the alley, but now she stopped. Henry was a very nice-looking young man with soft, puppy-dog brown eyes and a generous mouth. When he filled out, he was going to be a fine figure of manhood. "What kind of work do you do?"

"I'm a jeweler," he said. "And a silversmith. Want to see something?"

"Sure."

He pulled a silver watch and chain out of his vest pocket and held the watch up to the light. Milly's eyes widened when she saw the exquisite engraving and workmanship. "It's beautiful!"

"It was my father's," he said. "He taught me my trade. Look!"

He showed her a money clip and it was solid silver, delicately inlaid with beaded gold. Milly had never seen one so fine and she told him so. "You're very talented."

"You really mean that?"

"Of course."

"I'm going to make you something even if you are getting married to someone else," he decided out loud.

"I . . . I think you've done more than enough for me."

"I don't," he told her before he shyly took her hand, kissed the back of it, and whirled to rush away.

Milly watched the tall young man and her mouth formed a smile. Five minutes ago she'd felt like dirt, but this sweet boy had given her light and hope. Like an angel bearing gifts. An angel named Henry Fry.

Chapter 7

The Roark House cost Milly the outrageous sum of two dollars a night. But at least that included her meals, and Milly did not try to earn a reputation as a light or finicky eater. In fact, the Widow Roark thought her appetite decidedly unladylike.

"You'll get fat, Miss Taylor," she'd warned after the first day.

"No, I won't," Milly replied airily. "Because I refuse to sit around like some of these other ladies. I like to walk about town and hike up along the Truckee River."

"Unescorted?"

"Yes. The only people you see are families."

"You are very bold, Miss Taylor, and I heartily disapprove."

Milly did not say so outright, but she thought that Mrs. Roark could "disapprove" all she wished. Besides, the older woman was accustomed to the company of mostly spinsters and delicate, pampered young ladies trying to snag successful husbands. If the poor, proper thing had even a hint of Milly's background, she'd probably have fainted dead away.

And indeed, Milly did walk each day after checking

in at the Bonanza Mining Company office to see if her fiancé had arrived yet from Paiute Pass. Milly's favorite pastime was to hike up a well-traveled path along the rushing Truckee River until she was on ground high enough to see the vast Nevada deserts stretching out before her all the way to Utah. When the air was clearest in the morning, Milly could even see the shining tin roofs of buildings and mining operations on the Comstock Lode.

Occasionally, she would meet families hiking on the trail and exchange pleasantries with them. Often after such meetings, Milly would sit beside the river and dream of having her own family with Gus Luther. They had never discussed children, and she had the feeling he might bolt and run if she brought it up too soon, but there was always tomorrow.

It was on a pleasant September afternoon, when the aspen were just beginning to turn color, that Milly hiked far up into the mountains following the Truckee. She rounded a bend and abruptly came upon two prospectors who were panning the river. From the looks of them, they were hoping to earn enough "dust" to buy their next meals.

"Hey, lady," one of them said as he stepped out of the river with his dripping pan. "Come say hello."

Milly shook her head. She had to shout to be heard above the roar of the river. "I have to get back to town. I was just out for a walk. I haven't been this far upriver before and it's getting late in the afternoon."

The man was of average height, full-bearded, and wearing an old slouch hat, no shirt, and suspenders made of rope. His partner was tall and thin, with bad teeth and no shirt either to hide his narrow, shrunken chest.

"Ain't she the purty one, Ernie?" the tall one crowed, coming out of the water. "Maybe our luck ain't all going to be bad this week."

Milly swallowed and took a step back down the trail she'd followed. "Now you men just go back to work," she said, "and I wish you well. But I have to go."

The tall, thin one dropped his pan. He leered, and his rotting teeth were black and yellow. He started toward Milly trying to smile. "What's your name, pretty girl?"

Milly knew that she was in big trouble. She had previously met a family of hikers, but that had been over an hour ago and they had been returning to town. With the roar of the river in her ears, Milly knew that a cry for help would go unheeded.

"I have to get back to town," she said. "Now you just go back to panning for gold."

"Ain't much of any gold left in this river," the tall man said with his cold grin. "Might just as well have some fun together, purty girl."

Milly tried to fight down a rising panic. She had seen lust in more men than she cared to remember, but in this man's eyes she also saw cruelty. "Stay away from me!" she ordered, throwing her hands up.

"Get her, Hank!" Ernie shouted. "Before she runs!"

Hank charged, all long arms and legs. Milly whirled and ran. She had always been an extremely fast runner, but now she was wearing one of the pretty dresses that Ruby had given her and it bound her up. Looking back over her shoulder, Milly saw that Hank's long legs were churning and that she had no chance at all of outrunning him.

Milly spied a piece of driftwood caught in an eddy of the plunging Sierra river. It was a branch about three foot long and as thick as her forearm. She grabbed it out of the cold water and whirled to put her back up against a rock. She raised the branch.

"I'll brain you if you come any closer!"

Hank skidded to a halt. His mouth was hanging open, his sunken chest working like a faulty bellows. He panted, "Now you just put that stick down, little honey, and give old Hank a kiss."

"I'd rather kiss a dead fish!" Milly raged.

Hank's mouth twisted into a sneer. "You wait until I get between your legs, girl! Then I'll make you beg for it!"

Milly tried to speak, but found she could not. All she could do was to wait helplessly, trapped against the rock until Ernie overtook them.

"Well, well," Ernie said, gasping for breath. "We got a real she-lion trapped here, don't we."

"That we do," Hank said, licking his lips.

Milly fought off a sense of hopelessness. She might succeed in clubbing one of them, but not both. And in the end, they'd take her down and use her violently. And because they were animals, they would not let her go free to tell the law, but would use her until she was finished and then probably kill her and bury her in the soft riverbank soil.

"Listen," she gulped. "I've got some money down at my boardinghouse room. If you leave me alone, I'll give all of it to you."

"How much?" Hank demanded.

"Sixty dollars."

The two men laughed. "So you think we're stupid enough to go down there so's you can get help!"

"But I'll really give it to you!" she cried, knowing she would not and that only a pair of complete fools would be so gullible as to believe her desperate ruse.

"You'll 'give it to us,' all right," Hank said with a lecherous grin. "But it won't be money."

Milly knew that she was going to have to fight to the death. There was just no other choice. She was backed against a rock. The surging Truckee River was on her left and the canyon walls were on her right and beyond them was just high desert. Reno, far downriver, was beyond hope.

Hank drew a Bowie knife from a sheath on his belt. He took a step toward Milly, who lashed at him with the branch and missed his face by less than an inch.

Hank jumped back. "Good swing," he said, waving his big knife between them. "But the next time you swing, I'll come in fast with my knife and cut your throat open from ear to ear."

"No, you won't," Milly hissed, raising her club to her shoulder like an ax. "You won't do that until you've had your dirty fill of me."

Hank chuckled. "You're smart," he said, putting the knife back into its sheath. "I'll give you that much, you're smart and not just purty."

"Please," Milly begged. "Just leave me alone and go back to your prospecting. I won't tell the law what you said or wanted to do to a respectable woman."

"We mean to make you unrespectable real quick. And you'll like it," Ernie promised. "And you ain't never going to see the law again."

Ernie glanced sideways at his tall, cadaverous companion. "Hank, since we ain't going to shoot or cut her, how we gonna do this?"

"Grab us up some wood like she's got," Hank answered. "Then we'll rush her swinging."

"You're not men!" Milly cried, pressing up against the rock wall. "You're cowardly animals!"

"We're men," Hank said, waiting and leering while his companion hunted up sticks. "You're gonna find that out in a couple of minutes."

Milly tried to edge around the rock toward the riverside path, but Hank jumped to block her progress. "Why don't you drop that stick and make it easy on all of us? We're just wastin' our pleasurin' time."

Milly turned her eyes to the river. In this place, the canyon was narrow and the water swift and deep. White foam surged over rocks, and the river was littered with fallen branches and felled trees. Cold mist floated up toward lengthening shadows. Milly could not swim, but drowning seemed infinitely preferable to being raped over and over until her throat was slit.

Jump in now and take your slim chances, she thought, before the shorter one returns with the sticks.

Steeling herself, Milly feigned a rush to her right as if she was going to try and get back on the riverside path and race down to Reno. When Hank jumped that way, Milly twisted back around, took three running steps, and then threw herself in the river.

Its icy water tore her breath away. The raging river grabbed her like the fist of a giant and spun her underwater. Milly had the presence of mind to hold her breath as her arms and legs windmilled helplessly. She did not know which was was up or down, and she clawed at the current as if it were a wild animal trying to devour her in a single gulp.

She collided with a half-submerged tree. Breath exploded from her lungs and she felt herself being propelled into the air. For a frozen instant Milly hung over the river, and then she plunged back into the foaming water and was rolled over and over until she struck a rock and grabbed it with both hands. The rock was cold, slimy with moss, and impossibly slick, but she buried her fingernails into it, and then managed to even wrap her legs around it to keep from being swept away.

The rock was solid. Milly closed her eyes and clung to the rock as if it were the only thing left in the whole world. The Truckee's roar filled her eyes and she shivered violently, afraid to move even a muscle for fear she'd lose her grip and her life.

Milly waited. She was sure that she was going to die. Either the two prospectors would get a gun and shoot her to death from the shore, or else she'd weaken after dark, be torn from the rock by the current, and drown.

As the day ended, Milly thought of her past wasted life and she was filled with regrets. She'd lived hard and fast since she was fourteen, and had never known even a hint of what might be called love until she'd met Gus Luther. And maybe even *he* didn't love her as much as he lusted for her body. There was Longarm too. She could have loved him, but there was a part of the marshal that kept him from giving himself completely. No woman would ever own or hold Longarm.

"Miss Taylor!"

"Go away!" she cried into the darkness.

"Miss Taylor, I'm going to get you out of there! You got to grab this long branch and let me pull you over to shore."

Milly was so numb both physically and mentally that it took her the longest time to realize that the two prospectors had not known her name. With a start, she lifted her head from the rock and peered through the moonlight at Henry Fry. He was standing up to his waist in the river, a ten-foot-long branch in his fists.

"You got to help me!" Henry shouted. "You have to let loose of that rock and grab this branch."

Milly found that she could not force her body to obey her mind. Her fingers, arms, and legs would not release the boulder.

"Are you all right?" he cried.

She could not even nod her head.

"It's going to be all right!" he shouted, his voice echoing against the boom of the river. "You got to trust me."

First Milly retracted her fingernails from the moss, and then she unlocked one arm and one leg. Finally, she twisted around, stared at the branch that Henry extended some three feet from her fingertips, and lunged.

She caught the branch with one hand, fastened onto it, and then grabbed it with her other hand. The current grabbed her again and she felt herself swinging downriver. Milly heard Henry shout in alarm an instant before they were both torn downriver. Milly knew she was going to drown this time for sure.

Henry knew different. He grabbed Milly, and when a big log loomed out of the darkness, he grabbed for it with his free hand. For one heart-stopping moment, he and Miss Taylor were both almost torn under the log and hammered downriver, but Henry managed to pull them both up onto the log.

He grunted, "You got to help a little, Miss Taylor. Come on now!"

Milly stared at him in numb silence. His hair was plastered to his head and his skin was as pale as ice.

"Come on, Miss Taylor, we can do it!"

He sounded confident. He sounded as if he really believed they could escape this terrible current.

"All right, Henry."

A moment later, they were on top of the soggy, rotting log and inching their way to shore. Milly collapsed on the riverbank in a shivering heap and began to cry. Henry, after an awkward moment, enfolded her in his skinny arms and rocked her like a baby.

"It's going to be all right now," he said. "Miss Taylor, everything is going to be just fine."

"Two men," she stuttered, teeth clattering like dice in a tin cup. "They were going to rape me. One was real tall, taller than you and the other . . ."

"I'll take care of 'em," Henry vowed. "Not like the last time in the railroad coach. This time, I'll take care of 'em."

Milly clung to the young man. "Take care of me," she whispered.

"I'll do that too," he said, holding her very tight as the river boiled white foam and thunder.

Late the next afternoon, Henry peered out of the bushes at the pair of prospectors busily working the flanks of the Truckee with their pans. There was no mistaking that these were the two men that Miss Taylor had described the night before. No mistaking at all.

Henry watched them for several moments, and then he retreated into the bushes and circled around to where he'd seen their camp. The prospectors' weapons consisted of two old Navy Colt pistols and a Winchester rifle with a broken stock tightly bound by a parchmentlike strip of rawhide.

Henry was not a man who considered himself an expert with weapons. He'd never used a pistol much at all, but he had gone rabbit hunting with his father many times using a small-caliber rifle. He considered himself a fair rifle shot.

With the two prospectors totally absorbed with finding

gold, Henry took several moments to examine the Winchester. He soon determined that the rifle was loaded and how it cocked and fired. Putting the rifle to his shoulder, he felt the rawhide binding rub his shoulder as he sighted down the long, deadly barrel. The Winchester felt very heavy, but also very solid.

Henry took a deep breath. He mentally detached himself from his body and pretended he was a spirit floating overhead, observing—but not participating—in what was about to happen next. He walked out of the camp through the trees right up to the riverbank. The detached spirit of him admired how the colors of the blue sky brushed against the white water of the river. It even admired how the dying rays of sun glinted off a string of cheap brass conchos that decorated the tall man's hatband.

Henry said nothing as he raised the rifle and took aim on the tall man's sunken chest. The man was bent over and stirring his finger around and around in his ore pan, eyes hunting for flecks of gold. The shorter one was facing across the river, swirling water from his pan.

"You almost killed Miss Taylor," Henry said in a voice that could not possibly have been his own. "You wanted to take a lady and rape, then kill her. You are not worth the air you breathe."

The tall, thin man could not have heard those words, but something made him lift his eyes from his pan, and when he saw Henry with the rifle aimed at him, he dropped the pan and cried, "Don't! Please, mister, don't kill me!"

Henry shot him through the neck. He'd meant to hit him in the chest, but the man had started to dive into the river and so the bullet had entered his skinny neck. Even in the rushing water, you could see the blood turn the water crimson. The man folded over, hands grabbing at his throat, lips pulling away from rotting teeth in a death grin that lasted until he sank and the current spun his body away.

The shorter man was a little farther out in the river. He tried to whirl at the sound of the rifle, but lost his footing. He fell, surged to his feet, and managed to raise his ore pan to cover his face.

It didn't help. Henry missed once, then drilled a bull's-eye through the pan. When it spilled to the water, it showed the second man to be missing one eye as he sat down in the river, then stretched out on his back with his arms and legs outstretched as if he were crucified on the water. Then he rolled, and Henry shivered to see the back of the man's skull with fragments of bone and brain hanging out.

Henry hurled the Winchester into the cold river. He walked over to the water and squatted at its edge. He scooped cupped handfuls to his face, and then he stood up and did not move until he saw the bodies sweep around a canyon's bend. With luck, he thought, those bodies would float past Reno just after darkness and then be carried downriver far into the desert.

Henry Fry did not know where the Truckee River went, and he really did not care. It was time to go back to town. He would bathe, shave, and clean up before putting on his only suit and taking Miss Taylor out to dinner in order to celebrate his first order for silverwork. She was so beautiful and good that, as he headed back down the riverside trail, Henry knew that he would never even mention the two dead corpses now bobbing their way toward the deserts of Nevada.

Chapter 8

Longarm's eyes were bloodshot from cigar smoke and lack of sleep. Before him, resting on the green felt of the card table, were stacked over three hundred dollars' worth of his poker chips. They gave him reason to smile, but he had been playing for forty-six continuous hours and his mind was starting to thicken like cold custard.

"Mr. Long, I'll raise you a hundred dollars," the gambler across the table said to him, shoving in the very last chips he owned.

Because he and Longarm were the only two players who hadn't folded on the hand, and because Longarm knew his own mental processes were not at their best, he took his time and considered his next move carefully.

The gambler didn't appreciate that one damned bit. "Are you in or out?" he demanded to know.

Longarm studied his cards. He had three sevens. Not nearly a strong enough poker hand to bet another hundred dollars and call. And yet, something told him that the desperate gambler was bluffing.

Longarm squinted through the smoke of his cheroot and smiled wearily as he pushed a pile of chips forward to join the others in the pot. "Mr. Blevins," he drawled,

"I'm going to call your hand."

A nervous tic made the flesh twitch in the corner of Blevins's right eye. "Three of a kind," he said, not showing his hand.

"Me too," Longarm said. "Three sevens."

"Sonofabitch!" the gambler swore as he hurled his cards to the table to reveal he only held three fives.

Longarm expelled a deep breath and raked the pile in before him. His eyes stung and he felt awful, but the pot he'd just collected upped his Reno marathon winnings to about four hundred fifty dollars. It was one of the largest paydays he'd ever had, and it could not have come at a better time.

Longarm removed his Stetson, then raked all his chips into his hat. "Gentlemen, it's been a real pleasure."

"It hasn't been for us," one of the players grumbled without malice. "I'm sorry that I ever laid eyes on you, Mr. Long."

Two other players chuckled, and Longarm grinned. "I assure you," he said modestly, "it was more luck than skill. The last time I played in Denver, I couldn't draw a pair and lost several hundred dollars of badly needed vacation money."

All the players at the table were Reno businessmen, except for the gambler. Clint Blevins was young and a very skillful player, but he was too reckless. He also had not learned to control his anger and therefore his emotions. Whenever he'd drawn a very good hand, Longarm could read anticipation in the young gambler's eyes. That had been one of Longarm's edges in this game from the very start.

Blevins pulled out his gold pocket watch and chain. "I paid a hundred dollars for this in San Francisco. I'll bet it

84

against fifty dollars on the next hand, Mr. Long."

But Longarm shook his head. "Nope. About an hour ago I informed you gentlemen that I was quitting and I just have. Besides, I already own a fine gold watch and chain."

Blevins flushed with anger. "All right then. I'll place it at only twenty-five dollars' value against your chips!"

Longarm shook his head. "No," he said as he pushed out of his chair.

"Goddamn you!" Blevins shouted. "What kind of a man takes all our money and then leaves without giving anyone a chance to win at least part of it back!"

"A smart man," Longarm said as he finished dumping the big pile of poker chips into his hat. He hooked both thumbs into the pockets of his vest. "Now Mr. Blevins, I think you've managed to prove you're a very bad loser. Don't push this any further."

Instead of profiting by Longarm's stern warning, Blevins took even greater offense. Longarm's words were fuel for his already considerable fire, and he cried out as his hand shaded the gun on his hip, "I demand an apology!"

The other players shoved back their chairs so forcefully that one of them actually flipped over backward in his haste to remove himself from danger. When it was just Blevins and Longarm facing each other across from the table, Longarm shook his head.

"What are you shaking your damned head about?" the gambler demanded.

"You," Longarm replied. "I was just thinking that a man who can't lose with dignity ought not to gamble at all."

Blevins used his left hand to place his gold pocket watch and chain on the card table. "As you can see, it's worth every damned cent of one hundred dollars."

"It is," Longarm agreed, "if a man needs a pocket watch. But as *you* can see, I've already got a fine one."

Even as he was talking, Longarm reached up to his vest pocket and removed his watch. Then his fingers slipped into his other vest pocket as if to unfasten the gold chain. But instead, he withdrew a derringer attacked to the watch chain.

Blevins's eyes widened as he realized that he had been tricked and had a barrel pointed at his chest. His Adam's apple bobbed up and down and he licked his lips, which had suddenly gone very dry.

Longarm dropped his cheroot and ground it to death under his heel. "I want you to reach across your belly with your left hand and remove that six-gun from your holster, Mr. Blevins. Then place it on the table and step back."

"You going to shoot me? I'd be unarmed and it'd be murder, Mr. Long!"

"I know that," Longarm said. "I'm a United States marshal and I'm going to all this bother of explaining things just so I *don't* have to kill you."

"You're a federal marshal?"

"That's right."

"I don't see no badge."

"I'm on vacation," Longarm said lamely. "But I'm still a marshal and I know the law, so don't say another damn word."

"You gonna arrest me?"

"Put your gun on the table," Longarm ordered.

Blevins did as he was told.

"Now apologize for your ill-chosen words. The ones about what kind of a man would quit a winner."

Blevins flushed with humiliation but he stammered. "I . . . I was wrong to say that," he whispered. "A winner quits a winner."

"And what," Longarm asked, "does a loser do when he's beaten?"

Blevins shook his head in confusion. His eyes kept dropping to the derringer in Longarm's fist that was pointed at his chest. "I . . . I don't know!"

"A loser smiles and thanks the winner hoping he'll have another chance to redeem his losses some day. And then, when he has time alone, he tries to figure out exactly *why* he lost."

"Bad luck can't beat good luck," Blevins said, his voice bitter.

"That's right. But you have more than bad luck working against you," Longarm told the man, deciding the young fool might learn a valuable lesson. "I could read your thoughts as clear as I can read a book."

"The hell you say!" Blevins shouted in fury.

Longarm cocked the derringer. Realizing his mistake, Blevins took a panicky step back.

"I didn't mean it!" he cried, raising his hands up as if he were going to beg for his life. "Honest!"

"You don't have the temperament to be a gambler, boy. Cards and a bad temper are a deadly combination. Either you'll kill someone and get hanged, or else someone smarter and more reasoned than yourself will kill you. Find another calling."

Blevins wiped a sleeve across his brow. He was beginning to sweat profusely. "Are you all finished, Marshal?"

"I am. Now get out of here."

"What about my gun?"

87

"You'd be better off without one, but I'll leave it at the bar."

Blevins looked around at the other patrons of the saloon. He was trying desperately to muster up enough courage to say something that would save him face. But with that derringer aimed at his belly, he just couldn't do it and broke for the front door.

When he reached it, he whirled and said, "Maybe we'll meet again before you finish your damned vacation!"

"You'd better hope not," Longarm said as he carried his winnings over to the house cashier.

As the cashier pushed greenbacks at Longarm, he said, "You'd better watch your backtrail, Mr. Long. I've seen Blevins in action and he knows how to use a six-gun."

"Thanks," Longarm said. "I'll remember that."

Outside, Longarm looked up and down Virginia Street, and not seeing Blevins in wait, he went back to his hotel room, where he gathered his things and paid the overdue balance of his hotel bill.

"Is the stage station still at the south end of Virginia Street?"

The desk clerk nodded. "Yep. Used to be, when the Comstock was really booming, we had a stage rolling out of here every half hour. Nowadays, with ore production slowed up there, we only have three or four departures a day."

"Well," Longarm said, "I guess business is off everywhere."

"Virginia City is sure feeling it," the desk clerk said. "And so are we, but not near so bad."

The clerk counted Longarm's money. "You must have won some money in order to be able to pay your room bill."

"I did," Longarm said, as he grabbed his Winchester and saddlebags, then headed for the door. But on a whim, he stopped and said, "Do you know a fella named Gustav Luther? I understand he owns a mining company."

"Ha!" the desk clerk said harshly. "He don't own much of one."

Longarm started back toward the man. "What is that supposed to mean?"

"Gus Luther fancies himself a high roller, only he ain't. From what I hear, he has a rich father back in Boston and that's the only thing that is keeping him in business."

Longarm frowned. "You sound like you don't care for the man."

"That's right."

"Why?"

"Luther has a big mouth and he's a braggart. Always telling folks hereabouts how he's going to strike it rich at Paiute Pass. But he won't."

"How do you know that?"

The desk clerk shrugged. "I can't say for sure," he admitted, "but I've had men that worked for the Bonanza Mining Company tell me it's *borrasca*."

"What does that mean?"

"It's a Mexican word that means bad luck—bust. Just the opposite of bonanza."

"I see. How far away is Paiute Pass?"

"Eighty or ninety miles south. Why? Marshal, you're not thinking of going there, are you? It's hotter than hell and dry as sand."

"No," Longarm said, "I'm not thinking of going there. It's just that I know someone else who might."

"Well, I don't envy them," the desk clerk said with conviction. "Paiute Pass is a miserable place from what I hear, and the Bonanza Mining Company is its biggest employer. Hell, half the time, they can't even meet their own payroll."

Longarm was disturbed to hear this news. It did not portend well for Milly Taylor. On a hunch he said, "Other than the fact that he lives off his pa and is a braggart, anything else the matter with Gus Luther?"

"He's just a real ass, if you'll excuse my language. The man likes to throw his money around on the women. He dresses like an Eastern dandy with a derby hat and all, but I've seen him bust up men. He's no Eastern gentlemen when fists start to flying. He fights like he was taught to do it in the ring."

"I see."

The desk clerk leaned forward. "*Borrasca,*" he repeated. "It not only means no ore, but also bad luck. I'd sure change my mind if I was thinking about going there, Marshal Long."

"I appreciate your advice," Longarm said. "Where is the Bonanza Mining Company's office?"

"Just down the street. You can't miss it."

"Thanks."

Longarm headed for the Bonanza Mining Company not sure of exactly what intentions he had in mind. He knew that, if Milly Taylor had it in her mind to marry Gus Luther, she'd not appreciate hearing bad things about her fiancé. And yet, curiosity and genuine concern for the girl gave Longarm no other choice but to at least check out the man and his reputation.

As Longarm approached the Bonanza Mining Company office, he saw Milly leaving it.

"Milly!" he called, the weariness falling away at the mere sight of her. "Hey, over here!"

When Milly saw him she also lit up, and came hurrying over to give Longarm a hug. "I shouldn't be hugging you like this," she said with a laugh. "Not in front of the whole town when I'm engaged to be married to Mr. Luther."

"Aw," Longarm said, "this is just a friendly hug. Our real lovin', I'm sad to say, is in our past."

"Yes," she said, looking up to meet his eyes, "it most certainly is."

"I'm heading up to the Comstock Lode," Longarm explained.

"To find your old friend Jim Zack?"

"That's right."

"I hope he's still there."

"Me too," Longarm said. "You want to walk me down to the stage depot?"

Milly laughed. She looked terrific, happy, and excited when she said, "It just so happens that my fiancé is coming in on the stage from Paiute Pass."

"Then maybe I'll have the pleasure of his aquaintance," Longarm said, sticking out his right arm for her to take.

"That might not be such a good idea," Milly said, her smile fading.

"Why not?"

Milly sighed. "I just . . . well, Gustav can be a little short with people and he is a jealous man."

"Hmmm," Longarm mused, "maybe you're right. Might be better if he and I just remained strangers."

Milly nodded. She looked very relieved as she took Longarm's arm and they headed down Virginia Street.

They had not gone more than a block when a tall, slender young man overtook them. He was puffing, and appeared to have run some distance to catch up.

"Miss Taylor!"

When she turned and saw the young man, Milly took a deep breath. "Yes, Mr. Fry?"

He was Longarm's height, though considerably younger and leaner. Longarm saw him blush when he looked at Milly, then stammered, "I . . . I just wanted to wish you a good day."

Milly was clearly surprised and a little embarrassed. "Well, thank you, Mr. Fry."

He looked very directly into Longarm's eyes and said, "Marshal Long, it's good to see you again, sir."

Before Longarm could utter a word, the young man turned and hurried away. "Milly, what was that all about? And what was that 'again' business?"

"He's smitten with me," she said. "And he was riding that third-class coach I was on between Denver and Cheyenne."

"I see," Longarm said, recalling how Milly had almost been raped and no one had even tried to help her against the three he'd eventually had to shoot. "He's just a kid."

"I thought so too, the first time he approached me," Milly said. "But I found out differently."

"What does that mean?" Longarm asked, watching Fry hurry up the street.

"He . . . well, he sort of saved my life," Milly confessed. "Without him, I'd have drowned in the Truckee River."

"What!" Longarm stopped dead in his tracks. He turned to Milly and said, "Do you want to explain to me how that happened?"

In a few terse words, Milly told him all about how Henry Fry had rescued her from the two prospectors who'd wanted to rape and then kill her.

When she was finished, she said, "So although he might

look like a boy, he's quite a brave young man."

Longarm nodded. "If I'd known what he'd done, I'd have congratulated him."

"He'd just have been embarrassed."

"Yeah," Longarm said as they continued along toward the stage station, "I suppose he would have at that."

"So," Milly said as they arrived and Longarm got into line to buy himself a stage ride to the Comstock Lode, "you'll just pretend we don't know each other?"

"If that's the way you want it," Longarm said, feeling a little hurt.

"That *is* the way I want it," she said.

"Then that's the way that it will be."

Milly stayed with him until he bought his ticket. The clerk said, "Next coach leaves for Virginia City in one hour, sir."

"When does the stage arrive from Paiute Pass?" Milly asked.

The clerk glanced up at an old fly-specked clock on the opposite wall. "It should have been here about fifteen minutes ago. But then, she's normally a little late. We unhitch the team and send the coach right on up to the Comstock, so that's the one that you'll be taking," he said to Longarm.

"Sounds good. You ever hear of a man named Jim Zack?" Longarm winked. "Tall, good-lookin' fella like me."

"Nope," the ticket clerk said with a broad smile. "Any reason I should have?"

"Not really," Longarm said, paying his money and stepping out of line with his ticket.

Reading his disappointment, Milly squeezed his arm and said, "You'll find him."

"You bet I will," Longarm said. He heard the crack of

a whip and an instant later, he saw the stage from Paiute Pass rolling up Virginia Street chased by a cloud of dust.

"Good-bye," Milly said, kissing him quickly on the cheek. "And good luck, Marshal!"

"Same to you," Longarm said, meaning it with all his heart as he reluctantly turned his back on Milly and went over to lean against the stage station wall and have a cheroot before his stage left for Virginia City.

Chapter 9

Just as the stage from Paiute Pass arrived, Longarm saw the young man, Henry Fry, reappear. Fry rushed up to Milly, and although there was too much noise and commotion to hear what the fellow said to her, Longarm could see that Fry was very upset. He seemed to be pleading with Milly to go away with him.

Longarm frowned. It was obvious that Henry Fry was totally infatuated with Milly and he was trying to stop her from meeting her fiancé. Longarm debated whether or not he should go and help Milly get rid of kid. He decided that it would look even worse if Gustav Luther disembarked from the coach and saw two strangers arguing over Milly.

The moment the stage halted in from of the station, a large, ruggedly handsome man burst through the door. He was a little beefy with massive shoulders, a lantern jaw, and heavy brows. He was not quite as tall as Longarm, but would no doubt outweigh him. Longarm judged Gustav to be in his late twenties. He was dressed like a dandy with his tailored suit, white starched collar, and expensive derby hat. He even had a silver-tipped cane in one hand and a leather case in the other.

For Longarm, it was dislike at first sight. Had Gustav been any kind of a gentleman, he'd have at least waited for a woman passenger still inside the coach to be helped down first. But no, he charged out of the coach like a bull after a heifer and started up the street looking neither left nor right.

"Gustav!" Milly cried, breaking away from Henry Fry and running after the mining engineer. "Gustav!"

The man froze in mid-stride, and then he turned to see Milly rushing toward him. Instead of throwing out his arms and letting her jump into them, the bastard let his jaw drop, and then he frowned.

"Milly? What the hell are you doing in Reno?"

Longarm saw Milly break stride like a lung-shot deer. Saw her skid to a halt and her arms fall limply to her sides. Saw her joy crumble as her expression turned gray. Heard her cry, "Gustav? I came all the way from Denver to marry you!"

The big man looked around self-consciously. "Milly," he said, "I . . . I didn't recognize you dressed like that."

Longarm started forward. What he was seeing was Milly's spirit being ripped from her as surely as if the big sonofabitch had cut her chest open and torn out her heart.

"I . . . I'm glad to see you, Milly."

Longarm stopped. He turned slightly, not wanting to do anything drastic until he was sure that he knew exactly what was going on.

"You said we were going to marry," Milly said brokenly. "You said you loved me."

"I said a lot of things while we were together in Denver."

Longarm heard Milly choke. Then he heard something else, and it was the sound of running feet. And before

96

Longarm realized it, Henry Fry was attacking the loutish mine company owner.

Fry was a few inches taller than Gustav, but a good seventy pounds lighter. Even so, he attacked the far bigger man like a whirling dervish. His knobby fists were a blur, and Fry actually got three punches to Gustav's handsome face before the engineer blocked the next couple of punches and stepped back with surprise.

Gustav fingered his lower lip and his fingers came away with blood on them. He glared at Fry and hissed, "You might be crazy, but you are definitely going to get the beating of your goddamn life!"

"Come on!" Henry Fry challenged. "You don't deserve Miss Taylor. You aren't good enough for her!"

Milly tried to get between the two men, but Gustav roughly pushed her out of the way and then he raised his big fists. Fry came in windmilling, and Gustav parried each blow with infuriating ease. Then his left hand shot out, and twice Henry Fry's head snapped back violently and blood began to pour from his broken lips.

Longarm had to wince. It was going to be no contest, but Fry wasn't any quitter. He lowered his head and charged, but he was like a lamb going to slaughter. Longarm watched as Fry's knees buckled when he took a clubbing shot behind the right ear. How Fry remained on his feet was a miracle. But somehow he did, until Gustav laughed and drove a thundering uppercut to the young man's jaw.

Longarm heard bone crack. Fry cried out in pain and went down as if his legs had been chopped off at the knees. Gustav grabbed him by the shirtfront and hauled him to his feet. He drew back his fist, and would have caved in Fry's facial bones if Longarm had not grabbed the mining man by the wrist.

"That's enough!" Longarm shouted, hand dropping to his gun.

Gustav hurled the unconscious Henry Fry aside as if he were a rag doll. He whirled around and tried to pull away from Longarm, until the marshal brought his six-gun up and jammed it into his throat.

"Freeze or I'll blow you a new gullet," Longarm hissed.

Gustav froze. "Who the hell are you, his friend?"

"I'm a United States deputy marshal and I'm saving you from a murder charge."

"Let go of me!"

Longarm released Gustav's wrist. "If you've done that young man permanent damage, I'll see that you are arrested for assault and battery."

Gustav laughed, and it was not a pretty sound. He turned to Milly. "That fool attacked *me,* not the other way around. Isn't that right, Miss Taylor?"

"Yes," Milly said, kneeling beside the unconscious young jeweler. "But you didn't need to hurt poor Henry!"

"So, you *do* know him," Gustav said with a sneer. "What have you been doing, screwing him while you waited here for my return?"

Something in Longarm snapped and he drove his left fist up into the big man's solar plexus. Drove it with such force that Gustav actually lifted to his toes. It was a wicked blow and it had every ounce of anger and power that Longarm could muster. Few men could have stayed on their feet.

Gustav choked and grabbed his gut. He bent over, and it was all that Longarm could do not to pistol-whip the man to his knees.

"Marshal," Gustav croaked, "you've just made one hell of a mistake. I'll have your badge for this!"

"Then you'll have to go to Denver and dig it out from under my damned mattress," Longarm spat. He turned to Milly. "This big bastard isn't worth your time. Come away to the Comstock Lode with me."

She looked at Gustav. "Did you lie when you said that you wanted to marry me? Did you, Gustav?"

He glared at Longarm, pasty-faced and eyes burning with hatred. "Hell, no, I didn't lie!" he said. "These two sorry bastards aren't fit to . . ."

Longarm still had his gun in his right fist, and the knuckles of his left were stinging when he drove them into Gustav's leering face. The big man went down hard and he did not try to get up. Instead, he twisted around and glared up at Longarm.

"There will be another time, Marshal! A time when you won't be able to sucker-punch me."

"Make it now," Longarm challenged.

"I'll pick my time," Gustav said, climbing unsteadily to his feet and dusting off his expensive suit. "And I'll keep the girl."

Longarm turned to Milly. "He's no damned good."

"Marshal Long, will *you* marry me?"

"No, but . . ."

"Then leave me alone!" Milly cried. "I want a wedding ring and a family, not just another man looking for a good time until the money is gone."

Longarm shook his head. He holstered his gun and scooped up Henry Fry. Turning to the crowd of staring onlookers, he said, "Where's the nearest doctor's office?"

"Two blocks down on your left, Marshal."

"Luther, if you don't take care of Miss Taylor and make her a good husband, I'll come pay you a visit."

"Next time we meet up," Gustav vowed, "things will turn out differently."

The man drew his arm around Milly and glared at Longarm. "I can give her a home and the better things of life that someone like you can only dream about."

"Just be good to her," Longarm said, "or there will, by God, be an accounting."

Longarm hurried down the street with Henry Fry in his arms. When he reached the doctor's office, he laid Henry down on the man's examining table.

"My God!" the doctor exclaimed. "What happened to this young man? Did he get kicked in the face by a mule?"

"A jackass," Longarm gritted.

He dug twenty dollars out of his pocket and laid it beside the unconscious kid. "Here, Doc. Fix him up as best you can."

The doctor nodded, and put the money in his pants before he gingerly began to palpate Henry's rapidly swelling face. Longarm waited until the doctor pronounced that Henry's jaw was broken.

"I knew that already. Can it be fixed?"

"Oh, sure," the doctor said, wiping the blood from Henry's mouth and then seeing if the young man's front teeth were loose. "No loose teeth."

"It's a wonder," Longarm said, "that the kid still has his head attached to his shoulders, considering how hard he was hit in the face."

"I probably get one of these a month," the doctor said. "A broken jaw is inconvenient as hell, but a shattered cheekbone can be a whole lot worse if bone splinters puncture the sinus cavity."

Longarm didn't know or care what a "sinus cavity" was. His concern was for Henry Fry, as courageous a kid as he'd seen in a long, long time.

"He's a fine, brave young man," Longarm said, pulling another twenty dollars out of his Levi's. "Here. If the bill is less than this . . ."

"It won't be," the doctor said. "I'll have to do a lot of work on this young man after I get the jaw set. I just wish the young man was fatter."

"Why?"

"He'll be on a liquid diet for the next month."

Longarm clucked his tongue sympathetically. "Well, as you can see, he needs to add weight, not lose it."

Longarm then sighed. "Doc, there's a stagecoach waiting to take me to the Comstock Lode. But when that young man wakes up, you tell him to stay the hell away from Gustav Luther or that man will kill him the next time."

"Gustav beat this kid?"

"He was just warming up," Longarm said, remembering how Gustav had used his fists almost like a professional bare-knuckles fighter. "He's a mean one."

"You damn right he is," the doctor said. "I've had more than one of his beating victims on this table, and some were in a whole lot worse shape than this kid."

"I believe that," Longarm said, thinking about how he would probably have to fight the big man some day, and how he'd try to plant a boot in Gustav's crotch or a fist in his throat in order to end the fight quickly. The big man just had too much size, strength, and boxing skill to allow him to get up a full head of steam.

Longarm left the doctor's office and hurried back to the stage station. They were waiting for him with a fresh team of horses all harnessed and ready to go.

"Have a good trip, Marshal!" the ticket man hollered, stepping out to wave good-bye to the passengers.

"I intend to," Longarm said. "I'm on vacation, you know."

"You didn't look like you were on vacation when you lit into Gustav a few minutes ago."

"He needs to learn some humility," Longarm said, grabbing the door handle of the coach.

Longarm's smile widened when he took his seat in the dim coach and realized his only company was three Comstock-bound prostitutes.

"Ladies," he said, tipping his hat. "It's been my lucky day to win at cards and then have the pleasure of your lovely company."

The three chippies tittered. One of them, a big, handsome girl with black eyes and a bold look, said, "Are you really a marshal?"

"Yep. But like I said, I'm on vacation and I have just won a little money playin' poker."

The girls exchanged glances, and the black-haired one swung herself across the coach just as it lurched into motion. She spilled into Longarm's lap and wrapped her arms around his neck, steamy breasts bulging in his face. "We like to play poker too, mister."

"You do?"

"That's right."

"What kind of poker?"

"*Strip* poker," she breathed, starting to nibble Longarm's earlobe. "Can you get up for a game or two, Marshal?"

Longarm was sure that he could.

102

Chapter 10

Longarm knew that, when gold had first been discovered on the Comstock back in 1859, it had been in the form of a sticky, bluish mud that the miners cursed as they mucked out their sluice boxes and pans. After they finally realized that the damned blue mud was high-grade ore, a drunken celebrant named "Old Virginny" Finney had toppled from his burro, smashing a whiskey bottle on the ground while his jubilant companions guffawed hilariously.

Trying to retain some semblance of dignity, Finney had staggered to his feet, raised the neck of the shattered bottle in a toast, and shouted, "I hearby christen this strike Virginny!"

The name had stuck and during the next twenty years, the Comstock Lode had become the richest gold and silver strike ever discovered in the world. It had quickly eclipsed even the vast fortune panned out of the cold mountain streams tumbling off the western slopes of the Sierrra Nevada Mountains. Thousands of miners and prospectors who had been idle for years, after the Forty-Niner strike had petered out, streamed over to Nevada Territory from California. So rich was the Comstock

Lode that it had bought Nevada an early statehood, and had had a large part in financing the Civil War for the Union.

Longarm knew all this because he had been on the Comstock. Now, however, as he tucked in his shirttail and begged off on another game of strip poker, he found himself unable to enjoy the banter of the three prostitutes. Instead, he was thinking about Milly Taylor and wondering if Gustav Luther, that arrogant and mean-tempered sonofabitch, would really make Milly his wife.

Longarm was betting that the mining man would somehow weasel out of his marriage proposal. If that happened, Longarm was afraid that Milly might return to her old ways and have to support herself again in the saloons, dance halls, or dangerous brothels. Longarm was determined that he would not allow that to happen. If need be, he'd kidnap Milly and deliver her back to Cheyenne, where she could live with Ruby until someone realized what a diamond in the rough she really was and then offered to marry the pretty girl.

"What's the matter, Marshal," the big black-haired girl said to Longarm. "Too much lovin' worn you out?"

"Yeah," he admitted with a tired grin. "I think the three of you were in cahoots against me. I lost my pants before we even crossed out of the Reno city limits."

"We let you buy them back three times," the woman said slyly. "And you can't complain about the free personal services we threw in in the bargain."

One of the prostitutes dragged her dress up around her waist and spread her legs. She wasn't wearing any underclothing, and Longarm was thankful for the dimness as the woman hunched her hips while the other pair laughed uproariously.

"Last chance!" the woman said. "After we get to town, it'll be three dollars a poke, Marshal."

"I've had my fill," he said, slightly offended by their coarseness. Longarm could not help but hold them up to Milly, and they suffered by comparison. Milly might be a prostitute, but she had real class and dignity.

"We'd better leave him alone," the big girl said. "The marshal is all humped out and we've won enough of his money."

"Almost fifty dollars," Longarm conceded without any remorse. He was not a saver but instead a spender. And despite their crudeness, these girls were good-hearted. And unless he was wrong, Longarm knew that there would be many times when some lusty man screwed them, then beat them without paying them a cent. Things always evened out and these women always earned their money.

"Virginia City comin' up!" the stagecoach driver shouted.

Longarm stuck his head out the window and saw that the "Queen of the Comstock," as Virginia City was called, had indeed fallen on hard times. For one thing, the big mine on his right was closed down, and for another, there were also many shacks that appeared to be abandoned. The last time that Longarm had been here, every square inch of Sun Mountain's eastern slope had been claimed by miners, who often were forced to live like gophers in their little mine shafts. Now, he saw only a few hundred miners actively working their claims.

"Looks like the Consolidated Mine finally shut down," one of the prostitutes said, pointing out the opposite window.

"Damn!" the black-haired girl swore. "I sure hope

105

there's still some money to be made up here."

"There will be," another one said, "but we might have to drop our charges to a dollar."

"Not me," the black-haired one vowed. "Marshal, we're worth three bucks a screw, ain't we?"

"Damn right," Longarm said.

That pleased the girls. They forgot Longarm as the stage made its way up C Street toward the depot. Traffic was heavy on the main thoroughfare, and the three girls were shouting and hanging out the windows, exposing their breasts and egging on the ogling miners.

A freighter driving an ore wagon stopped and yelled, "Fresh meat, boys! How much are you chargin'!"

"Three dollars," the black-haired girl shouted.

"I'll take a poke here and now!"

Longarm shook his head as the girl piled out of the stage, jumped up on the wagon, and started tearing off the freighter's shirt to the delight of the spectators. The pair tumbled into the back of the ore wagon, and the team just kept plodding along.

"Minny has got some brass," one of the girls said.

But within minutes, Longarm was alone in the stage as the other two prostitutes, advertising that they were "fresh," were quickly paired up with eager samplers at three dollars a poke.

Longarm chuckled. Those girls knew how to make hay while the sun was shining. By nightfall, even at three dollars a throw, he would not be surprised if they had a hundred dollars between them—in addition to Longarm's money.

As soon as the stage halted before its station, Longarm climbed down. He shouldered his saddlebags and headed for the sheriff's office.

Sheriff Ed Pate was sitting with his young friend and deputy, talking about how the prices of Comstock mining stock kept going down.

"Five years ago I was worth about five thousand dollars in stock. Now I'm worth less than five hundred," the sheriff lamented.

"I'm worth a whole lot less than that," Longarm said, coming through the door.

Pate's melon-round face split into a wide grin. He stood up, a short man shaped like a marshmallow on toothpicks. But the man's looks were deceptive. Pate was a wicked fighter and amazingly strong. He had the arms and shoulders of a blacksmith and the tenacious fighting ability of a cornered badger. At five feet eight inches, but with well over two hundred pounds of solid muscle, Ed Pate was not a man to cross.

"Longarm!" Pate exclaimed, coming to his feet. "What the hell brings you up to the Comstock?"

"I'm on vacation."

"Come on!" Pate said with disbelief. "You mean Billy Vail is giving you a *paid* vacation?"

"That's right."

Pate winked at his deputy, a young fella named Dave, and they both grinned. Dave said, "I guess I'm going to have to start asking you for a paid vacation, Sheriff."

Pate made an obscene gesture and they all laughed. "Sit down, Longarm. Deputy, give the marshal a cup of coffee."

Longarm accepted the coffee, although he seemed to recall that it would be strong enough to float horseshoes. He sipped it and found out his memory wasn't failing.

"How you been, Ed?"

"I can't complain," the sheriff said. "The usual shootings and robberies, but fewer each year. We're both starting to worry about our jobs. The city council is sniffin' around like dogs after fresh meat as they try to cut their budget. I might lose Dave."

"That'd be a shame," Longarm said, for he knew that Dave was a good man, and that the sheriff thought very highly of his deputy and expected Dave to be his eventual replacement. "Dave, maybe I can get you on with the feds."

Dave tried not to look excited, but Longarm could see the hope that sprang into his eyes. "Do you mean it or are you just blowin' smoke, Marshal Long?"

"Well, I can't make any promises but it's possible," Longarm said. "Want me to ask when I return to Denver after vacation?"

Dave glanced at his sheriff. "Aw, I dunno. Things might get better up here one of these days."

"Bullshit, Dave," Pate said. "It wouldn't hurt for Longarm to at least ask."

"All right," Dave said with a relieved smile. "Thanks." He looked at the sheriff. "I guess I'll go and make the rounds and let you two jaw in peace."

When Dave was gone, Sheriff Pate said, "You couldn't do much better than to get Dave on with the feds."

"I know that. Do you really think he's going to lose his job?"

"Yep. But maybe not this year. We just had a pretty good strike come in down at the Bullfrog Mine. They hit a solid vein of ore at the twelve-hundred-foot level."

"Twelve-hundred-foot?"

"That's right. Down that deep, the temperatures run about a hundred and twenty-five degrees. At that level, the miners work fifteen minutes on, fifteen minutes off

108

in a little ice room drinking water and gasping like lapdogs."

"It must be a living hell," Longarm said, meaning it.

"I wouldn't go down there if it meant my life," Pate said. "The deeper they go, the hotter and more dangerous it gets. They keep hitting big reservoirs of scalding water. Longarm, have you ever seen one of those miners that has sent his pick through a wall into boiling water?"

"No."

"They look like hogs dipped in scalding brine. You can hear them screaming as they come up in the mining cages, and they don't stop screaming until they die. Their skin just falls off. It's a horrible death."

Longarm could well imagine. "Sheriff, I don't expect to stay more than a day or two up here before I'm heading for Lake Tahoe. I mean no offense, but I love the smell of cool pines, and the sight of that lake refreshes my spirits."

"Hell, if you jump in it, your balls will freeze and drop off."

Longarm chuckled. "That might well be, but I have a yen to smell the ponderosa and do some lake fishing."

"It doesn't sound bad," Pate admitted. "So why did you take this little detour up here?"

"I have a very good old friend that I am trying to find. Last I heard, he was living in Virginia City. I think you might have heard of him. He wasn't the shy or retiring kind of man, and I always thought he would make his mark."

"What is his name?"

"Jim Zack." Longarm leaned forward expectantly. "You ever heard of him?"

The sheriff's expression clouded. "Yeah, I sure have.

I helped send him to prison about six months ago."

"What!"

"I'm sorry," Pate said. "I knew Jim Zack pretty damn well. He owned a hotel and a saloon here in Virginia City. He had money and was a damn good fella to be around. I liked him and so did most everyone else."

"So what happened?"

"He married a rotten bitch named Sheila Ray, and that girl just wound him around her pretty finger. Next thing you know, she was running him here and there and his businesses were going to hell. He started drinking too much, and one night he broke into a mining office up here and stole about five thousand dollars' worth of gold nuggets and a few other valuables."

"Gold nuggets?" Longarm asked. "Why would anyone steal gold instead of cash?"

"It sure isn't as hard to break into a mining office as it is a bank. Besides, you can sell gold anyplace," the sheriff explained. "Maybe Jim figured that it would be impossible to identify."

"So how did you identify the stolen goods?"

"He took a few personal items as well," the sheriff said. "A money clip holding about fifty dollars cash. It was a beautiful piece of jewelry and anyone who'd seen Gustav Luther showing it off would know that—"

Longarm sat bolt upright. "Gustav Luther? The same sonofabitch who owns the Bonanza Mining Company with an office in Reno and an operation in Paiute Pass?"

"That's right. He also has some mining holdings up here on the Comstock Lode. They're *borrasca*—that means they don't pay."

"I know," Longarm said with more than a little agitation. "But why would my friend turn to petty theft?"

110

"It wasn't petty. And like I said, he got married to a woman with real expensive tastes. She milked Zack hard and he was starting to lose everything. Probably figured he was going to lose her as well if he didn't get some money to pay off his debts and turn things around."

"It sounds like he'd have been better off without that woman."

"Sure he would have," Sheriff Pate said, "but you try and tell that to a man who loves his wife, even if she is grinding his grapes and grinning all the while."

Longarm sighed. "How many years did Jim get?"

"Ten years in the Nevada State Prison just outside Carson City."

"Ten! For a first-time offense? That's mighty damned steep, isn't it?"

"Yeah," Pate said. "I thought he might get a year or two. He was drunk when we arrested him and offered no resistance. He said he didn't know how the gold and the money clip came to turn up in his desk, but they all say that, so the judge didn't take it into account. He was mighty tough on Jim. Everyone was kind of shocked."

Longarm stood up. "Do you know when the next Virginia and Truckee train heads down to Carson City? I want to visit the prison first thing tomorrow morning."

Pate extracted his pocket watch. "There's one leaving in about twenty minutes, but you just got up here."

"I'll be back," Longarm promised. "I'm sure I'll want to talk to Mrs. Zack."

"You can try."

"What's that supposed to mean?"

"Just that she's getting a divorce."

111

Longarm shook his head. "She sounds like a real gem."

"She's a man-killer, Longarm. Most beautiful thing you ever did see. She smiles at you and your dick turns to stone. But she's deadlier than a scorpion."

Longarm gulped down his coffee, choked a little because it was so acid, and came to his feet. "I reckon I'll be able to see Jim tomorrow, won't I?"

"Sure. Just show Warden Owens your badge and tell him that you're an old friend of mine. The warden is a good man. He'll bend the rules for a federal marshal."

"I left my . . . aw, never mind."

"What'd you leave?" Pate asked.

Longarm just couldn't tell the man he'd left his damned marshal's badge under his mattress in Denver.

"It's not important," Longarm said.

Pate walked him to the door. "This Jim Zack must have meant a lot to you, huh?"

"Yeah. We were friends when were both having some hard times. That's when you really get to know who your friends are."

"I agree," Pate said. "This Jim Zack thing has bothered me since it happened six months ago."

"Why?"

"Well, like I said, he was a fine man until he got married and that woman began to drive him to drink. He had everything and, frankly, could have married about any woman he'd wanted in this part of Nevada."

"A bad woman can always ruin a good man, and vice versa," Longarm added, thinking about Milly and that damned Gustav Luther.

"And you know what?" the sheriff asked as Longarm was starting to leave.

"What?"

"Luther is keeping company with Mrs. Zack when he comes up here on business."

Longarm's lip's drew back in anger. "He's *sleeping* with Jim's wife?"

"I expect he is," the sheriff said. "But like I said, the woman has control of all Jim's holdings now and so she's worth plenty. Gus Luther is a blood-sucking leech. I say it's a good match and I hope they screw each other into an early grave."

Longarm took a deep breath and expelled it slowly.

"What's the matter," Pate said. "You look madder than a teased polecat."

"I got a reason to be," Longarm said, thinking about how this news would square with Milly. How on earth could she compete with the rich, beautiful Mrs. Sheila Zack for Luther's affections?

The answer was very obvious. Milly could not. That meant that, even now, Milly was probably being used by Luther for his pleasure while the man had Sheila Zack, his Virginia City ball-buster, waiting for him on the Comstock.

"Damnation," Longarm muttered, wishing he'd decided to take this long-overdue vacation in New Orleans.

Chapter 11

Milly lay naked in the big four-poster bed and waited as Gustav undressed. She had been waiting for him all day long, just banging around in his fine home up on A Street. She'd cooked him a big dinner, but he hadn't returned until almost midnight.

"I thought you said that you were coming home for dinner," she said, trying to hide her anger and disappointment.

"I got tied up at the office," he snapped. "I been out of town for almost three weeks and there were a lot of loose ends down there that demanded immediate attention."

"Oh."

"You can't just drop in and expect me to be at your side constantly."

He unbuttoned his shirt to expose his hairy chest. Milly was surprised to see that he had put on a little weight since Denver.

"Milly," he said, kicking off his shoes. "I wish to God that you'd given me some warning before you came here."

"I thought it would be a surprise."

"It was that, all right."

Milly sat up in the bed, pulling the covers up to her neck. Gustav liked her in bed stark naked, but right now she felt more than just physically exposed. "Are you . . . upset that I came to Reno unannounced?"

"A little," he admitted. "First off, if I'd known you were coming, I'd have been here waiting when the train pulled in."

She smiled. "You would have?"

"Of course. But to be real honest, I wish you'd stayed in Denver. I was planning to come for you. I told you that, remember?"

"Things weren't going too good for me," Milly admitted. "I . . . well, I couldn't keep going the way I was. I had to stop."

"Stop what?"

Milly flushed. "You know."

Gustav snorted. "Hell, you were doing well enough, it seemed to me. I remember how it was the first time I had to pay."

"That's all past," she whispered. "I want to get married. Make you a home and a family."

He looked at her oddly. "Milly, I can't marry you right away."

"Why not!"

He unbuttoned his pants and tossed them on a chair. She saw that he was ready for her, his manhood strained against his underpants. He tore them off and advanced, lust in his eyes. "We can talk about this later."

"No!" she cried. "I want to know right now if you are going to marry me or not!"

He grabbed the coverlet and tore it from Milly's hands. "Sure I am," he breathed, eyes aflame with desire. "I just can't do it right away."

116

He grabbed her thighs and tried to pry them apart, but Milly pushed him away. "When! When are you going to marry me, Gustav!"

For a moment, she thought he was going to hit her with his doubled fists. His face contorted with rage and he grabbed her arm.

"Gus, if you hit me, you had better knock me out cold or I'll rip your eyes out!"

His cocked fist shook and then he unclenched it. His voice trembled when he said, "Milly, I'll marry you, but not for a while yet."

"When!" she demanded.

He took a deep breath. His hands dropped to her thighs and Milly felt him pulling them apart. She resisted until he said, "Before the year is out."

"Do you promise?" she asked, fighting against him with the last of her reserves.

"Yeah," he breathed, tearing her legs apart and driving his massive root into her body.

Milly gasped and wrapped her arms around the big man as he began to rut wildly. "Don't do me wrong," she begged, feeling her own passion begin to fire. "Please don't do me wrong, Gus!"

He growled something deep in his throat and Milly knew that he was mindless with desire. Gus felt like a stick of hot dynamite jamming in and out of her body, and his frantic lovemaking lifted Milly higher and higher until Gus exploded and filled her with a torrent of his hot seed.

"Ah, Milly," he panted, rolling off of her. "You got a power over me that I can't resist."

She was still riding her own wave of climax, and Milly's body kept twitching until he laid his hand on her womanhood and capped her fire.

Milly pressed her hand over his. "You marry me," she promised, "and I'll be yours for the taking as much and as often as you want. I'll be yours alone, Gus."

He chuckled. "Maybe you're like a pussycat that's been running wild and having wanton pleasure for too long but has finally found a home."

Milly's lips curved up at the corners. "That's a crazy way of putting it," she said, feeling his finger worm into her body and probe for the place that made her go mad.

He began to stir her again with his finger until Milly's heels began to rake back and forth across the covers. She reached for him. "Gus, don't start what you can't finish."

"I can finish," he said hoarsely. "Milly, go down on me."

Milly went down on the big man and as she took his root in her mouth, she prayed that he would not try and keep her down too much longer. But once she had his last name, then she'd have her respectability as Mrs. Luther and she'd finally be all right.

Gustav began to stiffen and moan. His thumbs pressed into Milly's temples hard enough to bring tears of pain to her eyes. Milly pushed the pain out of her mind and did what she believed no respectable woman would dream of doing as she took all of him.

The next day and the next Gustav was busy at work, leaving around nine o'clock in the morning and not returning until about the same hour in the evening. Each day, he asked Milly to stay in the house and not go outside.

"It would cause tongues to wag."

"I don't care about that," she said.

"Of course you do! You've told me at least a hundred times how you want to be respectable. How are you going to get respect if you're seen by everyone in town parading around during the daytime and then coming to roost in my bed?"

When Milly realized he had a point, Gustav smiled tolerantly and said, "Reno is the frontier, but its respectable ladies are still pretty Victorian, my dear."

"Well I can't stay locked up in this place forever!"

"I'm going up to Virginia City tomorrow," he announced.

"What!"

"I have an office and some holdings on the Comstock Lode," he said gruffly. "I should have been up there already, but I've stayed here an extra day because of you."

"Can't I go with you."

"No!"

"Please!" she begged. "Gus, I'm beginning to go crazy in this house. I can't exist here day after day."

He had started to pour them both a drink, but now he stopped. "You've *never* been in a house as nice as mine, have you?"

Milly had been in nicer homes. Some of her Denver clients had been very successful businessmen. One or two of them had even been bachelors and had taken her to their impressive homes after dark for a night of lovemaking. Those Denver mansions had put this one to shame, but Milly knew better than to tell this to her proud fiancé.

"This is a wonderful home," she said. "After we're married, I'd like to make a few changes but . . ."

119

"Nothing will change!"

Milly felt the sting of his words like a slap in the face. "But Gus, this will be my home too! Surely you can understand that I need to do a few things that will make it seem as if I belong here."

"Change the bedroom," he finally snapped. "Buy us a bedroom ceiling mirror so that I can watch when I mount you or when you go down on me."

Milly was hurt and offended. She realized that Gustav had already had a few drinks and that he was in an ugly and disagreeable mood. There was no sense in trying to reason with him when he was like this, so she dropped the subject.

"Here," he said, giving her a glass of good whiskey. "Let's toast to the future."

"To *our* future," she said.

He chuckled, but there was no warmth in his eyes or his smile, at least not for Milly. "Sure," he said, "to our future."

Milly drank. She should have been hopeful and happy, but she felt quite the opposite. Gustav was saying the right words, and when she had him in bed, he would tell her anything she wanted. But once he was satisfied, it was as if her hold had vanished. Then he became distant. Cold and even calculating.

"How long will you be in Virginia City?"

"No more than a couple of days."

"Promise."

"Yeah, yeah," he said irritably.

"After you get back from Virginia City," she said, "I'd like to talk about our wedding."

"What's to talk about?"

"Well, the guest list, of course."

120

He laughed in her face. "There will be no guest list unless it consists of those two sonsabitches that were at the stage station when I arrived. Especially that marshal. What did you say his name was? Custis Long?"

Milly swallowed nervously. Whenever her Gustav got on the subject of Longarm or Henry Fry, he became very upset and almost violent in his jealousy.

Before he could work himself up to a rage, Milly tossed down her drink and unbuttoned Gustav's trousers. She dropped to her knees before him and he forgot everything.

But Milly didn't. She thought of Longarm and even, she was surprised to admit, of young Henry Fry, the boy that had saved her from drowning in the treacherous Truckee River.

Henry Fry had been thinking of little else but Milly since his arrival in Reno and subsequent beating at the hands of Gustav Luther. He seemed to be sleepwalking through one day after the next. His broken jaw throbbed constantly, and it was all that Henry could do to swallow enough soup, milk, and strained food in order to keep up his strength.

Two days before, he'd read an article in the *Reno Evening Gazette* about a pair of bodies found floating in Pyramid Lake where the Truckee River finally emptied. The article went on to say that the bodies were decomposed beyond recognition, but that it appeared both men had been shot.

Henry wished that there had been a third body floating in Pyramid Lake, one belonging to Gustav Luther. As soon as he had been able to go outside, he'd removed a strap that was supposed to support his jaw, then headed off to find Milly.

It took Henry only a few hours to learn that Milly was staying in Luther's home and not coming out. Henry stayed near the house as much as he dared without seeming too conspicuous. His jaw ached like crazy and he felt like he'd been beaten in the face with a lead pipe, so he was unable to stay out more than a few hours each day.

But on the day that Gustav Luther left home with a suitcase in his fist, Henry felt his heart quicken with excitement. He saw Milly kiss the mining man good-bye, and then he followed Luther to the stage depot. Henry kept out of sight, and when Luther rolled out of town, Henry hurried up to the ticket man and said, "Where is that stage headed for?"

"Virginia City, then over the Divide and down into Gold Hill, Silver City, and on to Dayton. Then it doubles back west and rolls into Carson City and—"

"I suppose that Mr. Luther is going to the Comstock?"

"That's right," ticket man said, looking closely at Henry. "How come you're trying to talk with your mouth shut? Say, aren't you that young fella that Mr. Luther nearly . . ."

Henry did not bother to answer. He felt alive again with hope because Gustav Luther was gone and he'd left Miss Taylor behind and alone! Maybe just for a day or two, but enough time for Henry to safely visit and proclaim his love.

Fifteen minutes later, pale and trembling, he knocked on Milly's door. When she opened it, Henry removed his hat. "Hello," he wheezed through his clenched teeth. " 'Member me?"

"Henry!" she cried, pulling him into the house before the entire neighborhood saw the poor young jeweler. "What are you, crazy?"

He swallowed, bowed his head a little, and worked the short felt brim of his bowler with his fingers. "I had to say hello to you," he confessed. "To see if you're . . ."

"If I'm what?"

"Married!" he blurted out. Then Henry looked up into her eyes. Summoning up all of his courage, he said, "Please don't marry Mr. Luther! He's no good. Everyone says he's no good, Miss Taylor. He'll only bring you heartache."

It was quite a speech for Henry. The most words he'd spoken since getting his jaw broken. The words and the excitement made his jaw throb something awful, and Henry suddenly felt weak. He cradled his jaw in his hands knowing how pathetic he must appear.

"You dear man," Milly said, escorting Henry into Luther's parlor and sitting him down. "You look awful!"

"I *am* awful," he confessed. "I didn't even make it a good fight."

Milly knelt before Henry. She wanted to hug and console him, but just could not. She was betrothed. "Henry," she pleaded, "forget about Gustav and about me. We're to be married soon."

"But he's *bad*!" Henry exclaimed. "He's an awful man!"

Milly expelled a deep breath. "Maybe you're right. I . . . I don't know. Sometimes I feel so confused! I practically begged Longarm to marry me, but of course he wouldn't."

"I will," Henry said, without much hope that she'd accept.

123

"You would?"

"Uh-huh."

"Thanks," she told him with a big, happy smile. "But I'm taken."

Henry pushed himself to his feet. He was unaware that tears were clouding his vision. He felt dizzy and the room was swimming. He desperately needed some fresh air. But first, he had one last thing he must ask.

"Miss Taylor, if he don't marry you, would you marry me?"

Milly didn't know whether to laugh or to cry. "Yes," she said rashly. "I'd marry you if Gus wouldn't."

Henry straightened, and cuffed the tears from his eyes. "I'll wait," he vowed.

"Please don't come back," she begged. "If one of the neighbors should tell Gus that you came to visit ... well, I don't know what he might do."

Henry shuffled unsteadily toward the door. Milly came up behind him and impulsively kissed his cheek. "You deserve better than me," she said. "I'm no virgin and I've done some things that would ..."

He clamped his hands over both ears. "Stop it! You're the one I love."

Milly bit her lip. She did not trust her voice when she said, "Good-bye, Henry."

"Good-bye, Miss Taylor," he said, making a conscious decision right there and then to make two stops.

The first would be to a gunsmith, where he'd purchase a hideout, two-shot derringer. The second would be to buy a ticket for the next stage to Virginia City.

Chapter 12

Longarm stood outside the gates of the Nevada State Prison. The walls were of rock and stone, fifteen feet high, with barbed wire strung along the top and heavily armed guards ever vigilant in the guard towers.

"Marshal, even *you* will have to check your gun and your rifle," the prison gate guard said.

"Not a problem," Longarm told the man. "This isn't the first time I've paid a warden or some prisoner a visit."

The guard nodded. He wore a six-gun on his hip and cradled a scattergun in his hands. He looked plenty capable, and even eager to use both.

Longarm was patted down by a heavy-handed guard, and then allowed to pass into the heavily guarded prison. As always when he entered one of these places, he suddenly felt a stab of panic. There was just something very damned unnerving about going through two heavily armed and fortified gates without the company of Mr. Samuel Colt.

"This way," a guard said.

Longarm followed the shotgun-toting guard across the compound. The prisoners stared suspiciously at him, measuring his size, power, and toughness by the way he walked and held himself. In prison, toughness was everything. The strong survived and might even flourish, but it was always at the expense of the weak.

"How's things back in Colorado?" the guard asked when they passed into the administration building.

"About the the same."

"Still working for Chief Marshal Billy Vail?"

"Yep."

"He's a good one, I hear."

"The best."

"Go on in. Warden Owens will be in to see you in a couple of minutes."

"Thanks."

Longarm listened to the door close behind him. Then he took a seat and rested his eyes. The warden smoked good Cuban cigars. Longarm could smell their lingering aroma. He dug one of his own cheap cheroots out of his coat pocket, then decided not to light it because maybe the warden would offer him one of the expensive Cubans.

Longarm could hear the sounds of the prison through the warden's window. The shouts of the guards, the heavy steps of prisoners, even the rattle of chains and the grate of big keys in massive locks. Prison would be a terrible burden on a free spirit like Jim Zack.

In the few minutes that he had to wait, Longarm tried to remember what Jim had looked like. He was tall and good-looking, kind of cocky, and quick to laugh but also to take offense. He was the kind that the ladies went for in a big way. Longarm smiled privately as he remembered the many escapades that he and Jim Zack had gotten themselves into during those lean but devil-may-care years. Like the time that he and Jim . . .

"Marshal Long!" the warden said, pushing through the door. "I'm delighted to meet you."

"Sheriff Pate told me a good deal about you," Longarm said, coming to his feet and extending a hand. "I appreciate your taking a few minutes to meet with me."

The warden waved that aside. He was a tidy-looking man in a pressed suit, and his shoes were shined like a polished apple.

"Marshal, the fact that you've come all the way from Denver for this meeting is enough to raise my curiosity. Cigar?"

"Don't mind if I do," Longarm said as the warden selected a pair of fat, black Cubans out of a mahogany humidor. The warden had a little silver cigar-trimmer and nipped the tips off both ends, then presented one to Longarm as if it were a thing of beauty, something like a rose.

Longarm had a match ready, and when he lit his cigar and inhaled, it was with the same joy a kid might have sucking on a peppermint stick.

"Like it?"

"Warden, if I could afford these things, I'd smoke nothing else," Longarm said truthfully.

"Sit down," the warden said, "and tell me exactly what brought you all the way from Denver."

"Actually," Longarm said, feeling a little sheepish, "I'm here on vacation."

"Vacation!" The warden was so surprised that he almost dropped his Cuban.

"That's right," Longarm said. "I came to track down an old friend. One of the finest men whose company I've ever had the pleasure of enjoying."

The warden frowned. "But then why ..."

"His name is Jim Zack, and I just learned from Sheriff Pate up in Virginia City that he's one of your inmates."

The warden frowned as if his cigar had suddenly gone rank. "So you came to talk about Inmate Zack?"

"Yes, sir. Have you been having any trouble with him?"

"No," the warden said. "He's been a model prisoner. In fact, he doesn't fit the inmate mold, if you know what I mean."

"I do," Longarm said. "I had a real hard time believing that he would have stolen from that mining office and been stupid enough to have kept the evidence."

"The trial brought out that he was drunk," the warden explained. "If a man gets drunk, he makes real stupid mistakes."

"That's true," Longarm said, "and Jim did like to bend his elbow, but he was never a thief. And furthermore, I can't understand why he was sentenced so harshly for a first-time offense."

"Maybe it had to do with the fact that the judge was a friend of Gustav Luther, the fella who was robbed and who is now sparking Mrs. Zack."

Longarm bit back an unflattering comment. "I heard about that too. This whole thing is a mess, Warden. Any chance Jim might receive an early parole?"

"Sure," the warden said. "If Zack keeps his nose clean, he might be looking at about five years altogether. No promises, but given the circumstances, I think the parole board will let him out in another four and a half years."

"That's still a big chunk of a man's life," Longarm said, not a bit heartened at this piece of news. "Especially a man like Jim Zack."

The warden shrugged. "It's a big chunk of *any* man's life. We try to protect the weaker prisoners, but . . ."

"Jim is a pretty big man," Longarm said. "The Jim I knew wouldn't need much protection."

"Maybe your friend has changed a lot since you knew him," the warden said, avoiding Longarm's eyes. "Zack arrived here weighing about a hundred and fifty pounds."

"He's six-three!"

"He was a staggering drunk," the warden said flatly. "There wasn't a whole lot left of him by the time the trial was over. They said he refused to eat for near a week."

Longarm groaned softly. "Can I see him right now?"

The warden nodded. "Ordinarily, we only allow the prisoners to have visitors on Sunday afternoons. But seeing as you are a United States marshal and a friend of Sheriff Pate's, I'll make the exception."

"Thanks," Longarm said fervently. "I heard that Jim maintains his innocence. That's mostly what I want to talk to him about."

"You know they all claim to be innocent."

"Yeah, but . . ."

"Listen," the warden said, leaning forward across his desk. "Zack is is just a name and a number here. No special treatment can be given just because of his friends on the outside."

"I understand that," Longarm said, "but I'm a professional lawman, and you can be sure that I'm going to do all I can to prove that he was innocent of the charges."

129

"And I hope you do," the warden said. "From what I hear, this prisoner was misrepresented by a third-rate lawyer, and his wife couldn't wait to latch onto his hotel and other holdings."

"A man goes down fast when he mixes bad liquor and bad women," Longarm said.

The warden nodded solemnly and then he called for a guard. When the man arrived, Warden Owens ordered that Zack be brought to his office.

"It'll take about ten minutes," the warden explained. "Before he arrives, I'll leave you alone while I check on some things out in the front office. That way, you can have a little more time and some privacy. Take all the time you need. If I had you meet in the visitors' room, the other prisoners would hear about it and it would go hard on your poor friend."

"I can't thank you enough," Longarm said, coming to his feet and extending his hand with genuine gratitude.

The warden was of average stature, but he had an imposing presence and an easy way that Longarm appreciated. When the warden was gone, Longarm settled back to finish his expensive cigar. He tried to prepare himself for the shock of seeing his dear old friend in prison rags and in poor physical condition. And he tried to think of the many questions that would need to be asked.

When the door opened about ten minutes later, a guard escorted Jim Zack into the room. Longarm did not immediately turn around to face his old friend. He could hear Jim's ankle chains dragging across the floor.

"Hello, Jim," Longarm said, turning around and standing up.

130

Longarm did not know which one of them was more shocked. Jim because he had never expected to see his old friend again, especially as a United States marshal, or himself because the man he faced bore little resemblance to the wild Jim Zack of yesterday.

"Custis?"

"Yeah."

"*Marshal* Custis Long?"

Longarm nodded. He tried to smile but his face felt like dried mud, so brittle he was afraid it would crack to pieces. "Hello, Jim."

"Aw, damn," Zack whispered. "Custis, why'd you have to come and see me like this!"

Longarm laid his cigar down in an ashtray and went over to stand before his skeletal friend whose once-handsome face now appeared haggard and haunted. To his credit, Zack still looked at him eye to eye, but he seemed much smaller.

"I'm sorry you've fallen on such hard times, Jim. I come to see if I could help you somehow."

"You can't," Zack said, a trace of bitterness edging into his voice. "So it might be just better all the way around if you just got the hell out of this prison, Marshal, and forgot what you saw here and now."

"I can't rightly do that," Longarm said. "You know I never could walk out on a friend."

"We're not friends anymore! Neither one of us is anything like the wild young studs we once were." Jim's lip curled. "I never thought that you would stoop so low as to become a damned lawman."

Longarm knew that his old friend was trying to drive him away, and he was not buying it for a moment. "I understand that you were framed."

Zack snorted with derision. "You're a lawman. You ought to know that every inmate proclaims his innocence."

"Yeah, but every inmate isn't my friend," Longarm said. "If you really are innocent, tell me about it."

Zack pulled back, almost tripped on his ankle irons and chains, and spilled to the floor. He grabbed the warden's desk, spotted the smoking stump of Longarm's Cuban cigar, and jammed it into this mouth.

"Why waste our time?" he asked, inhaling deeply. "Why bother?"

"I told you," Longarm said, "I never walk on a friend. I won't help if you're guilty as charged, even though the sentence was too harsh, but nothing will stand between me and the truth if you are really innocent."

Zack blew a big, spinning smoke ring into Longarm's face. When the marshal did not retaliate with anger, Zack leaned heavily against the warden's desk and said, "It's simple. A Greek tragedy. I fell in love with a bad woman and when she broke my heart, I replaced her with drink."

"What about the theft that got you sentenced here?"

"I don't know how the gold and those things of Gustav Luther's ended up in my desk," Zack said. "That's the gospel truth."

"Could you have taken them while drunk? So drunk you don't remember?"

"No."

Longarm's voice hardened. "Jim, are you dead sure?"

"Yes!"

Longarm yanked one of his own cheroots out of his vest pocket and bit the tip off in anger. When he lit the damned thing, it tasted like a noxious weed in comparison with the warden's rich, black Cuban.

"All right," Longarm said, "let's get down to business because we don't have a hell of a lot of time. Tell me everything that you remember."

"Starting when?"

"Starting from when you first had a hint that your wife was screwing Gustav Luther."

Zack's eyebrows raised with surprise. "By damned, you don't beat around the bushes, do you, Marshal."

"I haven't got the time. I'm on a vacation and I'm expected back in about a week."

Zack's face fell. "Nothing good can possibly happen in a week."

"I'll stay on this until something good does happen," Longarm vowed. "I won't leave until I see justice done for you, Jim. That's a promise."

For the very first time since he had walked into the room, hope flared in Jim Zack's haunted eyes. Longarm saw it and it raised his own low spirits.

And as Jim began to tell his story, Longarm pledged that, one way or another, he was not going to let his old friend down.

Chapter 13

When Longarm arrived back on the Comstock Lode the next morning, he walked away from the V&T Railroad depot in Virginia City with a look of determination on his craggy face. The day before, he'd spent three hours talking to Jim Zack, and he was convinced of the man's innocence. It seemed very obvious to Longarm that Sheila Zack and Gustav Luther had conspired to frame poor Jim for a robbery that he had never committed.

It would have been ridiculously easy. After all, since the ore and the eye-catching money clip had both belonged to Luther, and since Luther was having an affair with Sheila Zack, there would have been no problem getting and placing the incriminating evidence. Add that to the fact that the judge presiding in the case was Luther's personal friend, and everything added up to a confused, bitter, but innocent man receiving an unusually harsh sentence.

All the way up from Carson City, Longarm had been debating where to begin in this case. At first, he thought to interview the judge and see if he could get the man to admit he had dealt Jim Zack an injustice. But on reflection, Longarm decided that was not likely. And because he had already confronted Gustav Luther at the Reno stage depot, it was obvious that a second meeting would be adversarial rather than productive.

That left only one natural choice for Longarm—Sheila Zack. She was, after all, the one who had destroyed poor Jim while taking up with Luther. She, more than anyone else, was profiting from her husband's wrongful conviction and severe prison term. The more that Longarm thought about it, the more he knew that he would have to figure some way to win Sheila's confidence, and then use her to discover the evidence that would prove her incarcerated husband's innocence.

Longarm went back to see his friend Sheriff Pate. In as few words as possible, he outlined the extent of his meeting with Jim Zack at the Nevada State Prison.

Longarm ended by saying, "He's as innocent of the robbery as we are, Sheriff. He told me that he had never even been inside Luther's office, nor had he ever even met the man."

"Well," the sheriff said, "I heard that statement at the trial. But the hard evidence was there to be seen by all."

"Who found the evidence?"

"Mrs. Zack, of course. But she was with her maid when they made the discovery. Since a wife can't testify against her husband, the maid testified that she found the ore and the money clip in Jim Zack's possession."

"How neat and tidy," Longarm said cynically. "All right, let's assume the maid was telling the truth. That still doesn't address the obvious fact that either Mrs. Zack or Luther himself planted the evidence."

"No," the sheriff admitted, "it doesn't. But you have to remember this as well, Longarm. When I arrested Jim

136

Zack, he was blind drunk. A raving maniac. Somehow, he got a bottle into my jail the night before his trial, and when he went on the witness stand he was still drunk."

"Then it was either his wife or Luther who slipped it through the jail bars."

"Yeah," the sheriff said. "That's the way Dave and I figured it happened. Damn shame too."

"Don't tell me. Jim lost his temper and started cursing the judge."

"That's right," the sheriff said. "He was far more effective convicting himself than any prosecutor."

Longarm clenched his fists in anger. "He got drunk and he got angry and mean in a county courtroom, Sheriff. I'm not excusing that, but it hardly warrants a ten-year prison sentence, does it?"

"No," Pate admitted, "it does not. So what are you going to do now?"

"I have to somehow work on Mrs. Zack. Gain her confidence and then . . ."

"She won't give you the time of the day," the sheriff told him. "Sheila Zack is only interested in men with money."

"I have some money," Longarm said. "Almost four hundred dollars. Well," he amended, remembering the three prostitutes and the money he'd been spending in Virginia City and Carson City, "closer to three hundred."

The sheriff chuckled. "That wouldn't impress a woman like Sheila Zack. Not even for a minute. It will impress her even less when she learns that you are a federal marshal trying to clear a dear old friend who just happens to be the man she and her lover framed."

Longarm frowned. "I see what you mean. She'd avoid me like the plague. So what do you think?"

The sheriff laced his fingers behind his head and leaned back in his desk chair. "I dunno. I suppose, if you're really serious about this, you'll have to change your appearance and pose as something other than a lawman."

"You think it might work?"

"I think that it's your only shot at getting the woman to trust you and hang herself."

Longarm didn't like the way this was shaping up, but try as he might, he could see no alternatives. Sheila Zack was the key, not Gustav Luther.

"I'd need your help, Sheriff."

"Not a chance," the lawman said. "If this thing explodes in your face, I'm not losing my job because I conspired to trick either of those two polecats. If you do this, you are on your own."

Longarm pulled a cheroot out of his pocket, bit off the tip, and spat it on the floor. "What happened to professional courtesy between fellow lawmen, not to mention friends?"

Sheriff Pate flushed with anger, but also with embarrassment. "All right," he said, "I'll help, but only in secret. Nothing that either one of those rattlesnakes can use to get me thrown out of office."

"Thanks!"

"But in return," the sheriff said, "I want you to promise to get Dave on with the feds back in Denver."

"I can't promise that!"

"Then I can't help you."

Longarm swore. "All right," he said, "I think that I can do it. I'll pull out all the stops."

"You'll be doing the feds a huge favor," the sheriff said. "He'll make a fine United States deputy marshal."

"I know that," Longarm said. "Now, can you tell me about Mrs. Zack and what I'm going to have to do to gain her confidence?"

The sheriff pursed his lips. "To start with, you're going to have to come up with a new name and face."

"Agreed. Then what?"

"A new suit of expensive clothes. Longarm, this is going to cost you every cent you own and then some."

"I'll gladly pay if I can get my friend out of that prison."

"Very well," the sheriff sighed, pulling a pencil and paper out of his desk. "I'll write you a note to our best tailor and haberdashery. I'll just tell them you are a friend and to give you their best. After that, you'll become, oh, Curtis Longman."

"Fair enough. What am I supposed to do for a living?"

"Nothing," the sheriff said. "You're supposed to be rich. You're a big Denver cattle rancher as well as an investor and a ladies' man. You've just arrived on the Comstock Lode in search of fun and business opportunities."

"Sounds good," Longarm said. "Anything else?"

"You like blondes with big jugs. More specifically, you like beautiful women who look like Sheila Zack."

Longarm foresaw a problem. "I won't make love to her. Not as long as she's still married to Jim."

"If you were lucky enough to have chance to make love to Sheila, only a saint could resist."

"I'm no saint," Longarm said. "But I make it a point to try to avoid sleeping with married women—especially the ones married to my friends."

"I understand and respect that," the sheriff said. "But that could be trouble. Then again, it might not."

139

"I don't get it."

"It's simple," the sheriff said. "Sheila filed for a divorce right after her husband was sent to prison. For all I know, it has already been granted. I imagine she delayed it just long enough to gain complete title to all of her husband's assets."

"Rather than make love to the viper, I'll most likely have a hard time not strangling her," Longarm said.

The sheriff just shook his head and chuckled. "I think you might change your mind about that once you've laid eyes on Sheila."

"That pretty, huh?"

"Pretty? Would you call a work of art just 'pretty'?"

"No."

"And neither would any sighted man call Sheila Zack, or Ray or whatever, 'pretty.'"

Longarm dragged his wallet out of his pants. He counted his money and it came to $314 and some change. After he divulged that figure to the sheriff, Pate suggested, "Buy a new suit, boots, hat, and haircut. She'll finish off the rest of that in about two days—if you're lucky."

"Then I'll work fast."

"I'm sure you will," the sheriff said with a lecherous wink. "I tell you something, I wish that I was in—or out of—your new boots if you bag that viper between the sheets."

"It won't give me any pleasure," Longarm gritted. "The only satisfaction that woman can give me is evidence that will put her and Gustav Luther in prison and get Jim out."

"Sure," the sheriff said. "Good luck. I'd stay off C Street if you can because there might be a few people here besides myself who will recognize you. Unless you shave off that big mustache."

There was a cracked mirror on the sheriff's wall, and Longarm walked over to study his reflection. He wiggled his upper lip and watched his long handlebar mustache twitch. "I'm not too sure that I can part with it. We are sorta attached."

"Yes you can," the sheriff said. "All you have to do is think about your poor friend facing another nine and a half years in the pen."

"You're right," Longarm said with determination. "I'll have the damned thing whacked off when I get shaved. I'll think cattle ranching, and after I get my hair cut and outfitted with new duds, I'm going to look like a whole new man."

"I can hardly wait to see it," the sheriff said. "And I wish you all the luck in the world."

Longarm headed for the door but stopped quite abruptly. "Sheriff?"

"Yeah?"

"How do I meet this woman? I can't just sashay up to her door and knock, then introduce myself, now can I?"

"No," Pate said thoughtfully, "I suppose you can't."

"Then what?"

Pate grabbed his hat and came to the door. "I'll take care of the introduction part," he promised. "You just get gussied up and then go pay the damned woman your respects this afternoon. She'll be expecting you."

"Thanks," Longarm said gratefully.

"Don't forget about getting Dave that federal marshal's job. I expect you to take him with you when you leave for Denver."

"You must be sure that the city council will cut your budget."

"They already have," the sheriff said wearily. "The chairman told me on the sly that Dave will be gone as of next week."

"You tell him yet?"

"No, and I won't until you are finished and ready to leave. Until then, he's on *my* payroll. But don't let him know that."

"I won't. Damned nice of you to do that for the kid."

"Professional courtesy," Pate growled as he pushed Longarm out the door in the direction of the nearest barber.

Chapter 14

Longarm glanced at his image in a window as he strolled along A Street toward the fine two-story wooden-frame house which Sheila Zack had robbed from her imprisoned husband. The reflection he saw was that of a stranger. He hardly recognized himself. Longarm's prized handlebar mustache was missing, as were his long, unshorn locks.

In place of his boots, he wore expensive new shoes, and his dark-blue suit was a perfect fit, stylishly accentuating his narrow waist and broad shoulders. Longarm knew that he made a striking figure, and when a pair of ladies passed him, they gave him more than a cursory glance. His jowls were shaved to a shine, and he'd had the barber pat them with a manly-smelling lotion.

My, my, he thought, I look like a lamb heading for the slaughter.

When he knocked on Sheila Zack's front door, Longarm heard someone call, "I'll get it, Amanda!"

Longarm had a bouquet of flowers, and as the sound of footsteps grew louder, he raised them to his face and inhaled their perfume. He wished he knew what kind of introduction the sheriff had secured for him, but that would have to be a surprise in what promised to be a very interesting game. Just before the door opened, Longarm reminded himself again that it was essential that he did not reveal the intense dislike and revulsion he felt for this woman.

When the door opened a crack, Longarm stared at a sliver of feminine beauty that even the sheriff's warning had not quite prepared him for.

"Yes?"

"My name is Mr. Curtis Longman. I believe you were told I might stop by."

"Mr. Longman," the woman said, opening the door wide and smiling, "what a pleasure to meet you."

Longarm was dazzled by her beauty and, had he not known better, he would have believed her sincerity because it was so very convincing. Sheila was taller than average, buxom as he'd been told, and possessing a face whose description would challenge Shakespeare. She quite took Longarm's breath away for an instant.

"Forgive me for staring," he said. "It's rare that I've encountered such beauty."

She actually blushed. Then she boldly said, "I was told that you were a rancher and investor, but not such a flatterer."

When he could not think of another thing to say, Longarm extended the flowers. "They pale in comparison to you, Mrs. Zack."

"Miss Ray," she corrected. "I'm no longer married."

"Oh." Longarm smiled as his eyes played with hers. "Neither am I."

"Won't you come inside?"

"Thank you." Longarm removed a new cream-colored Stetson, and Amanda arrived to take it and place it on a hall tree.

"Won't you join me in the parlor," Sheila said. "Amanda, please bring us some refreshments."

Sheila turned to Longarm. "Tea, coffee, or something stronger?"

"What will you have?"

Sheila raised her eyebrows. "Why not French champagne?"

"That would be perfect," he said after a moment of deliberation, "and well suited to what I hope we will look back upon as a great occasion."

"So do I," Sheila said, turning to lead him up the hallway and into the parlor with a very provocative swing to her shapely hips.

Longarm didn't see his surroundings because they paled in the company of their owner. It took him but an instant to see how this cold-hearted witch could easily have destroyed poor Jim. Longarm had no trouble believing that, once this woman had a man by the heartstrings, she would be able to jerk him about like a wooden puppet.

"So," she said, turning around and catching his eyes glued to her deliciously shaped bottom, "I understand that you are interested in buying a hotel?"

"If the price is right."

"The price is *very* right," she said. "Were you told anything about the property?"

"Not much." Longarm knew at once that she was talking about Jim's hotel. "Not even the number of rooms or the asking price."

"Well," Sheila said, taking a glass for herself and waiting until Amanda had served her guest, "let's drink to a mutually satisfying sale between you and me."

"Why not," he said.

The champagne was pale, cold, and delicious, like the woman herself. Longarm knew he should sip, but he gulped. Amanda poured another glass, and Longarm watched the way Sheila's lips caressed the rim of her glass. He could feel a traitorous stirring in his loins.

"Now then," he said, "about this hotel of yours."

"Yes," she said with a sensuous smile, "it has sixteen beds."

"Sixteen."

"Uh-huh."

"Good beds?"

"Very good."

Longarm finished his champagne. He could feel it at work, stoking a fire in his belly. Or maybe it was Sheila's eyes or lips and the fire was being stoked beneath his belly by six inches. "What, uh, about the rest of your hotel?"

She tossed her golden mane and took a seat in a leather man's chair that reminded Longarm of his grim purpose.

"The hotel is only about five years old," she said. "My former husband bought it from a man named Abe Waters. Mr. Waters had it built right after the last fire swept through the town. We've had quite a few, you know."

"Most mining towns do," he said. "Cripple Creek and our other Colorado mining towns suffer devastating fires every few years."

"We have a new pumper and our volunteer fire department has largely been replaced by professionals," she said, trying to reassure him. "I don't think you'll have to worry about fires anymore."

"I hope not," he said. "I trust that you have a clear title. One which is yours alone to convey?"

She raised her glass. "Well, actually, the land title was in both my name and that of my ex-husband. But I have an attorney who straightened that out."

"How?" Longarm asked bluntly. "Didn't your ex-husband, even though he is in prison, still have to formally convey full right of ownership to you?"

"You know about him in prison?"

"The sheriff told me."

"I see," Sheila said. "But of course that's exactly what he did."

Longarm nodded. He was afraid to press the point too hard for fear of arousing her suspicions, but he needed to know what her design would be. Also, it occurred to him that he could catch her breaking the law. Forging her ex-husband's name to a change in the title of ownership would become very strong leverage to use against Sheila.

"Tell me about yourself, Mr. Longman."

"Not much to tell," he said, not wanting to talk about his imaginary self. "I'd rather know about you."

She laughed. "But I asked first."

"All right." Longarm let his imagination run amok. "I was raised in Texas, but I hclpcd my father drive a big trail herd up to Abilene after the war. When we sold our herd, we learned that we could have gotten twice as much per head in beef-starved Denver. So my father kept his crew, and then we went back to Texas and used all our profits to collect a much bigger herd. We drove it all the way to Denver."

"That must have been a very exciting experience."

"Exciting?" Longarm smiled a little sadly. "It was hard and filled with danger. The herd was repeatedly attacked by Comanche Indians. By the time we reached

147

Denver, there were only seven us left and my father lay buried somewhere up beside the Pecos River."

"I'm sorry. How old were you?"

"Barely in my teens," Longarm said. "My mother had died years earlier of the cholera down near Houston."

"No brothers or sisters?"

"No."

She looked intently at him. "How is it that such a fine figure of a man as yourself has not married?"

"I lost her to Indians too," Longarm said, deciding that sounded better than to say he'd never married.

"How tragic!" Sheila raised her glass for a refill and while Amanda was at it, Longarm did the same.

"It's hard," Longarm agreed. "I've got all the money I'll ever need, but no one besides myself to spend it on."

"What a pity!"

"Yeah, ain't that the truth."

Sheila came out of her chair and was instantly at Longarm's side. She leaned close. "I hope we can become more than just two lonely people who consummated the sale of a hotel."

"Me too," he said, feeling his mouth go dry with desire.

Longarm decided that things could get out of hand real fast with a combination of Sheila and champagne. He was going to have to get some breathing space and gather his senses. He was going to have to stop thinking about how fantastic it might be to make love to this goddess, and return to thinking instead about tricking her into giving him the proof he needed to get poor Jim out of prison.

"Listen," he said, setting his glass down and then coming to his feet. "Maybe what we ought to do is to

148

go take a look at that hotel right now."

"Sure! Why not? Amanda, Mr. Longarm and I are going over to the hotel . . . oh, wait!"

"What is it?"

Sheila sighed. "I'm afraid I've an appointment today. In fact, Mr. Luther should be showing up any minute now."

"Mr. Luther?" Longarm said with a gulp.

"Yes," Sheila said brightly. "My good friend." There was a grandfather clock in the parlor and she turned to it.

"Mr. Luther's stage should have arrived ten or twenty minutes ago. It's always a little late, but when he arrives, we could all go over together."

Longarm had to quell a sudden panic. If Gustav Luther saw him it wouldn't matter if he was missing his mustache and had a new set of clothes and a new name. Gustav would recognize him instantly and the game would be over. He'd never get into Sheila Ray's confidence, and poor Jim would rot in prison for another nine and a half years.

"Actually," Longarm said quite abruptly, "I have another appointment myself. In fact, I'm late."

"Oh, no," she said, genuinely disappointed.

"I'm afraid so. But I'll return soon."

"What about dinner tonight with Mr. Luther and myself?"

"Not a . . . I'm sorry. I'm all tied up."

"But . . ."

"I'll be in touch," Longarm said quickly, diving past the woman and heading down the hallway. "I have some other business I have to attend to, but I promise that your hotel is at the head of my investment interests."

Sheila Ray hurried after him, high heels clicking on the marble tile of the hallway. "Are you sure we can't at least have dinner!"

"Positive."

"Then what about tomorrow?"

"I have to run down to Gold Hill," he lied. "But I promise that I'll return very soon."

Just as he was about to leave, Sheila grabbed his sleeve and pulled him up short. "Mr. Longman," she said, looking hurt and confused. "I really hope that I haven't said or done anything to offend you. And I don't understand . . ."

Longarm knew that he had to offer some explanation for his sudden change in behavior. "It's the champagne," he said.

"The champagne?"

"I can't drink the stuff. Even when it's vintage. It gives me . . . well, I regard you too highly to explain further."

Understanding at last flickered in her sky-blue eyes. "Oh, I see. I think."

"Yes," he said grimly. "That's why I *must* hurry off."

"Of course! You poor, poor man!"

"I'll be fine. And in a few days I *will* return."

"Please do," Sheila said breathlessly.

Longarm hurried out the door, one hand on his stomach and body slightly bent over. He knew that he made a sad appearance, and when he was rounding the first corner with his head down, he caught a glimpse of Gustav Luther rapidly striding toward Sheila Ray's house.

The big mining engineer was practically running and there was a look of unconcealed lust on his rugged

150

face. Longarm could read and understand the cause of that lust. And he knew that Gustav Luther, despite his promise to marry dear Milly Taylor, was going to have a very active night with the beautiful blond woman who lived alone on A Street.

Chapter 15

Longarm kept vigil on Sheila's house. He changed out of his fancy clothes back into his regular outfit, and pretended to work on the axle of a broken-down wagon parked a half block away in an abandoned lot. As anticipated, Gustav Luther did not reappear all that day. However, the following morning Longarm was rewarded by seeing the mining engineer leave Sheila Ray's home. Longarm followed the man first to his little mining office, then to the stage depot.

Longarm hoped that Gustav was either taking the stage back to Reno or else heading for Paiute Pass. Either way, it was essential that the man not be around Sheila Ray for a while if Longarm was to get anywhere proving Jim Zack innocent of the robbery charges.

It was Longarm's intention to wait near the stage unseen until Luther boarded, then to learn the man's destination. But intentions don't always work out as planned. Longarm blinked with surprise to see Henry Fry moving purposefully toward the engineer. From the young man's pale and determined expression, Longarm knew that Henry Fry was not going to exchange pleasantries. A moment later Henry's purpose became chillingly clear when Longarm saw that the young man was holding a derringer.

Longarm moved swiftly. He cut across the street toward the stage depot knowing that, if Gustav spotted him, the game was up. But Longarm also knew he had to stop Henry from killing the engineer. If Henry did that, he'd most likely be sentenced to hang. Longarm didn't want that to happen.

So focused on the mining engineer was Henry that he did not see Longarm until the marshal grabbed his arm and tore the derringer out of Henry's fist.

Longarm dragged the surprised jeweler off behind an empty stagecoach and hissed, "What the hell were you going to do!"

"What do you think," Henry snarled through clenched teeth and his broken jaw.

Longarm swore softly. "You'd be sentenced to hang for murder."

"I don't care."

"You'd better care," Longarm grated. "We're going to put Luther in prison rather than a coffin. Believe me, it's a far worse punishment."

Henry struggled with his anger and frustration. After a moment, he blinked, studied Longarm, and said, "Why'd you cut off your mustache?"

"Never mind that for the moment," Longarm answered, emptying the derringer into the dirt. "Were you really crazy enough to shoot Luther down in cold blood!"

"I was doing it for Miss Taylor!"

"You fool!"

"Oh, yeah, well, I killed two others that probably weren't as evil."

"I know," Longarm said, remembering what Milly had

154

told him about her narrow escape from the Truckee River. "But that was a lot different."

"Why?"

"Because they tried to rape and kill Milly!"

"Well, Luther is going to break her heart and kill her too! Only, he's going to take his time and do it slow!"

Longarm could see that Henry was not in a reasonable frame of mind. "All right," he said, dragging the young man off further away where they would not be overheard. "Listen to me. I'm going to send Luther to prison or to the morgue, *his* choice. But I'm going to do it so that justice is served and I won't put a noose around my own neck."

"How do you propose to do that?"

Longarm took a deep breath. "It's going to take a little doing, but I promise that it will happen. Do you want to do it my way, or do I have to drag you off to jail?"

"You don't leave me much choice," Henry said, snatching back his empty derringer.

"That's right."

"I'll help you," Henry said after a few moments. "But if your way fails, then I'll kill that sonofabitch, I swear I will, and I won't be stopped a second time."

Longarm scowled. "Some men are just bound and determined to get themselves in trouble. Come along with me while we talk."

The stagecoach rolled out of Virginia City with Gustav Luther looking as if he was going to collapse from weariness. It made Longarm wonder what Sheila was looking like, and he thought perhaps he would like to find out for himself.

"Could you tell me where that stage was bound?" Longarm asked the ticket man.

"Well, first it rolls down to Reno, then it doubles back

155

and heads for Franktown and then down to Carson City and Genoa before it . . ."

"Thanks," Longarm said, taking Henry's arm and leading him off down the street.

"Here's what you are going to do," Longarm said. "You're going to take the next stagecoach back to Reno and keep an eye on that man."

"I'll be happy to," Henry said ominously.

"But don't kill him!" Longarm grabbed the young man by the shoulders. "I promise that he'll get his due if you don't interfere. Will you swear not to shoot him?"

"All right," Henry said reluctantly. "But it won't be easy."

"Nothing worthwhile in life is quick or easy," Longarm said. "But putting a man like Gustav Luther behind bars will be the worst punishment we could inflict."

Henry nodded his head. "Yeah," he said, "a big dandy like that who thinks women live and breathe for the sight of him, sure. Prison would be real hard on Luther."

"Now you're making sense," Longarm said with relief. "So lay low. I'll stay up here a little while longer until I do what is necessary."

"Which is?"

"Get proof that Luther and a woman named Sheila Ray rigged a case of grand larceny in order to send an innocent man to prison. Then they consorted to rob that man of his assets."

"And that will get them a stiff prison sentence?"

"You bet it will," Longarm vowed.

A few minutes later, he left Henry at the stage depot and went back to a boarding house on B Street where he was staying. There he changed back into his new finery, and went to pay Sheila Ray a visit.

When she opened her door and saw him, Longarm had an unguarded moment where he saw the beautiful woman's rough edges. Sheila's blue eyes were ringed with dark circles and although she smiled in greeting, it was clear that she was exhausted. Longarm could only imagine what a strenuous night of lovemaking had taken place upstairs in the bedroom.

"Mr. Longman," she said, "what an unexpected pleasure! I didn't expect to see you for a few days."

"Well, my business in Gold Hill ended rather abruptly and I wanted to see you as soon as possible. Would another time be more convenient?"

"Of course not," she said not very convincingly as she led him up the hallway and back into the parlor.

"Would you like something besides champagne to drink?"

"How about coffee?"

"Me too," she said, calling for Amanda.

The maid took Sheila's order. She was a frumpy-looking woman with a habitually sour expression. In her mid-fifties, Amanda appeared drab and embittered. Longarm thought it might be because she was so unappealing in comparison with her lovely employer.

"Good morning, Amanda," Longarm said. "Thank you for the coffee."

The maid managed the slightest hint of a nod. She poured their coffee and marched out of the room.

"Is Amanda always so cheerful?" Longarm asked in jest.

"She's just angry all the time," Sheila said. "If she wasn't such a good cook and housekeeper, I'd have fired her after my husband left. He adored Amanda. Hired her over my objections and coddled

157

the damned woman. Why, he treated her almost like family!"

"How outrageous," Longarm said with mock concern.

"Yes," Sheila said. "I've been looking for someone to replace her and I think I've found just the person."

"Excellent!"

"She's from Reno. Mr. Luther referred her. An older woman but one who can actually seem pleasant."

"Is Amanda aware that she is about be out of a job?"

"I don't know," Sheila confessed. "She may look stupid, but she's not. And although I've tried to keep interviews and inquiries from her, I suspect that she does know she'll soon be out in the street."

Longarm nodded while his mind began to whirl with possibilities.

Sheila settled wearily into a leather chair and smiled at Longarm. "But you didn't come to discuss the trouble I'm having with my household help."

"No," he said. "I came to discuss business, but you do appear somewhat exhausted, Miss Ray. Difficult night?"

She blinked and her smile died. "What is *that* supposed to mean?"

"Insomnia," he said with feigned innocence. "My guess is that you did not sleep well."

"Yes," she said quickly, "I did sleep badly. Up most of the night."

"Too bad," he consoled. "Then I suppose that this is not a very good time to go see that hotel."

She wanted to sell it bad enough that she almost shook her head and resigned herself to taking him. But she just couldn't.

Placing her coffee on a chairside table, she said, "Mr. Longman, would you mind terribly if we waited until this

158

evening? I do feel very tired and I'm going to take a long nap."

"An excellent idea," Longarm said, sipping on his coffee. "I suppose that Mr. Luther might join us for dinner?"

"I'm afraid that he has gone back to Reno. This was just a quick business trip. After Reno, he has to hurry off to Paiute Pass, where he has mining interests."

"I'm sorry that I'm going to miss him," Longarm said.

"Yes. I think you and Mr. Luther would have much in common."

"Really?"

"Yes."

"Like what, for instance?"

"Like . . . oh, you're both big and successful men."

Longarm laughed outright. "Then we might very well realize it and become, well, competitive."

"But you have nothing to compete for," she told him.

Longarm placed his coffee cup down and walked over to Sheila. He pulled her gently to her feet and put his arms around her waist, then pressed her body to his own.

"Let's not kid ourselves about that, all right?"

Her eyes were round with surprise, and they stayed that way until Longarm kissed the viper's lovely mouth. Then she closed her eyes and melted against him. For a few moments, they were locked in a hard embrace and when it broke, Sheila was breathing heavily.

"I think we had better part for a little while, Mr. Longman," she whispered. "Although I'm not sure that I am going to be able to sleep now."

"Try," he urged. "You're going to need to be awake for tonight."

Sheila actually blushed just before Longarm placed his hand on her breast, then turned on his heel and went

159

out the door calling, "I'll be back at five o'clock!"

"So what kind of evidence do you expect that I can get out of Sheila this evening?" Longarm asked the sheriff while his young deputy listened intently. "Just a confidential confession won't send her and Luther to prison."

"That's right," the sheriff said. "It's going to take some physical evidence. Maybe a note or paper with a forgery."

"That's possible," Longarm said, "but it would be almost impossible to prove that Jim didn't steal that ore and money clip."

"What about her maid?" Dave said. "Doesn't she have a maid named Amanda and wouldn't that woman have probably seen something?"

Longarm snapped his fingers. "Dave, you and I think along the same lines. Yes! And even if Amanda did not witness the actual transfer of the ore and money clip to Jim's office, then at least she'd likely have overheard something!"

The sheriff nodded. "If you could get the woman to testify against them . . . but why should she?"

"Because," Longarm said, "she doted on Jim Zack and she despises Sheila Ray."

"How do you know that?" Dave asked.

"Because Sheila as much as told me. And if that wasn't enough, you can read the hatred in Amanda's eyes. And more. Sheila's going to replace Amanda, and Amanda probably knows it."

"Then it might work," the sheriff said. "When can you get to Amanda?"

Longarm steepled his fingertips. "I assume that the woman lives in a maid's quarters in that house. Correct?"

"Correct," the sheriff said.

"Then I'll pay her a late night visit."

"But . . . but how will you get in the house?"

Longarm winked. "I'll just wait until Sheila falls asleep and tiptoe down to the maid's quarters."

The sheriff and his deputy both reacted with surprise, and then they began to chuckle. Finally Dave said, "Rough bit of work, eh, Longarm?"

He grinned with anticipation. "Yes, especially considering that I am on vacation."

Chapter 16

Sheila stood in the lobby of the little two-story hotel with Longarm. Her eyes were bright and luminous for she had consumed a fair amount of wine during an expensive dinner which had set Longarm back a month's pay.

"Well," she said, "what do you think?"

"It's very nice," Longarm said, pivoting around in a full circle to study the hotel lobby.

"It was just repainted about eight months ago by Jim," she said. "He spent almost a thousand dollars in repairs. New curtains everywhere, a new furnace in the basement. A new roof that won't leak."

"It looks to be in very good condition," Longarm said.

He was impressed. The lobby was tastefully decorated in a soft green with heavy curtains, a polished hardwood floor with expensive throw rugs, and some very nice furniture for the guests.

"As you can easily see," Sheila told him, "we cater to the upper class. Visitors with money. No working-class miners or other riffraff who get drunk and want to destroy the place."

Longarm looked at a very impressive stairway with a gleaming mahogany railing. Sheila followed his eyes.

"There are eight rooms on this floor. One for the manager, of course."

"Of course."

"And eight more upstairs. They have all been redecorated. I chose all the new furnishings as well as the color patterns upstairs," Sheila said proudly.

"Then I'd like to see them," Longarm told her. "What I've seen down here is first class. You have wonderful taste, Miss Ray."

She blushed, genuinely flattered. "I rather think that I should have taken it up in a place like New York, Boston, or San Francisco," she told him. "I would probably have been extremely successful."

"Without question."

"Look," she said, taking his arm. "I painted this landscape. Do you like it?"

She led him over to a painting that was somewhat obscured by the stairwell. Longarm stared at an ornately framed landscape of what he thought was supposed to be Lake Tahoe with its blue water and heavily forested ring of mountains. In truth, it was a terrible oil painting. It revealed no talent, and he would have expected that it had been done by an unskilled child.

"Very nice!"

She beamed. "Oh, I knew you'd recognize it for its impressionistic qualities. Jim hated my paintings, even though he'd never come right out and say so. But Gustav is like you—he appreciates good art."

"I'm sure," Longarm said drily.

Sheila took his arm and led him up the stairs. She was fairly quivering with excitement. "Our Presidential Suite isn't occupied tonight so I can show it to you. I had complete charge of its decoration and I spared no expense to make it unforgettable."

"Then I am filled with anticipation, my dear."

She giggled and almost dragged him upstairs. When she opened the suite, Longarm stepped inside the most garish aberration imaginable. The room had been decorated in a cheap pseudo-Roman decor complete with plaster pillars and a four-foot statue of a centurion with his sword held aloft. At his feet lay a vanquished figure with his mouth grotesquely twisted in what Longarm supposed was a dying scream.

"Do you like it?" she asked eagerly.

"I'm never seen anything its equal," he told her truthfully as they ducked under a ridiculous grape arbor and beheld a Roman bath with gold fixtures and heavy velvet curtains the color of burgundy wine.

Longarm could feel her holding her breath waiting for more praise. "It's . . . it's unforgettable," he said.

"Oh," she breathed, "I knew that you'd love it!"

She took his hand and pulled him into a second room, which held a bed of massive proportions. It was suspended from the ceiling by gold braids, and over its head was a horrible painting of two Romans coupling in an amphitheater while a crowd cheered. It was either that, Longarm decided, or a dogfight in an open pit surrounded by frenzied bettors. The painting was so awful that Longarm just could not be sure.

"Do you like it?" she asked breathlessly.

"I've never seen anything like it."

She shivered like a puppy being praised and grabbed Longarm, then began to rip off his coat and shirt.

"Easy," he said, thinking about how much he'd paid for these clothes just so he could deceive this woman. "Easy."

"Easy, hell!" she panted, throwing herself onto the bed and clawing at her own clothes. "This room has always made me feel wild."

"Me too," he said, feeling wild to get the hell out of the monstrosity.

She was tearing off her dress when Longarm stepped back. "First business, then pleasure, Miss Ray."

"What!"

Longarm took a contract from the inside of his coat pocket that the sheriff had gotten a friendly attorney to draw up. It stated that Sheila was the sole owner of the hotel. "This is a sale contract for this hotel."

"Can't we talk money later?" she pleaded, already nearly undressed.

"No," he said sternly despite the fact that his insides were melting with lust. "What is your price?"

"Five thousand!"

"Agreed." Longarm whipped a pen from his pocket and smoothed the contract out on the bed. "Sign it and I'll deliver the money tomorrow."

She glanced at the contract, her breath coming fast. "Where's the price?"

Longarm found the blank space and filled it in with the words "FIVE THOUSAND DOLLARS CASH."

Sheila signed the contract with a flourish and then tore off the last of her undergarments. She twisted her head back and stared up at the bacchanalian scene she had created on canvas.

"Hurry, my Roman gladiator!"

Longarm had been called many things, but never a Roman gladiator. It didn't matter. He quickly undressed, and she grabbed his manhood and stuffed it into her

166

honeypot the way a starving man would stuff bread into his maw.

"Show me no mercy, Gladiator!"

"Right," Longarm gritted, thinking about his poor old friend rotting in prison.

Longarm took her hard and rough. He punished her with his thick rod until she cried out, but even as she did, Sheila was laughing and smiling. She was loving it.

For three hours Longarm took the woman until she whimpered and begged him to stop. He did, and then he had to practically dress her and carry her out of the hotel and back to her house.

It was long after midnight when Longarm, listening to Sheila's soft snoring, eased out of her bed, dressed, and then went down to the maid's quarters.

Amanda was snoring much louder than Sheila. Longarm found a candle, lit it, and then went over to clamp a hand over the woman's mouth. "Wake up!"

The maid tried to scream. Amanda would have screamed loud enough to rouse the dead if Longarm hadn't smothered her voice.

"I'm a United States marshal," he said, "and the only person in the world that Jim Zack can still call his true friend. Except maybe you. Do you want to listen and help him?"

Amanda nodded. Longarm hoped the woman was not going to prove deceptive. He removed his hand from her mouth. She stared up at him with a mixture of fear and loathing.

"Mr. Longman, if you try to take me by force, I will bite you!"

He shook his head. "Believe me, that is not my intention. What I need from you is certainly not related to the

167

flesh, but instead to justice. Justice for Jim Zack. I *am* his last friend and I know that he was framed on that robbery charge. Isn't that true?"

She gulped.

"Please," he begged, "you must have seen something. If you don't tell me the truth, then . . ."

"You said that you were a United States marshal. I want to see your badge."

"I don't have it with me."

"Then . . ."

"Sheriff Pate and his deputy will vouch for me. Now, will you help Jim Zack if we promise to protect you from harm?"

She nodded. "I can help. I ain't got a job here after next week anyhow. Sure!"

As ugly as the maid was, Longarm could have kissed her sour puss. "Get dressed. I'll be outside and we'll go visit the sheriff, and then all go find the judge that sentenced Jim."

Two hours later, a very unhappy judge sat in his pajamas and listened while Amanda told a shocking story of deceit. When it was all over, Longarm looked at the judge, then at the sheriff.

"Well, gentlemen," he said, "I don't think that there is much doubt that we have a creditable witness and that an innocent man has been imprisoned."

The judge drummed his stubby fingers on his desk. He leaned forward and glared at Amanda, who glared right back at him.

"Miss . . ."

"Watson. Amanda Watson."

"Well, Miss Watson."

"*Missus* Watson. I'm a widow."

"Whatever," the judge groused. "The point is this—you'll have to be willing to swear out a signed testimony stating exactly what you have told me about the night that Mr. Gustav Luther and Mrs. Sheila Zack planted the incriminating evidence that sent Mr. Zack to the Nevada State Prison."

"Her name is now Miss Ray," Amanda corrected. "She dumped Mr. Zack after she and that tawdry mining engineer started cattin' around behind Mr. Zack's back."

"Yes, well, never mind that. The point is, has Mr. Zack been wrongly accused and sentenced?"

"He's as innocent as a babe," Amanda declared. "I'll swear to that in court."

"And I have this contract for the sale of the hotel she illegally tried to sell me last night on her signature alone," Longarm said. "I checked at the county courthouse beforehand, and the property is registered in her husband's name."

"Let me see that," the judge demanded.

Longarm showed the judge the contract he had gotten Sheila to sign. When the judge had finished reading it, he said, "This is a legal document, properly drawn."

"Then at the very least, we have her for grand larceny," Longarm said.

"So it would seem," the judge agreed. "I'm really surprised and shocked by this evidence. Mrs. Zack is a very beautiful as well as intelligent woman."

"She's a greedy bitch!" Amanda snapped.

The judge looked pained. "All right, Sheriff," he said. "Come by my office tomorrow morning at nine o'clock sharp and I'll sign a warrant authorizing you to arrest both Miss Ray and Mr. Luther."

Longarm protested. "Time is of the essence, Your Honor! Can't you please go with us over there tonight and put that warrant in our hands?"

"In the middle of the night? Hell, no!"

"But it'll be daybreak in just three hours," Longarm argued.

"And I'll be sleeping," the judge snapped, pushing himself erect with a yawn. "Nine o'clock and not a minute before. Good night!"

Longarm knew that it would be futile and quite possibly dangerous to push this lazy, stubborn judge any harder. Apparently the sheriff had reached the same conclusion, for he said, "We'll see you then, Judge."

Outside, Longarm turned to Amanda. "Are you going back to your room?"

"No," she said. "I . . . I wouldn't feel right about it considering that I just squealed on her and Mr. Luther."

"You can come on over to my office," Sheriff Pate said. "Sleep on the cot. I've no prisoners to disturb you."

"You mean in a *cell?*"

The sheriff nodded. "It's just for a few hours. After that, Sheila Ray or whatever the hell her real name is will trade places with you."

Amanda liked the sound of that. She actually could smile, and she said, "Lead the way, Sheriff!"

Longarm went with them when the sheriff promised him free coffee. "I just wish the judge would have issued those warrants now instead of later."

"You told me Sheila would sleep late," the sheriff said with a sly wink.

"She will," Longarm said. "It's guaranteed."

Chapter 17

Milly awoke to hear a banging on the front door. She groaned and tried to ignore the sound, but it grew louder and louder. Finally, Milly roused herself enough to jab Gustav with her elbow.

"Someone is pounding on your front door."

Gustav groaned and opened one eye. "For crissakes, it's just getting light outside!"

"I know that. You know that. But whoever is downstairs beating on your door doesn't know it!"

Gustav swore. "Would you . . ."

"No," Milly said, "I won't go open it. Whoever is down there wants *you,* not me. So you'd better get up."

"Maybe they'll go away," Gustav said, closing his eyes.

But the banging downstairs, if anything, grew louder and more insistent. Finally, Milly piled out of bed, grabbed a wrapper, and headed for the staircase. "All right!" she yelled. "All right! I'm coming!"

Milly was furious with Gustav. "Next time, *you* answer your own door!"

Downstairs, the banging sounded even louder. Milly, still half asleep, almost tripped and went tumbling down the stairs. When she reached the front door, she shouted,

"Who the hell is it at this hour!"

"Sheila Ray! Open up!"

"Go away!" Milly yelled.

"I have to speak to Gustav!"

Milly yanked the door open to confront a stunningly beautiful woman. "Who are you?"

"Miss Sheila Ray," the woman said, her hair wild-looking and her expression worried and suspicious. "Who are *you*?"

"I'm Mr. Luther's fiancée," Milly said.

"Fiancée?" The beautiful blonde laughed coldly. "Honey, if Gustav marries anyone, it'll be *me,* not some chippie like you."

Milly launched herself at the woman. Her fingernails clawed Sheila's cheek and left three furrows of blood. The woman cried out in pain, then doubled up her fist and punched Milly in the side of the head, and the war was on as both women, screeching and clawing, crashed to the floor inside the front door.

Milly had been in fights before with other prostitutes, and although her opponent was a little bigger and stronger, Milly was so infuriated that she quickly took control of the fight. She managed to get the blonde under her, and then she sat up and pounded her lovely face until Sheila begged for mercy.

"Who are you!" Milly demanded, fists cocked and ready to rain down again on the blonde, whose lips were bleeding and whose marked and lumpy face was already starting to swell like a purple berry.

"I'm Miss Ray!" the woman cried. "Get off me! Gustav, help!"

Milly was just about to tell her that Gustav could not help when suddenly she heard him behind her. Milly twisted around, still sitting on the beaten woman.

"Gustav, who . . ."

Milly didn't have time to finish the question because Gustav's fist exploded against her jaw. One second she was furious and demanding and explanation; the very next moment she was plummeting into darkness.

Gustav grabbed Sheila and hauled her to her feet. The woman was crying and cursing. Gustav shook her violently. "What the hell!" he roared. "Are you crazy coming here!"

"I *had* to talk to you!" Sheila wailed. "Gustav, I think we're in big trouble! I think that Amanda has betrayed me and told the sheriff and Judge Wilson that we planted those gold nuggets and your money clip in Jim's desk."

"What!"

"I . . . it's a long story!" Sheila cried. "And my face, it's bleeding!"

Sheila staggered further into the house weeping. Gustav slammed the door. He knelt beside Milly, who was unconscious. Gustav shuddered because, in a terrible fit of anger, he'd struck the girl hard enough to kill her. Fortunately, she was alive, but now he was not at all sure what he was going to do with Milly. When she awakened, Gustav knew there would be hell to pay.

"I need a brandy," he said, stumbling past Sheila and going to his study.

"And I need a doctor!" Sheila wailed in pain and anger as she charged after him.

Gustav poured his brandy and tossed it down. He poured them both a brandy, and then he wet a rag and handed it to Sheila. "You look like you've been wrestling with a lion," he said, watching the woman cover her bloodied face with the wet rag.

Sheila stopped crying to glare at him. "You are the coldest-hearted sonofabitch I've *ever* known! Who is that woman!"

"She's nothing," Gustav said. "Just some tramp that I met in Denver and who followed me here looking for a wealthy husband who'd give her respectability and a few brats to raise."

"Why didn't you send her packing when she showed up at your door?"

"Because she's a wildcat in a fight—or in my bed," he said recklessly.

"You bastard!"

"Stop it!" he shouted. "What the hell is happening up in Virginia City!"

In a few broken words, Sheila related how she'd awakened to find Longman gone as well as her maid, Amanda. Confused and worried, she'd dressed and gone out only to see the pair, now accompanied by the sheriff, all going to pay a noctural visit to Judge Wilson.

"When I saw them together, I just panicked and ran to the stable and had my buggy hitched. Then I came here."

"Damn," Gustav muttered, shaking his head back and forth.

"Was I wrong to come running? What other reason could they have for getting together in the middle of the night!"

"None," Luther hissed. "Dammit, anyway! You were sleeping with the law?"

"I didn't know he was a lawman!" she cried. "I still don't for certain. He said his name was Curtis Longman and he—"

"Curtis Longman!"

"Yes." Sheila dabbed at her broken lips. "He said he was

174

a rancher and investor from Denver."

Gustav swore violently. "He's a United States marshal from Denver, you fool!"

"How do you know that for sure?"

"Describe this Longman fellow."

Sheila began to tremble. "Taller than you. Rugged and handsome. In his thirties."

"That is *definitely* Marshal Custis Long!" Gustav exploded. "And now he's on to us!"

"This is a nightmare," Sheila wailed, covering her disfigured face. "How was I to guess he was out to trap us when I sold him the hotel!"

"Oh, sweet mercy," Gustav muttered. "This whole thing is coming unraveled. I told you that hotel was still your husband's until we could get the court to change title. So why did you try and sell it?"

Sheila clamped her bloodied hands to her ears. "Stop yelling at me!"

Gustav glared at the woman. "You haven't the brains God gave a goose! And now, you're not even pretty with your face all marked up and misshapen."

Something snapped in Sheila. With a screech, she threw herself forward so abruptly that she caught Gustav by surprise as he was turning to go upstairs and pack.

"Ouch! Damn you!"

Gustav backhanded the woman to the floor. He continued upstairs and began to pack his bags. Sheila, dazed, came stumbling up to watch. "Where are you going?"

He whirled on her. "I'm getting the hell out of here before that marshal comes to arrest me, of course!"

"Take me with you."

"Hell, no!"

175

She threw herself at him. "Please! I swear I'll help you. And I'll treat you right."

He knocked her aside and sneered. "What more can you do than you already have?"

Sheila took a step back and her lips twisted into a threat. "If you don't take me with you, I'll tell the marshal everything."

Gustav finished packing. When he turned, Sheila was blocking the bedroom door, and he warned, "Get out of my way."

"No! Gustav, we have to stick together. If we keep our stories—"

"We're finished," he said, cutting her off. "I told you to fire that damned maid a long time ago. But you wouldn't do it."

"I'm sorry!"

Gustav dressed quickly saying, "Sorry won't keep us from going to the state prison in Carson City. Amanda has talked! We're finished."

"Gus, you aren't leaving me all alone to face the consequences. It was *your* idea that we frame Jim. Not mine!"

"Prove it," he said with a wicked grin. "You signed an illegal contract to sell a hotel you don't even own yet. That constitutes hard evidence that will be used against you. All they can get me for is fraud, and that won't be easy to prove. Not if I've got enough money to hire smart lawyers and file appeals."

Gustav grabbed up his bag. "Get out of my way, Missus Zack!"

Sheila's hand flew into her dress pocket, and Gustav lunged for her as the derringer came into view. They collided in the upstairs hallway and went hurtling into the rail.

The derringer roared between them and Gustav felt a

searing pain in his groin. He howled and hurled the woman away. Sheila struck the upstairs landing rail with such force that it broke, and she disappeared with a scream that abruptly ended with the sound of her body striking the floor.

Grabbing his crotch and doubled over in agony, Gustav collapsed to his knees. He inched over to the broken railing and peered down at Sheila, who lay in a rapidly expanding pool of her own blood.

"Oh, no," Gustav moaned, unbuttoning his pants and staring with horror down at the damage her bullet had wrought on its way between his legs.

Gustav had seen a lot of blood and pain, but at the sight of his own mangled manhood, he almost fainted. Gasping and trying to remain conscious, he cupped himself, then headed back into the bedroom. He tore sheets apart and pressed them to himself, ranting and cursing.

"Gotta get out of here," he whispered over and over. "Got to get money out of my office here and in Paiute Pass before I run!"

Somehow, he got the bleeding stopped. Every movement was an agony, especially descending the staircase. He passed by Sheila's body without a glance, but stopped beside the unconscious form of Milly Taylor.

"You were the best of them," he muttered.

Doubled up with pain and holding his satchel, Gustav Luther staggered out the door in the direction of his office. He would get into his safe, take whatever money was left, then take Sheila's buggy on down to Paiute Pass, where he had more money waiting.

He'd make it if he didn't bleed to death. There was, by his own reckoning, about a thousand dollars in his office safe at Paiute Pass. That, coupled with the money he had in his office up the street, would give him the means to escape to California, and then perhaps even to South America.

Or back to Boston! Yes, Gustav thought, back home where a family fortune awaited him. And a surgeon skilled enough to reconstruct his most prized piece of anatomy.

Gustav took hope as daybreak was unfolding. But no matter how great his pain, everything depended on getting out of Reno fast. For the stakes had risen quite dramatically. He had not really meant to push Sheila to her death, but what court would believe that considering the web of deceit that he and that foolish bitch had diabolically conceived on the Comstock Lode?

Chapter 18

By the time Longarm and the sheriff had gotten their damned warrant for Sheila Ray's arrest at nine o'clock, the woman was long gone. A quick stop at the livery revealed that the woman had raced out of town in the middle of the night in her buggy.

"She's bolted and run," Sheriff Pate had said, proclaiming the obvious. "She's gone to warn Gustav Luther."

"Maybe we can still catch her," Longarm had replied. "But I'll need a horse. In fact, two horses to relay down to Reno. With luck, I'll catch them both."

But when Longarm galloped into Reno and found Luther's house, he also found a crowd of morbid spectators. Spotting Milly being supported by Henry Fry, Longarm pushed through the crowd. He saw the livid purplish bruise on Milly's jaw.

"What happened?" he demanded.

Milly turned and threw her arms around Longarm. "It's awful," she said. "Gustav knocked me out cold and then he threw a woman off the upstairs balcony. She's dead."

"A pretty blonde?"

"Yes," Milly said. "She arrived at dawn and had to see Gustav. I tried to stop her and we had a fight. I got knocked

179

out, and they must have gone upstairs but then gotten into another fight. When I awakened . . .”

Milly squeezed her eyes shut. “It was awful. I wouldn’t wish that kind of a death on anyone.”

Longarm looked into the house. The local lawmen were prowling around inside. He turned back to Milly. “Has anyone said anything about where Luther might have headed?”

“I don’t know,” Milly said.

Longarm gently disengaged himself from her arms. “Take care of her,” he told Henry.

“For the rest of her life,” Henry vowed. He raised his chin and pushed out his chest. “I’m going to marry her, Marshal Long.”

Milly sniffled. “That’s right. I *did* promise I’d marry you if Gustav threw me over, didn’t I.”

“Yes, ma’am. And I’ll treat you like a lady. You’ll never go for wanting anything I can honestly provide.”

Milly managed a brave smile. She hugged Henry, and Longarm heard her whisper, “You’re a fine man, Henry. And I’ll promise to learn to love you for as long as we both shall live.”

Despite the grimness of the situation, Milly’s fervent pledge caused Longarm to smile. “You’re finally seeing things clearly,” he said to the girl. “You two take care of each other.”

“What about you?” Milly asked.

“I’m going to see if anyone knows where Gustav Luther ran after he killed Sheila Ray.”

When Longarm went inside and explained the reason for his intrusion, the sheriff was cooperative but not especially helpful. “We don’t know where Luther went,” he admitted. “I sent a deputy over to the man’s office, but

180

he was gone and the safe was empty. My guess is that he headed for California. Could have chosen any number of mountain passes."

"What have you done so far to catch the man?"

The sheriff frowned. "Marshal, so far I'm just finishing up with the poor victim's body. Later, I'll get to the issue of Gustav Luther and send telegrams to the officials in Sacramento and San Francisco as well as to Salt Lake City, Denver, and every other town that's got a telegraph office within five hundred miles of here."

"What about Paiute Pass?"

"No telegraph." The sheriff frowned. "Besides, why would he go down there?"

"Why not?"

"All right," the sheriff said with a deep sigh. "Next stage that goes down, I'll send a deputy. I think it's a waste of taxpayers' money, but I'll do it anyway."

Longarm nodded, but he was not pleased. "Thanks."

He started to turn, but then stopped and said, "May I take a look at the victim?"

"Sure, but it's not pretty."

Longarm walked over to Sheila and pulled up the blanket that covered her upper body. He ground his teeth and steeled his nerve. Less than twelve hours earlier he had been humping this beauty, and even though she was a cold-blooded viper, Sheila had not deserved such an awful fate.

The sheriff came over and said, "They must have had a hell of a fight. You can see how her face is all beaten to a pulp and her cheeks are scratched. Makes you wonder why a man would do a thing like that to any woman."

"Yes," Longarm agreed, deciding that it had been Milly who'd inflicted most of the scratches if not the facial pummeling.

Longarm went back outside to find that Milly and Henry were walking up the street. He hurried to catch up with them.

"Milly!"

She stopped and turned. Longarm said, "Do you have any idea where Gustav might have gone?"

"No. Not a clue."

"What about the woman? Did she arrive in a buggy?"

Milly frowned. "Come to think of it, I did see a buggy out in front when I opened the door. Why . . . do you think Gustav took her buggy?"

"Why not?"

Longarm strode back to the front of the house. The buggy tracks were fresh but pretty badly trampled by the spectators. No matter. They were easy enough to follow, and Longarm did follow them to the Bonanza Mining Company.

The sheriff had already told him that the office safe had been emptied, so Longarm did not even bother to go inside. Instead his eyes followed the buggy tracks, and they led toward Six Mile Canyon.

"He's going to Paiute Pass," Longarm muttered as he prodded his horse into a trot with a fresh animal trailing along behind.

It took Longarm the entire day to reel Gustav Luther into his sights. In the dying light of the sun, the mining man was pushing his poor carriage horse to its limits, but the ground was soft with sand this far south and Longarm was traveling light and fast.

He rode to within a quarter mile of the mining engineer before he was spotted. Luther used a whip to push his exhausted horse into a shambling run, but it didn't do much good. Longarm drew his six-gun, and quickly closed the distance between himself and the killer.

At seventy yards, Longarm fired a warning shot over Luther's head. "Pull that horse up!" he shouted. "You're under arrest for fraud, grand larceny, and murder!"

Luther had other plans for himself. He twisted around in the buggy seat, raised his six-gun, and began to fire. One of his shots put a hole in Longarm's fancy new Stetson, and another took a notch out of the right ear of his horse.

Longarm knew that he could not afford to wait and see if all six shots were going to be wide of their mark. Almost with resignation, he aimed and fired twice. His first bullet missed, but his second drilled Luther through his broad chest, and the man dropped his lines and toppled across the seat of the buggy.

Longarm galloped up and grabbed the bit of the carriage horse. He dragged it to a standstill, and looked down to see that Luther was still alive, but just barely.

Hopping into the carriage next to the dying man, Longarm peered into Luther's gray face and said, "Up until you killed Sheila, you'd have gotten out of this with little more than a slap on the wrist and maybe a light jail sentence."

The man glared up with defiance. "I didn't mean to kill her! She went crazy on me!"

Longarm noticed that Luther's pants were soaked with fresh blood. "Who shot you, Milly or Sheila?"

"Sheila! She shot off half my cock and one of my balls!"

Longarm shook his head, but he couldn't muster up much sympathy. "It just hasn't been your day, has it, Gustav."

"You . . . you bastard!"

Longarm picked up Luther's six-gun and shoved it behind his belt. "What shall we do with your body? Have you got enough money to get sent back to your rich folks in Boston?"

"No!" Luther cried, grasping Longarm's wrist with amazing strength. "Please. Not a word! If my father knew how I ended ... well, it'd kill him."

"He needs to know you're dead. After all, doesn't he send you money every month?"

"Yeah."

Longarm gave it just a moment of thought. "Reckon we we can spare him the sad details."

Luther relaxed. He even managed to grin. "I could have whipped your ass in a stand-up fistfight."

"Maybe," Longarm conceded. "But I dunno. Seems to me, Gustav, that most of your recent practice has been beating up women."

Luther choked in rage. An oath filled his throat, but it died on his lips.

Longarm shoved the body into the rear of the buggy. Then he tethered his riding horses to the vehicle. Taking up the lines, he turned the weary horse around and headed toward Carson City.

The very first thing he was going to do was visit the Nevada State Prison and win Jim Zack his freedom. Maybe they'd go up to Lake Tahoe for a little fishing before Longarm returned to Denver.

Sure, his two weeks' vacation was about up and he ought to be heading back to work, but he and Jim needed to spend a little time together. And besides, if Milly and Henry were going to be wed right away, Longarm was sort of hoping they'd both want him to be their best man.

Watch for

LONGARM ON THE BUTTERFIELD SPUR

172nd in the bold
LONGARM series from Jove

Coming in April!

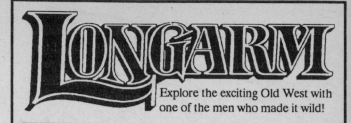